"Any hope or fear that the experimental novel was an aberration of the twentieth century is dashed by the appearance of Mark Z. Danielewski's *House of Leaves,* the first major experimental novel of the new millennium. And it's a monster. Dazzling."
—*The Washington Post Book World*

"An intricate, erudite, and deeply frightening book." —*The Wall Street Journal*

"A great novel. A phenomenal debut. Thrillingly alive, sublimely creepy, distressingly scary, breathtakingly intelligent—it renders most other fiction meaningless. One can imagine Thomas Pynchon, J. G. Ballard, Stephen King, and David Foster Wallace bowing at Danielewski's feet, choking with astonishment, surprise, laughter, awe."
—Bret Easton Ellis

"[Its] chills spark vertigo, its erudition brings on dislocating giddiness . . . *House of Leaves* is dizzying in every respect."
—*Entertainment Weekly*

"Stunning . . . What could have been a perfectly entertaining bit of literary horror is instead an assault on the nature of story."
—*Spin*

"This demonically brilliant book is impossible to ignore, put down, or persuasively conclude reading. In fact, when you purchase your copy you may reach a certain page and find me there, reduced in size like Vincent Price in *The Fly,* still trapped in the web of its malicious, beautiful pages."
—Jonathan Lethem, author of *Motherless Brooklyn*

"[A] tour de force first novel. [It] can keep you up at nights and make you never look at a closet in quite the same way again . . . Staggeringly good fun."
—*Chicago Sun-Times*

"A novelistic mosaic that simultaneously reads like a thriller and like a strange, dreamlike excursion into the subconscious."
—*The New York Times*

"If you can imagine that Peter Pan's enemy is not Captain Hook but Neverland itself, or that the whale that swallows Jonah is Moby-Dick, you'll begin to appreciate what this book is about. Anticipate it with dread, seize, and understand. A riveting reading experience."
—Gregory Maguire, author of *Wicked: The Life and Times of the Wicked Witch of the West*

"Grabs hold and won't let go . . . The reader races through the pages exactly as her mind races to find out what happens next."
—*The Village Voice*

"Like Melville's *Moby-Dick,* Joyce's *Ulysses,* and Nabokov's *Pale Fire,* Danielewski's *House of Leaves* is a grandly ambitious multi-layered work that simply knocks your socks off with its vast scope, erudition, formal inventiveness, and sheer storytelling skills."
—*San Diego Union-Tribune*

Mark Z. Danielewski's

House of Leaves

by

Zampanò

with introduction and notes by

Johnny Truant

2nd Edition

Pantheon Books New York

Published in the United States by Pantheon Books, a division of Random House, Inc., and simultaneously in Canada by Random House of Canada Limited, Toronto.

Pantheon Books and colophon are registered trademarks of Random House, Inc.

Permissions acknowledgments and illustration credits appear on pages 707–708.

Library of Congress Cataloging-in-Publication Data

Danielewski, Mark Z.
House of leaves / Mark Z. Danielewski.
p. cm.
ISBN 0-375-70376-4 (pbk)
ISBN 0-375-42052-5 (hc)
ISBN 0-375-41034-1 (hc/signed)
I. Title.
PS3554.A5596H68 2000 813'.54—dc21 99-36024 CIP

Random House Web Address: www.randomhouse.com
www.houseofleaves.com

Printed in the United States of America
~~First Edition~~
30

This novel is a work of fiction. Any references to real people, events, establishments, organizations or locales are intended only to give the fiction a sense of reality and authenticity. Other names, characters and incidents are either the product of the author's imagination or are used fictitiously, as are those fictionalized events and incidents which involve real persons and did not occur or are set in the future. — Ed.

A Note On This Edition

Full Color

- The word house in blue; minotaur and all ~~struck passages~~ in red.
- The only struck line in Chapter XXI appears in purple.
- Xxxxxxx and color plates.

2-Color

- Either house appears in blue or ~~struck passages~~ and the word minotaur appear in red.
- No Braille.
- Color or black & white plates.

Black & White

- Color is not used for the word house, minotaur, or ~~struck passages~~.
- No Braille.
- Black & white plates.

Incomplete

- No color.
- No Braille.
- Elements in the exhibits, appendices and index may be missing.

Contents

FOREWORD

The first edition of House of Leaves was privately distributed and did not contain Chapter 21, Appendix II, Appendix III, or the index. Every effort has been made to provide appropriate translations and accurately credit all sources. If we have failed in this endeavor, we apologize in advance and will gladly correct in subsequent printings all errors or omissions brought to our attention.

— The Editors

This is not for you.

<u>Introduction</u>

I still get nightmares. In fact I get them so often I should be used to them by now. I'm not. No one ever really gets used to nightmares.

For a while there I tried every pill imaginable. Anything to curb the fear. Excedrin PMs, Melatonin, L-tryptophan, Valium, Vicodin, quite a few members of the barbital family. A pretty extensive list, frequently mixed, often matched, with shots of bourbon, a few lung rasping bong hits, sometimes even the vaporous confidence-trip of cocaine. None of it helped. I think it's pretty safe to assume there's no lab sophisticated enough yet to synthesize the kind of chemicals I need. A Nobel Prize to the one who invents that puppy.

I'm so tired. Sleep's been stalking me for too long to remember. Inevitable I suppose. Sadly though, I'm not looking forward to the prospect. I say "sadly" because there was a time when I actually enjoyed sleeping. In fact I slept all the time. That was before my friend Lude woke me up at three in the morning and asked me to come over to his place. Who knows, if I hadn't heard the phone ring, would everything be different now? I think about that alot.

Actually, Lude had told me about the old man a month or so before that fateful evening. (Is that right? <u>fate</u>? It sure as hell wasn't <u>-ful</u>. Or was it exactly that?) I'd been in the throes of looking for an apartment after a little difficulty with a landlord who woke up one morning convinced he was Charles de Gaulle. I was so stunned by this announcement that before I could think twice I'd already told him how in my humble estimation he did not at all resemble an airport though the thought of a 757 landing on him was not at all disagreeable. I was promptly evicted. I could have put up a fight but the place was a nuthouse anyway and I was glad to leave. As it turned out Chuckie de Gaulle burnt the place to the ground a week later. Told the police a 757 had crashed into it.

During the following weeks, while I was couching it from Santa Monica to Silverlake looking for an apartment, Lude told me about this old guy who lived in his building. He had a first floor apartment peering out over a wide, overgrown courtyard. Supposedly, the old man had told Lude he would be dying soon. I didn't think much of it, though it wasn't exactly the kind of thing you forget either. At the time, I just figured Lude had been putting me on. He likes to exaggerate. I eventually found a studio in Hollywood and settled back into my mind numbing routine as an apprentice at a tattoo shop.

It was the end of '96. Nights were cold. I was getting over this woman named Clara English who had told me she wanted to date someone at the top of the food chain. So I demonstrated my unflagging devotion to her memory by immediately developing a heavy crush on this stripper who had Thumper tattooed right beneath her G-string, barely an inch from her shaved pussy or as she liked to call it—"The Happiest Place On Earth." Suffice it say, Lude & I spent the last hours of the year alone, scouting for new bars, new faces, driving recklessly through the canyons, doing our best to talk the high midnight heavens down with a whole lot of bullshit. We never did. Talk them down, I mean.

Then the old man died.

From what I can gather now, he was an American. Though as I would later find out, those who worked with him detected an accent even if they could never say for certain where it came from.

He called himself Zampanò. It was the name he put down on his apartment lease and on several other fragments I found. I never came across any sort of ID, whether a passport, license or other official document insinuating that yes, he indeed was An-Actual-&-Accounted-For person.

Who knows where his name really came from. Maybe it's authentic, maybe made up, maybe borrowed, a <u>nom de plume</u> or—my personal favorite—a <u>nom de guerre</u>.

As Lude told it, Zampanò had lived in the building for many years, and though he mostly kept to himself, he never failed to appear every morning and evening to walk around the courtyard, a wild place with knee high weeds and back then populated with over eighty stray cats. Apparently the cats liked the old man alot and though he offered no enticements, they would constantly rub up against his legs before darting back into the center of that dusty place.

Anyway, Lude had been out very late with some woman he'd met at his salon. It was just after seven when he finally stumbled back into the courtyard and despite a severe hangover immediately saw what was missing. Lude frequently came home early and always found the old guy working his way around the perimeter of all those weeds, occasionally resting on a sun beaten bench before taking another round. A single mother who got up every morning at six also noted Zampanò's absence. She went off to work, Lude went off to bed, but when dusk came and their old neighbor had still not appeared, both Lude and the single mother went to alert Flaze, the resident building manager.

Flaze is part Hispanic, part Samoan. A bit of a giant, you might say. 6'4", 245lbs, virtually no body fat. Vandals, junkies, you name it, they get near the building and Flaze will lunge at them like a pitbull raised in a crackhouse. And don't think he believes size & strength are invincible. If the interlopers are carrying, he'll show them his own gun collection and he'll draw on them too, faster than Billy The Kid. But as soon as Lude voiced his suspicions about the old man, pitbull & Billy The Kid went straight out the window. Flaze suddenly couldn't find the keys. He started muttering about calling the owner of the building. After twenty minutes, Lude was so fed up with this hemming & hawing he offered to handle the whole thing himself. Flaze immediately found the keys and with a big grin plopped them into Lude's outstretched hand.

Flaze told me later he'd never seen a dead body before and there was no question there would be a body and that just didn't sit well with Flaze. "We knew what we'd find," he said. "We knew that guy was dead."

The police found Zampanò just like Lude found him, lying face down on the floor. The paramedics said there was nothing unusual, just the way it goes, eighty some years and the inevitable kerplunk, the system goes down, lights blink out and there you have it, another body on the floor surrounded by things that don't mean much to anyone except to the one who can't take any of them along. Still, this was better than the prostitute the paramedics had seen earlier that day. She had been torn to pieces in a hotel room, parts of her used to paint the walls and ceiling red. Compared to that, this almost seemed pleasant.

The whole process took awhile. Police coming and going, paramedics attending to the body, for one thing making sure the old man was really dead; neighbors and eventually even Flaze poking their heads in to gawk, wonder or just graze on a scene that might someday resemble their own end. When it was finally over, it was very late. Lude stood alone in the apartment, the corpse gone, officials gone, even Flaze, the neighbors and other assorted snoops—all gone.

Not a soul in sight.

"Eighty fucking years old, alone in that pisshole," Lude had told me later. "I don't want to end up like that. No wife, no kids, no nobody at all. Not even one fucking friend." I must have laughed because Lude suddenly turned on me: "Hey Hoss, don't think young and squirting lots of come guarantees you shit. Look at yourself, working at a tattoo shop, falling for some stripper named Thumper." And he was sure right about one thing: Zampanò had no family, no friends and hardly a penny to his name.

The next day the landlord posted a notice of abandonment and a week later, after declaring that the contents of the apartment were worth less than $300, he called some charity to haul the stuff away. That was the night Lude made his awful discovery, right before the boys from Goodwill or wherever they came from swept in with their gloves and handtrucks.

When the phone rang, I was fast asleep. Anybody else I would have hung up on, but Lude's a good enough friend I actually dragged my ass out of bed at three in the morning and headed over to Franklin. He was waiting outside the gate with a wicked gleam in his eye.

I should have turned around right then. I should have known something was up, at the very least sensed the consequence lingering in the air, in the hour, in Lude's stare, in all of it, and fuck, I must have been some kind of moron to have been so oblivious to all those signs. The way Lude's keys rattled like bone-chimes as he opened the main gate; the hinges suddenly shrieking as if we weren't entering a crowded building but some ancient moss-eaten crypt. Or the way we padded down the dank hallway, buried in shadows, lamps above hung with spangles of light that I swear now must have been the work of gray, primitive spiders. Or probably most important of all, the way Lude whispered when he told me things, things I couldn't give a damn about back then but now, now, well my nights would be a great deal shorter if I didn't have to remember them.

Ever see yourself doing something in the past and no matter how many times you remember it you still want to scream stop, somehow redirect the action, reorder the present? I feel that way now, watching myself tugged stupidly along by inertia, my own inquisitiveness or whatever else, and it must have been something else, though what exactly I have no clue, maybe nothing, maybe nothing's all—a pretty meaningless combination of words, "nothing's all", but one I like just the same. It doesn't matter anyway. Whatever orders the path of all my yesterdays was strong enough that night to draw me past all those sleepers kept safely at bay from the living, locked behind their sturdy doors, until I stood at the end of the hall facing the last door on the left, an unremarkable door too, but still a door to the dead.

Lude, of course, had been unaware of the unsettling characteristics of our little journey to the back of the building. He had been recounting to me, in many ways dwelling upon, what had happened following the old man's death.

"Two things, Hoss," Lude muttered as the gate glided open. "Not that they make much difference." And as far as I can tell, he was right. They have very little to do with what follows. I include them only because they're part of the history surrounding Zampanò's death. Hopefully you'll be able to make sense of what I can represent though still fail to understand.

"The first peculiar thing," Lude told me, leading the way around a short flight of stairs. "Were the cats." Apparently in the months preceding the old man's death, the cats had begun to disappear. By the time he died they were all gone. "I saw one with its head ripped off and another with its guts strewn all over the sidewalk. Mostly though, they just vanished."

"The second peculiar thing, you'll see for yourself" Lude said, lowering his voice even more, as we slipped past the room of what looked suspiciously like a coven of musicians, all of them listening intently to headphones, passing around a spliff.

"Right next to the body," Lude continued. "I found these gouges in the hardwood floor, a good six or seven inches long. Very weird. But since the old man showed no sign of physical trauma, the cops let it go."

He stopped. We had reached the door. Now I shudder. Back then, I think I was elsewhere. More than likely daydreaming about Thumper. This will probably really wig you out, I don't care, but one night I even rented Bambi and got a hard on. That's how bad I had it for her. Thumper was something else and she sure beat the hell out of Clara English. Perhaps at that moment I was even thinking about what the two would look like in a cat fight. One thing's for sure though, when I heard Lude turn the bolt and open Zampanò's door, I lost sight of those dreams.

What hit me first was the smell. It wasn't a bad smell just incredibly strong. And it wasn't one thing either. It was extremely layered, a patina upon progressive patina of odor, the actual source of which had long since evaporated. Back then it had overwhelmed me, so much of it, cloying, bitter, rotten, even mean. These days I can no longer remember the smell only my reaction to it. Still if I had to give it a name, I think I would call it the scent of human history—a composite of sweat, urine, shit, blood, flesh and semen, as well as joy, sorrow, jealousy, rage, vengeance, fear, love, hope and a whole lot more. All of which probably sounds pretty ridiculous, especially since the abilities of my nose are not really relevant here. What's important though is that this smell was complex for a reason.

All the windows were nailed shut and sealed with caulking. The front entrance and courtyard doors all storm proofed. Even the vents were covered with duct tape. That said, this peculiar effort to eliminate any ventilation in the tiny apartment did not culminate with bars on the windows or multiple locks on the doors. Zampanò was not afraid of the outside world. As I've already pointed out, he walked around his courtyard and supposedly was even fearless enough to brave the LA public transportation system for an occasional trip to the beach (an adventure even I'm afraid to make). My best guess now is that he sealed his apartment in an effort to retain the various emanations of his things and himself.

Where his things were concerned, they ran the spectrum: tattered furniture, unused candles, ancient shoes (these in particular looking sad & wounded), ceramic bowls as well as glass jars and small wood boxes full of rivets, rubber bands, sea shells, matches, peanut shells, a thousand different kinds of elaborately shaped and colored buttons. One ancient beer stein held nothing more than discarded perfume bottles. As I discovered, the refrigerator wasn't empty but there wasn't any food in it either. Zampanò had crammed it full of strange, pale books.

Of course all of that's gone now. Long gone. The smell too. I'm left with only a few scattered mental snapshots: a battered Zippo lighter with Patent Pending printed on the bottom; the twining metal ridge, looking a little like some tiny spiral staircase, winding down into the bulbless interior of a light socket; and for some odd reason—what I remember most of all—a very old tube of chapstick with an amber like resin, hard & cracked. Which still isn't entirely accurate; though don't be misled into thinking I'm not trying to be accurate. There were, I admit, other things I recall about his place, they just don't seem relevant now. To my eye, it was all just junk, time having performed no economic alchemy there, which hardly mattered, as Lude hadn't called me over to root around in these particular and—to use one of those big words I would eventually learn in the ensuing months—deracinated details of Zampanò's life.

Sure enough, just as my friend had described, on the floor, in fact practically dead center, were the four marks, all of them longer than a hand, jagged bits of wood clawed up by something neither one of us cared to imagine. But that's not what Lude wanted me to see either. He was pointing at something else which hardly impressed me when I first glanced at its implacable shape.

Truth be told, I was still having a hard time taking my eyes off the scarred floor. I even reached out to touch the protruding splinters.

What did I know then? What do I know now? At least some of the horror I took away at four in the morning you now have before you, waiting for you a little like it waited for me that night, only without these few covering pages.

As I discovered, there were reams and reams of it. Endless snarls of words, sometimes twisting into meaning, sometimes into nothing at all, frequently breaking apart, always branching off into other pieces I'd come across later—on old napkins, the tattered edges of an envelope, once even on the back of a postage stamp; everything and anything but empty; each fragment completely covered with the creep of years and years of ink pronouncements; layered, crossed out, amended; handwritten, typed; legible, illegible; impenetrable, lucid; torn, stained, scotch taped; some bits crisp and clean, others faded, burnt or folded and refolded so many times the creases have obliterated whole passages of god knows what—sense? truth? deceit? a legacy of prophecy or lunacy or nothing of the kind?, and in the end achieving, designating, describing, recreating—find your own words; I have no more; or plenty more but why? and all to tell—what?

Lude didn't need to have the answer, but somehow he knew I would. Maybe that's why we were friends. Or maybe I'm wrong. Maybe he did need the answer, he just knew he wasn't the one who could find it. Maybe that's the real reason we were friends. But that's probably wrong too.

One thing's for sure, even without touching it, both of us slowly began to feel its heaviness, sensed something horrifying in its proportions, its silence, its stillness, even if it did seem to have been shoved almost carelessly to the side of the room. I think now if someone had said be careful, we would have. I know a moment came when I felt certain its resolute blackness was capable of anything, maybe even of slashing out, tearing up the floor, murdering Zampanò, murdering us, maybe even murdering you. And then the moment passed. Wonder and the way the unimaginable is sometimes suggested by the inanimate suddenly faded. The thing became only a thing.

So I took it home.

Back then—well it's way back then by now—you could have found me downing shots of whiskey at La Poubelle, annihilating my inner ear at Bar Deluxe or dining at Jones with some busty redhead I'd met at House of Blues, our conversation traversing wildly from clubs we knew well to clubs we'd like to know better. I sure as fuck wasn't bothered by old man Z's words. All those signs I just now finished telling you about quickly vanished in the light of subsequent days or had never been there to begin with, existing only in retrospect.

At first only curiosity drove me from one phrase to the next. Often a few days would pass before I'd pick up another mauled scrap, maybe even a week, but still I returned, for ten minutes, maybe twenty minutes, grazing over the scenes, the names, small connections starting to form, minor patterns evolving in those spare slivers of time.

I never read for more than an hour.

Of course curiosity killed the cat, and even if satisfaction supposedly brought it back, there's still that little problem with the man on the radio telling me more and more about some useless information. But I didn't care. I just turned the radio off.

And then one evening I looked over at my clock and discovered seven hours had passed. Lude had called but I hadn't noticed the phone ring. I was more than a little surprised when I found his message on my answering machine. That wasn't the last time I lost sense of time either. In fact it began to happen more often, dozens of hours just blinking by, lost in the twist of so many dangerous sentences.

Slowly but surely, I grew more and more disoriented, increasingly more detached from the world, something sad and awful straining around the edges of my mouth, surfacing in my eyes. I stopped going out at night. I stopped going out. Nothing could distract me. I felt like I was losing control. Something terrible was going to happen. Eventually something terrible did happen.

No one could reach me. Not Thumper, not even Lude. I nailed my windows shut, threw out the closet and bathroom doors, storm proofed everything, and locks, oh yes, I bought plenty of locks, chains too and a dozen measuring tapes, nailing all those straight to the floor and the walls. They looked suspiciously like lost metal roods or, from a different angle, the fragile ribs of some alien ship. However, unlike Zampanò, this wasn't about smell, this was about space. I wanted a closed, inviolate and most of all immutable space.

At least the measuring tapes should have helped.

They didn't.

Nothing did.

I just fixed myself some tea on the hot plate here. My stomach's gone. I can barely keep even this honey milked-up stuff down but I need the warmth. I'm in a hotel now. My studio's history. Alot these days is history.

I haven't even washed the blood off yet. Not all of it's mine either. Still caked around my fingers. Signs of it on my shirt. "What's happened here?" I keep asking myself. "What have I done?" What would you have done? I went straight for the guns and I loaded them and then I tried to decide what to do with them. The obvious thing was shoot something. After all, that's what guns are designed to do—shoot something. But who? Or what? I didn't have a clue. There were people and cars outside my hotel window. Midnight people I didn't know. Midnight cars I've never seen before. I could have shot them. I could have shot them all.

I threw up in my closet instead.

Of course, I have only my own immeasurable stupidity to blame for winding up here. The old man left plenty of clues and warnings. I was the fool to disregard them. Or was it the reverse: did I secretly enjoy them? At least I should have had some fucking inkling what I was getting into when I read this note, written just one day before he died:

> January 5, 1997
>
> Whoever finds and publishes this work shall be entitled to all proceeds. I ask only that my name take its rightful place. Perhaps you will even prosper. If, however, you discover that readers are less than sympathetic and choose to dismiss this enterprise out of hand, then may I suggest you drink plenty of wine and dance in the sheets of your wedding night, for whether you know it or not, now you truly are prosperous. They say truth stands the test of time. I can think of no greater comfort than knowing this document failed such a test.

Which back then meant absolutely nothing to me. I sure as hell didn't pause to think that some lousy words were going to land me in a shitty hotel room saturated with the stink of my own vomit.

After all, as I fast discovered, Zampanò's entire project is about a film which doesn't even exist. You can look, I have, but no matter how long you search you will never find <u>The Navidson Record</u> in theaters or video stores. Furthermore, most of what's said by famous people has been made up. I tried contacting all of them. Those that took the time to respond told me they had never heard of Will Navidson let alone Zampanò.

As for the books cited in the footnotes, a good portion of them are fictitious. For instance, Gavin Young's Shots In The Dark doesn't exist nor does The Works of Hubert Howe Bancroft, Volume XXVIII. On the other hand virtually any dimwit can go to a library and find W. M. Lindsay and H. J. Thomson's Ancient Lore in Medieval Latin Glossaries. There really was a "rebellion" on the 1973 Skylab mission but La Belle Nicoise et Le Beau Chien is made up as is, I assume, the bloody story of Quesada and Molino.

Add to this my own mistakes (and there's no doubt I'm responsible for plenty) as well as those errors Zampanò made which I failed to notice or correct, and you'll see why there's suddenly a whole lot here not to take too seriously.

In retrospect, I also realize there are probably numerous people who would have been better qualified to handle this work, scholars with PhDs from Ivy League schools and minds greater than any Alexandrian Library or World Net. Problem is those people were still in their universities, still on their net and nowhere near Whitley when an old man without friends or family finally died.

Zampanò, I've come to recognize now, was a very funny man. But his humor was that wry, desiccated kind soldiers whisper, all their jokes subsurface, their laughter amounting to little more than a tic in the corner of the mouth, told as they wait together in their outpost, slowly realizing that help's not going to reach them in time and come nightfall, no matter what they've done or what they try to say, slaughter will overrun them all. Carrion dawn for vultures.

See, the irony is it makes no difference that the documentary at the heart of this book is fiction. Zampanò knew from the get go that what's real or isn't real doesn't matter here. The consequences are the same.

I can suddenly imagine the cracked voice I never heard. Lips barely creasing into a smile. Eyes pinned on darkness:

"Irony? Irony can never be more than our own personal Maginot Line; the drawing of it, for the most part, purely arbitrary."

It's not surprising then that when it came to undermining his own work, the old man was superbly capable. False quotes or invented sources, however, all pale in comparison to his biggest joke.

Zampanò writes constantly about seeing. What we see, how we see and what in turn we can't see. Over and over again, in one form or another, he returns to the subject of light, space, shape, line, color, focus, tone, contrast, movement, rhythm, perspective and composition. None of which is surprising considering Zampanò's piece centers on a documentary film called <u>The Navidson Record</u> made by a Pulitzer Prize-winning photojournalist who must somehow capture the most difficult subject of all: the sight of darkness itself.

Odd, to say the least.

At first I figured Zampanò was just a bleak old dude, the kind who makes Itchy and Scratchy look like Calvin and Hobbes. His apartment, however, didn't come close to anything envisioned by Joel-Peter Witkin or what's routinely revealed on the news. Sure his place was eclectic but hardly grotesque or even that far out of the ordinary, until of course you took a more careful look and realized—hey why are all these candles unused? Why no clocks, none on the walls, not even on the corner of a dresser? And what's with these strange, pale books or the fact that there's hardly a goddamn bulb in the whole apartment, not even one in the refrigerator? Well that, of course, was Zampanò's greatest ironic gesture; love of love written by the broken hearted; love of life written by the dead: all this language of light, film and photography, and he hadn't seen a thing since the mid-fifties.

He was blind as a bat.

Almost half the books he owned were in Braille. Lude and Flaze both confirmed that over the years the old guy had had numerous readers visiting him during the day. Some of these came from community centers, the Braille Institute, or were just volunteers from USC, UCLA or Santa Monica College. No one I ever spoke with, however, claimed to know him well, though more than a few were willing to offer me their opinions.

One student believed he was certifiably mad. Another actress, who had spent a summer reading to him, thought Zampanò was a romantic. She had come over one morning and found him in "a terrible way."

"At first I assumed he was drunk, but the old guy never drank, not even a sip of wine. Didn't smoke either. He really lived a very austere life. Anyway he wasn't drunk, just really depressed. He started crying and asked me to leave. I fixed him some tea. Tears don't frighten me. Later he told me it was heart trouble. 'Just old heart-ache matters,' he said. Whoever she was, she must have been really special. He never told me her name."

As I eventually found out, Zampanò had seven names he would occasionally mention: Béatrice, Gabrielle, Anne-Marie, Dominique, Eliane, Isabelle and Claudine. He apparently only brought them up when he was disconsolate and for whatever reason dragged back into some dark tangled time. At least there's something more realistic about seven lovers than one mythological Helen. Even in his eighties, Zampanò sought out the company of the opposite sex. Coincidence had had no hand in arranging for all his readers to be female. As he openly admitted: "there is no greater comfort in my life than those soothing tones cradled in a woman's words."

Except maybe his own words.

Zampanò was in essence—to use another big word—a graphomaniac. He scribbled until he died and while he came close a few times, he never finished anything, especially the work he would unabashedly describe as either his masterpiece or his precious darling. Even the day before he failed to appear in that dusty courtyard, he was dictating long discursive passages, amending previously written pages and restructuring an entire chapter. His mind never ceased branching out into new territories. The woman who saw him for the last time, remarked that "whatever it was he could never quite address in himself prevented him from ever settling. Death finally saw to that."

With a little luck, you'll dismiss this labor, react as Zampanò had hoped, call it needlessly complicated, pointlessly obtuse, prolix—your word—, ridiculously conceived, and you'll believe all you've said, and then you'll put it aside—though even here, just that one word, "aside", makes me shudder, for what is ever really just put aside?—and you'll carry on, eat, drink, be merry and most of all you'll sleep well.

Then again there's a good chance you won't.

This much I'm certain of: it doesn't happen immediately. You'll finish and that will be that, until a moment will come, maybe in a month, maybe a year, maybe even several years. You'll be sick or feeling troubled or deeply in love or quietly uncertain or even content for the first time in your life. It won't matter. Out of the blue, beyond any cause you can trace, you'll suddenly realize things are not how you perceived them to be at all. For some reason, you will no longer be the person you believed you once were. You'll detect slow and subtle shifts going on all around you, more importantly shifts in you. Worse, you'll realize it's always been shifting, like a shimmer of sorts, a vast shimmer, only dark like a room. But you won't understand why or how. You'll have forgotten what granted you this awareness in the first place.

Old shelters—television, magazines, movies—won't protect you anymore. You might try scribbling in a journal, on a napkin, maybe even in the margins of this book. That's when you'll discover you no longer trust the very walls you always took for granted. Even the hallways you've walked a hundred times will feel longer, much longer, and the shadows, any shadow at all, will suddenly seem deeper, much, much, deeper.

You might try then, as I did, to find a sky so full of stars it will blind you again. Only no sky can blind you now. Even with all that iridescent magic up there, your eye will no longer linger on the light, it will no longer trace constellations. You'll care only about the darkness and you'll watch it for hours, for days, maybe even for years, trying in vain to believe you're some kind of indispensable, universe-appointed sentinel, as if just by looking you could actually keep it all at bay. It will get so bad you'll be afraid to look away, you'll be afraid to sleep.

Then no matter where you are, in a crowded restaurant or on some desolate street or even in the comforts of your own home, you'll watch yourself dismantle every assurance you ever lived by. You'll stand aside as a great complexity intrudes, tearing apart, piece by piece, all of your carefully conceived denials, whether deliberate or unconscious. And then for better or worse you'll turn, unable to resist, though try to resist you still will, fighting with everything you've got not to face the thing you most dread, what is now, what will be, what has always come before, the creature you truly are, the creature we all are, buried in the nameless black of a name.

And then the nightmares will begin.

— Johnny Truant
October 31, 1998
Hollywood, CA

Muss es sein?

The Navidson Record

I

I saw a film today, oh boy . . .

— The Beatles

While enthusiasts and detractors will continue to empty entire dictionaries attempting to describe or deride it, "authenticity" still remains the word most likely to stir a debate. In fact, this leading obsession—to validate or invalidate the reels and tapes—invariably brings up a collateral and more general concern: whether or not, with the advent of digital technology, image has forsaken its once unimpeachable hold on the truth.[1]

For the most part, skeptics call the whole effort a hoax but grudgingly admit *The Navidson Record* is a hoax of exceptional quality. Unfortunately out of those who accept its validity many tend to swear allegiance to tabloid-UFO sightings. Clearly it is not easy to appear credible when after vouching for the film's verity, the discourse suddenly switches to why Elvis is still alive and probably wintering in the Florida Keys.[2] One thing remains certain: any controversy surrounding Billy Meyer's film on flying saucers[3] has been supplanted by the house on Ash Tree Lane.

Though many continue to devote substantial time and energy to the antinomies of fact or fiction, representation or artifice, document or prank, as of late the more interesting material dwells exclusively on the interpretation of events within the film. This direction seems more promising, even if the house itself, like Melville's behemoth, remains resistant to summation.

Much like its subject, *The Navidson Record* itself is also uneasily contained—whether by category or lection. If finally catalogued as a gothic tale, contemporary urban folkmyth, or merely a ghost story, as some have called it, the documentary will still, sooner or later, slip the limits of any one of those genres. Too many important things in *The Navidson Record* jut out past the borders. Where one might expect horror, the supernatural, or traditional paroxysms of dread and fear, one discovers disturbing sadness, a sequence on radioactive isotopes, or even laughter over a *Simpsons* episode.

In the 17th century, England's greatest topographer of worlds satanic and divine warned that hell was nothing less than "Regions of sorrow, doleful shades, where peace/ And rest can never dwell, hope never

---

[1]A topic more carefully considered in Chapter IX.

[2]See Daniel Bowler's "Resurrection on Ash Tree Lane: Elvis, Christmas Past, and Other Non-Entities" published in *The House* (New York: Little Brown, 1995), p. 167-244 in which he examines the inherent contradiction of any claim alleging resurrection as well as the existence of that place.

[3]Or for that matter the Cottingley Fairies, Kirlian photography, Ted Serios' thoughtography or Alexander Gardner's photograph of the Union dead.

comes/ That comes to all" thus echoing the words copied down by hell's most famous tourist: "*Dinanzi a me non fuor cose create/ Se non etterne, e io etterna duro./ Lasciate ogni speranza, voi ch'entrate*."[4]

Even today many people still feel *The Navidson Record*, in spite of all its existential refinements and contemporary allusions, continues to reflect those exact sentiments. In fact a few eager intellectuals have already begun to treat the film as a warning in and of itself, perfectly suited for hanging whole above the gates of such schools as Architectonics, Popomo, Consequentialism, Neo-Plasticism, Phenomenology, Information Theory, Marxism, Biosemiotics, to say nothing of psychology, medicine, New Age spirituality, art and even Neo-Minimalism. Will Navidson, however, remains stalwart in his insistence that his documentary should be taken literally. As he himself says, ". . . all this, don't take it as anything else *but* this. And if one day you find yourself passing by that house, don't stop, don't slow down, just keep going. There's nothing there. Beware."

Considering how the film ends, it is not surprising that more than a handful of people have decided to heed his advice.

The Navidson Record did not first appear as it does today. Nearly seven years ago what surfaced was "The Five and a Half Minute Hallway"—a five and a half minute optical illusion barely exceeding the abilities of any NYU film school graduate. The problem, of course, was the accompanying statement that claimed all of it was true.

In one continuous shot, Navidson, whom we never actually see, momentarily focuses on a doorway on the north wall of his living room before climbing outside of the house through a window to the east of that door, where he trips slightly in the flower bed, redirects the camera from the ground to the exterior white clapboard, then moves right, crawling back inside the house through a second window, this time to the west of that door, where we hear him grunt slightly as he knocks his head on the sill, eliciting light laughter from those in the room, presumably Karen, his brother Tom, and his friend Billy Reston—though like Navidson, they too never appear on camera—before finally returning us to the starting point, thus completely circling the doorway and so proving, beyond a shadow of a doubt, that insulation or siding is the only possible thing this doorway could lead to, which is when all laughter stops, as Navidson's hand appears in frame and pulls open the door, revealing a narrow black hallway at least ten feet long, prompting Navidson to re-investigate, once again leading us on another circumambulation of this strange passageway, climbing in and out of the windows, pointing the camera to where the hallway should extend but finding nothing more than his own backyard—no ten foot protuberance, just rose bushes, a muddy dart gun, and the translucent summer air—in essence an exercise in disbelief which despite his best intentions still takes Navidson back inside to that impossible hallway, until as the camera begins

---

[4]That first bit comes from Milton's Paradise Lost, Book I, lines 65-67. The second from Dante's Inferno, Canto III, lines 7-9. In 1939, some guy named John D. Sinclair from the Oxford University Press translated the Italian as follows: "Before me nothing was created but eternal things and I endure eternally. Abandon every hope, ye that enter."[5]

[5]In an effort to limit confusion, Mr. Truant's footnotes will appear in Courier font while Zampanò's will appear in Times. We also wish to note here that we have never actually met Mr. Truant. All matters regarding the publication were addressed in letters or in rare instances over the phone. — The Editors

to move closer, threatening this time to actually enter it, Karen snaps, "Don't you dare go in there again, Navy," to which Tom adds, "Yeah, not such a hot idea," thus arresting Navidson at the threshold, though he still puts his hand inside, finally retracting and inspecting it, as if by seeing alone there might be something more to feel, Reston wanting to know if in fact his friend does sense something different, and Navidson providing the matter-of-fact answer which also serves as the conclusion, however abrupt, to this bizarre short: "It's freezing in there."

Dissemination of "The Five and a Half Minute Hallway" seemed driven by curiosity alone. No one ever officially distributed it and so it never appeared in film festivals or commercial film circles. Rather, VHS copies were passed around by hand, a series of progressively degenerating dubs of a home video revealing a truly bizarre house with notably very few details about the owners or for that matter the author of the piece.

Less than a year later another short surfaced. It was even more hotly sought after than "The Five and a Half Minute Hallway" and resulted in some fervent quests for Navidson and the house itself, all of which, for one reason or another, failed. Unlike the first, this short was not a continuous shot, prompting many to speculate that the eight minutes making up "Exploration #4" were in fact bits of a much larger whole.

The structure of "Exploration #4" is highly discontinuous, jarring, and as evidenced by many poor edits, even hurried. The first shot catches Navidson mid-phrase. He is tired, depressed and pale. "—days, I think. And, I . . . I don't know." [Drink of something; unclear what.] "Actually I'd like to burn it down. Can't think clearly enough to do it though." [Laughs] "And now . . . this."

The next shot jumps to Karen and Tom arguing over whether or not to "go in after him." At this point it remains unclear to whom they are referring.

There are several more shots.

Trees in winter.

Blood on the kitchen floor.

One shot of a child (Daisy) crying.

Then back to Navidson: "Nothing but this tape which I've seen enough times, it's more like a memory than anything else. And I still don't know: was he right or just out of his mind?"

Followed by three more shots.

Dark hallways.

Windowless rooms.

Stairs.

Then a new voice: "I'm lost. Out of food. Low on water. No sense of direction. Oh god . . ." The speaker is a bearded, broad shouldered man with frantic eyes. He speaks rapidly and appears short of breath: "Holloway Roberts. Born in Menomonie, Wisconsin. Bachelor's from U. Mass. There's something here. It's following me. No, it's *stalking* me. I've been stalked by it for days but for some reason it's not attacking. It's waiting, waiting for something. I don't know what. Holloway Roberts. Menomonie, Wisconsin. I'm not alone here. I'm not alone."

Thus bringing to an end this strange abstract which as the release of *The Navidson Record* revealed was sparingly incomplete.

Then for two years nothing. Few clues about who any of these people were, though eventually a number of photographers in the news community did recognize the author as none other than Will Navidson, the prize-winning photojournalist who won the Pulitzer for his picture of a dying girl in Sudan. Unfortunately this discovery only generated a few months of heated speculation, before, in the absence of press, corroboration, the location of the house or for that matter any comment by Navidson himself, interest died out. Most people just wrote it off as some kind of weird hoax, or, because of the unusual conceit, an aberrant UFO sighting. Nevertheless the deteriorating dubs did circulate and in some trendy academic circles a debate began: was the subject a haunted house? What did Holloway mean by "lost"? How could anyone be lost in a house for days anyway? Furthermore, what was someone with Navidson's credentials doing creating two strange shorts like these? And again, was this artifice or reality?

Certainly a good deal of the debate was sustained by a bit of old fashioned cultural elitism. People talked about the Navidson pieces because they were lucky enough to have seen them. Lee Sinclair suspects a majority of professors, students, SoHo artists and avant-garde filmmakers who spoke—and even wrote—so knowingly about the tapes, more than likely had never even viewed one frame: "There just weren't that many copies available."[6]

While "The Five and a Half Minute Hallway" and "Exploration #4" have been respectively called a "teaser" and a "trailer", they are also, in their own right, peculiar cinematic moments. On a purely symbolic level, they afford a vast potential for examination: the compression of space, the power of the imagination to decompress that space, the house as trope for the unlimited and the unknowable etc., etc. On a strictly visceral level, they provide ample shocks and curiosities. However, the most unnerving aspect about both pieces is their ability to convince us that everything really happened, some of which can be attributed to the verifiable elements (Holloway Roberts, Will Navidson et al.), but most of which must be chalked up to the starkness of the production—the absence of make-up, expensive sound tracks, or crane shots. Except for framing, editing, and in some cases sub-titles,[7] there is virtually no room for creative intrusion.

Who would have suspected that almost three years after "The Five and a Half Minute Hallway" began appearing on VHS, Miramax would quietly release *The Navidson Record* in a limited run and almost immediately unsettle audiences everywhere. Since the opening three years ago last April[8] in New York and Los Angeles, *The Navidson Record* has been screened nationwide, and while hardly a blockbuster, the film continues to generate revenues as well as interest. Film periodicals frequently publish reviews, critiques and letters. Books devoted entirely to *The Navidson Record* now appear with some regularity. Numerous professors have made *The Navidson Record* required viewing for their seminars, while many universities already claim that dozens of students from a variety of departments have completed doctoral dissertations on the film. Comments and references frequently appear in *Harper's, The New Yorker*, *Esquire*, *American Heritage, Vanity Fair, Spin* as well as on late night television. Interest abroad is equally intense. Japan, France and

---

[6]Lee Sinclair's "Degenerate" in *Twentieth Century Dub, Dub* edited by Tony Ross (New York: CCD Zeuxis Press, 1994), p. 57-91.

[7]Arguably interpretive, especially in the case of Holloway's garbled patter where even the subtitles appear as incomprehensible onomatopoeia or just question marks.

[8]i.e. 1993.

Norway have all responded with awards but to this day the spectral Navidson has yet to appear let alone accept any one of these. Even the garrulous Weinstein brothers remain unusually reticent about the film and its creator.

Interview magazine quoted Harvey Weinstein as saying, "It is what it is."[9]

The Navidson Record now stands as part of this country's cultural experience and yet in spite of the fact that hundreds of thousands of people have seen it, the film continues to remain an enigma. Some insist it must be true, others believe it is a trick on par with the Orson Welles radio romp *The War of the Worlds*. Others could care less, admitting that either way *The Navidson Record* is a pretty good tale. Still many more have never even heard of it.

These days, with the unlikely prospect of any sort of post-release resolution or revelation, Navidson's film seems destined to achieve at most cult status. Good story telling alone will guarantee a healthy sliver of popularity in the years to come but its inherent strangeness will permanently bar it from any mainstream interest.

---

[9]Mirjana Gortchakova's "Home Front" in *Gentleman's Quarterly*, v. 65, October 1995, p. 224.

II

The labours of men of genius, however erroneously directed, scarcely ever fail in ultimately turning to the solid advantage of mankind.

— Mary Shelley

The Navidson Record actually contains two films: the one Navidson made, which everyone remembers, and the one he set out to make, which very few people ever detect. While easily overshadowed by the finished film, the filmmaker's original intentions provide an early context in which to view the peculiar properties of the house later on.

In many ways, the opening of *The Navidson Record*, shot back in April of 1990, remains one of the more disturbing sequences because it so effectively denies itself even the slightest premonition about what will soon take place on Ash Tree Lane.

Not once during those initial minutes does Navidson indicate he knows anything about the impending nightmare he and his entire family are about to face. He is wholly innocent, and the nature of the house, at least for a little while, lies beyond his imagination let alone his suspicions.

Of course not everyone remains in accordance with this assessment. Dr. Isaiah Rosen believes, "Navidson's a fraud from frame one and his early posturing puts the entire work at risk."[10] Rosen assumes the beginning is just a case of "bad acting" performed by a man who has already envisioned the rest of the film. Consequently Rosen seriously undervalues the importance of Navidson's initial intentions.

All too often major discoveries are the unintended outcome of experiments or explorations aimed at achieving entirely different results. In Navidson's case, it is impossible to disregard his primary goal, especially since it served as progenitor or at the very least the "near origin" to all that followed. Rosen's presumptions[11] lead him to dismiss the cause for the result, thereby losing sight of the complex and rewarding relationship which exists between the two.

"It's funny," Navidson tells us at the outset. "I just want to create a record of how Karen and I bought a small house in the country and moved into it with our children. Sort of see how everything turns out. No gunfire, famine, or flies. Just lots of toothpaste, gardening and people stuff. Which is how I got the Guggenheim Fellowship and the NEA Media Arts Grant.

[10]Isaiah Rosen, Ph.D., *Flawed Performances: A Consideration of the Actors in the Navidson Opus* (Baltimore: Eddie Hapax Press, 1995), p. 73.

[11]`Not the first and definitely not the last time Zampanò implies that` `The Navidson Record exists.`

Maybe because of my past they're expecting something different, but I just thought it would be nice to see how people move into a place and start to inhabit it. Settle in, maybe put down roots, interact, hopefully understand each other a little better. Personally, I just want to create a cozy little outpost for me and my family. A place to drink lemonade on the porch and watch the sun set."

Which is almost literally how *The Navidson Record* begins, with Will Navidson relaxing on the porch of his small, old-style heritage house, enjoying a glass of lemonade, watching the sun turn the first few minutes of daytime into gold. Despite Rosen's claim, nothing about him seems particularly devious or false. Nor does he appear to be acting. In fact he is a disarmingly pleasant man, lean, attractive, slowly edging through his 40s,[12] determined once and for all to stay in and explore the quieter side of life.

At least initially he succeeds, providing us with pristine glimpses of the Virginia countryside, the rural neighborhood, purple hills born on the fringe of night, before moving past these establishing shots and focusing more closely on the process of moving into the house itself, unrolling pale blue oriental rugs, arranging and rearranging furniture, unpacking crates, replacing light bulbs and hanging pictures, including one of his own prize-winning photographs. In this way, Navidson not only reveals how each room is occupied, but how everyone has helped apply his or her own personal texture.

At one point, Navidson takes a break to interview his two children. These shots are also impeccably composed. Son and daughter bathed in sunlight. Their warmly lit faces framed against a cool backdrop of green lawn and trees.

His five year old daughter Daisy approves of their new house. "It's nice here," she giggles shyly, though she is not too shy to point out the absence of stores like "Bloomydales."

Chad who is three years older than Daisy is a little more self-conscious, even serious. Too often his response has been misread by those aware of the film's ending. It is important to realize, however, that at this point in time Chad has no sense what the future holds. He is merely expressing anxieties natural for a boy his age who has just been uprooted from his home in the city and deposited in a vastly different environment.

As he tells his father, what he misses most is the sound of traffic. It seems the noise made by trucks and taxi cabs created for him a kind of evening lullaby. Now he finds it difficult to fall asleep in the quiet.

"What about the sound of crickets?" Navidson asks.

Chad shakes his head.

"It's not the same. I dunno. Sometimes it's just silent . . . No sound at all."

"Does that scare you?"

Chad nods.

"Why?" asks his father.

"It's like something's waiting."

"What?"

Chad shrugs. "I dunno Daddy. I just like the sound of traffic."[13]

---

[12]In his article "Years of Those" in *The New Republic,* v. 213, November 20, 1995, p. 33-39, Helmut Kereincrazch puts Navidson's age at forty-eight.

[13]The question of lengthy narrative descriptions in what is purportedly a critical exegesis is addressed in Chapter 5; footnote 67. — Ed.

Of course, Navidson's pastoral take on his family's move hardly reflects the far more complicated and significant impetus behind his project—namely his foundering relationship with longtime companion Karen Green. While both have been perfectly content not to marry, Navidson's constant assignments abroad have led to increased alienation and untold personal difficulties. After nearly eleven years of constant departures and brief returns, Karen has made it clear that Navidson must either give up his professional habits or lose his family. Ultimately unable to make this choice, he compromises by turning reconciliation into a subject for documentation.

None of this, however, is immediately apparent. In fact it requires some willful amnesia of the more compelling sequences ahead, if we are to detect the subtle valences operating between Will and Karen; or as Donna York phrased it, "the way they talk to each other, the way they look after each other, and of course the way they don't."[14]

Navidson, we learn, began his project by mounting a number of Hi 8s around the house and equipping them with motion detectors to turn them on and off whenever someone enters or leaves the room. With the exception of the three bathrooms, there are cameras in every corner of the house. Navidson also keeps on hand two 16mm Arriflexes and his usual battery of 35mm cameras.

Nevertheless, as everyone knows, Navidson's project is pretty crude. Nothing, for instance, like the constant eye of CCTV systems routinely installed in local banks or the lavish equipment and multiple camera operators required on MTV's *Real World*. The whole effort would seem very home movie-ish at best were it not for the fact that Navidson is an exceptionally gifted photographer who understands how one sixtieth of a second can yield an image worth more than twenty-four hours of continuous footage. He is not interested in showing all the coverage or attempting to capture some kind of catholic or otherwise mythical view. Instead he hunts for moments, pearls of the particular, an unexpected phone call, a burst of laughter, or some snippet of conversation which might elicit from us an emotional spark and perhaps even a bit of human understanding.

More often than not, the near wordless fragments Navidson selects reveal what explication could only approximate. Two such instances seem especially sublime, and because they are so short and easy to miss, it is worth reiterating their content here.

In the first one, we see Navidson climbing to the top of the stairs with a crate full of Karen's things. Their bedroom is still cluttered with lamps in bubble wrap and assorted unpacked suitcases and garbage bags full of clothes. Nothing hangs on the walls. Their bed is not made. Navidson finds some room on top of a bureau to set down his load. He is about to leave when some invisible impulse stops him. He takes Karen's jewelry box out of the crate, lifts the hand-carved horn lid, and removes the inner tray. Unfortunately, whatever he sees inside is invisible to the camera.

When Karen walks in carrying a basket stuffed with bedsheets and pillow cases, Navidson has already turned his attention to an old hairbrush lying next to some perfume bottles.

"What are you doing?" she immediately asks.

[14]Donna York's "In Twain" in *Redbook*, v. 186, January 1996, p. 50.

"This is nice," he says, removing a big clump of her blonde hair from the tines and tossing it into the wastebasket.

"Give me that," Karen demands. "Just you watch, one day I'll go bald, then won't you be sorry you threw that away."

"No," Navidson replies with a grin.

It is unnecessary to dwell here on the multiple ways in which these few seconds demonstrate how much Navidson values Karen,[15] except to highlight how despite his sarcasm and apparent disregard for her things the scene itself represents the exact opposite. Using image and exquisitely controlled edits, Navidson has in effect preserved her hair, called into question his own behavior and perhaps in some ways contradicted his own closing remark, which as Samuel T. Glade has pointed out could refer to either "watch," "bald," or "sorry" or all three.[16] Even better, Navidson has permitted the action and subtlety of the composition to represent the profound sentiments at work without the molestations of some ill-conceived voice-over or manipulative soundtrack.

In keeping with this approach, the second moment also does without explanations or disingenuous musical cues. Navidson simply concentrates on Karen Green. Once a model with the Ford Agency in New York, she has since put behind her the life of Milan fashion shoots and Venetian Masques in order to raise her two children. Considering how beautiful she appears on the dreadful Hi 8 tapes, it is hardly surprising editors frequently relied on slides of her pouty lips, high cheek bones, and hazel eyes to sell their magazines.

Early on, Navidson gave Karen a Hi 8 which he asked her to treat like a journal. Her video entries—which Navidson promised to view only after the film was shot and then only if she agreed—reveal a thirty-seven year old woman who worries about leaving the city, growing old, keeping trim, and staying happy. Nevertheless, despite their purely confessional content, it is not a journal entry but rather an unguarded moment captured on one of the house Hi 8s that demonstrates Karen's almost bewildering dependence on Navidson.

Karen sits with Chad and Daisy in the living room. The children are in the midst of a candle-making project which involves several empty egg cartons, a dozen long lengths of wick, a bucket of plaster of Paris and a jar full of crystal wax. Using a pair of red handled scissors, Daisy cuts the wicks down to three inch pieces and then presses them down into an egg cup which Chad in turn fills with a layer of plaster followed by a layer of the tiny wax beads. The result is some kind of candle with plenty of goop to go around, most of it ending up on the children's hands. Karen helps brush the hair out of her daughter's eyes lest she try to do it herself and end up smearing plaster all over her face. And yet even though Karen keeps Chad from overfilling the molds or Daisy from hurting herself with the scissors,

---

[15]See "The Heart's Device" by Frances Leiderstahl in *Science,* v. 265 August 5, 1994, p. 741; Joel Watkin's "Jewelry Box, Perfume, and Hair" in *Mademoiselle,* v. 101 May, 1995, p. 178-181; as well as Hardy Taintic's more ironic piece "Adult Letters and Family Jewels" *The American Scholar,* v. 65 spring 1996, p. 219-241.

[16]Samuel T. Glade's "Omens & Signs" in *Notes From Tomorrow* ed. Lisbeth Bailey (Delaware: Taema Essay Publications, 1996).

she still cannot resist looking out the window every couple of minutes. The sound of a passing truck causes her to glance away. Even if there is no sound, the weight of a hundred seconds always turns her head.

Though clearly a matter of opinion, Karen's gaze seems just as lost as it is "surfeit with love and longing."[17] The reasons are in part answered when at last Navidson's car pulls into the driveway. Karen hardly attempts to contain her relief. She instantly leaps up from the mini candle factory and dashes from the room. Seconds later—no doubt thinking better of herself—she returns.

"Daisy, hold off using the scissors until I get back."

"Mommy!" Daisy shrills.

"You heard what I said. Chad keep an eye on your sister."

"Mommy!" Daisy squealing even louder.

"Daisy, mommy also wants you to look after your brother."

This seems to appease the little girl, and she actually settles down, smugly eyeing Chad even as she continues to snip wicks.

Strangely enough, by the time Karen reaches Navidson in the foyer, she has quite effectively masked all her eagerness to see him. Her indifference is highly instructive. In that peculiar contradiction that serves as connective tissue in so many relationships, it is possible to see that she loves Navidson almost as much as she has no room for him.

"Hey, the water heater's on the fritz," she manages to say.

"When did that happen?"

She accepts his brief kiss.

"I guess last night."[18]

---

[17]Max C. Garten's "100 Looks" in *Vogue*, v. 185, October 1995, p. 248.

[18]I got up this morning to take a shower and guess what? No fucking hot water. A pretty evil discovery especially when you're depending on that watery wake-up call, me being massively dehydrated from a long night drunk my road-dog Lude and I winged our way onto last night. As I'm remembering it now, we somehow ended up at this joint on Pico, and soon thereafter found ourselves in conversation with some girls wearing black cowboy hats, supposedly lost in their own private-blend of brain-hatching euphoria—Thank you Herbal Ecstasy—prompting us to put a little Verbal Ecstasy on them which would, as it turned out, ultimately lead them giggling into the night.

I've forgotten now what we did exactly to get the whole thing rolling. I think Lude started giving one of them a trim, whipping out his scissors which he always has on hand, like old gunslingers I guess always had on hand their Colts—there he goes, snipping locks & bangs, doing a great fucking job too, but hey he's a pro, and all of it in the dark too, on a barstool, surrounded by dozens of who knows who, fingers & steel clicking away, tiny bits of hair spitting off into the surrounding turmoil, the girls all nervous until they see he really is the shit and then they're immediately chirping "me, next" & "do me" which is too easy to remark upon, so instead Lude & I remark upon something else which this time round is all about some insane adventure I supposedly had when I was a Pit Boxer. Mind you I'd never heard that term before nor had Lude. Lude just made it up and I went with it.

"Aw come on, they don't want to hear about that," I said with about as much reluctance as I could reasonably feign.

"No Hoss, you're wrong," Lude insisted. "You must."

"Very well," I said, starting then to recall for everyone how at the lonely age of nineteen I had climbed off a barge in Galveston.

"Actually I escaped," I improvised. "See, I still owed my crazy Russian Captain a thousand dollars for a wager I'd lost in Singapore. He wanted to murder me so I practically had to run the whole way to Houston."

"Don't forget to tell them about the birds," Lude winked. He was just throwing shit at me, something he loved doing, keeping me on my toes.

"Sure," I mumbled, stretching for an explanation. "This barge I'd been on was loaded with dates and pounds of hash and an incredible number of exotic birds, all of it, of course, illegal to transport, but what did I know? It didn't exactly affect me. And anyway, I wasn't sticking around. So I reach Houston and the first thing that happens, some twerp comes up and tries to rob me."

Lude frowned. He clearly wasn't pleased with what I'd just done to his birds.

I ignored him and continued.

"This guy just walked straight over and told me to give him all my money. I didn't have a dime on me but it wasn't like this weasely sonofabitch had a weapon or anything. So I slugged him. Down he went. But not for long. A second later he pops up again and you know what? he's smiling, and then this other guy joins him, much bigger, and he was smiling too and shaking my hand, congratulating me. They'd been searching all day for a Pit Boxer, pay was two hundred dollars a night and apparently I'd just made the grade. This weasely sonofabitch was the head interviewer. His partner referred to him as Punching Bag."

By now the girls were crowding around me & Lude, sucking down more drinks and all in all falling into the rhythm of the story. Carefully, I led them through that first night, describing the ring with its dirt floor surrounded by hordes of folk come to bet a few dollars and watch guys hurt—hurt themselves, hurt someone else. Gloves were not an option in this kind of fighting. Miraculously, I made it through alive. I actually won my first two fights. A couple of bruises, a cut cheek, but I walked with two hundred bucks and Punching Bag forked for ribs and beer and even let me crash on his couch. Not bad. So I continued. In fact, for a whole month I did this twice a week.

"See the scar on his eyebrow there—" Lude pointed, giving the girls one of those all knowing completely over-the-top nods.

"Is that how you broke your front tooth too?" a girl with a ruby pin in her cowboy hat blurted out, though as soon as she said it, I could see she felt bad about mentioning my busted incisor.

"I'm getting to that," I said with a smile.

Why not work the tooth into it too?, I thought.

After three-four weeks, I continued, I had enough dough to pay back the Captain and even keep a bit for myself. I was pretty tired of the whole thing anyway.

The fights were bad enough. "And incidentally I'd won every one," I added. Lude scoffed. "But having to be wary all the time around the likes of Punching Bag & his partner, that was by far the worst aspect. Also, as it turned out, the place I was staying in was a whorehouse, full of these sad girls, who between their own senseless rounds would talk about the simplest, most inconsequential things. I liked it better on the barge, even with the Captain and his murderous moods.

"Well my last night, the twerp pulls me aside and suggests I bet my dough on myself. I tell him I don't want to because I could lose. 'You stupid fucking kid,' he spits at me. 'You've won every fight so far.' 'Yeah,' I say. 'So?' 'Well figure it out. It's not because you're any good. They've all been fixed. I find some lump, pay him fifty bucks to swing and dive. We make a killing on the bets. You won last week, you won the week before, you'll win tonight. I'm just trying to help you out here.'

"So being the stupid kid I was I bet all the money I had and walked into the ring. Who do you think was there waiting from me?"

I gave everyone a chance to come up with their own answer while I drained my glass of beer, but no one had a clue who I was about to fight. Even Lude was a step behind. Of course, that depends on how you look at it: he was also fondling the ass of a girl with a tourmaline in her cowboy hat while she in turn, or so it appeared to me, was caressing the inside of his thigh.

"In the middle of all those Houston losers, all of 'em screaming odds, screaming money, licking their gums for blood, stood Punching Bag, fists all taped up and not even the flicker of a smile or the slightest bit of recognition in his eye. Boy, let me tell you, he turned out to be a mean-spirited remorseless S.O.B. That first round he knocked me down twice. The second round I almost didn't get up.

"All month long, he and his partner had been boosting the numbers on me so that when Punching Bag—and at this point he was the long shot—slaughtered me, they'd walk with a small fortune. Or run. Me though, a dumb nineteen year old who'd wandered into Galveston after three months at sea, I was going to lose my money and wind up in a hospital. Maybe worse. Since the fights were just three rounds long, I only had one more left to do something. His partner threw a bucket of ice water in my face and told me to crawl out there and get it over with.

"As I wobbled to my feet, I shook my head, and saying it loud enough so he could hear me, but not so loud so he'd think I was selling something, I said that it was all too bad because I'd been planning to use my money to buy a shipment of some stuff worth at least a thousand percent on the street.

"Well, the next round, the last round I should say, Punching Bag broke my tooth. I was out. They'd both originally planned to ditch me but my little gambit had worked. After what the partner had heard me say, which I'm sure he shared as soon as he could with Punching Bag, they dragged me along, dumped some whiskey into me in their truck and then started grilling me about that stuff I'd been babbling about, trying to find out what was worth a thousand percent.

"Now I was in a bad way, more than a little afraid that they'd do something really evil if they found out I'd been bullshitting them. Still, if I stayed in Houston I'd probably be lynched by the bettors who by now had figured out something was sour which could only mean one thing to them (all explanations to the grave): Punching Bag & his partner and me were to blame. I had to think fast and besides, I still wanted my money back, so—"

By now even Lude was hooked. They all were. The girls all engrossed and smiling and still shimmying closer, as if maybe by touching me they could find out for sure if I was for real. Lude knew it was pure crap but he had no clue where I was heading. To tell you the truth neither did I. So I took my best shot.

"I pointed them to the barge. I hadn't figured out what I'd do once we got there but I knew the ship was leaving with the tide early next morning so we had to hurry. Luckily we arrived in time and I immediately went off to find the Captain who as soon as he saw me grabbed me by the throat. Somehow between gasps, I succeeded in telling him about Punching Bag & his partner and their money—all their money which included my money most of which was in essence the Captain's money. That got the bastard listening. A few minutes later, he sauntered over to the duo, poured them coffee mugs full of vodka, and in his incomprehensible accent, began going on and on about pure New Guinea value.

"Punching Bag had no idea what this idiot was talking about, neither did I for that matter, but an hour and two bottles of vodka later, he came to the conclusion that the Captain must be talking about drugs. After all the Captain kept mentioning euphoria, Spanish explorers and paradise, even though he refused to show Punching Bag the tiniest bit of anything tangible, vaguely referring to custom officials and the constant threat of confiscation and jail.

"Now here was the clincher. While he's babbling on, this van drives up and a guy no one has ever seen before or ever will see again gets out, gives the Captain a thousand dollars, takes one crate and then drives off. Just like that, and boy does that do it. Without even examining what he's buying, Punching Bag hands over five g's. The Captain, keeping his word, immediately loads five crates into the back of Punching Bag's truck.

"I'm sure the twerp would of inspected them right on the spot, except suddenly in the distance we all start hearing police sirens or harbor patrol sirens or some such shit. They weren't after us, but Punching Bag & his partner still got spooked and took off as fast as they could.

"Even after we got out to sea, the Captain was still laughing. I wasn't though. The bastard wouldn't give me any of my money. By his way of thinking—and him explaining this to me in that incomprehensible accent of his—I owed him for saving my life, not to mention transporting my sorry ass all the way to Florida, where I finally did end up going, nearly dying in a cold water place called the Devil's Ear which is an altogether different story.

"Still it wasn't so bad, especially when I think now and then about Punching Bag & his partner. I mean I wonder what they did, what they said, when they finally tore open all those crates and discovered all those fucking birds. Over fifty Birds of Paradise.

"A few months later I did read somewhere how Houston Police busted two known felons trying to unload a bunch of exotic birds at a zoo."

Which was pretty much how that story ended or at least the story I told last night. Maybe not verbatim but close.

Unfortunately nothing happened with the girls. They just ran off giggling into the night. No digits, no dates, not even their names, leaving me feeling dumb and sad, a bit like a broken thermos—fine on the outside, but on the inside nothing but busted glass. And why I'm going on about any of this right now is beyond me. I've never even seen a Bird of Paradise. And I sure as hell have never boxed or been on a barge. In fact just looking at this story makes me feel a little queasy all of a sudden. I mean how fake it is. Just sorta doesn't sit right with me. It's like there's something else, something beyond it all, a greater story still looming in the twilight, which for some reason I'm unable to see.

Anyway I didn't mean to wander into all this. I was telling you about the shower. That's what I wanted to deal with. As you probably know, finding out there's no warm water is a particularly unpleasant discovery simply because it's not something you figure out immediately. You have to let the water run awhile and even though it remains icy, part of you still refuses to believe it won't change, especially if you

What both these moments reveal is how much Will and Karen need each other and yet how difficult they find handling and communicating those feelings.

Unfortunately, critics have been less than sympathetic. Following the release of *The Navidson Record*, neither Karen nor Navidson's reputation escaped unscathed. Karen, in particular, was decimated by a vituperative stream of accusations from the tabloids, reputable reviewers, and even an estranged sister. Leslie Buckman blows high the roof beams when she calls "Karen Green a cold bitch, plain and simple. A high-fashion model, not much smarter than a radiator, who grew up thinking life revolved around club owners, cocaine and credit card limits. Watching her burble on about her weight, her children, or how much she needs Navidson made me want to retch. How can she say she loves a man when she's incapable of anything even remotely resembling commitment? Did I say she was a cold bitch? She's also a slut."[19]

Buckman is not alone in her opinion. Dale Corrdigan has also pointed out that Karen was anything but a lovely housewife: "Karen hardly gave up the promiscuous behavior that marked her 20s. She only became more discreet."[20]

In retrospect, the rabid speculation over Karen's infidelities seems driven by a principally sexist culture, especially since so little attention was paid to Navidson's role in their relationship. As David Liddel once

---

wait a little longer or open up the valve a little more. So you wait but no matter how many minutes run by, you still see no steam, you still feel no heat.

Maybe a cold shower would of been good for me. The thought crossed my mind but I was already too freezing to try for even a quick one. I don't even know why I was freezing. It was pretty warm in my place. Even warmer outside. Not even my big brown corduroy coat helped.

Later I spotted some workers in back tackling the water heater. One of them, snorting on a dirty handkerchief, covered in tatts, Manson crucified on his back, told me it would be fixed by evening. It's not.

Now I'm sure you're wondering something. Is it just coincidence that this cold water predicament of mine also appears in this chapter?

Not at all. Zampanò only wrote "heater." The word "water" back there—I added that.

Now there's an admission, eh?

Hey, not fair, you cry.

Hey, hey, fuck you, I say.

Wow, am I mad right now. Clearly a nerve's been hit somewhere but I don't how, why or by what. I sure don't believe it's because of some crummy made-up story or a lousy (water) heater.

Can't follow the feeling.

If only any of it were true. I mean we'd all be so lucky to wind up a punching bag and still find our crates full of Birds of Paradise.

No such luck with this crate.

Let the cold water run.

It's gotta warm up eventually.

Right?

[19]"Lie Lexicon and Feminine Wiles" by Leslie Buckman published in *All In The Name Of Feminism: A Collection Of Essays* ed. Nadine Muestopher (Cambridge, Massachusetts: Shtrön Press, 1995), p. 344.

[20]Dale Corrdigan, "Blurbs." *Glamour*, v. 94, April 1996, p. 256.

exclaimed: "If he has horns, who's to say he doesn't have hooves?"[21] Fortunately unlike the biased treatment offered by the media, Navidson does not hesitate to constantly include in his film evidence of his own failings. In fact as of late, many have called into question the accuracy of this self-portrait, observing that Navidson may have gone too far out of his way to cast himself in a less than favorable light.[22]

Not only does Navidson reveal through Karen, Chad, and Daisy how he spent the last decade perfecting a career in distance, where taking off on a moment's notice to shoot Alaskan fishing boats was something his family had to just accept, even if that three day trip slowly evolved into weeks and even months, he also, by way of the film, admits to carrying around his own alienating and intensely private obsessions.

As it turns out though, the first hint concerning these dark broodings does not come from him but from Karen. Navidson's early Hi 8 journal entries are so easy and mild they rarely, if ever, allude to deeper troubles. Only Karen, staring straight into that little lens, brings up the problem.

"He mentioned Delial again," she says in an extremely clipped tone. "I've warned him if he's not going to tell me who she is he better damn not bring her up. Part of this move south was supposed to be about putting the past and all that behind us. He's been pretty good but I guess he can't control his dreams. Last night, I wasn't sleeping very well. I was cold. It's the middle of May but I felt like I was lying in a freezer. I got up to get a blanket and when I came back he was talking in his sleep: 'Delial.' Just like that. Out of the blue. And I'm certain because he said her name twice. Almost shouted it."

As it turns out, Karen was not the only one who was kept in the dark about Delial. Even friends and fellow photojournalists who had heard Navidson use the name before never received any sort of explanation. No one had any idea who she was or why it was she haunted his thoughts and conversation like some albatross.[23]

That said, while the first sequence certainly hints at a number of underlying tensions in the Navidson/Green family, all brought into relief by this chapter, it is crucial not to lose sight of the prevailing sense of bliss still evoked in those opening minutes. After a couple of nights, Chad no longer has trouble sleeping. After a couple of days, Daisy's nipped finger heals. The heater is easily repaired. Even both parents enjoy a private moment where their hands can playfully unlock and interlock, Will finally putting his arm around Karen as she, letting out a heart-stirring sigh, rests her head on his shoulder.

In fact it is rare to behold such radiant optimism in anything these days, let alone in films, each frame so replete with promise and hope. Navidson clearly cherishes these bucolic, near idyllic impressions of a new world. Of course, nostalgia's role in shaping the final cut must not be forgotten, especially since within a year these pieces were all Navidson had

---

[21]"A Horny Duo" by David Liddel, *Utne Reader*, July/August 1993, p. 78.

[22]Ascencion Gerson's "The Vanity of Self-Loathing" in *Collected Essays on Self-Portraiture* ed. Haldor Nervene (Honolulu: University of Hawaii Press, 1995), p. 58.

[23]Since the revelation, there has been a proliferation of material on the subject. Chapter XIX deals exclusively with the subject. See also Chris Ho's "What's in a name?" *Afterimage,* v. 31, December, 1993; Dennis Stake's *Delial* (Indianapolis: Bedeutungswandel Press, 1995); Jennifer Caps' *Delial, Beatrice, and Dulcinea* (Englewood Cliffs, N.J.: Thumos Inc., 1996); Lester Breman's "Tis but a Name" in *Ebony,* no. 6, May 1994, p. 76; and Tab Fulrest's *Ancient Devotions* (Berkeley: University of California Press, 1995).

left—Karen and the children a mere blur racing down the staircase, the pointillism of their pets' paw prints caught on the dew covered lawn, or the house itself, an indefinite shimmer, sitting quietly on the corner of Succoth and Ash Tree Lane, bathed in afternoon light.

III

It is no accident that the photographer
becomes a photographer any more than
the lion tamer becomes a lion tamer.

— Dorothea Lange

וַיֹּאמֶר מֹשֶׁה אֶל־הָאֱלֹהִים מִי אָנֹכִי כִּי אֵלֵךְ אֶל־פַּרְעֹה
וְכִי אוֹצִיא אֶת־בְּנֵי יִשְׂרָאֵל מִמִּצְרָיִם׃

— Exodus 3. 11[24]

Why Navidson? Why not someone else?

When the great Florentine howls, "*Ma io perchè venirvi? o chi 'l concede?/ Io non Enëa, io non Paulo sono,*"[25] Homer's rival calls him a

---

[24]"But Moses said to God, 'Who am I that I should go to Pharaoh and free the Israelites from Egypt?' " — Ed.

[25]Dante again. Again translated by Sinclair. Canto II; lines 31-32: "But I, why should I go there, and who grants it? I am not Aeneas; I am not Paul."

A question I'm often asking myself these days. Though not the Aeneas/Paul part.

The simple answer I know: Lude woke me up at three in the morning to check out some dead guy's stuff.

Of course, it's not really all that simple. Typically when Lude calls me late at night it's because there's some party he wants to hit. He's the kind of guy who thinks sublime is something you choke on after a shot of tequila. Maybe he's right.

Not that this matters, someone once told me Lude's real name is Harry, maybe he did, though no one I know has ever called him that.

Lude knows every bar, club and gatekeeper at every bar and club. Hollywood has always been mother's milk to Lude. Mother's tongue. Whatever. Unlike me, he never needs to translate, interpret or learn in LA. He knows. He knows the drinks, the addresses and most important of all he can usually tell the difference between the women who are out to talk and those out to do something a little more interesting which always interests Lude.

Despite a nose that others have described as a bee-battered, Lude's always surrounded by very attractive women which is pretty much the norm for hair stylists—and photographers—especially if they're good and Lude is that. Beautiful women are always drawn to men they think will keep them beautiful.

During the past two years, he and I have spent a good deal of time wandering all over this odd city. We both thrive in the late hours, appreciate its sad taste and never get in the way of each other's dreams, even though Lude just wants more money, better parties and prettier girls and I want something else. I'm not even sure what to call it anymore except I know it feels roomy and it's drenched in sunlight and it's weightless and I know it's not cheap.

Probably not even real.

Who can guess why Lude and I have ended up friends. I think it's mainly because he recognizes that I'm game for any mis-step he has in mind and he enjoys the company. Of course publicly, Lude likes to throw me plenty of props, invariably focusing on the disjointed life I've led. He's still impressed—and in turn likes to impress others—with the fact that at the age of thirteen I went to work in Alaska and by the time I was eighteen had already slept in a whorehouse in Rome. Most of all though he loves the stories. Especially the way I tell them to the girls we meet. (I already got into that a little with the whole riff on boxing and Birds of Paradise and some guy named Punching Bag.) But they're only stories, the way I tell them I mean. I actually have a whole bunch.

Take the scars for instance.

There are a number of variations on that one. The most popular is my two year stint in a Japanese Martial Arts Cult, made up entirely of Koreans living in Idaho, who on the last day of my initiation into their now-defunct brotherhood made me pick up a scalding metal wok using only my bare forearms. In the past the wok has been heated in a kiln; recently it's been full of red hot coals. The story's an absolute crock of shit, or should I say a wok of shit—sorry; I know, I know I should learn to crawl before I walk; sorry again; I mean for not being sorry the first time or for that matter the second time—but, you see, it's so hard to argue with all those whirls of melted flesh.

"Show them your arms, Johnny" Lude will say, in his most offhand over-the-top manner.

"Aw come on. Well, alright just this once." I roll up my left sleeve and then, taking my time, I roll up the right one.

"He got that in a cult in Indiana."

"Idaho," I correct him. And it goes on from there.

I'm sure most women know it's bull but hey, they're entertained. I also think it's somewhat of a relief not to hear the true story. I mean you look at the horror sweeping all the way up from my wrists to my elbows, and you have to take a deep breath and ask yourself, do I really want to know what happened there? In my experience, most people don't. They usually look away. My stories actually help them look away.

Maybe they even help me look away.

But I guess that's nothing new. We all create stories to protect ourselves.

It's March now. Late March. Three months have gone by since Lude called me up that night. Three months since I dragged away a black, unremarkable, paint spattered trunk, which as I quickly found out was one of those old cedar lined jobbers, built in Utica, NY, special thanks to the C. M. Clapp Company, complete with rusted latches, rotting leather handles and a lifetime of digressions and disappointments.

To date, I've counted over two hundred rejection letters from various literary journals, publishing houses, even a few words of discouragement from prominent professors in east coast universities. No one wanted the old man's words—except me.

coward and orders him to get moving because the powers above have taken a personal interest in his salvation.

For hell's cartographer, the answer is mildly satisfying. For Navidson, however, there is no answer at all. During "Exploration #4" he even asks aloud, "How the fuck did I end up here?" The house responds with resounding silence. No divine attention. Not even an amaurotic guide.

Some have suggested that the horrors Navidson encountered in that house were merely manifestations of his own troubled psyche. Dr. Iben Van Pollit in his book *The Incident* claims the entire house is a physical incarnation of Navidson's psychological pain: "I often wonder how things might have turned out if Will Navidson had, how shall we say, done a little bit of house cleaning."[26]

While Pollit is not alone in asserting that Navidson's psychology profoundly influenced the nature of those rooms and hallways, few believe it conjured up that place. The reason is simple: Navidson was not the first to live in the house and encounter its peril. As the Navidsons' real estate agent Alicia Rosenbaum eventually revealed, the house on Ash Tree Lane has had more than a few occupants, approximately .37 owners every year, most of whom were traumatized in some way. Considering the house was supposedly built back in 1720, quite a few people have slept and suffered within those walls. If the house were indeed the product of psychological agonies, it would have to be the collective product of every inhabitant's agonies.

It is no great coincidence then that eventually someone with a camera and a zest for the dangerous would show up at this Mead Hall and confront

---

What can I say, I'm a sucker for abandoned stuff, misplaced stuff, forgotten stuff, any old stuff which despite the light of progress and all that, still vanishes every day like shadows at noon, goings unheralded, passings unmourned, well, you get the drift.

As a counselor once told me—a Counselor For Disaffected Youth, I might add: "You like that crap because it reminds you of you." Couldn't of said it better or put it more bluntly. Don't even disagree with it either. Seems pretty dead on and probably has everything to do with the fact that when I was ten my father died and almost nine years later my crazy Shakespearean mother followed him, a story I've already lived and really don't need to retell here.

Still for whatever reason, and this my Counselor For Disaffected Youth could never explain, accepting his analysis hardly altered the way I felt.

I just glanced over at the trunk. The first time I saw it, I mean when I discovered what was inside, it appalled me. Like I was staring at the old guy's corpse. Now it's just a trunk. Of course, I also remember thinking I was going to toss it by the end of the week. That was before I started reading. Long before I began putting it all together.

You know this is still the simple answer.
I guess the complicated one I don't feel like getting into.

[26]Regrettably, Pollit's proclivity to pun and write jokes frequently detracts from his otherwise lucid analysis. *The Incident* (Chicago: Adlai Publishing, 1995), p. 108, is a remarkable example of brilliant scholarship and exemplary synthesis of research and thought. There are also some pretty good illustrations. Unfortunately almost everything he concludes is wrong.

the terror at the door. Fortunately for audiences everywhere, that someone possessed extraordinary visual talents.

Navidson's troubles may not have created the house but they did ultimately shape the way he faced it.

Navidson's childhood was fairly bleak. His father was a St. Louis salesman who worked for a string of large electronics corporations, shuttling his family around the mid-west every two or three years. He was also an alcoholic and prone toward violent outbursts or disappearing for long periods of time.[27]

Navidson's mother was no better. She soon left them all to pursue a career as an actress and ended up living with a string of not so productive producers. Purportedly in her own words, all she ever wanted to do was "bring down the house." Navidson's father died of congestive heart failure but his mother just vanished. She was last seen in a Los Angeles bar smoking cigarettes and talking about moonlight and why you could find so much of it in Hollywood. Neither Will nor his twin brother Tom ever heard from her again.[28]

Because the enormous narcissism of their parents deprived Will and Tom of suitable role models, both brothers learned to identify with absence. Consequently, even if something beneficial fortuitously entered their lives they immediately treated it as temporary. By the time they were teenagers they were already accustomed to a discontinuous lifestyle marked by constant threats of abandonment and the lack of any emotional stability. Unfortunately, "accustomed to" here is really synonymous with "damaged by."[29]

Perhaps one reason Navidson became so enamored with photography was the way it gave permanence to moments that were often so fleeting.

---

[27]Michelle Nadine Goetz recalls how on one occasion Navidson's father climbed onto the hood of the family's recently purchased car, used a thermos to crack up the windshield, then marched back into the kitchen, picked up a pan full of sizzling pork chops and threw it against the wall. (See the Goetz interview published in *The Denver Post*, May 14, 1986, B-4). Terry Borowska, who used to babysit both brothers, remembers how every so often Navidson's father would vanish, sometimes for up to five weeks at a time, without telling his family where he was going or when he might return. Inevitably when he did come back—typically after midnight, or early in the morning, sitting in his truck, waiting for them to wake up since he had either left his key or lost it—there would be a few days of warmth and reconciliation. Eventually though, Tony Navidson would return to his own moods and his own needs, forcing Will and Tom to realize they were better off just trying to keep clear of their father. (See Borowska's interview published in *The St. Louis Post-Dispatch,* September 27, 1992, D-3, column one.)

[28]A selection of personal interviews with Adam Zobol, Anthony Freed and Anastasia Cullman. September 8-11, 1994.

[29]Rita Mistopolis M.D., in her book *Black Heart, Blue Heart* (Provo, Utah: Brigham Young University Press, 1984), p. 245, describes the seriousness of emotional deprivation:

> It is not difficult to understand how children who have suffered from malnutrition or starvation need food and plenty of care if their bodies are to recover so they can go on to lead normal lives. If, however, the starvation is severe enough, the damage will be permanent and they will suffer physical impairments for the rest of their lives. Likewise, children who are deprived of emotional nurturing require care and love if their sense of security and self-confidence is to be restored. However, if love is minimal and abuse high, the damage will be permanent and the children will suffer *emotional* impairments for the rest of their lives.

Nevertheless, not even ten thousand photographs can secure a world, and so while Navidson may have worked harder, taken greater risks and become increasingly more successful, he was ultimately misled in feeling that his labor could make up for the love he was deprived of as a child and the ultimate sense of security such love bestows.

For this reason, we should again revisit Navidson on his porch, his gaze fixed, his delicate fingers wrapped around a glass of lemonade. "I just thought it would be nice to see how people move into a place and start to inhabit it," he calmly announces. "Settle in, maybe put down roots, interact, hopefully understand each other a little better. Personally, I just want to create a cozy little outpost for me and my family." A pretty innocuous and laconic rumination and yet it contains one particularly nettlesome word.

By definition "outpost" means a base, military or other, which while safe inside functions principally to provide protection from hostile forces found on the outside. This has always seemed a bizarre word to choose to describe a small house in the Virginia countryside,[30] but it does shed some light on why Navidson undertook this project in the first place. More than just snapping a few pictures and recording daily events with a few Hi 8s, Navidson wanted to use images to create an outpost set against the transience of the world. No wonder he found it so impossible to give up his professional occupation. In his mind abandoning photography meant submitting to loss.

Therefore to revisit our first two questions:

Why Navidson?

Considering the practically preadamite history of the house, it was inevitable someone *like* Navidson would eventually enter those rooms.

Why not someone else?

Considering his own history, talent and emotional background, only Navidson could have gone as deep as he did and still have successfully brought that vision back.[31]

---

[30]Keillor Ross in his article "Legal Zoning" for *Atlantic Monthly,* v. 278, September 1996, p. 43, does not wish to discount the possibility of irony: "After all Navidson has just moved from the extremely populated confines of New York City and is now only poking fun at the relative wilderness of this suburb." Ross makes a good point, except for the fact that Navidson is a man who understands the meaning of outpost and his tone seems too straight forward to imply any kind of jest.

[31]Zampanò. This chapter first appeared as "The Matter Of Why" in *LA Weekly*, May 19, 1994.

IV

Faith, sir, as to that matter, I don't believe one half of it myself.

— Diedrich Knickerbocker

In early June of 1990, the Navidsons flew to Seattle for a wedding. When they returned, something in the house had changed. Though they had only been away for four days, the change was enormous. It was not, however, obvious—like for instance a fire, a robbery, or an act of vandalism. Quite the contrary, the horror was atypical. No one could deny there had been an intrusion, but it was so odd no one knew how to respond. On video, we see Navidson acting almost amused while Karen simply draws both hands to her face as if she were about to pray. Their children, Chad and Daisy, just run through it, playing, giggling, completely oblivious to the deeper implications.

What took place amounts to a strange spatial violation which has already been described in a number of ways—namely surprising, unsettling, disturbing but most of all uncanny. In German the word for 'uncanny' is 'unheimlich' which Heidegger in his book *Sein und Zeit* thought worthy of some consideration:

> *Daß die Angst als Grundbefindlichkeit in solcher Weise erschließt, dafür ist weider die alltägliche Daseinsauslegung und Rede der unvoreingenommenste Beleg. Befindlichkeit, so wurde früher gesagt, macht offenbar »wie einem ist«. In der Angst is einem »unheimlich«. Darin kommt zunächst die eigentümliche Unbestimmtheit dessen, wobei sich das Dasein in der Angst befindet, zum Ausdruck: das Nichts und Nirgends. Unheimlichkeit meint aber dabei zugleich das Nichtzuhause-sein. Bei der ersten phänomenalen Anzeige der Grundverfassung des Daseins und der Klärung des existenzialen Sinnes von In-Sein im Unterschied von der kategorialen Bedeutung der »Inwendigkeit« wurde das In-Sein bestimmt als Wohnen bei . . ., Vertrautsein mit . . . Dieser Charakter des In-Seins wurde dann konkreter sichtbar gemach durch die alltägliche Öffentlichkeit des Man, das die beruhigte Selbstsicherheit, das selbstverständliche »Zuhause-sein« in die durchschnittliche Alltäglichkeit des Daseins*

bringt. Die Angst dagegen holt das Dasein aus seinem verfallenden Aufgehen in der »Welt« zurück. Die alltägliche Vertrautheit bricht in sich Zusammen. Das Dasein ist vereinzelt, das jedoch als In-der-Welt-sein. Das In-Sein kommt in den existenzialen »Modus« des Un-zuhause. Nichts anderes meint die Rede von der »Unheimlichkeit.«[32]

---

[32]Declared Martin Heidegger's *Sein und Zeit* (Frankfurt Am Main: Vittorio Klostermann, 1977), p. 250-251.[33]

[33]And here's the English, thanks to John Macquarrie and Edward Robinsons' translation of Heidegger's Being and Time, Harper & Row, 1962, page 233. A real bitch to find:

> In anxiety one feels uncanny. Here the peculiar indefiniteness of that which Dasein finds itself alongside in anxiety, comes proximally to expression: the "nothing and nowhere". But here "uncanniness" also means "not-being-at home." [das Nicht-zuhause-sein]. In our first indication of the phenomenal character of Dasein's basic state and in our clarification of the existential meaning of "Being-in" as distinguished from the categorial signification of 'insideness', Being-in was defined as "residing alongside . . .", "Being-familiar with . . ." This character of Being-in was then brought to view more concretely through the everyday publicness of the "they", which brings tranquilized self-assurance—'Being-at-home', with all its obviousness—into the average everydayness of Dasein. On the other hand, as Dasein falls, anxiety brings it back from its absorption in the 'world'. Everyday familiarity collapses. Dasein has been individualized, but individualized as Being-in-the-world. Being-in enters into the existential 'mode' of the "not-at-home". Nothing else is meant by our talk about 'uncanniness'.

Which only goes to prove the existence of crack back in the early twentieth century. Certainly this geezer must of gotten hung up on a pretty wicked rock habit to start spouting such nonsense. Crazier still, I've just now been wondering if something about this passage may have actually affected me, which I know doesn't exactly follow, especially since that would imply something in it really does make sense, and I just got finished calling it non-sense.

I don't know.

The point is, when I copied down the German a week ago, I was fine. Then last night I found the translation and this morning, when I went into work, I didn't feel at all myself. It's probably just a coincidence—I mean that there's some kind of connection between my state of mind and The Navidson Record or even a few arcane sentences on existence penned by a former Nazi tweaking on who knows what. More than likely, it's something entirely else, the real root lying in my already strange mood fluctuations, though I guess those are pretty recent too, rocking back and forth between wishful thinking and some private agony until the bar breaks. I've no fucking clue.

das Nicht-zuhause-sein
[not-being-at-home.]
That part's definitely true.

These days, I'm an apprentice at a tattoo shop on Sunset. I answer phones, schedule consultations and clean up. Any idiot could handle it. In fact the job's reserved for idiots. This afternoon though, how do I explain it?, something's really off. I'm off. I can't do a fucking thing. I just keep staring at all the ink we have, that wild variety of color, everything from rootbeer, midnight blue and cochineal to mauve, light doe, lilac, south sea green, maize, even pelican black, all lined up in these plastic caps, like tiny transparent thimbles—and needles too, my eyes catching on all those carefully preserved points and we have hundreds, mostly #12 sharps, many singles, though plenty in two, three, four, five, six and seven needle groups, even a fourteen round shader.

It depends on what you need.

I don't know what I need but for no apparent reason I'm going terribly south. Nothing has happened, absolutely nothing, but I'm still having problems breathing. The air in the Shop is admittedly thick with the steady smell of sweat, isopropyl alcohol, Benz-all, all that solution for the ultrasonic cleaner, even solder and flux, but that's not it either.

Of course no one notices. My boss, a retinue of his friends, some new inductee who's just put down $150 for a rose, keep up the chatter, pretty loud chatter too, though never quite enough to drown out the most important sound of all: the single, insistent buzz of an original "J" tattoo machine logging yet another hundred stabs a minute in the dimple of some chunky ass.

I get a glass of water. I walk out into the hallway. That's a mistake. I should of stayed near people. The comfort of company and all that. Instead I'm alone, running through a quick mental check list: food poisoning? (stomach's fine) withdrawals? (haven't been on a gak or Ecstasy diet for several months, and while I didn't smoke any pot this morning—my usual ritual—I know THC doesn't create any lasting physical dependencies). And then out of the be-fucking-lue, everything gets substantially darker. Not pitch black mind you. Not even power failure black. More like a cloud passing over the sun. Make that a storm. Though there is no storm. No clouds. It's a bright day and anyway I'm inside.

I wish that had been all. Just a slight decrease in illumination and a little breathing difficulty. Could still blame that on a blown fuse or some aberrant drug related flashback. But then my nostrils flare with the scent of something bitter & foul, something inhuman, reeking with so much rot & years, telling me in the language of nausea that I'm not alone.

Something's behind me.

Of course, I deny it.

It's impossible to deny.

I wanna puke.

To get a better idea try this: focus on these words, and whatever you do don't let your eyes wander past the perimeter of this page. Now imagine just beyond your peripheral vision, maybe behind you, maybe to the side of you, maybe even in front of you, but right where you can't see it, something is quietly closing in on you, so quiet in fact you can only hear it as silence. Find those pockets without sound. That's where it is. Right at this moment. But don't look. Keep your eyes here. Now take a deep breath. Go ahead take an even deeper one. Only this time as you start to exhale try to imagine how fast it will happen, how hard it's gonna hit you, how many times it will stab your jugular with its teeth or are they nails?, don't worry, that particular detail doesn't matter, because before you have time to even process that you should be moving, you should be running, you should at the very least be flinging up your arms—you sure as hell should be getting rid of this book—you won't have time to even scream.

Don't look.

I didn't.

Of course I looked.

I looked so fucking fast I should of ended up wearing one of those neck braces for whiplash.

My hands had gone all clammy. My face was burning up. Who knows how much adrenaline had just been dumped into my system. Before I turned, it felt exactly as if in fact I had turned and at that instant caught sight of some tremendous beast crouched off in the shadows, muscles a twitch from firing its great mass forward, ragged claws slowly extending, digging into the linoleum, even as its eyes are dilating, beyond the point of reason, completely obliterating the iris, and by that widening fire, the glowing furnace of witness, a camera lucida, with me in silhouette, like some silly Hand shadow twitching about upside down, is that right?, or am I getting confused?, either way registering at last the sign it must have been waiting for: my own recognition of exactly what has been awaiting me all along—except that when I finally do turn, jerking around like the scared-shitless shit-for-brains I am, I discover only a deserted corridor, or was it merely a recently deserted corridor?, this thing, whatever it had been, obviously beyond the grasp of my imagination or for that matter my emotions, having departed into alcoves of darkness, seeping into corners & floors, cracks & outlets, gone even to the walls. Lights now normal. The smell history. Though my fingers still tremble and I've yet to stop choking on large irregular gulps of air, as I keep spinning around like a stupid top spinning around on top of nothing, looking everywhere, even though there's absolutely nothing, nothing anywhere.

I actually thought I was going to fall, and then just as abruptly as I'd been possessed by this fear, it left me and I fell back into control.

When I re-enter the Shop things are still askew but they at least seem manageable.

The phone has been ringing. Nine times and counting, my boss announces. He's clearly annoyed. More annoyed when I express some surprise over his ability to count that high.

I pick up before he can start yammering at me about my attitude.

The call's for me. Lude's on a pay phone in the valley with important info. Apparently, there's some significant doings at some significant club. He tells me he can guest list my boss and any cohorts I deem worthy. Sure, I say, but I'm still shaken and quickly lose hold of the details when I realize I've just forgotten something else as well, something very important, which by the time I hang up, no matter how hard I try, I can no longer remember what I'd meant to remember when whatever it was had first entered my head.

Or had it?

Maybe it hadn't entered my head at all. Maybe it had just brushed past me, like someone easing by in a dark room, the face lost in shadow,

Nevertheless regardless of how extensive his analysis is here, Heidegger still fails to point out that *unheimlich* when used as an adverb means "dreadfully," "awfully," "heaps of," and "an awful lot of." Largeness has always been a condition of the weird and unsafe; it is overwhelming, too much or too big. Thus that which is uncanny or *unheimlich* is neither homey nor protective, nor comforting nor familiar. It is alien, exposed, and unsettling, or in other words, the perfect description of the house on Ash Tree Lane.

In their absence, the Navidsons' home had become something else, and while not exactly sinister or even threatening, the change still destroyed any sense of security or well-being.

Upstairs, in the master bedroom, we discover along with Will and Karen a plain, white door with a glass knob. It does not, however, open into the children's room but into a space resembling a walk-in closet. However unlike other closets in the house, this one lacks outlets, sockets, switches, shelves, a rod on which to hang things, or even some decorative molding. Instead, the walls are perfectly smooth and almost pure black—'almost' because there is a slightly grey quality to the surface. The space cannot be more than five feet wide and at most four feet long. On the opposite end, a second door, identical to the first one opens up into the children's bedroom.

Navidson immediately asks whether or not they overlooked the room. This seems ridiculous at first until one considers how the impact of such an implausible piece of reality could force anyone to question their own perceptions. Karen, however, manages to dig up some photos which clearly show a bedroom wall without a door.

The next question is whether or not someone could have broken in and in four days constructed the peculiar addition. Improbable, to say the least.

Their final thought is that someone came in and uncovered it. Just installed two doors. But why? And for that matter, to quote Rilke, *Wer?*[34]

Navidson does check the Hi 8s but discovers that the motion sensors were never triggered. Only their exit and re-entrance exists on tape. Virtually a week seamlessly elided, showing us the family as they depart from a house without that strange interior space present only to return a fraction of a second later to find it already in place, almost as if it had been there all along.

---

my thoughts lost in another conversation, though something in her movement or perfume is disturbingly familiar, though how familiar is impossible to tell because by the time I realize she's someone I should know she's already gone, deep into the din, beyond the bar, taking with her any chance of recognition. Though she hasn't left. She's still there. Embracing shadows.

Is that it?

Had I been thinking of a woman?

I don't know.

I hope it doesn't matter.

I have a terrifying feeling it does.

[34]Neatly translated as "Who?" which I happened to find in this poem "Orpheus, Eurydice, Hermes." The book's called The Selected Poetry of Rainer Maria Rilke, edited and translated by Stephen Mitchell. 1989. See page 53, Vintage International.

Since the discovery occurred in the evening, the Navidsons' inquiry must wait until morning. And so while Chad and Daisy sleep, we watch Karen and Will suffer through a restless night. Hillary, their one year old Siberian husky, and Mallory, their tabby cat, lie on either side of the 24″ Sony television unperturbed by the new closet or the flicker from the tube or the drone from the speakers—Letterman, new revelations regarding the Iran-Contra affair, reruns, the traffic of information assuring everyone that the rest of the world is still out there, continuing on as usual, even if two new doors now stand open, providing a view across a new space of darkness, from parent's room to children's room, where a tiny nightlight of the Star Ship Enterprise burns like some North Star.

It is a beautiful shot. In fact, the composition and elegant balance of colours, not to mention the lush contrast of lights and darks, are so exquisite they temporarily distract us from any questions concerning the house or events unfolding there. It seems a perfect example of Navidson's unparalleled talent and illustrates why few, if any, could have accomplished what he did, especially toward the end.

The following day both Karen and Will pursue the most rational course: they acquire the architectural blueprints from their local real estate office. As might have been expected, these blueprints are not actual building plans but were drawn up in 1981 when former owners sought permission from the town's zoning board to construct an ell. The ell, however, was ultimately never built as the owners soon sold the property, claiming they needed something "a little smaller." Though the designs, as they appear on screen, do not show a room or closet, they do confirm the existence of a strange crawl space, roughly four feet wide, running between both bedrooms.[35]

Alicia Rosenbaum, the real estate agent responsible for selling the Navidsons the house, gives the camera a bewildered shrug when Karen asks if she has any idea who could be responsible for "this outrage." Unable to say anything useful, Mrs. Rosenbaum finally asks if they want to call the police, which amusingly enough they do.

That afternoon, two officers arrive, examine the closet and try to hide the fact that *this* has to be the weirdest call they have ever made. As Sheriff Axnard says, "We'll file a report but other than that, well I don't know what more we can do. Better I guess t'have been a victim of a crazy carpenter than some robber" which even strikes Karen and Navidson as a little funny.

With all obvious options exhausted, Navidson returns to the building plans. At first this seems pretty innocent until he gets out a measuring tape. Idly at first, he starts comparing the dimensions indicated in the plans with those he personally takes. Very soon he realizes not everything adds up. Something, in fact, is very wrong. Navidson repeatedly tacks back and forth from his 25′ Stanley Power Lock to the cold blue pages spread out on his bed, until he finally mutters aloud: "This better be a case of bad math."

An incongruous cut presents us with the title card: **1/4″**

Outside the house, Navidson climbs up a ladder to the second story. Not an easy ascent he casually confesses to us, explaining how a troublesome skin condition he has had since childhood has recently begun to flare up around his toes. Wincing slightly at what we can assume is at least moderate pain, he reaches the top rung where using a 100′ Empire

[35] In Appendix II-A, Mr. Truant provides a sketch of this floor plan on the back of an envelope. — Ed.

fiberglass tape with a hand crank, he proceeds to measure the distance from the far end of the master bedroom to the far end of the children's bedroom. The total comes to 32′ 9 3/4″ which the house plans corroborate—plus or minus an inch. The puzzling part comes when Navidson measures the internal space. He carefully notes the length of the new area, the length of both bedrooms and then factors in the width of all the walls. The result is anything but comforting. In fact it is impossible.

32′ 10″ exactly.

The width of the house inside would appear to exceed the width of the house as measured from the outside by 1/4″.

Certain that he has miscalculated, Navidson drills through the outer walls to measure their width precisely. Finally, with Karen's help, he fastens the end of some fishing line to the edge of the outer wall, runs it through the drilled hole, stretches it across the master bedroom, the new space, the children's bedroom and then runs it through a hole drilled through the opposite wall. He double checks his work, makes sure the line is straight, level and taut and then marks it. The measurement is still the same.

32′ 10″ exactly.

Using the same line, Navidson goes outside, stretches the fishing line from one side of the house to the other only to find it is a quarter of an inch too long.

Exactly.

The impossible is one thing when considered as a purely intellectual conceit. After all, it is not so large a problem when one can puzzle over an Escher print and then close the book. It is quite another thing when one faces a physical reality the mind and body cannot accept.

Karen refuses the knowledge. A reluctant Eve who prefers tangerines to apples. "I don't care," she tells Navidson. "Stop drilling holes in my walls." Undeterred, Navidson continues his quest, even though repeated attempts at measuring the house continue to reveal the quarter-inch anomaly. Karen gets quieter and quieter, Navidson's mood darkens, and responding like finely tuned weathervanes the children react to the change in parental weather by hiding in other parts of the house. Frustration edges into Navidson's voice. No matter how hard he tries—and Navidson tries six consecutive times in six consecutive segments—he cannot slaughter that tiny sliver of space. Another night passes and that quarter of an inch still survives.

Where narratives in film and fiction often rely on virtually immediate reactions, reality is far more insistent and infinitely (literally) more patient. Just as insidious poisons in the water table can take years before their effects are felt, the consequences of the impossible are likewise not so instantly apparent.

Morning means orange juice, *The New York Times*, NPR, a squabble over the children's right to eat sugared cereal. The dishwasher moans, the toaster pops. We watch Karen scan the classifieds as Navidson toys with his coffee. He adds sugar, milk, stirs it all up, stirs it again, and then as an afterthought adds more sugar, a little more milk. The liquid rises to the rim and then by a fraction exceeds even this limit. Only it does not spill. It holds—a bulge of coffee arcing tragically over china, preserved by the physics of surface tension, rhyme to some unspeakable magic, though as everyone knows, coffee miracles never last long. The morning wake-up call wobbles, splits, and then abruptly slips over the edge, now a Nile of caffeine wending past glass and politics until there is nothing more than a brown blot on the morning paper.[36]

When Navidson looks up Karen is watching him.

"I called Tom," he tells her.

She understands him well enough not to say a thing.

"He knows I'm insane," he continues. "And besides he builds houses for a living."

"Did you talk to him?" she carefully asks.

"Left a message."

The next card simply reads: **Tom**.

Tom is Will Navidson's fraternal twin brother. Neither one has said much to the other in over eight years. "Navy's successful, Tom's not," Karen explains in the film. "There's been a lot of resentment over the years. I guess it's always been there, except when they lived at home. It was different then. They kind of looked after each other more."

Two days later, Tom arrives. Karen greets him with a big hug and a Hi 8. He is an affable, overweight giant of a man who has an innate ability to amuse. The children immediately take to him. They love his laugh, not to mention his McDonalds french fries.

" My own brother who I haven't talked to in years calls me up at four in the morning and tells me he needs my tools. Go figure."

"That means you're family" Karen says happily, leading the way to Navidson's study where she has already set out clean towels and made up the hideaway.

---

[36]Easily that whole bit from "coffee arcing tragically" down to "the mourning paper" could have been cut. You wouldn't of noticed the absence. I probably wouldn't of either. But that doesn't change the fact that I can't do it. Get rid of it, I mean. What's gained in economy doesn't really seem to make up for what you lose of Zampanò, the old man himself, coming a little more into focus, especially where digressions like these are concerned.

I can't tell you why exactly but more and more these days I'm struck by the fact that everything Zampanò had is really gone, including the bowl of betel nuts left on his mantle or the battered shotgun bearing the initials RLB under his bed—Flaze appropriated that goody; the shotgun, not the bed—or even the curiously preserved bud of a white rose hidden in the drawer of his nightstand. By now his apartment has been scrubbed with Clorox, repainted, probably rented out to someone else. His body's either molding in the ground or reduced to ash. Nothing else remains of him but this.

So you see from my perspective, having to decide between old man Z and his story is an artificial, maybe even dangerous choice, and one I'm obviously not comfortable making. The way I figure it, if there's something you find irksome—go ahead and skip it. I couldn't care less how you read any of this. His wandering passages are staying, along with all his oddly canted phrases and even some warped bits in the plot. There's just too much at stake. It may be the wrong decision, but fuck it, it's mine.

Zampanò himself probably would of insisted on corrections and edits, he was his own harshest critic, but I've come to believe errors, especially written errors, are often the only markers left by a solitary life: to sacrifice them is to lose the angles of personality, the riddle of a soul. In this case a very old soul. A very old riddle.

"Usually when you want a level you ask a neighbor or go to the hardware store. Count on Will Navidson to call Lowell, Massachusetts. Where is he?"

As it turns out Navidson has gone to the hardware store to pick up a few items.

In the film, Tom and Navidson's first encounter has almost nothing to do with each other. Instead of addressing any interpersonal issues, we find them both huddled over a Cowley level mirror transit, alternately taking turns peering across the house, the line of sight floating a few feet above the floor, occasionally interrupted when Hillary or Mallory in some keystone chase race around the children's beds. Tom believes they will account for the quarter inch discrepancy with a perfectly level measurement.

Later on, out in the backyard, Tom lights up a joint of marijuana. The drug clearly bothers Navidson but he says nothing. Tom knows his brother disapproves but refuses to alter his behavior. Based on their body language and the way both of them avoid looking directly at each other, not to speak of the space between their words, the last eight years continues to haunt them.

"Hey, at least I'm an acquaintance of Bill's now" Tom finally says, exhaling a thin stream of smoke. "Not a drop of booze in over two years."

At first glance, it seems hard to believe these two men are even related let alone brothers. Tom is content if there happens to be a game on and a soft place from which to watch it. Navidson works out every day, devours volumes of esoteric criticism, and constantly attaches the world around him to one thing: photography. Tom gets by, Navidson succeeds. Tom just wants to be, Navidson must become. And yet despite such obvious differences, anyone who looks past Tom's wide grin and considers his eyes will find surprisingly deep pools of sorrow. Which is how we know they are brothers, because like Tom, Navidson's eyes share the same water.

Either way the moment and opportunity for some kind of fraternal healing disappears when Tom makes an important discovery: Navidson was wrong. The interior of the house exceeds the exterior not by 1/4″ but by 5/16″.

No matter how many legal pads, napkins, or newspaper margins they fill with notes or equations, they cannot account for that fraction. One incontrovertible fact stands in their way: the exterior measurement *must* equal the internal measurement. Physics depends on a universe infinitely centred on an equal sign. As science writer and sometime theologian David Conte wrote: "God for all intents and purposes is an equal sign, and at least up until now, something humanity has always been able to believe in is that the universe adds up."[37]

On this point, both brothers agree. The problem must lie with their measuring techniques or with some unseen mitigating factor: air temperature, mis-calibrated instruments, warped floors, something, anything. But after a day and a half passes without a solution, they both decide to look for help. Tom calls Lowell and postpones his construction obligations. Navidson calls an old friend who teaches engineering at UVA.

[37]Look at David Conte's "All Thing Being Equal" in *Maclean's*, v. 107, n. 14, 1994, p. 102. Also see Martin Gardner's "The Vanishing Area Paradox" which appeared in his "Mathematical Games" column in *Scientific America*, May 1961.

Early the following morning, both brothers head off for Charlottesville.

Navidson is not the only one who knows people in the vicinity. Karen's friend Audrie McCullogh drives down from Washington, D.C. to catch up and help construct some bookshelves. Thus as Will and Tom set out to find an answer, two old friends put an enigma on hold, stir up some vodka tonics, and enjoy the rhythm of working with brackets and pine.

Edith Skourja has written an impressive forty page essay entitled *Riddles Without* on this one episode. While most of it focuses on what Skourja refers to as "the political posture" of both women—Karen as ex-model; Audrie as travel agent—one particular passage yields an elegant perspective into the whys and ways people confront unanswered questions:

> Riddles: they either delight or torment. Their delight lies in solutions. Answers provide bright moments of comprehension perfectly suited for children who still inhabit a world where solutions are readily available. Implicit in the riddle's form is a promise that the rest of the world resolves just as easily. And so riddles comfort the child's mind which spins wildly before the onslaught of so much information and so many subsequent questions.
>
> The adult world, however, produces riddles of a different variety. They do not have answers and are often called enigmas or paradoxes. Still the old hint of the riddle's form corrupts these questions by re-echoing the most fundamental lesson: there must be an answer. From there comes torment.
>
> It is not uncharacteristic to encounter adults who detest riddles. A variety of reasons may lie behind their reaction but a significant one is the rejection of the adolescent belief in answers. These adults are often the same ones who say "grow up" and "face the facts." They are offended by the incongruities of yesterday's riddles with answers when compared to today's riddles without.
>
> It is beneficial to consider the origins of "riddle." The Old English *rǣdelse* means "opinion, conjure" which is related to the Old English *rǣdon* "to interpret" in turn belonging to the same etymological history of "read." "Riddling" is an offshoot of "reading" calling to mind the participatory nature of that act—to interpret—which is all the adult world has left when faced with the unsolvable.
>
> "To read" actually comes from the Latin *reri* "to calculate, to think" which is not only the progenitor of "read" but of "reason" as well, both of which hail from the Greek *arariskein* "to fit." Aside from giving us "reason," *arariskein* also gives us an unlikely sibling, Latin *arma* meaning "weapons." It seems that "to fit" the world or to make sense of it requires either reason or arms. Charmingly enough Karen

> Green and Audrie McCullogh "fit it" with a bookshelf.
>
> As we all know, both reason and weapons will eventually be resorted to. At least though for now—before the explorations, before the bloodshed—a drill, a hammer, and a Phillips screwdriver suffice.
>
> Karen refers to her books as her "newly found day to day comfort." By assembling a stronghold for them, she provides a pleasant balance between the known and the unknown. Here stands one warm, solid, and colorful wall of volume after volume of history, poetry, photo albums, and pulp. And though irony eventually subsumes this moment, for now at least it remains uncommented upon and thus wholly innocent. Karen simply removes a photo album, as anyone might do, and causes all the books to fall like dominos along the length of the shelf. However instead of tumbling to the floor, they are soundly stopped, eliciting a smile from both women and this profound remark by Karen: "No better book ends than two walls."
>
> Lessons from a library.[38]

Skourja's analysis, especially concerning the inherent innocence of Karen's project, sheds some light on the value of patience.

Walter Joseph Adeltine argues that Skourja forms a dishonest partnership with the shelf building segment: "Riddle me this—Riddle me that—Is all elegant crap. This is not a confrontation with the unknown but a flat-out case of denial."[39] What Adeltine himself denies is the need to face some problems with patience, to wait instead of bumble, or as Tolstoy wrote: "*Dans le doute, mon cher . . . abstiens-toi.*"[40]

Gibbons when working on *The Decline and Fall of the Roman Empire* would go on long walks before sitting down to write. Walking was a time to organize his thoughts, focus and relax. Karen's shelf building serves the same purpose as Gibbon's retreats outside. Maturity, one discovers, has everything to do with the acceptance of "not knowing." Of course not knowing hardly prevents the approaching chaos.

Tum vero omne mihi visum considere in ignis Ilium:
Delenda est Carthago.[41]

---

[38]Edith Skourja's "Riddles Without" in *Riddles Within*, ed. Amon Whitten (Chicago: Sphinx Press, 1994), p. 17-57.

[39]Walter Joseph Adeltine "Crap," *New Perspectives Quarterly*, v. 11, winter 1994, p. 30.

[40]Something like "When in doubt, friend, do nothing." War and Peace by Leo Tolstoy, 1982, Penguin Classics in New York, p. 885.

[41]Know what, Latin's way out of my league. I can find people who speak Spanish, French, Hebrew, Italian and even German but the Roman tongue's not exactly thriving in the streets of LA.

A girl named Amber Rightacre suggested it might have something to do with the destruction of Carthage.[42] She's the one who translated and sourced the previous Tolstoy phrase. I've actually never read War and Peace but she had, and get this, she read it to Zampanò.

I guess you might say in a round about way the old man introduced us.

Anyway since that episode in the tattoo shop, I haven't gone out as much, though to tell you the truth I'm no longer convinced anything happened. I keep cornering myself with questions: did I really experience some sort of decapacitating seizure, I mean in-? Or did I invent it? Maybe I just got a little creative with a residual hangover or a stupid head rush?

Whatever the truth is, I've been spending more and more time riddling through Zampanò's bits—riddling also means sifting; as in passing corn, gravel or cinders through a coarse sieve; a certain coed taught me that. Not only have I found journals packed with bibliographies and snaking etymologies and strange little, I don't know what you'd call them, aphorisms??? epiphanies???, I also came across this notepad crammed with names and telephone numbers. Zampanò's readers. Easily over a hundred of them, though as I quickly discovered more than a few of the numbers are now defunct and very few of the names have last names and for whatever reason those that do are unlisted. I left a couple of messages on some machines and then somewhere on page three, Ms. Rightacre picked up. I told her about my inheritance and she immediately agreed to meet me for a drink.

Amber, it turns out, was quite a number; a quarter French and a quarter Native American with naturally black hair, dark blue eyes and a beautiful belly, long and flat and thin, with a slender twine of silver piercing her navel. A barbed wire tattoo in blue & red encircled her ankle. Whether Zampanò knew it or not, she was a sight I'm sure he was sorry to miss.

"He loved to brag about how uneducated he was," Amber told me. "'I never even went to high school' he would say. "'Good, that makes me smarter than you.' We talked like that a little, but most of the time, I just read to him. He insisted on Tolstoy. Said I read Tolstoy better than anyone else. I think that was mainly because I could manage the French passages okay, my Canadian background and all."

After a few more drinks, we ambled over to the Viper. Lude was hanging out at the door and walked us in. Much to my surprise, Amber grabbed my arm as we headed up the stairs. This thing we shared in common seemed to have created a surprisingly intense bond. Lude listened to us for a while, hastening to add at every pause that he was the one who'd found the damn thing, in fact he was the one who'd called me, he'd even seen Amber around his building a few times, but because he hadn't taken the time to read any of the text he could never address the particulars of our conversation. Amber and I were lost to a different world, a deeper history. Lude knew the play. He ordered a drink on my tab and went in search of other entertainment.

When I eventually got around to asking Amber to describe Zampanò, she just called him "imperceivable and alone, though not I think so lonely." Then the first band came on and we stopped talking. Afterwards, Amber was the one who resumed the conversation, stepping a little closer, her elbow grazing mine. "I never got the idea he had a family," she continued. "I asked him once—and I remember this very clearly—I asked him if he had any children. He said he didn't have any children any more. Then he added: 'Of course, you're all my children,' which was strange since I was the only one there. But the way he looked at me with those blank eyes—" she shuddered and quickly folded her arms as if she'd just gotten cold. "It was like that tiny place of his was suddenly full of faces and he could see them all, even speak to them.

It made me real uneasy, like I was surrounded by ghosts. Do you believe in ghosts?"

I told her I didn't know.

She smiled.

"I'm a Virgo, what about you?"

We ordered another round of drinks, the next band came up, but we didn't stay to hear them finish. As we walked to her place—it turned out she lived nearby, right above Sunset Plaza in fact—she kept returning to the old man, a trace of her own obsession mingling with the drift of her thoughts.

"So not so lonely," she murmured. "I mean with all those ghosts, me and his other children, whoever they were, though actually, hmmm I forgot about this, I don't know why, I mean it was why I finally stopped going over there. When he blinked, his eyelids, this is kind of weird, but they stayed closed a little bit longer than a blink, like he was consciously closing them, or about to sleep, and I always wondered for a fraction of a second if they would ever open again. Maybe they wouldn't, maybe he was going to go to sleep or maybe even die, and looking at his face then, so serene and peaceful made me sad, and I guess I take back what I said before, because with his eyes closed he didn't look alone, then he looked lonely, terribly lonely, and that made me feel real sad and it made me feel lonely too. I stopped going there after a while. But you know what, not visiting him made me feel guilty. I think I still feel guilty about just dropping out on him like that."

We stopped talking about Zampanò then. She paged her friend Christina who took less than twenty minutes to come over. There were no introductions. We just sat down on the floor and snorted lines of coke off a CD case, gulped down a bottle of wine and then used it to play spin the bottle. They kissed each other first, then they both kissed me, and then we forgot about the bottle, and I even managed to forget about Zampanò, about this, and about how much that attack in the tattoo shop had put me on edge. Two kisses in one kiss was all it took, a comfort, a warmth, perhaps temporary, perhaps false, but reassuring nonetheless, and mine, and theirs, ours, all three of us giggling, insane giggles and laughter with still more kisses on the way, and I remember a brief instant then, out of the blue, when I suddenly glimpsed my own father, a rare but oddly peaceful recollection, as if he actually approved of my play in the way he himself had always laughed and played, always laughing, surrendering to its ease, especially when he soared in great updrafts of light, burning off distant plateaus of bistre & sage, throwing him up like an angel, high above the red earth, deep into the sparkling blank, the tender sky that never once let him down, preserving his attachment to youth, propriety and kindness, his plane almost, but never quite, outracing his whoops of joy, trailing him in his sudden turn to the wind, followed then by a near vertical climb up to the angles of the sun, and I was barely eight and still with him and yes, that <u>was</u> the thought that flickered madly through me, a brief instant of communion, possessing me with warmth and ageless ease, causing me to smile again and relax as if memory alone could lift the heart like the wind lifts a wing, and so I renewed my kisses with even greater enthusiasm, caressing and in turn devouring their dark lips, dark with wine and fleeting love, an ancient memory love had promised but finally never gave, until there were too many kisses to count or remember, and the memory of love proved not love at all and needed a replacement, which our bodies found, and then the giggles subsided, and the laughter dimmed, and darkness enfolded all of us and we gave away our childhood for nothing and we died and condoms littered the floor and Christina

Karen's project is one mechanism against the uncanny or that which is "un-home-like." She remains watchful and willing to let the bizarre dimensions of her house gestate within her. She challenges its irregularity by introducing normalcy: her friend's presence, bookshelves, peaceful conversation. In this respect, Karen acts as the quintessential gatherer. She keeps close to the homestead and while she may not forage for berries and mushrooms she does accumulate tiny bits of sense.

Navidson and Tom, on the other hand, are classic hunters. They select weapons (tools; reason) and they track their prey (a solution). Billy Reston is the one they hope will help them achieve their goal. He is a gruff man, frequently caustic and more like a drill sergeant than a tenured professor. He is also a paraplegic who has spent almost half his life in an aluminum wheelchair. Navidson was barely twenty-seven when he first met Reston. Actually it was a photograph that brought them together. Navidson had been on assignment in India, taking pictures of trains, rail workers, engineers, whatever caught his attention. The piece was supposed to capture the clamor of industry outside of Hyderabad. What ended up plastered on the pages of more than a few newspapers, however, was a photograph of a black American engineer desperately trying to out run a falling high voltage wire. The cable had been cut when an inexperienced crane operator had swung wide of a freight car and accidentally collided with an electrical pole. The wood had instantly splintered, tearing in half one of the power cables which descended toward the helpless Billy Reston, spitting sparks, and lashing the air like Nag or Nagaina.[43]

---

threw up in the sink and Amber chuckled a little and kissed me a little more, but in a way that told me it was time to leave.

And so only now, days later, as I give these moments shape here, do I re-encounter what my high briefly withheld; the covering memory permanently hitched to everything preceding it and so prohibiting all of it, those memories, the good ones, no matter how different, how blissful, eclipsed by the jack-knifed trailer across the highway, the tractor truck lodged in the stony ditch off the shoulder, oily smoke billowing up into the night, and hardly deterred by the pin prick drizzle, the fire itself crawling up from the punctured fuel tanks, stripping the paint, melting the tires and blackening the shattered glass, the windshield struck from within, each jagged line telling the story of a broken heart which no ten year old boy should ever have to recollect let alone see, even if it is only in half-tone, the ink, all of it, over and over again, finally gathered on his delicate finger tips, as if by tracing the picture printed in the newspaper, he could in some way retract the details of death, smooth away the cab where the man he saw and loved like a god, agonized and died with no word of his own, illegible or otherwise, no god at all, and so by dissolving the black sky bring back the blue. But he never did. He only wore through one newspaper after another which was when the officials responsible for the custody of parentless children decided something was gravely wrong with him and sent him away, making sure he had no more clippings and all the ink, all that remained of his father, was washed from my hands.

[42]In an effort to keep the translations as literal as possible, both Latin phrases read as follows: "Then in fact all of Troy seemed to me to sink into flames" (Aeneid II, 624) and "Carthage must be destroyed." — Ed.

[43]Nag and Nagaina were the names of the two cobras in Rudyard Kipling's The Jungle Book. Eventually both were defeated by the mongoose Rikki-Tikki-Tavi.

That very photograph hangs on Reston's office wall. It captures the mixture of fear and disbelief on Reston's face as he suddenly finds himself running for his life. One moment he was casually scanning the yard, thinking about lunch, and in the next he was about to die. His stride is stretched, back toes trying to push him out of the way, hands reaching for something, anything, to pull him out of the way. But he is too late. That serpentine shape surrounds him, moving much too fast for any last ditch effort at escape. As Fred de Stabenrath remarked in April 1954, "*Les jeux sont fait. Nous sommes fucked*."[44]

Tom takes a hard look at this remarkable 11 x 14 black and white print. "That was the last time I had legs," Reston tells him. "Right before that ugly snake bit 'em off. I used to hate the picture and then I sort of became grateful for it. Now when anyone walks into my office they don't have to think about asking me how I ended up in this here chariot. They can see for themselves. Thank you Navy. You bastard. Rikki-Tikki-Tavi with a Nikon."

Eventually the chat subsides and the three men get down to business. Reston's response is simple, rational, and exactly what both brothers came to hear: "There's no question the problem's with your equipment. I'd have to check out Tom's stuff myself but I'm willing to bet university money there's something a little outta whack with it. I've got a few things you can borrow: a Stanley Beacon level and a laser distance meter." He grins at Navidson. "The meter's even a Leica. That should put this ghost in the grave fast. But if it doesn't, I'll come out and measure your place myself and I'll charge you for my time too."

Both Will and Tom chuckle, perhaps feeling a little foolish. Reston shakes his head.

"If you ask me Navy, you've got a little too much time on your hands. You'd probably be better off if you just took your family for a nice long drive."

On their way back, Navidson points the Hi 8 toward the darkening horizon.

For a while neither brother says a word.

Will breaks the silence first: "Funny how all it took was a fraction of an inch to get us in a car together."

"Pretty strange."

"Thanks for coming Tom."

"Like there was really a chance I'd say no."

A pause. Again Navidson speaks up.

"I almost wonder if I got tangled up in all this measuring stuff just so I'd have some pretext to call you."

---

[44]Fred de Stabenrath purportedly exclaimed this right before he was ki [xxxxxxxxxxxxxxxxxxxxxxxxx
xxxxxxxxxxxxxxxxxxxxxxxxxxxxxxxxxxxxxxxxxxxxxxxxxxxxxxxxxxxxxxxxxxxxxxxxxxxxxxxx
xxxxxxxxxxxxxxxxxxxxxxxxxxxxxxxxxxxxpart missingxxxxxxxxxxxxxxxxxxxxxxxxxxxxxxxxxxx
xxxxxxxxxxxxxxxxxxxxxxxxxxxxxxxxxxxxxxxxxxxxxxxxxxxxxxxxxxxxxxxxxxxxxxxxxxxxxxxxx
xxxxxxxxxxxxxxxxxxxxxxxxxxxxxxxxxxxxxxxxxxxxxxxxxxxxxxxxxxxxxxxxxxxxxxxxxxxxxxxxx][45]

[45]Zampanò left the rest of this footnote buried beneath a particularly dark spill of ink. At least I'm assuming it's ink. Maybe it's not. Maybe it's something else. But then that's not really important. In some cases, I've managed to recover the lost text (see Chapter Nine). Here, however, I failed. Five lines gone along with the rest of Mr. Stabenrath.

Despite his best efforts, Tom cannot hold back a laugh: "You know I hate to tell you this but there are simpler reasons you could of come up with."

"You're telling me," Navidson says, shaking his head.

Rain starts splashing down on the windshield and lightning cracks across the sky. Another pause follows.

This time, Tom breaks the silence: "Did you hear the one about the guy on the tightrope?"

Navidson grins: "I'm glad to see some things never change."

"Hey this one's true. There was this twenty-five year old guy walking a tightrope across a deep river gorge while half way around the world another twenty-five year old guy was getting a blow job from a seventy year old woman, but get this, at the exact same moment both men were thinking the exact same thought. You know what it was?"

"No clue."

Tom gives his brother a wink.

"Don't look down."

And thus as one storm begins to ravage the Virginias, another one just as easily dissipates and vanishes in a flood of bad jokes and old stories.

When confronting the spatial disparity in the house, Karen set her mind on familiar things while Navidson went in search of a solution. The children, however, just accepted it. They raced through the closet. They played in it. They inhabited it. They denied the paradox by swallowing it whole. Paradox, after all, is two irreconcilable truths. But children do not know the laws of the world well enough yet to fear the ramifications of the irreconcilable. There are certainly no primal associations with spatial anomalies.

Similar to the ingenuous opening sequence of *The Navidson Record*, seeing these two giddy children romp around is an equally unsettling experience, perhaps because their state of naïveté is so appealing to us, even seductive, offering such a simple resolution to an enigma. Unfortunately, denial also means ignoring the possibility of peril.

That possibility, however, seems at least momentarily irrelevant when we cut to Will and Tom hauling Billy Reston's equipment upstairs, the authority of their tools quickly subduing any sense of threat.

Just watching the two brothers use the Stanley Beacon level to establish the distance they will need to measure communicates comfort. When they then turn their attention to the Leica meter it is nearly impossible not to at last expect some kind of resolution to this confounding problem. In fact Tom's crossed fingers as the Class 2 laser finally fires a tiny red dot across the width of the house manages to succinctly represent our own sympathies.

As the results are not immediate, we wait along with the whole family as the internal computer calibrates the dimension. Navidson captures these seconds in 16mm. His Arriflex, already pre-focused and left running, spools in 24 frames per second as Daisy and Chad sit on their beds in the background, Hillary and Mallory linger in the foreground near Tom, while Karen and Audrie stand off to the right near the newly created bookshelves.

Suddenly Navidson lets out a hoot. It appears the discrepancy has finally been eliminated.

Tom peers over his shoulder, "Good-bye Mr. Fraction."

"One more time" Navidson says. "One more time. Just to make sure."

Oddly enough, a slight draft keeps easing one of the closet doors shut. It has an eerie effect because each time the door closes we lose sight of the children.

"Hey would you mind propping that open with something?' Navidson asks his brother.

Tom turns to Karen's shelves and reaches for the largest volume he can find. A novel. Just as with Karen, its removal causes an immediate domino effect. Only this time, as the books topple into each other, the last few do not stop at the wall as they had previously done but fall instead to the floor, revealing at least a foot between the end of the shelf and the plaster.

Tom thinks nothing of it.

"Sorry," he mumbles and leans over to pick up the scattered books.

Which is exactly when Karen screams.

V

Raju welcomed the intrusion—something to relieve the loneliness of the place.

— R. K. Narayan

It is impossible to appreciate the importance of space in *The Navidson Record* without first taking into account the significance of echoes. However, before even beginning a cursory examination of their literal and thematic presence in the film, echoes reverberating within the word itself need to be distinguished.

Generally speaking, echo has two coextensive histories: the mythological one and the scientific one.[46] Each provides a slightly different perspective on the inherent meaning of recurrence, especially when that repetition is imperfect.

To illustrate the multiple resonances found in an echo, the Greeks conjured up the story of a beautiful mountain nymph. Her name was Echo and she made the mistake of helping Zeus succeed in one of his sexual conquests. Hera found out and punished Echo, making it impossible for her to say anything except the last words spoken to her. Soon after, Echo fell in love with Narcissus whose obsession with himself caused her to pine away until only her voice remained. Another lesser known version of this myth has Pan falling in love with Echo. Echo, however, rejects his amorous offers and Pan, being the god of civility and restraint, tears her to pisces, burying all of her except her voice. *Adonta ta melê.*⊕ In both cases, unfulfilled love results in the total negation of Echo's body and the near negation of her voice.[48]

But Echo is an insurgent. Despite the divine constraints imposed upon her, she still manages to subvert the gods' ruling. After all, her repetitions are far from digital, much closer to analog. Echo colours the words with faint traces of sorrow (The Narcissus myth) or accusation (The Pan myth) never present in the original. As Ovid recognized in his *Metamorphoses:*

---

[46]David Eric Katz argues for a third: the epistemological one. Of course, the implication that the current categories of myth and science ignore the reverberation of knowledge itself is not true. Katz's treatment of repetition, however, is still highly rewarding. His list of examples in Table iii are particularly impressive. See *The Third Beside You: An Analysis of the Epistemological Echo* by David Eric Katz (Oxford: Oxford University Press, 1982).

⊕*Adonta ta* . . . = "Her still singing limbs."[47]

[47]`Note that luckily in this chapter, Zampanò penciled many of the translations for these Greek and Latin quotations into the margins. I've gone ahead and turned them into footnotes.`

[48]Ivan Largo Stilets, *Greek Mythology Again* (Boston: Biloquist Press, 1995), p. 343-497; as well as Ovid's *Metamorphoses*, III. 356-410.

Spreta latet silvis pudibundaque frondibus ora protegit et solis ex illo vivit in antris; sed tamen haeret amor crescitque dolore repulsae; extenuant vigiles corpus miserabile curae adducitque cutem macies et in aera sucus corporis omnis abit; vox tantum atque ossa supersunt: vox manet, ossa ferunt lapidis traxisse figuram. Inde latet silvis nulloque in monte videtur, omnibus auditur: sonus est, qui vivit in illa.[P]

To repeat: her voice has life. It possesses a quality not present in the original, revealing how a nymph can return a different and more meaningful story, in spite of telling the same story.[49]

[P]Eloquently translated by Horace Gregory as: "So she was turned away/ To hide her face, her lips, her guilt among the trees,/ Even their leaves, to haunt caves of the forest,/ To feed her love on melancholy sorrow/ Which, sleepless, turned her body to a shade,/ First pale and wrinkled, then a sheet of air,/ Then bones, which some say turned to thin-worn rocks; / And last her voice remained. Vanished in forest,/ Far from her usual walks on hills and valleys,/ She's heard by all who call; her voice has life." *The Metamorphoses* by Ovid. (New York: A Mentor Book, 1958), p. 97.

[49]Literary marvel Miguel de Cervantes set down this compelling passage in his *Don Quixote* (Part One, Chapter Nine) :

> . . . la verdad, cuya madre es la historia, émula del tiempo, depósito de las acciones, testigo de lo pasado, ejemplo y aviso de lo presente, advertencia de lo por venir.[51]

Much later, a yet untried disciple of arms had the rare pleasure of meeting the extraordinary Pierre Menard in a Paris café following the second world war. Reportedly Menard expounded on his distinct distaste for Madelines but never mentioned the passage (and echo of *Don Quixote*) he had penned before the war which had subsequently earned him a fair amount of literary fame:

> . . . la verdad, cuya madre es la historia, émula del tiempo, depósito de las acciones, testigo de lo pasado, ejemplo y aviso de lo presente, advertencia de lo por venir.

This exquisite variation on the passage by the "ingenious layman" is far too dense to unpack here. Suffice it to say Menard's nuances are so fine they are nearly undetectable, though talk with the Framer and you will immediately see how haunted they are by sorrow, accusation, and sarcasm.[50]

[50]Exactly! How the fuck do you write about "exquisite variation" when both passages are exactly the same?

I'm sure the late hour has helped, add to that the dim light in my room, or how poorly I've been sleeping, going to sleep but not really resting, if that's possible, though let me tell you, sitting alone, awake to nothing else but this odd murmuring, like listening to the penitent pray—you know it's a prayer but you miss the words—or better yet listening to a bitter curse, realizing a whole lot wrong's being ushered into the world but still missing the words, me like that, listening in my way by comparing in his way both Spanish fragments, both written out on brown leaves of paper, or no, that's not right, not brown, more like, oh I don't know, yes brown but in the failing light appearing almost colored or the memory of a color, somehow violent, or close to that, or not at all, as I just kept reading both pieces over and over again, trying to detect at least one differing accent or

In his own befuddled way, John Hollander has given the world a beautiful and strange reflection on love and longing. To read his marvelous dialogue on echo[52] is to find its author standing perfectly still in the middle of the sidewalk, eyes wild with a cascade of internal reckonings, lips acting out some unintelligible discourse, inaudible to the numerous students who race by him, noting his mad appearance and quite rightly offering him a wide berth as they escape into someone else's class.[53]

Hollander begins with a virtual catalogue of literal echoes. For example, the Latin "*decem iam annos aetatem trivi in Cicerone*" echoed by the Greek "*one*!"♂ Or "*Musarum studia*" (Latin) described by the echo as "*dia*" (Greek).☿ Or Narcissus' rejection "*Emoriar, quam sit tibi copia*

---

letter, wanting to detect at least one differing accent or letter, getting almost desperate in that pursuit, only to repeatedly discover perfect similitude, though how can that be, right? if it were perfect it wouldn't be similar it would be identical, and you know what? I've lost this sentence, I can't even finish it, don't know how—

Here's the point: the more I focused in on the words the farther I seemed from my room. No sense where either, until all of a sudden along the edges of my tongue, towards the back of my mouth, I started to taste something extremely bitter, almost metallic. I began to gag. I didn't gag, but I was certain I would. Then I got a whiff of that same something awful I'd detected outside of the Shop in the hall. Faint as hell at first until I knew I'd smelled it and then it wasn't faint at all. A whole lot of rot was suddenly packed up my nose, slowly creeping down my throat, closing it off. I started to throw up, watery chunks of vomit flying everywhere, sluicing out of me onto the floor, splashing onto the wall, even onto this. Except I only coughed. I didn't cough. I lightly cleared my throat and then the smell was gone and so was the taste. I was back in my room again, looking around in the dim light, jittery, disoriented but hardly fooled.

I put the fragments back in the trunk. Walked the perimeter of my room. Glass of bourbon. A toke on a blunt. There we go. Bring on the haze. But who am I kidding? I can still see what's happening. My line of defense has not only failed, it failed long ago. Don't ask me to define the line either or why exactly it's needed or even what it stands in defense against. I haven't the foggiest idea.

This much though I'm sure of: I'm alone in hostile territories with no clue why they're hostile or how to get back to safe havens, an Old Haven, a lost haven, the temperature dropping, the hour heaving & pitching towards a profound darkness, while before me my idiotic amaurotic Guide laughs, actually cackles is more like it, lost in his own litany of inside jokes, completely out of his head, out of focus too, zonules of Zinn, among other things, having snapped long ago like piano wires, leaving me with absolutely no sound way to determine where the hell I'm going, though right now going to hell seems like a pretty sound bet.

[51]Which Anthony Bonner translates as ". . . truth, whose mother is history, who is the rival of time, depository of deeds, witness of the past, example and lesson to the present, and warning to the future." — Ed.

[52]See John Hollander's *The Figure of Echo* (Berkeley: University of California Press, 1981).

[53]Kelly Chamotto makes mention of Hollander in her essay "Mid-Sentence, Mid-Stream" in *Glorious Garrulous Graphomania* ed. T. N Joseph Truslow (Iowa City: University of Iowa Press, 1989), p. 345.

♂ "I've spent ten years on Cicero" "Ass!"

☿ "The Muses' studies" "divine ones."

nostri" to which Echo responds "*sit tibi copia nostri.*"☾ On page 4, he even provides a woodcut from Athanasius Kircher's *Neue Hall -und Thonkunst* (Nördlingen, 1684) illustrating an artificial echo machine designed to exchange "*clamore*" for four echoes: "*amore,*" "*more,*" "*ore,*" and finally "*re.*" ♃ Nor does Hollander stop there. His slim volume abounds with examples of textual transfiguration, though in an effort to keep from repeating the entire book, let this heart-wrenching interchange serve as a final example:

> *Chi dara fine al gran dolore?*
> *L'ore.*∞

While *The Figure of Echo* takes special delight in clever word games, Hollander knows better than to limit his examination there. Echo may live in metaphors, puns and the suffix—*solis ex illo vivit in antris*Ω—but her range extends far beyond those literal walls. For instance, the rabbinical *bat kol* means "daughter of a voice" which in modern Hebrew serves as a rough equivalent for the word "echo." Milton knew it: "God so commanded, and left that Command/ Sole Daughter of his voice."[55] So did Wordsworth: "stern Daughter of the Voice of God." Quoting from Henry Reynold's *Mythomystes* (1632), Hollander evidences religious appropriation of the ancient myth (page 16):

> This *Winde* is (as the before-mentioned Iamblicus, by consent of his other fellow-*Cabalists* sayes) the Symbole of the Breath of God; and Ecco, the reflection of this divine breath, or spirit upon us; or (as they interpret it) *the daughter of the divine voice;* which through the beatifying splendor it shedds and diffuses through the Soule, is justly worthy to be reverenced and adored by us. This *Ecco* descending upon a Narcissus, or such a Soule as (impurely and vitiously affected) slights, and stops his eares to the Divine voice, or shutts his harte from divine Inspirations, through his being enamour'd of not himselfe, but his owne shadow meerely . . . he becomes thence . . . an earthy, weake, worthlesse thing, and fit sacrifize for only eternall oblivion . . .

Thus Echo suddenly assumes the role of god's messenger, a female Mercury or perhaps even Prometheus, decked in talaria, with lamp in hand, descending on fortunate humanity.

☾Narcissus: "May I die before I give you power over me." Echo: "I give you power over me."

♃"O outcry" returns as "love," "delays," "hours" and "king."

∞ "Who will put an end to this great sadness?" "The hours passing"

Ω "Literature's rocky caves"[54]

[54]"From that time on she lived in lonely caves." — Ed.

[55]John Milton's *Paradise Lost,* IX, 653-54.

In 1989, however, the noted southern theologian Hanson Edwin Rose dramatically revised this reading. In a series of lectures delivered at Chapel Hill, Rose referred to "God's Grand Utterance" as "The Biggest Bang Of Them All." After discussing in depth the difference between the Hebrew *davhar* and the Greek *logos*, Rose took a careful accounting of St. John, chapter 1, Verse 1—"In the beginning was the Word, and the Word was with God, and the Word was God." It was a virtuoso performance but one that surely would have been relegated to those dusty shelves already burdened with a thousand years of seminary discourse had he not summed up his ruminations with this incendiary and still infamous conclusion: "Look to the sky, look to yourself and remember: we are only god's echoes and god is Narcissus."[56]

Rose's pronouncement recalls another equally important meditation:

> Why did god create a dual universe?
> So he might say,
> "Be not like me. I am alone."
> And it might be heard.[57]

There is not time or room to adequately address the complexity inherent in this passage, aside from noting how the voice is returned—or figuratively echoed—not with an actual word but with the mere understanding that it was received, listened to, or as the text explicitly states "heard." What the passage occludes, no doubt on purpose, is how such an understanding might be attained.

Interestingly enough, for all its marvelous observation, *The Figure of Echo* contains a startling error, one which performs a poetic modulation on a voice sounded over a century ago. While discussing Wordsworth's poem "The Power of Sound" Hollander quotes on page 19 the following few lines:

> Ye Voices, and ye Shadows
> And Images of voice—to hound and horn
> From rocky steep and rock-bestudded meadows
> Flung back, and in the sky's blue *care* reborn —
>
> [Italics added for emphasis]

Perhaps it is simply a typographical error committed by the publisher. Or perhaps the publisher was dutifully transcribing an error committed by Hollander himself, not just a scholar but a poet as well, who in that tiny slip where an "r" replaced a "v" and an "s" miraculously vanished reveals his own relation to the meaning of echo. A meaning Wordsworth did not share. Consider the original text:

---

[56]Hanson Edwin Rose, *Creationist Myths* (Detroit, Michigan: Pneuma Publications, 1989), p. 219.

[57]`These lines have a familiar ring though I've no clue why or where I've heard them before.`[58]

[58]Though we were ultimately unsuccessful, all efforts were made to determine who wrote the above verse. We apologize for this inconsistency. Anyone who can provide legitimate proof of authorship will be credited in future editions. — Ed.

Ye Voices, and ye Shadows
And Images of voice—to hound and horn
From rocky steep and rock-bestudded meadows
Flung back, and, in the sky's blue *caves* reborn —[59]

[Italics added for emphasis]

While Wordsworth's poetics retain the literal properties and stay within the canonical jurisdiction of Echo, Hollander's find something else, not exactly 'religious'—that would be hyperbole—but 'compassionate', which as an echo of humanity suggests the profoundest return of all.

Aside from recurrence, revision, and commensurate symbolic reference, echoes also reveal emptiness. Since objects always muffle or impede acoustic reflection, only empty places can create echoes of lasting clarity.

Ironically, hollowness only increases the eerie quality of otherness inherent in any echo. Delay and fragmented repetition create a sense of another inhabiting a necessarily deserted place. Strange then how something so uncanny and outside of the self, even ghostly as some have suggested, can at the same time also contain a resilient comfort: the assurance that even if it is imaginary and at best the product of a wall, there is still something else out there, something to stake out in the face of nothingness.

Hollander is wrong when he writes on page 55:

> The apparent echoing of solitary words . . . [reminds] us . . . that acoustical echoing in empty places can be a very common auditory emblem, redolent of gothic novels as it may be, of isolation and often of unwilling solitude. This is no doubt a case of natural echoes conforming to echo's mythographic mocking, rather than affirming, role. In an empty hall that should be comfortably inhabited, echoes of our voices and motions mock our very presence in the hollow space.

It is not by accident that choirs singing Psalms are most always recorded with ample reverb. Divinity seems defined by echo. Whether the Vienna Boys Choir or monks chanting away on some chart climbing CD, the hallowed always seems to abide in the province of the hollow. The reason for this is not too complex. An echo, while implying an enormity of a space, at the same time also defines it, limits it, and even temporarily inhabits it.

When a pebble falls down a well, it is gratifying to hear the eventual plunk. If, however, the pebble only slips into darkness and vanishes without a sound, the effect is disquieting. In the case of a verbal echo, the

---

[59]William Wordsworth, *The Poems Of William Wordsworth,* ed. Nowell Charles Smith, M.A. vol. 1. (London: Methuen and Co., 1908), p. 395. Also of some interest is Alice May Williams letter to the observers at Mount Wilson (CAT. #0005) in which she writes: "I beleive that sky opens & closes on certain periods, When you see all that cloud covering the sky right up, & over. Those clouds are called. Blinds, shutters, & verandahs. Somtimes that sky opens underneath." See *No One May Ever Have The Same Knowledge Again: Letters to Mount Wilson Observatory 1915-1935,* edited and transcribed by Sarah Simons (West Covina, California: Society For the Diffusion of Useful Information Press, 1993), p. 11.

spoken word acts as the pebble and the subsequent repetition serves as "the plunk." In this way, speaking can result in a form of "seeing."

For all its merits, Hollander's book only devotes five pages to the actual physics of sound. While this is not the place to dwell on the beautiful and complex properties of reflection, in order to even dimly comprehend the shape of the Navidson house it is still critical to recognize how the laws of physics in tandem with echo's mythic inheritance serve to enhance echo's interpretive strength.

The descriptive ability of the audible is easily designated with the following formula:

⊙ Sound + Time = Acoustic Light

As most people know who are versed in this century's technological effects, exact distances can be determined by timing the duration of a sound's round trip between the deflecting object and its point of origin. This principle serves as the basis for all the radar, sonar and ultrasonics used every day around the world by air traffic controllers, fishermen, and obstetricians. By using sound or electromagnetic waves, visible blips may be produced on a screen, indicating either a 747, a school of salmon, or the barely pumping heart of a fetus.

Of course echolocation has never belonged exclusively to technology. *Microchiroptera* (bats), *Cetacean* (porpoises and toothed whales), *Delphinis delphis* (dolphins) as well as certain mammals (flying foxes) and birds (oilbirds) all use sound to create extremely accurate acoustic images. However, unlike their human counterparts, neither bats nor dolphins require an intermediary screen to interpret the echoes. They simply "see" the shape of sound.

Bats, for example, create frequency modulated [FM] images by producing constant-frequency signals [0.5 to 100+ ms] and FM signals [0.5 to 10 ms] in their larynx. The respondent echoes are then translated into nerve discharges in the auditory cortex, enabling the bat not only to determine an insect's velocity and direction (through synaptic interpretation of Doppler shifts) but pinpoint its location to within a fraction of a millimeter.[60]

As Michael J. Buckingham noted in the mid-80s, imaging performed by the human eye is neither active nor passive. The eye does not need to produce a signal to see nor does an object have to produce a signal in order to be seen. An object merely needs to be illuminated. Based on these observations, the already mentioned formula reflects a more accurate understanding of vision with the following refinement:

⊙ Sound + Time = Acoustic Touch

As Gloucester murmured, "I see it feelingly."[61]

Unfortunately, humans lack the sophisticated neural hardware present in bats and whales. The blind must rely on the feeble light of fingertips and the painful shape of a cracked shin. Echolocation comes down to the crude assessment of simple sound modulations, whether in the dull reply of

---

[60]See D. R. Griffin, *Listening in the Dark* (1986).

[61]*King Lear*, IV, vi, 147.

a tapping cane or the low, eerie flutter in one simple word—perhaps your word—flung down empty hallways long past midnight.[62]

---

[62]You don't need me to point out the intensely personal nature of this passage. Frankly I'd of rec'd a quick skip past the whole echo ramble were it not for those six lines, especially the last bit "— perhaps your word —" conjuring up, at least for me, one of those deep piercing reactions, the kind that just misses a ventricle, the old man making his way—feeling his way—around the walls of another evening, a slow and tedious progress but one which begins to yield, somehow, the story of his own creature darkness, taking me completely by surprise, a sudden charge from out of the dullest moment, jaws lunging open, claws protracting, and just so you understand where I'm coming from, I consider ". . . long past midnight" one claw and "empty hallways" another.

Don't worry Lude didn't buy it either but at least he bought a couple of rounds.

Two nights ago, we were checking out the Sky Bar, hemorrhaging dough on drinks, but Lude could only cough hard and then laugh real coronary like: "Hoss, a claw's made of bone just like a stilt's made of steel."

"Sure" I said.

But it was loud there and the crowd kept both of us from hearing correctly. And while I wanted to believe Lude's basics, I couldn't. There was something just so awful in the old man's utterance. I felt a terrible empathy for him then, living in that tiny place, permeated with the odor of age, useless blinks against the darkness. His word—my word, maybe even your word—added to this, and ringing inside me like some awful dream, over and over again, modulating slightly, slowly pitching my own defenses into something entirely different, until the music of that recurrence drew into relief my own scars drawn long ago, over two decades ago, and with more than a claw, a stiletto or even an ancient Samuel O'Reilly @ 1891, and these scars torn, ripped, bleeding and stuttering—for they are first of all his scars—the kind only bars of an EKG can accurately remember, a more precise if incomplete history, Q waves deflecting downward at what must be considered the commencement of the QRS complex, telling the story of a past infarction, that awful endurance and eventual letting go, the failure which began it all in the first place, probably right after one burning maze but still years ahead of the Other loss, a horrible violence, before the coming of that great Whale, before the final drift, nod, macking skid, twist and topple—his own burning—years before the long rest, coming along in its own way, its own nightmare, perhaps even in the folds of another unprotected sleep (so I like to imagine), silvering wings fragmenting then scattering like fish scales flung on the jet stream, above the clouds and every epic venture still suggested in those delicate, light-cradled borders—Other Lands—sweeping the world like a whisper, a hand, even if salmon scales still slip through words as easily as palmed prisms of salt will always slip through fingers, shimmering, raining, confused, and no matter how spectacular forever unable to prevent his fall, down through the silver, the salmon, away from the gold and the myriad of games held in just that word, suggesting it might have even been Spanish gold, though this makes no differance, still tumbling in rem-, dying and -embered, even? or never, in a different light, and not waking this time, before the hit, but sleeping right through it, the slamming into the ground, at terminal velocity too, the pound, the bounce, What kind of ground-air emergency code would that mark mean? the opposition of L's? Not understood? Probably just X marks the spot: Unable To

The study of architectural acoustics focuses on the rich interplay between sound and interior design. Consider, for example, how an enclosed space will naturally increase sound pressure and raise the frequency. Even though they are usually difficult to calculate, resonance frequencies, also known as eigenfrequencies or natural frequencies, can be easily determined for a perfectly rectangular room with hard smooth walls. The following formula describes the resonance frequencies [*f*] in a room

---

Proceed—then in the awful second arc and second descent, after the sound, the realization of what Sleep has just now delivered, that bloody handmaiden, this time her toiling fingers wet with boiling deformation, oozing in the mutilations of birth, heartless & unholy, black with afterbirth, miscreated changeling and foul, what no one beside him could prevent, but rather might have even caused, and mine too, this unread trauma, driving him to consciousness with a scream, not even a word, a scream, and even that never heard, so not a scream but the clutch of life held by will alone, no 911, no call at all, just his own misunderstanding of the reality that had broken into the Hall, the silence then of a woman and an only son, describing in an agonizing hour all it takes to let go, broken, bleeding, ragged, twisted, savaged, torn and dying too, so permanently wronged, though for how many years gone untold, unseen, reminiscent of another silver shape, so removed and yet so dear, kept on a cold gold chain, years on, this fistful of twitching injured life, finally recovering on its own until eventually like a seed conceived, born and grown, the story of its injured beat survives long enough to destroy and devour by the simple telling of its fall, all his hope, his home, his only love, the very color of his flesh and the dark marrow of his bone.

"You okay Truant?" Lude asked.

But I saw a strange glimmer everywhere, confined to the sharp oscillations of yellow & blue, as if my retinal view suddenly included along with the reflective blessings of light, an unearthly collusion with scent & sound, registering all possibilities of harm, every threat, every move, even with all that grinning and meeting and din.

A thousand and one possible claws.

Of course, Lude didn't see it. He was blind. Maybe even right. We drove down Sunset and soon veered south into the flats. A party somewhere. An important gathering of E heads and coke heads. Lude would never feel how "empty hallways long past midnight" could slice inside of you, though I'm not so sure he wasn't sliced up just the same. Not seeing the rip doesn't mean you automatically get to keep clear of the Hey-I'm-Bleeding part. To feel though, you have to care and as we walked out onto the blue-lit patio and discovered a motorcycle sputtering up oil and bubbles from the bottom of the pool while on the diving board two men shoved flakes of ice up a woman's bleeding nostrils, her shirt off, her bra nearly transparent, I knew Lude would never care much about the dead. And maybe he was right. Maybe some things are best left untouched. Of course he didn't know the dead like I did. And so when he absconded with a bottle of Jack from the kitchen, I did my best to join him. Obliterate my own cavities and graves.

But come morning, despite my headache and the vomit on my shirt, I knew I'd failed.

Inside me, a long dark hallway already caressed the other music of a single word, and what's worse, despite the amazements of chemicals, continued to grow.

with a length of *L*, width of *W*, and height of *H*, where the velocity of sound equals *c* :

$$f = {}^{c}/_{2} \left[({}^{n}/_{L})^2 + ({}^{m}/_{W})^2 + ({}^{p}/_{H})^2 \right]^{1/2} \text{Hz}$$

Notice that if L, W, and H all equal ∞, *f* will equal 0.

Along with resonance frequencies, the study of sound also takes into account wave acoustics, ray acoustics, diffusion, and steady-state pressure level, as well as sound absorption and transmission through walls. A careful examination of the dynamics involved in sound absorption reveals how incident sound waves are converted to energy. (In the case of porous material, the subsurface lattice of interstices translates sound waves into heat.) Nevertheless, above and beyond the details of frequency shifts and volume fluctuations—the physics of 'otherness'—what matters most is a sound's delay.[63]

Point of fact, the human ear cannot distinguish one sound wave from the same sound wave if it returns in less than 50 milliseconds. Therefore for anyone to hear a reverberation requires a certain amount of space. At 68 degrees Fahrenheit sound travels at approximately 1,130ft per second. A reflective surface must stand at least 56 1/2ft away in order for a person to detect the doubling of her voice.[64]

In other words, to hear an echo, regardless of whether eyes are open or closed, is to have already "seen" a sizable space.

Myth makes Echo the subject of longing and desire. Physics makes Echo the subject of distance and design. Where emotion and reason are concerned both claims are accurate.

And where there is no Echo there is no description of space or love.

There is only silence.[65]

---

[63]Further attention should probably be given to sabins and Transmission Loss as described by TL = 10 log 1/ τ dB, where τ= a transmission coefficient and a high TL indicates a high sound insulation. Unfortunately, one could write several lengthy books on sound alone in *The Navidson Record.* Oddly enough, with the sole exception of Kellog Pequity's article on acoustic impedance in Navidson's house (*Science*, April 1995, p. 43), nothing else has been rendered on this particularly resonant topic. On the subject of acoustic coefficience, however, see Ned Noi's "Echo's Verse" in *Science News,* v. 143, February 6, 1993, p. 85.

[64]Parallel surfaces will create a flutter echo, though frequently a splay of as little as 16mm (5/8 inch) can prevent the multiple repetitions.

[65]There is something more at work here, some sort of antithetical reasoning and proof making, and what about light?, all of which actually made sense to me at a certain hour before midnight or at least came close to making sense. Problem was Lude interrupted my thoughts when he came over and after much discussion (not to mention shots of tequila and a nice haircut) convinced me to share a bag of mushrooms with him and in spite of getting violently ill in the aisle of a certain 7-Eleven (me; not him) led me to an after hours party where I soon became engrossed in a green-eyed brunette (Lucy) who had no intention of letting our dance end at the club, and yet even in our sheet twisting, lightless dance on my floor, her own features, those pale legs, soft arms, the fragile collar bone tracing a shadow of (—can't write the word—), invariably became entwined and permanently??? entangled, even entirely replaced??? by images of a completely different woman; relatively new, or not new at

all, but for reasons unknown to me still continuing to endure as a center to my thoughts; her—

—first encountered in the company of Lude and my boss at a place my boss likes to call The Ghost. The problem is that in his mind The Ghost actually refers to two places: The Garden of Eden on La Brea and The Rainbow Bar & Grill on Sunset. How or why this came about is impossible to trace. Private nomenclature seems to rapidly develop in tight set-upon circles, though truth be told we were only set-upon on a good day, and tight here should be taken pretty loosely.

How then, you ask, do you know what's being referred to when The Ghost gets mentioned?

You don't.

You just end up at one or the other. Often the Rainbow. Though not always the Rainbow. You see, how my boss defines The Ghost varies from day to day, depending mostly on his moods and appetites. Consequently, the previously mentioned "pretty loosely" should probably be struck and re-stated as "very, very loosely."

Anyway, what I'm about to tell you happened on one of those rare evenings when we actually all got together. My boss was chattering incessantly about his junk days in London and how he'd contemplated sobriety and what those contemplations had been like. Eventually he detoured into long winded non-stories about his Art School experiences in Detroit,—lots of "Hey, my thing for that whole time thing was really a kinda art thing or something"—which was about when I hauled out my pad of sketches, because no matter what you made of his BS you still couldn't fault him for his work. He was one of best, and every tatted local knew it.

Truth be known, I'd been waiting for this chance for a while, keen on getting his out-of-the-Shop perspective on my efforts, and what efforts they were—diligent designs sketched over the months, intended someday to live in skin, each image carefully wrapped and coiled in colors of cinnabar, lemon, celadon and indigo, incarnated in the scales of dragons, the bark of ancient roods, shields welded by generations cast aside in the oily umber of shadow & blood not to speak of lifeless trees prevailing against indifferent skies or colossal vessels asleep in prehistoric sediment, miles beneath even the faintest suggestion of light—at least that's how I would describe them—every one meticulously rendered on tracing paper, cracking like fire whenever touched, a multitude of pages, which my boss briefly examined before handing them back to me.

"Take up typing," he grunted.

Well that's nice, I thought.

At least the next step was clear.

Some act of violence would be necessary.

And so it was that before another synapse could fire within my bad-off labyrinthine brain, he was already lying on the floor. Or I should say his mangled body was lying on the floor. His head remained in my hands. Twisted off like a cap. Not as difficult as I'd imagined. The first turn definitely the toughest, necessitating the breaking of cervical vertebrae and the snapping of the spinal cord, but after that, another six or so turns, and voilà—the head was off. Nothing could be easier. Time to go bowling.

My boss smiled. Said hello.

But he wasn't smiling or saying hello to me.

Somehow she was already standing there, right in front of him, right in front of me, talking to him, reminiscing, touching his shoulder, even winking at me and Lude.

Wow. Out of nowhere. Out of the blue.

Where had she come from? Or for that matter, when?

Of course my boss didn't introduce her. He just left me to gape. I couldn't even imagine twisting off his head for a second time as that would of meant losing sight of her. Which I found myself quite unwilling to do.

Fortunately, after that evening, she began dropping by the Shop alot, always wearing these daisy sunglasses and each time taking me completely off guard.

She still drives me nuts. Just thinking of her now and I'm lost, lost in the smell of her, the way of her and everything she conjures up inside me, a mad rush of folly & oddly muted lusts, sensations sublimated faster than I can follow, into— oh hell I don't know what into, I probably shouldn't even be using a word like sublimate, but that's beside the point, her hair reminding me of a shiny gold desert wind brazed in a hot August sun, hips curving like coastal norths, tits rising and falling beneath her blue sweatshirt the way an ocean will do long after the storm has passed. (She's always a little out of breath when she climbs the flight of stairs leading up to the Shop.) One glance at her, even now in the glass of my mind, and I want to take off, travel with her, who knows where either, somewhere, my desire suddenly informed by something deeper, even unknown, pouring into me, drawn off some peculiar reserve, tracing thoughts of the drive she and I would take, lungs full of that pine rasping air, outracing something unpleasant, something burning, in fact the entire coast along with tens of thousands of acres of inland forest is burning but we're leaving, we're getting away, we're free, our hands battered by the clutch of holding on—I don't know what to, but holding just the same—and cheeks streaked with wind tears; and now that I think of it I guess we are on a motorcycle, a Triumph?, isn't that what Lude always talks about buying?, ascending into colder but brighter climes, and I don't know anything about bikes let alone how to drive one. And there I go again. She does that to me. Like I already said, drives me nuts.

"Hello?"

That was the first word she ever said to me in the Shop. Not like "Hi" either. More like "Hello, is anyone home?" hence the question mark. I wasn't even looking at her when she said it, just staring blankly down at my equally blank pad of tracing paper, probably thinking something similar to all those ridiculous, sappy thoughts I just now recounted, about road trips and forest fires and motorcycles, remembering her, even though she was right there in front of me, only a few feet away.

"Hey asshole," my boss shouted. "Hang up her fucking pants. What's the matter with you?"

Something would have to be done about him.

But before I could hurl him through the plate glass window into the traffic below, she smiled and handed me her bright pink flip-flops & white Adidas sweats. My boss was lucky. This magnificent creature had just saved his life.

Gratefully I received her clothes, lifting them from her fingers tips like they were some sacred vesture bestowed upon me by the Virgin Mary herself. The hard part, I found, was trying not to stare too long at her legs. Very tricky to do. Next to impossible, especially with her just standing there in a black G-string, her bare feet sweating on the naked floor.

I did my best to smile in a way that would conceal my awe.

"Thank you," I said, thinking I should kneel.

"Thank you," she insisted.

Those were the next two words she ever said to me, and wow, I don't know why but her voice went off in my head like a symphony. A great symphony. A sweet symphony. A great-fucking-sweet symphony. I don't know what I'm saying. I know absolutely shit about symphonies.

"What's your name?" The total suddenly climbing to an impossible six words.

"Johnny," I mumbled, promptly earning four more words. And just like that.

"Nice to meet you," she said in a way that almost sounded like a psalm. And then even though she clearly enjoyed the effect she was having on me, she turned away with a wink, leaving me to ponder and perhaps pray.

At least I had her ten words: "hello thank you what's your name nice to meet you." Ten whole fucking words. Wow. Wow. Wow. And hard as this may be for you to believe, I really was reeling. Even after she left the Shop an hour or so later, I was still giving serious thought to petitioning all major religions in order to have her deified.

In fact I was so caught up in the thought of her, there was even a moment where I failed to recognize my boss. I had absolutely no clue who he was. I just stared at him thinking to myself, "Who's this dumb mutant and how the hell did he get up here?" which it turns out I didn't think at all but accidentally said aloud, causing all sorts of mayhem to ensue, not worth delving into now.

Quick note here: if this crush—slash—swooning stuff is hard for you to stomach; if you've never had a similar experience, then you should come to grips with the fact that you've got a TV dinner for a heart and might want to consider climbing inside a microwave and turning it on high for at least an hour, which if you do consider only goes to show what kind of idiot you truly are because microwaves are way too small for anyone, let alone you, to climb into.

Quick second note: if that last paragraph didn't apply to you, you may skip it and proceed to this next part.

As for her real name, I still don't know it. She's a stripper at some place near the airport. She has a dozen names. The first time she came into the Shop, she wanted one of her tattoos retouched. "Just an inch away from my perfectly shaved pussy," she announced very matter-a-factly, only to add somewhat coyly, slipping two fingers beneath her G-string and pulling it aside; no need to wink now: "The Happiest Place On Earth."

Suffice it to say, the second I saw that rabbit the second I started calling her Thumper.

I do admit it seems a little strange, even to me, to realize that even after four months I'm still swept up in her. Lude sure as hell doesn't understand it. One— because I've fallen for a stripper: "'fuck a' and 'fall for' have very different meanings, Hoss. The first one you do as much as you can. The second one you never ever, ever do."; and two— because she's older than me: "If you're gonna reel for a stripper," he advises. "You should at least reel for a young one. They're sexier and not as bent." Which is true, she does have a good six years on me, but what can I say? I'm taken; I love how enthralled she remains by this festival of living, nothing reserved or even remotely ashamed about who she is or what she does, always talking blue streak to my boss about her three year old child, her boyfriend, her boyfriends, the hand jobs she gets extra for, eleven years of sobriety, her words always winding up the way it feels to wake up wide awake, everything about her awakening at every moment, alive to the world and its quirky opportunities, a sudden rite of spring, Thumper's spring, though spring's already sprung, rabbit rabbit, and now April's ruling April's looming April's fooling, around, in yet another round, for this year's ruling April fool.

Yeah I know, I know. This shit's getting ridiculous.

Even worse, I feel like I could continue in that vein for years, maybe even decades.

And yet, listen to this, to date I've hardly said a word to her. Don't have a decent explanation for my silence either. Maybe it's my boss and his guard dog glare. Maybe it's her. I suspect it's her. Every time she visits (though I admit there haven't been that many visits), she overwhelms me. It doesn't matter that she always gives me a wink and sometimes even a full throated laugh when I call her "Thumper", "Hi Thumper" "Bye Thumper" the only words I can really muster, she still really only exists for me as a strange mixture of daydream and present day edge, by which I mean something without a past or a future, an icon or idyll of sorts, for some reason forbidden to me, but seductive beyond belief and probably relief, her image feeling permanently fixed within me, but not new, more like it's been there all along, even if I know that's not true, and come last night going so far as to entwine, entangle and finally completely replace her with the (—can't write the word—) of—

—Thumper's flashing eyes, her aching lips, her heart-ending moans, those I had imagined, an ongoing list, so minute and distracting that long after, when the sheets were gathered, wet with sex, cold with rest, I did not know who lay beside me (——) and seeing this stranger, the vessel of my dreams, I withdrew to the toilet, to the shower, to my table, enough racket and detachment to communicate an unfair request, but poor her she heard it and without a word dressed, and without a smile requested a brush, and without a kiss left, leaving me alone to return to this passage where I discovered the beginnings of a sense long since taken and strewn, leading me away on what I guess amounts to another hopeless digression.

Perhaps when I'm finished I'll remember what I'd hoped to say in the first place.[66]

[66]Mr. Truant declined to comment further on this particular passage. — Ed.

As tape and film reveal, in the month following the expansion of the walls bracketing the book shelves, Billy Reston made several trips to the house where despite all efforts to the contrary, he continued to confirm the confounding impossibility of an interior dimension greater than an exterior one.

Navidson skillfully captures Reston's mental frustration by focusing on the physical impediments his friend must face within a house not designed with the disabled in mind. Since the area in question is in the master bedroom, Reston must make his way upstairs each time he wishes to inspect the area.

On the first visit, Tom volunteers to try and carry him.

"That won't be necessary" Reston grunts, effortlessly swinging out of his chair and dragging himself up to the second story using only his arms.

"You got a pair of guns there, don't you partner."

The engineer is only slightly winded.

"Too bad you forgot your chair," Tom adds dryly.

Reston looks up in disbelief, a little surprised, maybe even a bit shocked, and then bursts out laughing.

"Well, and fuck you."

In the end, Navidson is the one who hauls up the wheelchair.[67]

Still, no matter how many times Reston wheels from the children's bedroom to the master bedroom or how carefully he examines the strange closet space, the bookshelves, or the various tools Tom and Will have been measuring the house with, he can provide no reasonable explanation for what he keeps referring to as "a goddamn spatial rape."

---

[67]Yesterday I managed to get Maus Fife-Harris on the phone. She's a UC Irvine PhD candidate in Comp Lit who apparently always objected to the large chunks of narrative Zampanò kept asking her to write down. "I told him all those passages were inappropriate for a critical work, and if he were in my class I'd mark him down for it. But he'd just chuckle and continue. It bothered me a little but the guy wasn't my student and he was blind and old, so why should I care? Still, I did care, so I'd always protest when he asked me to write down a new bit of narrative. 'Why won't you listen to me?' I demanded one time. 'You're writing like a freshman.' And he replied—I remember this very distinctly: 'We always look for doctors but sometimes we're lucky to find a frosh.' And then he chuckled again and pressed on." Not a bad way to respond to this whole fucking book, if you ask me.

By June—as the date on the Hi 8 tape indicates—the problem still remains unsolved. Tom, however, realizes he cannot afford to stay any longer and asks Reston to give him a lift to Charlottesville where he can catch a ride up to Dulles.

It is a bright summer morning when we watch Tom emerge from the house. He gives Karen a quick kiss good-bye and then kneels down to present Chad and Daisy with a set of neon yellow dart guns.

"Remember kids," he tells them sternly. "Don't shoot each other. Aim at the fragile, expensive stuff."

Navidson gives his brother a lasting hug.

"I'll miss you, man."

"You got a phone," Tom grins.

"It even rings," Navidson adds without missing a beat.

While there is no question the tone of this exchange is jocular and perhaps even slightly combative, what matters most here is unspoken. The way Tom's cheeks burn with a sudden flush of color. Or the way Navidson quickly tries to wipe something from his eyes. Certainly the long, lingering shot of Tom as he tosses his duffel bag in the back of Reston's van, waving the camera good-bye, reveals to us just how much affection Navidson feels for his brother.

Strangely enough, following Tom's departure, communication between Navidson and Karen begins to radically deteriorate.

An unusual quiet descends on the house.

Karen refuses to speak about the anomaly. She brews coffee, calls her mother in New York, brews more coffee, and keeps track of the real estate market in the classifieds.

Frustrated by her unwillingness to discuss the implications of their strange living quarters, Navidson retreats to the downstairs study, reviewing photographs, tapes, even—as a few stills reveal—compiling a list of possible experts, government agencies, newspapers, periodicals, and television shows they might want to approach.

At least both he and Karen agree on one thing: they want the children to stay out of the house. Unfortunately, since neither Chad nor Daisy has had a real opportunity to make any new friends in Virginia, they keep to themselves, romping around the backyard, shouting, screaming, stinging each other with darts until eventually they drift farther and farther out into the neighborhood for increasingly longer spates of time.

Neither Karen nor Navidson seems to notice.

The alienation of their children finally becomes apparent to both of them one evening in the middle of July.

Karen is upstairs, sitting on the bed playing with a deck of Tarot cards. Navidson is downstairs in his study examining several slides returned from the lab. News of Oliver North's annulled conviction plays on the TV. In the background, we can hear Chad and Daisy squealing about something, their voices peeling through the house, the strained music of their play threatening at any instant to turn into a brawl.

With superb cross-cutting, Navidson depicts how both he and Karen react to the next moment. Karen has drawn another card from the deck but instead of adding it to the cross slowly forming before her crossed legs, the occult image hangs unseen in the air, frozen between her two fingers, Karen's eyes already diverted, concentrating on a sound, a new sound, almost out of reach, but reaching her just the same. Navidson is much closer. His children's cries immediately tell him that they are way out of bounds.

Karen has only just started to head downstairs, calling out for Chad and Daisy, her agitation and panic increasing with every step, when Navidson bolts out of the study and races for the living room.

The terrifying implication of their children's shouts is now impossible to miss. No room in the house exceeds a length of twenty-five feet, let alone fifty feet, let alone fifty-six and a half feet, and yet Chad and Daisy's voices are echoing, each call responding with an entirely separate answer.

In the living room, Navidson discovers the echoes emanating from a dark doorless hallway which has appeared out of nowhere in the west wall.[68] Without hesitating, Navidson plunges in after them. Unfortunately the living room Hi 8 cannot follow him nor for that matter can Karen. She freezes on the threshold, unable to push herself into the darkness toward the faint flicker of light within. Fortunately, she does not have to wait too long. Navidson soon reappears with Chad and Daisy in each arm, both of them still clutching a homemade candle, their faces lit like sprites on a winter's eve.

This is the first sign of Karen's chronic disability. Up until now there has never been even the slightest indication that she suffers from crippling claustrophobia. By the time Navidson and the two children are safe and sound in the living room, Karen is drenched in sweat. She hugs and holds them as if they had just narrowly avoided some terrible fate, even though neither Chad nor Daisy seems particularly disturbed by their little adventure. In fact, they want to go back. Perhaps because of Karen's evident distress, Navidson agrees to at least temporarily make this new addition to their house off limits.

For the rest of the night, Karen keeps a tight grip on Navidson. Even when they finally slip into bed, she is still holding his hand.

"Navy, promise me you won't go in there again."

"Let's see if it's even here in the morning."

"It will be."

She lays her head down flat on his chest and begins to cry.

"I love you so much. Please promise me. Please."

Whether it is the lasting flush of terror still in Karen's cheeks or her absolute need for him, so markedly different from her frequently aloof posture, Navidson cradles her in his arms like a child and promises.

Since the release of *The Navidson Record,* Virginia Posah has written extensively about Karen Green's adolescent years. Posah's thin volume entitled *Wishing Well* (Cambridge, Massachusetts: Harvard University Press, 1996) represents one of the few works which while based on the Navidsons' experience still manages to stand on its own merits outside of the film.

Along with an exceptional background in everything ranging from Kate Chopin, Sylvia Plath, Toni Morrison, *Autobiography of a*

---

[68]There's a problem here concerning the location of "The Five and a Half Minute Hallway." Initially the doorway was supposed to be on the north wall of the living room (page 4), but now, as you can see for yourself, that position has changed. Maybe it's a mistake. Maybe there's some underlying logic to the shift. Fuck if I know. Your guess is as good as mine.

Schizophrenic Girl: The True Story of "Renee", Francesca Block's Weetzie Bat books to Mary Pipher's *Reviving Ophelia* and more importantly Carol Gilligan's landmark work *In a Different Voice: Psychological Theory and Women's Development,* Posah has spent hundreds of hours researching the early life of Karen Green, analyzing the cultural forces shaping her personality, ultimately uncovering a remarkable difference between the child she once was and the woman she eventually became. In her introduction (page xv), Posah provides this brief overview:

> When Diderot told the teenage Sophie Volland "You all die at fifteen" he could have been speaking to Karen Green who at fifteen did die.
>
> To behold Karen as a child is nearly as ghostly an experience as the house itself. Old family films capture her athletic zeal, her unguarded smiles, the tomboy spirit which sends her racing through the muddy flats of a recently drained pond. She's awkward, a little clumsy, but rarely self-conscious, even when covered in mud.
>
> Former teachers claim she frequently expressed a desire to be president, a nuclear physicist, a surgeon, even a professional hockey player. All her choices reflected unattenuated self-confidence—a remarkably healthy sign for a thirteen year old girl.
>
> Along with superb class work, she excelled in extra-curricular activities. She loved planning surprise parties, working on school productions, and even on occasion taking on a schoolyard bully with a bout of fists. Karen Green was exuberant, feisty, charming, independent, spontaneous, sweet, and most of all fearless.
>
> By the time she turned fifteen, all of that was gone. She hardly spoke in class. She refused to function in any sort of school event, and rather than discuss her feelings she deferred the world with a hard and perfectly practiced smile.
>
> Apparently—if her sister is to be believed—Karen spent every night of her fourteenth year composing that smile in front of a blue plastic handled mirror. Tragically her creation proved flawless and though her near aphonia should have alarmed any adept teacher or guidance counselor, it was invariably rewarded with the pyritic prize of high school popularity.

Though Posah goes on to discuss the cultural aspects and consequences of beauty, these details in particular are most disturbing, especially in light of the fact that little of their history appears in the film.

Considering the substantial coverage present in *The Navidson Record*, it is unsettling to discover such a glaring omission. In spite of the enormous quantity of home footage obviously available, for some reason calamities of the past still do not appear. Clearly Karen's personal life, to say nothing of his own life, caused Navidson too much anxiety to portray either one particularly well in his film. Rather than delve into the pathology of Karen's claustrophobia, Navidson chose instead to focus strictly on the house.[69]

Of course by the following morning, Karen has already molded her desperation into a familiar pose of indifference.

She does not seem to care when they discover the hallway has not vanished. She keeps her arms folded, no longer clinging to Navidson's hand or stroking her children.

---

[69]Fortunately a few years before *The Navidson Record* was made Karen took part in a study which promised to evaluate and possibly treat her fear. After the film became something of a phenomenon, those results surfaced and were eventually published in a number of periodicals. The *Anomic Mag* based out of Berkeley (v. 87, n. 7, April, 1995) offered the most comprehensive account of that study as it pertained to Karen Green:

> . . . Subject #0027-00-8785 (Karen Green) suffers severe panic attacks when confronting dark, enclosed spaces, usually windowless and unknown (e.g. a dark room in an unfamiliar building). The attacks are consistently characterized by (1) accelerated heart rate (2) sweating (3) trembling (4) sensation of suffocation (5) feeling of choking (6) chest pain (7) severe dizziness (8) derealization (feelings of unreality) and eventual depersonalization (being detached from oneself) (9) culmination in an intense fear of dying. See DSM-IV "Criteria for Panic Attack." . . . Diagnosis—subject suffers from Specific Phobia (formally known as Simple Phobia); Situational type. See DSM-IV "Diagnostic criteria for 300.29 Specific Phobia." . . . Because behavioral-cognitive techniques have thus far failed to modify perspectives on anxiety-provoking stimuli, subject was considered ideal for current pharmacotherapy study . . . Initially subject received between 100-200 mg/ day of Tofranil (Imipramine) but with no improvement switched early on to a ß-adrenergic blocker (Propranolol). An increase in vivid nightmares caused her to switch again to the MAOI (Monoamine Oxidase Inhibitor) Tranylcypromine. Still dissatisfied with the results, subject switched to the SSRI (Selective Serotonin Reuptake Inhibitor) Fluoxetine, commonly known as Prozac. Subject responded well and soon showed increased tolerance when intentionally exposed to enclosed, dark spaces. Unfortunately moderate weight gain and orgasmic dysfunction caused the subject to drop out of the study . . . Subject apparently relies now on her own phobia avoidance mechanisms, choosing to stay clear of enclosed, unknown spaces (i.e. elevators, basements, unfamiliar closets etc., etc.), though occasionally when attacks become "more frequent" . . . she returns to Prozac for short periods of time . . . See David Kahn's article "Simple Phobias: The Failure of Pharmacological Intervention"; also see subject's results on Sheehan Clinician Rated Anxiety Scale as well as Sheehan Phobia Scale.[70]

While the report seems fairly comprehensive, there is admittedly one point which remains utterly perplexing. Other publications repeat verbatim the ambiguous phrasing but still fail to shed light on the exact meaning of those six words: "occasionally when attacks become 'more frequent.' " At least the implication seems clear, vicissitudes in Karen's life, whatever those may be, affect her sensitivity to space. In her article "Significant (OT)Her" published in *The Psychology Quarterly* (v. 142, n. 17, December 1995, p. 453) Celine Berezin, M.D. observes that "Karen's attacks, which I suspect stem from early adolescent betrayal, increase proportionally with the level of intimacy—or even the threat of potential intimacy—she experiences whether with Will Navidson or even her children."

Also see Steve Sokol and Julia Carter's *Women Who Can't Love: When a Woman's Fear Makes Her Run from Commitment and What a Smart Man Can Do About It* (New Hampshire: T. Devans and Company, 1978).

[70]See Exhibit Six.

She removes herself from her family's company by saying very little, while at the same time maintaining a semblance of participation with a smile.

Virginia Posah is right. Karen's smile is tragic because, in spite of its meaning, it succeeds in remaining so utterly beautiful.

The Five and a Half Minute Hallway in *The Navidson Record* differs slightly from the bootleg copy which appeared in 1990. For one thing, in addition to the continuous circumambulating shot, a wider selection of shots has made the coverage of the sequence much more thorough and fluid. For another, the hallway has shrunk. This was impossible to see in the VHS copy because there was no point of comparison. Now, however, it is perfectly clear that the hallway which was well over sixty feet deep when the children entered it is now a little less than ten feet.

Context also significantly alters "The Five and a Half Minute Hallway." A greater sense of the Navidsons and their friends and how they all interact with the house adds the greatest amount of depth to this quietly evolving enigma. Their personalities almost crowd that place and suddenly too, as an abrupt jump cut redelivers Tom from Massachusetts and Billy Reston from Charlottesville, the UVA professor once again wheeling around the periphery of the angle, unable to take his eyes off the strange, dark corridor.

Unlike *The Twilight Zone,* however, or some other like cousin where understanding comes neat and fast (i.e. This is clearly a door to another dimension! or This is a passage to another world—with directions!) the hallway offers no answers. The monolith in *2001* seems the most appropriate cinematic analog, incontrovertibly there but virtually inviolate to interpretation.[71] Similarly the hallway also remains meaningless, though it is most assuredly not without effect. As Navidson threatens to reenter it for a closer inspection, Karen reiterates her previous plea and injunction with a sharp and abrupt rise in pitch.

The ensuing tension is more than temporary.

Navidson has always been an adventurer willing to risk his personal safety in the name of achievement. Karen, on the other hand, remains the standard bearer of responsibility and is categorically against risks especially those which might endanger her family or her happiness. Tom also shies from danger, preferring to turn over a problem to someone else, ideally a police officer, fireman, or other state paid official. Without sound or movement but by presence alone, the hallway creates a serious rift in the Navidson household.

Bazine Naodook suggests that the hallway exudes a "conflict creating force": "It's those oily walls radiating badness which maneuver Karen and Will into that nonsensical fight."[72] Naodook's argument reveals a rather tedious mind. She feels a need to invent some non-existent "dark-force" to account for all ill will instead of recognizing the dangerous influence the unknown naturally has on everyone.

A couple of weeks pass. Karen privately puzzles over the experience but says very little. The only indication that the hallway has in some way intruded on her thoughts is her newfound interest in Feng Shui. In the film,

---

[71]Consider Drew Bluth's "Summer's Passage" in *Architectural Digest,* v. 50, n. 10, October 1993, p. 30.
[72]Bazine Naodook's *The Bad Bodhi Wall* (Marina Del Rey: Bix Oikofoe Publishing House, 1995), p. 91.

we can make out a number of books lying around the house, including *The Elements of Feng Shui* by Kwok Man-Ho and Joanne O'Brien (Element Books: Shaftesbury, 1991), *Feng Shui Handbook: A Practical Guide to Chinese Geomancy and Environmental Harmony* by Derek Walters (Aquarian Press, 1991), *Interior Design with Feng Shui* by Sarah Rosbach (Rider: London, 1987) and *The I Ching or Book of Changes, 3rd Edition* translated by Richard Wilhelm (Routledge & Kegan Paul, 1968).

There is a particularly tender moment as Chad sits with his mother in the kitchen. She is busily determining the Kua number (a calculation based on the year of birth) for everyone in the family, while he is carefully making a peanut butter and honey sandwich.

"Mommy" Chad says quietly after a while.

"Hmm?"

"How do I get to become President when I grow up?"

Karen looks up from her notebook. Quite unexpectedly, and with the simplest question, her son has managed to move her.

"You study hard at school and keep doing what you're doing, then you can be whatever you want."

Chad smiles.

"When I'm President, can I make you Vice President?"

Karen's eyes shine with affection. Putting aside her Feng Shui studies, she reaches over and gives Chad a big kiss on his forehead.

"How about Secretary of Defense?"

During all this, Tom earns his keep by installing a door to close off the hallway. First, he mounts a wood frame using some of the tools he brought from Lowell and a few more he rented from the local hardware store. Then he hangs a single door with 24-gauge hot-dipped, galvanized steel skins and an acoustical performance rating coded at ASTM E413-70T-STC 28. Last but not least, he puts in four Schlage dead bolts and colour codes the four separate keys: red, yellow, green, and blue.

For a while Daisy keeps him company, though it remains hard to determine whether she is more transfixed by Tom or the hallway. At one point she walks up to the threshold and lets out a little yelp, but the cry just flattens and dies in the narrow corridor.

Tom seems noticeably relieved when he finally shuts the door and turns over the four locks. Unfortunately as he twists the last key, the accompanying sound contains a familiar ring. He grips the red kye and tries it again. As the dead bolt glances the strike plate, the resulting click creates an unexpected and very unwelcome echo.

Slowly, Tom unlocks the door and peers inside.

Somehow, and for whatever reason, the thing has grown again.

Intermittently, Navidson opens the door himself and stares down the hallway, sometimes using a flashlight, sometimes just studying the darkness itself.

"What do you do with that?" Navidson asks his brother one evening.

"Move," Tom replies.

Sadly, even with the unnatural darkness now locked behind a steel door, Karen and Navidson still continue to say very little to each other, their own feelings seemingly as impossible for them to address as the meaning of the hallway itself.

Chad accompanies his mother to town as she searches for various Feng Shui objects guaranteed to change the energy of the home, while Daisy follows her father around the house as he paces from room to room, talking vehemently on the phone with Reston, trying to come up with a feasible and acceptable way to investigate the phenomenon lurking in his living room, until finally, in the middle of all this, he lifts his daughter onto his shoulders. Unfortunately as soon as Karen returns, Navidson sets Daisy back down on the floor and retreats to the study to continue his discussions alone.

With domestic tensions proving a little too much to stomach, Tom escapes to the garage where he works for a while on a doll house he has started to build for Daisy,[73] until eventually he takes a break, drifting out to the backyard to get high and hot in the sun, pointedly walking around the patch of lawn the hallway should for all intents and purposes occupy. Before long, both Chad and Daisy are sidling up to this great bear snoring under a tree, and even though they start to tie his shoe laces together, tickle his nostrils with long blades of grass, or use a mirror to focus the sun on his nose, Tom remains remarkably patient. He almost seems to enjoy their mischief, growling, yawning, playing along, putting both of them in a headlock, Chad and Daisy laughing hysterically, until finally all three are exhausted and snoozing into dusk.

Considering the complexity of Karen and Navidson's relationship, it is fortunate our understanding of their problems is not left entirely up to interpretation. Some of their respective views and feelings are revealed in their video journal entries.

"Sex, sex, sex," Karen whispers into her camcorder. "It was like we just met when we got here. The kids would go out and we'd fuck in the kitchen, in the shower. We even did it in the garage. But ever since that closet thing appeared I can't. I don't know why. It terrifies me."

On the same subject, Navidson offers a similar view: "When we first moved here, Karen was like a college co-ed. Anywhere, anytime. Now all of a sudden, she refuses to be touched. I kiss her, she practically starts to cry. And it all started when we got back from Seattle." ⌜⌟

But the division between them is not just physical.

Karen again: "Doesn't he see I don't want him going in there because I love him. You don't need to be a genius to realize there's something really bad about that place. Navy, don't you see that?"

Navidson: "The only thing I want to do is go in there but she's adamant that I don't and I love her so I won't but, well, it's just killing me. Maybe because I know this is all about her, her fears, her anxieties. She hasn't even given a thought to what I care about."

Until finally the lack of physical intimacy and emotional understanding leads both of them to make privately voiced ultimatums.

Karen: "But I will say this, if he goes in there, I'm outta here. Kids and all."

---

[73]See Lewis Marsano's "Tom's 1865 Shelter" in *This Old House,* September/October 1995, p. 87.

⌜⌟Nor does it seem to help that Navidson and Karen both have among their books Erica Jong's *Fear of Flying* (New York: Holt, Rinehart & Winston, 1973), Anne Hooper's *The Ultimate Sex Book : A Therapist's Guide to the Programs and Techniques That Will Enhance Your Relationship and Transform Your Life* (DK Publishing, 1992), X.Y.'s *Broken Daisy-Chains* (Seattle: Town Over All Press, 1989), Chris Allen's *1001 Sex Secrets Every Man Should Know* (New York: Avon Books, 1995) as well as Chris Allen's *1001 Sex Secrets Every Woman Should Know* (New York: Avon Books, 1995).

Navidson: "If she keeps up this cold front, you bet I'm going in there."

Then one night in early August __________[74] and the equally famous __________ drop in for dinner. It is a complete coincidence that they happened to be in D.C. at the same time, but neither one seems to mind the presence of the other. As __________ said, "Any friend of Navy's is a friend of mine." Navidson and Karen have known both of them for quite a few years, so the evening is light hearted and filled with plenty of amusing stories. Clearly Karen and Navidson relish the chance to reminisce a little about some good times when things seemed a lot less complicated.

Perhaps a little star struck, Tom says very little. There is plenty of opportunity for a glass of wine but he proves himself by keeping to water, though he does excuse himself from the table once to smoke a joint outside. (Much to Tom's surprise and delight, __________ joins him.)

As the evening progresses, __________ harps a little on Navidson's new found domesticity: "No more Crazy Navy, eh? Are those days gone for good? I remember when you'd party all night, shoot all morning, and then spend the rest of the day developing your film—in a closet with just a bucket and a bulb if you had to. I'm willing to bet you don't even have a darkroom here." Which is just a little too much for Navidson to bear: "Here __________, you wanna see a darkroom, I'll show you a darkroom." "Don't you dare, Navy!" Karen immediately cries. "Come on Karen, they're our friends," Navidson says, leading the two celebrities into the living room where he instructs them to look out the window so they can see for themselves his ordinary backyard. Satisfied that they understand nothing but trees and lawn could possibly lie on the other side of the wall, he retrieves the four coloured keys hidden in the antique basinet in the foyer. Everyone is pretty tipsy and the general mood is so friendly and easy it seems impossible to disturb. Which of course all changes when Navidson unlocks the door and reveals the hallway.

__________ takes one look at that dark place and retreats into the kitchen. Ten minutes later __________ is gone. __________ steps up to the threshold, points Navidson's flashlight at the walls and floor and then retires to the bathroom. A little later __________ is also gone.

Karen is so enraged by the whole incident, she makes Navidson sleep on the couch with his "beloved hallway."

No surprise, Navidson fails to fall asleep.

He tosses around for an hour until he finally gets up and goes off in search of his camera.

A title card reads: **Exploration A**

The time stamp on Navidson's camcorder indicates that it is exactly 3:19 A.M.

"Call me impetuous or just curious," we hear him mutter as he shoves his sore feet into a pair of boots. "But a little look around isn't going to hurt."

Without ceremony, he unlocks the door and slips across the threshold, taking with him only a Hi 8, a MagLite, and his 35mm Nikon. The commentary he provides us with remains very spare: "Cold. Wow, really cold! Walls are dark. Similar to the closet space upstairs." Within a few

---

[74]Zampanò provided the blanks but never filled them in.

seconds he reaches the end. The hallway cannot be more than seventy feet long. "That's it. Nothing else. No big deal. Over this Karen and I have been fighting." Except as Navidson swings around, he suddenly discovers a new doorway to the right.   It was not there before.

"What the . . . ?"

Navidson carefully nudges his flashlight into this new darkness and discovers an even longer corridor. "This one's easily . . . I'd say a hundred feet." A few seconds later, he comes across a still larger corridor branching off to the left. It is at least fifteen feet wide with a ceiling well over ten feet high. The length of this one, however, is impossible to estimate as Navidson's flashlight proves useless against the darkness ahead, dying long before it can ever come close to determining an end.

Navidson pushes ahead, moving deeper and deeper into the house, eventually passing a number of doorways leading off into alternate passageways or chambers. "Here's a door. No lock. Hmmm . . . a room, not very big. Empty. No windows. No switches. No outlets. Heading back to the corridor. Leaving the room. It seems colder now. Maybe I'm just getting colder. Here's another door. Unlocked. Another room. Again no windows. Continuing on."

Flashlight and camera skitter across ceiling and floor in loose harmony, stabbing into small rooms, alcoves, or spaces reminiscent of closets, though no shirts hang there. Still, no matter how far Navidson proceeds down this particular passageway, his light never comes close to touching the punctuation point promised by the converging perspective lines, sliding on and on and on, spawning one space after another, a constant stream of corners and walls, all of them unreadable and perfectly smooth.

Finally, Navidson stops in front of an entrance much larger than the rest. It arcs high above his head and yawns into an undisturbed blackness. His flashlight finds the floor but no walls and, for the first time, no ceiling.

Only now do we begin to see how big Navidson's house really is.

Something should be said here about Navidson's hand. Out of all the footage he personally shoots, there rarely exists a shake, tremble, jerk, or even a case of poor framing. His camera, no matter the circumstances, manages to view the world—even this world—with a remarkable steadiness as well as a highly refined aesthetic sensibility.

Comparisons immediately make Navidson's strengths apparent. Holloway Roberts' tape is virtually unwatchable: tilted frames, out of focus, shakes, horrible lighting and finally oblivion when faced with danger. Likewise Karen and Tom's tapes reflect their inexperience and can only be considered for content. Only the images Navidson shoots capture the otherness inherent in that place. Undeniably Navidson's experience as a photojournalist gives him an advantage over the rest when focusing on something that is as terrifying as it is threatening. But, of course, there is more at work here than just the courage to stand and focus. There is also the courage to face and shape the subject in an extremely original manner.[75]

---

[75]See Liza Speen's *Images Of Dark*; Brassaï's *Paris By Night*; the tenderly encountered history of rooms in Andrew Bush's *Bonnettstown*; work of O. Winston Link and Karekin Goekjian; as well as some of the photographs by Lucien Aigner, Osbert Lam, Cas Oorthuys, Floris M. Neusüss, Ashim Ghosh, Annette Lemieux, Irèna Ionesco, Cindy Sherman, Edmund Teske, Andreas Feininger, John Vachon, Tetsuya Ichimura, Sandy Skoglund, Yasuhiro Ishimoto, Beaumont Newhall, James Alinder, Robert Rauschenberg, Miyako Ishiuchi, Alfred Eisenstaedt, Sebastião Ribeiro Salgado, Alfred Stieglitz, Robert Adams, Sol

Libsohn, Huynh Cong ("Nick") Ut, Lester Talkington, William Henry Jackson, Edward Weston, William Baker, Yousuf Karsh, Adam Clark Vroman, Julia Margaret Cameron, George Barnard, Lennart Nilsson, Herb Ritts, Nancy Burson ("Untitled, 1993"), Bragaglia, Henri Cartier-Bresson ("Place de l'Europe"), William Wegman, Gordon Parks, Alvin Langdon Coburn, Edward Ruscha, Herbert Pointing, Simpson Kalisher, Bob Adelman, Volkhard Hofer ("Natural Buildings, 1991"), Lee Friedlander, Mark Edwards, Harry Callahan, Robert Frank, Baltimore *Sun* photographer Aubrey Bodine, Charles Gatewood, Ferenc Berko, Leland Rice, Joan Lyons, Robert D'Alessandro, Victor Keppler, Larry Fink, Bevan Davies, Lotte Jacobi, Burk Uzzle, George Washington Wilson, Julia Margaret Cameron, Carleton Watkins, Edward S. Curtis, Eve Arnold, Michael Lesy (*Wisconsin Death Trip*), Aaron Siskind, Kelly Wise, Cornell Capa, Bert Stern, James Van Der Zee, Leonard Freed, Philip Perkis, Keith Smith, Burt Glin, Bill Brandt, László Moholy-Nagy, Lennart Arthur Rothstein, Louis Stettner, Ray K. Metzker, Edward W. Quigley, Jim Bengston, Richard Prince, Walter Chappell, Paz Errazuriz, Rosamond Wolff Purcell, E. J. Marey, Gary Winogrand, Alexander Gardner, Wynn Bullock, Neal Slavin, Lew Thomas, Patrick Nagatani, Donald Blumberg, David Plowden, Ernestine Ruben, Will McBride, David Vestal, Jerry Burchard, George Gardner, Galina Sankova, Frank Gohlke, Olivia Parker, Charles Traub, Ashvin Mehta, Walter Rosenblum, Bruce Gilden, Imogen Cunningham, Barbara Crane, Lewis Baltz, Roger Minick, George Krause, Saul Leiter, William Horeis, Ed Douglas, John Baldessari, Charles Harbutt, Greg McGregor, Liliane Decock, Lilo Raymond, Hiro, Don Worth, Peter Magubane, Brett Weston, Jill Freedman, Joanne Leonard, Larry Clark, Nancy Rexroth, Jack Manning, Ben Shahn, Marie Cosindas, Robert Demachy, Aleksandra Macijauskas, Andreas Serrano, Les Krims, Heinrich Tönnies, George Rodger, Art Sinsabaugh, Arnold Genthe, Frank Majore, Gertrude Käsebier, Charles Négre, Harold Edgerton, Shomei Tomatsu, Roy Decarava, Samuel Bourne, Giuseppe Primoli, Paul Strand, Lewis Hine, William Eggleston, Frank Sutcliffe, Diane Arbus, Daniel Ibis, Raja Lala Deen Dayal, Ralph Eugene Meatyard, Walker Evans, Mary Ellen Mark, Timothy O'Sullivan, Jacob A. Riis, Ian Isaacs, David Epstein, Karl Struss, Sally Mann, P.H. Emerson, Ansel Adams, Liu Ban Nong, Berencie Abbot, Susan Lipper, Dorthea Lange, James Balog, Doris Ulmann, William Henry Fox Talbot, John Thomson, Phillippe Halsman, Morris Engel, Christophe Yve, Thomas Annan, Alexander Rodchenko, Eliot Elisofon, Eugène Atget, Clarence John Laughlin, Arthur Leipzig, F. Holland Day, Jack English, Alice Austen, Bruce Davidson, Eudora Welty, Jimmy Hare, Ruth Orkin, Masahiko Yoshioka, Paul Outerbridge, Jr., Jerry N. Uelsmann, Louis Jacques Mandè Daguerre, Emmet Gowin, Cary Wasserman, Susan Meiselas, Naomi Savage, Henry Peach Robinson, Sandra Eleta, Boris Ignatovich, Eva Rubinstein, Weegee (Arthur Fellig), Benjamin Stone, André Kertész, Stephen Shore, Lee Miller, Sid Grossman, Donigan Cumming, Jack Welpott, David Sims, Detlef Orlopp ("Untitled"), Margaret Bourke-White, Dmitri Kessel, Val Telberg, Patt Blue, Francisco Infante, Jed Fielding, John Heartfield, Eliot Porter, Gabriele and Helmut Nothhelfer, Francis Bruguière, Jerome Liebling, Eugene Richards, Werner Bischof, Martin Munkacsi, Bruno Barbey, Linda Connor, Oliver Gagliani, Arno Rafael Minkkinen, Richard Margolis, Judith Golden, Philip Trager, Scott Hyde, Willard Van Dyke, Eileen Cowin, Nadar (Gaspard Felix Tournachon), Roger Mertin, Lucas Samaras, Raoul Hausmann, Vilem Kriz, Lisette Model, Robert Leverant, Josef Sudek, Glen Luchford, Edna Bullock, Susan Rankaitis, Gail Skoff, Frank Hurley, Bank Langmore, Carrie Mae Weems, Michael Bishop, Albert and Jean Seeberger, John Gutmann, Kipton Kumler, Joel Sternfeld, Derek Bennett, William Clift, Erica Lennard, Arthur Siegel, Marcia Resnick, Clarence H. White, Fritz Henle, Julio Etchart, Fritz Goro, E.J. Bellocq, Nathan Lyons, Ralph Gibson, Leon Levinstein, Elaine Mayes, Arthur Tess, William Larson, Duane Michals, Benno Friedman, Eve Sonneman, Mark Cohen, Joyce Tenneson, John Pfahl, Doug Prince, Albert Sands Southworth and Josiah Johnson Hawes, Robert W. Fichter, George A. Tice, John Collier, Anton Bruehl, Paul Martin, Tina Barney, Bob Willoughby, Steven Szabo, Paul Caponigro, Gilles Peress, Robert Heinecken, Wright Morris, Inez van Lamsweerde, Peter Hujar, Inge Morath, Judith Joy Ross, Judy Dater, Melissa Shook, Bea Nettles, Dmitri Baltermants, Karl Blossfeldt, Alexander Liberman, Wolfgang Tillmans, Hans Namuth, Bill Burke, Marion Palfi, Jan Groover, Peter Keetman ("Porcelain Hands, 1958"), Henry Wessel, Jr., Syl Labrot, Gilles Ehrmann, Tana Hoban, Martine Franck, John Dominis, Ilse Bing, Jo Ann Callis, Lou Bernstein, Vinoodh Matadin, Todd Webb, Andre Gelpke ("Chiffre 389506: Inkognito, 1993"), Thomas F. Barrow, Robert Cumming, Josef Ehm, Mark Yavno, Tod Papageorge, Ruth Bernhard, Charles Sheeler, Tina Modotti, Zofia Rydet, M. Alvarez Bravo, William Henry Jackson, Peeter Tooming, Betty Hahn, T. S. Nagarajan, Meridel Rubinstein, Romano Cagnoni, Robert Mapplethorpe, Albert Renger-Patzsch, Stasys Zvirgzdas, Geoff Winningham, Thomas Joshua Cooper, Erich Hartmann, Oscar Bailey, Herbert List, Mirella Ricciardi, Franco Fontana, Art Kane, Georgij Zelma, Sergei Mikhailovich Prokudin-Gorskii, Mario Sorrenti, Craig McDean, René Burri, David Douglas Duncan, Tazio Secchiaroli, Joseph D. Jachna, Richard Baltauss, Richard Misrach, Yoshihiko Ito, Minor White, Ellen Auerbach, Izis, Deborah Turbeville, Arnold Newman,

Tzachi Ostrovsky, Joel-Peter Witkin, Adam Fuss, Inge Osswald, Enzo Ragazzini, Bill Owens, Soyna Noskowiak, David Lawrence Levinthal, Mariana Yampolsky, Juergen Teller, Nancy Honey, Elliott Erwitt, Bill Witt, Taizo Ichinose, Nicholas Nixon, Allen A. Dutton, Henry Callahan, Joel Meyrowitz, Willaim A. Garnett, Ulf Sjöstedt, Hiroshi Sugimoto, Toni Frissell, John Blakemore, Roman Vishniac, Debbie Fleming Caffery, Raúl Corrales, Gyorgy Kepes, Joe Deal, David P. Bayles, Michael Snow, Aleksander Krzywoblocki, Paul Bowen, Laura Gilpin, Andy Warhol, Tuija Lydia Elisabeth Lindström-Caudwell, Corinne Day, Kristen McMenamy, Danny Lyon, Erich Salomon, Désiré Charnay, Paul Kwilecki, Carol Beckwith, George Citcherson ("Sailing Ships in an Ice Field, 1869"), W. Eugene Smith, William Klein, José Ortiz-Echagüe, Eadweard Muybridge, and David Octavius Hill, August Sander (*Antlitz der Zeit*), Herbert Bayer, Man Ray, Alex Webb, Frances B. Johnston, Russell Lee, Suzy Lake, Jack Delano, Diane Cook, Heinrich Zille, Lyalya Kuznetsova, Miodrag Djordjevi, Terry Fincher, Joel Meyerowitz, John R. Gossage, Barbara Morgan, Édouard Boubat, Horst P. Horst, Hippolyte Bayard, Albert Kahn, Karen Helen Knorr, Carlotta M. Corpon, Abigail Heyman, Marion Post Wolcott, Lillian Bassman, Henry Holmes Smith, Constantine Manos, Gjon Mili, Michael Nichols, Roger Fenton, Adolph de Meyer, Van Deren Coke, Barbara Astman, Richard Kirstel, William Notman, Kenneth Josephson, Louise Dahl-Wolfe, Josef Koudelka, Sarah E. Charlesworth, Erwin Blumenfeld, Jacques Henri Lartigue, Pirkle Jones, Edward Steichen, George Hurrell, Steve Fitch, Lady Hawarden, Helmar Lerski, Oscar Gustave Rejlander, John Thomson, Irving Penn, and Jane Evelyn Atwood (photographs of children at the National School for Blind Youth). Not to mention Suze Randall, Art Wolfe, Charles and Rita Summers, Tom and Pat Leeson, Michael H. Francis, John Botkin, Dan Blackburn, Barbara Ess, Erwin and Peggy Bauer, Peter Arnold, Gerald Lacz, James Wojcik, Dan Borris, Melanie Acevedo, Micheal McLaughlin, Darrin Haddad, William Vazquez, J. Michael Myers, Rosa & Rosa, Patricia McDonough, Aldo Rossi, Mark Weiss, Craig Cutler, David Barry, Chris Sanders, Neil Brown, James Schnepf, Kevin Wilkes, Ron Simmons, Chip Clark, Ron Kerbo, Kevin Downey, Nick Nichols; also Erik Aeder, Drew Kampion, Les Walker, Rob Gilley, Don King, Jeff Hornbaker, Alexander Gallardo, Russell Hoover, Jeff Flindt, Chris Van Lennep, Mike Moir, Brent Humble, Ivan Ferrer, Don James, John Callahan, Bill Morris, Kimiro Kondo, Leonard Brady, Fred Swegles, Eric Baeseman, Tsuchiya, Darrell Wong, Warren Bolster, Joseph Libby, Russell Hoover, Peter Frieden, Craig Peterson, Ted Grambeau, Gordinho, Steve Wilkings, Mike Foley, Kevin Welsh, LeRoy Grannis, John Bilderback, Craig Fineman, Michael Grosswendt, Craig Huglin, Seamas Mercado, John Heath "Doc" Ball, Tom Boyle, Rob Keith, Vince Cavataio, Jeff Divine, Aaron Loyd, Chris Dyball, Steve Fox, George Greenough, Aaron Loyd, Ron Stoner, Jason Childs, Kin Kimoto, Chris Dyball, Bob Barbour, John Witzig, Ben Siegfried, Ron Romanosky, Brian Bielmann, Dave Bjorn, John Severson, Martin Thick (see his profound shot of Dana Fisher cradling a chimpanze rescued from a meat vendor in Zaire), Doug Cockwell, Art Brewer, Fred Swegles, Erik Hans, Mike Balzer, John Scott, Rob Brown, Bernie Baker, William Sharp, Randy Johnson, Nick Pugay, Tom Servais, Dennis Junor, Eric Baeseman, Sylvain Cazenave, Woody Woodworth, and of course, J.C. Hemment, David "Chim" Seymour, Vu Ngoc Tong, William Dinwiddie, James Burton, Marv Wolf, London Thorne, John Gallo, Nguyen Huy, Leonidas Stanson, Pham Co Phac, Kadel & Herbert, Underwood & Underwood, James H. Hare, Tran Oai Dung, Lucian S. Kirtland, Edmond Ratisbonne, Pham Tranh, Luong Tan Tuc, George Strock, Joe Rosenthal, Ralph Morse, Ho Van De, Nguyen Nhut Hoa, Nguyen Van Chien, Nguyen Van Thang, Phung Quang Liem, Truong Phu Thien, John Florea, George Silk, Carl Mydans, Pham Van Kuong, Nguyen Khac Tam, Vu Hung Dung, Nguyen Van Nang, Yevgeny Khaldei, To Dinh, Ho Ca, Hank Walker, Tran Ngoc Dang, Vo Duc Hiep, Trinh Dinh Hy, Howard Breedlove, Nguyen Van Thuan, Vu Hanh, Ly Van Cao, Burr McIntosh, Ho Van Tu, Helen Levitt, Robert Capa, Ly Eng, Mathew Brady, Sau Van, Thoi Huu, Leng, Thong Veasna, Nguyen Luong Nam, Huynh Van Huu, Ngoc Huong, Alan Hirons, Lek, George J. Denoncourt II, Hoang Chau, Eric Weigand, Pham Vu Binh, Gilles Caron, Tran Binh Khuol, Jerald Kringle, Le Duy Que, Thanh Tinh, Frederick Sommer, Nguyen Van Thuy, Robert Moeser, Chhim Sarath, Duong Thanh Van, Howard Nurenberger, Vo Ngoc Khanh, Dang Van Hang, James Pardue, Bui Dinh Tuy, Doug Clifford, Tran Xuan Hy, Nguyen Van Tha, Keizaburo Shimamoto, Nguyen Van Ung, Bob Hodierne, Nguyen Viet Hien, Dinh De, Sun Heang, Tea "Moonface" Kim Heang, Lyng Nhan, Charles Chellappah, The Dinh, Nguyen Van Nhu, Ngoc Nhu, John Andescavage, Nguyen Van Huong, Francis Bailly, Georg Gensluckner, Vo Van Luong, James Denis Gill, Huynh Van Dung, Nguyen Than Hien, Terrence Khoo, Paul Schutzer, Vo Van Quy, Malcolm Browne, Le Khac Tam, Huynh Van Huong, Do Van Nhan, Franz Dalma, Kyoichi Sawada, Willy Mettler, James Lohr, Le Kia, Sam Kai Faye, Frank Lee, Nguyen Van Man, Joseph Tourtelot, Doan Phi Hung, Ty Many, Nguyen Ngoc Tu, Le Thi Nang, Nguyen Van Chien, Doug Woods, Glen Rasmussen, Hiromichi Mine, Duong Cong Thien, Bernard B. Fall, Randall Reimer, Luong Nghia Dung, Bill Hackwell, Pen, Nguyen Duc Thanh, Chea Ho, Jerry Wyngarden, Vantha, Chip Maury, J.

As Navidson takes his first step through that immense arch, he is suddenly a long way away from the warm light of the living room. In fact his creep into that place resembles the eerie faith required for any deep sea exploration, the beam of his flashlight scratching at nothing but the invariant blackness.

Navidson keeps his attention focused on the floor ahead of him, and no doubt because he keeps looking down, the floor begins to assume a new meaning. It can no longer be taken for granted. Perhaps something lies beneath it. Perhaps it will open up into some deep fissure.

Suddenly immutable silence rushes in to replace what had momentarily shattered it.

Navidson freezes, unsure whether or not he really just heard something growl.

"I better be able to find my way back," he finally whispers, which though probably muttered in jest suddenly catches him off guard.

Navidson swiftly turns around. Much to his horror, he can no longer see the arch let alone the wall. He has walked beyond the range of his light. In fact, no matter where he points the flashlight, the only thing he can perceive is oily darkness. Even worse, his panicked turn and the subsequent absence of any landmarks has made it impossible for him to remember which direction he just came from.

"Oh god" he blurts, creating odd repeats in the distance.

He twists around again.

"Hey!" he shouts, spawning a multitude of a's, then rotates forty-five degrees and yells "Balls!" a long moment of silence follows before he hears the faint halls racing back through the dark. After several more such turns, he discovers a loud "easy" returns a z with the least amount of delay. This is the direction he decides on, and within less than a minute the beam from his flashlight finds something more than darkness.

Quickening his pace slightly, Navidson reaches the wall and the safety he perceives there. He now faces another decision: left or right. This time, before going anywhere, he reaches into his pocket and places a penny

---

Gonzales, Pierre Jahan, Catherine Leroy, Leonard Hekel, Kim Van Tuoc, W.B. Bass Jr., Sean Flynn, Heng Ho, Dana Stone, Nguyen Dung, Landon K. Thorne II, Gerard Hebert, Michel Laurent, Robert Jackson Ellison, Put Sophan, Nguyen Trung Dinh, Huynh Van Tri, Neil K. Hulbert, James McJunkin, Le Dinh Du, Chhor Vuthi, Claude Arpin-Pont, Raymond Martinoff, Jean Peraud, Nguyen Huong Nam, Dickey Chapelle, Lanh Daunh Rar, Bryan Grigsby, Henri Huet, Huynh Thang My, Peter Ronald Van Thiel, Everette Dixie Reese, Jerry A. Rose, Oliver E. Noonan, Kim Savath, Bernard Moran, Kuoy Sarun, Do Van Vu, Nguyen Man Hieu, Charles Richard Eggleston, Sain Hel, Nguyen Oanh Liet, Dick Durance, Vu Van Giang, Bernard Kolenberg, Sou Vichith, Ronald D. Gallagher, Dan Dodd, Francois Sully, Kent Potter, Alfred Batungbacal, Dieter Bellendorf, Nick Mills, Ronald L. Haeberle, Terry Reynolds, Leroy Massie, Sam Castan, Al Chang, Philip R. Boehme. And finally Eddie Adams, Charles Hoff, Larry Burrows, and Don McCullin ("American soldiers tending wounded child in a cellar of a house by candlelight, 1968").[76]

[76]Alison Adrian Burns, another Zampanò reader, told me this list was entirely random. With the possible exception of Brassaï, Speen, Bush and Link, Zampanò was not very familiar with photographers. "We just picked the names out of some books and magazines he had lying around," Burns told me. "I'd describe a picture or two and he'd say no or he'd say fine. A few times he just told me to choose a page and point. Hey, whatever he wanted to do. That was what I was there for. Sometimes though he just wanted to hear about the LA scene, what was happening, what wasn't, the gloss, the names of clubs and bars. That sort of thing. As far as I know, that list never got written down."

at his feet. Relying on this marker, he heads left for a while. When a minute passes and he has still failed to find the entrance, he returns to the penny. Now he moves off to the right and very quickly comes across a doorway, only this one, as we can see, is much smaller and has a different shape than the one he originally came through. He decides to keep walking. When a minute passes and he still has not found the arch, he stops.

"Think, Navy, think," he whispers to himself, his voice edged slightly with fear.

Again that faint growl returns, rolling through the darkness like thunder.

Navidson quickly does an about face and returns to the doorway. Only now he discovers that the penny he left behind, which should have been at least a hundred feet further, lies directly before him. Even stranger, the doorway is no longer the doorway but the arch he had been looking for all along.

Unfortunately as he steps through it, he immediately sees how drastically everything has changed. The corridor is now much narrower and ends very quickly in a T. He has no idea which way to go, and when a third growl ripples through that place, this time significantly louder, Navidson panics and starts to run.

His sprint, however, lasts only a few seconds. He realizes quickly enough that it is a useless, even dangerous, course of action. Catching his breath and doing his best to calm his frayed nerves, he tries to come up with a better plan.

"Karen!" he finally shouts, a flurry of air-in's almost instantly swallowed in front of him. "Tom!" he tries, briefly catching hold of the -om's as they too start to vanish, though before doing so completely, Navidson momentarily detects in the last -om a slightly higher pitch entwined in his own voice.

He waits a moment, and not hearing anything else, shouts again: "I'm in here!" giving rise to tripping nn-ear's reverberating and fading, until in the next to last instant a sharp cry comes back to him, a child's cry, calling out for him, drawing him to the right.

By shouting "I'm here" and following the add-ee's singing off the walls, Navidson slowly begins to make his way through an incredibly complex and frequently disorienting series of turns. Eventually after backtracking several times and making numerous wrong choices, occasionally descending into disturbing territories of silence, the voice begins to grow noticeably louder, until finally Navidson slips around a corner, certain he has found his way out. Instead though, he encounters only more darkness and this time greater quiet. His breathing quickens. He is uncertain which way to go. Obviously he is afraid. And then quite abruptly he steps to the right through a low passageway and discovers a corridor terminating in warm yellow light, lamp light, with a tiny silhouette standing in the doorway, tugging her daddy home with a cry.

Emerging into the safety of his own living room, Navidson immediately scoops Daisy up in his arms and gives her a big hug.

"I had a nightmare," she says with a very serious nod.

Similar to the Khumbu Icefall at the base of Mount Everest where blue seracs and chasms change unexpectedly throughout the day and night, Navidson is the first one to discover how that place also seems to constantly change. Unlike the Icefall, however, not even a single hairline fracture appears in those walls. Absolutely nothing visible to the eye provides a reason for or even evidence of those terrifying shifts which can in a matter of moments reconstitute a simple path into an extremely complicated one.[77]

---

[77]"nothing visible to the eye provides a reason"—a fitting phrase for what's happened.

And to think my day actually started off pretty well.

I woke up having had an almost wet-dream about Thumper. She was doing this crazy Margaretha Geertruida Zelle dance, veil after colored veil thrown aside, though oddly enough never landing, rather flying around her as if she were in the middle of some kind of gentle twister, these sheer sheets of fabric continuing to encircle her, even as she removes more and more of them, allowing me only momentary glimpses of her body, her smooth skin, her mouth, her waist, her—ah yes, I get a glimpse of that too, and I'm moving towards her, moving past all that interference, certain that with every step I take I'll soon have her, after all she's almost taken everything off, no she <u>has</u> taken everything off, her knees are spreading apart, just a few more veils to get past and I'll be able to see her, not just bits & pieces of her, but all of her, no longer molested by all this nonsense, in fact I'm there already which means I'm about to enter her which apparently is enough to blow the circuit, hit the switch, prohibit that sublime and much anticipated conclusion, leaving me blind in the daylight stream pouring through my window.

Fuck.

I go off to cuff in the shower. At least the water's hot and there's enough steam to fog the mirror. Afterwards, I pack my pipe and light up. Wake & Bake. More like Wash & Bake. Half a bowl of cereal and a shot of bourbon later, I'm there, my friendly haze having finally arrived. I'm ready for work.

Parking's easy to find. On Vista. I jog up to Sunset, even jog up the stairs, practically skipping past the By Appointment Only sign. Why skipping? Because as I step into the Shop I know I'm not even one minute late, which is not usually the case for me. The expression on my boss's face reveals just how astonishing an achievement this is. I couldn't care less about him. I want to see Thumper. I want to find out if she's really wearing any of that diaphanous rainbow fabric I was dreaming about.

Of course she's not there, but that doesn't get me down. I'm still optimistic she'll arrive. And if not today, why fuck, tomorrow's just another day away.

A sentiment I could almost sing.

I immediately sit down at the side counter and start working, mainly because I don't want to deal with my boss which could mean jeopardizing my good mood. Of course he couldn't care less about me or my mood. He approaches, clearing his throat. He will talk, he will ruin everything, except it suddenly penetrates that chalky material he actually insists on calling his brain, that I'm building his precious points, and sure enough this insight prohibits his trap from opening and he leaves me alone.

Points are basically clusters of needles used to shade the skin. They are necessary because a single point amounts to a prick not much bigger than this period ".". Okay, maybe a little bigger. Anyway, five needles go into what's called a 5, seven for 7's and so on—all soldered together towards the base.

I actually enjoy making them. There's something pleasant about concentrating on the subtle details, the precision required, constantly checking and re-checking to assure yourself that yes indeed the sharps are level, in the correct arrangement, ready at last to be fixed in place with dots of hot solder. Then I re-check all my re-checking: the points must not be too close nor too far apart nor skewed in any way, and only then, if I'm satisfied, which I usually am—though take heed "usually" does not always mean "always"—will I scrub the shafts and put them aside to be sterilized later in the ultrasound or Autoclave.

My boss may think I can't draw worth shit but he knows I build needles better than anyone. He calls me all the time on my tardiness, my tendency to drift & moither and of course the odds that I'll ever get to tattoo anything—"Johnny, nothing you do, (shaking his head) no one's ever gonna wanna make permanent, unless they're crazy, and let me tell you something Johnny, crazies never pay"—but about my needle making I've never heard him complain once.

Anyway, a couple of hours whiz by. I'm finishing up a batch of 5's—my boss's cluster of choice—when he finally speaks, telling me to pull some bottles of black and purple ink and fill a few caps while I'm at it. We keep the stuff in a storeroom in back. It's a sizable space, big enough to fit a small work table in. You have to climb eight pretty steep steps to reach it. That's where we stock all the extras, and we have extras for almost everything, except light bulbs. For some reason my boss hasn't picked up any extra light bulbs in a while. Today, of course, I flick the switch, and FLASH! BLAM! POP!, okay scratch the blam, the storeroom bulb burns out. I recommence flicking, as if such insistent, highly repetitive and at this point pointless action could actually resurrect the light. It doesn't. The switch has been rendered meaningless, forcing me to feel my way around in the dark. I keep the door open so I can see okay, but it still takes me awhile to negotiate the shadows before I can locate the caps and ink.

By now, the sweet effects of my dream, to say nothing of the soft thrumming delivered care of alcohol and Oregon bud, have worn off, though I still continue to think about Thumper, slowly coming to grips with the fact that she won't be visiting today. This causes my spirits to drop substantially, until I realize I have no way of knowing that for certain. After all, there's still half a day left. No, she's not coming. I know it. I can feel it in my gut. That's okay. Tomorrow's—aw, fuck that.

I start filling caps with purple, concentrating on its texture, the strange hue, imagining I can actually observe the rapid pulse of its bandwidth. These are stupid thoughts, and as if to confirm that sentiment, darkness pushes in on me. Suddenly the slash of light on my hands looks sharp enough to cut me. Real sharp. Move and it will cut me. I do move and guess what? I start to bleed. The laceration isn't deep but important stuff has been struck, leaking over the table and floor. Lost.

I don't have long.

Except I'm not bleeding though I am breathing hard. Real hard. I don't need to touch my face to know there are now beads of sweat slipping off my forehead, flicking off my eyelids, streaming down the back of my neck. Cold as hands. Hands of the dead. Something terrible is going on here. Going extremely wrong. Get out, I think. I want to get out. But I can't move.

Then as if this were nothing but a grim prelude, shit really starts to happen.

There's that awful taste again, sharp as rust, wrapping around my tongue.

Worse, I'm no longer alone.

Impossible.

Not impossible.

This time it's human.

Maybe not.

Extremely long fingers.

A sucking sound too. Sucking on teeth, teeth already torn from the gums.

I don't know how I know this.

But it's already too late, I've seen the eyes. The eyes. They have no whites. I haven't seen this. The way they glisten they glisten red. Then it begins reaching for me, slowly unfolding itself out of its corner, mad meat all of it, but I understand. These eyes are full of blood.

Except I'm only looking at shadows and shelves.

Of course, I'm alone.

And then behind me, the door closes.

The rest is in pieces. A scream, a howl, a roar. All's warping, or splintering. That makes no sense. There's a terrible banging. The air's rank with stench. At least that's not a mystery. I know the source. Boy, do I ever. I've shit myself. Pissed myself too. I can't believe it. Urine soaking into my pants, fecal matter running down the back of my legs, I'm caught in it, must run and hide from it, but I still can't move. In fact, the more I try to escape, the less I can breathe. The more I try to hold on, the less I can focus. Something's leaving me. Parts of me.

Everything falls apart.

Stories heard but not recalled.

Letters too.

Words filling my head. Fragmenting like artillery shells. Shrapnel, like syllables, flying everywhere. Terrible syllables. Sharp. Cracked. Traveling at murderous speed. Tearing through it all in a very, very bad perhaps even irreparable way.

Known.

Some.

Call.

Is.

Air.

Am?

Incoherent—yes.

Without meaning—I'm afraid not.

The shape of a shape of a shape of a face dis(as)sembling right before my eyes. What wail embattled break. Like a hawk. Another Maldon or no Maldon at all, on snowy days, or not snowy at all, far beyond the edge of any reasonable awareness. This is what it feels like to be really afraid. Though of course it doesn't. None of this can truly approach the reality of that fear, there in the midst of all that bedlam, like the sound of a heart or some other unholy blast, desperate & dying, slamming, no banging into the thin wall of my inner ear, paper thin in fact, attempting to shatter inside what had already been shattered long ago.

I should be dead.

Why am I still here?

And as that question appears—concise, in order, properly accented—I see I'm holding onto the tray loaded with all those caps and bottles of black and purple ink. Not only that but I'm already walking as fast as I can through the doorway. The door is open though I did not

After putting his daughter back to bed, Navidson finds Karen standing in the entrance to their room.

---

open it. I stub my toe. I'm falling down the stairs, tripping over myself, hurling the tray in the air, the caps, the ink, all of it, floating now above me, as my hands, independent of anything I might have thought to suggest, reach up to protect my head. Something hisses and slashes out at the back of my neck. It doesn't matter. Down I go, head first, somersaulting down those eight pretty steep steps, a wild blur, leaving me to passively note the pain spots as they happen: shoulders, hip, elbows, even as I also, at the same time, remain dimly aware of so much ink coming down like a bad rain, splattering around me, everywhere, covering me, even the tray hitting me, though that doesn't hurt, the caps scattering across the floor, and of course the accompanying racket, telling my boss, telling them all, whoever else was there— What? not that it was over, it wasn't, not yet.

The wind's knocked out of me. It's not coming back. Here's where I die, I think. And it's true, I'm possessed by the premonition of what will be, what has to be, my inevitable asphyxiation. At least that's what they see, my boss and crew, as they come running to the back, called there by all that clatter & mess. What they can't see though is the omen seen in a fall, my fall, as I'm doused in black ink, my hands now completely covered, and see the floor is black, and—have you anticipated this or should I be more explicit?—jet on jet; for a blinding instant I have watched my hand vanish, in fact all of me has vanished, one hell of a disappearing act too, the already foreseen dissolution of the self, lost without contrast, slipping into oblivion, until mid-gasp I catch sight of my reflection in the back of the tray, the ghost in the way: seems I'm not gone, not quite. My face has been splattered with purple, as have my arms, granting contrast, and thus defining me, marking me, and at least for the moment, preserving me.

Suddenly I can breathe and with each breath the terror rapidly dissipates.

My boss, however, is scared shitless.

"Jesus Christ Johnny," he says. "Are you okay? What happened?"

Can't you see I've shit myself, I think to shout. But now I see that I haven't. Except for the ink blotting my threads, my pants are bone dry.

I mumble something about how much my toe hurts.

He takes that to mean I'm alright and won't try to sue him from a wheelchair.

Later a patron points out the long, bloody scratch on the back of my neck.

I'm unable to respond.

Now though, I realize what I should of said—in the spirit of the dark; in the spirit of the staircase —

"Known some call is air am."

Which is to say —

"I am not what I used to be."[78]

[78]Though Mr. Truant's asides may often seem impenetrable, they are not without rhyme or reason. The reader who wishes to interpret Mr. Truant on his or her own may disregard this note. Those, however, who feel they would profit from a better understanding of his past may wish to proceed ahead and read his father's obituary in Appendix II-D as well as those letters written by his institutionalized mother in Appendix II-E. — Ed.

"What's the matter," she murmurs, still half-asleep.

"Go back to sleep. Daisy just had a bad dream."

Navidson starts to go back downstairs.

"I'm sorry Navy," Karen says quietly. "I'm sorry I got so mad. It's not your fault. That thing just scares me. Come back to bed."

And as they later confide in separate video entries, that night, for the first time in weeks, they made love again, their descriptions running the gamut of anything from "gentle" and "comforting" to "familiar" and "very satisfying." Their bodies had repaired what words never tried to, and at least for a little while they felt close again.

The next morning, with harmony now restored, Navidson cannot bring himself to tell Karen about his visit. Fortunately having nearly gotten lost inside his own house has for the moment diminished his appetite for its darkness. He promises to turn over the initial investigation to Billy Reston: "Then we'll call *The New York Times*, Larry King, whoever, and we'll move. End of story." Karen responds to his offer with kisses, clinging to his hand, a stability of sorts once again returning to their lives.

Still the compromise is far from satisfying. As Karen records on her Hi 8: "I told Navy I'll stay for the first look in there but I've also called Mom. I want to get out of here as soon as possible."

Navidson admits in his: "I feel lousy about lying to Karen. But I think it's unreasonable of her to expect me not to investigate. She knows who I am. I think —"

At which point, the study door suddenly swings open and Daisy, wearing a red and gold dress, barges in and begins tugging on her father's sleeve.

"Come play with me Daddy."

Navidson lifts his daughter onto his lap.

"Okay. What do you want to play?"

"I don't know," she shrugs. "Always."

"What's always?"

But before she can answer, he starts tickling her around the neck and Daisy dissolves into bursts of delight.

Despite the tremendous amount of material generated by Exploration A, no one has ever commented on the game Daisy wants to play with her father, perhaps because everyone assumes it is either a request "to play always" or just a childish neologism.

Then again, "always" slightly mispronounces "hallways."

It also echoes it.

VI

[Animals] lack a symbolic identity and the self-consciousness that goes with it. They merely act and move reflexively as they are driven by their instincts. If they pause at all, it is only a physical pause; inside they are anonymous, and even their faces have no name. They live in a world without time, pulsating, as it were, in a state of dumb being . . . The knowledge of death is reflective and conceptual, and animals are spared it. They live and they disappear with the same thoughtlessness: a few minutes of fear, a few seconds of anguish, and it is over. But to live a whole lifetime with the fate of death haunting one's dreams and even the most sun-filled days—that's something else.

— Ernest Becker

While the pragmatic space of animals is a function of inborn instincts, man has to learn what orientation he needs in order to act.

— Christian Norberg-Schulz

When Hillary, the grey coated Siberian husky, appears at the end of *The Navidson Record,* he is no longer a puppy. A couple of years have passed. Something forever watchful has taken up residence in his eyes. He may be playful with those he knows but whenever strangers wander too close they invariably hear a growl rising from somewhere deep in his throat, a little like distant thunder, warning them away.[79]

Mallory, the tabby cat, vanishes completely, and no mention is made about what happened to him. His disappearance remains a mystery.

One thing however is certain: the house played a very small part in both their histories.

The incident took place on August 11th, 1990 a week after Will Navidson's secret exploration of the hallway. Saturday morning cartoons blare from the kitchen television, Chad and Daisy munch down their breakfast, and Karen stands outside smoking a cigarette, talking on the phone with Audrie McCullogh, her shelf building accomplice. The topic of the moment is Feng Shui and all it has failed to do. "No matter how many ceramic turtles or wooden ducks, goldfish, celestial dragons, or bronze lions I put in this goddamn house," she rants. "It still keeps throwing off this awful energy. I need to find a psychic. Or an exorcist. Or a really good real-estate agent." Meanwhile in the living room, Tom helps Navidson take some still shots of the hallway using a strobe.

Suddenly, somewhere in the house, there is a loud yowl and bark. An instant later Mallory comes screaming into the living room with Hillary nipping at his tail. It is not the first time they have involved themselves in such a routine. The only exception is that on this occasion, after dashing up and over the sofa, both puppy and cat head straight down the hallway and disappear into the darkness. Navidson probably would have gone in after them had he not instantly heard barks outside followed by Karen's shouts accusing him of letting the animals out when on that day they were supposed to stay in.

"What the hell?" we hear Navidson mutter loudly.

Sure enough Hillary and Mallory are in the backyard. Mallory up a tree, Hillary howling grandly over his achievement.

For something so startling, it seems surprising how little has been made of this event. Bernard Porch in his four thousand page treatise on *The Navidson Record* devotes only a third of a sentence to the subject: ", (strange how the house won't support the presence of animals)."[80] Mary Widmunt leaves us with just one terse question: "So what's the deal with the pets?"[81] Even Navidson himself, the consummate investigator, never revisits the subject.

Who knows what might have been discovered if he had.

Regardless, Holloway soon arrives and any understanding that might have been gained by further analyzing the strange relationship between animals and the house is passed over in favor of human exploration.[82]

Endnotes

[79]See Selwyn Hyrkas' "The End of City Life" in *Interview*, v. 25 October 1995, p. 54.
[80]Bernard Porch's *All In All* (Cambridge: Harvard University Press, 1995), p. 1,302.
[81]Mary Widmunt's "The Echo of Dark" in *Gotta Go* (Baton Rouge: Louisiana State University Press, 1994), p. 59.
[82]Strange how Zampanò also fails to comment on the inability of animals to wander those corridors. I believe there's a great deal of significance in this discovery. Unfortunately, Zampanò never returns to the matter and while I would like to offer you my own interpretation I am a little high and alot drunk, trying to determine what set me off in the first place on this private little home-bound binge.

For one thing, Thumper came into the Shop today.

Ever since I fell down the stairs, things have changed there. My boss kind of tiptoes around me, playing all low key and far off, his demeanor probably matching his old junkie days. Even his friends keep their distance, everyone for the most part just leaving me alone to sketch and solder, though I'm sketching far less these days, I mean, with all this writing. Anyway, Thumper's actually been by a few times but my incomprehensible shyness persists, forbidding me to ever summon up more than an occasional intelligible sentence. Recently though I did get this crazy idea: I decided to go out on a limb and show her that sappy little bit I wrote about her—you know with all that coastal norths and August-sun scent-of-pine-trees stuff, even the Lucy part. I just put it in an envelope and carried it around with me until she dropped by and then handed it to her without a word.

I don't know what I expected, but she opened it right on the spot and read it and then laughed and then my boss grabbed it and he sort of winced—"Now look who's the dumb mutant" he shuddered—and that was that. Thumper handed me her flip flops and Adidas sweat pants and stretched out on the chair. I felt like such an idiot. Lude had warned me I'd be certifiable if I showed it to her. Maybe I am. I actually believed it would touch her in some absurd way. But to hear her laugh like that really fucked me up. I should of stayed away from such flights of fancy, stuck to my regular made-up stories.

I did my best to hide in the back, though I was too scared to go too far back because of the storeroom.

Then right before she left, Thumper came over and handed me her card.

"Call me some time," she said with a wink. "You're cute."

My life instantly changed.

I thought.

I told Lude. He told me to call her at once.

I waited.

Then I re-considered, then I postponed.

Finally, at exactly twenty-two past three in the morning, I dialed. It was a beeper. I punched in my number.

She's a stripper I reasoned. Strippers live late.

An hour passed. I started drinking. I'm still drinking. She hasn't called. She isn't going to call.

I feel dead. Hillary and Mallory, I suddenly envy them. I wonder if Navidson did too. I bet Zampanò envied them. I need to get away. Zampanò liked animals. Far away. All those cats he would talk to in that weedy courtyard. At dawn. At night. So many shades slinking out from under that dusty place like years, his years, could they be like my years too? though certainly not so many, not like him, years and years of them, always rubbing up against his legs, and I see it all so clearly now, static announcements that yes! hmmm, how shocking, they still are there, disconnected but vital, the way memories reveal their life by simply appearing, sprinting out from under the shadows, paws!-patter-paws-paws!, pausing then to rub against our legs, zap! senile sparks perhaps but ah yes still there, and I'm thinking, has another missing year resolved in song?— though let me not get too far from myself, they were after all only cats, quadruped mice-devouring mote-chasing shades, Felis catus, with very little to remind them of themselves or their past or even their tomorrows, especially when the present burns hot with play, their pursuits and their fear, a bright flash to pursue (sun a star on a nothing's back), a dark slash to escape (there are always predators . . .), the spry interplay of hidden things and visible wings flung upon that great black sail of rods and cones, thin and fractionary, a covenant of light, ark for the instant, echoing out the dark and the Other, harmonizing with the crack-brack-crisp-tricks of every broken leaf of grass or displaced stick, and so thrust by shadow and the vague hope of color into a rhapsody of motion and meaning, albeit momentary, pupil pulling wider, wider still, and darker, receiving all of it, and even more of it, though still only beholding some of it, until in the frenzy of reception, this mote-clawing hawk-fearing shade loses itself in temporary madness, leaping, springing, flinging itself after it all, as if it were possessed (and it is); as if that kind of physical response could approximate the witnessed world, which it can't, though very little matters enough to prevent the try—all of which is to say, in the end, they are only cats but cats to talk to just the same before in their own weaving and wending, they Kilkenny-disappear, just as they first appeared, out of nowhere, vanishing back into the nowhere, tales from some great story we will never see but one day just might imagine (which in the gray of gentler eves will prove far more than any of us could ever need; "enough," we will shout, "enough!" our bellies full, our hearts full, our ages full; fullness and greater fullness and even more fullness; how then we will laugh and forget how the imagining has already left us) slinking back into that place of urban barley, grass, fennel and wheat, or just plain hay, golden hay, where—Hey! Hey! Hey-hey! Hay days gone by, bye-bye, gone way way away. And what of dogs you ask? Well, there are no dogs except for the Pekinese but that's another story, one I won't, I cannot tell. It's too dark and difficult and without whim, and if you didn't notice I'm in a whimsical (inconsequential) frame of mind right now, talking (scribbling?) aimlessly and strangely about cats, enjoying all the rules in this School of Whim, the play of it,—Where Have I Moved? What Have I Muttered? Who Have I Met?—the frolic and the drift, as I go thinking now, tripping really, over the notion of eighty or more of Zampanò's dusty cats (for no particular/relevant reason) which must implicitly mean that no, it cannot be raining cats and dogs, due to the dust, so much of it, on the ground, about the weeds, in the air, so therefore/ ergo/ thus (∴): no dogs, no Pekinese, just the courtyard,

Zampanò's courtyard, on a mad lost-noon day, wild with years and pounce and sun, even if another day would find Zampanò elsewhere, far from the sun, this sun, flung face down on his ill-swept floor, without so much as a clue, "No trauma, just old age" the paramedics would say, though they could never explain—no one could—what they found near where he lay, four of them, six or seven inches long and half an inch deep, splintering the wood, left by some terrible awe-full thing, signature in script of steel or claws, though not Santa, Zampanò died after Christmas after all, but no myth either, for I saw the impossible marks near the trunk, touched them, even caught some splinters in my fingertips, some of their unexpected sadness and mourning, which though dug out later with a safety pin, I swear still fester beneath my skin, reminding me in a peculiar way of him, just like other splinters I still carry, though these much much deeper, having never been worked out by the body but quite the contrary worked <u>into</u> the body, by now long since buried, calcified and fused to my very bones, taking me further from the warm frolic of years, reminding me of much colder days, Where I Left Death, or thought I had—I am tripping—overcast in tones December gray, recalling names,—I have tripped—swept in Ohio sleet and rain, ruled by a man with a beard rougher than horse hide and hands harder than horn, who called me beast because I was his boy though he wasn't my father, which is another story, another place I'm here to avoid, as I'm certain there are places you too have sought to avoid, just as one of Zampanò's early readers also found a story she wanted to avoid, though she finally told me it, or at least some of it, how she'd departed from the old man's apartment at nightfall, having just endured hours of speech on comfort, death and legend, not to speak of mothers & daughters and birds & bees and fathers & sons and cats & dogs, all of it distressing her, saddening her, confusing her, and thus leaving her completely unprepared for the memory she was about to find, abruptly returning from her childhood in Santa Cruz, even as she was trying to reorient herself in a familiar setting and the comforting routine of a long walk back to her car,—it had been raining there; pouring in fact; though not on Franklin & Whitley—suddenly noticing the unnatural heaviness of a shadow slipping free from the burnt dusk, though not a shadow at all, later translating this as the sight of an enormous creature trespassing on the curve of a Northern California night, like the shadow she saw hiding in the bottom turn of Zampanò's stairwell, moving too, towards her, and so causing her to panic and scramble into the comforts offered by a local bar—or that night scramble through the gate of Zampanò's building—away from all that gloom, until only many hours and many drinks later could she finally fall asleep, her hangover the following day leaving her—"gratefully," she said—with only a fleeting memory of something white with ropes of sea smoke and one terrifying flash of blue, which was more, she told me, than she could usually share even if—which she wouldn't share—she knew it still wasn't even the half of it.

And so now, in the shadow of unspoken events, I watch Zampanò's courtyard darken.

Everything whimsical has left.

I try to study the light-going carefully. From my room. In the glass of my memory. In the moonstream of my imagination. The weeds, the windows, every bench.

But the old man is not there, and the cats are all gone.

Something else has taken their place. Something I am unable to see. Waiting.

I'm afraid.
It is hungry. It is immortal.

Worse, it knows nothing of whim.

VII

But all this—the mysterious, far-reaching hair-line trail, the absence of sun from the sky, the tremendous cold, and the strangeness and weirdness of it all—made no impression on the man. It was not because he was long used to it. He was a newcomer in the land, a chechaquo, and this was his first winter. The trouble with him was that he was without imagination.

— Jack London
"To Build A Fire"

Holloway Roberts arrives carrying a rifle. In fact in the very first shot we see of him, he emerges from a truck holding a Weatherby 300 magnum.

Even without weapons though, Holloway would still be an intimidating man. He is broad and powerful with a thick beard and deeply creased brow. Dissatisfaction motivates him, and at forty-eight, he still drives himself harder than any man half his age. Consequently, when he steps onto Navidson's front lawn, arms folded, eyes scrutinizing the house, bees flying near his boots, he looks less like a guest and more like some conquistador landing on new shores, preparing for war.

Born in Menomonie, Wisconsin, Holloway Roberts has made a career as a professional hunter and explorer. As travel writer Aramis Garcia Pineda commented: "He is confident, leads well, and possesses a remarkable amount of brassball courage. Over the past some have resented his strength and drive but most agree the sense of security one feels in his presence—especially in life-threatening situations—makes tolerating the irritating sides of his character well worth it."[83]

When Navidson told Reston how Karen had explicitly asked him not to explore the hallway—and presumably Navidson described the discoveries he made during Exploration A—the first person Reston called was Holloway.

Reston had met Holloway four years earlier at a symposium on arctic gear design held at Northwestern University. Holloway was one of the speakers invited to represent explorers. Not only did he clearly articulate the problems with current equipment, he also focused on what was needed to correct the problems. Though a fairly humorless speech, its conciseness impressed many people there, especially Reston who bought the man a drink. A sort of friendship soon developed.[84] "I always thought he was

---

[83]See Aramis Garcia Pineda's "More Than Meets The Eye" in *Field and Stream,* v. 100, January 1996, p. 39-47.

[84]Leezel Brant's "Billy Reston's Friends For Life" in *Backpacker,* v. 23, February 1995, p. 7.

rock solid," Reston said much later in **The Reston Interview**. "Just look at his C.V. Never for a moment did I suspect he was capable of that."[85]

As it turned out, as soon as Holloway saw the tape of "The Five and Half Minute Hallway", which Reston had sent him, he was more than willing to participate in an investigation. [5½] Within a week he had arrived at the house, along with two employees: Jed Leeder and Kirby "Wax" Hook.

As we learn in *The Navidson Record*, Jed Leeder lives in Seattle, though he was originally from Vineland, New Jersey. He had actually been on his way to becoming a career truck driver when a trans-continental job took him all the way to Washington. It was there that he discovered the great outdoors was not just some myth conjured up in a magazine. He was twenty-seven when he first saw the Cascades. One look was all he needed. Love at first sight. He quit his job on the spot and started selling camping gear. Six years later he is still a long way from Vineland, and as we can see for ourselves, his passion for the Pacific Northwest and the great outdoors only seems to have grown more intense.

Consummately shy, almost to the point of frailty, Jed possesses an uncanny sense of direction and remarkable endurance. Even Holloway concedes that Jed would probably out distance him in a packless climb. When he is not trekking, Jed loves drinking coffee, watching the tide turn, and listening to Lyle Lovett with his fiancée. "She's from Texas," he tells us very softly. "I think that's where we're going to get married."[86]

Wax Hook could not be more different. At twenty-six, he is the youngest member of the Holloway team. Born in Aspen, Colorado, he grew up on mountain faces and in cave shafts. Before he could walk he knew where to drive a piton and before he could talk he had a whole vocabulary of knots under his fingers. If there is such a thing as a climbing prodigy, Wax is it. By the time he dropped out of high school, he had climbed more peaks than most climbers have claimed in a lifetime. In one clip, he tells us how he plans to eventually make a solo ascent of Everest's North Face: "And I'll tell you this, more than a few people are bettin' I'll do it."

When Wax was twenty-three, Holloway hired him as a guide. For the next three years, Wax helped Holloway and Jed lead teams up Mt. McKinley, down into Ellison's Cave in Georgia, or across some Nepalese cwm. The pay was not much to brag about but the experience was worth plenty.

Wax sometimes gets a little out of hand. He likes to drink, get laid, and most of all boast about how much he drank and how many times he got laid. But he never brags about climbing. Booze and women are one thing but "a rocky face is always better than you and if you make it down alive you're grateful you had a good trip."[87]

"This though has to be the weirdest," Wax later tells Navidson, right before making his last foray down the hallway. "When Holloway asked me

---

[85]See Exhibit Four for the complete transcript of The Reston Interview.

[5½]Gabriel Reller in his book *Beyond The Grasp of Commercial Media* (Athens, Ohio: Ohio University Press, 1995) suggests that the appearance of the first short entitled "The Five and a Half Minute Hallway" originated here: "Holloway probably copied the tape, gave it to a couple of friends, who in turn passed it along to others. Eventually it found its way to the academic set" (p. 252).

[86]See also Susan Wright's "Leeder of the Pack" in *Outdoor Life,* v. 195, June 1995, p. 28.

[87]Bentley Harper's "Hook, Line and Sinker" in *Sierra,* v. 81, July/August 1996, p. 42.

if I wanted to explore a house I thought he was cracked. But whatever Holloway does is interesting to me, so sure I went for it, and sure enough this *is* the weirdest!"

On the day Holloway and his team arrive at Ash Tree Lane, Navidson and Tom are there to greet them at the door. Karen says a brief hello and leaves to pick the children up from school. Reston makes the necessary introductions and then after everyone has gathered in the living room, Navidson begins to explain what he knows about the hallway.

He shows them a map he drew based on his first visit. Tellingly, this hardly strikes Tom as news. While Navidson does his best to impress upon everyone the dangers posed by the tremendous size of that place as well as the need to record in detail every part of the exploration, Tom passes out xerox copies of his brother's diagram.

Jed finds it difficult to stop smiling while Wax finds it difficult to stop laughing. Holloway keeps throwing glances at Reston. In spite of the tape he saw, Holloway seems convinced that Navidson has more than a few loose wing nuts jangling around in his cerebral cortex. But when the four dead bolts are at last unlocked and the hallway door drawn open, the icy darkness instantly slaughters every smile and glance.

Newt Kuellster suspects the first view of that place irreparably altered something in Holloway: "His face loses color, something even close to panic suffuses his system. Suddenly he sees what fortune has plopped on his plate and how famous and rich it could make him, and he wants it. He wants all of it, immediately, no matter the cost."[88] Studying Holloway's reaction, it is almost impossible to deny how serious he gets staring down the hallway. "How far back does it go?" he finally asks.

"You're about to find out," Navidson replies, sizing up the man, a half-smile on his lips. "Just be careful of the shifts."

From the first time they shake hands on the doorstep, it is obvious to us Navidson and Holloway dislike each other. Neither one says anything critical but both men bristle in each other's presence. Holloway is probably a little unnerved by Navidson's distinguished career. Navidson, no doubt, is privately incensed that he must ask another man to explore his own house. Holloway does not make this intrusion any easier. He is cocky and following Navidson's little introduction immediately starts calling the shots.

In earlier years, Navidson would have probably paid little attention to Karen and headed down those corridors by himself—danger be damned. Yet as has already been discussed, the move to Virginia was about repairing their crumbling relationship. Karen would refrain from relying on other men to mollify her insecurities if Navidson curbed his own risk-lust and gave domesticity a real shot. After all, as Karen later intimated, their home was supposed to bring them closer together.[89] The appearance of the hallway, however, tests those informal vows. Navidson finds himself constantly itching to leave his family for that place just as Karen discovers old patterns surfacing in herself.

Later that evening, Holloway places his hand on Karen's back and makes her laugh with a line the camera never hears. Navidson immediately

---

[88]See Newt Kuellster's "The Five and a Half Minute Holloway" in *The Holloway Question* (San Francisco: Metalambino Inc., 1996), p. 532; as well as Tiffany Balter's "Gone Away" in *People,* v. 43, May 15, 1995, p. 89.

[89]See Chapter XIII.

bumps Holloway aside with his shoulder, revealing, for one thing, his own easily underestimated strength. Navidson, however, reserves his glare for Karen. She laughs it off but the uneasy energy released recalls Leslie Buckman and Dale Corrdigan's accusations.[90]

Yet even after Navidson's interjection, Holloway still finds it difficult to keep his eyes off of Karen. Her flirting hardly helps. She is bright, extremely sexual, and just as Navidson has always enjoyed danger, she has always thrived on attention.

Karen brings the men beers and they go outside with her and light her cigarettes. It matters very little what they say, her eyes always flash, she gives them that famous smile, and sure enough soon they are all doting on her.

Navidson confides to his Hi 8,"I can't tell you how much I'd like to deviate that fucker's [Holloway's] septum." And then later on mutters somewhat enigmatically: "For that I should throw her out." Still aside from these comments and the strong nudge he gave Holloway, Navidson refrains from openly displaying any other signs of jealousy or rage.

Unfortunately he also refrains from openly considering the significance of these feelings. The closest he comes appears in a Hi 8 journal entry spliced in following his encounter with Holloway. On camera, Navidson treats what he refers to as "his rotten feet." As we can clearly see, the tops are puffy and in some places as red as clay. Furthermore, all his toe nails are horribly cracked, disfigured, and yellow. "Perpetuated," Navidson informs us. "By a nasty fungus two decades worth of doctors finally ended up calling S-T-R-E-S-S." Sitting by himself on the edge of the tub, blood stained socks draped over the edge, he carefully spreads a silky ointment around what he glibly calls his "light fantastic toe." It is one of the more naked moments of Navidson, and especially considering its placement in the sequence, seems to reveal in a non-verbal way some of the anxiety Karen's flirtation with Holloway has provoked in him.

All of which becomes pretty irrelevant as Holloway soon spends most of his hours leading his team down that lightless hallway.

Frequently treatment of the first three explorations has concentrated on the physical aspects of the house. Florencia Calzatti, however, has shown in her compelling book *The Fraying of the American Family* (New York: Arcade Publishing, 1995)—no longer in print—how these invasions begin to strip the Navidsons of any existing cohesion. It is an interesting examination of the complex variables implicit in any intrusion. Unfortunately understanding Calzatti's work is not at all easy, as she makes her case using a peculiar idiom no reader will find readily comprehensible

---

[90]Refer to footnotes 19 and 20 concerning Karen's infidelities. Perhaps it also should be noted here that for all his wanderings Navidson was pointedly not promiscuous. Good looks, intelligence, and fame did not combine to create an adulterous lifestyle. Iona Panofsky in "Saints, Sinners, and Photojournalists" *Fortune,* v. 111, March 18, 1985, p. 20, attributes Navidson's genius to his "monk-like existence." However, Australian native, Ryan Murray in his book *Wilder Ways* (Sydney: Outback Works, 1996) calls Navidson's monastic habits "a sure sign of unresolved oedipal anxieties, repressed homosexuality, and a disturbed sense of self. Considering the time he spent away from home coupled with the kind of offers he got from the most exotic and tantalizing women (not even including those from his numerous female assistants), his refusal proves a nauseating absence of character. Make no mistake about it: over here his kind enter a bar with a smile and leave with a barstool for a hat." An odd thing to say considering Navidson drank freely in every Australian bar he ever visited and on the one occasion when he was attacked by two drunks, purportedly angry over all the attention the waitresses were lavishing on him, both inebriates left bruised and bleeding. (*The Wall Street Journal,* March 29, 1985, p. 31, column 3.)

(e.g. She never refers to Holloway as anything but "the stranger"; Jed and Wax appear as only "the instruments"; and the house is encoded as "the patient"). No doubt inspired by Calzatti, a small group of other writers, including the poet Elfor O'Halloran, have continued to mull over the dynamics brought on by Holloway's arrival.[91]

Without focusing too closely on the fine filigree of detail presented in these pieces—a book in itself—it is worthwhile, however briefly, to track the narrative events of the three explorations and recite to some degree how they effect the Navidsons.

For **Exploration #1**, Holloway, Jed and Wax enter the hallway equipped with Hi 8s, down parkas, hats, Gortex gloves, powerful halogen lamps, extra batteries, and a radio to keep in contact with Navidson, Tom and Reston. Navidson ties one end of some fishing line to the hallway door and then hands the spool to Holloway.

"There's almost two miles of line here," he tells him. "Don't let go of it."

Karen says nothing when she hears Navidson make this comment, though she does get up abruptly to go out to the backyard and smoke a cigarette. It is particularly eerie to watch Holloway and his team disappear down the long hallway, while just outside Karen paces back and forth in the light of a September day, oblivious of the space she repeatedly crosses though for whatever reason cannot penetrate.[92]

An hour later, Holloway, Jed, and Wax return. When their Hi 8 tapes are replayed in the living room, we watch along with everyone else how a series of lefts eventually leads them to the apparently endless corridor which, again to the left, offers entrance into that huge space where Navidson almost got lost. Though Holloway's ability to shoot this trip hardly compares to the expertise evident in Navidson's Exploration A, it is still thrilling to follow the trio as they investigate the darkness.

As they quickly discover, the void above them is not infinite. Their flashlights, much more powerful than Navidson's, illuminate a ceiling at least two hundred feet high. A little later, at least fifteen hundred feet away, they discover an opposing wall. What no one is prepared for, however, is the even larger entrance waiting for them, opening into an even greater void.

Two things keep them from proceeding further. One—Holloway runs out of fishing line. In fact, he briefly considers setting the spool down, when two—he hears the growl Navidson had warned them about. A little rattled by the sound, Holloway decides to turn back in order to better consider their next move. As Navidson foretold, they soon see for themselves how all the walls have shifted (though not as severely as they had for Navidson). Fortunately, the changes have not severed the fishing line and the three men find their way back to the living room with relative ease.

Exploration #2 takes place the following day. This time Holloway carries with him four spools of fishing line, several flares, and some

---

[91]Consider Bingham Arzumanian's "Stranger in a Hall" *Journal of Psychoanalysis*, v.14 April 12, 1996, p. 142; Yvonne Hunsucker's "Counseling, Relief, and Introjection" *Medicine,* v.2 July 18, 1996, p. 56; Curtis Melchor's "The Surgical Hand" *Internal Medicine,* v.8 September 30, 1996, p. 93; and Elfor O'Halloran's "Invasive Cures" *Homeopathic Alternatives,* October 31, 1996, p. 28.

[92]See Jeffrey Neblett's "The Illusion of Intimacy and Depth" *Ladies' Home Journal,* v. 111, January 1994, p. 90-93.

neon markers. He virtually ignores Navidson, putting Wax in charge of a 35mm camera and instructing Jed on how to collect scratchings from all the walls they pass along the way. Reston provides the dozen or so sample jars.

Though Exploration #2 ends up lasting over eight hours, Holloway, Jed, Wax only hear the growl once and the resulting shifts are negligible. The first hallway seems narrower, the ceiling a little lower, and while some of the rooms they pass look larger, for the most part everything has remained the same. It is almost as if continued use deters the growl and preserves the path they walk.

Aside from feeling generally incensed by what he perceives as Holloway's postured authority, Navidson almost goes berserk listening to the discoveries on the radio. Reston and Tom try to cheer him up and to Navidson's credit he tries to act cheerful, but when Jed announces they have crossed what he names the Anteroom and entered what Holloway starts calling the Great Hall, Navidson finds it increasingly more difficult to conjure even a smile.

Radio psychologist Fannie Lamkins believes this is a clear cut example of the classic male struggle for dominance:

> It's bad enough to hear the Great Hall has a ceiling at least five hundred feet high with a span that may approach a mile, but when Holloway radios that they've found a staircase in the center which is over two hundred feet in diameter and spirals down into nothing, Navidson has to hand Reston the radio, unable to muster another word of support. He has been deprived of the right to name what he inherently understands as his own.[93]

Lamkins sees Navidson's willingness to obey Karen's injunction as a sacrifice on par with scarification, "though invisible to Karen."[94]

After Holloway's team returns, Jed tries to describe the staircase: "It was enormous. We dropped a few flares down it but never heard them hit bottom. I mean in that place, it being so empty and cold and still and all, you really can hear a pin drop, but the darkness just swallowed the flares right up." Wax nods, and then adds with a shake of his head: "It's so deep, man, it's like it's almost dream like."

This last comment is actually not uncommon, especially for individuals who find themselves confronting vast tenebrific spaces. Back in the mid-60s, American cavers tackled the Sotano de las Golondrinas, an incredible 1,092ft hole in Mexico's Sierra Madre Oriental. They used rope, rappel racks, and mechanical ascenders to make the descent. Later on, one of the cavers described his experience: "I was suspended in a giant dome with thousands of birds circling in small groups near the vague blackcloth of the far walls. Moving slowly down the rope, I had the feeling that I was

[93]Fannie Lamkins' "Eleven Minute Shrink," KLAT, Buffalo, New York, June 24, 1994.

[94]Ibid. Florencia Calzatti also sees Karen's edict as violent, though she ultimately considers it of great value: "A needed rite to reinvigorate and strengthen the couple's personal bonds." *The Fraying of the American Family,* p. 249.

descending into an illusion and would soon become part of it as the distances became unrelatable and entirely unreal."[95]

When Holloway plays back the Hi 8s for everyone, Navidson's frustrations get the best of him. He leaves the room. It hardly helps that Karen stays, entirely engrossed in Holloway's presentation and the ghostly if inadequate images of a banister frozen on the monitor. Tom, actually, pulls her aside and tries to convince her to let Navidson lead the next exploration.

"Tom," she replies defensively. "Nothing's stopping Navy. If he wants to go, he can go. But then I go too. That's our deal. He knows that. You know that."

Tom seems a little shocked by her anger, until Karen directs his attention to Chad and Daisy, sitting in the kitchen, working hard at not doing their homework.

"Look at them," she whispers. "Navy's had a lifetime of wandering and danger. He can let someone else take over now. It won't kill him, but losing him would kill them. It would kill me too. I want to grow old, Tom. I want to grow old with him. Is that such an awful thing?"

Her words clearly register with Tom, who perhaps also perceives what a great toll his brother's death would have on him as well.[96]

When he sees Navidson next, Tom tells him to go find his son.

Based on what we can tell from *The Navidson Record,* it appears Chad soon got fed up with his class assignment and took off down the street with Hillary, determined to explore his own dark. Navidson had to look for almost an hour before he finally found him. Chad it turned out was in the park filling a jar full of fireflies. Instead of scolding him, Navidson helped out.

By ten, they had returned home with jars full of light and hands sticky with ice cream.

Exploration #3 ends up lasting almost twenty hours. Relying primarily on the team's radio transmissions interspersed with a few clips from the Hi 8s, Navidson relates how Holloway, Jed, and Wax take forty-five minutes to reach the Spiral Staircase only to spend the next seven hours walking down it. When they at last stop, a dropped flare still does not illuminate or sound a bottom. Jed notes that the diameter has also increased from two hundred feet to well over five hundred feet. It takes them over eleven hours to return.

Unlike the two previous explorations, this intrusion brings them face to face with the consequences of the immensity of that place. All three men come back cold, depleted, their muscles aching, their enthusiasm gone.

"I got some vertigo," Jed confesses. "I had to step way back from the edge and sit down. That was a first for me." Wax is more cavalier, claiming to have felt no fear, though for some reason he is more exhausted than the rest. Holloway remains the most stoic, keeping any doubts to himself, adding only that the experience is beyond the power of any Hi 8 or 35mm camera: "It's impossible to photograph what we saw."[97]

---

[95]*Planet Earth: Underground Worlds* by Donald Dale Jackson and The Editors of Time-Life Books (Alexandra, Virginia: Time-Life Books, 1982), p. 149.

[96]Both Bingham Arzumanian and Curtis Melchor's pieces have offered valuable insight into the nature of Tom's alignment with Karen. Also see Chapter XI.

[97]Marjorie Preece uses this one line to launch into her powerfully observed essay "The Loss of Authority: Holloway's Challenge" *Kaos Journal,* v. 32, September, 1996, p. 44. Preece wonderfully shows how

Even after seeing Navidson's accomplished shots, it is hard to disagree with Holloway. The darkness recreated in a lab or television set does not begin to tell the true story. Whether chemical clots determining black or video grey approximating absence, the images still remain two dimensional. In order to have a third dimension, depth cues are required, which in the case of the stairway means more light. The flares, however, barely illuminate the size of that bore. In fact they are easily extinguished by the very thing they are supposed to expose. Only knowledge illuminates that bottomless place, disclosing the deep ultimately absent in all the tapes and stills—those strange *cartes de visites.* It is unfortunate that Holloway's images cannot even be counted as approximations of that vast abrupt, where as Rilke wrote, "*aber da, an diesem schwarzen Felle/ wird dein stärkstes Schauen aufgelöst.*"[98]

Holloway's assertion that the camera is impotent within the house "helps establish him—at least for a little while—as the tribe's head."

[98]No idea. Actually, Lude had a German friend named Kyrie, a tall blonde haired beauty who spoke Chinese, Japanese and French, drank beer by the quart, trained for triathlons when she wasn't playing competitive squash, made six figures a year as a corporate consultant and loved to fuck. Lude took heed when I told him I needed a German translation and introduced us.

As it turned out, I'd met her before, about five or so months ago. It had actually been a little tricky. I was leering about, pretty obliterated in the arms of drink, hours of drink actually, feeling like days of drink, when this monstrous guy loomed up in front of me, grumbling insensibly about bad behavior, something concerning too much talk with too much gesture, gestures towards her, that much of the grumble, the "her" bit, I understood. He meant Kyrie of course who even back then was a blonde haired beauty, writing my name in Japanese and assigning all sorts of portentous things to it, things I was hoping to lead or was it follow? elsewhere, when this prehistoric shithead, reeking of money and ignorance, interposed himself, cursing, spitting and threatening, in fact so loud & mean Kyrie had to interpose herself, which only made matters worse. He reached over her and hit me in the forehead with the heel of his hand. Not hard, more like a shove, but a strong enough shove to push me back a few feet.

"Well look at that," I remember hollering. "He has an opposable thumb."

The monster wasn't amused. It didn't matter. The alcohol in me had already quickened and fled. I stood there tingling all over, a dangerous clarity returning to me, ancient bloodlines colluding under what I imagine now must of been the very aegis of Mars, my fingers itching to weld into themselves, while directly beneath my sternum a hammer struck the timeless bell of war, a call to arms, though all of it still held back by what? words I guess, or rather a voice, though whose I have no clue.

He was twice my size, bigger and stronger. That should of mattered. For some reason it didn't. Odds were he'd rip me to pieces, probably even try to stomp me, and yet part of me still wanted to find out for sure. Luckily, the alcohol returned. I got wobbly and then I got scared.

Lude was yelling at me.

"You got a death wish Truant?"

Which was the thing that scared me.

'Cause maybe I did.

Five months or so later, Lude arranged for me to meet Kyrie at Union. I was late by an hour. I had an excuse. Every time I tried to open my door, my heart started racing for a bypass. I had to sit down and wait for the thumping to calm. This went on for almost fifty minutes, until I finally just gave up, gritted my teeth and charged out into the night.

Of course I recognized Kyrie immediately and she recognized me. She was getting ready to leave when I arrived. I apologized and begged her to stay, making up some lame excuse about police trying to save a guy in my building who'd stuck his head in a microwave. She looked wonderful and her voice was soft and offered me something Thumper had taken away when she hadn't called me back. She even wrote down on a napkin the glyph she'd created for me half a year ago to reflect my name and nature.

Before I could order a drink, a Jack and Coke, she told me her boyfriend was out of town, working on some construction site in Poland, single handedly dislodging supertankers stuck in dry dock in Gdansk or something. It was a dirty job but someone had to do it, and what's more he wasn't going to be back for a few more weeks. Before I even took a sip of my drink, Kyrie was complaining about all the people filtering in around us and then as I finished my drink in one long gulp, she suggested we go for a drive in her new 2 door BMW Coupe.

"Sure" I said, feeling vaguely uneasy about wandering too far from where I lived, which I realized, as I took a second to think that out, was absolutely absurd. What the fuck was happening to me? My apartment's a dump. There's nothing there for me. Not even sleep. Cat naps are fine but for some reason deep REM is getting more and more difficult to achieve. Definitely not a good thing.

Fortunately, I was falling under the spell of Kyrie's blue eyes, like sea ice, almost inhuman, reminding me again—as she herself had already pointed out—that she was alone, Gdansk Man more than half a world spinning world away.

In the parking lot, we slipped into her bucket seats and quickly swallowed two tabs of Ecstasy.

Kyrie took over from there.

At nearly ninety miles per hour, she zipped us up to that windy edge known to some as Mullholland, a sinuous road running the ridge of the Santa Monica mountains, where she then proceeded to pump her vehicle in and out of turns, sometimes dropping down to fifty miles per hour only to immediately gun it back up to ninety again, fast, slow, fast-fast, slow, sometimes a wide turn, sometimes a quick one. She preferred the tighter ones, the sharp controlled jerks, swinging left to right, before driving back to the right, only so she could do it all over again, until after enough speed and enough wind and more distance than I'd been prepared to expect, taking me to parts of this city I rarely think of and never visit, she dipped down into some slower offshoot, a lane of lightless coves, not stopping there either, but pushing further on until she finally found the secluded spot she'd been heading for all along, overlooking the city, far from anyone, pedestrian or home, and yet directly beneath a street lamp, which as far as I could tell, was the only street lamp around for miles.

Seems all that twittering light flooding down through the sunroof really turned her on.

I can't remember the inane things I started babbling about then. I know it didn't really matter. She wasn't listening. She just yanked up on the emergency brake, dropped her seat back and told me to lie on top of her, on top of those leather pants of hers, extremely expensive leather pants mind you, her hands immediately guiding mine over those soft slightly oily folds, positioning my fingers on the shiny metal tab, small and round like a tear, then murmuring a murmur so inaudible that even though I could feel her lips tremble against my ear, she seemed far, far away—"pinch it" she'd said, which I did, lightly, until she also said "pull it" which I also did, gently, parting the teeth, one at a time, down, under and beneath, the longest unzipping of my life, all the way from right beneath her perfectly oval navel to the tiny tattoo, a Japanese sign, the meaning of which I never guessed, marking her lower back, and not a stitch of underwear to get in the way, the rest very guessable though don't underestimate the danger which I guess really wasn't so dangerous after all.

We never even kissed or looked into each other's eyes. Our lips just trespassed on those inner labyrinths hidden deep within our ears, filled them with the private music of wicked words, hers in many languages, mine in the off color of my only tongue, until as our tones shifted, and our consonants spun and squealed, rattled faster, hesitated, raced harder, syllables soon melting with groans, or moans finding purchase in new words, or old words, or made-up words, until we gathered up our heat and refused to release it, enjoying too much the dark language we had suddenly stumbled upon, craved to, carved to, not a communication really but a channeling of our rumored desires, hers for all I know gone to Black Forests and wolves, mine banging back to a familiar form, that great revenant mystery I still could only hear the shape of, which in spite of our separate lusts and individual cries still continued to drive us deeper into stranger tones, our mutual desire to keep gripping the burn fueled by sound, hers screeching, mine—I didn't hear mine—only hers, probably counter-pointing mine, a high-pitched cry, then a whisper dropping unexpectedly to practically a bark, a grunt, whatever, no sense any more, and suddenly no more curves either, just the straight away, some line crossed, where every fractured sound already spoken finally compacts into one long agonizing word, easily exceeding a hundred letters, even thunder, anticipating the inevitable letting go, when the heat is ultimately too much to bear, threatening to burn, scar, tear it all apart, yet tempting enough to hold onto for even one second more, to extend it all, if we can, as if by getting that much closer to the heat, that much more enveloped, would prove . . .—which when we did clutch, hold, postpone, did in fact prove too much after all, seconds too much, and impossible to refuse, so blowing all of everything apart, shivers and shakes and deep in her throat a thousand letters crashing in a long unmodulated fall, resonating deep within my cochlea and down the cochlear nerve, a last fit of fury describing in lasting detail the shape of things already come.

Too bad dark languages rarely survive.

As quickly as they're invented, they die, unable to penetrate much, explore anything or even connect. Terribly beautiful but more often than not inadequate. So I guess it's no surprise that what I recall now with the most clarity is actually pretty odd.

When Kyrie dropped me off, she burped.

At the time I thought it was kind of cute but I guess "man eater" did cross my mind. Then as I opened the door, she burst into tears. All she was in that $85,000 car could not exclude the little girl. She said something about Gdansk Man's disinterest in her, in fucking her, in even touching her, running away to Poland, and then she apologized, blamed the drugs still roaming around in her veins and told me to get out.

Resistance to representation, however, is not the only difficulty posed by those replicating chambers and corridors. As Karen discovers, the whole house defies any normal means of determining direction.

Apparently while Karen had been struggling with the explorers' invasion of her home, her mother had managed to acquire the number of a Feng Shui master in Manhattan. After a long conversation with this expert, Karen is relieved to learn she has been putting all the ceramic animals, crystals, and plants in the wrong places. She is still told to use the Pau Kua table, *I Ching*, and the Lo Shu magic square, but to do so with the assistance of a compass. Since much of Feng Shui, especially in the Compass School, relies on auspicious and inauspicious directions, it is crucial to get an accurate reading on how the house sits in relationship to points north, south, east, and west.

Karen immediately goes out and buys a compass—this while the men are in the midst of Exploration #2. Upon returning home, however, she is astonished to find the compass refuses to settle on any one direction inside the house. Assuming it must be broken, she drives back to town and exchanges it for a new one. Apparently this time she tests it in the store. Satisfied, she returns to the house only to discover that once again the compass is useless.[100]

No matter what room she stands in, whether in the back or the front, upstairs or downstairs, the needle never stays still. North it seems has no authority there. Tom confirms the strange phenomenon, and during Exploration #3 Holloway, who up till then has relied solely on neon arrows and fishing line to mark their path, demonstrates how the same holds true for a compass read within those ash-like halls.

"I'll be damned," Holloway grunts as he stares at the twitching needle.[101]

"I guess all we've got now is your sense of direction," Wax jokingly tells Jed, which as Luther Shepard wrote: "Only helps to emphasize how real the threat was of getting lost in there."[102]

She was still crying when she drove off.

In the end, the whole thing had been so frantic and fast and strange and even sad in some ways, I completely forgot to ask her about the German phrase.[99] I suppose I could call her (Lude has her number) but for some reason these days dialing seven let alone eleven numbers feels like an infinite stretch. The phone's right in front of me but it's out of reach. When it rings at four AM I don't answer it. All I have to do is extend my hand but I can't run that far. Sleep never really arrives. Not even rest. There's no satisfaction anymore. Morning shrinks space but leaves no message.

[99]"But here within this thick black pelt, your strongest gaze will be absorbed and utterly disappear." As translated by Stephen Mitchell. — Ed.

[100]Rosemary Park considers Karen's dilemma highly emblematic of the absence of cultural polarities: "In this case, Karen's inability to determine a direction is not a fault but a challenge, requiring tools more capable than compasses and reference points more accurate than magnetic fields." See "Impossible Directions" in *Inside Out* (San Francisco: Urban B-light, 1995), p. 91.

[101]Devon Lettau wrote an amusing if ultimately pointless essay on the compass' behavior. He asserted that the minute fluctuations of the needle proved the house was nothing less than a vestibule for pure energy which if harnessed correctly could supply the world with unlimited power. See *The Faraday Conclusion* (Boston: Maxwell Press, 1996). Rosie O'Donnell, however, offered a different perspective when she wryly remarked on *Entertainment Tonight*: "The fact that Holloway waited that long to use a compass only goes to show how men—even explorers—still refuse to ask for directions."

[102]See Luther Shepard's chapter entitled "The Compass School" in *The Complete Feng Shui Guide for The Navidson Record* (New York: Barnes & Noble, 1996), p. 387.

In light of this new development and in preparation for Exploration #4, Tom makes several trips into town to purchase more fishing line, neon markers, and anything else that might serve to mark the team's path. Since Holloway's plan is to spend at least five nights inside, Tom also picks up extra food and water. On one of these excursions, he even takes Daisy and Chad along. No Hi 8 records their trip but the way Chad and Daisy relate to their mother the details of their shopping spree reveals how fond they have become of their uncle.

Unfortunately, Tom also has to buy a ticket back to Massachusetts. With the exception of a few weeks in July, he has not worked in over three months. As Tom explains to Karen and Navidson, "the time's come for me to put ass in gear and get on with my life." He also tells them the time has come for them to contact the media and find a new house.

Originally Tom had intended to leave right after Exploration #3 but when Navidson begs him to stay through Exploration #4, he agrees.

Reston also sticks around. He had briefly considered taking a leave of absence from the university but managed instead to somehow arrange for a week off, despite the fact that it is late September and the fall semester has already begun. He and Tom both live at the house, Tom in the study,[103] Reston crashing on the pull-out in the living room, while Holloway, Jed, and Wax—at least up until Exploration #4—stay at a local motel.

From all the clips leading up to Exploration #4, we can see how both Navidson and Holloway expect to gain a great deal of fame and fortune. Even if Holloway's team does not reach the bottom of the staircase, both men agree their story will guarantee them national attention as well as research grants and speaking opportunities. Holloway's company will more than likely thrive, to say nothing of the reputations of all those involved.

This kind of talk, on the day before Exploration #4 is scheduled to start, actually manages to bring Navidson and Holloway a little closer together. There is still a good deal of unspecified tension between them but Holloway warms to discussions of success, especially to the idea of, to use Navidson's words, "going down in history." Perhaps Holloway imagines himself joining Navidson's world, what he perceives as a place for the esteemed, secure, and remembered. Nevertheless, what these short clips do not show is the paranoia growing within him. As we are well aware, future events will ultimately reveal how much Holloway feared Navidson would get rid of him and thus deprive him of the recognition he had a spent a lifetime trying to obtain, the recognition the house seemed to promise.

Of course, Karen will have nothing to do with such talk. Upon hearing what the men are discussing, she angrily withdraws to the periphery of the house. She clearly despises anything that might suggest a longer, more protracted relationship with the oddities of their home. Daisy, on the other hand, keeps close to Navidson, picking at tiny scabs on her wrists, always sitting on her father's shoulders or when that proves impossible on Tom's. Chad turns out to be the most problematic. He spends more and more time outside by himself, and that afternoon returns home from school with a bruised eye and swollen nose.

---

[103]Neekisha Dedic's "The Study: Tom's Place" Diss. Boston University, 1996, examines the meaning of "study" when juxtaposed with the ritual of territory, sleep, and memory.

Navidson breaks off his conversation with Holloway to find out what happened. Chad, however, refuses to speak.[104]

---

[104]Which is not really a good response. And you know changing the details or changing the subject can be just the same as refusing to speak. I guess I've been guilty of those two things for a long time now, especially the first one, always shifting and re-shifting details, smoothing out the edges, removing the corners, colorizing the whole thing or if need be de-colorizing, sometimes even flying in a whole chorus of cartoon characters, complete with slapstick Biff! Blam! Pow! antics,—this time leave in the blam—which may have some appeal, can't underrate the amusement factor there, even though it's so far from the truth it might as well be a cartoon because it certainly isn't what happened, no Bugs Bunny there, no Thumper, no Biff! Blam! Pow! either, no nothing of the kind. And fuck, now I know exactly where I'm going, a place I've already managed to avoid twice, the first time with a fictive tooth improv, the second time with that quick dart north to Santa Cruz and the troubles of a girl I barely know, though here I am again, right at this moment too, again heading straight for it, which I suppose I could still resist. I am resisting. Maybe not. I mean I could always just stop, do something else, light up a joint, get swollen on booze. In fact doing virtually anything at all, aside from this, would keep me from relating the real story behind my broken tooth, though I don't know if I want to, not relate that story I mean, not anymore. I actually think it would do me some good to tell it, put it down here, at least some of it, so I can see the truth of it, see the details, revisit that taste, that time, and maybe re-evaluate or re-understand or re- I don't know.

Besides, I can always burn it when I'm done.

After my father died I was shipped around to a number of foster homes. I was trouble wherever I went. No one knew what to do with me. Eventually—though it did take awhile—I ended up with Raymond and his family. He was a former marine with, as I've already described, a beard rougher than horse hide and hands harder than horn. He was also a total control freak. No matter the means, no matter the cost, he was going to be in control. And everyone knew if push came to shove he was as likely to die for it as he was to kill for it.

I was twelve years old.

What did I know?

I pushed.

I pushed all the time.

Then one night, late at night, much closer to dawn than dusk, while ice still gathered outside along the window frames and tessellated walks, I woke up to find Raymond squatting on my bed, wearing his black dirt-covered boots, chewing on a big chunk of beef jerky, jabbing me in the face with his fingers, murdering all remnants of sterno or park dreams.

"Beast," he said when he was satisfied sleep was completely dead. "Let's get an understanding going. You're not really in this family but you're living with this family, been living'n us for near a year, so what does that make you?"

I didn't answer. The smart move.

"That makes you a guest, and being a guest means you act like a guest. Not like some kind of barnyard animal. If that doesn't suit you, then I'll treat you like an animal which'll have to suit you. And what I'm saying 'bout your behavior don't just go for here either. It goes for that school too. I don't want no more problems. You clear?"

Again I didn't say anything.

He leaned closer, forcing on me that rank smell of meat clinging to his teeth. "If you understand that, then you and I aren't going to cross no more." Which was all he said, though he squatted there on my bed for a while longer.

The next day I fought in the schoolyard until my knuckles were bloody. And then I fought the following day and the day after that. A whole week, fifteen faceless assailants racing after me right when school rang out, mostly eighth graders but a few ninth graders too, always bigger than me, telling me no seventh grade newcomer ever gets a say back, but I always said back, I bounced all of it right back, back-off whenever they gave me even the slightest bit of shit, and they finally hurt me for doing it, hurt me enough to make me give up and die, just curl up and cry, kicking the ground, my face all puffy, balls bashed and ribs battered, though something would always just pick me up from that fetal hold, maybe in the end it was all the nothing I had to hold, and it would throw me again after whoever was winning or just wanted to go next.

After the tenth fight, something really poisonous got inside me and turned off all the pain. I didn't even register a hit or cut anymore. I heard the blow but it never made it far enough along my nerves for me to even feel. As if all the feel-meters had blown. So I just kept hacking back, spending everything I was against what I still didn't know.

This one kid, he must have been fourteen too, hit me twice and figured I was down for good. I clawed up his face pretty bad then, enough for the blood to get in his eyes, and I don't think he expected it was ever going to get to that. I mean there were rivulets on his parka and on alot of the snow and he kind of froze up, frightened I guess, I don't know, but I apparently fractured his jaw and loosened a couple of his teeth then, split three of my knuckles too. Gloves were not an option in this kind of fighting.

Anyway, he's the kid that got me expelled, but since the fight had taken place after school, it took all the next day for the administrators to put the pieces together. In the meantime, I fought three more times. Right at noon recess. Friends of the ninth grader came after me. I couldn't punch too well with my broken knuckles and they kept pushing me down and kicking me. Some teachers finally pulled them off, but not before I got my thumb in one of the kid's eyes. I heard he had blood in it for weeks.

When I got home Raymond was waiting for me. His wife had called him at the site and told him what had happened. Over the last week, Raymond had seen the bruises and cuts on my hands but since the school hadn't called and I wasn't saying anything, he didn't say anything either.

No one asked me what happened. Raymond just told me to get in the truck. I asked him where we were going. Even a question from me made him mad. He yelled at his daughters to go to their room.

"I'm taking you to the hospital," he finally whispered.

But we didn't go directly to the hospital.

Raymond took me somewhere else first, where I lost half my tooth, and alot more too I guess, on the outskirts, in an ice covered place, surrounded by barbed wire and willows, where monuments of rust, seldom touched, lie frozen alongside fence posts and no one ever comes near enough to hear the hawks cry.

Holloway, for his part, does not permit these domestic tensions and concomitant stresses to distract him from his preparations. The ever oblique Leon Robbins in attempting to adequately evaluate these efforts has gone so far as to suggest that "Operation" would in fact be a far more appropriate word than "Exploration":

> Holloway in many ways resembles a conscientious medical practitioner in pre-op. Take for example how meticulously he reviews his team's supplies the evening before—what I like to call—"Operation #4." He makes sure flashlights are all securely mounted on helmets and Hi 8s properly attached to chest harnesses. He personally checks, re-checks, packs, and re-packs all the tents, sleeping bags, thermal blankets, chemical heat packs, food, water, and First-Aid kits. Most of all, he confirms that they have ample amounts of neon markers, lightsticks (12 hours), ultra high intensity lightsticks (5 minutes), spools of 4 lb test/ 3,100 yard monofilament fishing line, flares, extra flash lights, including a pumper light (hand generator), extra batteries, extra parts for the radios, and one altimeter (which like the compass will fail to function).[105]

Robbins' medical analogy may be a little misguided, but his emphasis on Holloway's deliberate and careful planning reminds one of the technical demands required in this journey—whether an "Operation" or "Exploration."

After all, spending a night in an enclosed lightless place is very uncommon, even in the world of caving. The Lechugilla Crystal Cavern in New Mexico is one exception. Typically Lech visits last twenty-four to thirty-six hours.[106] Holloway, however, expects to take at least four, possibly five nights exploring the Spiral Staircase.

Despite the detailed preparations and Holloway's infectious determination, everyone is still a little nervous. Five nights is a long time to remain in freezing temperatures and complete darkness. No one knows what to expect.

Though Wax puts his faith in Jed's unerring sense of direction, Jed admits to some pre-exploration apprehensions: "How can I know where to go when I don't know where we are? I mean, really, where is that place in relation to here, to us, to everything? Where?"

Holloway tries to make sure everyone stays as busy as bees, and in an effort to keep them focused, creates a simple set of priorities: "We're taking pictures. We're collecting samples. We're trying to reach the bottom of the stairs. Who knows, if we do that then maybe we'll even discover something before Navidson starts all the hoopla involved with raising

---

[105]Leon Robbins' *Operation #4: The Art of Internal Medicine* (Philadelphia: University of Pennsylvania, 1996), p. 479.

[106]See "The Crystal Cavern" chapter in Michael Ray Taylor's *Cave Passages* (New York: Scribner, 1996).

money and organizing large scale explorations." Jed and Wax both nod, unaware of the darker implications inherent in what Holloway has just uttered.

As Gavin Young later writes: "Who could have predicted that those two words 'discover something' would prove the seeds to such unfortunate destruction? The problem, of course, was that the certain 'something' Holloway so adamantly sought to locate never existed per se in that place to begin with."[107]

Unlike Explorations #1 thru #3, for Exploration #4 Holloway decides to take along his rifle. When Navidson asks him "what the hell" he plans to shoot, Holloway replies: "Just in case."

By this point, Navidson has settled on the belief that the persistent growl is probably just a sound generated when the house alters its internal layout. Holloway, however, is not at all in accordance with this assessment. Furthermore, as he pointedly reminds Navidson, he is the team captain and the one responsible for everyone's safety: "With all due respect, since I'm also the one actually going in there, your notions don't really hold much water with me." Wax and Jed do not object. They are accustomed to Holloway carrying some sort of firearm. The inclusion of the Weatherby hardly causes them any concern.

Jed just shrugs.

Wax though proves a little more fractious.

"I mean what if you're wrong?" he asks Navidson. "What if that sound's not from the wall's shifting but coming from something else, some kind of thing? You wanna leave us defenseless?"

Navidson drops the subject.

The question of weapons aside, another big point of concern that comes up is communication. During Exploration #3 the team discovered just how quickly all their transmissions deteriorated. Without a cost effective way of rectifying the problem—obviously buying thousands of feet of audio cable would be impossible—Holloway settled the issue by simply announcing that they should just plan on losing radio contact by the first night. "After that, it'll be four to five days on our own. Not ideal but we'll manage."

That evening, Holloway, Jed, and Wax move from their motel and camp out in the living room with Reston. Navidson briefs Holloway for the last time on the most efficacious way to handle the cameras. Jed makes a brief call to his fiancée in Seattle and then helps Reston organize the sample jars. Tom in an effort to cheer up a bruised and unnaturally quiet Chad winds up reading both him and Daisy a long bedtime story.

Somehow Wax ends up alone with Karen.[108]

If Holloway's hand on Karen had upset Navidson, it is hard to imagine what his reaction would have been had he walked in on this particular moment. However when he finally did see the tape so much had happened, Navidson, by his own admission, felt nothing. "I'm surprised, I

---

[107]Gavin Young, *Shots In The Dark* (Stanford: University of California Press, 1995), p. 151.

[108]Again Florencia Calzatti's *The Fraying of the American Family* proves full of valuable insight. In particular see "Chapter Seven: The Last Straw" where she decries the absolute absurdity of end-series items: "There is no such thing as the last straw. There is only hay."

guess" he says in **The Last Interview**. "But there's no rage. Just regret. I actually laughed a little. I'd been watching Holloway all the time, feeling insecure by this guy's strength and courage and all that, and I never even thought about the kid. (He shakes his head.) Anyway, I betrayed her when I went in there the first time and so she betrayed me. People always say how two people were meant for each other. Well we weren't but somehow we ended up together anyway and had two incredible children. It's too bad. I love her. I wish it didn't have to turn out like this."[109]

The clip of Karen and Wax did not appear in the first release print of *The Navidson Record* but apparently was edited in a few months later. Miramax never commented on the inclusion nor did anyone else. It is a little strange Karen did not erase the tape in the wall mounted camcorder. Perhaps she forgot it was there or planned to destroy it later. Then again perhaps she wanted Navidson to see it.

Regardless of her intentions, the shot catches Karen and Wax alone in the kitchen. She picks at a bowl of popcorn, he helps himself to another beer. Their conversation circles tediously around Wax's girlfriends, intermittently returning to his desire to get married *someday*. Karen keeps telling him that he is young, he should have fun, keep living, stop worrying about settling down. For some reason both of them speak very softly.

On the counter, someone has left a copy of the map Navidson drew following Exploration A. Karen occasionally glances over at it.

"Did you do that?" she finally asks.

"Nah, I can't draw."

"Oh," she says, letting the syllable hang in the air like a question.

Wax shrugs.

"I actually don't know who made it. I thought your old Navy man did."

Based on the film, it is impossible for us to tell if Holloway, Jed, or Wax were ever explicitly told not to mention to Karen Navidson's illegal excursion. Wax, however, does not seem to recognize any trespass in his admission.

Karen does not look at the map again. She just smiles and takes a sip of Wax's beer. They continue talking, more about Wax's girl troubles, another round of "don't worry, keep living, you're young" and then out of nowhere Wax leans over and kisses Karen on the lips. It lasts less than a second and clearly shocks her, but when he leans over and kisses her again she does not resist. In fact the kiss turns into something more than a kiss, Karen's hunger almost exceeding Wax's. But when he knocks over his beer in an effort to get still closer, Karen pulls away, glances once at the liquid spilling onto the floor and quickly walks out of the room. Wax starts to follow her but realizes before he takes a second step that the game is already over. He cleans up the mess instead.

A few months later Navidson saw the kiss.

By that time Karen was gone along with everyone else.

Nothing mattered.

[109]See Exhibit Four for the complete transcript of The Last Interview.

VIII

SOS . . . A wireless code-signal summoning assistance in extreme distress, used esp. by ships at sea. The letters are arbitrarily chosen as being easy to transmit and distinguish. The signal was recommended at the Radio Telegraph Conference in 1906 and officially adopted at the Radio Telegraph Convention in 1908 (See G. G. Blake <u>*Hist. Radio Telegr*</u>*., 1926, 111-12).*

— The Oxford English Dictionary

• • • – – – • • •

Billy Reston glides into frame, paying no attention to the equipment which Navidson over the last few weeks has been setting up in the living room, including though not limited to, three monitors, two 3/4″ decks, a VHS machine, a Quadra Mac, two Zip drives, an Epson colour printer, an old PC, at least six radio transmitters and receivers, heavy spools of electrical cord, video cable, one 16mm Arriflex, one 16mm Bolex, a Minolta Super 8, as well as additional flashlights, flares, rope, fishing line (anything from braided Dacron to 40 lb multi-strand steel), boxes of extra batteries, assorted tools, compasses twitching to the odd polarities in the house, and a broken megaphone, not to mention surrounding shelves

•

already loaded with sample jars, graphs, books, and even an old microscope.

Instead Reston concentrates all his energies on the radios, monitoring Holloway as he makes his way through the Great Hall. Exploration #4 is underway and will mark the team's second attempt to reach the bottom of the staircase.

"We hear you fine, Billy" Holloway replies in a wash of white noise.

Reston tries to improve the signal. This time Holloway's voice comes in a little clearer.

•

"We're continuing down. Will try you again in fifteen minutes. Over and out."

The obvious choice would have been to structure the segment around Holloway's journey but clearly nothing about Navidson is obvious. He keeps his camera trained on Billy who serves now as the expedition's base commander. In grainy 7298 (probably pushed one T-stop), Navidson captures this crippled man expertly maneuvering his wheelchair from radio to tape recorder to computer, his attention never wavering from the team's progress.

✓

By concentrating on Reston at the beginning of Exploration #4, Navidson provides a perfect counterpoint to the murky world Holloway navigates. Confining us to the comforts of a well-lit home gives our varied imaginations a chance to fill the adjacent darkness with questions and demons. It also further increases our identification with Navidson, who like us, wants nothing more than to penetrate first hand the mystery of that place. Other directors might have intercut shots of the 'Base Camp' or 'Command Post'[110] with Holloway's tapes but Navidson refuses to view Exploration #4 in any other way except from Reston's vantage point. As Frizell Clary writes, "Before personally permitting us the sight of such species of Cimmerian dark, Navidson wants us to experience, like he already has, a sequence dedicated solely to the much more revealing details of waiting."[111]

Naguib Paredes, however, goes one step further than Clary, passing over questions concerning the structure of anticipation in favor of a slightly different, but perhaps more acute analysis of Navidson's strategy: "First and foremost, this restricted perspective subtly and somewhat cunningly allows Navidson to materialize his own feelings in Reston, a man with fearsome intelligence and energy but who is nonetheless—and tragically I might add—physically handicapped. Not by chance does Navidson shoot Reston's wheelchair in the photographic idiom of a prison: spokes for bars, seat like a cell, glimmering brake resembling some kind of lock. Thus in the manner of such images, Navidson can represent for us his own increasing frustration."[112]

As predicted, by the first night Holloway and the team start to lose radio contact. Navidson reacts by focusing on a family of copper-verdigris coffee cups taking up residence on the floor like settlers on the range while nearby a pile of sunflower seed shells rises out of a bowl like a volcano born on some unseen plate in the Pacific. In the background, the ever-present hiss of the radios continues to fill the room like some high untouch-

able wind. Considering the grand way these moments are photographed, it almost appears as if Navidson is trying through even the most quotidian objects and events to evoke for us some sense of Holloway's epic progress. That or participate in it. Perhaps even challenge it.[113]

---

[110]`There's something weird going on here, as if Zampanò can't quite make up his mind whether this is all an exploration (i.e. 'Base Camp') or a war (i.e. 'Command Post')?`

[111]Frizell Clary's *Tick-Tock-Fade: The Representation of Time in Film Narrative* (Delaware: Tame An Essay Publications, 1996), p. 64.

[112]Naguib Paredes' *Cinematic Projections* (Boston: Faber and Faber, 1995), p. 84.

[113]Navidson's camera work is an infinitely complex topic. Edwin Minamide in *Objects of a Thousand Facets* (Bismark, North Dakota: Shive Stuart Press, 1994), p. 421, asserts that such "resonant images," especially those in this instance, conjure up what Holloway could never have achieved: "The fact that Navidson can photograph even the dirtiest blue mugs in a way that reminds us of pilgrims on a quest proves he is the necessary narrator without whom there would be no film; no understanding of the house." Yuriy Pleak in *Semiotic Rivalry* (Casper, Wyoming: Hazard United, 1995), p. 105, disagrees, claiming Navidson's lush colors and steady pans only reveal his competitiveness and bitterness toward Holloway: "He seeks to eclipse the team's historical descent with his own limited art." Mace Roger-Court, however, finds *In These Things I Find,* Series #18 (Great Falls, Montana: Ash Otter Range Press, 1995) that Navidson's posture is highly instructive and even enlightening: "His lonely coffee cups, his volcanic bowl

Time passes. There are long conversations, there are long silences. Sometimes Navidson and Tom play Go. Sometimes one reads aloud to Daisy[114] while the other assists Chad with some role-playing game on the family computer.[115] Periodically Tom goes outside to smoke a joint of marijuana while his brother jots down notes in some now lost journal. Karen keeps clear of the living room, entering only once to retrieve the coffee cups and empty the bowl of sunflower seed shells. When Navidson's camera finds her, she is usually on the phone in the kitchen, the TV volume on high, whispering to her mother, closing the door.

But even as the days lose themselves in night and find themselves again come dawn only to drag on to yet more hours of lightless passage, Billy Reston remains vigilant. As Navidson shows us, he never loses focus, rarely leaves his post, and constantly monitors the radios, never forgetting the peril Holloway and the team are in.

Janice Whitman was right when she noted another extraordinary quality: "Aside from the natural force of his character, his exemplary intellect, and the constant show of concern for those participating in Exploration #4, what I'm still most struck by is [Reston's] matter of fact treatment of this twisting labyrinth extending into nowhere. He does not seem confounded by its impossibility or at all paralyzed by doubt."[116] Belief is one of Reston's greatest strengths. He has an almost animal like ability to accept the world as it comes to him. Perhaps one overcast morning in Hyderabad, India he had stood rooted to the ground for one second too long because he did not really believe an electrical pole had fallen and an ugly lash of death was now whipping toward him. Reston had paid a high price for that disbelief: he would never walk up stairs again and he would never fuck.[117] At least he would also never doubt again.

---

of shells, the maze like way equipment and furniture are arranged, all reveal how the everyday can contain objects emblematic of what's lyrical and what's epic in our lives. Navidson shows us how a sudden sense of the world, of who or where we are or even what we do not have can be found in even the most ordinary things."

[114]Ascher Blootz in her pithy piece "Bedtime Stories" (*Seattle Weekly*, October 13, 1994, p. 37) claims the book Tom reads to Daisy is Maurice Sendak's *Where The Wild Things Are.* Gene D. Hart in his letter entitled "A Blootz Bedtime Story" (*Seattle Weekly*, October 20, 1994, p. 7) disagrees: "After repeatedly viewing this sequence, frame by frame, I am still unable to determine whether or not she's right. The cover is constantly blocked by Tom's arm and his whisper consistently evades the range of the microphone. That said I'm quite fond of Blootz's claim, for whether she's right or wrong, she is certainly appropriate."

[115]See Corning Qureshy's essay "D & D, *Myst,* and Other Future Paths" in *MIND GAMES* ed. Mario Aceytuno (Rapid City, South Dakota: Fortson Press, 1996); M. Slade's "Pawns, Bishops & Castles" http://cdip.ucsd.edu/; as well as Lucy T. Wickramasinghe's "Apple of Knowledge vs. Windows of Light: The Macintosh-Microsoft Debate" in *Gestures*, v.2, November 1996, p. 164-171.

[116]Janice Whitman's *Red Cross Faith* (Princeton, NJ: Princeton University Press, 1994), p. 235.

[117]Though this chapter was originally typed, there were also a number of handwritten corrections. "make love" wasn't crossed out but

"FUCK" was still scratched in above it. As I've been doing my best to incorporate most of these amendments, I didn't think it fair to

suddenly exclude this one even if it did mean a pretty radical shift in tone.

By now you've probably noticed that except when safely contained by quotes, Zampanò always steers clear of such questionable four-letter language. This instance in particular proves that beneath all that cool pseudo-academic hogwash lurked a very passionate man who knew how important it was to say "fuck" now and then, and say it loud too, relish its syllabic sweetness, its immigrant pride, a great American epic word really, starting at the lower lip, often the very front of the lower lip, before racing all the way to the back of the throat, where it finishes with a great blast, the concussive force of the K catching up then with the hush of the F already on its way, thus loading it with plenty of offense and edge and certainly ambiguity. FUCK. A great by-the-bootstrap prayer or curse if you prefer, depending on how you look at it, or use it, suited perfectly for hurling at the skies or at the world, or sometimes, if said just right, for uttering with enough love and fire, the woman beside you melts inside herself, immersed in all that word-heat.

Holy fuck, what was that all about?

"Love and fire"? "word-heat"?

Who the hell is thinking up this shit?

Maybe Zampanò just wrote "fuck" because he wasn't saying fuck before when he could fuck and now as he waited in that hole on Whitley he wished he would of lived a little differently. Or then again maybe he just needed a word strong enough to push back his doubts, a word strong enough to obliterate, at least temporarily, the certain vision of his own death, definitely necessary for those times when he was working his way around the courtyard, trying to stretch his limbs, keep his heart pumping, a few remaining cats still rubbing up against his withered legs, reminding him of the years he missed, the old color, the old light. The perfect occasion, if you ask me, to say "fuck." Though if he did say it no one there ever heard him.

Of course, fuck you, you may have a better idea. I went ahead and paged Thumper again. Again she didn't call me back. Then this morning, I discovered a message on my machine. It startled me. I couldn't remember hearing the phone ring. Turned out some girl named Ashley wanted to see me, but I had no idea who she was. When I finally rolled into the Shop, I was a good three hours late. My boss flew off the handle. Put me on probation. Said I was an ass hair away from getting fired, and no he didn't care anymore how well I made needles.

Unfortunately, I'm not too hopeful about improving my punctuality. You wouldn't believe how much harder it's getting for me to just leave my studio. It's really sad. In fact these days the only thing that gets me outside is when I say: Fuck. Fuck. Fuck. Fuck you. Fuck me. Fuck this. Fuck. Fuck. Fuck. —

All the images Navidson finds during this period are beautifully concise. Every angle he chooses describes the agony of the wait, whether a shot of Tom sleeping on the couch, Reston listening more and more intently to the nonsense coming over the radio, or Karen watching them from the foyer, for the first time smoking a cigarette inside the house. Even the occasional shot of Navidson himself, pacing around the living room, communicates the impatience he feels over being denied this extraordinary opportunity. He has done his best to keep from resenting Karen, but clearly feels it just the same. Not once are they shown talking together. For that matter not once are they shown in the same frame together.

Eventually the entire segment becomes a composition of strain. Jump cuts increase. People stop speaking to each another. A single shot never includes more than one person. Everything seems to be on the verge of breaking apart, whether between Navidson and Karen, the family as a whole, or even the expedition itself. On the seventh day there is still no sign of the team. By the seventh night, Reston begins to fear the worst, and then in the early A.M. hours of the eighth day everyone hears the worst. The radio remains an incomprehensible buzz of static, but from somewhere in the house, rising up like some strange black oil, there comes a faint knocking. Chad and Daisy actually detect it first, but by the time they reach their parent's bedroom, Karen is already up with the light on, listening intently to this new disturbance.

It sounds exactly like someone rapping his knuckles against the wall: three quick knocks followed by three slow knocks, followed by three more quick knocks. Over and over again.

Despite a rapid search of the upstairs and downstairs, no one can locate the source, even though every room resonates with the distress signal. Then Tom presses his ear against the living room wall.

"Bro', don't ask me how, but it's coming from in there. In fact, for a second it sounded like it was right on the other side."

• • • - - - - • • •

Ironically enough, it is the call for assistance that eliminates the jump cuts and reintegrates everyone again into a single frame. Navidson has finally been granted the opportunity he has been waiting for all along. Consequently, with Navidson suddenly in charge now, declaring his intent to lead a rescue attempt, the sequence immediately starts to resolve with the elimination of visual tensions. Karen, however, is furious. "Why don't we just call the police?" she demands. "Why does it have to be the great Will Navidson who goes to the rescue?" Her question is a good one, but unfortunately it only has one answer: because he *is* the great Will Navidson.

Considering the circumstances, it does seem a little ludicrous for Karen to expect a man who has thrived his whole life under shell fire and napalm to turn his back on Holloway and go drink lemonade on the porch. Furthermore, as Navidson points out, "They've been in there almost eight days with water for six. It's three in the morning. We don't have time to get officials involved or a search party organized. We have to go now." Then adding in a half-mumble: "I waited too long with Delial. I'm not going to do it again."

The name "Delial" and its adamantine mystery stops Karen cold. Without saying another word, she sits down on the couch and waits for Navidson to finish organizing all the equipment they will need.

It takes only thirty minutes to assemble the necessary supplies. The hope is that they will locate Holloway's team nearby. If not, the plan is for Reston to go as far as the stairway where he will establish a camp and

•

handle the radios, serving as a relay between the living room command post and Navidson and Tom who will continue on down the stairs. As far as photographic equipment is concerned, everyone wears a Hi 8 in a chest harness. (Short two cameras, Navidson has to take down one of the wall mounted Hi 8s from his study and another one from the upstairs hall.) He also brings his 35mm Nikon equipped with a powerful Metz strobe, as well as the 16mm Arriflex, which Reston volunteers to carry in his lap. Karen unhappily takes over the task of manning the radios. A Hi 8 captures her sitting in the living room, watching the men fade into the darkness of the hallway. There are in fact three quick shots of her, the last two as she calls her mother to report Navidson's departure as well as his mention of Delial. At first the phone is busy, then it rings.

- - • • •

Navidson names this sequence **SOS** which aside from referring to the distress signal sent by Holloway's team also informs another aspect of the work. At the same time he was mapping out the personal and domestic tensions escalating in the house, Navidson was also editing the footage in accordance to a very specific cadence. Tasha K. Wheelston was the first to discover this carefully created structure:

> At first I thought I was seeing things but after I watched SOS more carefully I realized it was true: Navidson had not just filmed the distress call, he had literally incorporated it into the sequence. Observe how Navidson alternates between three shots with short durations and three shots with longer durations. He begins with three quick angles of Reston, followed by three long shots of the living room (and these are in fact just that — long shots taken from the
>
> •
>
> foyer), followed again by three short shots and so on. Content has on a few occasions interfered with the rhythm but the pattern of three-short three-long three-short is unmistakable.[118]

[118]Tasha K. Wheelston's "M.O.S.: Literal Distress," *Film Quarterly*, v. 48, fall 1994, p. 2-11.

Thus while representing the emergency signal sent by Holloway's team, Navidson also uses the dissonance implicit in his home-bound wait—the impatience, frustration, and increasing familial alienation—to figuratively and now literally send out his own cry for help.

The irony comes when we realize that Navidson fashioned this piece long after the Holloway disaster occurred but before he made his last plunge into that place. In other words his SOS is entirely without hope. It either comes too late or too early. Navidson, however, knew what he was doing. It is not by accident that the last two short shots of SOS show Karen on the phone, thus providing an acoustic message hidden within the already established visual one: three busy signals, three rings.

In other words:

.

. . . - - -

.

(or)

.

SO?[119]

---

[119]Pretty bitter but I've said the same thing myself more than a few times. In fact that word helped me make it through those months in Alaska. Maybe even got me there to begin with. The woman at the agency had to have known I wasn't close to sixteen, more like thirteen going on thirty-three, but she approved my application anyway. I like to imagine she was thinking to herself "Boy does this kid look young" and then because she was tired or really didn't care or because my tooth was split and I looked mean, she answered herself with "So?" and went ahead and secured my place at the canning factory.

Those were the days, let me tell you. Obscene twelve hour days cradled in the arms of stupefying beauty. Tents on the beach, out there on the Homer Spit, making me, not to mention the rest of us, honorary

.

spit rats.

Nothing to ever compare it to again either. An awful juxtaposition of fish bones & can-grime and the stench of too many aching lives & ragged fingers set against an unreachable and ever present beyond, a life-taking wind, more pure than even glacier water. And just as some water is too cold to drink, that air was almost too

.

bright to breathe, raking in over ten thousand teeth of range pine, while bald eagles soared the days away like gods, even if they scavenged the mornings like rats, hopping around on gut-wet docks with the sea at their backs always calling out like a blue-black taste of something more.

Nothing about the job itself could have kept you there, hour upon hour upon even more hours, bent to the bench, steaming over the dead,

.

gouging for halibut cheeks, slabs of salmon, enduring countless mosquito bites, even bee stings—my strange fortune—and always in the ruin of so many curses from the Filipinos, the White Trash, the Blacks, the Haitians, a low grade-grumbling which is the business of canning. The wage was good but it sure as hell wasn't enough to lock you down. Not after one week, let alone two weeks, let alone three months of the same

▫

mind-numbing gut-heaving shit.

You had to find something else.

For me it was the word "So?" And I learned it the hard way, in fact right at the very start of that summer.

I'd been invited out on a fishing boat, a real wreck of a thing but supposedly as seaworthy as they get. Well, we hadn't been gone for

.

more than a few hours when a storm suddenly came up, split the seams and filled the hull with water. The pumps worked fine but only for about ten minutes. Tops. The coast guard came to the rescue but they took an hour to reach us. At the very least. By then the boat had already sunk. Fortunately we had a life raft to cower in and almost everyone survived. Almost. One guy didn't. An old Haitian. At least sixteen

.

years old. He was a friend too or at least on his way to becoming a friend. Some line had gotten tangled around his ankle and he was dragged down with the wreck. Even when his head went under, we could all hear him scream. Even though I know we couldn't.

Back on shore everyone was pretty messed up, but the owner/captain was by far the worst off. He ended up drunk for a week, though the only thing he ever said was "So?"

The boat's gone. "So?"

Your mate's dead. "So?"

Hey at least you're alive. "So?"

An awful word but it does harden you.

It hardened me.

▫

Somehow—though I don't remember exactly how—I ended up telling my boss a little about that summer. Even Thumper tuned in. This was the first time she'd paid any real attention to me and it felt great. In fact by the time I finished, since the day was almost over anyway and we were locking up, she let me walk her out.

"You're alright Johnny," she said in a way that actually made me feel alright. At least for a little while.

We kept talking and walked a little longer and then on a whim decided to get some Thai food at a small place on the north side of Sunset. She saying "Are you hungry?" Me using the word "starving." Her insisting we get a quick bite.

Even if I hadn't been starving, I would of eaten the world just to

be with her. Everything about her shimmered. Just watching her drink a glass of water, the way she'd crush an ice cube between her teeth, made me go a little crazy. Even the way her hands held the glass, and she has beautiful hands, launched me into all kinds of imaginings, which I really didn't have time for because the moment we sat down, she started telling me about some new guy she was seeing, a trainer or something for a cadre of wanna-be never-be boxers. Apparently, he could make her come harder than she had in years.

I suppose that might of made me feel bad but it didn't. One of the reasons I like Thumper is because she's so open and uninhabited, I mean uninhibited, about everything. Maybe I've said that already. Doesn't matter. Where she's concerned I'm happy to repeat myself.

"It takes more than just being good," she told me. "Don't get me wrong: I love oral sex, especially if the guy knows what he's doing. Though if you treat my clit like a doorbell, the door's not going to open." She crushed another cube of ice. "Recently though, it's like I need to be thinking something really different and out there to get me crazy. For a while, money made my wet. I'm older now. Anyway this guy said he was going to slap my ass and I said sure. For whatever reason I hadn't done that before. You done it?" She didn't wait for my answer. "So he got behind me, and he's got a nice cock, and I love the sound his thighs make when they snap up against my ass, but it wasn't going to make me come, even with me touching myself. That's when he smacked me. I could hardly feel it the first time. He was being kind of timid. So

I told him to do it harder. Maybe I'm nuts, I don't know, but he whacked me hard the next time and I just started to go off. Told him to do it again and each time I got worked. Finally when I did come, I came really—" and she held out the "reeeal"—"hard. Saw in the mirror later I had a handprint right on my ass cheek. I guess you could say these days I like handprints. He said his palm stung." She laughed over that one.

When our food arrived, I began telling her about Clara English, another story altogether, Christina & Amber, Kyrie, Lucy and even the Ashley I have no clue about, which also made her laugh. That's when I decided not to bring up my unreturned pages. I didn't want to get all petty with her, even though secretly I did want to know why she never called me back. Instead I made a plan to stick exclusively to the

subject of sex, flirt with her that way, make up some insane stories, maybe even elaborate on the Alaska thing, make her laugh some more, all of which was fine and good until for some reason, out of the blue, I changed the plan and started to tell her about Zampanò and the trunk and my crazy attacks. She stopped laughing. She even stopped crushing ice. She just listened to me for a half hour, an hour, I don't know how long, a long time. And you know the more I talked the more I felt some of the pain and panic inside me ease up a notch.

In retrospect it was pretty weird. I mean there I was wandering into all this personal stuff. I wasn't even sharing most of it with her either. I mean not as much as I've been putting down here, that's for

sure. There's just too much of it anyway, always running parallel, is that the right word?, to the old man and his book, briefly appearing, maybe even intruding, then disappearing again; sometimes pale, sometimes bleeding, sometimes rough, sometimes textureless; frequently angry, frightened, sorry, fragile or desperate, communicated in moments of motion, smell and sound, more often than not in skewed grammar, a mad rush broken up by eidetic recollections, another type of signal I suppose, once stitched into the simplest cries for help flung high above the rust and circling kites or radioed when the Gulf waters of Alaska finally swept over and buried the deck for good—Here Come Dots . . .—or even carried to a stranger place where letters let alone visits never register, swallowed whole and echoless, in a German homonym for the

whispered Word, taken, lost, gone, until there's nothing left to examine there either, let alone explore, all of which fractured in my head, even if it was hardly present in the words I spoke, though at the very least these painful remnants were made more bearable in the presence of Thumper.

At one point I managed to get past all those private images and

just glance at her eyes. She wasn't looking around at people or fixing on silverware or tracking some wandering noodle dangling off her plate. She was just looking straight at me, and without any malice either. She was wide open, taking in everything I told her without judgment, just listening, listening to the way I phrased it all, listening to how I felt. That's when something really painful tore through me, like some old, powerful root, the kind you see in mountains sometimes splitting

apart chunks of granite as big as small homes, only instead of granite this thing was splitting me apart. My chest hurt and I felt funny all over, having no idea what it was, this root or the feeling, until I suddenly realized I was going to start sobbing. Now I haven't cried since I was twelve, so I had no intention of starting at twenty-five, especially in some fucking Thai restaurant.

So I swallowed up.

I killed it.

I changed the subject.

A little while later, when we said goodnight, Thumper gave me a big, sweet hug. Almost as if to say she knew where I'd just been.

"You're alright Johnny," she said for the second time that night. "Don't worry so much. You're still young. You'll be fine."

And then as she put her jeep into gear, she smiled: "Come down and see me at work some time. If you want my opinion, you just need to get out of the house."

IX

Hic labor ille domus et inextricabilis error

— Virgil

laboriosus exitus domus

— Ascensius

laboriosa ad entrandum

— Nicholas Trevet[x]

---

[x]"Here is the toil of that house, and the inextricable wandering" *Aeneid* 6. 27. "The house difficult of exit" (Ascensius (Paris 1501)); "difficult to enter" (Trevet (Basel 1490)).[135] See H. J. Thomson's "Fragments of Ancient Scholia on Virgil Preserved in Latin Glossaries" in W. M. Lindsay and H. J. Thomson's *Ancient Lore in Medieval Latin Glossaries* (London: St. Andrews University Publications, 1921).[120]

[120]In fact all of this was quoted directly from Penelope Reed Doob's The Idea of the Labyrinth: From Classical Antiquity through the Middle Ages (Ithaca: Cornell University Press, 1990) p. 21, 97, 145 and 227. A perfect example of how Zampanò likes to obscure the secondary sources he's using in order to appear more versed in primary documents. Actually a woman by the name of Tatiana turned me onto that bit of info. She'd been one of Zampanò's scribes and—"lucky for me" she told me over the phone—still had, among other things, some of the old book lists he'd requested from the library.

I do have to say though getting over to her place was no easy accomplishment. I had trouble just walking out my door. Things are definitely deteriorating. Even reaching for the latch made me feel sick to my stomach. I also experienced this awful tightening across my chest, my temples instantly registering a rise in pulse rate. And that's not the half of it. Unfortunately I don't think I can do justice to how truly strange this all is, a paradox of sorts, since on one hand I'm laughing at myself, mocking the irrational nature of my anxiety, what I continue in fact to perceive as a complete absurdity—"I mean Johnny what do you really have to be afraid of?"— while on the other hand, and at the same time mind you, finding myself absolutely terrified, if not of something in particular—there were no particulars as far as I could see—then of the reaction itself, as undeniable & unimpeachable as Zampanò's black trunk.

I know it makes no sense but there you have it: what should have negated the other only seemed to amplify it instead.

Fortunately, or not fortunate at all, Thumper's advice continued to echo in my head. I accepted the risk of cardiac arrest, muttered a flurry of fucks and charged out into the day, determined to meet Tatiana and retrieve the material.

Of course I was fine.

Except as I started walking down the sidewalk, I watched a truck veer from its lane, flatten a stop sign, desperately try to slow, momentarily redirect itself, and then in spite of all the brakes on that monster, all the accompanying smoke and ear puncturing shrieks, it still barreled straight into me. Suddenly I understood what it meant to be weightless, flying through the air, no longer ruled by that happy dyad of gravity &

mass until I was, landing on the roof of a parked car, which turned out to be my car, a good fifteen feet away, hearing the thud but not actually feeling it. I even momentarily blacked out, but came to just in time to watch the truck, still hurtling towards me until it was actually slamming into me, causing me to think, and you're not going to believe this—"I can't believe this asshole just totaled my fucking car! Of all the cars on this street and he had to fucking trash mine!" even as all that steel was grinding into me, instantly pulverizing my legs, my pelvis, the metal from the grill wedging forward like kitchen knives, severing me from the waist down.

People started screaming.

Though not about me.

Something to do with the truck.

It was leaking all over the place.

Gas.

It had caught fire. I was going to burn.

Except it wasn't gas.

It was milk.

Only there was no milk. There was no gas. No leak either. There weren't even any people. Certainly none who were screaming. And there sure as hell wasn't any truck. I was alone. My street was empty. A tree fell on me. So heavy, it took a crane to lift it. Not even a crane could lift it. There are no trees on my block.

This has got to stop.

I have to go.

I did go.

When I reached Tatiana's place, she'd just gotten back from the gym and her brown legs glistened with sweat. She wore black Spandex shorts and a pink athletic halter top which was very tight but still could not conceal the ample size of her breasts. I said "hello" and then explained again how I had come into possession of the old man's papers and why in my effort to straighten them all out I needed to trace some of his references. She happily handed over the reading lists she'd compiled on his behalf and even dug up a few notes she'd made relating to the etymology of "labor."

When she offered me a drink, I jokingly suggested a Jack and Coke. I guess she didn't understand my sense of humor or understood it perfectly. She appeared with the drink and poured herself one as well. We spoke for another hour, ended up finishing all the Jack, and then right out of the blue she said, "I won't let you fuck me." Time to get going, I thought, and began to stand up. Not that I'd expected anything mind you. "But if you want, you can come on me," she added. I sat back down and before I could think of something to say, she had tugged off her top and stretched herself out in the middle of the floor. Her tits were round, hard and perfectly fake. As I straddled her, she unbuttoned my pants. Then she reached for some extremely aromatic oil sitting on her coffee table. She squeezed hard enough to release a thin stream. It dripped off of me, a warm rain spilling down over her toned belly and large brown nipples. Pleased with what she'd done, she settled back to watch me stroke & grind myself into my own hands.

At one point she bit down on her lower lip and it amped me up even more. When she started to caress her own breasts, small groans of pleasure rising up from her throat, I felt the come in my balls begin to boil. However only when I got ready to climax did I lose sight of her, my eyes slamming shut, something I believe now she'd been waiting for, a temporary instant of darkness, where vulnerable and blind to everything but my own pleasure, she could reach up beneath me and press the tip

[K]Having already discussed in Chapter V how echoes serve as an effective means to evaluate physical, emotional, and thematic distances present in *The Navidson Record*, it is now necessary to remark upon their descriptive limitations. In essence echoes are confined to large spaces. However, in order to consider how distances within the Navidson house are radically distorted, we must address the more complex ideation of convolution, interference, confusion, and even decentric ideas of design and construction. In other words the concept of a labyrinth.

It would be fantastic if based on footage from *The Navidson Record* someone were able to reconstruct a *bauplan*[JL] for the house. Of course this is an impossibility, not only due to the wall-shifts but also the film's constant destruction of continuity, frequent jump cuts prohibiting any sort of accurate mapmaking. Consequently, in lieu of a schematic, the film offers instead a schismatic rendering of empty rooms, long hallways, and dead ends, perpetually promising but forever eluding the finality of an immutable layout.

Curiously enough, if we can look to history to provide us with some context, the reasons for building labyrinths have varied substantially over the ages.[122] For example, the English hedgerow maze at Longleat was designed to amuse garden party attendants, while Amenemhet III of the XII dynasty in Egypt built for his mortuary temple a labyrinth near lake Moeris to protect his soul. ~~Most famous of all, however, was the labyrinth Daedalus constructed for King Minos. It served as a prison. Purportedly located on the island of Crete in the city of Knossos, the maze was built to~~

---

of an oil soaked finger against my asshole, circling, rubbing, until finally she pushed hard enough to exceed the threshold of resistance, slipping inside me and knowing exactly where to go too, heading straight for the prostate, the P spot, the LOUD button on this pumping stereophonic fuck system I never knew I had, initiating an almost unbearable scream for (and of) pleasure, endorphins spitting through my brain at an unheard of rate, as muscles in my groin (almost) painfully contracted in a handful of heart stomping spasms—not something I could say I was exactly prepared for. I exploded. A stream of white flying across her tits, strings of the stuff dripping off her nipples, collecting in pools around her neck, some of it leading as far as her face, one gob of it on her chin, another on her lower lip. She smiled, started to gently rub my semen into her black skin and then opened her mouth as if to sigh, only she didn't sigh, no sound, not even a breath, just her moon bright teeth, and finally her tongue licking first her upper lip before turning to her lower lip, where, smiling, her eyes focused on mine, watching me watching her, she licked up and finally swallowed my come.

[JL]So sorry.[121]

[121]German for "building plan." — Ed.

[122]For further insight into mazes, consider Paolo Santarcangeli's *Livre des labyrinthes;* Russ Craim's "The Surviving Web" in *Daedalus*, summer 1995; Hermann Kern's *Labirinti;* W. H. Matthews' *Mazes and Labyrinths;* Stella Pinicker's *Double-Axe;* Rodney Castleden's *The Knossos Labyrinth;* Harold Sieber's *Inadequate Thread*; W. W. R. Ball's "Mathematical Recreations and Essays"; Robinson Ferrel Smith's *Complex Knots—No Simple Solutions*; O. B. Hardison Jr.'s *Entering The Maze;* and Patricia Flynn's *Jejunum and Ileum.*

incarcerate the Minotaur, a creature born from an illicit encounter between the queen and a bull. As most school children learn, this monster devoured more than a dozen Athenian youths every few years before Theseus eventually slew it.[123]

123

At the
risk of stating the
obvious
no woman can mate with a
bull and produce a child.

Recognizing this simple scientific fact,
I am led to a somewhat interesting
suspicion: King Minos did not build the
labyrinth to imprison a monster but to
conceal a deformed
child—his child.

While the Minotaur has often been depicted as a creature with the body of a bull but the torso of a man—centaur like—the myth describes the Minotaur as simply having the head of a bull and the body of a man,[127] or in other words, a man with a deformed face. I believe pride would not allow Minos to accept that the heir to the throne had a horrendous appearance. Consequently, he dissolved the right of ascension by publicly accusing his wife Pasiphaë of fornicating with a male bovine.

Having enough conscience to keep from murdering his own flesh and blood, Minos had a labyrinth constructed, complicated enough to keep his son from ever escaping but without bars to suggest a prison. (It is interesting to note how the myth states most of the Athenian youth "fed" to the Minotaur actually starved to death in the labyrinth, thus indicating their deaths had more to do with the complexity of the maze and less to do with the presumed ferocity of the Minotaur.)

I am convinced Minos' maze really serves as a trope for repression. My published thoughts on this subject (see "Birth Defects in Knossos" Sonny Won't Wait Flyer, Santa Cruz, 1968)[124] inspired the playwright Taggert Chiclitz to author a play called *The Minotaur* for The Seattle Repertory Company.[126] As only eight people, including the doorman, got a chance to see the production, I produce here a brief summary:

Chiclitz begins his play with Minos entering the labyrinth late one evening to speak to his son. As it turns out, the Minotaur is a gentle and misunderstood creature, while the so-called Athenian youth are convicted criminals who were already sentenced to death back in Greece. Usually King Minos has them secretly executed and then publicly claims their deaths were caused by the terrifying Minotaur thus ensuring that the residents of Knossos will never get too close to the labyrinth. Unfortunately this time, one of the criminals had escaped into the maze,

However, even as Holloway Roberts, Jed Leeder, and Wax Hook make their way further down the stairway in **Exploration #4**, the purpose of that vast place still continues to elude them. Is it merely an aberration of physics? Some kind of warp in space? Or just a topiary labyrinth on a much grander scale? Perhaps it serves a funereal purpose? Conceals a secret? Protects something? Imprisons or hides some kind of monster? Or, for that matter, imprisons or hides an innocent? As the Holloway team soon discovers, answers to these questions are not exactly forthcoming.[129]

~~encountered Mint (as Chiclitz refers to the Minotaur) and nearly murdered him. Had Minos himself not rushed in and killed the criminal, his son would have perished. ¶Suffice it to say Minos is furious. He has caught himself caring for his son and the resulting guilt and sorrow incenses him to no end.¶ As the play progresses, the King slowly sees past his son's deformities, eventually discovering an elegiac spirit, an artistic sentiment and most importantly a visionary understanding of the world. Soon a deep paternal love grows in the King's heart and he begins to conceive of a way to reintroduce the Minotaur back into society.¶ Sadly, the stories the King has spread throughout the world concerning this terrifying beast prove the seeds of tragedy. Soon enough, a bruiser named Theseus arrives (Chiclitz describes him as a drunken, virtually retarded, frat boy) who without a second thought hacks the Minotaur into little pieces.¶ In one of the play'smost moving scenes, King Minos, with tears streaming down his face, publicly commends Theseus' courage. The crowd believes the tears are a sign of gratitude while we the audience understand they are tears of loss. The king's heart breaks, and while he will go on to be an extremely just ruler, it is a justice forever informed by the deepest kind of agony.[128]~~

```
Note: Struck passages indicate what Zampanò tried to get rid of, but
which I, with a little bit of turpentine and a good old magnifying glass
managed to resurrect.
```

124~~"Violent Prejudice in Knossos" by Zampanò in Sonny Will Wait Flyer, Santa Cruz, 1969.~~[125]

125I've no idea why these titles and cited sources are different. It seems much too deliberate to be an error, but since I haven't been able to find the "flyer" I don't know for certain. I did call Ashley back, left message, even though I still don't remember her.

126~~*The Minotaur* by Taggert Chiclitz, put on at The Hey Zeus Theater by The Seattle Repertory Company on April 14, 1972.~~

127~~W. H. Matthews writes "A similar small labyrinth, with a central Theseus-Minotaur design, is to be found on the wall of the church of San Michele Maggiore at Pavia. It is thought to be of tenth century construction. This is one of the few cases where the Minotaur is represented with a human head and a beast's body — as a sort of Centaur, in fact." See his book *Mazes & Labyrinths: Their History & Development* (New York: Dover Publications, Inc., 1970), p. 56. Also see Fig. 40 on p. 53.~~

128~~Even in *Metamorphoses* Ovid notes how Minos, in his old age, feared young men.~~

> ~~*Qui, dum fuit integer aevi, terruerat magnas ipso quoque nomine gentes; tunc erat invalidus, Deïonidenque iuventae robore Miletum Phoeboque parente superbum pertimuit, credensque suis insurgere regnis, haut tamen est patriis arcere penatibus ausus.*~~

~~("When Minos was in golden middle age/ All nations feared the mention of his name,/ But now he'd grown so impotent, so feeble/ He shied away from proud young Miletus,/ The forward son of Phoebus and Deione;/ Though Minos half-suspected Miletus/ Had eyes upon his throne and framed a plot/ To make a palace revolution, he feared to act,/ To sign the papers for his deportation." Horace Gregory p. 258-259.) Perhaps Miletus reminded Minos of his slain son and out of guilt he cowered in the presence of his youth.~~

129Strictly as an aside, Jacques Derrida once made a few remarks on the question of structure and centrality.

It is too complex to adequately address here; for some, however, this mention alone may prove useful when considering the meaning of 'play', 'origins', and 'ends'—especially when applied to the Navidson house:

> Ce centre avait pour fonction non seulement d'orienter et d'équilibrer, d'organiser la structure—on ne peut en effet penser une structure inorganisée—mais de faire surtout que le principe d'organisation de la structure limite ce que nous pourrions appeler le *jeu*[137] de la structure. Sans doute le centre d'une structure, en orientant et en organisant la cohérence du système, permet-il le jeu des éléments à l'intérieur de la forme totale. Et aujourd'hui encore une structure privée de tout centre repésente l'impensable lui-même.

And later on:

> C'est pourquoi, pour une pensée classique de la structure, le centre peut être dit, paradoxalement, *dans* la structure et *hors de* la structure. Il est au centre de la totalité et pourtant, puisque le centre ne lui appartient pas, la totalité *a son centre ailleurs.* Le centre n'est pas le centre.[130]

See Derrida's *L'écriture et la différence* (Paris: Editions du Seuil, 1967), p. 409-410.

[130]Here's the English. The best I can do:

> The function of [a] center was not only to orient, balance, and organize the structure—one cannot in fact conceive of an unorganized structure—but above all to make sure that the organizing principle of the structure would limit what we might call the *play* of the structure. By orienting and organizing the coherence of the system, the center of a structure permits the play of its elements inside the total form. And even today the notion of a structure lacking any center represents the unthinkable itself.

And later on:

> This is why classical thought concerning structure could say that the center is, paradoxically, *within* the structure and *outside* it. The center is at the center of the totality, and yet, since the center does not belong to the totality (is not part of the totality), the totality *has its center elsewhere*. The center is not the center.[131]

Something like that. From Jacques Derrida's "Structure, Sign, and Play in the Discourse of the Human Sciences" in Writing and Difference translated by Alan Bass. Chicago. University of Chicago Press. 1978. p. 278-279.

[131]Conversely Christian Norberg-Schulz writes:

Penelope Reed Doob avoids the tangled discussion of purpose by cleverly drawing a distinction between those who walk within a labyrinth and those who stand outside of it:

> [M]aze-treaders, whose vision ahead and behind is severely constricted and fragmented, suffer confusion, whereas maze-viewers who see the pattern whole, from above or in a diagram, are dazzled by its complex artistry. What you see depends on where you stand, and thus, at one and the same time, labyrinths are single (there is one physical structure) and double: they simul-

---

> In terms of spontaneous perception, man's space is 'subjectively centered.' The development of schemata, however, does not only mean that the notion of centre is established as a means of general organization, but that certain centres are 'externalized' as points of reference in the environment. This need is so strong that man since remote times has thought of the whole world as being centralized. In many legends the 'centre of the world' is concretized as a tree or a pillar symbolizing a vertical *axis mundi.* Mountains were also looked upon as points where sky and earth meet. The ancient Greeks placed the 'navel' of the world (*omphalos*) in Delphi, while the Romans considered their Capitol as *caput mundi.* For Islam *ka'aba* is still the centre of the world. Eliade points out that in most beliefs it is difficult to reach the centre. It is an ideal goal, which one can only attain after a 'hard journey.' To 'reach the centre is to achieve a consecration, an initiation. To the profane and illusory existence of yesterday, there succeeds a new existence, real, lasting and powerful.' But Eliade also points out that 'every life, even the least eventful, can be taken as the journey through a labyrinth.'[132]

See Christian Norberg-Schulz's *Existence, Space & Architecture* (New York: Praeger Publishers, 1971), p. 18 in which he quotes from Mircea Eliade's *Patterns in Comparative Religion*, trans. R. Sheed (London: Sheed and Ward, 1958), p. 380-382.

[132]What Derrida and Norberg-Schulz neglect to consider is the ordering will of gravitation or how between any two particles of matter exists an attractive force (this relationship usually represented as G with a value of $6.670 \mathbf{X} 10^{-11}$ N-m^2 / kg^2). Gravity, as opposed to gravitation, applies specifically to the earth's effect on other bodies and has had as much to say about humanity's sense of centre as Derrida and Norberg-Schulz. Gravity informs words like 'balance', 'above', 'below', and even 'rest'. Thanks to the slight waver of endolymph on the ampullary crest in the semicircular duct or the rise and fall of cilia on maculae in the utricle and saccule, gravity speaks a language comprehensible long before the words describing it are ever spoken or learned. Albert Einstein's work on this matter is also worth studying, though it is important not to forget how Navidson's house ultimately confounds even the labyrinth of the inner ear.[133]

[133]`This gets at a Lissitzky and Escher theme which Zampanò seems to constantly suggest without ever really bringing right out into the open. At least that's how it strikes me. Pages 30, 356 and 441, however, kind of contradict this. Though not really.`

> taneously incorporate order and disorder, clarity and confusion, unity and multiplicity, artistry and chaos. They may be perceived as a path (a linear but circuitous passage to a goal) or as a pattern (a complete symmetrical design) . . . Our perception of labyrinths is thus intrinsically unstable: change your perspective and the labyrinth seems to change.[134]

Unfortunately the dichotomy between those who participate inside and those who view from the outside breaks down when considering the house, simply because no one ever sees that labyrinth in its entirety. Therefore comprehension of its intricacies must always be derived from within.

This not only applies to the house but to the film itself. From the outset of *The Navidson Record*, we are involved in a labyrinth, meandering from one celluloid cell to the next, trying to peek around the next edit in hopes of finding a solution, a centre, a sense of whole, only to discover another sequence, leading in a completely different direction, a continually devolving discourse, promising the possibility of discovery while all along dissolving into chaotic ambiguities too blurry to ever completely comprehend.[135]

In order to fully appreciate the way the ambages unwind, twist only to rewind, and then open up again, whether in Navidson's house or the film—*quae itinerum ambages occursusque ac recursus inexplicabiles* [136]—we should look to the etymological inheritance of a word like 'labyrinth'. The Latin *labor* is akin to the root *labi* meaning to slip or slide backwards[137] though the commonly perceived meaning suggests difficulty and work. Implicit in 'labyrinth' is a required effort to keep from slipping or falling; in other words stopping. We cannot relax within those walls, we have to struggle past them. Hugh of Saint Victor has gone so far as to suggest that the antithesis of labyrinth—that which contains work—is Noah's ark[138]—in other words that which contains rest.×

---

[134]Penelope Reed Doob, *The Idea Of The Labyrinth: from Classical Antiquity through the Middle Ages* (Ithaca: Cornell University Press, 1990), p.1 ×

[135]At least, as Daniel Hortz lamented, "By granting all involved the right to wander (e.g. daydream, free associate, phantasize [sic] etc., etc.; see Gaston Bachelard) that which is discursive will inevitably re-appropriate the heterogeneity of the disparate and thus with such an unanticipated and unreconciled gesture bring about a re-assessment of self." ~~Or in other words, like the house, the film itself captures us and prohibits us at the same time as it frees us, to wander, and so first misleads us, inevitably, drawing us from the us, thus, only in the end to lead us, necessarily, for where else could we have really gone?, back again to the us and hence back to ourselves.~~ See Daniel Hortz's *Understanding The Self: The Maze of You* (Boston: Garden Press, 1995), p. 261.[129]

[136]["Passages that wind, advance and retreat in a bewilderingly intricate manner." — Ed.] Pliny also wrote when describing the Egyptian maze: "*sed crebis foribus inditis ad fallendos occursus redeundumque in errores eosdem.*" ["Doors are let into the walls at frequent intervals to suggest deceptively the way ahead and to force the visitor to go back upon the very same tracks that he has already followed in his wanderings."—Ed.] K

[137]*Labi* is also probably cognate with "sleep."[134]

[138]See Chapter Six, footnote 82, Tom's Story as well as footnote 249. — Ed.

If the work demanded by any labyrinth means penetrating or escaping it, the question of process becomes extremely relevant. For instance, one way out of any maze is to simply keep one hand on a wall and walk in one direction. Eventually the exit will be found. Unfortunately, where the house is concerned, this approach would probably require an infinite amount of time and resources. It cannot be forgotten that the problem posed by exhaustion—a result of labor—is an inextricable part of any encounter with a sophisticated maze. In order to escape then, we have to remember we cannot ponder all paths but must decode only those necessary to get out. We must be quick and anything but exhaustive. Yet, as Seneca warned in his *Epistulae morales* 44, going too fast also incurs certain risks:

Quod evenit in labyrintho properantibus:
ipsa illos velocitas inplicat.[139]

Unfortunately, the anfractuosity of some labyrinths may actually prohibit a permanent solution. More confounding still, its complexity may exceed the imagination of even the designer.[140] Therefore anyone lost within must recognize that no one, not even a god or an Other, comprehends the entire maze and so therefore can never offer a definitive answer. Navidson's house seems a perfect example. Due to the wall-shifts and extraordinary size, any way out remains singular and applicable only to those on that path at that particular time. All solutions then are necessarily personal.[141]

---

[139][This is what happens when you hurry through a maze: the faster you go, the worse you are entangled. — Ed.] Words worth taking to heart, especially when taking into account Pascal's remark, found in Paul de Man's *Allegories of Reading:* "Si on lit trop vite où trop doucement, on n'entend rien." [If one reads too quickly or too slowly, one understands nothing. — Ed.] [135]

[140]"*. . . ita Daedalus implet innumeras errore vias vixque ipse reverti ad limen potuit: tanta est fallacia tecti.*" Ovid, *Metamorphoses* VIII. l. 166-168. ["So Daedalus made those innumerable winding passages, and was himself scarce able to find his way back to the place of entry, so deceptive was the enclosure he had built." Horace Gregory, however, offers a slightly different translation: "So Daedalus designed his winding maze;/ And as one entered it, only a wary mind/ Could find an exit to the world again —/ Such was the cleverness of that strange arbour." p. 220. — Ed.] ~~Or in other words: shy from the sky. No answer lies there. It cannot care, especially for what it no longer knows. Treat that place as a thing unto itself, independent of all else, and confront it on those terms. You alone must find the way. No one else can help you. Every way is different. And if you do lose yourself at least take solace in the absolute certainty that you will perish.~~ ×

[141]I'm not sure why but I feel like I understand this on an entirely different level. What I mean to say is that the weird encounter with Tatiana seems to have helped me somehow. As if getting off was all I needed to diminish some of this dread and panic. I guess Thumper was right. Of course the downside is that this new discovery has left me practically beside myself, by which I mean priapic.

Last night, I made the rounds. I called Tatiana but she wasn't home. Amber's machine picked up but I didn't leave a message. Then as the hours lengthened and a particular heaviness crept in on me, I thought about Thumper. In fact I almost went down to where she works, to that place where I could be alone with the failing light and shadow play, where I could peek in ease, unhurried, unmolested, a notion which as suddenly as it crossed my mind suddenly—and for no apparent reason either—made me feel terribly uncomfortable. I called Lude instead. He gave me Kyrie's number. No answer. Not even a machine picked up. I called Lude back and an hour later we were losing ourselves in pints of cider at Red.

For some reason I had with me a little bit Zampanò wrote about Natasha (See Appendix F). I found it some months ago and immediately assumed she was an old love of his, which of course may still be true. Since then, however, I've begun to believe that Zampanò's Natasha also lives in Tolstoy's guerrulous pages. (Yes, amazingly enough, I finally did get around to reading War and Peace.)

Anyway, that evening, as coincidence would have it, a certain Natasha was dining on vegetables and wine. Rumor was—or so Lude confided; I've always loved the way Lude could 'confide' a rumor—her mother was famous but had been killed in a boating accident, unless you believed another rumor—which Lude also confided—that her father was the one who had been killed in a boating accident though he was not famous.

What did it matter?

Either way, Natasha was gorgeous.

Tolstoy's prophecy brought to life.

Lude and I quarreled over who would approach her first. Truth be known I didn't have the courage. A few pints later though, I watched Lude weave over to her table. He had every advantage. He knew her. Could say 'hello' and not appear obscene. I watched, my glass permanently fixed to my mouth so I could drink continuously—though breathing proved a bit tricky.

Lude was laughing, Natasha smiling, her friends working on their vegetables, their wine. But Lude stayed too long. I could see it in the way she started looking at her friends, her plate, everywhere but at him. And then Lude said something. No doubt an attempt to save the sitch. Little did I know I was the one being sacrificed, that is until he started pointing over at the counter, at me. And then suddenly she was looking over at the counter, at me. And neither one of them was smiling. I lifted the base of my glass high enough to eclipse my face and paid no mind to the stream of cider spilling from either side, foaming in my lap. When I lowered my deception I saw Natasha hand Lude back a piece of paper he had just given her. Her smile was curt. She said very little. He continued the charade, smiled quickly and departed.

"Sorry Hoss," Lude said as he sat down, unaware that the scene had turned me to stone.

"You didn't just tell her that I wrote that for her, did you?" I finally stuttered.

"You bet. Hey, she liked it. Just not enough to dump her boyfriend."

"I didn't write that. A blind man wrote it," I yelled at him, but it was too late. I finished my drink, and with my head down, got the hell out of there, leaving Lude behind to endure Natasha's pointed inattention.

Heading east, I passed by Muse and stopped in at El Coyote where I drank tequila shots until an Australian gal started telling me about kangaroos and the Great Barrier Reef and then ordered something else, potent and green. A while ago, over a year? two years? she had seen a gathering there of very, very famous people speaking censorially of things most perverse. She told me this with great glee, her breasts bouncing around like giant pacmen. Who cared. Fine by me. Did she want to hear about Natasha? Or at least what a blind man wrote?

When I finally walked outside, I had no idea where I was, orange lights burning like sunspots, initiating weird riots in my head, while in the ink beyond a chorus of coyotes howled, or was that the traffic? and no sense of time either. We stumbled together to a corner and that's when the car pulled over, a white car? VW Rabbit? maybe/maybe not? I strained to see what this was all about, my Australian gal giggling, both pacmen going crazy, she lived right around here somewhere but wasn't that funny, she couldn't remember exactly where, and me not caring, just squinting, staring at the white? car as the window rolled down and a lovely face appeared, tired perhaps, uncertain too, but bright nonetheless with a wry smile on those sweet lips—Natasha leaning out of her car, "I guess love fades pretty fast, huh?"[142] winking at me then, even as I shook my head, as if that kind of emphatic shaking could actually prove something, like just how possible it is to fall so suddenly so hard, though for it to ever mean anything you have to remember, and I would remember, I would definitely remember, which I kept telling myself as that white? car, her car?, sped off, bye-bye Natasha, whoever you are, wondering then if I would ever see her again, sensing I wouldn't, hoping senses were wrong but still not knowing; Love At First Sight having been written by a blind man, albeit sly, passionate too?, the blind man of all blind men, me,—don't know why I just wrote that—though I would still love her despite being unblind, even if I had all of a sudden started dreaming then of someone I'd never met before, or had known all along, no, not even Thumper—wow, am I wandering—maybe Natasha after all, so vague, so familiar, so strange, but who really and why? though at least this much I could safely assume to be true, comforting really, a wild ode mentioned at New West hotel over wine infusions, light, lit, lofted on very entertaining moods, yawning in return, open nights, inviting everyone's song, with me losing myself in such a dream, over and over again too, until that Australian gal shook my arm, shook it hard—

"Hey, where are you?"

"Lost" I muttered and started to laugh and then she laughed and I don't remember the rest. I don't remember her door, all those stairs to the second story, the clatter we made making our way down the hall, never turning on the lights, the hall lights or her room lights, falling onto the futon on her floor. I can't even remember how all our clothes came off, I couldn't get her bra off, she finally had to do that, her white bra, ahh the clasp was in front and I'd been struggling with the back, which was when she let the pacmen out and ate me alive.

Yeah I know, the dots here don't really connect. After all, how does one go from a piece of poetry to a heart wrenching beauty to the details of a drunken one night stand? I mean even if you could connect those dots, which I don't think you can, what kind of picture would you really draw?

There was something about her pussy. I do remember that. In fact it was amazing how hairy it was, thick coils of black hair, covering her, hiding her, though when fingered & licked still parting so readily for the feel of her, the taste of her, as she continued to sit on top of me, just straddling my mouth, and all the time easing slightly back, pushing slightly forward, even when her legs began to tremble, still wanting me to keep exploring her like that, with my fingers and my lips and my tongue, the layers of her warmth, the sweet folds of her darkness, over and over and over again.

The rest I'm sure I don't remember though I know it went on like that for a while.

Up in the sky-high,
Off to the side-eye,
All of us now sigh,
Right down the drain-ae.

Just a ditty. I guess.

As with previous explorations, Exploration #4 can also be considered a personal journey. While some portions of the house, like the Great Hall for instance, seem to offer a communal experience, many inter-communicating passageways encountered by individual members, even with only a glance, will never be re-encountered by anyone else again. Therefore, in spite of, as well as in light of, future investigations, Holloway's descent remains singular.

When his team finally does reach the bottom of the stairway, they have already spent three nights in that hideous darkness, their sleeping bags and tents successfully insulating their bodies from the cold, but nothing protecting their hearts from what Jed refers to as "the heaviness" which always seemed to him to be crouching, ready to spring, just a few feet away. While everyone enjoys some sense of elation upon reaching the last step, in truth they have only brought to a conclusion an already experienced aspect of the house. None of them are at all prepared for the consequences of the now unfamiliar.

On the morning of the fourth day, the three men agree to explore a new series of rooms. As Holloway says, "We've come a long way. Let's see if there's anything down here." Wax and Jed do not object, and soon enough, they are all wending their way through the maze.

As usual, Holloway orders numerous stops to procure wall samples. Jed has become quite handy with his chisel and hammer, cutting out small amounts of the black-ashen substance which he deposits into one of the many sample jars Reston equipped him with. As had been the case even on the stairway, Holloway personally takes responsibility for marking their path. He constantly tacks neon arrows to the wall, sprays neon paint on corners, and metes out plenty of fishing line wherever the path becomes

---

Later, I don't even know how much later, she said we'd been great and she felt great even though I didn't. I didn't even know where I was, who she was, or how we'd done what she said we'd done. I had to get out, but fuck the sun hurt my eyes, it split my head open, I dropped her number before I reached the corner, then spent a quarter of an hour looking for my car. Something was beginning to make me feel panicky and bad again. Maybe it was to have been that lost, to lose sense, even a little bit about some event, and was I losing more than I knew, larger events? greater sense? In fact all I had to hold onto at that moment as I cautiously pointed the old car to that place I had the gall to still call a home—never again—was her face, that wry smile, Natasha's, seen but unknown, found in a restaurant, lost on a street corner, gone in a wind of traffic—as in "to wind something up." I looked at my hands. I was holding onto the steering wheel so tightly, all my knuckles were shiny points of white, and my blinker was on, CLICK-click CLICK-click CLICK-click, so certain, so plain, so clear, and yet for all its mechanical conviction, blinking me in the wrong direction.

142

especially complicated and twisted.□

Oddly enough, however, the farther Holloway goes the more infrequently he stops to take samples or mark their path. Obviously deaf to Seneca's words.

Jed is the first to voice some concern over how quickly their team leader is moving: "You know where you're going, Holloway?" But Holloway just scowls and keeps pushing forward, in what appears to be a determined effort to find something, something different, something defining, or at least some kind of indication of an outsideness to that place. At one point Holloway even succeeds in scratching, stabbing, and ultimately kicking a hole in a wall, only to discover another windowless room with a doorway leading to another hallway spawning yet another endless series of empty rooms and passageways, all with walls potentially hiding and thus hinting at a possible exterior, though invariably winding up as just another border to another interior. As Gerard Eysenck famously described it: "Insides and in-ness never inside out."[143]

[144]Not only are there no hot-air registers, return air vents, or radiators, cast iron or other, or cooling systems—condenser, reheat coils, heating convector, damper, concentrator, dilute solution, heat exchanger, absorber, evaporator, solution pump, evaporator recirculating pump—or any type of ducts, whether spiral lock-seam/standing rib design, double-wall duct, and Loloss™ Tee, flat oval, or round duct with perforated inner liner, insulation, and outer shell; no HVAC system at all, even a crude air distribution system—there are no windows—no water supplies,

This desire for exteriority is no doubt further amplified by the utter blankness found within. Nothing there provides a reason to linger. In part because not one object, let alone fixture or other manner of finish work has ever been discovered there.[144] Back in 1771, Sir Joshua Reynolds in his *Discourses On Art* argued against the importance of the particular, calling into question, for example, "minute attention to the discriminations of Drapery . . . the cloathing is neither Woollen, nor linen, nor silk, sattin or velvet: it is drapery: it is nothing more."[145] Such global appraisal seems perfectly suited for Navidson's house which despite its corridors and rooms of various sizes is nothing more than corridors and rooms, even if sometimes, as John Updike once observed in the course of translating the labyrinth: "The galleries seem straight but curve furtively."

Of course rooms, corridors, and the occasional spiral staircase are themselves subject to patterns of arrangement. In some cases particular patterns. However, considering the constant shifts, the seemingly endless

---

□Aside from the practical aspect of fishing line—a readily available and cheap way to map progress through that complicated maze—there are of course obvious mythological resonances. ~~Minos' daughter, Ariadne, supplied Theseus with a thread which he used to escape the labyrinth.~~ Thread has repeatedly served as a metaphor for an umbilical cord, for life, and for destiny. The Greek Fates (called Moerae) or the Roman Fates (called Fata or Parcae) spun the thread of life and also cut it off. Curiously in Orphic cults, thread symbolized semen.

[143]Gerard Eysenck's "Break Through (not a) Breakthrough: Heuristic Hallways In The Holloway Venture." *Proceedings from The Navidson Record Semiotic Conference Tentatively Entitled Three Blind Mice and the Rest As Well.* American Federation of Architects. June 8, 1993. Reprinted in Fisker and Weinberg, 1996.

[145]See Joshua Reynolds' *Discourses on Art* (1771) (New York: Collier, 1961).

redefinition of route, even the absurd way the first hallway leads away from the living room only to return, through a series of lefts, back to where the living room should be but clearly is not; describes a layout in no way reminiscent of any modern floorplans let alone historical experiments in design.[146]

Sebastiano Pérouse de Montclos, however, has written a sizable examination on the changes within the house, positing that they in fact follow Andrea Palladio's structural derivations.

By way of a quick summary, Palladian grammar seeks to organize space through a series of strict rules. As Palladio proved, it was possible to use his system to generate a number of layouts such as Villa Badoer, Villa Emo, Villa Ragona, Villa Poiana, and of course Villa Zeno. In essence there are only eight steps:

1. Grid definition
2. Exterior-wall definition
3. Room layout
4. Interior-wall realignment
5. Principal entrances—porticos and exterior wall inflections
6. Exterior ornamentation—columns
7. Windows and Doors
8. Termination[149]

Pérouse de Montclos relies on these steps to delineate how Navidson's house was (1.0) first established (2.0) limited (3.0) sub-divided and (4.0) so on. He attempts to convince the reader that the constant refiguration of doorways and walls represents a kind of geological loop in the process of working out all possible forms, most likely *ad infinitum*, but never settling because, as he states in his conclusion, "unoccupied space will never cease to change simply because nothing forbids it to do so. The continuous internal alterations only prove that such a house is necessarily uninhabited."[150]

[144]Not only are there no hot-air registers, return air vents, or radiators, cast iron or other, or cooling systems—condenser, reheat coils, heating convector, damper, concentrator, dilute solution, heat exchanger, absorber, evaporator, solution pump, evaporator recirculating pump—or any type of ducts, whether spiral lock-seam\standing rib design, double-wall duct, and LolossTM Tee, flat oval, or round duct with perforated inner liner, insulation, and outer shell; no HVAC system at all, even a crude air distribution system—there are no windows—no water supplies,

[146]For example, there is nothing about the house that even remotely resembles 20th century works whether in the style of Post-Modern, Late-Modern, Brutalism, Neo-Expressionism, Wrightian, The New Formalism, Miesian, the International Style, Streamline Moderne, Art Deco, the Pueblo Style, the Spanish Colonial, to name but a few, with examples such as the Western Savings and Loan Association in Superstition, Arizona, Animal Crackers in Highland Park, Illinois, Pacific Design Center in Los Angeles, or Mineries Condominium in Venice, Wurster Hall in Berkeley, Katselas House in Pittsburgh, Dulles International Airport, Greene House in Norman Oklahoma, Chicago Harold Washington Library, the Watts Towers in South Central, Barcelona National Theatre, New Town of Seaside Florida, Tugendhat House, Rue de Laeken in Brussels, Richmond Riverside in Richmond Surrey, the staircase hall in the Athens, Georgia News Building, the Tsukuba Center Building in Ibaraki, the Digital House, Hiroshima City Museum of Contemporary Art, the interior of the Judge Institute of Management Studies in Cambridge, Maison à Bordeaux, TGV Railway Station in Lyon-Satolas, the post-modernism of the Wexner Center for Visual Arts in Columbus, Ohio, Palazzo Hotel in Fukuoka, National Geographic Society in Washington, D.C., the Amon Carter Museum in Fort Worth, Texas, Sainsbury Wing of the National Gallery, Pyramid at the Louvre, New Building at Staatsgalerie Stuttgart, J. Paul Getty Museum in Malibu, Palace of Abraxas at Marne-La-Vallée, Piazza d'Italie in New Orleans, AT&T Building in New York, the modernism of Carré d'Art, Lloyds Building in London, the Boston John F. Kennedy Library complex, Nave of Vuokseeniska Church in Finland, head office of the Enso-Gutzeit Company, Administrative Center of Säynätsalo, the Eames House, the Baker dormitory at MIT, inside the TWA terminal at Kennedy Airport, The National Theatre in London, Hull House Association Uptown Center in Chicago, Hektoen Laboratory also in Chicago, Fitzpatrick House in the Hollywood Hills, Graduate Center at Harvard University, Pan-Pacific Auditorium in Los Angeles, General Motors Testing Laboratory in Phoenix Arizona, Bullock's Wilshire Department Store in Los Angeles, Casino Building in New York, Hotel Franciscan in Albuquerque New Mexico, La Fonda Hotel in Santa Fe, or Santa Barbara County Courthouse, the Neff or Sherwood House in California, Exterior of the Secondary Modern School, Maisons Jaoul, Notre-Dame-du-Haut near Belfort, The Unité d'Habitation in Marseilles, The Farnsworth House in Plano, Illinois, The Alumni Memorial Hall at Illinois Institute of Technology, Guggenheim Museum in New York, or nothing of the traditionalism of Lawn Road Flats in Hampstead, the Zimbabwe House and Battersea Power Station in London, Choir of the Anglican cathedral in Liverpool or Memorial to the Missing of the Somme near Aras, Viceroy's house in New Delhi, Gledstone Hall in Yorkshire, Finsbury Circus facade, Castle Drogo near Drewsteignton Devon, Casa del Fascio in Como, Villa

[149]For an exemplary look at Palladian grammar in action, see William J. Mitchell's *The Logic of Architecture: Design, Computation, and Cognition* (Cambridge, Massachusetts: The MIT Press, 1994), p. 152-181. As well as Andrea Palladio's *The Four Books of Architecture* (1570) trans. Isaac Ware (New York: Dover, 1965).

[150]Sebastiano Pérouse de Montclos' *Palladian Grammar and Metaphysical Appropriations: Navidson's Villa Malcontenta* (Englewood Cliffs: Prentice-Hall, 1996), p. 2,865. Also see Aristides Quine's *Concatenating Corbusier*

Thus, as well as prompting formal inquiries into the ever elusive internal shape of the house and the rules governing those shifts, Sebastiano Pérouse de Montclos also broaches a much more commonly discussed matter: the question of occupation. Though few will ever agree on the meaning of the configurations or the absence of style in that place, no one has yet to disagree that the labyrinth is still a house.[151] Therefore the question soon arises whether or not it is someone's house. Though if so whose? Whose was it or even whose *is* it? Thus giving voice to another suspicion: could the owner still be there? Questions which echo the snippet of gospel Navidson alludes to in his letter to Karen[152]—St. John, chapter 14—where Jesus says:

> In my Father's house are many rooms: if it *were* not *so*, I would have told you. I go to prepare a place for you . . .

Something to be taken literally as well as ironically.[153]

drains, bathtubs, urinals, sinks, drinking fountains, water heaters, or coolers, expansion tanks, pressure relief valves, flow control, branch vent, downspout, soil stacks, or waste stacks, or fire protection equipment: smoke detectors, sprinklers, flow detectors, dry pipe valve, O.S. & Y. Gate valve, water motor alarm, visual annunciation devices, hose rack and hose reel whether a 2 1/2" or 1 1/2" valve, foam systems, gaseous suppression systems; nor any sign of daisy-chain wiring or star wiring or electrical metallic tubing (EMT), rigid conduit, wireways, bus ducts, underfloor ducts,

(New York: American Elsevier, 1996) in which Quine applies Corbusier's Five Points to the Navidson house, thereby proving, in his mind, the limitations and hence irrelevance of Palladian grammar. While these conclusions are somewhat questionable, they are not without merit. In particular, Quine's treatment of the Villa Savoye and the Domino House deserves special attention. Finally consider Gisele Urbanati Rowan Lell's far more controversial piece "Polypod Or Polylith?: The Navidson Creation As Mechanistic/ Linguistic Model" in *Abaku Banner Catalogue,* v. 198, January 1996, p. 515-597, in which she treats the "house-shifts" as evidence of polylithic dynamics and hence structure. For a point of reference see Greenfield and Schneider's "Building a Tree Structure. The Development of Hierarchical Complexity and Interrupted Strategies in Children's Construction Activity" in *Developmental Psychology,* 13, 1977, p. 299-313.

[151]Which also happens to maintain a curious set of constants. Consider —

Temperature: 32˚F ± 8.
Light: absent.
Silence: complete*
Air Movement (i.e. breezes, drafts etc.): none
True North: DNE

*With the exception of the 'growl'.

[152]See Chapter XVII.

[153]Also not to be forgotten is the terror Jacob feels when he encounters the territories of the divine: "How dreadful is this place! this is none other but the house of God, and this is the gate of heaven." (Genesis 28:17)

Philibert de l'Orme, Pierre Lescot, Gilles le Breton, Pirro Ligorio, Andrea Palladio, Martini Bassi, Galeazzo Alessi, Domenico Fontana, Giacomo Barozzi da Vignola, Jacopo Tatti Sansovino, Michele Sanmicheli, Michelangelo Buonarroti, Giulio Romano, Baldassare Peruzzi, Raffaello Sanzio, Antonia da Sangallo the Younger, Antonia da Sangallo the Elder, Donato Bramante, Filarete, Leonardo da Vinci, Leon Battista Alberti, Filippo Brunelleschi, Simon of Cologne, Juan Guas, Juan Gil de Hontañón, Arnolfo di Cambio, Lorenzo Maitani, Benedikt Ried, Konrad Heinzelmann, Nicolaus Eseler, Jörg Ganghofer, Ulrich von Ensingen, Wentzel Roriczer, Heinrich von Brunsberg, Hans von Burghausen, Peter Parler, Diogo Arruda, Diogo Boytac, William Wynford, Robert Janyns, Henry Yevele, Henry de Reynes, William the Englishman, William of Sens, Jean de Loubinère, Bishop Bernard de Castanet (P), Jean d'Orbais, Abbot Suger (P), Nicola Pisano, Pedro Petriz, Gunzo, Apollodorus of Damascus, Severus, Celer, Daedalus— though here the names of the authors of buildings have begun to fade into the names of Patrons (P), whether Bishops, Kings, Emperors, Dynasties, eventually myth, and finally time—148

[148]See Exhibit One.

It is not surprising then that when Holloway's team finally begins the long trek back, they discover the staircase is much farther away than they had anticipated, as if in their absence the distances had stretched. They are forced to camp for a fourth night thus necessitating strict rationing of food, water, and light (i.e. batteries). On the morning of the fifth day, they reach the stairs and begin the long climb up. Aside from the fact that the diameter of the Spiral Staircase is now more than seven hundred and fifty feet wide, the ascent moves fairly quickly.

During the walk down, Holloway had prudently decided to leave provisions along the way, thus lightening their load and at the same time allocating needed supplies for their return. Though Holloway had initially estimated they would need no more than eight hours to reach the first of these caches, it ends up taking them nearly twelve hours. At last at their destination, they quickly set up camp and collapse in their tents. Oddly enough, despite their exhaustion, all of them find it very difficult to fall asleep.

On the sixth day, they still make an early start. The knowledge that they are heading back keeps Wax and Jed's spirits elevated. Holloway, however, remains uncharacteristically sallow, revealing what critic Melisa Tao Janis calls "a sign of [his] deepening, atrabilious obsession with the unpresent."[154]

Nevertheless, the climb still proceeds smoothly, until Holloway discovers the remains of one of their foot long neon markers barely clinging to the wall. It has been badly mauled, half of the fabric torn away by some unimaginable claw. Even worse their next cache has been gutted. Only traces of the plastic water jug remain along with a few scattered pieces of PowerBars. Fuel for the campfire stove has completely disappeared.

"That's nice," Wax murmurs.

"Holy shit!" Jed hisses.

Emily O'Shaugnessy points out in *The Chicago Entropy Journal* the importance of this discovery: "Here at last are the first signs—evidenced ironically enough by the expurgation of a neon sign and the team's provisions—of the house's powerful ability to exorcise any and all things from its midst."[F]

---

[154]Melisa Tao Janis' "Hollow Newel Ruminations" in *The Anti-Present Trunk*, ed. by Philippa Frake (Oxford: Phaidon, 1995), p. 293.

[F] Emily O'Shaugnessy, "Metaphysical Emetic" in *Chicago Entropy Journal*, Memphis, Tennessee, v.182, n. 17, May, 1996.

Mairea in Noormarkku, Central Station in Milan, the New York City World's Fair Interior of the Finnish Pavilion, lobby of the Stockholm Concert House, Stockholm City Library, Woodland Crematorium, Police Headquarters in Copenhagen, Helsinki railway station, Villa Hvitträsk near Helsinki, Grundtvig Church in Copenhagen, Villa Savoye in Poissy, 25 rue Vavin in Paris, 62 rue Des Belles Feuilles also in Paris, Notre-Dame du Raincy, 25 bis, rue Franklin, Paris again, Chateau of Voisins, Rochefort-en-Yvelines, New Chancellery in Berlin, The Festival House near Dresden, the Schröder House, Utrecht, The Bauhaus in Dessau, or the expressionism of the Fagus Factory near Hildesheim, Amsterdam's Scheepvarthuis, Rheinhalle in Düsseldorf, the Chilehaus in Hamburg, Einstein Tower in Berlin, Schocken Department Store in Suttgart, Auditorium of the Grosses Schauspielhaus in Berlin, The Glass Pavilion in Cologne, Bresau's Centennial Hall, I.G.-Farben Dye Factory, Höchst, the Völkerschlacht Memorial in Leipzig, Haus Wiegand in Berlin, AEG Turbine Factory also in Berlin, the Stuttgart Railway Station, Leipziger Platz facade and the National Bank of Germany in Berlin, the American Radiator Building in New York, the Nebraska State Capitol, the Jefferson Memorial in Washington, D.C., Villa Vizcaya in Miami, Cathedral of St. John the Divine in New York, or Fallingwater, Administration Building at the S.C. Johnson Wax Factory, plan for the Tokyo Imperial Hotel or Taliesin East, the Robie House, the Winslow House, Warren Hickox House, or History Faculty Building in Cambridge, the Pompidou Center in Paris, the David B. Gamble House, The Seagram Building in New York, the Portland public service buiding, or the Art Nouveau of the cathedral of the Sagrada Familia in Barcelona, the Assembly building at Chandigarh in India, Casa Milá in Barcelona, the Majolikahaus and the Secession building in Vienna, the Greek Theatre at Park Güell, Casa Batllo, and Casa Vicens in Barcelona, and the staircase of the Tassel House in Brussels, Central Rotunda at the International Exhibition of Decorative Arts in Turin, Palazzo Castiglioni in Milan, the Elvira Photographic Studio in Munich, the Stoclet House in Brussels, The Imperial and Royal Post Office Savings Bank in Vienna, Darmstadt Artist's Colony, Library Facade of Glasgow School of Art, Paris Metro station entrance, Castel Béranger also in Paris, Maison du Peuple in Brussels, the Exchange in Amsterdam, the staircase of the Van Eetvelde House and Hôtel Solvay in Brussels, or anything of the Bungaloid style, the Mission Style, the Western Slick Style or the Prairie Style, whether the Crocker House in Pasadena, the Town and Gown Club in Berkeley, or the Goodrich House in Tucson, or any evidence of 19th century modes, whether stylistically enunciated as Jacobethan Revival, Late Gothic, Neo-Classical Revival, Georgian Revival, Second Renaissance Revival, Beaux-Arts Classicism, Chateauesque, Richardsonian Romanesque, the Shingle Style, Eastlake Style, Queen Anne Style, Stick Style, Second Empire, High Victorian Italianate, High

drains, bathtubs, urinals, sinks, drinking fountains, water heaters, or coolers, expansion tanks, pressure relief valves, flow control, branch vent, downspout, soil stacks, or waste stacks, or fire protection equipment: smoke detectors, sprinklers, flow detectors, dry pipe valve, O.S. & Y. Gate valve, water motor alarm, visual annunciation devices, hose rack and hose reel whether a 2 1/2" or 1 1/2" valve, foam systems, gaseous suppression systems; nor any sign of daisy-chain wiring or star wiring or electrical metallic tubing (EMT), rigid conduit, wireways, bus ducts, underfloor ducts,

Holloway Roberts is not nearly as analytical. He responds as a hunter and the image that fills the frame is a weapon. Kneeling beside his pack, we watch as he pulls out his Weatherby 300 magnum and carefully inspects both the bolt and the scope mounts before loading five 180 grain Nosler Partition® rounds in the magazine. As he chambers a sixth round, a glimmer of joy flickers across Holloway's features, as if finally something about that place has begun to make sense.

Fueled by the discovery, Holloway insists on exploring at least some of the immediate hallways branching off the staircase. Soon enough he is stalking doorways, leading the dancing moon of Jed's flashlight with the barrel of his rifle, and always listening. Corners, however, only reveal more corners, and Jed's light only targets ashen walls, though soon enough they all begin to detect that inimitable growl,[155] like calving glaciers, far off in the distance, which at least in the mind's eye, inhabits a thin line where rooms and passageways must finally concede to become a horizon.

a cellular floor, a raised floor, or for that matter wire of any sort, No. 36 to No. 0000 (#4/0), or electrical boxes—3 duct junction boxes etc., etc.— or plug-in receptacles, 3-prong grounded duplex or other, pots or pans or cans, or switch plates, switches, whether swing pole, dimmer or remote, or circuit breakers or fuses, whether lead, tin, copper, silver, etc., etc., with a voltage class from 12, 24, 125, 250, 600, 5000+, or even lights, whether electrical discharge, incandescent, or combustion, no flame arc or gas-filled, tipless, inside frosted, decorative, general service, 10,000 watt aviation pic-

"The growl almost always comes like the rustle of a high mountain wind on the trees," Navidson explained later. "You hear it first in the distance, a gentle rumble, slowly growing louder as it descends, until finally it's all around you, sweeping over you, and then past you, until it's gone, a mile away, two miles away, impossible to follow."[156]

Esther Newhost in her essay "Music as Place in *The Navidson Record*" provides an interesting interpretation of this sound: "Goethe once remarked in a letter to Johann Peter Eckermann [March 23, 1829]: 'I call architecture frozen music.'[157] The unfreezing of form in the Navidson house releases that music. Unfortunately, since it contains all the harmonies of time and change, only the immortal may savor it. Mortals cannot help but fear those curmurring walls. After all do they not still sing the song of our end?"[158]

For Holloway, it is impossible to merely accept the growl as a quality of that place anymore. Upon seeing the torn marker and their lost water, he seems to transfigure the eerie sound into an utterance made by some definitive creature, thus providing him

Ventura, Francois
Hurtado Izquierdo,
Leonardo de Figueroa,
James Gibbs, Carlo
Fontana, Thomas Archer,
Nicholas Hawksmoor,
John Vanbrugh, William
Talman, Christopher
Wren, Matthäus Daniel
Pöppelmann, Joseph
Schmuzer, Peter Thum,
Dominikus
Zimmermann, Cosmas
Damian Asam, Egid
Quirin, Balthasar
Neumann, Jakob
Prandtauer, Johann
Santini Aichel, Lucas von
Hildebrandt, Joseph
Emanuel Fischer von
Erlach, Johann Bernhard
Fischer von Erlach,
Emmanuel Héré de
Corny, Germain
Boffrand, Jules Hardouin-
Mansart, Louis Le Vau,
G.B. Vaccarini, Andrea
Palma, Andrea Giganti,
Tommaso Napoli,
Ferdinando Fuga,
Domenico Antonio
Vaccaro, Cosimo
Fanzago, Carlo Francesco
Dotti, Francesco Maria
Ricchino, Galeazzo
Alessi,
Bartolommeo
Bianco, Turin
Guarino Guarini,
Filippo Juvarra,
Bernardo Vittone,
Nicola Salvi, Carlo
Fontana,
Alessandro Specchi,
Andrea Pozzo,
Pietro da Cortona,
Francesco
Borromini, Giovanni
Battista Montano,
Gianlorenzo
Bernini, Inigo Jones,
Robert Smythson,
Jacob van Campen,
Bonifaz Wolmut, Aleviso
Novi, Jakob Wolf,
Alberlin Tretsch, Konrad
Krebs, Alonso de
Avarrubias, Enrique Egas,
Jacques Lemercier,
Solomon de Brosse,
François Mansart,

155In describing the Egyptian labyrinth, Pliny noted how "when the doors open there is a terrifying rumble of thunder within." ×

156The Last Interview.

157*Ich die Baukunst eine erstarrte Musik nenne.*

158Esther Newhost's "Music as Place in *The Navidson Record*" in *The Many Wall Fugue*, ed. Eugenio Rosch & Joshua Scholfield (Farnborough: Greg International, 1994), p. 47.

Victorian Gothic, the Octagon Mode, the Renaissance Revival, the Italian Villa Style, Romanesque Revival, Early Gothic Revival, Egyptian Revival, Greek Revival, such as University Club in Portland Oregon, Calvary Episcopal in Pittsburgh, the Minneapolis Institute of Arts, Germantown Cricket Club in Pennsylvania, All Souls Unitarian Church in Washington, D.C., Detroit Public Library or the Racquet and Tennis Club in New York, Metropolitan Museum of Art, Riverside County Courthouse in California, the Kimball House in Chicago, the Gresham House in Galveston, Texas, Cheney Building in Hartford Connecticut, Pioneer Building in Seattle, House House in Austin, Texas, Bookstaver House in Middletown Rhodes Island, Double House on Twenty-First Street in San Fancisco, Brownlee House in Bonham, Texas, Los Angeles Heritage Society, Sagamore Hill in Oyster Bay, Cram House in Middletown Rhode Island, House of San Luis Obispo, City Hall in Philadelphia, Gallatin House in Sacramento, Blagen Block and Marks House in Portland, Langworthy House in Dubuque, Iowa, Cedar Point in Swansboro, North Carolina, Haughwout Building in New York City, Farmers' and Mechanics' Bank in Philadelphia, Calvert Station in Baltimore, Jarrad House in New Brunswick, New Jersey, Old Stone Church in Cleveland, Church of Assumption in St. Paul, Minnesota, Rotch House in New Bedford, Massachusetts, St. James in Willmington, North Carolina, Philadelphia's Moyamensing Prison, Medical College of Virginia in Richmond, Lyle-Hunnicutt House in Athens, Georgia, Montgomery County Courthouse in Dayton, Ohio, which is not to exclude the non-presence of other 19th century examples such as the Pennsylvania station, exterior and concourse, Villard Houses in New York, the Boston Public Library, Court of Honor at the Chicago World's Fair, the St. Louis Wainwright Building, the Buffalo's Guaranty Building, Watts Sherman House in Newport Rhode Island, Boston Trinity Church, Ames Gate Lodge in North Easton, the Philadelphia Provident Life and Trust Company, Pennsylvania Academy of Fine Arts, Nott Memorial Library in Schenectady, New York, saloon in the Breakers, Boston City Hall, or Greek and gothic presence in the New York City Trinity Church, Philadelphia Girard College for Orphans, the Washington, D.C. Smithsonian Institute, Boston Tremont House, Philadelphia Merchant's Exchange, Ohio State Capitol, The Singer's Hall in Bavaria, Washington, D.C. Treasury Building, the Palais de Justice in Brussels, Empress Josephine's bedroom at Château of Malmaison, the Academy of Science in Athens, the Royal Pavilion in Brighton, Moscow Historical Museum, the New Admiralty in St. Petersburg, the grand staircase of the Paris Opéra, the St. Petersburg Exchange, Thorwaldsen Museum, Senate Square in Helsinki, Florence Cathedral, Milan's Galleria Vittorio Emanuele II, Palazzo di Giustizia in Rome, Conova Mausoleum near Possagno, Padua's Caffé Pedrocchi, the Parliament House in Vienna, the Dresden Opera

a cellular floor, a raised floor, or for that matter wire of any sort, No. 36 to No. 0000 (#4/0), or electrical boxes—3 duct junction boxes etc., etc.—or plug-in receptacles, 3-prong grounded duplex or other, pots or pans or cans, or switch plates, switches, whether swing pole, dimmer or remote, or circuit breakers or fuses, whether lead, tin, copper, silver, etc., etc., with a voltage class from 12, 24, 125, 250, 600, 5000+, or even lights, whether electrical discharge, incandescent, or combustion, no flame arc or gas-filled, tipless, inside frosted, decorative, general service, 10,000 watt aviation pic

with something concrete to pursue. Holloway almost seems drunk as he rushes after the sound, failing to lay down any fishing line or hang neon markers, rarely even stopping to rest.

Jed and Wax do not draw the same conclusion as Holloway. They realize, and quite accurately too, that even though they are traveling farther and farther away from the staircase, they are not getting any closer to the source of the growl. They insist on turning around. Holloway first promises to investigate just a little while longer, then resorts to goading, calling them anything from "fucking pussies" and "cowards" to "jack-holes" and "come-guzzling shit-eating cunts." Suffice it to say this last comment does not steel Wax and Jed's resolve to hunt the great beast.

They both stop.

Enough is enough. They are tired and more than a little concerned. Their bodies ache from the constant cold. Their nerves have been eviscerated by the constant darkness. They are low on battery power (i.e. light), neon markers, and fishing line. Furthermore, the destroyed cache of supplies could indicate their other caches are in jeopardy. If that proves to be the case, they will not have enough water to even make it back within radio range of Navidson.

"We're heading home now," Jed snaps.

"Fuck you," Holloway barks. "I give the orders here, and I say no one's going anywhere yet." Which considering the circumstances are pretty bizarre words to be hearing in such regions of dark.

"Look dude," Wax tries, doing his best to lure Holloway over to their side of sense. "Let's just check in so we can resupply and, you know . . . uh . . . get more guns."

"I will not abort this mission" Holloway responds sharply, jabbing an angry finger at the twenty-six year old from Aspen, Colorado.

Easily as much attention has been given to Holloway's use of the word "abort" as to Navidson's use of the word "outpost." The implication in "abort" is the failure to attain a goal—the prey not killed, the peak not climbed. As if there could have been a final objective in that place. Initially Holloway's only goal was to reach the bottom of the staircase (which he achieved). Whether it was the growl or the expurgating qualities of the house or something entirely else, Holloway decided to redefine that goal mid-way. Jed and Wax, however, understand that to begin hunting some elusive presence now is just the same as suicide. Without another word, they both turn around and start heading back to the stairs.

Holloway refuses to follow them. For a while, he rants and raves, screaming profanities at a blue streak, until finally and abruptly, he just storms off by himself, vanishing into the blackness. It is another peculiar event which is over almost before it starts. A sudden enfilade of "fuck you's" and "shit-heads" followed by silence.[159]

Back on the staircase, Jed and Wax wait for Holloway to cool off and return. When several hours pass and there is still no sign of him, they make a brief foray into the area, calling out his name, doing everything in their power to locate him and bring him back. Not only do they not find him, they do not come across a single neon marker or even a shred of fishing line. Holloway has run off blind.

We watch as Jed and Wax make camp and try to force themselves to sleep for a few hours. Perhaps they hope time will magically reunite the team. But the morning of the seventh day only brings more of the same. No sign of Holloway, a terrifying shortage of supplies, and a very ugly decision to make.

Hank Leblarnard has devoted several pages on the guilt both men suffered when they decided to head back without Holloway.[160] Nupart Jhunisdakazcriddle also analyzes the tragic nature of their action, pointing out that in the end, "Holloway chose his course. Jed and Wax waited for him and even made a

ture studio, projection, signal, Christmas tree, arc projector, photoflood, mercury, sodium, glow, sun, flash, black light, water cooled, germicidal, purple x, ozone, fluorescent, Slimline, Lumiline, Circline, rough service, Q coated, Bonus A-line, 75,000 watt, Quartzline, special service, DVY, DFC, iodine cycle, axial quartz, halogen cycle, bi-post, heat, brooder, red bowl therapy, silver neck brooder, quartz infrared, bent-end infrared, iodine cycle infrared, RSC base, red filter, Marc 300, Lucalox, multi-vapor, e-bulb mercury, 1,500 watt multi-vapor, Watt-Miser II, Magicube,

---

159This is not the first time individuals exposed to total darkness in an unknown space have suffered adverse psychological effects. Consider what happened to an explorer entering the Sarawak Chamber discovered in the Mulu mountains in Borneo. This chamber measures 2,300ft long, 1,300ft wide, averages a height of 230ft, and is large enough to contain over 17 football fields. When first entering the chamber, the party of explorers kept close to a wall assuming incorrectly that they were following a long, winding passageway. It was only when they chose to return by striking straight out into that blackness—expecting to run into the opposite wall—that they discovered the monstrous size of that cavern: "So the trio marched out into the dark expanse, maintaining a compass course through a maze of blocks and boulders until they reached a level, sandy plain, the signature of an underground chamber. The sudden awareness of the immensity of the black void caused one of the cavers to suffer an acute attack of agoraphobia, the fear of open spaces. None of the three would later reveal who panicked, since silence on such matters is an unwritten law among cavers." *Planet Earth: Underground Worlds* p. 26-27.

Of course, Holloway's reactions exceed a perfectly understandable case of agoraphobia.

160Hank Leblarnard's *Grief's Explorations* (Atlanta: More Blue Publications, 1994).

Robert Smirke, William
Wilkins, Sir John Soane,
Richard Payne Knight,
Humphry Repton, John
Nash, Gustave Eiffel,
Ferdinand Dutert, J.C.A.
Alphand, Victor Baltard,
Jean-Louise-Charles
Garnier, Joseph Auguste-
Emile Vaudremer, Leon
Vaudoyer, Louis-Joseph
Duc, Pierre-Francois-
Henri Labrouste, Jacque-
Ignace Hittorff, A.F.T.
Chalgrin, Charles Percier,
Francois-Léonard
Fontaine, Benjamin
Latrobe, George Hadfield,
Etienne Hallet, William
Thornton, Charles
Bulfinch, Thomas
Jefferson, Peter Harrison,
Charles Cameron, Matvei
Feodorovich Kazakow,
Giacomo Quarenghi, Ivan
Yegorovich Starov, Vasili
Ivanovich Bazhenov,
Fredrik Magnus Piper,
Carl August Ehrensvärd,
Louis-Joseph Le Lorrain,
Jakub Kubicki, Christian
Piotr Aigner, Dominik
Merlini, Friedrich Gilly,
Heinrich Jussow, Pierre-
Michel d'Ixnard, Wilhelm
von Erdmannsdorf,
Giuseppe
Piermarini,
Michelangelo
Simonetti, Pietro
Camporese, Claude-
Nicolas Ledoux,
Etienne-Louis
Boullée, Charles de
Wailly, Marie-
Joseph Peyre, Victor
Louis, Pierre
Rousseau, Jacques-
Germain Soufflot,
Jacques Gabriel,
John Wood, George
Dance, James
Wyatt, James Gandon,
William Chambers,
Robert Adam, William
Kent, Carlo Marchionni,
Giovanni Battista
Piranesi, Niccolò Nasoni,
Mateus Vicente de
Oliveira, Johann Friedrich
Ludwig, Rodriguez Tizón

noble effort to find him. At 5:02 A.M., as the Hi 8 testifies, their only option was to return without him."[161]

As Jed and Wax resume their climb back up the Spiral Staircase, they discover every neon marker they left behind has been torn apart. Furthermore the higher they get, the more the markers have been devoured. Around this time, Jed also begins to notice how more than a few of his buttons have vanished. Strips of velcro have fallen off his parka, shoe laces have shredded forcing him to bind his boots together with duck tape. Amazingly enough, even his pack frame has "crumbled"—the word Jed uses.

"It's kind of scary" Wax mutters in the middle of a long ramble. "Like you stop thinking about something and it vanishes. You forget you have pocket zippers and pow they're gone. Don't take nothing for granted here."

Jed keeps wondering aloud: "Where the hell is [Holloway]?" and silence keeps trying to mean an answer.

An hour later, Jed and Wax reach another cache, placed out of the way against the wall at the far end of a stair, near the entrance to some unexplored corridor. Nothing remains of the food and fuel but the jug of water is perfectly intact. Wax is back for a second chug, when the crack of a rifle drops him to the floor, blood immediately gushing from his left armpit.

"Oh my god! Oh my god!" Wax screams. "My arm—Oh god Jed help me, I'm bleeding!" Jed immediately crouches next to Wax's side and applies pressure to the wound. Moments later, Holloway emerges from the dark corridor with his rifle in hand. He seems just as shocked by the sight of these two as he is by the sight of the stairs.

"How the hell did I get here?" he blurts out incoherently. "I thought it was that, that thing. Fuck. It *was* that thing. I'm sure of it. That awful fucking . . . fuck, fuck."

"Don't stand there. Help him!" Jed yells. This seems to snap Holloway out of his trance—at least for a little while. He helps Jed peal off Wax's jacket and treat the wound. Fortunately they are not unprepared. Jed has a medical supply kit loaded with gauze, ace bandages, disinfectant, ointments, and some painkillers. He forces two pills into Wax's mouth but the ensuing cut

House, Befreiungshalle near Kelheim, Walhalla across the Danube, Feldherrnhalle in Munich, Berlin National Galerie or Bauakademie or the staircase in the Altes Museum or Schauspielhaus, nor the gothic revival of the campanile of Wesminster cathedral, New Scottland Yard, Standen in Sussex, the house at Cragside in Northumberland or Newnham College in Cambridge, or Leyswood in Sussex, the Crystal Palace or the Law Courts in London, the chapel at Keble college, Albert Memorial in Kensington Gardens, or the Saloon of the Reform Club, Elmes' St. George's Hall in Liverpool, Taylorian Institution at the Ashmolean Museum in Oxford, Edinburgh Royal College of Physicians, British Museum in London, Devon Luscombe Castle, Cumberland Terrace in Regent's Park, the Paris Grand Palais or Gare du Quai d'Orsay or the staircase at the Nouvelle Sorbonne or the Opéra or St-Augustin or Fontaine St-Michel or Parc des Buttes-Chaumont, the Marseilles Cathedral, the Paris Bibliothèque Nationale, the Salle de Harlay in the Palais de Justice, or the reading room at the Bibliothèque Ste-Geneviève, Gare du Nord, Ecole des Beaux-Arts, St-Vincent de Paul, Church of the Madeleine, rue de Rivoli, the arc du Carrousel, nor anything like 18th century classicism of the Washington, D.C. Supreme Court Chamber, the staircase vestibule in the D.C. capitol and the capitol itself, Baltimore Roman Catholic Cathedral, bank of Pennsylvania, the University of Virginia Jefferson Library, Monticello near Charlottesville, First Baptist Meeting House in Providence Rhode Island, Drayton Hall in Charleston, King's Chapel in Boston, or examples of the Jeffersonian Classicism or the Adam Style, such as Pavilion VII at the University of Virginia, Estouteville in Albemarle County, Clay Hill in Harrodsburg Kentucky, Nickels-Sortwell House in Wiscasset, Maine, Ware-Sibley House in Augusta, Georgia, or the Congregational Church in Tallmadge Ohio, or the Dalton House in Newburyport, Massachusetts, Sheremetev Palace near Moscow, Cameron Gallery in Tsarskow Seloe, the Catherine Hall in the St. Petersburg Tauride Palace, Leningrad Academy of Fine Arts, Copenhagen Amalienborg Palace, Lazienki Palace near Warsaw, the mock Gothic castle of Löwenburg at Schloss Wilhelmshöhe, the Brandenburg Gate in Berlin, mosque in the garden of Schwetzingen near Mannheim, Villa Hamilton near Dessau, Milan's Palazzo Serbelloni, the Sale delle Muse in the Vatican, the Boston Massachusetts State House, Paris Barrière de la Villette, the Director's house at the saltworks of Arc-et-Senans near Besancon, Paris Pantheon, or La Solitude in Stuttgart, Rue de la Pépinière, Château at Montmusard near Dijon, the breakfast room of Sir John Soane's Museum, or the French Neo-Classicism of the Hameau at Versailles, the staircase of the theatre at Bordeaux, the anatomy theatre in the Paris School of Surgery, chambers for the mausoleum of the Prince of Wales, entrance and colonnade of the Hôtel de Salm, Syon House in Middlesex, Versailles St. Symphorien, or Petit Trianon, or London Lin-

ture studio, projection, signal, Christmas tree, arc projector, photoflood, mercury, sodium, glow, sun, flash, black light, water cooled, germicidal, purple x, ozone, fluorescent, Slimline, Lumiline, Circline, rough service, Q coated, Bonus A-line, 75,000 watt, Quartzline, special service, DVY, DFC, iodine cycle, axial quartz, halogen cycle, bi-post, heat, brooder, red bowl therapy, silver neck brooder, quartz infrared, bent-end infrared, iodine cycle infrared, RSC base, red filter, Marc 300, Lucalox, multi-vapor, e-bulb mercury, 1,500 watt multi-vapor, Watt-Miser II, Magicube,

[161] Nupart Jhunisdakazcriddle's *Killing Badly, Dying Wise* (London: Apophrades Press, 1996), p. 92.

shows that only some of Wax's agony has subsided.

Jed starts to tell Holloway what they will have to do in order to carry Wax the remainder of the way up.

"Are you crazy?" Holloway suddenly shouts. "I can't go back now. I just shot someone."

"What the hell are you talking about?" Jed tries to say as calmly as possible. "It was an accident."

Holloway sits down. "It doesn't matter. I'll go to jail. I'll lose everything. I have to think."

"Are you kidding me? He'll die if you don't help me carry him!"

"I can't go to prison," Holloway mumbles, more to himself now than to either Wax or Jed. "I just can't."

"Don't be ridiculous," Jed says, starting to raise his voice. "You're not gonna go to jail. But if you sit there and let Wax die, for that they'll lock you up for life. And I'll make sure they throw away the fucking key. Now get up and help me."

Flash Bar, Flip-Flash, GE-500, composite, discharge forward lighting, Precise, 35.5 lumens, white Lucalox, standby Lucalox, high output Lucalox, Halarc 32 watt, Halarc 100 watt, Staybright XL, high intensity Biax, metal halide, to say nothing of communication systems such as public address, intercom, radio, TV, CCTV, SATV, VSAT, telephone (PAX or PBX etc., etc.) or data, signal multimedia designs, or BAS, BMS, BMAS automation; there are not even any moldings or other stylistic signatures such as casings, baseboards, or finished floors, linoleum, cement, whether

Holloway does struggle to his feet, but instead of giving Jed a hand, he just walks away, disappearing once again into that impenetrable curtain of black, leaving Jed to carry and care for Wax by himself. For whatever reason, departure suddenly became Holloway's only choice. *Une solution politique honorable.*[162]

Jed does not get very far with Wax before two bullets smash into a nearby wall. Holloway's helmet light reveals that he is standing on the opposite side of the stairway.

Jed instantly turns off his flashlight and with Wax on his back scrambles up a few stairs. Then by rapidly clicking his flashlight on and off, he discovers a narrow hallway branching off the stairway into unseen depths. Unfortunately another shot instantly answers this fractionary bit of vision, the bang echoing over and over again through the pitch.

As we can see Jed does succeed in dragging Wax into this new corridor, the next Hi 8 clip capturing him with his flashlight back on, moving through a series of tiny rooms. Occasionally we hear the faint crack of a rifle shot in the distance, causing Jed to push ahead even faster, darting through as many chambers as possible, until his breath rasps painfully in and out of his lungs and he is forced to put his friend down, unable for the moment to go any farther.

Jed just slides to the floor, turns off his light, and starts to sob.

---

[162] "An honorable political solution"—and as usual, pretentious as all fuck. Why French? Why not English? It also doesn't make much sense. Nothing about Holloway's choice or Jed's request seems even remotely political.

Benjamin Latrobe, Petrus
Josephus Hubertus
Cuypers, Joseph Poelaert,
Ernst Ziller, Theophilus
Eduard Hansen, Hans
Christian Hansen,
Vladimir Ossipovich
Sherwood, Konstantin
Andreevich Thon, Osip
Beauvais, Afanasy
Grigoryev, Domenico
Gilardi, Vasili Petrovich
Stasov, Auguste Ricard de
Montferrand, Karl
Ivanovich Rossi, Adrian
Dmitrievich Zakharov,
Thomas de Thomon,
Andrei Nikiforovich
Voronikhin, Antonio
Corazzi, Johan Albrecht
Ehrenström, Bertel
Thorwaldsen, Carl
Ludwig Engel, Christian
Heinrich Grosch, Gottlieb
Birkner Bindesbøll,
Christian Frederick
Hansen, Emilio de Fabris,
Camillo Boito, Pietro
Estense Selvatico,
Guglielmo Calderini,
Gaetano Koch, Marion
Crawford, Giuseppe
Mengoni, Giuseppe
Valadier, Raffaello Stern,
Braccio Nuovo,
Alessandro
Antonelli, Carlo
Amati, Antonio
Niccolini, Pietro
Bianchi, Giuseppe
Jappelli, Antonio
Selva, Eduard
Riedel, Georg von
Dollmann, Julius
Raschdorf, Paul
Wallot, Gottfried
Semper, Fredrich
von Gärtner, Leo
von Klenze, Karl
Fredrich Schinkel,
Heinrich Hübsch,
John Francis
Bentley, Philip Webb,
Basil Champneys, Richard
Norman Shaw, Owen
Jones, Sir Joseph Paxton,
George Edmund Street,
Augustus Welby
Northmore Pugin, E.M.
Barry, Sir Charles Barry,
Charles Robert Cockerell,

At 3:31 A.M. the camera blips on again. Jed has moved Wax to another room. Realizing the camcorder may be his only chance to provide an explanation for what happened, Jed now speaks directly into it, reiterating the events leading up to Holloway's break with reality and how exhausted, pursued, and ultimately lost, Jed has still somehow managed to carry, drag, and push Wax to a relatively safe place. Unfortunately, he no longer has any idea where they are: "So much for my sense of direction. I've spent the last hour looking for a way back to the staircase. No luck. The radio is useless. If help doesn't come soon, he'll die. I'll die."

Barely caught in the frame, we can just make out Jed's fist rapping incessantly against the floor, which as it turns out, has the exact same timbre as those knocks heard back in the living room. Alan P. Winnett, however, remarks on one notable difference:

> Curiously enough, despite the similarity of intonation and pitch, the pattern does not even remotely resemble the three short – three long – three short SOS signal heard by the Navidsons. Carlos Avital has suggested the house itself not only carried the signal an incredible distance but interpreted it as well. Marla Hulbert disagrees, positing that the rhythm of the knocking hardly matters: "By the eighth day, the absence of any word from Holloway's team was already a distress signal in and of itself."[163]

Regardless of its meaning and the reasons behind its transfiguration, Jed only produces this strange tattoo for a short time before returning to the needs of his badly wounded friend.[164]

coln's Inn Fields, the Consols Office in the Bank of England, the plan of Fonthill Abbey, the Cupola Room at Heaton Hall, the Dublin Four Courts, the Somerset House in London, the Casino at Marino House in Dublin, the Pagoda at Kew Gardens, Stowe House portico at Buckinghamshire, drawing room at 20 St. James' Square, Middlesex Syon House, Marble Hall at Kedleston, Temple of Ancient Virtue in the Stowe Elysian Fields, staircase at 44 Berkeley Square, Holkham Hall in Norfolk, the cupola room in Kensington Palace, Tempietto Diruto at Villa Albani Rome, entrance front to S. Maria del Priorato also in Rome, Ancient Mausoleum from *Prima Parte di Architetture e Prospettive*, or the Baroque expansion indicated by the cascade of steps at Bom Jesus do Monte near Braga, or royal palace at Queluz, the Royal Library at the University of Coimbra, the palace-convent of Mafra near Lisbon, Salamanca Plaza Mayor, cathedral of Santiago de Compostela, cathedral at Murcia, Granada cathedral, the transparente in Toledo cathedral, octagonal pavilion at Orleans House, St Martin-in-the-Fields, Radcliffe Library in Oxford, the Wieskirche, chapel of Würzburg Residenz, or Stepney St. George-in-the-East, St. George's, Bloomsbury London, Oxfordshire Blenheim Palace, the mirror room of the Amlienburg in Munich, the Yorkshire Mausoleum at Castle Howard, Chatsworth Derbyshire, the painted hall at the Greenwich Royal Hospital, Rome's interior dome of S. Carlo alle quattro Fontane, or the Salon de la Guerre in Versailles, St. Paul's Cathedral, Piazza S. Pietro, Wren's Sheldonian Theatre in Oxford, the abbey church at Ottobeuren, or the German rococo of the Zwinger, Wallpavillon Dresden, St. John Nepomuk in Munich, the high altar at the abbey church of Weltenburg, the staircase at the Residenz Würzburg or the church at Vierzehnheiligen, the monastery of Melk in Austria, staircase at Pommersfelden, the upper Belvedere, Imperial Library of the Hofburg, Karlskirche in Vienna, the Ancestral Hall at Schloss Frain in Moravia, or French rococo like the Salon de la Princesse at Hôtel de Soubise in Paris, not even just the interior chapel at Versailles, domed oval saloon at Vaux-le-Vicomte, Paris Hôtel Lambert, S. Agata in Catania, the Syracuse cathedral, the ballroom at the Palazzo Gangi in Palermo, the majolica cloister at S. Chiara or the Piazza del Gesù in Naples, or even the uncompleted Palazzo Donn'Anna, or the interior of the Gesuiti in Venice, the plan of the University Genoa, the Royal Palace at Stupinigi, the Superga near Turin, or the staircase at the Palazzo Madama, or the dome of S. Lorenzo in Turin, or the interior of the dome of the Cappella della SS. Sindone, or the Trevi Fountain or the facade of S. Maria Maggiore or the Spanish steps or the frescoes on the nave vault of S. Ignazio in Rome, or also in Rome the interior of S. Maria in Via Lata, Pietro da Cortona's SS. Luca e Martina, Villa Sacchetti del Pigneto, Piazza Navona, Fontana del Moro, S. Ivo dell Sapienza, facade of the Oratory of the Congregration of St. Philip Neri, chapel ceiling at the Collegio di Propa-

Flash Bar, Flip-Flash, GE-500, composite, discharge forward lighting, Precise, 35.5 lumens, white Lucalox, standby Lucalox, high output Lucalox, Halarc 32 watt, Halarc 100 watt, Staybright XL, high intensity Biax, metal halide, to say nothing of communication systems such as public address, intercom, radio, TV, CCTV, SATV, VSAT, telephone (PAX or PBX etc., etc.) or data, signal multimedia designs, or BAS, BMS, BMAS automation; there are not even any moldings or other stylistic signatures such as casings, basedboards, or finished floors, linoleum, cement, whether

[163]Alan P. Winnett's *Heaven's Door* (Lincoln: University of Nebraska Press, 1996), p. 452. Also see Carlos Avital's widely read though somewhat prolix pamphlet *Acoustic Intervention* (Boston: Berklee College of Music, 1994) as well as Marla Hulbert's "Knock Knock, Who Cares?" in *The Phenomenology of Coincidence in The Navidson Record* (Minneapolis: University of Minnesota Press, 1996).

[164]Once, in the dining hall of a certain boarding school—it was my second and nothing fancy—I met a ghost. I'd been talking with two friends, but due to

all the seven o'clock din, the place being packed with fellow gorgers, it was almost impossible to hear much of what anyone said, unless you shouted, and we weren't shouting because our conversation had to be kept secret. Not that what we said offered a whole lot of anything new. Not even variation.

Girls.

That was all. One word to pretty much sum up the whole of all we cared about. Week in, week out. Where to meet them. What to say to them. How not to need them. That was unattractive. Girls could never know you needed them, which was why our conversation had to be kept secret, because that's all it was about: needing them.

Back then, I was living life like a ghost, though not the ghost I'm about to tell you about. I was all numb & stupid and dazed too I guess, a pretty spooky silentiary for matters I knew by heart but could never quite translate for anyone I knew let alone myself. I constantly craved the comforts of feminine attention, even though the thought of actually getting a girlfriend, one who was into me and wanted to be with me, seemed about as real as any dozen of the myths I'd been reading about in class.

At least the same guy who explained my attachment to junk, The Counselor For Disaffected You—I mean Youth—, helped me see how influenced I remained by my past. Unfortunately it was a lesson delivered tongue in cheek, as he ultimately believed I'd made most of my past up just to impress him.

About one thing he was right, my mother wasn't actually dead yet. Telling everyone she was though made my life far less complicated. I don't think anyone at the boarding school, including my friends, teachers, certainly not my counselor, ever found out the truth, which was fine with me. That's the way I liked it.

My arms, however, were another story. It's kinda funny, but despite my current professional occupation, I don't have any tattoos. Just the scars, the biggest ones of course being the ones you know about, this strange seething melt running from the inside of both elbows all the way up to the end of both wrists, where—I might as well tell you—a skillet of sizzling corn oil unloaded its lasting wrath on my efforts to keep it from the kitchen floor. "You tried to catch it all," my mother had often said of that afternoon when I was only four. See, not nearly as dramatic as a Japanese Martial Arts Cult run by Koreans in Indiana. I mean Idaho. Just a dropped pan. That's all.

As for the rest of the scars, there are too many to start babbling on about here, jagged half-moon reminders on my shoulders and shins, plenty stippled on my bones, a solemn

fast setting, coloured, fiber reinforced, self-leveling, mortar, high early-strength, sand mix, silica sand, plastic, hydraulic, or sheet vinyl, tile, cork tile, terrazo, rubber, carpeting, epoxy, ceramic & stone, slate, aputitsiarvaq, or marble, whether white—Danby Imperial, Colorado Yule, or Carrara—or black or green; or hardwood, whether overlay, strip flooring with alternate joints, or herringbone, inlaid, basket weave, Arenberg, Chantilly, or Versailles parquet; in fact no wood anywhere, whether redwood, treated western hemlock, yellow pine, cedar, wood-polymer, Engelmann spruce,

Grosvenor Goodhue,
James Gamble Rogers,
Ralph Adams Cram, John
F. Staub, Diego Suarez,
Burrall Hoffmann, Paul
Chalfin, John Russell
Pope, Henry Bacon, John
Bakewell, Arthur Brown,
Horace Trumbauer, Henry
Mather Greene, John
Lyman Silsbee, Frances
Berenguer y Mestres, Luis
Domenech y Montaner,
Antoni Gaudi i Cornet,
Raimond D'Aronco,
Giuseppe Sommaruga,
Otto Wagner, Henri van
de Velde, Theodor Lipps,
August Endell, Ernst
Ludwig Haus, C.F.A.
Voysey, Charles Harrison
Townsend, Herman
Muthesius, Charles
Rennie Mackintosh,
Charles Plumet, Jules
Lavirotte, Frantz
Jourdain, Georges
Chedanne, Xavier
Schoellkopf, Hector
Guimard, Henrik Petrus
Berlage, Paul Hankar,
Victor Horta, Paul
Sédille, Jules Saulnier,
Cass Gilbert, John
Smithmeyer, Paul Pelz,
Stanford White,
William Rutherford
Mead, Charles
Atwood, Charles
Follen McKim,
Louis Henry
Sullivan, Daniel
Burnham, John
Root, William Le
Baron Jenney, Frank
Furness, Henry Van
Brunt, William
Ware, John Sturgis,
Charles Brigham,
Edward Potter,
Peter B. Wright,
Richard Morris
Hunt, Arthur Gilman,
Gridley Bryant, Alfred B.
Mullet, James Renwick,
Richard Upjohn, Thomas
Ustick Walter, Thomas
Cole, Isaiah Rogers,
Alexander Jackson Davis,
Ithiel Town, Robert Mills,
William Strickland,

ganda Fide or the S. Carlo alle Quattro Fontane, Scala Regia in the Vatican, S. Andrea al Quirinale, nor even elements of the Renaissance as evinced by the Great Hall at the Hatfield House in Hertfordshire, Longleat, Hardwick Hall in Derbyshire, the Gate of Honour at Gonville and Caius College in Cambridge, Burghley House in Northamptonshire, Meat Hall in Haarlem, the House Ten Bosch at Maarssen, the Mauritshuis at the Hague, the Antwerp town hall, the arcaded loggia of the Belvedere in Prgaue, Wawel Cathedral in Cracow, the town hall at Augsburg, Schloss Johannesburg, Aschaffenburg, the court facade of the Ottheinrichsbau of the Schloss at Heidelberg, the Jesuit church of St. Michael in Munich, court of Altes Schloss in Stuttgart, Escorial, the Portal of Pardon, Granada, palace courtyard for Charles V at Alhambra, Granada, the Royal Hospital at Santiago de Compostela, the Queen's House in Greenwich, the Bourbon chapel at St-Denis, chateau pf Maisons-Lafittem the church of the College of the Sorbonne, the Palazzo Corner della Ca'-Grande in Venice, or the Francois I gallery at Fontainebleau, Place des Vosges in Paris, gateway of the chateau at Anet, the Petit Chateau at Chantilly, the Chateau de Chambord, Square Court of the Louvre, Courtyard of the Chateau of Ancy-le-Franc, the Medici Chapel, the open staircase at Blois, the interior of Il Redentore in Venice, or Villa Rotonda near Vicenza, Palazza Chiericati, Villa Barbaro, S. Maria, Vicoforte di Mondovi, Palazzo Farnese, Caprarola, the Strada Nuova in Genoa, the hemicycle of Villa Giulia, Villa Garzoni, Pontecasale, library of S. Marco in Venice, the Loggetta at the base of the Campanile, Cappella Pellegrini in Verona, Rome's S. Maria Degli Angeli, the giant order of the Rome Capitol, staircase of the Laurentian Library in Florence, or Mantua's Palazzo Ducale or Palazzo del Tè, or Palazzo Farnese or Palazzo Massimi or Villa Farnesina or Villa Madama in Rome, or S. Maria della Consolazione in Todi, Belvedere Court, S. Pietro in Montorio, or Palazzo della Cancelleria in Rome, S. Maria delle Grazie in Milan, Cappella del Perdono, Palazzo Ducale, Urbino, Palazzo Medici-Riccardi in Florence, the Pienxa Piazza, Rimini Tempio Malatestiano, Mantua's S. Andrea, Florence's S. Spirito or Pazzi Chapel, to say nothing of the lack of even a gothic signature, whether like the church of Sta Maria de Vitória at Batalha, the Cristo Monastery at Tomar, the palace of Bellver near Palma de Mallorca, cathedral at Palma de Mallorca, the Seville cathedral, Ca' d'Oro in Venice, Siena's Palazzo Pubblico, Venice's Piazzetta, the Doges' Palace Facade, or the nave of the Milan Cathedral, Orvieto cathedral, or the Florence cathedral, or the upper church of S. Francesco at Assisi, cathedral and castle of the Teutonic Order at Marienwerder Poland, the town hall at Louvain, St. Barbara in Kuttenberg, the Vladislav Hall in the Hradcany Castle in Prague, St Lorenz in Nuremberg, the Starsbourg cathedral, the Ulm cathedral, Vienna Cathedral, interior of the Aarchen cathedral, the Prague cathedral, the choir vaulting of the church of

fast setting, coloured, fiber reinforced, self-leveling, mortar, high early-strength, sand mix, silica sand, plastic, hydraulic, or sheet vinyl, tile, cork tile, terrazo, rubber, carpeting, epoxy, ceramic & stone, slate, aputisiarvaq, or marble, whether white—Danby Imperial, Colorado Yule, or Carrara—or black or green; or hardwood, whether overlay, strip flooring with alternate joints, or herringbone, inlaid, basket weave, Arenberg, Chantilly, or Versailles parquet; in fact no wood anywhere, whether redwood, treated western hemlock, yellow pine, cedar, wood-polymer, Engelmann spruce,

---

white one intersecting my eyebrow, another obvious one still evident in my broken, now discolored front tooth, a central incisor to be more precise, and some even deeper than all of the above, telling a tale much longer than anyone has ever heard or probably ever will hear. All of it true too, though of course scars are much harder to read. Their complex inflections do not resemble the reductive ease of any tattoo, no matter how extensive, colorful or elaborate the design. Scars are the paler pain of survival, received unwillingly and displayed in the language of injury.

My Counselor For Disaffected Youth had no idea what kept me going—though he never phrased it exactly like that. He just asked me how, in light of all my stories, I'd still managed to sustain myself. I couldn't answer him. I know one thing though, whenever I felt particularly bad I'd instantly cling to a favorite daydream, one I was willing to revisit constantly, a pretty vivid one too, of a girl, a certain girl, though one I'd yet to meet or even see, whose eyes would sparkle just like the Northern sky I would describe for her when once while sitting on a splintered deck heaving on top of the black-pitch deck of the world, I beheld all the light not of this world.

Which was when, as I was briefly revisiting this same daydream in the presence of my two friends, I heard a voice in my ear—the ghost—softly saying my name.

By the way, this is what got me on this whole jag in the first place. The knocking in the house returning this vivid recollection.

"Johnny" she said in a sigh even more gentle than a whisper.

I looked around. No one sitting at my table was saying anything even remotely like my name. Quite the contrary, their voices were pitched in some egregiously felt debate over something having to do with scoring, the details of which I know I'll never recall, thrown up amidst the equally loud banter of a hundred plates, glasses, knives and forks clattering here and there, and yes everywhere, serving to quickly dispel my illusion until it happened again—

reincarnation, phobia, ascent to godhood, paranoia, desert, reverse affirmation of spiritual perdurability, ibid, ibid, ibid, ibid, title, totemic assumption, submarine, absence of past, vision, psychosis, technology, ibid, serial killer or aliens. All of which *The Navidson Record* bravely refuses to indulge."[167]

"Johnny."

For an instant then, I understood she was my ghost, a seventeen year old with gold braided hair, as wild as a will-o'-the-wisp, encountered many years ago, maybe even in another life, now encountered again, and perhaps here too to find me and restore me to some former self lost on some day no boy can ever really remember—something I write now not really even understanding though liking the sound of it just the same.

"He's so dreamy. I just love the way he smiles when he talks, even if he doesn't say that much."

Which was when I realized, a moment later, that this Ghost was none other than the domed ceiling, rising above the dining hall, somehow carrying with particular vividness, from the far wall to my wall, in one magnificent arc, the confession of a girl I would never see or hear again, a confession I could not even respond to—except here, if this counts.

Sadly enough, my understanding of the rare acoustic dynamics in that hall came a fraction of a second too late, coinciding with the end of dinner, the voice vanishing as suddenly as it appeared, lost in a cumulative leaving, so that even as I continued to scan the distant edge of the dining room or the line forming to deposit trays, I could never find the girl whose expressions or even gestures might match such sentiments.

Of course, ghostly voices don't just have to rely exclusively on domed ceilings. They don't even have to be just voices.

I finally hooked up with Ashley. I went over to her place yesterday morning. Early. She lives in Venice. Her eyebrows look like flakes of sunlight. Her smile, I'm sure, burnt Rome to the ground. And for the life of me I didn't know who she was or where we'd met. For a moment I wondered if she was that voice. But before she said even a word, she held my hand and led me through her house to a patio overgrown with banana trees and rubber plants. Black, decomposing leaves covered the ground but a large hammock hung above it all.

We sat down together and I wanted to talk. I wanted to ask her who she was, where we'd met, been before, but she just smiled and held my hand as we sat down on the hammock and started to swing above all those dead leaves. She kissed

pecan, southern magnolia, Colorado spruce, alpine fir, american beech, northern red oak, Canada Hemlock, red maple, sugar maple, eastern white pine, butternut hickory, shagbark hickory, american plane tree, eastern black walnut, ponderosa pine, white fir, northern catalpa, common bald cypress, american sweet gum, bur oak, California live oak, mahogany, Douglas fir, eastern cottonwood; nor any sign of a subfloor, sheathing, drywall, any kind of insulating material, polyicynene or other; sills, sill plates, sill sealer, rebar, anchor bolts, let alone footings or foundation walls; or

Edwin Lutyens, Giovanni Muzio, Angiolo Mazzoni, Giuseppe Pagano, O. Frezzotti, Marcello Piacentini, Pio Piacentini, Antonio Sant'Elia, Cesare Bazzani, Povl Baumann, Kay Fisker, G.B. Hagen, Edvard Thomsen, Carl Petersen, Lars Sonck, Sigfrid Ericson, Herman Gesellius, Armas Lindgren, Kaare Klint, Peder Vilhelm Jensen-Klint, Lars Israel Wahlman, Ragnar Östberg, Martin Nyrop, Roger-Henri Expert, Paul Tournon, André Lurcat, Robert Mallet-Stevens, Pierre Chareau, Henri Sauvage, Tony Garnier, Francois Hennebique, Auguste Perret, René Sergent, Arthur Davis, Charles-Frédéric Mewès, Walter Johannes Krüger, Albert Speer, Heinrich Tessenow, Emil Fahrenkamp, Gerrit Rietveld, Willem Marinus Dudok, J.J.P. Oud, Adolf Loos, László Moholy-Nagy, Theo van Doesburg, Hannes Meyer, Walter Gropius, Johan van der Mey, Michel de Klerk, Fritz Höger, Otto Bartning, Dominikus Böhm, Eric Mendelsohn, Bruno Taut, Max Berg, Hans Poelzig, Bruno Schmitz, Peter Behrens, Paul Bonatz, Fritz Schumacher, Theodor Fischer, Alfred Messel, Ludwig Hoffman, William Lescase, George Howe, Albert Kahn, William Van Alen, Paul Gmelin, Stephen F. Voorhees, Andrew C. Mackenzie, Ralph Thomas Walker, John Mead Howells, Washington Roebling, Raymond Hood, Cass Gilbert, Bertram

[167] In her elegantly executed piece entitled "Vertical Influence" reproduced in *Origins of Faith* (Cambridge, Mass.: The Belknap Press of Harvard University Press, 1996) p. 261, Candida Hayashi writes: "For that matter, what of literary hauntings? Poe's *The Fall of the House of Usher*, Shirley Jackson's *The Haunting*, Charles Brockden Brown's *Wieland*, Walker Percy's *The Moviegoer*, Stephen King's "The Breathing Method" in *Different Seasons*

the Holy Cross, choir of Cologne cathedral, Oxford New College, or Harlech Castle in Gwynnedd North Wales, Stokesay Castle in Shropshire, the Great Hall of Penhurst Place in Kent, the King's College Chapel in Cambridge, Westminster Hall in the Palace of Westminster, the vaulting of Henry VII chapel at Westminster, St Stephen's chapel, interior at Gloucester cathedral, or the interior octagon at Ely cathedral, the north porch of St. Mary Redcliffe in Bristol, the Exeter cathedral, vault at the Wells cathedral, Westminster Abbey, St Hugh's choir vaults in Lincoln cathedral, Palacio del Infantado at Guadalajara, the Canterbury cathedral, Rouen's Palais de Justice, the house of Jacques Coeur at Bourges, Bristol cathedral, Albi cathedral's Flamboyant south porch, the church of St-Maclou in Rouen, the Paris Sainte-Chapelle, the church of St-Urbain, Sées cathedral, Notre-Dame, Amiens cathedral, Reims cathedral, Laon cathedral, Soissons cathedral, or the nave of Noyon cathedral, or even the ambulatory of St. Denis, nor for that matter elements of the Carolingian and Romanesque such as the Pisa baptistery or cathedral or the cathedral at Lucca, or the Leaning Tower of Pisa, S. Miniato al Monte or the baptistery in Florence, S. Ambrogio in Milan, the campanile and baptistery of the Parma cathedral, Salamanca's Old Cathedral, the cloister of Sto Domingo de Silos, fortified walls of Ávila, kitchen at Fontevrault Abbey, Angers, church and monastery at Loarre, St-Gilles-du-Gard in Provence, cathedral of Autun, Poitiers' Notre-Dame-la-Grande, abbey church of La Madeleine in Vézelay, Angoulême's cathedral, abbey church at Cluny, cathedral of Santiago de Compostela, St-Serin in Toulouse, Portico de la Glória, Santiago de Compostela, Conques Ste-Foy, the staircase of the chapter-house in Beverley, the interior of the chapter-house in Bristol, the Durham cathedral, St John's Chapel, White Tower, Tower of London, Winchester cathedral, Lincoln cathedral, the abbey church of Notre-Dame, Jumièges, Florence's S. Miniato al Monte, Dijon St-Bénigne, ambulatory of St-Philibert in Tournus, St. Mark's cathedral in Venice, St. Basil's cathedral in Moscow, abbey church of Maria Laach, cathedral of Trier, Basilica of S. Apollinare Nuovo, Ravenna, the dome of the Palatine chapel, interior of cathedral, Speyer, St. Michael in Hildesheim, the Great Mosque at Córdoba, S. Maria Naranco, All Staints, Earls Barton, St Lawrence, Bradford-on-Avon, church at Corvey on the Weser, the gateway at the monastery of Lorsch, plan for the monastery at St Gall, interior of the oratory in Germigny-des-Prés, or at the very least not even remnants of early Christian and Byzantine architectural conceits, whether the Cathedral of S. Front, Périgueux, cathedral of Monreale Sicily, interior of the Palatine Chapel in Palermo, the church of Transfiguration, Kizhi, Hagia Sophia in Kiev, hillside churches in Mistra Greece, Katholikon, Hosios Lukas, or church of Theotokos, mosaic of Christ Pantocrator in the dome of the church of Domition, Daphni, S. Vitale or S. Apollinare in Classe in Ravenna, Constantinople's

pecan, southern magnolia, Colorado spruce, alpine fir, american beech, northern red oak, Canada Hemlock, red maple, sugar maple, eastern white pine, butternut hickory, shagbark hickory, american plane tree, eastern black walnut, ponderosa pine, white fir, northern catalpa, common bald cypress, american sweet gum, bur oak, California live oak, mahogany, Douglas fir, eastern cottonwood; nor any sign of a subfloor, sheathing, drywall, any kind of insulating material, polyvinyene or other; sills, sill plates, sill sealer, rebar, anchor bolts, let alone footings or foundation walls; or

Wax, for his part, tries to be brave, forcing a smile for the camera, even if it is impossible to miss how pale he looks or misunderstand the meaning of his request—"Jed, man, I'm so thirsty"—especially since a few seconds earlier he had swallowed a big gulp of water.

---

me once and then suddenly sneezed, a tiny beautiful sneeze, which made her smile even more and my heart started hurting because I couldn't share her happiness, not knowing what it was, or why it was or who for that matter I was—to her. So I lay there hurting, even when she sat on top of me, covering me in the folds of her dress, and her with no underwear and me doing nothing as her hands briefly unbuttoned my jeans and pulled me out of my underwear, placing me where it was rough and dry, until she sank down without a gasp, and then it was wet, and she was wet, and we were wet, rocking together beneath a small patch of overcast sky, brightening fast, her eyes watching the day come, one hand kneading her dress, the other hand under her dress needing herself, her blonde hair covering her face, her knees tightening around my ribs, until she finally met that calendrical coming without a sound—the only sign—and then even though I had not come, she kissed me for the last time and climbed out of the hammock and went inside.

Before I left she told me our story: where we'd met—Texas—kissed, but never made love and this had confused her and haunted her and she had needed to do it before she got married which was in four months to a man she loved who made a living manufacturing TNT exclusively for a highway construction firm up in Colorado where he frequently went on business trips and where one night, drunk, angry and disappointed he had invited a hooker back to his motel room and so on and who cared and what was I doing there anyway? I left, considered jerking off, finally got around to it back at my place though in order to pop I had to think of Thumper. It didn't help. I was still hurting, abandoned, drank three glasses of bourbon and fumed on some weed, then came here, thinking of voices, real and imagined, of ghosts, my ghost, of her, at long last, in this idiotic footnote, when she gently pushed me out her door and I said quietly "Ashley" causing her to stop pushing me and ask "yes?" her eyes bright with something she saw that I could never see though what she saw was me, and me not caring though now at least knowing the

The Exorcist, John Carpenter's *The Thing*, *Labyrinth*, *Raiders of the Lost Ark*, *Das Boot*, *Taxi Driver*, *Crimes and Misdemeanors*, *Repulsion*, *Fantastic Voyage*, *Forbidden Planet*, *C'est arrivé près de chez vous*, or even *The Abyss*. I hasten to point out that each one of the above mentioned movies ultimately resorts to some form of delusion, whether

No stranger to shock,|| Jed immediately raises Wax's legs to increase blood flow to the head, uses pocket heaters and a solar blanket to keep him warm, and never stops reassuring him, smiling, telling jokes, promising a hundred happy endings. A difficult task under any circumstances. Nearly impossible when those guttural cries soon find them, the walls too thin to hold any of it back, sounds too obscene to be shut out, Holloway screaming like some rabid animal, no longer a man but a creature stirred by fear, pain, and rage.

"At least he's far off," Jed whispers in an effort to console Wax.

But the sound of distance brings little comfort to either one.

bricks, whether split paver or red bullnose, or wall studs, firestopping, or braces, nor evidence of floor joists, end joists, or ledgers, bridgings, girders, double plate, gable studs, ceiling joists, rafters, king posts, struts, side posts, ridge beams, collar ties, gussets, furring strips, or bed molding (at least the stairs offer some detail: risers, treads, two large newel posts, one at the top and one at the bottom, capped and connected with a single, curved banister supported by countless balusters) though among other things no wallpaper, veneer plaster, Baldwin locks, any sign of glass,

---

`truth and telling her the truth: "I've never been to Texas."`

||The following definition is from *Medicine for Mountaineering*, 3rd edition. Edited by James A. Wilkerson, M.D. (Seattle: The Mountaineers, 1985), p. 43:

> "Mild shock results from loss of ten to twenty percent of blood volume. The patient appears pale and his skin feels cool, first over the extremities and later over the trunk. As shock becomes more severe, the patient often complains of feeling cold and he is often thirsty. A rapid pulse and reduced blood pressure may be present. However, the absence of these signs does not indicate shock is not present since they may appear rather late, particularly in previously healthy young adults.
>
> "Moderate shock results from loss of twenty to forty percent of the blood volume. The signs characteristic of mild shock are present and may become more severe. The pulse is typically fast and weak or 'thready.' In addition, blood flow to the kidneys is reduced as the available blood is shunted to the heart and brain and the urinary output declines. A urinary volume of less than 30 cc per hour is a late indication of moderate shock. In contrast to the dark, concentrated urine observed with dehydration, the urine is usually a light color.
>
> "Severe shock results from loss of more than forty percent of the blood volume and is characterized by signs of reduced blood flow to the brain and heart. Reduced cerebral blood flow initially produces restlessness and agitation, which is followed by confusion, stupor and eventually coma and death. Diminished blood flow to the heart can produce abnormalities of the cardiac rhythm."

as well as "Tebular" in *More Tales*, Steve Erickson's *Days Between Stations*, John Fante's *The Road to Los Angeles*, not to mention Henri Bosco's *L'Antiquaire*, Salman Rushdie's *Satanic Verses*, B. Walton's *Cave of Danger*, Jean Genet's *Notre-Dame des Fleurs*, Richard Fariña's *Been Down So Long It Looks Like Up To Me*, John Gardner's *October Light*, many stories by Lovecraft, Pynchon's gator patrol in *V*, Borges' "The Garden of Forking Paths" in *Ficciones*, Conrad's *Heart of Darkness*, Lawrence Weschler's *Mr. Wilson's*

der Rohe, Philip Johnson, Hans Hollein, Rem Koolhaas, John S. Chase, Harvey B. Gantt, Robert Venturi, James Stirling, Norman Foster, Richard Rogers, Renzo Piano, Alvar Aalto, Lou Switzer, Roberta Washington, J. Max Bond Jr., Robert Kennard, Luigi Nervi, Jørn Utzon, Eero Saarinen, Buckminster Fuller, Louis Kahn, Roderick Lincoln Knox, Paul Rudolph, James M. Whitley, William N. Whitley, R. Joyce Whitley, Paul G. Devrouax, Charles Duke, Marshall E. Purnell, Robert P. Madison, Sir Leslie Martin, Harry L. Overstreet, Sir Denys Lasdun, Sir Basil Spence, Peter Smithson, James Gowan, Gordon Matta-Clark, Howard F. Sims, Harold R. Varner, Roger W. Margerum, Harry Simmons Jr., Wendell J. Campbell, Susan M. Campbell, James Stirling, Oscar Niemeyer, Norma Merrick Sklarek, Le Corbusier, Frank Lloyd Wright, William J. Stanley, Ivenue Love-Stanley, Vernon A. Williams, Leslie A. Williams, Cornelius Henderson, Paul Revere Williams, Boris Mikhailovich Iofan, Vladimir Alekssevich Shchuko, V.G. Gelfreikh, Ilya Golosov, Konstantin Melnikov, Moses McKissack, William S. Pittman, John A. Lankford, El Lissitzky, Aleksandr, and Viktor Vesnin, Serge Chermayeff, Charles Holden, Sir John Burnet, Edwin Rickards, H.V. Lanchester, Wilhelm Kreis, Giles Gilbert Scott, Frederick Gibberd, Sir

Hagia Sophia, Ravenna's interior of the Mausoleum of Galla Placidia, Rome's S. Stefano Rotondo or S. Maria Maggiore or S. Clemente, or Milan's S. Lorenzo, or even the plan of Old St Peter's, nor the slightest trace of classical foundations whether Greek, Hellenistic, or Roman, as might be exemplified by the Temple of Jupiter, Diocletian's palace at Spalato, the gateway to the market at Miletus, Algeria's Timgad with its Arch of Trajan, apartment housing in Ostia, Trajan's Market in Rome, also in Rome, the Baths of Diocletian, the Basilica of Maxentius, Baths of Caracalla, the Temple of Venus, near the Golden House of Nero, Hadrian's Mausoleum, the Mausoleum of Caecilia Metella on the Via Appia, the Canopus of Hadrian's villa, the interior of the Pantheon, Hadrian's villa at Tivoli, or the Piazza d'Oro with peristyle court and pavilions, or the Flavian Palace, the Villa of the Mysteries in Pompeii, plan of the Villa Jovis at Capri, Arch of Tiberius at Orange, France, Trajan's column in Rome, the Imperial Forum, Temple of Mars Ultor, Forum Augustum, Forum of Nerva, the Forum Romanum with the arch of Septimius Severus, the Arch of Titus and the Temple of Castor and Pollux, or in Spain the aqueduct at Segovia, or back in Rome the theatre of Marcellus, the Colosseum, the sanctuary of Fortuna Primigenia, Praeneste with its axonometric reconstruction, the Temple of Vesta at Tivoli, the Forum Boarium in Rome, the Maison Carrée at Nîmes, or the House of the Vettii in Pompeii, the walls of Herculaneum, the terrace of Naxian Lions on Delos, the Tower of the Winds in Athens, the Stoa of Attalus in the agora of Athens, the plan for the city of Pergamum or city center of Miletus or the Bouleuterion in Miletus, or the Temple of Apollo at Didyma, Temple of Athena Polias at Priene, Mausoleum at Halicarnassus, the theatre at Epidaurus, the Choragic Monument of Lysicrates in Athens as well as the Temple of Olympian Zeus, or the tholos at Delphi, or the Temple of Apollo at Bassae, or the Erechtheion on the Acropolis, the Porpylaea on the Acropolis, the Parthenon with its Panathenaic frieze, Athen's acropolis, the temple of Aphaia at Aegina, the Temple of Olympian Zeus at Acragas, the Temple of Hera or Poseidon or Neptune at Paestum, the Temple of Apollo at Corinth, the shrine of Anubis at the Temple of Hatshepsut, Deir al Bahari, or the Lion Gate at Mycenae, or the palace at Mycenae, the palace of Tiryns, the Palace of Minos, Knossos, Crete—which seems like a good place to end though it cannot end there, especially when there is still the Great Zimbabwe Enclosure, the Giza pyramids of Mykerinos, Cheops and Chefren, to say nothing of Ireland's New Grange passage grave, France's Essé gallery grave, Malta's Ggantija temple complex, Scotland's Skara Brae's settlement, the Lascaux cave, the Laussel prehistoric rock-cut Venus, or the notion of the Terra Armata hut which is also a good place to end though of course it cannot end there either—[147]

Perhaps[165]

bricks, whether split paver or red bullnose, or wall studs, firestopping, or braces, nor evidence of floor joists, end joists, or ledgers, bridgings, girders, double plate, gable studs, ceiling joists, rafters, king posts, struts, side posts, ridge beams, collar ties, gussets, furring strips, or bed molding (at least the stairs offer some detail: risers, treads, two large newel posts, one at the top and one at the bottom, capped and connected with a single, curved banister supported by countless balusters) though among other things no wallpaper, veneer plaster, Baldwin locks, any sign of glass,

here

is as good a place as any to consider some of the ghosts haunting *The Navidson Record.* And since more than a handful of people have pointed out similarities between Navidson's film and various commercial productions, it seems worthwhile to at least briefly examine what distinguishes documentaries from Hollywood releases.[166]

In his essay "Critical Condition" published in *Simple Themes* (University of Washington Press, 1995) Brendan Beinhorn declared that Navidson's house, when the explorers were within it, was in a state of severe shock. "However *without* them, it is completely dead. Humanity serves as its life blood. Humanity's end would mark the house's end." A statement which provoked sociologist Sondra Staff to claim "Critical Condition" was "just another sheaf of Beinhorn bullshit." (A lecture delivered at Our Lady of the Lake University of San Antonio on June 26, 1996.)

[165]Mr. Truant refused to reveal whether the following bizarre textual layout is Zampanò's or his own. — Ed.

[166]In his essay "It Makes No Difference" *Film Quarterly* v.8, July, 1995, p. 68, Daniel Rosenblum wrote: "In response to the suggestion that the names of the ghosts haunting Navidson's house are none other than *The Shining*, *Vertigo*, *2001*, *Brazil*, *Lawrence of Arabia*, *Poltergeist*, *Amityville Horror*, *Night of the Living Dead*,

whether clear, reflective, insulated, heat-resistant, switchable, tinted, bad-guy, antique; or even tin-plated steel, factory-painted steel, brass; or even a single nail or screw, whether sheet-metal, particleboard, drywall, concrete, drive, aluminum, silicon bronze, solid brass, mechanically galvanized, yellow-zinc plated, stainless steel, epoxy coated, black finish, Durocoat; to say nothing of the sheer absence of anything that might suggest a roof, whether pitched, gable, hip, lean-to, flat, sawtooth, monitor, ogee, bell, dome, helm, sloped, hip-and-valley, conical, pavilion, rotunda,

---

168Aside from cinematic, literary, architectural, or even philosophical ghosts, history also offers a few of its own. Consider two famous expeditions where those involved confronted the unknown under circumstances of deprivation and fear only to soon find themselves caught in a squall of terrible violence.

I.

On September 20th, 1519 Ferdinand Magellan embarked from Sanlúcar de Barrameda to sail around the globe. The voyage would once and for all prove the world was round and revolutionize people's thoughts on navigation and trade, but the journey would also be dangerous, replete with enough horror and hardship that in the end it would cost Magellan his life.

In March of 1520 when Magellan's five vessels reached Patagonia and sailed into the Bay of St. Julian, things were far from harmonious. Fierce winter weather, a shortage of stores, not to mention the anxiety brought on by the uncertainty of the future, had caused tensions among the sailors to increase, until on or around April Fools Day, which also happened to be Easter Day, Captain Gaspar Quesada of the *Concepcion* and his servant Luiz de Molino planned and executed a mutiny, resulting in the death of at least one officer and the wounding of many more.[169] Unfortunately for Quesada, he never stopped to consider that a man who could marshal an expedition to circle the globe could probably marshal men to retaliate with great ferocity. This gross underestimation of his opponent cost Quesada his life.

Like a general, Magellan rallied those men still loyal to him to retake the commandeered ships. The combination of his will and his tactical acumen made his success, especially in retrospect, seem inevitable. The mutineer Mendoza of the *Victoria* was stabbed in the throat. The *Santo Antonia* was stormed, and by morning the *Concepcion* had surrendered. Forty-eight hours after the mutiny had begun, Magellan was again in control. He sentenced all the mutineers to death and then in an act of calculated good-will suspended the sentence, choosing instead to concentrate maritime law and his own ire on the three directly responsible for the uprising: Mendoza's corpse was drawn and quartered, Juan de Cartagena was marooned on a barren shore and Quesada was executed.

Quesada, however, was not hung, shot or even forced to walk the plank. Magellan had a better idea. Molino, Quesada's trusty servant, was granted clemency if he agreed to execute his master. Molino accepted the duty and

Cabinet of Wonder, Jim Kalin's *One Worm*, Sartre's *Huis Clos*, or *Les Mouches*, Jules Verne's *Journey to the Center of the Earth*, Lem's *Solaris*, Ayn Rand's *The Fountainhead*, "The Turn of the Screw" by Henry James, Nathaniel Hawthorne's "Young Goodman Brown" or *The House of Seven Gables*, or *The Lion, the Witch and the Wardrobe* by C. S. Lewis? To say nothing of *Brodsky & Utkin*, Frida Kahlo's "Blue House" in Coyoacán, Diego Rivera's "Nocturnal Landscape: Paisaje Nocturno" (1947), Rachel Whiteread's *House* or Charles Ray's *Ink Box*, Bill Viola's *Room for St. John of the Cross* or more words by Robert Venturi, Aldo van Eyck, James Joyce, Paolo Portoghesi, Herman Melville, Otto Friedrich Bollnow (*Mensch und Raum*, 1963), and Maurice Merleau-Ponty (*The Phenomenology of Perception*, 1962, in which he declares "depth is the most 'existential' of all dimensions")? To all of it, I have only one carefully devised response: Ptooey!"168

147Of course, it is impossible to consider any sort of construction, whether of homes, factories, shops, stores, department stores, market halls, conservatories, exhibition buildings, railway stations, warehouses, and office buildings, exchanges and banks, hotels, prisons, hospitals, museums, libraries, theatres, churches, bridges, airports, town halls, law courts, ministries, and public offices. Houses of parliament, monuments, parks, even towns, and cities, public works etc., etc., without paying heed to such names as Thomas Hall Beeby, Ricardo Bofill, John Simpson, Steven Holl, Léon Krier, Richard Neutra, Andres Duany, and Elizabeth Plater-Zyberk, Ramon Fortet, Daniel Libeskind, Quinlan Terry, Allan Greenberg, Jane B. Drew, Robin Seifert, Frank Gehry, Jean Willerval, Arat Isozaki, Kisho Kurokawa, Gisue and Mojgan Hariri, John Outram, Zaha Hadid, Peter Eisenmann, Richard Meier, John Hejduk, Aldo Rossi, Herman Hertzberger, Louis E. Fry Sr., Louis E. Fry Jr., Louis E. Fry III, Santiago Calatrava, I. M. Pei, Recardo Scofidio, Harry G. Robinson III, Terry Farrell, Bernard Tschumi, Charles F. McAfee, Eva Vecsei, the Coop Himmelblau, Cheryl L. McAfee, Charles Eames, Simon Rodia, Ray Eames, Ricardo Bofill, Donald L. Stull, M. David Lee, Michael Graves, Elizabeth Diller, Charles Moore, Bruno Taut, Robert Traynham Coles, Mies van

whether clear, reflective, insulated, heat-
resistant, switchable, tinted, bad-guy,
antique; or even tin-plated steel, factory-
painted steel, brass; or even a single nail or
screw, whether sheet-metal, particleboard,
drywall, concrete, drive, aluminum, silicon
bronze, solid brass, mechanically galvanized, yellow-zinc plated, stainless steel,
epoxy coated, black finish, Durocoat; to
say nothing of the sheer absence of anything that might suggest a roof, whether
pitched, gable, hip, lean-to, flat, sawtooth,
monitor, ogee, bell, dome, helm, sloped,
hip-and-valley, conical, pavilion, rotunda,

---

together both men were set in a shallop and directed back to their ship, the *Trinidad*, to fulfill their destiny.[171]

Like Magellan, Holloway led an expedition into the unknown. Like Magellan, Holloway faced a mutiny. And like the captain who meted out a penalty of death, Holloway also centred the cross-hairs upon those who had spurned his leadership. However unlike Magellan, Holloway's course was in fact doomed, thus necessitating a look at Henry Hudson's fate.

II.

By April of 1610, Hudson left England in his fourth attempt to find the northwest passage. He headed west across arctic waters and eventually ended up in what is known today as the Hudson Bay. Despite its innocuous sounding name, back in 1610 the bay was Hell in ice. Edgar M. Bacon in his book *Henry Hudson* (New York: G.P. Putnam's Sons, 1907) writes the following:

> On the first of November the ship was brought to a bay or inlet far down into the south-west, and hauled aground; and there by the tenth of the month she was frozen in. Discontent was no longer expressed in whispers. The men were aware that the provisions, laid in for a limited number of months, were running to an end, and they murmured that they had not been taken back for winter quarters to Digges Island, where such stores of wild fowl had been seen, instead of beating about for months in *"a labyrinth without end."*
>
> [italics added for emphasis]

This labyrinth of blue ice drifting in water cold enough to kill a man in a couple of minutes tested and finally outstripped the resolve of Hudson's crew. Where Magellan's men could fish or at least enjoy the cove of some habitable shore, Hudson's men could only stare at shores of ice.[180]

Inevitably, whispers rose to shouts until finally shouts followed action. Hudson, along with his son and seven others, was forced into a shallop without food and water. They were never heard from again, lost in that *labyrinth with*

imperial, or mansard; no westwork, ziggurat, brise-soleil, trompe l'oeil etc., fenestration, tierceron rib, coffering, tholos, strapwork, stoa, egg-and-tongue, sala terrena, absidiole, rotunda, revetments, reredos, flying buttresses, retablo, herm, belvedere, pavillon, pastas, narthex, lunettes, dormers, cottage orné, pendentives, cheek-walls, cavetto, abutment, nor vaulted chambers, whether quadripartite or lierne vaults, or Mihrab domes, turrets, minarets, minbars, porticoes, peristyles, tablinums, compluviums, impluviums, atriums, alas, excedras, androns, fauces, pos-

---

out end. [170]

Like Hudson, Holloway found himself with men who, short on reserves and faith, insisted on turning back. Like Hudson, Holloway resisted. Unlike Hudson, Holloway went willingly into that labyrinth.

Fortunately for audiences everywhere, only Hudson's final moments continue to remain a mystery.

[169]While mutiny is not terribly common today, consider the 1973 Skylab mission where astronauts openly rebelled against a mission controller they felt was too imperious. The incident never resulted in violence, but it does emphasize how despite constant contact with the society at home, plenty of food, water, and warmth, and only a slight risk of getting lost, tensions among explorers can still surface and even escalate.

Holloway's expedition had none of the amenities Skylab enjoyed. 1) There was no radio contact; 2) they had very little sense of where they were; 3) they were almost out of food and water; 4) they were operating in freezing conditions; and 5) they suffered the implicit threat of that 'growl'.[155]

[170]Also see *The Works of Hubert Howe Bancroft, Volume XXVIII* (San Francisco: The History Company, Publishers, 1886).

[171]Taken from Zampanò's journal: "As often as I have lingered on Hudson in his shallop, I have in the late hours turned my thoughts to Quesada and Molino's journey across those shallow waters, wondering aloud what they said, what they thought, what gods came to keep them or leave them, and what in those dark waves they finally saw of themselves? Perhaps because history has little to do with those minutes, the scene survives only in verse: *The Song of Quesada and Molino* by [XXXX].[172] I include it here in its entirety."[175]

Then:

"Forgive me please for including this. An old man's mind is just as likely to wander as a young man's, but where a young man will forgive the stray,[177] an old man will cut it out. Youth always tries to fill the void, an old man learns to live with it. It took me twenty years to unlearn the fortunes found in a swerve. Perhaps this is no news to you but then I have killed many men and I have both legs and I don't think I ever quite equaled the bald gnome Error who comes from his cave with featherless ankles to feast on the mighty dead."[173]

[172]Illegible.

[173]You got me.[176] Gnome aside, I don't even know how to take "I've killed many men." Irony? A confession? As I already said "You got me."[174]

[174]For reasons entirely his own, Mr. Truant de-struck the last six lines in footnote 171. — Ed.

[175]See Appendix E.

[176]See Appendix B.

[177]~~For instance, youth's peripatetic travails in *The PXXXXXXX Poems*; a perfect example why errors should be hastily excised.~~[178]

imperial, or mansard; no westwork, ziggurat, brise-soleil, trompe l'oeil etc., fenestration, tierceron rib, coffering, tholos,
strapwork, stoa, egg-and-tongue, sala terrena, absidiole, rotunda, revetments, reredos, flying buttresses, retablo, herm,
belvedere, pavilion, pastas, narthex,
lunettes, dormers, cottage orné, pendentives, cheek-walls, cavetto, abutment, nor
vaulted chambers, whether quadripartite
or lierne vaults, or Mihrab domes, turrets,
minarets, minbars, porticoes, peristyles,
tablinums, compluviums, impluviums, atriums, alas, excedras, androns, fauces, pos

[178]i.e. The Pelican Poems.[179]

[179]See Appendix II-B. — Ed.

[180]Though written almost two hundred years after Hudson's doomed voyage, it is hard not to think of Coleridge's *The Rime Of The Ancient Mariner*, especially this fabled moment—

With sloping masts and dripping prow,
As who pursued with yell and blow
Still treads the shadow of his foe,
And forward bends his head,
The ship drove fast, loud roared the blast,
And southward aye we fled.
And now there came both mist and snow,
And it grew wondrous cold:
And ice, mast-high, came floating by,
As green as Emerald.

The land of ice, and
of fearful sounds
where no living thing
was to be seen.

And through the drifts the snowy clifts
Did send a dismal sheen:
Nor shapes of men nor beasts we ken —
The ice was all between.

The ice was here, the ice was there,
The ice was all around:
It cracked and growled, and roared and howled,
Like noises in a swound!

Till a grèat sea-bird
called the Albatross...

At length did cross an Albatross,
Through the fog it came . . .

This was not some feverish world concocted in a state of delirium but a very real place which Hudson had faced despite the evident terror it inflicted upon everyone, especially his crew. Nor was such terror vanquished by the modern age. Consider the diary entry made in 1915 by Reginald James, expedition physicist for Shackleton's *Endurance* which was trapped and finally crushed by pack ice off the coast of Antarctica in the Weddell Sea: "A terrible night with the ship sullen dark against the sky & the noise of the pressure against her . . . seeming like the cries of a living creature." See also Simon Alcazaba's *Historic Conditions* (Cleveland: Annwyl Co., Inc., 1963) as well as Jack Denton Scott's "Journey Into Silence" *Playboy,* August 1973, p. 102.

For one thing, Hollywood films rely on sets, actors, expensive film stock, and lush effects to recreate a story. Production value coupled with the cultural saturation of trade gossip help ensure a modicum of disbelief, thus reaffirming for the audience, that no matter how moving, riveting, or terrifying a film may be, it is still only entertainment. Documentaries, however, rely on interviews, inferior equipment, and virtually no effects to document real events.[181] Audiences are not allowed the safety net of disbelief and so must turn to more challenging mechanisms of interpretation which, as is sometimes the case, may lead to denial and aversion.[182]

[182]Obviously, the tradition of documentary filmmaking is a long and valuable one, especially when considering those contributions made by Robert Flaherty, Herbert Kline, Ernest B. Schoedsack, Paul Rotha, Mary Lampson, Stuart Legg, D. W. Griffith, Henri Storck, John Ernest, Burton Benjamin, Jean Epstein, Jan Kucera, Heinz Seilman, Alberto Cavalcanti, Merian Cooper, Jerome Hill, Walter Heynowski, Leo Seltzer, Bonnie Sherr Klein, Edgard Morin, Boris Barnet, Leacock, Skanata, Rouch, Paul Strand, Jill Godmilow, Jerzy Hoffman, Ion Bostan, Tadeusz Jaworski, Carol Reed, Micahel Rubbo, Humphrey Jennings, Shirley Clark, Ilya Trauberg, Marianne Szemes, Pat Jackson, Alan Winton King, Arthur Barron, Jacques-Yves Cousteau, Krsto Skanata, Mikhail Slutsky, Agoston Kollanyi, Barbara Kopple, Marvin Lichtner, Erwin Leiser, Julia Reichert, Graeme Ferguson, James Klein, Edward R. Murrow, Noel Coward, Nevena Toshava, Basil Wright, Adrian Brunel, Willard Van Dyke, Joris Ivens, Anatole Litvak, Ben Maddow, Walt Disney,

Livia Gyaramathy, Henri-George Clouzot, Brian Desmond Hurst, Pursia Djordjevic, Jan Lomnicki, Esther Shub, Warren Wallace, Edmund Bert Gerrard, Tom Haydon, David Lean, Eric Nussbaum, Jerry Bruck Jr., Savel Stiopul, William Wyler, Bruce Herschensohn, Ante Babaja, Ellen Hovde, David Loeb Weiss, Thorold Dickinson, Ilya Kopalin, Robert Drew, Henri Cartier-Bresson, Max Fleischer, Luis Buñel, Cesare Zavattini, Arthur Elton, Yuli Raizman, Shuker, Jerzy Bossak, Barron, Keith Merrill, Philippe Mora, George M. Williamson, Eugene Jones, Robin Spry, Kirsten Johnson, Kroitor, Haskell Wexler, Jersey, John Ferno, Dick Robinson, Hans Bertram, D. A. Pennebaker, Angelo Spaveni, Dr. Fritz Hippler, Jean Vigo, Gregori Kozintsev, Rouman Grigorov, Michael Latham, Nicholas Webster, Sergei Yutkevitch, Walter Ruttmann, Frederick Wiseman, Perrault, Elmar Klos, David Elstein, Kazimierz Karabasz, Istvan Timar, Sid Knigtsen, Jürgen Böttcher, Leni Riefenstahl, Leonid Varlamov, Takahiko Ismura, Walon Green, Roman Karmen, Joseph Krumgold, Douglas Leiterman, Hristo

ticums, peristylums, vestibules, arcades, apses, naves, naos, pronaos, opisthodomos, nymphaeum, internal crepidoma, courtyards, paradegrounds, bailey, demilune, caponiere, tenaille, flank, postern, rampart, face, bastion, embrasure, curtain, keep, brattice, merlon, or battlement; nor—obviously—pilasters, pillars, friezes, entablatures, architraves, facades, pediments, stylobates, triglyphs, scotia, torus, fillets, finials, and flutes, capitals, whether Ionic, Doric, or Corinthian, with volutes, abacuses, rosettes, acanthus leaf, or metopes, guttas, mutules, acroterions, dentils, or

[181]Consider Stephen Mamber's definition of cinema vérité which seems an almost exact description of how Navidson made his film:

> Cinema vérité is a strict discipline only because it is in many ways so simple, so "direct." The filmmaker attempts to eliminate as much as possible the barriers between subject and audience. These barriers are technical (large crews, studio sets, tripod-mounted equipment, special lights, costumes and makeup), procedural (scripting, acting, directing), and structural (standard editing devices, traditional forms of melodrama, suspense, etc.) Cinema vérité is a practical working method based upon a faith of unmanipulated reality, a refusal to tamper with life as it presents itself. Any kind of cinema is a process of selection, but there is (or should be) all the difference in the world between the cinema-vérité aesthetic and the methods of fictional and traditional documentary film.

Stephen Mamber, *Cinema Vérité in America: Studies in Uncontrolled Documentary* (Cambridge, Massachusetts: The MIT Press, 1974), p. 4.

While in the past, live footage was limited to the aftermath—the oral histories given by survivors or photographs taken by pedestrians—these days the proliferation of affordable video cameras and tapes has created more of an opportunity for someone to record a plane wreck or bank robbery as it is actually taking place.

Of course, no documentary is ever entirely absolved from at least the suspicion that the mise-en-scene may have been carefully designed, actions staged, or lines written and rehearsed—much of which these days is openly carried out under the appellation of "reenactment."

By now it is common knowledge that Flaherty recreated certain scenes in *Nanook* for the camera. Similar accusations have been made against shows like *America's Funniest Home Videos.* For the most part, professionals in the field do their best to police, or at least critique, the latest films, well aware that to lose the public's trust would mean the death rattle for an already besieged art form.

ticums, peristylums, vestibules, arcades, apses, naves, naos, pronaos, opisthodomos, nymphaeum, internal crepidoma, courtyards, paradegrounds, bailey, demilune, caponiere, tenaille, flank, postern, rampart, face, bastion, embrasure, curtain, keep, brattice, merlon, or battlement; nor—obviously—pilasters, pillars, friezes, entablatures, architraves, facades, pediments, stylobates, triglyphs, scotia, torus, fillets, finials, and flutes, capitals, whether Ionic, Doric, or Corinthian, with volutes, abacuses, rosettes, acanthus leaf, or metopes, guttas, mutules, acroterions, dentils, or

[183] Without whom culture would not possess such works as *Scott's Antarctic Expedition, The Memphis Belle, Gimme Shelter, Painters Painting, How Life Begins, The Ramparts We Watch, Millhouse, An American Family, Chang, L'Hippocampe, Cinema Eye, A Married Couple, This Week, La Sang Des Bêtes, We Are The Marines, Crisis: Behind a Presidential Commitment, Ten Days That Shook The World, A Labor of Love, Underground, Turkish, Valley Town, The Quiet One, Voyage Au Congo, Feuertaufe, The Bridge, Johnny Cash, On the Pole, Komsomol, Cathy Come Home, Rain, Der Ewige Jude, Drifters, Cops, The Henry Miller Odyssey, Berlin—Symphony Of A Big City, The Titicut Follies, The Weavers: Wasn't That a Time!, Triumph Of The Will, Olympia, La Sortie des usines Lumière, Vanishing Wilderness, Las Hurdes, Secrets Of Life, New Earth, Contact, Leningrad At Combat, Mourir à Madrid, 101 Acts of Love, The 400 Million, L'Arrivée d'un train, Brother Can You Spare A Dime?, Jazz on a Summer Day, The British Empire, La Vie Est À Nous, Riens Que Les Heures, Louisiana Story, Salesman, In Heaven There Is No Beer?, Regards sur la folie, The True Glory, Imagine: John Lennon, Hearts And Minds, The Face of Britain, Chronique d'un été, Sixty Minutes, Paris in the Twenties, Antonia, In Which We Serve, Housing Problems, The Feeling Of Rejection, Hollywood, Enough To Eat, Decisions, World Without Sun, The Making Of The President, The Song of the Shirt, North Sea, The Dream of Wild Horses, The Chelsea Girls, On Any Sunday, The Great American Novel, Imperial Valley, Images d'Ostende, Queros: The Shape of Survival, The Mills of God, Le Chagrin Et La Pitié, Marc & Ann, Edna the Inebriate Woman, The Spanish Earth, Land Where the Blues Began, Sexual Customs in Scandanavia, Always for Pleasure, The Hellstrom Chronicle, The River, Hotel Terminus:*

Currently, the greatest threat comes from the area of digital manipulation.

In 1990 in *The New York Times*, Andy Grundberg wrote:

Kovachev, Will Roberts, Josef von Sternberg, René Clément, Connie Field, Roy Boulting, Jack Glen and Lothar Wolff, Lipscomb, Alain Resnais, Karl Gass, Ruspoli, Jean Grémillon, Lionel Rogosin, Marcel Ophüls, Louis Lumière, Fred Friendly, Koenig, Georges Franju, John Huston, Bunny Peters Dana, Yuli Stroyanov, Jim Brown, Brault, Raymond Depardon, Michael Apted, Cinda Firestone, Louis de Rochemont, George Rouquier, James Algar, Frederick Wiseman, Harry Watt, Erik Barnouw, Jean Renoir, Robert Snyder, Jerry Blumenthal, Jennifer Rohrer, Gualtiero Jacopetti, Yulia Solntseva, Dziga Vertov, Robert Flaxman, Edgar Anstey, Sergei Eisenstein, Ralph Steiner, George Stoney, Gheorghe Vitandis, Léon Poirier, Heinz Sielman, John Korty, Helen Whitney, John Whitmore, Budd Boeticher, Janus Majewski, Howard Smith-Sarah Kernochan, J. B. Holmes, Peter Davis, Jeremy Sanford, Charlotte Zwerin, Amalie Rothschild, Emile de Antonio, Thor Heyerdahl, Jonathan Danam Christian Blackwood, Herbert Kline, Siegfried Kracauer, Richard T. Heffron, Robert Gardner, Alexander Petrovich Dovzhenko, Eric Haims, Beryl Fox, Robert Vas, Morton Silverstein, Andy Warhol, Abe Osheroff, William Richert, Frédéric Rossif, Jean Painlevé, Arthur R. Dubs, Kon Ichikawa, Chris Marker, Vsevolod Pudovkin, John Pett, Al Di Lauro, Garson Kanin, Denys Colomb de Daunant, John Cohen, Sergei Gerasimov, Nicolai van der Heyde, Y. Avdeyenko, Michael Lindsay Hogg, David Helpern Jr., Bruce Weber, Bert Haanstra, Harold Mantell, Roger Graef, Frank Capra, Ján Kadár, Seymour Stern, Marc Allégret, M. C. Von Hellen, Andrew and Annelie Thorndike, Ken Burns, Susan Clayton, Jonas Mekas, Charles Guggenheim, Alan Lomax, Pare Lorentz, Yelizaveta Svilova, Gil Kofman, Les Blank, Tony Richardson, Jozsef Csoke, Joseph Strick, Lindsay Anderson, George Greenough, James Algar, Murray Lerner, Karel Reisz, Michael Powell, Bert Stern, David Wolper, Herman van der Horst, Albert and David Maysles, Arthur Baron, Gerhard Scheumann, Craig Gilbert, Garson Kanin, Sidney Meyers, Wladislaw Slesicki, Bruce Brown—[183]

modillions, or even trefoil, Tudor, stilted, horeshoe, ogee, lancet, or equilateral arches, most probably resembling basket handle though without any sign of a keystone, pier, spandrel, voussoir, springer, or import.

~~Picture that. In your dreams.~~

"In the future, readers of newspapers and magazines will probably view news pictures more as illustrations than as reportage, since they will be well aware that they can no longer distinguish between a genuine image and one that has been manipulated. Even if news photographers and editors resist the temptations of electronic manipulation, as they are likely to do, the credibility of all reproduced images will be diminished by a climate of reduced expectations. In short, photographs will not seem as real as they once did."[184]

[184] Andy Grundberg, "Ask It No Questions: The Camera Can Lie," *The New York Times,* August 12, 1990, Section 2, 1, 29. All of which reiterates in many ways what Marshall McLuhan already anticipated when he wrote: "To say 'the camera cannot lie' is merely to underline the multiple deceits that are now practiced in its name."

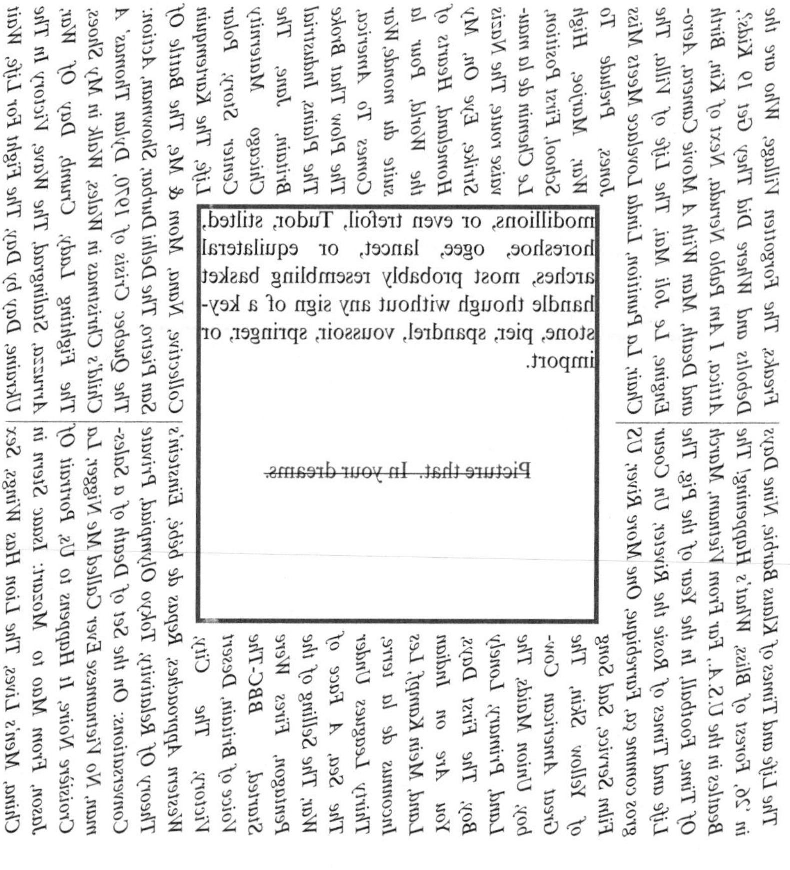

Also in 1990, Associated Press executive, Vincent Alabiso, acknowledged the power of digital technology and condemned its use to falsify images:

"The electronic darkroom is a highly sophisticated photo editing tool. It takes us out of a chemical darkroom where subtle printing techniques such as burning and dodging have long been accepted as journalistically sound. Today these terms are replaced by 'image manipulation' and 'enhancement.' In a time when such broad terms could be misconstrued we need to set limits and restate some basic tenets.

"The content of photographs will NEVER be changed or manipulated in any way."

A year later, the NPPA (National Press Photographers Association) also recognized the power of electronic imaging techniques:

"As journalists we believe the guiding principle of our profession is accuracy: therefore, we believe it is wrong to alter the content of a photograph in a way that deceives the public.

"As photojournalists, we have the responsibility to document society and to preserve its images as a matter of historical record. It is clear that the emerging electronic technologies provide new challenges to the integrity of photographic images. The technology enables the manipulation of the content of an image in such a way that the change is virtually undetectable. In light of this, we, the National Press Photographers Associations, reaffirm the basis of our ethics: Accurate representation is the benchmark of our profession."[185]

Then in 1992, MIT professor William J. Mitchell offered this powerful summation:

"Protagonists of the institutions of journalism, with their interest in being trusted, of the legal system, with their need for provably reliable evidence, and of science, with their foundational faith in the recording instrument, may well fight hard to maintain the hegemony of the standard photographic image—but others will see the emergence of digital imaging as a welcome opportunity to expose the aporias in photography's construction of the visual world, to deconstruct the very ideas of photographic objectivity and closure, and to resist what has become an increasingly sclerotic pictorial tradition."[W]

[185]See chapter 20 in Howard Chapnick's *Truth Needs No Ally: Inside Photojournalism* (University of Missouri Press, 1994).

[W] William J. Mitchell's *The Reconfigured Eye: Visual Truth In The Post-Photographic Era* (Cambridge, Massachusetts: The MIT Press, 1994), p. 8.

Ironically, the very technology that instructs us to mistrust the image also creates the means by which to accredit it.

ing for Fidel, Corral, Universe, Mechanics Of The Brain, Warrendale, Mondo Cane, Ai, The World at War, I'm A Stranger Here Myself, Diaries, Notes & Sketches, The Johnstown Flood, The Battle Of Midway, Seig Im Western, Hôtel Des Invalides, Dreams and Nightmares, The Man Alive Reports, Finnis Terrae, Guernica, Moana, A Propos De Neice, Inside Nazi Germany, Le Mystère Picasso, Common Threads: Stories from the Quilt, Grey Gardens, Here Comes Everybody, The Children Must Learn, Requiem For 500,000, Target For Tonight, Let's Get Lost, Old, Borrowed, Years of Lightning, Day of Drums, Stag, Patria O Muerte, The Jerry Springer Show, Let It Be, Song of Ceylon, The End Of The Road, Animal Life In The Antarctic, Sandstone, The Civil War, A Time for Burning, Gap-Toothed Women, The Vanishing Prairie, The Way Ahead, On The Bowery, Shipyard, Africa, Feldzug In Polen, 28-Up, The Savage Eye, Hiroshima-Nagasaki—August, 1945, Pathé-Faits Divers, Borinage, Youth Terror: The View from Behind the Gun Coal Face, Children At School, The Anderson Platoon, The Living Desert, Public Defender, Les Charmes De L'Existence, Harry Tomorrow, Nuit Et Brouillard, Harlan County U.S.A., The Challenge, Echoes, Don't Look Back, America's Funniest Home Videos, Junkyard by the Sea, La Bataille Du Rail, Victory Through Air Power, Le Mystère Koumiko, Arrivée des Congressistes, On the Road to Button Bay, Jane, City Of Gold, "Atomic Power", Jungle Cat, CNN, A Stravinsky Portrait, Autobiography of a Jeep, Domestic Wildlife, Fillmore, Shoah, The Kon-Tiki, Black Fantasy, Law and Order, Basic Training, Traces of Death, Report From The Aleutians, Happy Mother's Day, C'est surtout pas de l'amour—Un film sur la pornographie, Hoop Dreams, Night of the Dragon, Cavedwellers, The Endless Summer—K

As author Murphy Gruner once remarked:

"Just as is true with Chandler's Marlowe, the viewer is won over simply because the shirts are rumpled, the soles are worn, and there's that ever present hat. These days nothing deserves our faith less than the slick and expensive. Which is how video and film technology comes to us: rumpled or slick.

"Rumpled Technology —capital M for Marlowe—hails from Good Guys, Radio Shack or Fry's Electronics. It is cheap, available and very dangerous. One needs only to consider *The George Holliday Rodney King Video* to recognize the power of such low-end technology. Furthermore, as the recording time for tapes and digital disks increases, as battery life is extended, and as camera size is reduced, the larger the window will grow for capturing events as they occur.

"Slick Technology — capital S for Slick— is the opposite: expensive, cumbersome, and time consuming. But it too is also very powerful. Digital manipulation allows for the creation of almost anything the imagination can come up with, all in the safe confines of an editing suite, equipped with 24 hour catering and an on site masseuse."[186]

[186] Murphy Gruner's *Document Detectives* (New York: Pantheon, 1995), p. 37.[187]

[187] ~~One can imagine a group of Documentary Detectives whose sole purpose is to uphold Truth & Truth~~ » ~~by guaranteeing the the authenticity of all works. Their seal of approval would create a sense of public faith which could only be maintained if said Documentary Detectives were as fierce as pit bulls and as scrupulous as saints. Of course, this is more the kind of thing a novelist or playwright would deal with, and as I am pointedly not a novelist or a playwright I will leave that tale to someone else —~~

» Or TNT. Truth And Truth therefore becoming another name for the nitrating of toluene or $C_7H_5N_3O_6$—not to be confused with $C_{16}H_{10}N_2O_2$—in other words one word: trinitrotoluene. TNT[188] telegraphing a weird coalition of sense. On one hand transcendent and lasting and on the other violent and extremely flammable.

As Grundberg, Alabiso and Mitchell contend, this impressive ability to manipulate images must someday permanently deracinate film and video from its now sacrosanct position as "eyewitness." The perversion of image will make *The Rodney King Video* inadmissible in a
court of law . ¶Inc redible as it may
seem, Los Angele s Mayor Bradley'
s statement— "Ou r eyes did not
deceive us. We sa w what we saw
and what we saw w as a crime."—will
seem ludicrous. Tr uth will once ag
ain revert to the sh ady territories of
the word and hum anity's abilities to
judge its peculiar m odalities. Nor is
this a particularly original predic-
tion. Anything fro m Michael Crich-
ton's *Rising Sun*, to Delgado's *Card*
Tricks, or Lisa Ma rie "Slit Slit" Bad
er's *Confession of a* *Porn Star* delve
into the increasing ly protean nature
of a digital univer se.¶ In his article
"True Grit", Anth ony Lane at *Th*
e New Yorker clai ms "grittiness is
the most difficult e lement to constru
ct and will always e lude the finest stu
dio magician. Grit, however, does no
t elude Navidson." ¶Consider the savage scene captured on grainy 16mm film of a tourist eaten alive by lions in a wildlife preserve in Angola (*Traces of Death*) and compare it to the ridiculous and costly comedy *Eraser* in which several villains are dismembered by alligators.[190]

---

[188]Which also stands for Technological Neural Transmitters (TNT)[189] — another pun and another story altogether.

[189]Or what as Lude once pointed out also means Tits And Tail. i.e. also explosive. i.e. orgasmic. i.e. a sudden procreating pun which turns everything into something entirely else, which now as I catch up with myself, where I've gone and where I haven't gone and what I better get back to, may very well have not been a pun at all but plain and simple just the bifurcation of truth, with an ampersand tossed in for unity. A sperm twixt another form of similar unity, and look there's an echo at haand. The articulation of conflict may very well be a better thing upon which to stand—Truth & Truth 'z all, after all, or not at all. In other words, just as Zampanò wrote it.[196]

[190]Jennifer Kale told me she'd visited Zampanò around seven times: "He liked me to teach him filmic words. You know, film crit kind of stuff. Straight out of Christian Metz and the rest of that crew. He also liked me to read him some of the jokes I'd gotten on the Internet. Mostly though I just described movies I'd recently seen." <u>Eraser</u> was one of them.

William J. Mitchell offers an alternate description of "grit" when he highlights Barthe's observation that reality incorporates "seemingly functionless detail 'because it is there' to signal that 'this is indeed an unfiltered sample of the real.'[191]"[192]

Kenneth Turan, however, disagrees with Lane's conclusion: "Navidson has still relied on F/X. Don't fool yourself into thinking any of this stuff's true. Grit's just grit, and the room stretching is all care of Industrial Light & Magic."

Ella Taylor, Charles Champlin, Todd McCarthy, Annette Insdorf, G. O. Pilfer, and Janet Maslin, all sidestep the issue with a sentence or two. However, even serious aficionados of documentaries or "live-footage," despite expressing wonder over the numerous details suggesting the veracity of *The Navidson Record,* cannot get past the absolute physical absurdity of the house.

---

[191]Roland Barthes' "The Reality Effect," in *French Literary Theory Today* ed. Tzvetan Todorov (Cambridge: Cambridge University Press, 1982), p. 11-17.
[192]William J. Mitchell's *The Reconfigured Eye: Visual Truth In The Post-Photographic Era,* p. 27.

As Sonny Beauregard quipped: "Were it not for the fact that this is a supreme gothic tale, we'd have bought the whole thing hook-line-and-sinker."[193]

[193]Sonny Beauregard's "Worst of Times" *The San Francisco Chronicle*, July 4, 1995. C-7, column 2. Difficult to ignore here is the matter of that recent and most disturbing piece of work *La Belle Nicoise et Le Beau Chien*. As many already know, the film portrayed the murder of a little girl in such comic reality it was instantly hailed as the belle of the ball in the palace of the grotesque, receiving awards at Sundance and Cannes, earning international distribution deals, and enjoying the canonical company of David Lynch, Luis Buñuel, Hieronymus Bosch, Charles Baudelaire, and even the Marquis De Sade, until of course it was discovered that there really was such a little Lithuanian girl and she really was murdered and by none other than the wealthy filmmaker himself. It was a slickly produced snuff film sold as an art house flick. Emir Kusturica's *Underground* finally replaced *Nicoise* as the winner of the Cannes Palm d'Or; an equally absurd and terrifying film though gratefully fictive. About Yugoslavia.

The Navidson Record looks like a gritty, shoestring documentary. *La Belle Nicoise et Le Beau Chien* looks like a lushly executed piece of cinema. Both pieces are similar in one way: what one could believe one doubts, *Nicoise* because one depends upon the moral sense of the filmmaker, *The Navidson Record* because one depends upon the moral sense of the world. Both are assumptions neither film deserves. As Murphy Gruner might have observed: "Rumpled vs. Slick. Your choice."

Perhaps the best argument for the authenticity of *The Navidson Record* does not come from film critics, university scholars, or festival panel members but rather from the I.R.S. Even a cursory glance at Will Navidson's tax statements or for that matter Karen's, Tom's or Billy Reston's, proves the impossibility of digital manipulation.[194]

They just never had enough money.

Sonny Beauregard conservatively estimates the special effects in *The Navidson Record* would cost a minimum of six and a half million dollars. Taking into account the total received for the Guggenheim Fellowship, the NEA Grant, everyone's credit limit on Visa, Mastercard, Amex etc., etc., not to mention savings and equity, Navidson comes up five and a half million dollars short. Beauregard again: "Considering the cost of special effects these days, it is inconceivable how Navidson could have created his house."

[194]The records were made public in the Phillip Newharte article "The House The I.R.S. Didn't Build" published in *Seattle Photo Zine* v.12, 118, p.92-156.

Strangely then, the best argument for fact is the absolute unaffordability of fiction. Thus it would appear the ghost haunting *The Navidson Record*, continually bashing against the door, is none other than the recurring threat of its own reality.[195]

---

[195]Despite claiming in Chapter One that "the more interesting material dwells exclusively on the interpretation of events within the film," Zampanò has still wandered into his own discussion of "the antinomies of fact or fiction, representation or artifice, document or prank" within The Navidson Record.[196] I have no idea whether it's on purpose or not. Sometimes I'm certain it is. Other times I'm sure it's just one big fucking train wreck.

[196]195 (cont.) Which, in case you didn't realize, has everything to do with the story of Connaught B. N. S. Cape who observed four asses winnow the air . . . for as we know there can only be one conclusion, no matter the labor, the lasting trace, the letters or even the faith—no daytime, no starlight, not even a flashlight to the rescue—just, that's it, so long folks, one grand kerplunk, even if Mr. Cape really did come across four donkeys winnowing the air with their hooves . . .

Thoughts blazing through my mind while I was walking the aisles at the Virgin Megastore, trying to remember a tune to some words, changing my mind to open the door instead, some door, I don't know which one either except maybe one of the ones inside me, which was when I found Hailey, disturbed face, incredible body, only eighteen, smoking like a steel mill, breath like the homeless but eyes bright and pure and she had an incredible body and I said hello and on a whim invited her over to my place to listen to some of the CD's I'd just bought, convinced she'd decline, surprised when she accepted, so over she came, and we put on the music and smoked a bowl and called Pink Dot though they didn't arrive with our sandwiches and beer until we were already out of our clothes and under the covers and coming like judgment day (i.e. for the second time) and then we ate and drank and Hailey smiled and her face seemed less disturbed and her smile was naked and gentle and peaceful and as I felt myself drift off next to her, I wanted her to fall asleep next to me, but Hailey didn't understand and for some reason when I woke up a little later, she was already gone, leaving neither a note nor a number.

A few days later, I heard her on KROQ's Love Line, this time drenched in purple rain, describing to Doctor Drew and Adam Carolla how I—"this guy in a real stale studio with books and writing everywhere, everywhere! and weird drawings all over his walls too, all in black. I couldn't understand any of it."—had dozed off only to start screaming and yelling terrible things in his sleep, about blood and mutilations and other crazy %&#@, which had scared her and had it been wrong of her to leave even though when he'd been awake he'd seemed alright?

An ugly shiver ripped up my back then. All this time I'd believed the cavorting and drinking and sex had done away with that terrible onslaught of fear. Clearly I was wrong. I'd only pushed it off into another place. My stomach turned. Screaming things was bad enough, but the thought that I'd also frightened someone I felt only tenderness for made it far worse.

Did I scream every night? What did I say? And why in the hell couldn't I remember any of it in the morning?

I checked to make sure my door was locked. Returned a second later to put on the chain. I need more locks. My heart started hammering. I retreated to the corner of my room but that didn't help. Fuck, fuck, fuck—wasn't helping either. Better go to the bathroom, try some water on the face, try anything. Only I couldn't budge. Something was approaching. I could hear it outside. I could feel the vibrations. It was about to splinter its way through the Hall door, my door, Walker in Darkness, from whose face earth and heaven long ago fled.

Then the walls crack.

All my windows shatter.

A terrible roar.

More like a howl more like a shriek.

My eardrums strain and split.

The chain snaps.

I'm desperately trying to crawl away, but it's too late. Nothing can be done now.

That awful stench returns and with it comes a scene, filling my place, painting it all anew, but with what? And what kind of brushes are being used? What sort of paint? And why that smell?

Oh no.

How do I know this?

I cannot know this.

The floor beneath me fails into a void.

Except before I fall what's happening now only reverts to what was supposed to have happened which in the end never happened at all. The walls have remained, the glass has held and the only thing that vanished was my own horror, subsiding in that chaotic wake always left by even the most rational things.

Here then was the darker side of whim.

I tried to relax.

I tried to forget.

I imagined some world-weary travelers camped on the side of some desolate road, in some desolate land, telling a story to allay their doubts, encircle their fears with distraction, laughter and song, a collective illusion of vision spun above their portable hearth of tinder & wood, their eyes gleaming with divine magic, born where perspective lines finally collude, or so they think. Except those stars are never born on such far away horizons as that. The light in fact comes from their own gathering and their own conversation, surrounding and sustaining the fire they have built and kept alive through the night, until inevitably, come morning, cold and dull, the songs are all sung, the stories lost or taken, soup eaten, embers dark. Not even the seeds of one pun are left to capriciously turn the mind aside and tropos is at the center of "trope" and it means "turn."

Though here's a song they might of sung:

> Mad woman on another tour;
> Everything she is she spits on the floor.
> An old man tells me she's sicker than the rest.
> God I've never been afraid like this.

Heart may still be the fire in hearth but I'm suddenly too cold to continue, and besides, there's no hearth here anyway and it's the end of June. Thursday. Almost noon. And all the buttons on my corduroy coat are gone. I don't know why. I'm sorry Hailey.[197] I don't know what to do.

Eventually Jed tries again to carry Wax toward what he hopes is home. He also attempts periodically to signal Navidson on the radio though never gets a response. Regrettably very little footage exists from this part of the voyage. Battery levels are running low and there is not much desire on Jed's part to exert any energy towards memorializing what seems more and more like a trek toward his own end.

The penultimate clip finds Jed huddled next to Wax in a very small room. Wax is silent, Jed completely exhausted. It is remarkable how faced with his own death, Jed still refuses to leave his friend. He tells the camera he will go no further, even though the growl seems to be closing in around them.

In the final shot, Jed focuses the camera on the door. Something is on the other side, hammering against it, over and over again. Whatever comes for those who are never seen again has come from[198] him, and Jed can do nothing but focus the camera on the hinges as the door slowly begins to give way. ▷

The locks may have held, the chain too, but my room still stinks of gore, a flood of entrails spread from wall to wall, the hacked remains of hooves and hands, matted hair and bone, used to paint the ceiling, drench the floor. The chopping must have gone on for days to leave only this. Not even the flies settle for long. Connaught B. N. S. Cape has been murdered along with his donkeys but nobody knows by whom.

For as we know, there cannot be an escape.

I'm too far from here to know anything or anyone anymore.

I don't even know myself.

[197]Following the release of the first edition over the Internet, several responses were received by e-mail including this one:

> I think Johnny was a little off here. I wanted to write and tell you about it. We actually had a pretty rad time (though his screams were really weird and definately scarred me.) He was very sweet and really gentle and kinda crude too but we still had a lot of fun. It did hurt my feelings the part about my breath. Tell him Ive been brushing my teeth more and trying to quit smoking. But one part he didn't mention. He said the nicest things about my wrists. I was sorry to hear he disappeared. Do you know what happened to him?
>
> — Hailey. February 13, 1999.

—Ed.

[198]Typo. Should read "for".

▷ (No punctuation point should appear here) See also Saul Steinberg's *The Labyrinth* (New York: Harper & Brothers, 1960).K

Bibliography

Architecture:

Brand, Stewart. *How Buildings Learn: What Happens After They're Built.* New York: Viking, 1994.

Jordan, R. Furneaux. *A Concise History of Western Architecture.* London: Thames and Hudson Limited, 1969.

Kostof, Spiro. *A History of Architecture: Settings and Rituals.* Oxford: Oxford University Press, 1995.

Pothorn, Herbert. *Architectural Styles: An Historical Guide to World Design.* New York: Facts On File Publications, 1982.

Prevsner, Nikolaus. *A History of Building Types.* Princeton, N.J.: Princeton University Press, 1976.

Prost, Antoine and Gérard Vincent, eds. *A History of Private Life: Riddles of Identity in Modern Times.* Trans. Arthur Goldhammer. Cambridge: The Belknap Press of Harvard University Press, 1991.

Prussin, Labelle. *African Nomadic Architecture: Space, Place, and Gender.* Smithsonian Institution Press, 1995.

Travis, Jack, ed. *African American Architecture In Current Practice.* New York: Princeton Architectural Press, Inc. 1991.

Watkin, David. *A History of Western Architecture.* 2nd ed. London: Laurence King Publishing, 1996.

Whiffen, Marcus. *American Architecture Since 1780.* Cambridge: The MIT Press, 1992.

Wu, Nelson Ikon. *Chinese and Indian Architecture: The City of Man, the Mountain of God, and the Realm of the Immortals.* New York: George Braziller, Inc., 1963.

Film:

Too numerous to list here.

X

Every house is an architecturally structured "path": the specific possibilities of movement and the drives toward movement as one proceeds from the entrance through the sequence of spatial entities have been pre-determined by the architectural structuring of that space and one experiences the space accordingly. But at the same time, in its relation to the surrounding space, it is a "goal", and we either advance toward this goal or depart from it.

— Dagobert Frey
Grundlegung zu einer vergleichenden Kunstwissenschaft

Karen may lose herself in resentment and fear, but the Navidson we see seems joyful, even euphoric, as he sets out with Reston and his brother to rescue Holloway and his team. It is almost as if entrance let alone a purpose—any purpose—in the face of those endless and lightless regions is reason enough to rejoice.

Using 16mm motion picture (colour and B/W) and 35mm stills, Navidson for the first time begins to capture the size and sense of that place. Author Denise Lowery writes the following evocative impression of how Navidson photographs the Anteroom:

> The hot red flame spits out light, catching on Tom, entwining in the spokes of Reston's wheelchair, casting Shape Changers and Dragons on a nearby wall. But even this watery dance succeeds in only illuminating a tiny portion of a corner. Navidson, Tom and Reston continue forward beneath those gables of gloom and walls buttressed with shadow, lighting more flares, penetrating this world with their halogen lamps, until finally what seemed undefinable comes forth out of the shimmering blank, implacable and now nothing less than obvious and undeniable—as if there never could have been a question about the shape, there never could have been a moment when only the imagination succeeded in prodding those inky folds, coming up with its own sense, something far more perverse and contorted and heavy with things much stranger and colder than even this brief shadow play performed in the irregular burn of sulfur—mythic and inhuman, flickering, shifting, and finally dying around the men's continuous progress.[199]

[199]See chapter ten of Denise Lowery's *Sketches: The Process of Entry* (Fayetteville, Arkansas: University of Arkansas Press, 1996).

Of course, the Great Hall dwarfs even this chamber. As Holloway reported in Exploration #2, its span approaches one mile, making it practically impossible to illuminate. Instead the trio slips straight through the black, carefully marking their way with ample fishing line, until the way ahead suddenly reveals an even greater darkness, pitted in the centre of that immense, incomprehensible space.

In one photograph of the Great Hall, we find Reston in the foreground holding a flare, the light barely licking an ashen wall rising above him into inky oblivion, while in the background Tom stands surrounded by flares which just as ineffectually confront the impenetrable wall of nothingness looming around the Spiral Staircase.

As Chris Thayil remarks: "The Great Hall feels like the inside of some preternatural hull designed to travel vast seas never before observed in this world."[200]

---

[200]Chris Thayil's "Travel's Legacy" in *National Geographic,* v. 189, May 1996, p. 36-53.

Since rescuing Holloway's team is the prime objective, Navidson takes very few photographs. Luckily for us, however, the beginning of this sequence relies almost entirely on these scarce but breathtaking stills instead of the far more abundant but vastly inferior video tapes, which are used here mainly to provide sound.

Eventually when they realize Holloway and his team are nowhere near the Great Hall, the plan becomes for Reston to set up camp at the top of the stairway while Navidson and Tom continue on below.

Switching to Hi 8, we follow Navidson and Reston as they react to Tom's announcement.

"Bullshit," Navidson barks at his brother.

"Navy, I can't go down there," Tom stammers.

"What's that supposed to mean? You're just giving up on them?"

Fortunately, by barely touching his friend's arm, Billy Reston forces Navidson to take a good hard look at his brother. As we can see for ourselves, he is pale, out of breath, and in spite of the cold, sweating profusely. Clearly in no condition to go any further let alone tackle the profound depths of that staircase.

Navidson takes a deep breath. "Sorry Tom, I didn't mean to snap at you like that."

Tom says nothing.

"Do you think you can stay here with Billy or do you want to head home? You'll have to make it back on your own."

"I'll stay here."

"With Billy?" Reston responds. "What's that supposed to mean? The hell if you think I'm letting you go on alone."

But Navidson has already started down the Spiral Staircase.

"I should sue the bastards who designed this house," Reston shouts after him. "Haven't they heard of handicap ramps?"

The dark minutes start to slide by. Based on Holloway's descent, Navidson had estimated the stairway was an incredible thirteen miles down. Less than five minutes later, however, Tom and Reston hear a shout. Peering over the banister, they discover Navidson with a lightstick in his hand standing at the bottom—no more than 100ft down. Tom immediately assumes they have stumbled upon the wrong set of stairs.

Further investigation by Navidson, though, reveals the remnants of neon trail markers left by Holloway's team.

Without another word, Reston swings out of his chair and starts down the stairs. Less than twenty minutes later he reaches the last step.

Navidson knows he has no choice but to accept Reston's participation, and heads back up to retrieve the wheelchair and the rest of their gear.

Amazingly enough, Tom seems fine camping near the staircase.

Both Navidson and Reston hope his presence will enable them to maintain radio contact for a much longer time than Holloway could. Even if they both know the house will still eventually devour their signal.

As Navidson and Reston head out into the labyrinth, they occasionally come upon pieces of neon marker and shreds of various types of fishing line. Not even multi-strand steel line seems immune to the diminishing effects of that place.

"It looks like its impossible to leave a lasting trace here," Navidson observes.

"The woman you never want to meet," quips Reston, always managing to keep his wheelchair a little ahead of Navidson.

Soon, however, Reston begins to suffer from nausea, and even vomits. Navidson asks him if he is sick. Reston shakes his head.

"No, it's more . . . shit, I haven't felt this way since I went fishing for marlin."

Navidson speculates Reston's sea sickness or his "*mal de mer*," as he calls it, may have something to do with the changing nature of the house: "Everything here is constantly shifting. It took Holloway, Jed, and Wax almost four days to reach the bottom of the staircase, and yet we made it down in five minutes. The thing collapsed like an accordion." Then looking over at his friend: "You realize if it expands again, you're in deep shit."

"Considering our supplies," Reston shoots back. "I'd say we'd both be in deep shit."

As was already mentioned in Chapter III, some critics believe the house's mutations reflect the psychology of anyone who enters it. Dr. Haugeland asserts that the extraordinary absence of sensory information forces the individual to manufacture his or her own data.[201] Ruby Dahl, in her stupendous study of space, calls the house on Ash Tree Lane "a solipsistic heightener," arguing that "the house, the halls, and the rooms all become the self—collapsing, expanding, tilting, closing, but always in perfect relation to the mental state of the individual."[202]

[201]Missing. — Ed.

[202]Ibid. Curiously Dahl fails to consider why the house never opens into what is necessarily outside of itself.

If one accepts Dahl's reading, then it follows that Holloway's creature comes from Holloway's mind not the house; the tiny room Wax finds himself trapped within reflects his own state of exhaustion and despair; and Navidson's rapid descent reflects his own knowledge that the Spiral Staircase is *not* bottomless. As Dr. Haugeland observes:

> The epistemology of the house remains entirely commensurate with its size. After all, one always approaches the unknown with greater caution the first time around. Thus it appears far more expansive than it literally is. Knowledge of the terrain on a second visit dramatically contracts this sense of distance.
>
> Who has never gone for a walk through some unfamiliar park and felt that it was huge, only to return a second time to discover that the park is in fact much smaller than initially perceived?

When revisiting places we once frequented as children, it is not unusual to observe how much smaller everything seems. This experience has too often been attributed to the physical differences between a child and an adult. In fact it has more to do with epistemological dimensions than with bodily dimensions: knowledge is hot water on wool. It shrinks time and space.

(Admittedly there is the matter where boredom, due to repetition, *stretches* time and space. I will deal specifically with this problem in a later chapter entitled "Ennui."[203])

When Holloway's team traveled down the stairway, they had no idea if they would find a bottom. Navidson, however, knows the stairs are finite and therefore has far less anxiety about the descent.

---

[203] See also Dr. Helen Hodge's *American Psychology: The Ownership Of Self* (Lexington: University of Kentucky Press, 1996), p. 297 where she writes:

> What is boredom? Endless repetitions, like, for example, Navidson's corridors and rooms, which are consistently devoid of any *Myst*-like discoveries `[see Chad; p. 99.]` thus causing us to lose interest. What then makes anything exciting? or better yet: what *is* exciting? While the degree varies, we are always excited by anything that engages us, influences us or more simply involves us. In those endlessly repetitive hallways and stairs, there is nothing for us to connect with. That permanently foreign place does not excite us. It bores us. And that is that, except for the fact that there is no such thing as boredom. Boredom is really a psychic defense protecting us from ourselves, from complete paralysis, by repressing, among other things, the meaning of that place, which in this case is and always has been horror.

See also Otto Fenichel's 1934 essay "The Psychology of Boredom" in which he describes boredom as "an unpleasurable experience of a lack of impulse." Kierkegaard goes a little further, remarking that "Boredom, extinction, is precisely a continuity of nothingness." While William Wordsworth in his preface for *Lyrical Ballads* (1802) writes:

> The subject is indeed important! For the human mind is capable of being excited without the application of gross and violent stimulants; and he must have a very faint perception of its beauty and dignity who does not know this, and who does not further know, that one being is elevated above another, in proportion as he possesses this capability . . . [A] multitude of causes, unknown to former times, are now acting with a combined force to blunt the discriminating powers of the mind, and unfitting it for all voluntary exertion to reduce it to a state of almost savage torpor. The most effective of these causes are the great national events which are daily taking place, and the increasing accumulation of men in cities, where the uniformity of their occupations produces a craving for extraordinary incident, which the rapid communication of intelligence hourly gratifies. To this tendency of life and manners the literature and theatrical exhibitions of the country have conformed themselves.

See Sean Healy's *Boredom, Self and Culture* (Rutherford, N.J.: Fairleigh Dickinson University Press, 1984); Patricia Meyer Spacks' *Boredom: The Literary History of a State of Mind* (Chicago: University of Chicago Press, 1995); and finally Celine Arlesey's *Perversity In Dullness . . . and Vice-Versa* (Denver: Blederbiss Press, 1968).

Unlike the real world, Navidson's journey into the house is not just figuratively but literally shortened.[204]

[204] Missing. — Ed.

This theme of structures altered by perception is not uniquely observed in *The Navidson Record.* Almost thirty years ago, Günter Nitschke described what he termed "experienced or concrete space":

> It has a centre which is perceiving man, and it therefore has an excellent system of directions which changes with the movements of the human body; it is limited and in no sense neutral, in other words it is finite, heterogeneous, subjectively defined and perceived; distances and directions are fixed relative to man . . .[205]

---

[205]Günter Nitschke's "Anatomie der gelebten Umwelt" (*Bauen + Wohnen* , September 1968).[206]

[206]`Which you are quite right to observe makes no sense at all.`

Christian Norberg-Schulz objects; condemning subjective architectural experiences for the seemingly absurd conclusion it suggests, mainly that "architecture comes into being only when experienced."[207]

[207]Christian Norberg-Schulz, *Existence, Space & Architecture*, p. 13.

Norberg-Schulz asserts: “Architectural space certainly exists independently of the casual perceiver, and has centres and directions of its own.” Focusing on the constructions of any civilization, whether ancient or modern, it is hard to disagree with him. It is only when focusing on Navidson’s house that these assertions begin to blur.

Can Navidson's house exist without the experience of itself?

Is it possible to think of that place as "unshaped" by human perceptions?

Especially since everyone entering there finds a vision almost completely—though pointedly not completely—different from anyone else's?

Even Michael Leonard, who had never heard of Navidson's house, professed a belief in the "psychological dimensions of space." Leonard claimed people create a "*sensation* of space" where the final result "in the perceptual process is a single sensation—a 'feeling' about that particular place . . ."[208]

[208]Michael Leonard's "Humanizing Space," *Progressive Architecture,* April 1969.

In his book *The Image of the City*, Kevin Lynch suggested emotional cognition of all environment was rooted in history, or at least *personal* history:

> [Environmental image, a generalized mental picture of the exterior physical world] is the product both of immediate sensation and of *the memory of past experience*, and it is used to interpret information and to guide action.[209]
>
> [Italics added for emphasis]

[209]Kevin Lynch's *The Image of the City* (Cambridge, Massachusetts: The MIT Press, 1960), p. 4.

Or as Jean Piaget insisted: "It is quite obvious that the perception of space involves a gradual construction and certainly does not exist ready-made at the outset of mental development."[210] Like Leonard's attention to *sensation* and Piaget's emphasis on constructed perception, Lynch's emphasis on the importance of the past allows him to introduce a certain degree of subjectivity to the question of space and more precisely architecture.

---

[210]J. Piaget and B. Inhelder's *The Child's Conception of Geometry* (New York: Basic Books, 1960), p. 6.

Where Navidson's house is concerned, subjectivity seems more a matter of degree. The Infinite Corridor, the Anteroom, the Great Hall, and the Spiral Staircase, exist for all, though their respective size and even layout sometimes changes. Other areas of that place, however, never seem to replicate the same pattern twice, or so the film repeatedly demonstrates.

No doubt speculation will continue for a long time over what force alters and orders the dimensions of that place. But even if the shifts turn out to be some kind of absurd interactive Rorschach test resulting from some peculiar and as yet undiscovered law of physics, Reston's nausea still reflects how the often disturbing disorientation experienced within that place, whether acting directly upon the inner ear or the inner labyrinth of the psyche, can have physiological consequences.[211]

---

[211]No doubt about that. My fear's gotten worse. Hearing Hailey describing my screams on the radio like that has really upset me. I no longer wake up tired. I wake up tired and afraid. I wonder if the morning rasp in my voice is just from sleep or rather some inarticulate attempt to name my horror. I'm suspicious of the dreams I cannot remember, the words only others can hear. I've also noticed the inside of my cheeks are now all mutilated, lumps of pink flesh dangling in the wet dark, probably from grinding, gritting and so much pointless chewing. My teeth ache. My head aches. My stomach's a mess.

I went to see a Dr. Ogelmeyer a few days ago and told him everything I could think of about my attacks and the awful anxiety that haunts my every hour. He made an appointment for me with another doctor and then prescribed some medication. The whole thing lasted less than half an hour and including the prescription cost close to a hundred and seventy-five dollars.

I tore up the appointment card and when I got back to my studio I grabbed my radio/ CD player and put it out on the street with a For Sale sign on it. An hour later, some guy driving an Infiniti pulled over and bought it for forty-five dollars. Next, I took all my CDs to Aaron's on Highland and got almost a hundred dollars.

I had no choice. I need the money. I also need the quiet.

As of now, I still haven't taken the medicine. It's a low-grade sedative of some kind. Ten flakes of chalk-blue. I hate them. Perhaps when night comes I'll change my mind. I arrange them in a tidy line on the kitchen counter. But night finally does come and even though my fear ratchets towards the more severe, I fear those pills even more.

Ever since leaving the labyrinth, having had to endure all those convolutions, those incomplete suggestions, the maddening departures and inconclusive nature of the whole fucking chapter, I've craved space, light and some kind of clarity. Any kind of clarity. I just don't know how to find it, though staring over at those awful tablets only amps my resolve to do something, anything.

Funny as it sounds—especially considering the amounts of drugs I've been proud to consume—those pills, like dots, raised & particular, look more and more like some kind of secret Braille spelling out the end of my life.

Perhaps if I had insurance; if one hundred and seventy-five dollars meant I was twenty-five over my deductible, I'd think differently. But it's not and so I don't.

As far as I can see, there's no place for me in this country's system of health, and even if there were I'm not sure it would make a difference. Something I considered over and over again while I was sitting in that stark office, barely looking at the National Geographic or People magazines, just waiting on the bustle of procedure and paper work, until the time came, quite a bit of time too, when I had to answer a call, a call made by a nurse, who led me down a hall and then another hall and still another hall, until I found myself alone in a cramped sour smelling room, where I waited again, this time on a slightly different set of procedures and routines carried out by these white draped ministers of medicine, Dr.Ogelmeyer & friends, who by their very absence forced me to wonder what would happen if I were really unhealthy, as unhealthy as I am now poor, how much longer would I have to wait, how much more cramped and sour would this room be, and if I wanted to leave would I? Could I? Perhaps I wouldn't even know how to leave. Incarcerated forever within the corridors of some awful facility. 5051. Protective custody. Or just as terrifying: no 5051, no protective custody. Left to wander alone the equally ferocious and infernal corridors of indigence.

To put it politely: no fucking way.
I know what it means to go mad.
I'll die before I go there.
But first I have to find out if that's where I'm really heading.
I've got to stop blinking in the face of my fear.
I must hear what I scream.
I must remember what I dream.

I pick up the sedatives, these Zs without Z, and one by one crush them between my fingers, letting the dust fall to the floor. Next I locate all the alcohol I have buried around my studio and pour it down the sink. Then I root out every seed and bud of pot and flush it down the toilet along with the numbers of all suppliers. I eventually find a few tabs of old acid as well as some Ecstasy hidden in a bag of rice. These I also toss.

The consumption of MDMA, aka Ecstasy, aka E, aka X, has been known to bring on epilepsy especially when taken in large quantities. Eight months ago, I ingested more than my fair share, mostly White Angels, though I also went ahead and invited to the party a slew of Canaries, Stickmen, Snowballs, Hurricanes, Hallways, Butterflies, Tasmanian Devils and Mitsubishis, which was a month long party, all of it pretty much preceding Thanksgiving, and a different story altogether.

There are so many stories . . .

Perhaps I'll be lucky and discover this awful dread that gnaws on me day and night is nothing more than the shock wave caused by too many crude chemicals rioting in my skull for too long. Perhaps by cleaning out my system I'll come to a clearing where I can ease myself into peace.

Then again perhaps in finding my clearing I'll only make myself an easier prey for the real terror that tracks me, waiting beyond the perimeter, past the tall grass, the brush, that stand of trees, cloaked in shadow and rot, but with enough presence to resurrect within me a whole set of ancient reflexes, ordering a non-existent protrusion at the base of my spine to twitch, my pupils already dilating, adrenaline flowing, even as instinct commands me to run.

But by then it will already be too late. The distance far too great to cover. As if there ever really was a place to hide.

At least I'll have a gun.

I'll buy a gun.

Then I'll crouch and I will wait.

Outside shots are fired. Lots. In fact one sounds like an artillery cannon going off. Suddenly the city's at war and I'm confused. When I go to my window a spray of light sets me straight, though the revelation is not without irony.

Somehow the date escaped me.

It's July 4th.

This country's birthday. Wow.

Which I realize means I forgot my own birthday. A day that came and passed, it turns out, in of all places Hailey's arms. How about that, I can remember the beginnings of a nation that doesn't give a flying fuck about me, would possibly even strangle me if given half the chance, but I can't remember my own beginnings—and I'm probably the only one alive willing to at least attempt on my behalf that tricky flying fuck maneuver.

Which might be worth some sort of smile, if I hadn't already come to realize that irony is a Maginot Line drawn by the already condemned—which oddly enough still does make me smile.

Fortunately Reston's nausea does not last long, and he and Navidson can spend the rest of the day pushing deeper and deeper into the labyrinth.

Initially, they follow the scant remains of the first team and then continue on by following their instincts. Based on the fact that there was very little evidence of the first team's descent remaining on the stairs, Navidson determines that the neon markers and fishing line last at most six days before they are entirely consumed by the house.

When they finally make camp, both men are disheartened and exhausted. Nevertheless, each agrees to alternately serve as watch. Navidson takes the first shift, spending his time removing the dark blotched gauze around his toes—clearly a painful process—before reapplying ointment and a fresh dressing. Reston spends his time tinkering with his chair and the mount on the Arriflex.

Except for their own restlessness, neither one hears anything during the night.

Toward the end of their second day inside (making this the ninth day since Holloway's team set out into the house), both men seem uncertain whether to continue or return.

It is only as they are making camp for the second night that Navidson hears something. A voice, maybe a cry, but so fleeting were it not for Reston's confirmation, it probably would have been shrugged off as just a high note of the imagination.

Leaving most of their equipment behind, the two men head out in pursuit of the sound. For forty minutes they hear nothing and are about to give up when their ears are again rewarded with another distant cry. Based on the rapidly changing video time stamp, we can see another three hours passes as they weave in and out of more rooms and corridors, often moving very quickly, though never failing to mark their course with neon arrows and ample amounts of fishing line.

At one point, Navidson manages to get Tom on the radio, only to learn that there is something the matter with Karen. Unfortunately, the signal decays before he can get more details. Finally, Reston stops his wheelchair and jabs a finger at a wall. On Hi 8, we witness his gruff assertion: "How we get through it, I don't have a clue. But that crying's coming from the other side."

Searching out more hallways, more turns, Navidson eventually leads the way down a narrow corridor ending with a door. Navidson and Reston open it only to discover another corridor ending with another door. Slowly they make their way through a gauntlet of what must be close to fifty doors (it is impossible to calculate the exact number due to the jump cuts), until Navidson discovers for the first and only time a door without a door knob. Even stranger, as he tries to push the door open, he discovers it is locked. Reston's expression communicates nothing but incredulity.[212]

---

[212]See Gaston Bachelard's *La Poétique de L'Espace* (Paris: Presses Universitaires de France, 1978), p. 78, where he observes:

> Françoise Minkowska a exposé une collection particulièrement émouvante de dessins d'enfants polonais ou juifs qui ont subi les sévices de l'occupation allemande pendant la dernière guerre. Telle enfant qui a vécu caché, à la moindre alerte, dans une armoire, dessine longtemps après les heures maudites, des maisons étroites, froides et fermées. Et c'est ainsi que Françoise Minkowska parle de "maisons immobiles," de maisons immobilisées dans leur raideur: "Cette raideur et cette immobilité se retrouvent aussi bien à la *fumée* que dans les rideaux des fenêtres. Les arbres autour d'elle sont *droits*, ont l'air de la garder."...
>
> A un détail, la grande psychologue qu'était Françoise Minkowska reconnaissait le mouvement de la maison. Dans la maison dessinée par un enfant de huit ans, Françoise Minkowska note qu'à la porte, il y a "une poignée; on y entre, on y habite." Ce n'est pas simplement une maison-construction, "c'est une maison-habitation." La poignée de la porte désigne évidemment une fonctionnalité. La kinesthésie est marquée par ce signe, si souvent oublié dans les dessins des enfants "rigides."
>
> Remarquons bien que la "poignée" de la porte ne pourrait guère être dessinée à l'échelle de la maison. C'est sa fonction qui prime tout souci de

grandeur. Elle traduit une fonction d'ouverture. Seul un esprit logique peut objecter qu'elle sert aussi bien à fermer qu'à ouvrir. Dans le règne des valeurs, la clef ferme plus qu'elle n'ouvre. La poignée ouvre plus qu'elle ne ferme.[213]

See also Anne Balif's article in which she quotes Dr. F. Minkowska's comments on *De Van Gogh et Seurat aux dessins d'enfants,* illustrated catalogue of an exhibition held at the *Musèe Pedagogique* (Paris) 1949.

213"I recall that Françoise Minkowska organized an unusually moving exhibition of drawings by Polish and Jewish children who had suffered the cruelties of the German occupation during the last war. One child, who had been hidden in a closet every time there was an alert, continued to draw narrow, cold, closed houses long after those evil times were over. These are what Mme. Minkowska calls 'motionless' houses, houses that have become motionless in their rigidity. ' This rigidity and motionlessness are present in the *smoke* as well as in the window curtains. The surrounding trees are quite straight and give the impression of *standing* guard over the house.' . . .

"Often a simple detail suffices for Mme. Minkowska, a distinguished psychologist, to recognize the way the house functions. In one house, drawn by an eight-year-old child, she notes that there is 'a knob on the door; people go in the house, they live there.' It is not merely a constructed house, it is also a house that is 'lived-in.' Quite obviously the door-knob has a functional significance. This is the kinesthetic sign, so frequently forgotten in the drawings of 'tense' children.

"Naturally too, the door-knob could hardly be drawn in scale with the house, its function taking precedence over any question of size. For it expresses the function of opening, and only a logical mind could object that it is used to close as well as to open the door. In the domain of values, on the other hand, a key closes more often than it opens, whereas the door-knob opens more often than it closes." As translated by Maria Jolas in Gaston Bachelard's The Poetics of Space (Boston, Massachusetts: Beacon Press, 1994), p. 72-73. — Ed.

As Navidson pulls away to re-examine the obstacle, he hears a whimper coming from the other side. Taking two steps back, he throws his shoulder into the door. It bends but does not give way. He tries again and again, each hit straining the bolt and hinges, until the fourth hit, at last, tears the hinges free, pops whatever bolt held it in place, and sends the door cracking to the floor.

Reston keeps the chair mounted Arriflex trained on Navidson and while the focus is slightly soft, as the door breaks loose, the frame gracefully accepts Jed's ashen features as he faces what he has come to believe is his final moment.

This whole sequence amounts to a pretty ratty collection of cuts alternating between Jed's Hi 8 and an equally poor view from the 16mm camera and Navidson and Reston's Hi 8s. Nevertheless what matters most here is adequately captured: the alchemy of social contact as Jed's rasp of terror almost instantly transforms itself into laughter and sobs of relief. In a scattering of seconds, a thirty-three year old man from Vineland, New Jersey, who loves to drink Seattle coffee and listen to Lyle Lovett with his fiancée, learns his sentence has been remitted.

He will live.

As diligent as any close analysis of the Zapruder film, similar frame by frame examination carried out countless times by too many critics to name here[214] reveals how a fraction of a second later one bullet pierced his upper lip, blasted through the maxillary bone, dislodging even fragmenting the central teeth, (Reel 10; Frame 192) and then in the following frame (Reel 10; Frame 193) obliterated the back side of his head, chunks of occipital lobe and parietal bone spewn out in an instantly senseless pattern uselessly preserved in celluloid light (Reel 10; Frames 194, 195, 196, 197, 198, 199, 200, 201, 202, 203, 204, & 205). Ample information perhaps to track the trajectories of individual skull bits and blood droplets, determine destinations, even origins, but not nearly enough information to actually ever reassemble the shatter. Here then—

[214]Though still see Danton Blake's *Violent Verses: Cinema's Treatment of Death* (Indianapolis: Hackett, 1996).

the after

math

of meaning.

A life

time

finished between

the space of

two frames.

The dark line where the

eye persists in seeing

something that was never there

To[215] begin with

[215]Typo. "T" should read "t" with a period following "with."

Ken Burns has used this particular moment to illustrate why *The Navidson Record* is so beyond Hollywood: "Not only is it gritty and dirty and raw, but look how the zoom claws after the fleeting fact. Watch how the frame does not, cannot anticipate the action. Jed's in the lower left hand corner of the frame! Nothing's predetermined or foreseen. It's all painfully present which is why it's so painfully real."[216]

[216]As you probably guessed, not only has Ken Burns never made any such comment, he's also never heard of The Navidson Record let alone Zampanò.

Jed crumples, his moment of joy stolen by a pinkie worth of lead, leaving him dead on the floor, a black pool of blood spilling out of him.

In the next shots—mostly from the Hi 8s—we watch Navidson dragging Wax and Jed out of harm's way while trying at the same time to get Tom on the radio.

Reston returns fire with an HK .45.

"Since when did you bring a gun?" Navidson asks, crouching near the door.

"Are you kidding me? This place is *scary*."

Another shot explodes in the tiny room.

Reston wheels back to the edge of the doorway and squeezes off three more rounds. This time there is no return fire. He reloads. A few more seconds pass.

"I can't see a fucking thing," Reston whispers.

Which is true: neither one of their flashlights can effectively penetrate that far into the black.

Navidson grabs his backpack and pulls out his Nikon and the Metz strobe with its parabolic mirror.

Thanks to this powerful flash, the Hi 8 can now capture a shadow in the distance. The stills, however, are even more clear, revealing that the shadow is really the blur of a man,

standing
dead
centre

with
a
rifle
in
his
hand.

Then just as the strobe captures him lifting the weapon, presumably now aiming at the blinding flash, we hear a series of sharp cracks. Neither Navidson nor Reston have any idea where these sounds are coming from, though gratefully the stills reveal what is happening:

all those doors

behind

the
man

are
slamming
shut,

one

after

another

after

another,

which still does not prevent the figure from firing.

"Awwwwwwwwwwww shit!" Reston shouts.

But Navidson keeps his Nikon steady and focused, the motor chewing up a whole roll of film as the flash angrily slashes out at the prevailing darkness, ultimately capturing

this
dark
form

vanishing

behind
a
closing

door,

even though a hole
the size of a fist
punches through
the muntin,

the
round
powerful
enough to propel
the bullet into
the second
door,

though

not

powerful

enough

to do more

than

splinter

a

panel,

before this damage along with even the sound from the blast

disappears behind the roar of more slamming doors,

the last one finally hammering shut, leaving

the
room

saturated in silence.

Navidson sprints down the corridor to the first door but can find no way to lock it.

"He's alive" Reston whispers. "Navy, come here. Jed's breathing."

The camera captures Navidson's P.O.V. as he returns to the dying young man.

"It doesn't matter Rest. He's still dead."

Whereupon Navidson's eye quickly pans from the thoughtless splatter of grey matter and blood to more pressing things, the groan of the living calling him away from the sigh of the dead.

Despite his shoulder wound and loss of blood, Wax is still very much alive. As we can see, a fever—probably due to the onset of an infection—has marooned him in a delirium and although his rescuers are now at hand his eyes remain fixed on a horizon that is both empty and meaningless. Navidson's shot of Jed, though brief, is not nearly as short as this shot of Wax.

In the next segment, taken at least fifteen minutes later at a new location, we see Navidson elevating Wax's legs, cleaning the wound, and gently feeding him half a tablet of a painkiller, probably meperidine.[217]

[217] i.e. Demerol.

Reston, meanwhile, finishes converting their two-man tent into a makeshift stretcher. Having already arranged the tent poles in a way that will provide the most support, he now uses some pack straps to create two handles which will enable Navidson to carry the rear end more easily.

"What about Jed?" Reston asks, as he begins securing the front end of the stretcher to the back of his wheelchair.

"We'll leave his pack and mine behind."

"Some habits die hard, huh?"

"Or they don't die," replies Navidson.[218]

---

[218] A bit of dialogue which of course only makes sense when Navidson's history is taken into account.[219]

[219] `See page 332-333.`

A little later, Navidson gets Tom on the radio and tells him to meet them at the bottom of the stairs.

XI

La poëte au cachot, débraillé, maladif,
Roulant un manuscrit sous son pied convulsif,
Mesure d'un regard que la terreur enflamme
L'escalier de vertige où s'abîme son âme.

— Charles Baudelaire[220]

While Karen stayed home and Will Navidson headed for the front line, Tom spent two nights in no man's land. He even brought his bag and papers, though in the long run the effects of the weed would not exactly comfort him.

More than likely when Tom first stepped foot in that place, every instinct in his body screamed at him to immediately get out, race back to the living room, daylight, the happy median of his life. Unfortunately it was not an impulse he could obey as he was needed near the Spiral Staircase in order to maintain radio contact.

By his own admission, Tom is nothing like his brother. He has neither the fierce ambition nor the compulsion for risk taking. If both brothers paid the same price for their parents' narcissism, Will relied on aggression to anchor the world while Tom passively accepted whatever the world would give or take away. Consequently Tom won no awards, achieved no fame, held no job for more than a year or two, remained in no relationship for longer than a few months, could not settle down in a city for longer than a few years, and ultimately had no place or direction to call his own. He drifted, bending to daily pressures, never protesting when he was deprived of what he should have rightfully claimed as his own. And in this sad trip downstream, Tom dulled the pain with alcohol and a few joints a day—what he called his "friendly haze."

Ironically though, Tom is better liked than Will. Physically as well as emotionally, Tom has far fewer edges than his famous brother. He is soft, easy-going and exudes a kind of peacefulness typically reserved for Buddhist monks.

---

[220]`Something about the terror of the staircase.`[221]

[221]"The poet, sick, and with his chest half bare/ Tramples a manuscript in his dark stall,/ Gazing with terror at the yawning stair/ Down which his spirit finally must fall." As translated by Roy Campbell. — Ed.

Anne Kligman's essay on Tom is nearly poetic in its brevity. In only one and a half pages, she condenses fifty-three interviews with Tom's friends, all of whom speak warmly and generously of a man they admittedly did not know all that well but nonetheless valued and in some cases appeared to genuinely love. Will Navidson, on the other hand, is respected by thousands but "has never commanded the kind of gut-level affection felt for his twin brother."[222]

A great deal of exegesis exists on the unique relationship between these two brothers. Though not the first to make the comparison, Eta Ruccalla's treatment of Will & Tom as contemporary Esau & Jacob has become the academic standard. Ruccalla finds the biblical tale of twins wrestling over birthright and paternal blessing the ideal mirror in which to view Will & Tom, "who like Jacob and Esau sadly come to share the same conclusion— *yipparedu*.[223] "[224]

Incredible as it may seem, Ruccalla's nine hundred page book is not one page too long. As she says herself, "To adequately analyze the history of Esau and Jacob is to painstakingly exfoliate, layer by layer, the most delicate mille-feuille."[225]

Of course it is also an act that could in the end deprive the reader of all taste for the subject. Ruccalla accepts this risk, recognizing that an investment in such a complex, and without exception, time consuming

---

[222]Anne Kligman's "The Short List" in *Paris Review*, spring, 1995, p. 43-44.

[223]"[They] shall be separated." — Ed.

[224]Eta Ruccalla's exemplary *Not True, Man: Mi Ata Beni?* (Portland: Hineini Press, May 1995), p. 97. It probably should be noted that while Ruccalla equates Jacob with Navidson, "the clean-shaven intellectual aggressively claiming his birthright," and Esau with Tom, "unkempt and slightly lethargic, lumbering through life like some obtuse water buffalo," Nam Eurtton in her piece "All Accurate" in *Panegyric,* v. 18, July 30, 1994 draws the opposite conclusion: "Isn't Navidson a hunter like Esau, actively shooting with his camera? And doesn't Tom's calm, in fact a Zen-like calm, make him much more similar to Jacob?"

Note: Regardless of your take on who's Navidson and who's Tom, here's a quick summary for those unfamiliar with this biblical story about twins. Esau's a hairy, dim-witted hunter. Jacob's a smooth-skinned, cunning intellectual. Daddy Isaac dotes on Esau because the kid always brings him venison. When the time finally comes for the paternal blessing, Isaac promises to give it to Esau as soon as he brings him some meat. Well while Esau's off hunting, Jacob, with help from his mother, covers his hands with goat hair so they resemble Esau's and then approaches his blind father with a bowl full of stew. The ruse works and Isaac thinking the son before him is Esau blesses Jacob instead. When Esau returns, Isaac figures out what's happened but tells Esau he has no second blessing for him. Esau bawls like a baby and vows to kill Jacob. Jacob runs off and meets god. Years later the brothers meet up again, make up, but don't hang together for long. It's actually pretty sad. See Genesis, chapters 25-33.

[225]Eta Ruccalla's *Not True, Man: Mi Ata Beni?* p. 3.

array of ideas will in the end yield a taste far superior to anything experienced casually.

In the chapter entitled "*Va-yachol, Va-yesht, Va-yakom, Va-yelech, Va-yivaz*" Ruccalla reevaluates the meaning of birthright by treating its significance as nothing more than[226]

---

[226]What follows here is hopelessly incomplete. Denise Neiman who is now married and lives in Tel Aviv claims to have worked on this section when it was intact.

"The whole thing was really quite brilliant," she told me over the phone. "I helped him a little with the Hebrew but he really didn't need my assistance, except to write down what he said, this incredible analysis about parental blessings, sibling rivalry, birthright, and all the time quoting from memory entire passages from the most obscure books. He possessed a pretty uncanny ability to recite verbatim almost anything he'd read, and let me tell you, he'd read alot. Incredible character.

"It took us about two weeks to write everything he had to say about Esau and Jacob. Then I read it back to him. He made corrections, and we eventually got around to a second draft which I felt was pretty polished." She took a deep breath. I could hear a baby crying in the background.

"Then one day I arrived at his place and the pages had vanished. Also all his fingers were bandaged. He mumbled something about falling, scraping up his hands. At first, he ignored me when I asked him about our work, but when I persisted he muttered something like 'What difference does it make? They're dead anyway, right? Or not-alive, however you want to look at it.' I told him I didn't understand. So he just said it was 'too personal' 'an unrealized theme' 'poorly executed' 'a complete mess.'

"He did grunt something about there never having been a blessing to begin with, which I thought was pretty interesting. No birthright, all of it a misleading ploy, both brothers fools, and as for the comparison to the Navilson [sic] twins he suddenly claimed it was justifiable only if you could compare any pair of siblings to Israel and his brother.

"Zampanò was clearly upset, so I tried fixing him something to eat. He eventually came around and we read some books on meteors.

"I figured that was that, except when I went to the bathroom I found the pages. Or I should say I found what was left of them. He had torn them to shreds. They were in the wastebasket, some strewn on the floor, no doubt a fair share lost down the toilet.

"As I started to pick them up, I also discovered that most of the pieces were stained with blood. I never learned what seizure caused him to rip it all apart but for whatever reason I was overcome by my own impulse to save what was left, not for me really, but for him.

"I stuffed all the crumpled bits into my pockets and later transferred them to a manila envelope which I placed at the bottom of that chest. I guess I hoped he'd find it one day and realize his mistake."

Unfortunately Zampanò never did. Though for what it's worth I did. Bits of blood-stained paper, just like Denise Neiman said, all suggesting the

rzzzzzzzzzzzzzzzzzzzzzzzzzzz

but the Lord Yahweh—that too oft accused literalist —instructs Rebekah in the subtler ways of language by using irony:

> And the Lord said unto her, Two nations *are* in thy womb, and two manner of people shall be separated from thy bowels; and *the one* people shall be stronger than *the other* people; and the elder shall serve the younger.
>
> And when her days to be delivered were fulfilled, behold, <u>*there were* twins in her womb</u>.
>
> (Genesis 25: 23-24)
>
> [Chalmer's underline]

On one hand Yahweh announces a hierarchy of age and on the other hand claims the children are the same age.[227]

rzzzzzzzzzzzzzzzzzzzzzzzzzzz

Esau comes from the root *ash* meaning "to hurry" while *Ya'akov* comes from the root *akav* which means "to delay" or "to restrain."[228] (i.e. Esau entered the world first; Jacob last.) But *Esau* is also connected to *asah* meaning "to cover" while Jacob derives from *aqab* meaning "heel" (i.e. Esau was covered in hair; Jacob born clutching Esau's heel, restraining him.[229])

At least Freed Kashon convincingly objects to Ruccalla's comparison when he points out how really Holloway, not Tom, is the hairy one: "His beard, surly appearance, and even his profession as a hunter make Holloway the perfect Esau. The tension between Navidson and Holloway is also more on par with the tension between Jacob and his brother."[230]

---

same theme but somehow never quite fitting back together.

On more than a few occasions I even considered excluding all this. In the end though, I opted to transcribe the pieces which I figured had enough on them to have some meaning even if that meant not meaning much to me.

One thing's for sure: it did disturb me. There's just something so creepy about all the violence and blood. I mean over what? <u>This</u>? Arcane, obtuse and way over-the-top wanna-be scholarship? Is that what got to him? Or was it something else?

Maybe it really <u>was</u> too personal. Maybe he had a brother. A son. Maybe he had two sons. Who knows. But here it is. All that's left. Incoherent scrap.

Too bad so much of his life had to slip between the lines of even his own words.

---

[227]Tobias Chalmer's *J's Ironic Postures* (London University Press, 1954), p. 92. Chalmer, however, fails to take into account Genesis 25:25-26.

[228]Norman J. Cohen's *Self, Struggle & Change: Family Conflict Stories in Genesis and Their Healing Insights for Our Lives* (Woodstock, Vermont: Jewish Lights Publishing, 1995), p. 98.

[229]Robert Davidson's *Genesis 12-50* (Cambridge: Cambridge University Press, 1979), p. 122.

[230]Freed Kashon's *Esau* (Birmingham, Alabama: Maavar Yabbok Press, 1996), p. 159.

rzzzzzzzzzzzzzzzzzzzzzzzzzz

The degree of Esau and Jacob's struggle is emphasized by the word *vayitrozzu* which comes from the root *rzz* meaning "to tear apart, to shatter." The comparison falters, however, when one realizes Will and Tom never indulged in such a violent struggle.

rzzzzzzzzzzzzzzzzzzzzzzzzzz

During their childhood, Tom and Will were seldom apart. They gave each other support, encouragement, and the strength to persevere in the face of parental indifference.[231] Of course their intertwining adolescent years eventually unraveled as they reached adulthood, Will pursuing photography and fame in an attempt to fill the emotional void, Tom drifting into an unremarkable and for the most part internal existence.

rzzzzzzzzzzzzzzzzzzzzzzzzzz

Tom, however, never hid behind the adjunct meaning of a career. He never acquired the rhetoric of achievement. In fact his life never moved much beyond the here and now.

Nevertheless, in spite of a brutal struggle with alcoholism, Tom did manage to preserve his sense of humor, and in his twelve-step program, inspired many admirers who to this day speak highly of him.

Of the hard times that came his way, he experienced the greatest grief during those eight years when he was estranged from his brother or in his words "when the old rug was pulled out from under old Tom." It is hardly a coincidence that during this period he succumbed to chemical dependencies, went on unemployment, and prematurely ended a budding relationship with a young schoolteacher. *The Navidson Record* never explains what came between Tom and Will, though it implies Tom envied Navy's success and was increasingly dissatisfied with his own accomplishments.[232]

rzzzzzzzzzzzzzzzzzzzzzzzzzz

In his article "Brothers In Arms No More" published in *The Village Voice,* Carlos Brillant observes that Tom and Will's estrangement began with the birth of Chad: "While it's complete speculation on my part, I wonder if the large amount of energy required to raise a family pulled Will's attention away from his brother. Suddenly Tom discovered his brother—his only supporter and sympathizer—was devoting more and more time to his son. Tom may have felt abandoned."[233]

Annabelle Whitten echoes these sentiments when she points out how Tom occasionally referred to himself as "orphaned at the

[231]Terry Borowska interview.

[232]Personal interviews with Damion Searle, Annabelle Whitten and Isaac Hodge. February 5-23, 1995.

[233]Lost.

age of forty."[234] The year Tom (and Will for that matter) turned forty was the year Chad was born.

rzzzzzzzzzzzzzzzzzzzzzzzzzz

Ironically enough, Tom's presence in the house on Ash Tree Lane only served to help Will and Karen get along. As Whitten states: "Tom's desire to reacquire his lost parental figures transmuted Navidson into father and Karen into mother, thus offering one explanation why Tom frequently sought to reduce tension between both."[235]

Of course as Nam Eurtton argued, "Why? Because Tom's a nice guy."[236]

rzzzzzzzzzzzzzzzzzzzzzzzzzz

Esau's blessing was stolen with a mask. Tom wears no mask, Will wears a camera. But as Nietzsche wrote, "Every profound spirit needs a mask."[237]

rzzzzzzzzzzzzzzzzzzzzzzzzzz

And yet, despite the triumph of Jacob's ruse, he should have heeded this admonition: "Cursed be he that maketh the blind to wander out of the way" (Deuteronomy 27:18). And Jacob was indeed cursed, forced to wrestle for the rest of his life with this question of self-worth.[238]

Navidson was no different.[239]

rzzzzzzzzzzzzzzzzzzzzzzzzzz

≠

rzzzzzzzzzzzzzzzzzzzzzzzzzz

"To me, Tom seemed an incredibly peaceful man. Plain, decent but most of all peaceful."[240]

rzzzzzzzzzzzzzzzzzzzzzzzzzz

Here Ruccalla's analysis unexpectedly rereads the meaning of Esau's lost inheritance, sublimely uncovering an unspoken history, veiled in irony and blankness, yet still describing how one brother could not have succeeded without the other. Cain may not have been his brother's keeper but Esau certainly was[241]

rzzzzzzzzzzzzzzzzzzzzzzzzzz

" . . . a cunning hunter"
"of the field"

---

[234]Lost.

[235]Ibid., 112.

[236]Nam Eurtton's "All Accurate" p. 176.

[237]Of some note is the strange typo which appears in the Aaron Stern text: "But the blind Isaac repeated his question, 'Are you really my son Esau?' to which the chosen one replied 'Annie' meaning 'I am.' "

Aaron Stern's *All God's Children: Genesis* (New York: Hesed Press, 1964), p. 62.

[238]From the Robert Davidson commentary: "Jacob wrestled with an unidentified 'man' who turned out to be God, wrestled and lived to tell the tale. Gathered into the story are so many curious elements that we can only assume that here is a story which has taken many centuries to reach its present form, and which has assimilated material, some of it very primitive, which goes back long before the time of Jacob. It is like an old house which has had additions built on to it, and has been restored and renovated more than once during the passing years." p. 184.

[239]Lost.

[240]Ibid.

[241]Ibid.

"plain man, dwelling in tents."[242]

rzzzzzzzzzzzzzzzzzzzzzzzzzzz

This then is the meaning of Esau

rzzzzzzzzzzzzzzzzzzzzzzzzzzz

As Scholem writes: "Frank's ultimate vision of the future was based upon the still unrevealed laws of the Torah of *atzilut* which he promised his disciples would take effect once they had 'come to Esau,' that is, when the passage through the 'abyss' with its unmitigated destruction and negation was finally accomplished."[245]

rzzzzzzzzzzzzzzzzzzzzzzzzzzz

But as a great Hasidic maxim reminds us: "The Messiah will not come until the tears of Esau have ceased."[246]

rzzzzzzzzzzzzzzzzzzzzzzzzzzz

and so returns to Tom and Will Navidson, divided by experience, endowed with different talents and dispositions, yet still brothers and "naught without the other."

As Ruccalla states in her concluding chapter: "While the differences are there, like the serpents of the Caduceus, these two brothers have always been and always will be inextricably intertwined; and just like the Caduceus, their shared history creates a meaning and that meaning is health."[247]

rzzzzzzzzzzzzzzzzzzzzzzzzzzz

By the end of the first night, Tom has begun to feel the terrible strain of that place. At one point he even threatens to abandon his post. He does not. His devotion to his brother triumphs over his own fears. Remaining by the radio, "[Tom] gnaws on boredom like a dog gnawing on a bone while all the time eyeing fear like a mongoose."[248]

Fortunately for us, some trace of this struggle survives on his Hi 8 where Tom recorded an eclectic, sometimes funny, sometimes bizarre history of thoughts passing away in the atrocity of that darkness.

[242]See Genesis 27:24[243]

[243]`Wrong. See Genesis 27:29.`[244]

[244]Mr. Truant also appears to be in error. The correct reference is Genesis 25:27. — Ed.

[245]Gershom Scholem's *The Messianic Idea in Judaism* (New York: Schocken Books, 1971), p. 133. In taking the time to consider Frank's work, Scholem does not fail to also point out Frank's questionable character: "Jacob Frank (1726-91) will always be remembered as one of the most frightening phenomena in the whole Jewish history: a religious leader who, whether for purely self-interested motives or otherwise, was in all his actions a truly corrupt and degenerate individual." p. 126.

[246]`Lost.`

[247]Eta Ruccalla, p. 897.

But it also means [`Rest missing.`]

[248]Ibid., p. 249.

Tom's Story

[Transcript]

Day 1: 10:38

[Outside Tom's tent; breath frosting in the air]

Who am I kidding? A place like this has to be haunted. That's what happened to Holloway and his team—the ghosts got 'em. That's what will happen to Navy and me. The ghosts will get us. Except he's with Reston. He's not alone. I'm alone. That just figures. Ghosts always go first for the one who's alone. In fact, I bet they're here right now. Lurking.

Day 1: 12:06

[In order to maintain contact, it was necessary to set up the radio outside of the tent]

Radio (Navidson): Tom, we found another neon marker. Most of it's gone. Just a shred. We're laying down line and proceeding.

Tom into radio: Okay Navy. See any ghosts?

Radio (Navidson): Nothing. You a little spooked?

Tom: Lighting up a fat one.

Radio (Navidson): If it gets too much for you, go back. We'll be alright.

Tom: Fuck yourself Navy.

Radio (Navidson): What?

Tom: Doesn't he go around autographing lightbulbs?

Radio (Navidson): Who?

Tom: Watt.

Radio (Navidson): What?

Tom: Nevermind. Over. Out. Whatever.

[Changing channels]

Tom: Karen, this is Tom.

Radio (Karen): I would hope so. How's Navy?

Tom: He's fine. Found another marker.

Radio (Karen): And Billy?

Tom: Fine too.

Radio (Karen): How are you managing?

Tom: Me? I'm cold, I'm scared shitless, and I feel like I'm about to be eaten alive at any moment.

Otherwise, I'd say I'm fine.

Day 1: 15:46

[Inside tent]

Okay, Mr. Monster. I know you're there and you're planning to eat me and there's nothing I can do about that, but I should warn you I've lived for years on fast food, greasy fries, more than a few polyurethane shakes. I smoke a lot of weed too. Got a pair of lungs blacker than road tar. My point being, Mr. Monster, I don't taste so good.

Day 1: 18:38

[Outside tent]

This is ridiculous. I don't belong here. No one belongs here. Fuck you Navy for bringing me here. I'm a slob. I like lots of food. These things I consider accomplishments. I am not a hero. I am not an adventurer. I am Tom the slow, Tom the chunky, Tom the stoned, Tom about to be eaten by Mr. Monster. Where are you Mr. Monster, you stinking bastard? Sleeping on the job?

Day 1: 21:09

[Outside tent]

I'm sick. I'm freezing to death. I'm going.
[He throws up]
This is not fun. This isn't fair.
[Pause]
I think there's a game on tonight.

Day 1: 23:41

[Outside tent]

Tom: What kind of voices?

Radio (Karen): Daisy doesn't know. Chad said they sounded like a few people, but he couldn't understand what they were saying.

Tom: Book me a flight to the Bahamas.

Radio (Karen): Are you kidding, book a flight for the whole family. This is absurd.

Tom: Where's that bottle of bourbon when you need it? [Pause] Hey, I better sign off. Don't want a bunch of dead batteries on my hands.

Radio (Karen): Tell him I love him, Tom.

Tom: I already did.

Day 2: 00:11

[Outside tent; smoking a joint]

I call this "A Little Bedtime Story For Tom."

A long time ago, there was this captain and he was out sailing the high seas when one of his crew spotted a pirate ship on the horizon. Right before the battle began, the captain cried out, "Bring me my red shirt!" It was a long fight but in the end the Captain and his crew were victorious. The next day three pirate ships appeared. Once again the captain cried out, "Bring me my red shirt!" and once again the captain and his men defeated the pirates. That evening everyone was sitting around, resting, and taking care of their wounds, when an ensign asked the captain why he always put on his red shirt before battle. The captain calmly replied, "I wear the red shirt so that if I'm wounded, no one will see the blood. That way everyone will continue to fight on unafraid." All the men were moved by this great display of courage.

Well the next day, ten pirate ships were spotted. The men turned to their captain and waited for him to give his usual command. Calm as ever, the Captain cried out, "Bring me my brown pants."

Day 2: 10:57

[Inside tent]

Radio (Navidson): Tom? [Static] Tom, you read me?

Tom: (Going outside to the radio) What time is it? (Looking at his watch) 11 AM! Jesus, did I sleep well.

Radio (Navidson): Still no sign, except for [Static] markers [Static] over.

Tom: Say again Navy. You're fading.

Day 2: 12:03

[Outside tent]

This punker gets on a bus and takes a seat. His hair's all green, he's got brightly colored tattoos covering his arms and piercings all over his face. Feathers hang from each earlobe. Across the aisle sits an old man who proceeds to stare at him for the next fifteen miles. Eventually the punker gets pretty unnerved and blurts out:

"Hey man, didn't you do anything crazy when you were young?"

Without missing a beat, the old man replies:

"Yeah when I was in the Navy, I got drunk one night in Singapore and had sex with a Bird of Paradise. I was just wondering if you were my son."

Day 2: 13:27

[Outside tent]

I feel like I'm in a goddamned refrigerator, that's what. So what I want to know is, where's all the goddamn food? God knows I could use a drink.

Day 2: 14:11

[Inside tent]

A monk joins an abbey ready to dedicate his life to copying ancient books by hand. After the first day though, he reports to the head priest. He's concerned that all the monks have been copying from copies made from still more copies.

"If someone makes a mistake," he points out. "It would be impossible to detect. Even worse the error would continue to be made."

A bit startled, the priest decides that he better check their latest effort against the original which is kept in a vault beneath the abbey. A place only he has access to.

Well two days, then three days pass without the priest resurfacing. Finally the new monk decides to see if the old guy's alright. When he gets down there though, he discovers the priest hunched over both a newly copied book and the ancient original text. He is sobbing and by the look of things has been sobbing for a long time.

"Father?" the monk whispers.

"Oh Lord Jesus," the priest wails. "The word is 'celebrate.'"

Day 2: 15:29

[Outside tent; smoking a joint; coughing; coughing again]

Did you expect oration Mr. Monster? Or maybe just a little expectoration?

[Coughs and spits]

Navy taught me that one.

Day 2: 15:49

[Outside tent]

Tom: Hey, uh, Karen, I've got a bit of the munchies going on here. Do you think you could order me a Pizza.

Radio (Karen): What?!

Tom: When the delivery boy comes to the door just tell him to take it to the fat guy at the end of the hall. Two miles down on the left.

Radio (Karen): [Pause] Tom, maybe you should come back.

Tom: No maybe about it. Is there any lemon meringue left?

Day 2: 16:01

[Inside tent]

There once was a poor man who walked around without shoes. His feet were covered in calluses. One day a rich man felt sorry for the poor man and bought him a pair of Nikes. The poor man was extremely grateful and wore the shoes constantly. Well after a year or so, the shoes fell apart. So the poor man had to go back to running around barefoot, only now all his calluses were gone and his feet got all cut up and soon the cuts became infected and the man got sick and eventually, after they cut off his legs, he died.

I call that particular story "Love, Death & Nike." A real cheer me up story for Mr. Monster. That's right! All for you. Oh and something else: fuck you Mr. Monster.

Day 2: 16:42

[Outside tent]

The seven dwarves went to the Vatican and when the Pope answered the door, Dopey stepped forward: "Your Excellency," he said. "I wonder if you could tell me if there are any dwarf nuns in Rome?"

"No Dopey, there aren't," the Pope replied.

Behind Dopey, the six dwarves started to titter.

"Well, are there any dwarf nuns in Italy?" Dopey persisted.

"No, none in Italy," the Pope answered a little more sternly.

A few of the dwarves now began to laugh more openly.

"Well, are there any dwarf nuns in Europe?"

This time the Pope was much more firm.

"Dopey, there are no dwarf nuns in Europe."

By this point, all the dwarves were laughing aloud and rolling around on the ground.

"Pope," Dopey demanded. "Are there any dwarf nuns in the whole world?"

"No Dopey," the Pope snapped. "There are no dwarf nuns anywhere in the world."

Whereupon the six dwarves started jumping up and down chanting, "Dopey fucked a penguin! Dopey fucked a penguin!"

Day 2: 17:16

[Outside tent]

Here's a riddle: who makes a better house? A framer? A welder? A form builder? Give up? A grave maker! 'Cause his house lasts until judgment day! Okay that's a stupid joke. An old Sunday school joke, actually.

Day 2: 18:28

[Inside tent]

Now Mr. Monster looks like a frog, a little gribbbb-it frog when suddenly oooooh, little frog has become a . . . uh . . . piglet.

[By carefully positioning his halogen lamp, Tom is able to cast hand shadows on the back wall of his tent. He conjures up a whole menagerie of creatures.]

Yes a piggy wiggy creature just oinking along when . . . uh-oh an elephant! Look at that, the piglet has turned into an elephant. Jesus and look at the size of that elephant, it could . . . ooops, well I'll be, it's turned into a woodpecker, oh, now it's a snail, hmmm or how about a praying mantis, a sea urchin, a dove maybe, a tiger, or even this . . . a wascawwy wabbit, and then all of a sudden . . . oh no Mr. Monster, don't do that . . . but Mr. Monster does, turning into a dragon. Yup, that's right folks, a mean, no game playing, flesh eating dragon. And you say you want to eat me? Sure, sure . . . Except for one thing, just when Mr. Monster thinks he's gonna turn Tom the hefty into Tom the short rib, Tom unleashes his secret weapon.

[As the dragon on the tent wall turns toward Tom and opens its mouth, Tom gets ready to turn off the halogen with his foot.]

Ah ha, Mr. Monster! Bye-Bye baby!

[Click. Black.][249]

---

[249]Taking into account Chapter Six, only Tom's creatures, born out of the absence of light, shaped with his bare hands, seem able to exist in that place, though all of them are as mutable as letters, as permanent as fame, a strange little bestiary lamenting nothing, instructing no one, revealing the outline of lives really only visible to the imagination.

And tonight as I copied this scene down, I began to feel very bad. Maybe because Tom's antics only temporarily transform that place into something other than itself, though even that transformation is not without its own peculiar horror; for no matter how many creatures he flings on the wall of his tent, no matter how large or how real they may appear, they still all perish in a flood of darkness. No Noah's ark. Nothing safe. No way to survive. Which may have had something to do with my outburst at the Shop today.

I was in some weird kind of jittery daze. Everyone was there, Thumper, my boss, the usual visitants, along with some depraved biker who was in the middle of getting an octopus carved into his deltoid. He kept blathering on about the permanence of ink which I guess really got to me because I started howling, and loud too—real loud—spit sputtering off my lips, snot shooting out of my nose.

"Permanent?" I shouted. "Are you fucking loopy, man?"

Everyone was shocked. The biker could have taught me a thing or two about the impermanence or at least the destructibility of flesh—in this case my flesh—but he was also shocked. Thumper came to my rescue, quickly escorting me outside and ordering me to take the day off: "I don't know what you're getting messed up in Johnny but it's fucking you up bad." Then she touched my arm and I immediately wanted to tell her everything. Right then and there. I <u>needed</u> to tell her everything. Unfortunately, there was no question in my mind that she would think I was certifiable if I started rattling on about animals and Hand shadows, mutable as letters, as permanent as fame, a strange be— aww fuck, the hell with the rest. I choked down the words. Maybe I am certifiable. I came here instead. Which in an odd and round about way brings me to the Pekinese, the dog story I mentioned a ways back but didn't want to discuss. Well, I've changed my mind. The Pekinese belongs here. With Tom's Hand shadows.

It happened last December, a month before I'd ever heard of Zampanò, on the tail end of what had proved to be a rather dramatic November, All Souls Day commencing with Lude's acquisition of a great deal of Ecstasy, a portion of which he sold to me at bulk rate.

"Hoss, this is our pass to paradise," Lude had told me, and of course he was right.

Who cared if it was fall, it felt like spring. Lude led the way, zipping from club to bar, crashing Bel Air fêtes, desert raves and any after hours open house Malibu mansion madness we could find out about. Remarkably, no matter how zealously guarded these events were—velvet ropes as impossible to transcend as concertina wire without a hand grenade—the pills were our hand grenades. Velvet blown aside with the release of just one tab. They got us in everywhere. Even if noses were already bloody with coke, lungs black with Cannabis or throats dry with bourbon. X was still something else entirely, a spine shivering departure from the regular banquet, offering plenty of love-simulated bliss-bloated diversions. And so it happened that that month—Novem nine and all mine November—Lude disappeared into his own bower of bentdom, while I wandered off and promptly found my own.

Not too long afterwards, Lude made a great show of sharing with me his official and most prodigious tally for that month. Something which, for some reason, I felt compelled to write down.

LUDE'S LIST

11/1 — Monique. 36. On her washing machine. She came during the rinse cycle. He came during the spin cycle. Drier broken.
11/3 — Morning: Tonya. 23. Hispanic. Twice.
Evening: Nina. 34. Leather choker. Thigh high boots.
11/4 — Sparkle. 32. In a gazebo above the party.
11/5 — Kelly. 29. Dancer. In some host's sauna.
11/6 — Gina. 22. Said "please" before making the weirdest requests.
11/8 — Jennifer. 20. Naked at midnight on the diving platform at USC.
11/9 — Caroline. 21. Swedish. On her Nordic track.
Later, some guy dating Monique (11/1) caught up with Lude. Turned out he only wanted some E.
11/10 — Susan. 19. Surprised him with a golden shower. He surprised her with a raincoat.
11/11 — Evening: Brooke. 25.
Midnight: Marin. 22. Poured champagne all over the bed and told him to sleep in the wet spot.
11/12 — Noon: Alison 24-28????
Evening: ????? 23. Did it in wet suits. Neoprene smeared with Astroglide. She kept calling him O'Neil.
11/13 — Holly. 24-34???? Vietnamese.
11/14 — Dawn. 19. Leslie. 19. Melissa. 19. From San Diego. They went to The Pleasure Chest together and bought a vibrating dildo for the first time.

11/19 — Cindy. 20. Waitress. "I get bored when I can't use my mouth."
11/20 — Erin. 21. Jewish. In a changing stall at The Gap.
11/21 — Betsy. 36. After sex, wanted a pearl necklace. Lude told her he was broke.
11/22 — Michelle. 20. Catholic. Informed him that all anal sex requires is Vaseline and a pillow. She had both.
11/25 — Stephanie. 18. Black.
11/27 — Alicia. 23. On top of her stereo speakers. Big speakers. Big woofers. Apparently very intense. Plenty of woofing.
11/28 — Thanksgiving. Dana. 28. Navel pierced. Nipples pierced. Clitoral hood pierced. Danced for Lude on her bed, then masturbated until she came. An hour later, sex. He couldn't come for the second time. She called a girlfriend. They 69'd and then played Russian Blow Job—a variation on Russian Roulette. Lude was the gun, they took turns, thirty seconds at a time (he timed); Dana's girlfriend lost (or won; depending on your tastes).[YN]

[YN] 100 tabs of X;
12 AA batteries;
half a dozen tubes of KY jelly;
4 boxes of condoms (ribbed and ultra thin; all w/ Nonoxynol-9);
3 loads of laundry;
2 wet suits;
and 1 bottle of champagne.

Quite a month.

Note: This section also elicited several e-mails:

> Lude was such a jerk and a shitty fuck. You can tell him that.
>
> — Clarissa
> April 13, 1999
>
> Lude was so much fun. Give him my new number: 323 _____- _____. Do you know what happened to him? Did he leave LA?
>
> And what about Johnny? What was all that crazy stuff in the introduction about guns and blood? I mean if it wasn't his blood, whose was it?
>
> — Natalie
> May 30, 1999
>
> Hey kids, it takes two to tango.
>
> — Bethami
> June 6, 1999

— Ed.

Though clearly not as epic as Lude's, I too had my encounters that November.

Three.

Gabriella was the first. Her body was covered by a terrible birthmark which ran from her collar bone across one breast, over her belly and down both her legs. You could see traces of it on her wrists and ankles. But you couldn't feel it. It was textureless. Purely a visual shift. At first she turned out the lights but after a while it didn't matter. She was gorgeous and gentle and I was sad to see her go. She left for Milan the following morning.

Barbara came next. She'd been spending alot of time at the Playboy Mansion. Said she didn't want to be a centerfold but liked the atmosphere there. When we got on her bed, she tore my shirt open. I could hear the buttons skitter across her floor. By midnight she was saying she loved me. She said it so many times, I stopped counting. By morning, despite numerous hints, she couldn't remember my name.

And then I hooked up with Clara English. For just one night but at least it had started off well. Plenty of drinks, the buzz happy thrum of our newly ingested X-ray vision, lap dances for both of us at Crazy Girls, and then back to her place for a whole lot of fucking, only there wasn't that much fucking before there were a whole lot more hesitations and even tears set off by a series of interior tics I couldn't see. My fault for asking to see. I shouldn't have been curious. Should have left the blinders on. Probably could have made it through the tears. But I didn't. I pulled out the old Question Mark (QM) and Clara English didn't even think to answer with a joke. She didn't even conjure up some ridiculous story. She just took one sentence to tell me about the rape.

That stopped the tears. Replaced now by well practiced meanness. I guess I can't blame her. Who knew how I was going to respond to that kind of confession, though she didn't exactly give me the chance to respond. Suddenly she hated me for knowing, even though she'd been the one to tell me. Though I had asked. I had asked. When I called her the next day, she said she was finished fucking around with guys who belonged in a zoo. She hung up before I could ask her if she saw me with the cats or the birds.

I guess I still think about her. Fixed smile. Those removed gestures. That terrified gaze whenever it wasn't lost to something dull, angry and broken, an image that invariably returns me to the same question: can Clara English ever recover or is she permanently wounded, damned to stagger under years devoid of meaning & love until finally the day comes when she stumbles and is swept away?

I haven't seen her since. Maybe she's already been swept away. Now though when I look at Lude's list I don't see what I wrote down back then. I pencil in additional thoughts. They're made up of course. All of them born out of Clara's memory.

Strange.

Back then November had seemed like nothing but fun. The drugs robbing it of any consequence. The sex erasing all motives. Now, however, thorns have surfaced. Sharp thorns. My blissful bower's fallen, overrun by weeds and deadly vines. So is Lude's. Spiked with hurt. Heavy with poisonous bloom.

LUDE'S LIST REVISITED

Monique	—	Husband recently left her.
Tonya	—	An ex- and a restraining order.
Nina	—	Silence.
Sparkle	—	Rage.
Kelly	—	When she was only eleven, her mother had forced her to perform oral sex on her.
Gina	—	Hiding from a stalker. Her fourth.
Caroline	—	Grew up in a commune. Had her first abortion when she was twelve.
Susan	—	Said "Who cares" two dozen telling times. Hole in the roof of her mouth from too much cocaine.
Brooke	—	Numb.
Marin	—	Uncle would come over and finger her.
Alison	—	Father killed when she was eighteen.
Leslie	—	Raped by gym coach when she was fourteen.
Dawn	—	Date raped last year.
Melissa	—	Ex-boyfriend used to hit her. She finally had to get a nose job.
Erin	—	Walked in on her mother screwing her boyfriend.
Betsy	—	A reduction left jagged scars running around her nipples and through both breasts. Ashamed before. Ashamed now.
Michelle	—	Engaged.
Alicia	—	Lost her virginity to her father.
Dana	—	Prostitute.

And as for my list, my Gabriella and Barbara, to say nothing of Amber & Christina, Lucy, Kyrie, Tatiana, the Australian gal, Ashley, Hailey and I suppose others—yes there have been others—who's to say. Scratch in your own guesses. No doubt your postils will be happier than mine, though if they are, you clearly don't know what the fuck you're talking about. Then again, maybe I'm wrong. Maybe you have got it right. I mean if you've lasted this far, maybe you do know what I'm talking about. Maybe even better than me.

People frequently comment on the emptiness in one night stands, but emptiness here has always been just another word for darkness. Blind encounters writing sonnets no one can ever read. Desire and pain communicated in the vague language of sex.

None of which made sense to me until much later when I realized everything I thought I'd retained of my encounters added up to so very little, hardly enduring, just shadows of love outlining nothing at all.

Which I guess finally brings me to the story I've been meaning to tell all along, one that still haunts me today, about the wounded and where I still fear they finally end up.

The story of my Pekinese.

By the time December came around, I'd run out of E and energy. For at least a week, I was hung over with no sense of what lay ahead, plenty of untraceable guilt and a mounting sense of despair. One thing was sure though, I needed rest.

Lude didn't care. A 10 PM call and an hour later he was dragging me to the Opium Den, into the harangue of voices and amplified rhythms, all of it mixing, on ice, with a combination of cheap bourbon and better bourbon, though surprisingly little talk or smiles; feast to famine; or was it the other way around?, until towards the end of the night, Lude, noticing my isolation but secure in his own AM plans, pointed across the room —

"I think she's a porn star" he yelled at me, though the music turned his yell into a whisper. I glanced over at the bar and immediately knew who he was talking about. There were plenty of girls milling around, ordering cosmopolitans and beers, but she stood out, literally, from all the rest. Not height wise, mind you. She couldn't have been more than 5'5". A petite figure, platinum hair, way too much eyeliner, nails as long as kitchen knives and lips stuffed with god knows how many layers of tissue collected from the ass of some cadaver. But her tits, they were what told the whole story: enormous, and that's an understatement. We're talking DDDD, entire seas sacrificed to fill those saline sacks, Red Sea on the left, the Dead Sea on the right. Given the right storm, they could probably take out coastal townships with no guarantees for inland villages either.

"Go talk to her" Lude urged me.

"What do I say?" I yelled/whispered. Bewildered.

"Ask her how big they are."

I did go up and talk to her and we talked for a while though never about her tits which constantly drew my eyes into their orbit no matter how hard I tried to resist—moon and sea tied together. Turned out she liked to listen to country music or Pantera, depending on her mood, which at that moment was completely unreadable, her bloodshot eyes flashing out at me from beneath all that liner, sad? drunk? dry? or just permanently red? After a good twenty minutes of talk, talk interpolated with countless conversation ends, huge uncomfortable gaps where I always expected her to cough and excuse herself which for whatever reason she never did, waiting for me to continue our conversation—could anyone call that a conversation? "What kind of music do you like?" "Country." [Long pause] "Really, country? hmmm?" [Long pause] "And Pantera." "Country and Pantera? Really? hmmmm?"—on and on like that until finally, after twenty minutes, the club started closing down and bouncers began herding people towards the exits. And we walked out together. She'd come with a girlfriend who she waved goodbye to outside, ignoring me, though after the wave, suddenly returning to me, asking me to escort her to her truck.

As we waited for the light to change, she told me her name was Johnnie, though some people called her Sled, though her real name was Rachel. This is a simple telling of a much more difficult series of questions, the answers to which, in retrospect, were more than likely all made up. Then as the light changed and we crossed to the east side of Vine, we found on the corner a black bug-eyed Pekinese without tags. It was dirty, scared and obviously without owner, snot pouring out of its pug nose, every part of it trembling as it cowered on that grimy sidewalk, motionless, finally, after how many hours, how many days, at a loss where to go. All directions leading to the same place anyway. Its own end.

"Oh my poor baby" Johnnie cooed, those cold and indifferent spaces in our talk suddenly full of affection and concern, though the notes seemed wrong, not dissonant or flat or played at an improper tempo, just wrong, the melody somehow robbed of itself, meaning not another melody either, just something else. At least that's how it sounds now. Back then I hardly noticed.

Still, I was the one who picked up the frightened thing, cradling its small head in the crook of my arm, wiping some of the snot off on the sleeve of my buttonless corduroy coat, deciding as I did this—making a mess of myself—to take it home with me. To hell with the cramped space. I wasn't going to let this animal die. Not after it had snotted on my coat and sighed in my arms. But Johnnie wanted the poor thing.

"What kind of place do you have?" she asked. "A studio," I replied. "No way," she said, growing increasingly more emphatic and insistent, even if all this was spoken in that strange melody, not exactly atonal, I don't know, just wrong. So despite my instincts I relented. After all, she had a home in the valley, a yard, the kind of place dogs are meant to have. "A happy pet land," she called it, and really, considering the hole I inhabited, there was no argument. I handed Johnnie the poor Pekinese and together we placed it in the truck.

"Call me the momma to all strays," she said and gave me a weird smile.

Johnnie ended up giving me a lift back to my place. Oddly enough, when we pulled up in front of my building, I didn't ask her in. She seemed grateful. But I hadn't ducked the invitation on her behalf. Something seemed wrong, very wrong. Maybe it was the vacancy I had begun to taste, brought on by November—Novem ovum nine and all mine. Or maybe it was her, the salt full breasts, the deformed mouth, the fresco of makeup, her entire figure so perfect(ly grotesque) and all at the age of twenty-four, or so she had told me, though she probably was closer to six thousand years old.

Something about her frightened me. The knotted fingers. That blank stare, permanently fixed on some strange slate bare continent lost deep beneath ancient seas, her seas, dark, red, dead. Maybe not. Maybe it was that Pekinese pup, hungry and abandoned, suddenly rescued, suddenly with hope; a projection of myself? my own place in the way of straydom? Maybe. Who knows the real answer, but I'll tell you this, I sure as hell wasn't thinking then about Johnnie's tits or her lips or the positions, the absurd positions, we could have made together. I was thinking only about the Pekinese, its safety, its future. The Pekinese and me: a contract of concern. I rubbed the top of its ears, stroked its back and then I climbed out of the truck and said goodbye.

As Johnnie pulled away, she smiled again, that weird all wrong smile. For a moment, I watched her tail lights trail down the street, still feeling uncertain but a little relieved, until as I turned to go inside, I heard the thump. The one I remember even now, so clearly, an eerie and awful sound. Not too loud. Slightly hollow in fact, amounting to just that—a thump. Like that. Thump. I looked down the street. Her truck was gone but behind it, in its wake, something dark rolled into the light of a street lamp. Something Johnnie had thrown out her window as she passed the parked cars. I jogged down the block, feeling more than a little uneasy, until as I approached that clump of something on the side of the road, I discovered much to my dismay all my uneasiness confirmed.

To this day I don't know why she did it: my abandoned Pekinese, found on Vine, bug eyed, with snot pouring out of its pug nose, re-found not too far from my front door, that very same night, lying next to a car with half its head caved in, an eye broken and oozing vitreous jelly, tongue caught (and partially severed) in its snapped jaws. She

Day 2: 19:04

[Outside tent; smoking another joint]

Enough. I've had enough. Man, this is just not fair.

Day 2: 20:03

[Outside tent]

Radio (Navidson): [Static] We hear something [Noise] going [Noise] —ter it.

Tom: Good luck bro'.

[Silence]

Day 2: 21:54

[Outside tent]

Radio (Karen): I'm scared Tom.

Tom: What's the matter? Are the kids alright?

---

must have thrown it with tremendous force too. In truth an almost unimaginable amount of force.

I tried to picture those claw like hands grabbing this poor creature by the neck and hurling it out her window. Had she even looked at what she held? Had she even glanced back?

Later in the week Lude told me he'd been wrong. She wasn't a porn star. She was someone else. Someone he didn't know. Did I know? I don't know why I didn't tell him. Probably because his real question was had I fucked her, and what could have been further from the truth? Me, staring down at that lifeless dog, not a speck of blood mind you, just a shadow looking alot like some kind of a charcoal drawing, featureless & still, floating in a pool of yellow lamp light. I couldn't even say anything, not a cry, a shout or a word. I couldn't feel anything either, shock alone possessing me, depriving me of any emotional meaning, finally leaving me in a mad debate over what to do with the body: bury it, take it to the pound, throw the thing in a garbage can. I couldn't decide anything. So I just crouched there, my knees burning, finally filling with enough of that distant pain that tells all of us, especially in our sleep, that the time has come to move. But I wanted to give this dog a name first and lists skipped through my mind, endless lists, which in the end ran out. There was no name. I was too late. And so I just stood up and left. Call me an asshole (and fuck you too) my Pekinese friend was gone. Ant food now. At the very least—I reasoned—the body was close enough to the curb. The street sweeper would get it in the morning.

Another mother to all strays.

Radio (Karen): No, they're okay. I mean I think they're okay. Daisy, stays in her room. Chad prefers being outside. Who can argue with that. It's something else.

Tom: What?

Radio (Karen): All my Feng Shui— Oh Christ, this whole thing doesn't make any sense. How are Navy and Billy doing? Have they found anything? When are they coming back?

Tom: They heard someone crying. I didn't get it all 'cause the reception was so poor. From what I can gather, they're fine.

Radio (Karen): Well, I'm not. I don't like being here alone, Tom. In fact I'm fucking fed up with being alone. [She starts crying] I don't like being scared all the time. Wondering if he's going to be alright, then wondering if I'm going to be alright if he's not, knowing I won't be. I'm so tired of being frightened like this. I've had enough Tom. I really have. After this, I'm leaving. I'm taking the kids and I'm going. This wasn't necessary. It could have been avoided. We didn't need to go through all this.

Tom: [Gently] Karen, Karen, wait a minute. Just back up for a second. First, tell me what you were saying about your Feng Shui stuff.

Radio (Karen): [Pause] The objects. I put all these objects around the house. You remember, to improve the energy, or some such shit.

Tom: Sure. Crystals and bullfrogs, goldfish and dragons.

Radio (Karen): Tom, they're all gone.

Tom: What do you mean?

Radio (Karen): [Crying harder] They disappeared.

Tom: Hey Karen. Come on. Did you ask Daisy and Chad? Maybe they took them?

Radio (Karen): Tom, they're the ones who told me. They wanted to know why I'd gotten rid of it all.

Day 2: 22:19
[Outside tent]

Radio (Navidson): How's Karen [Static]?

Tom: Not so good, Navy. She's pretty scared. You should get back here.

Radio (Navidson): Wh[Static]? [Static] [Static] [Static] [Static]ear you.

Tom: Navy? Navy?

[Static]

Day 2: 23:07
[Outside tent]

This is such bullshit. You hear me Mr. Monster . . . BULLSHIT!

What kind of house do you got here anyway? No lights, no central heating, not even any plumbing! I've been shitting in a corner and pissing on a wall for two days.

[Getting louder]

Doesn't that irk you a little, Mr. Monster? I've been shitting in your corner. I've been pissing on your wall.

[Then softer]

Of course, the piss has dried up. And the crap just vanishes. You gobble it all up don't you? Turtles, shit, it doesn't matter to you.

[Loud again]

Indiscriminate bastard! Doesn't it make you sick? It makes me sick. Makes me wanna retch.

[Long series of echoes]

Day 3: 00:49

[Outside tent; reaching into his ziploc bag for the last joint]

And all through the house not a creature was stirring not even a mouse. Not even you Mr. Monster. Just Tom, poor ol' Tom, who was doing plenty of stirring around this house until finally he went stir crazy wishing there was a creature any creature—even a mouse.

Day 3: 00:54

[Outside tent]

Radio (Navidson): [Bang] We're in shit now . . . [Static]

Tom: Navy, what's happening? I can barely hear you.

Radio (Navidson): Jed's been shot, he's bleed [Static]

Tom: Shot? By who?!

Radio:

[Pop-Pop-Pop]

Reston: I can't see a fucking thing.

[crack . . . crack . . . crack
. . . cracK]

Reston: Awwwwwwwwwww shit!

[. . . cracK -BANG- craCK . . . craCK
crACK.cRACK.cRACK.CRACK.CRACK.]

Tom: What the hell was that?!

Radio (Navidson): Tom [Static] [Static]. I'm gonna [Static] [Static] [Static] [Static] Wax. We have to—shit— [Static . . .]

Tom: I'm losing you Navy.

Radio (Navidson): [Static]

Tom: Navy, do you read me? Over.

Day 3: 01:28
[Outside tent]

Radio (Navidson): [Static] it's probably gonna take us a good eight hours to make it back to the stairs. Tom, I need you to meet me at the bottom [Static] We need help. We can't carry them up ourselves. Also, you're [Static] [Static] [Static] [Static]eed to [Static] a doctor [Static]

[Static . . .]

Day 3: 07:39
[Outside tent]

[Tom looks down the Spiral Staircase, ignites a lightstick and drops it.]

Are you down there, Mr. Monster?

[Below, the lightstick flickers and dies. Tom recoils.]

No way. Not gonna happen, Navy. I've been alone in this shithole for almost three days and now you want me to go down <u>there</u> alone? No way.

[Tom descends a few steps, then quickly retreats]

No can do.

[Tom tries again, makes it down to the first flight]

There that's not so bad. Fuck you, Mr. Monster! Yeah, FUCK YOU!!!

[Then as Tom starts down the second flight, the stairs suddenly stretch and drop ten feet. Tom looks up and sees the circular shape of the stairwell bend into an ellipse before snapping back to a circle again.]

[Tom's breathing gets noticeably more rapid.]

You <u>are</u> here, aren't you Mr. Monster?

[A pause. And then out of nowhere comes that growl. More like a roar. Almost deafening. As if it originated right next to Tom.]

[Tom panics and sprints back up the stairs. The shot from the camcorder instantly becomes an incoherent blur of walls, banisters, and the dim light thrown by the halogen.]

[A minute later, Tom reaches the top.]

Day 3: 07:53

[Outside tent]

Tom: Karen . . .
Radio (Karen): Are you alright?
Tom: I'm coming in.

A Short Analysis of Tom's Story

How does one approach this quirky sequence? What does it reveal about Tom? What does it say about *The Navidson Record* ?

For one thing, Navidson edited this segment months later. No doubt, what would soon take place deeply influenced the way he treated the material. As Nietzsche wrote, "It is our future that lays down the law of our today."

All throughout Tom's Story, Navidson tenderly focuses on Tom's mirth and his ability to play in the halls of hell, those dolorous mansions of Isolation, Fear, and Doubt. He captures his brother trying to help Karen and him with their foundering relationship, and he reveals Tom's surprising strength in the face of such utter darkness and cold.

There is nothing hasty about Tom's Story. Navidson has clearly put an enormous amount of work into these few minutes. Despite obvious technological limitations, the cuts are clean and sound beautifully balanced with the rhythm and order of every shot only serving to intensify even the most ordinary moment.

This is a labor of love, a set piece sibling to Karen's short film on Navidson.

Perhaps because Tom's antics are so amusing and so completely permeated with warmth, we could easily miss how hand shadows, an abundance of bad jokes and the birth of "Mr. Monster" ultimately come to mean Sorrow.

If Sorrow is *deep regret over someone loved*, there is nothing but regret here, as if Navidson with his great eye had for the first time seen what over the years he never should have missed.

Or should have missed
all along.

XII

Not every cave search has a Terry Tarkington who knows the cave like his own home. Six months earlier three boys had vanished from the face of the earth near a similar Missouri cave they had been exploring. Despite weeklong search operations of incredible extent, they remain missing to this day.

— William R. Halliday, M.D.
American Caves and Caving

When Navidson and Reston finally reach the foot of the stairway,
Tom is not there.

It is almost noon on the third day of the rescue attempt. Reston's gloves are torn; his hands are blistered and bleeding. Wax's breathing is shallow and inconsistent. Jed's body weighs heavily on Navidson. All of which, bad as it is, is made even more unbearable when Navidson realizes his brother has not come down the stairs to meet them.

"We'll manage Navy," Reston says, trying to console his friend.
"I shouldn't be surprised," Navidson says gruffly. "This is Tom. This is what Tom does best. He lets you down."

Which is when the rope slaps down on the floor.

After making his unsuccessful bid to reach the bottom of the Spiral Staircase, Tom had retraced his way back to the living room where he began to construct a light gurney out of scrap wood. Karen helped out by going to town to purchase additional parts, including a pulley and extra rope.

Navidson was wrong. Tom may not have gone down those stairs
but the alternative he came up with was far better.

Within minutes Navidson and Reston are hoisting Wax up the 100ft shaft. As a safety precaution, Navidson ties the end of the rope around the bottom banister. Thus if something should happen, causing them to lose their hold on the rope, the stretcher would still stop short of hitting the bottom by several feet.

A few seconds later, a quarter clatters on the floor, indicating that Wax has safely reached the top and the stretcher can be re-lowered and readied for the next load.

Jed is next. Hand over hand, Navidson and Reston haul the body upwards, the excess rope gathering in coils around their feet. As Tom does not operate a Hi 8 during this sequence, we can only imagine what his reaction was as he struggled to lift the corpse over the railing. Nonetheless, a minute later, a second quarter clatters on the floor. Reston goes next.

Navidson double-checks to make sure the end of the rope is still securely tied to the last banister and then begins hoisting his friend up the shaft.

"You are one heavy bastard," Navidson grunts.

Reston lights a green flare and gives Navidson a big toothy grin: "Going up like the fourth of July."

At first everything seems to be proceeding smoothly. Slowly but surely, Navidson draws more and more slack rope down onto the floor, steadily lifting Reston up through the bore of those stairs. Then about half way up, something strange happens: the excess rope at Navidson's feet starts to vanish while the rope he holds begins to slip across his fingers and palms with enough speed to leave a burning gash. Navidson finally has to let go. Reston, however, does not fall. In fact, Reston's ascent only accelerates, marked by the burning green light he still holds in his hand.

But if Navidson is no longer holding onto the rope, what could possibly
be pulling Reston to the

top?

Then as the stairway starts getting darker and darker and as that faintly illuminated circle above—the proverbial light at the end of the tunnel—starts getting smaller and smaller, the answer becomes clear:

Navidson is
s
in
k
i
ng
.
.

O r   t h e   s t a i r w a y   i s
t
r
e
t
c
h
i
n

e x p a n d i n g,

dropping,

and as it slips,

d

r

a

g

g

i

n

g

Reston

up

with

it.

Then at a certain point, the depth of the stairway begins to exceed the length of the rope. By the time Reston reaches the top the rope has gone taut, but the stairway still continues to stretch. Realizing what is about to happen, Navidson makes a desperate grab for the only remaining thread connecting him to home, but he is too late. About ten feet above the last banister

the

r

o

p

e

sn-

-ps[...]

[...]Time has accelerated and I've done nothing to mark its passage. Yesterday seemed like the beginning of July but somehow today finds me mid-way through August. When I went to work everyone got incredibly uncomfortable and drifted away. My boss looked stunned. He finally asked me what I was doing and I just shrugged and told him I was about to start building needles.

"Johnny, are you alright?" he said in a very sincere and concerned tone, without even a note of sarcasm, which was probably the weirdest part.

"Sort of, I guess," I replied.

"I had to hire someone else, Johnny," he said very quietly, pointing over to a young blonde woman already in the process of cleaning out the back storeroom. "You've been gone for three weeks."

I heard myself mutter "I have?" even though I knew I'd been away, it just hadn't seemed that long, but of course it had been that long, I just hadn't been able to make it in or even call. I hadn't been able to make it anywhere for that matter and I pretty much kept the phone unplugged.

"I'm so sorry," I blurted, suddenly feeling very bad, because I'd let my boss down and I could see he was a pretty decent guy after all, though at the same time feeling also a little relieved about the news of my replacement. It made everything seem a little lighter.

My boss handed me my last check and then wrote down a number.

"Get yourself in a program man. You look like shit."

He didn't even ask if I was strung out, he just assumed it and somehow that struck me as funny, although I held off from laughing until I got outside. A hooker in silver slippers quickened by me.

Back in my studio, I discovered a message from Kyrie. I'd thrown her number out weeks ago. I'd thrown everyone's number out. Nothing could be done. I was gone from everyone. I erased her message and returned to the house.

In the back of my mind, I understood I would need money soon, but for some reason that didn't bother me. I still had my Visa card, and since selling my CD player, I'd further improved on that resulting silence by insulating my room with egg cartons and limiting the sun's glare with strips of tinfoil stapled to pieces of cardboard placed over my windows, all of which helps me feel a little safer.

Mostly the clock tells me the time, though I suspect the hands run intermittently fast and slow, so I'm never sure of the exact hour. It doesn't matter. I'm no longer tied to anyone's schedule.

As a precaution, I've also nailed a number of measuring tapes along the floor and crisscrossed a few of them up and down the walls. That way I can tell for sure if there are any shifts. So far the dimensions of my room remain true to the mark.

Sadly enough, despite all this—even six weeks without alcohol, drugs or sex—the attacks persist. Mostly now when I'm sleeping. I suddenly jerk awake, unable to breathe, bound in ribbons of darkness, drenched in sweat, my heart dying to top two hundred. I've no recollection what vision has made me so apoplectic, but it feels like the hinges must have finally failed, whatever was trying to get in, at last succeeding, instantly tearing into me, and though I'm still conscious, slashing my throat with those long fingers and ripping my ribs out one by one with its brutal jaws.

On a few occasions, these episodes have caused me to dry heave, my system wrenching up stomach acid in response to all the fear and confusion. Maybe I have an ulcer. Maybe I have a tumor. Right now the only thing that keeps me going is some misunderstood desire to finish The Navidson Record. It's almost as if I believe questions about the house will eventually return answers about myself, though if this is true, and it may very well not be, when the answers arrive the questions are already lost.

For example, on my way back from the Shop, something strange surfaced. I say "strange" because it doesn't seem connected to anything—nothing my boss said or Navidson did or anything else immediately on my mind. I was just driving towards my place and all of a sudden I realized I was wrong. I'd been to Texas though not the state. And what's more the memory came back to me with extraordinary vividness, as clean and crisp as a rare LA day, which usually happens in winter, when the wind's high and the haze loosens its hold on the hills so the line between earth and sky suddenly comes alive with the shape of leaves, thousands of them on a thousand branches, flung up against an opaline sky—

—An eccentric gay millionaire from Norway who owned a colonial house in a Cleveland suburb and a tea shop in Kent. Mr. Tex Geisa. A friend of a friend of a passing someone I knew having passed along an invitation: come to Tex's for an English tea, four sharp, on one unremarkable Saturday in April. I was almost eighteen.

The someone had flaked at the last minute but having nothing better to do I'd gone on alone, only to find there, seated in a wicker chair, listening to Tex, nibbling on her scone . . . Strange how clarity can come at such a time and place, so unexpectedly, so out of the blue, though who's firing the bolt?, a memory in this case, shot out of the August sun, Apollo invisible in all that light, unless you have a smoked glass which I didn't, having only those weird sea stories, Tex delivering one after another in his equally strange monotone, strangely reminiscent of something else, whirlpools, polar bears, storms and sinking ships, one sinking ship after another, in fact that was the conclusion to every single story he told, so that we, his strange audience, learned not to wonder about the end but paid more attention to the tale preceding the end, those distinguishing events before the inevitable rush of icy water, whirlpools, polar bears and good ol' ignis fatuus, perilous to chase, ideal to incarnate, especially when you're the one pursued by the inevitable ending, an ending Tex had at that moment been relating—deckwood on fire, the ship tilting, giving way to the pursuit of the sea, water extinguishing the flames in a burst of steam, an unnoticed hiss, especially in that sounding out of death, a grinding relentless roar, which like a growl in fact, overwhelms the pumps, fills up deck after deck with the Indian Ocean, leaving those on board with no place else to go, I remember, no I don't remember any of it anymore, I never heard the rest, I had gone off to piss, flushing the toilet, a roar there too, grinding, taking everything down in what could, yes it really could be described as a growl, but leaving Tex's sinking ship and that sound for the garden where who should I find but . . . my memory, except I realize now my ship, isn't Tex's ship, the one I'm seeing now, not remembering but something else, resembling icy meadows and scrambles for a raft and loss . . . though not the same, a completely different story after all, built upon story after story, so many, how many?, stories high, but building what? and why?—like for instance, why—the approaching "it" proving momentarily vague—did it have to leave Longyearbyen, Norway and head North in the dead of summer? Up there summer means day, a constant ebb of days flowing into more days, nothing but constant light washing over all that ice and water, creating strange ice blinks on the horizon, flashing out a code, a distress signal?—maybe; or some other prehistoric meaning?—maybe; or nothing at all?—also maybe; nothing's all; where monoliths of ice cloaked in the haar, suddenly rise up from the water, threatening to smash through the reinforced steel hull, until an instant before impact the monstrous ice vanishes and those who feared it become yet another victim to a looming mirage, caused by temperature changes frequent in summer, not to mention the chiding of the more experienced hands drunk on cold air and Bokkøl beer . . . Welcome to The Atrocity, a 412ft, 13,692 ton vessel carrying two cargoes within its holds, one secret, the other extremely flammable, like TNT, and though the sailors are pleasant enough and some married and with children and though the captain turns out to be a kind agent of art history, especially where the works of Turner, de Vos and Goya are concerned, that strange cargo could have cared less when towards the bow, in the first engine room, sparks from a blown fuse suddenly found a puddle of oil, an unhappy mistake any old mop could have corrected, should have, but it's too late, the sparks from the fuse having spun wildly out into space, tiny embers, falling, cooling, gone, except for one which has with just one flickering kiss transformed the greasy shadow into a living Hand of angry yellow, suddenly washing over and through that room, across the threshold, past the open door, who left it open? and out into the corridors, heat building, sucking in the air, eating it, until the air comes in a wind, whistling through the corridors like the voice of god—not my description but the captain's—and they all heard it even before the ugly black smoke confirmed the panic curdling in all of their guts: a fire loose and spreading with terrifying speed to other decks leaving the captain only one choice: order water on board, which he does, except he has misjudged the fire, no one could have imagined it would move that fast, so much fire and therefore more water needed, too much water, let loose now across the decks, an even mightier presence drowning out the flames and the hiss in its own terrifying roar, not the voice of god, but whose?, and when the captain hears that sound, he knows what will happen next, they all know what will happen next even before the thought, their thoughts, describe what their bodies have already begun to prepare for, the chthonic expectation which commanded the thought in the first place— . . . sos.sos.sos . . . SOS . . . SOS . . . SOS . . . sos.sos.sos . . . —way way too late, though who knew they'd all be so long, long gone by the time the spotter planes arrived, though they all fear it, a fear growing from that growl loose inside! their ship, tearing, slashing, hurling anyone aside who dares hesitate before it, bow before it, pray before it . . . breaking some, ripping apart others, burying all of them, and it's still only water, gutting the inside, destroying the pumps, impotent things impossibly set against transporting outside that which has always waited outside but now on gaining entrance, on finding itself inside, has started to make an outside of the whole—there is no more inside—and the decks tilt to the starboard side, all that awesome weight rocking the ship, driving the hull down towards deeper water, closing the gap between the deck rail and the surface of the sea, until the physics of tugawar intercede, keel and ballast fighting back against the violent heave, driving The

Atrocity away from this final starboard plunge, heading back up, that's right, righting itself, a recorrection promising balance, outside and inside again, except the rock and roll away from the sea proves a useless challenge . . . the monstrous war of ice water below also heads away from the starboard side of the ship and as the captain's deck for a brief instant levels out, the water within also levels out, everyone hopes for a pause, though really the water never stops, following through on the powerful surge away from the starboard side, heading now towards the port side—Sosososososos—past the center—Sosososososos—coalescing into a wave—Sosososososos . . . useless, obviously—and the captain knows it, hearing their death before the actual impact reverberates through the hull—and there never really had been time for lifeboats . . . —the wave beneath them pounding into the port side, this time powerful enough to drive the ship all the way over, burying the rail of the top deck beneath water, then the stack, letting all of the sea within, banishing the inside once and for all, and though some fathers still make for the lifeboats, it's all useless, a theatrical gesture born out of habit and habit is never hope, though some actually might have survived—habit does have its place—had there been a little more time, sinking time, except what was flammable below, now explodes, an angry Hand punching through bulkhead and hull, where a reciprocal nearly maternal Hand reaches up from the darkness below and drags all of them down, captain, deck hands, fathers, loners and of course sons—though no daughters—so many of them trapped inside it now, tons of dark steel, slicing down into the blackness, vanishing in under twelve minutes from the midnight sun, so much sun and glistening light, sparking signals to the horizon, reminiscent of a message written once upon a time, a long, long time ago, though now no more, lost, or am I wrong again? never written at all, let alone before . . . unlawful hopes? . . . retroactive crimes? . . . unknowable rapes? an attempt to conceal the Hand that never set a word upon this page, or any page, nor ever was for that matter, no Hand at all, though I still know the message, I think, in all those blinks of light upon the ice, inferring something from what is not there or ever was to begin with, otherwise who's left to catch the signs? crack the codes? even if the message is ultimately preternatural and unsympathetic . . . especially since right now in that place where The Atrocity sunk without a trace there is no sympathy, just blind blinks of light upon the ice, a mockery of meaning where meaning had never been needed before, there away from the towering glacial peaks near Nordaustlandet, a flat plate of water with only a few solitary bubbles and even those gone soon enough, long gone by the time the spotter plane flies over this mirror of sky, the only distinguishing mark, a hole of blinding light, rising and descending with the hours, though never disappearing, so that even as the plane's tiny shadow races across the whisper of old storms, or is it the approach of a new storm?, something foretold in those thousands and thousands of cat paws, reflection draws a second shadow on the vault of heaven . . . The Atrocity is lost along with its secret cargo and all aboard . . . shhhhhhhhhhhh . . . and who would ever know of the pocket of air in that second hold where one man hid, having sealed the doors, creating a momentary bit of inside, a place to live in, to breathe in, a man who survived the blast and the water and instead lived to feel another kind of death, a closing in of such impenetrable darkness, far blacker than any Haitian night or recounted murder, though he did find a flashlight, not much against the darkness he could hear outside and nothing against the cold rushing in as this great coffin plummeted downwards, pressure building though not enough to kill him before the ship hit a shelf of rock and rested, knocks in the hull like divers knocking with hammers—though, he knows, there are no divers only air bubbles and creaks lying about the future. He drops the flashlight, the bulb breaks, nothing to see anyway, losing air, losing his sense of his home, his daughters, his five blonde daughters and . . . and . . . he feels the shelf of rock give way and suddenly the ship rushes down again, no rock now, no earth, so black, and nothing to stop this final descent . . . except maybe the shelf of rock didn't give way, maybe the ship hasn't moved at all, maybe what he feels now is only his own fall as the air runs out and the cold closes in for good and I've lost sight of him, I'm not even sure if he really had five blonde daughters, I'm losing any sense of who he was, no name, no history, only the awful panic he felt, universal to us all, as he sunk inside that thing, down into the unyielding waters, until peace finally did follow panic, a sad and mournful peace but somewhat pleasant after all, even though he lay there alone, chest heaving, yes, understanding home, understanding hope, and losing all of it, all long long gone a long long time ago . . . shhhhhhhhhhhhh . . . when next to him, not a foot away, lay Something he never saw, no one saw, for he had come upon the secret when he escaped into this cargo hold but never knew it, though it might have saved him, saved us all for that matter, but it's gone, letters of salt read by the sea . . . and I too have lost <u>The Atrocity</u> . . . and the sun pours in on me, surfaces once transparent now reflect, like a sea of a different sort, and I forget my ship, or I lose sight of it, or is that the same thing? to a time long before I saw in my own holds two cargoes, one a secret, the other extremely flammable, the flammable put there by invisible hands for invisible reasons . . . when I remembered her in the garden where she wandered away from all those ugly ends in the Indian Ocean, far from my arctic one, and found flowers and a fountain, perfume and a breeze, a warm breeze . . . Not Texas but Tex's, Tex's tea, where I met Ashley—Ashley, Ashley, Ashley . . . the sun could make you sneeze—only back then her hair was dyed neon green, matching her Doc boots, a match made in heaven, both of us together, talking and talking, at first timidly and then responding more avidly to the obvious attraction both of us could feel until she gave me her number and I wrote down my number, my first name and my last name, which was how, years later, she finally found the right number to call and she kissed me and I kissed her and we kissed for a while more until she invited me home and I said no. I had fallen in love with her, flash of gold and sunlight and Rome, and I wanted to wait, in three days call her, court her, marry her, impregnate her and fill our house with five blonde daughters, until . . . oh no, where have I gone now? horror but not horror but another kind of -orro-? or both, or I'm not sure, suddenly flooding through me, what back then had only been weeks away, in fact right around the corner from there, a legacy of leaving, fast approaching: excrement—let go . . . —urine—let go . . . —and burst conjunctiva—letting go streaks of red tears. All I could hold but in the end not save. Of course I lost everything. I lost her number, I lost her, and then in a fugue of erasure, I lost the memory of her, so that by the time she called she was gone along with the kisses and the promise and all that hope. Even after our strange reunion in the hammock suspended over strewn & decomposing leaves from a banana tree, later followed by an even stranger goodbye, she was still long, long gone. I know I am too late. I'm lost inside and no longer convinced there's a way out. Bye-bye Ashley and goodbye to the one you knew before I found him and had to let him go.

(Considering this was a 7/16" dynamic kernmantle cord it is not difficult to imagine the sort of force acting upon it.)[250]

[250]Breaks at 6,000 to 7,000 pounds. — Ed.

Above him, Navidson hears a faint cry and then nothing. Not even
the tiniest hole of light.

In The Reston Interview, we learn from Billy how the pulley at the top was torn from the banister. Luckily, Tom managed to grab him as well as the rope before "the whole kit and caboodle" plummeted back down the shaft. "It took us a few minutes to get our bearings," Reston tells the camera. "We still weren't sure what happened."

For the final shot of this section, Navidson loads his Arriflex with a 100ft of high-speed tungsten, uses a five minute ultra high intensity lightstick to illuminate the area, and rolls his Hi 8 to record sound.

"For almost an hour," he begins. "I waited, rested, kept hoping something would change. It didn't. Eventually I started going over my stuff, trying to figure out what exactly to do next. Then all of a sudden I heard something clatter behind me. I turned around and there lying on the floor, just off to the side here, was the third quarter. [He holds up the coin] If Tom dropped it say a few minutes after Reston reached the top, then it's been falling for at least fifty minutes. I'm too muddled to do the math but it doesn't take a genius to realize I'm an impossible distance down.[251]

[251]If $D_{ft}=16t^2$ where time is calculated in seconds, the quarter would have to have fallen 27,273 miles exceeding even the earth's circumference at the equator by 2,371 miles. Calculating at 32 ft/sec^2 the number climbs even higher to 54,545 miles. An "impossible distance" indeed.[252]

[252]This formula isn't entirely accurate. A more precise calculation can be made by [fill in later][253]

[253]Mr. Truant never completed this note. — Ed.

"I don't know how I'm going to get back. The radio's dead. If I can find my pack and Jed's, I'll have water and food for at least three days with maybe four days worth of batteries. But what will that do? *Non gratum anus rodentum.*[254] Hell."

[254]"Not worth a rat's ass." — Ed.

The film runs out here,

leaving nothing else behind but an unremarkable

white

screen

XIII

~~The Minotaur~~[123]

Alarga en la pradera una pausada
Sombra, pero ya el hecho de nombrarlo
Y de conjecturar su circunstancia
Lo hace ficción del arte y no criatura
Viviente de las que andan por la tierra.

— Jorge Luis Borges[255]

THE WAIT

1.

Teppet C. Brookes had seen plenty of children's drawings in her life. Having taught all grades from kindergarten through sixth grade, she was familiar with a vast array of stick figures, objects, and plots. This was not the first time she had seen a wolf, a tiger, or a dragon. The problem was that these wolves did not just stalk quietly through cadmium woods; their teeth drew madder and rose from each other's throats. The tigers did not just sleep on clover; they clawed Sunday red and indigo from celadon hills. And the dragon with its terrible emerald tail and ruby glare did not merely threaten; it incinerated everything around it with a happy blossom of heliotrope and gamboge.

And yet even these violent fantasies were nothing compared to what lay in wait at the centre of the drawing.

The week before Navidson set out on the rescue attempt, Brookes had asked her third grade class to draw a picture of their house. The one Chad handed in had no chimney, windows, or even a door. In fact, it was nothing more than a black square filling ninety percent of the page. Furthermore, several layers of black crayon and pencil had been applied so that not even a speck of the paper beneath could show through. In the thin margins, Chad had added the marauding creatures.

It was an extremely odd image and stuck with Brookes. She knew Chad had recently moved to Virginia and had already been involved in several scuffles in the school playground. Though she was hardly satisfied with her conclusion, she decided the picture reflected the stress caused by the move and the new surroundings. But she also made a note to keep an eye on him as the year progressed.

She would not have to wait that long.

---

[255] ". . . a slow shadow spreads across the prairie,/ but still, the act of naming it, of guessing/ what is its nature and its circumstances/ creates a fiction, not a living creature,/not one of those who wander on the earth." As translated by Alastair Reid. — Ed.

Brookes usually went straight home after school, but that Friday, quite by chance, she wandered into the kindergarten classroom. A number of drawings hung on the wall. One in particular caught her eye. The same wolves, the same tigers, the same dragon, and at the centre, though this time only two-thirds the size of the page, an impenetrable square, composed of several layers of black and cobalt blue crayon, with not even the slightest speck of white showing through.

That picture had been drawn by Daisy.

Though Brookes lacked a formal degree in psychology, two decades of teaching, nearly half of it at Sawatch Elementary, had exposed her to enough child abuse to last a lifetime. She was familiar with the signs and not just the obvious ones like malnutrition, abrasion, or unnatural shyness. She had learned to read behavior patterns, eating habits, and even drawings. That said, she still had never encountered such a striking similarity between a five year old girl and her eight year old brother. The collective artistry was appalling. "Now heck, I've survived two bad marriages and seen my share of evil along the way. I don't get fazed by much, but let me tell you just seeing those pictures gave me the willies."[256]

Teppet C. Brookes could have contacted the Department of Children's Services. She could have even called the Navidsons and requested a consultation. That Monday, however, when neither Chad nor Daisy showed up at school, she decided to pay the Navidsons a little visit herself. Willies or not, curiosity got the best of her: "Truth be told, I just had to take a gander at the place that had inspired those drawings."[257]

2.

During her lunch break, Brookes climbed into her Ford Bronco and made the fifteen minute drive to Ash Tree Lane. "I thought the house was nice and quaint on the outside. I was expecting something else I guess. To tell you the truth, I almost drove off but since I'd made the drive, I decided I should at least introduce myself. I had a good excuse. I wanted to know why both kids were not in school. And heck, if it was Chicken Pox, I've had mine, so that was no matter."[259]

Brookes recalls looking at her watch as she walked toward the front door: "It was close to one. I knocked or rang the door bell, I don't remember. Then I heard the screams. Wails. I've heard that kind of grief before. I started banging real hard. A second later an Afro-American man in a wheelchair opened the door. He seemed surprised to see me, like he was expecting someone else. I could tell he was in pretty bad shape, his hands all ripped up and bleeding. I didn't know what to say so I told him I was from the school. He just nodded and told me he was waiting for the ambulance and would I mind giving him a hand."

Brookes was hardly prepared for the slaughterhouse she was about to enter: a woman sobbing in the living room, a big man holding her, two bodies in the kitchen surrounded by blood, and on the staircase Chad sitting next to his little sister Daisy who kept quietly singing to no one in particular words no one else could understand—"ba. dah. ba-ba."

---

[256]Teppet C. Brookes' *The Places I've Seen* as told to Emily Lucy Gates (San Francisco: Russian Hill Press, 1996), p. 37-69.

[257]Ibid., p. 38.[258]

[258]`Also refer back to footnote 212 dealing with Françoise Minkowska.`

[259]Teppet C. Brookes' *The Places I've Seen*, p. 142.

Brookes lasted five minutes, crossing herself too many times to help anyone. Fortunately the sheriff, the paramedics, and an ambulance soon arrived. "I had entered a war zone and I have to be honest, it overwhelmed me. I could tell my blood pressure was rising. You know sometimes you go into something thinking you're going to make all the difference. You're going to save the situation. Make it right. But that was too much for me. It was real humbling. [Starts to cry] I never saw the kids after that. Though I still have their drawings."[260]

3.

In some respects, the distillate of crayon and colour traced out by the hands of two children captures the awfulness at the heart of that house better than anything caught on film or tape, those shallow lines and imperfect shapes narrating the light seeping away from their lives. Brookes, however, is not the only one to have seen those drawings. Chad and Daisy's room is full of them, the monstrous black square getting progressively larger and darker, until in Chad's case, not even the barest margin survives.

Karen knows her kids are in trouble. A clip of Hi 8 catches her telling them that as soon as their father returns she will take them all to "grandma's."

Unfortunately, when Navidson, Tom and Reston disappear down that hallway early Saturday morning, Karen is put in an impossible situation: torn between monitoring the radios and looking after Chad and Daisy. In the end, separation from Navidson proves more painful. Karen keeps by the radios.

For a while Daisy and Chad try to coax their mother to even briefly abandon her post. When that fails, they hang around the living room. Karen's inability to concentrate on them, however, soon drives both children away. A few times, Karen asks them to at least keep together. Daisy, however, insists on hiding in her room where she can play endlessly with her prized Spanish doll and the doll house Tom finally finished for her, while Chad prefers to escape outside, disappearing into the summoning woods, sometimes with Hillary, often now without, always well beyond the range of any camera, his adventures and anger passing away unobserved.

That Saturday night Chad and Daisy have to put themselves to sleep. Then around ten o'clock, we watch as both children come racing down into the living room, claiming to have heard voices. Karen, however, has heard nothing more than the ever present hiss of the radios, occasionally interrupted by Tom calling in from the Great Hall. Even after she checks out their bedroom, she is unable to detect any unusual sounds. At least Chad and Daisy's obvious fear momentarily snaps Karen out of her obsession. She leaves the radios and spends an hour tucking her children into bed.

Dr. Lon Lew believes the house enabled Karen to slowly break down her reliance on Navidson, allowing her a greater and more permanent distance: "Her children's fear coupled with their need for her further separated Karen from Navidson. Sadly, it's not the healthiest way to proceed. She merely replaced one dependency for another without confronting what lay at the heart of both."[261]

Then on Sunday evening, both children ask her what happened to all her Feng Shui objects. We watch as they lead her from room to room,

---

[260]"The Navidson Legacy" *Winter's Grave,* PBS, September 8, 1996.

[261]Dr. Lon Lew's "Adding In to Dependent" *Psychology Today,* v. 27, March/April 1994, p. 32.

pointing out the absent tiger, the absent marble horses, and even the absent vase. Karen is shocked. In the kitchen, she has to sit down, on the verge of a panic attack. Her breathing has quickened, her face is covered in sweat. Fortunately, the episode only lasts a couple of minutes.

Along with several other critics, Gail Kalt dwells on Karen's choice of words during her conversation with Tom on the radio when she refers to Feng Shui as "some such shit."

> Karen has begun to deconstruct her various mechanisms of denial. She does not continue to insist on the ineffectual science of Feng Shui. She recognizes that the key to her misery lies in the still unexplored fissure between herself and Navidson. Without knowing it she has already begun her slow turn to face the meaning, or at least one meaning, of the darkness dwelling in the depths of her house.[262]

Certainly Karen's step away from denial is made more evident when right after her talk with Tom she gathers up any remaining items having to do with Feng Shui and throws them in a box. David N. Braer in his thesis "House Cleaning" notes how Karen not only adds to this collection the books already mentioned in Chapter V but also includes the Bible, several New Age manuals, her tarot cards, and strangest of all a small hand mirror.[263] Then after depositing the box in the garage, she looks in on her children one more time, comforting them with an open invitation to sleep in the living room with her if they like. They do not join her but the grateful tone of their murmurs seems to suggest they will now sleep better.

Helen Agallway asserts that by "Monday, October 8th, Karen has made up her mind to depart. When Tom reappears in the living room and informs her that Navidson is only hours away from getting back, she keeps the children home from school because she has every intention of leaving for New York that day."[264]

Upon returning from town with bundles of rope, the pulleys, and several trolley wheels, Karen begins packing and orders the children to try to do the same. She is in fact in the middle of frantically removing several winter coats and shoes from the foyer closet when Tom races out of the hallway, pushing the gurney in front of him, tears gushing from his eyes.

4.

When Karen sees Wax her hand flies to her mouth, though it hardly prevents the cry.[265] Reston emerges from the hallway next, the growl

---

[262]Gail Kalt's "The Loss of Faith—(Thank God!)" *Grand Street,* v. 54, fall 1195, p. 118.

[263]David N. Braer's "House Cleaning" Diss. University of Tennessee, 1996, p. 104.

[264]Helen Agallway's "The Process of Leaving" Diss. Indiana University, 1995, p. 241.

[265]Many have complained that The Holloway Tape as well as the two untitled sequences frequently identified as "The Wait" and "The Evacuation" are incomprehensible. Poor resolution, focus, and sound (with the exception of the interviews shot afterward in 16mm) further exacerbate the difficulties posed by so many jarring cuts and a general chronological jumble. That said, it is crucial to recognize how poor quality and general incoherence is not a reflection of the creator's state of mind. Quite the contrary, Navidson brilliantly used these stylistic discrepancies to further drive home the overwhelming horror and dislocation experienced by his family during "The Evacuation." For other books devoted specifically to reconstructing

growing louder behind him, threatening to follow him into the living room. Frantically, he slams the door and bolts all four locks, which no doubt thanks to the door's acoustic rating actually seems to keep that terrible sound at bay.

Karen, however, starts shouting: "What are you doing? Billy? What about Navy? Where's Navy?"

Even though he is still crying, Tom tries to pull her away from the door, "We lost him."

"He's dead?" Karen's voice cracks.

"I don't think so," Tom shakes his head. "But he's still down there. Way down."

"Well then go in and get him! Go in and get your brother!" Then starting to shriek, "You can't just leave him there."

But Tom remains motionless, and when Karen finally looks him in the face and beholds the measure of his fear and grief, she crumples into a fit of sobs. Reston goes to the foyer and calls an ambulance.

Meanwhile, Wax, who has been temporarily left alone in the kitchen, quietly groans on the stretcher. Next to him lies Jed's body. Unfortunately Tom did not realize how much blood had soaked into Jed's clothes. Blind with his own sorrow, he unknowingly covered the linoleum with a smear of red when he set the corpse down. He even stepped in the blood and tracked footprints across the carpet as he lurched back to the living room to console Karen.

Perhaps inevitably, all the commotion draws the children out of their room.

Chad catches sight of the body first. There is something particularly disquieting about watching the way he and Daisy walk slowly toward Jed and then over to Wax's side. They both seem so removed. Almost in a daze.

"Where's our daddy?" Chad finally asks him. But Wax is delirious.

"What. I need what-er."

Together Chad and Daisy fill a glass from the sink. Wax, however, is far too weak to sit up let alone drink. They end up dribbling small drops of water on his cracked lips.

A few seconds later there is a loud banging on the front door. Reston wheels over and opens it. He expects to see the paramedics but finds instead a woman in her late 40s with almost perfectly grey hair. Chad and Daisy retreat to the staircase. They too step in the blood, their feet leaving small red imprints on the floor. Chad's teacher fails to utter even one word or offer any sort of assistance. Tom continues to sit with Karen, until eventually her muted cries join the wail of sirens rapidly approaching their house on Ash Tree Lane.

5.

While *The Navidson Record* clearly states that Wax Hook survived, it does not dwell on any of the details following his departure. Numerous articles published after the film's release, however, reveal that he was almost immediately rushed by helicopter to a hospital in Washington, D.C. where he was placed in an I.C.U. There doctors discovered that fragments from the coracoid process and scapula spine had turned his trapezius, delta

---

the narrative see *The Navidson Record: The Novelization* (Los Angeles: Goal Gothum Publication, 1994); Thorton J. Cannon Jr.'s *The Navidson Record: Action and Chronologies* (Portland: Penny Brook Press, 1996); and Esther Hartline's *Thru Lines* (New York: Dutton, 1995).

and infraspinous muscles to hamburger. Miraculously though, the bullet and bone shrapnel had only grazed the subclavian artery. Wax eventually recovered and after a long period of rehabilitation returned to a life of outdoor activities, even though it is doubtful he will ever climb Everest now let alone attempt to solo the North Face. By his own admission, Wax also keeps clear of caves not to mention his own closet.[266]

Even as Wax was loaded into the ambulance, police began an investigation into Jed Leeder's death. Reston provided them with a copy of the tape from his Hi 8 showing Holloway shooting Wax and Jed. To the police, the murder appeared to have taken place in nothing more than a dark hallway. As APBs went out, patrolmen began a statewide search which would ultimately last several weeks. That afternoon, Karen also insisted on introducing the authorities to that all consuming ash-walled maze. Perhaps she thought they would attempt to locate Navidson. The results were hardly satisfying.

In The Reston Interview, Billy shakes his head and even laughs softly:

> It wasn't a bad idea. Tom and I'd had enough too. Karen just expected too much, especially from a town that has one sheriff and a handful of deputies. When the sheriff came over, Karen immediately dragged him over to the hallway, handed him a flashlight and the end of a spool of Monel fishing line. He looked at her like she was nuts, but then I think he got a little spooked too. At that point in time, no one was about to go in there with him. Karen because of her claustrophobia. Tom, well he was already going to the bottom of a bottle. And me, I was trying to fix my wheelchair. It was all bent from when I came up on the pulley. Even so though, I mean even if my chair had been fine, going back would have been hard. Anyway Sheriff Oxy, Axard, Axnard, I think that was his name, Sheriff Axnard went in there by himself. He walked ten feet in and then walked straight back out, thanked us and left. He never said a word about where he'd been and he never came back. He spent a good amount of time looking for Holloway everywhere else but never in the house.

Right after the release of *The Navidson Record*, Sheriff Josiah Axnard was accosted by numerous reporters. One clip captures the Sheriff in the process of climbing into his squad car: "For once and for all, that house was completely searched and Holloway Roberts was not in it." Six months later the Sheriff consented to an interview on National Public Radio (April 18, 1994) where he told a slightly different story. He confessed to

---

[266]See *U.S. News & World Report,* v. 121, December 30, 1996, p. 84; *Premiere,* v. 6, May 1993, p. 68-70; *Life,* v. 17, July 1994, p. 26-32; *Climbing,* November 1, 1995, p. 44; *Details,* December 1995, p. 118.

walking down "an unfamiliar hallway." "It's not there no more," he continued. "I checked. Nothing unusual there now but . . . but back then there was . . . there was a corridor on the south wall. Cold, no lights and goin' on into nowhere. It creeped me like I never been creeped before, like I was standing in a gigantic grave and I remember then, clearly, like it was yesterday, thinking to myself 'If Holloway's in here I don't need to worry. He's gone. He's long gone.' "[267]

6. That night Karen stays in the living room, crying off and on, leaving the hallway door open, even though, as she explains to Reston, standing a foot too close will cause her to experience heart palpitations and tremors. Reston, however, badly in need of some shut eye almost immediately falls into a deep sleep on the couch.

There is one particularly horrible moment when the phone rings and Karen answers on speaker. It is Jed Leeder's fiancée calling from Seattle, still unaware of what has happened. At first Karen tries to keep the news to herself but when the woman begins to detect the lie, Karen tells her the truth. A panicked shout cracks over the speaker phone and then decays into terrified cries. Abruptly the line goes dead. Karen waits for the woman to call back but the phone does not ring again.

Of course during all this, the children are once again abandoned, left to look after each other, with no one around to help translate the horror of the afternoon. They hide in their room, rarely saying a thing. Not even Tom makes an appearance to even temporarily contest their fears with the soothing lyric of a bedtime story about otters, eagles, and the occasional tiger.

When Tom had returned from the grave, he was convinced he had lost his brother. Both he and Reston had heard the great Spiral Staircase yawn beneath them, and Reston's Hi 8 had even caught a glimpse of Navidson's light sinking, finally vanishing into the deep like a failing star.

As Billy explains in The Reston Interview: "Tom felt like a part of him had been ripped away. I'd never seen him act like that. He started shaking and tears just kept welling up in his eyes. I tried to tell him the stairway could shrink just like it had stretched, and he kept agreeing with me, and nodding, but that didn't stop the tears. It was terrifying to watch. He loved his brother that much."

After watching the paramedics take Wax away, we follow Tom's retreat to the study where he manages to locate among his things the last bit of a joint. Smoking it, however, offers absolutely no relief. He is no longer crying but his hands still shake. He takes several deep breaths and then as

---

[267]Nor is that the first time the word "grave" appears in reference to the house in *The Navidson Record.* When Reston suggests Navidson use the Leica distance meter, he adds, "That should put this ghost in the grave fast." Holloway in Exploration #3 mutters: "Cold as a grave." Also in the same segment Wax grunts a variation, "I feel like I'm in a coffin." In one of her Hi 8 journal entries, Karen tries to make light of her situation when she remarks: "It's like having a giant catacomb for a family room." Tom in Tom's Story tells the "grave-maker" joke, while Reston, during the rescue attempt, admits to Navidson: "You know, I feel like I'm in a grave." To which Navidson responds, "Makes you wonder what gets buried here." "Well judging by the size," Reston replies. "It must be the giant from Jack and the fucking Beanstalk." Giant indeed.[268]

[268]On several occasions, Zampanò also uses the word "grave."[269]

[269]See Index. — Ed.

Karen is getting ready to show Sheriff Axnard the hallway, he steals a sip of bourbon.[270]

Regrettably, Tom fails to stop at a sip. A few hours later he has finished off the whole fifth as well as half a bottle of wine. He might have spent all night drinking had exhaustion not caught up with me. Of course, the following morning does nothing to erase yesterday's events. Tom attempts to recover lost ground by accompanying Reston back to the Great Hall. Much to their surprise, however, they discover the hallway now terminates thirty feet in, nor are there any doors or alternate hallways branching off it. Karen returns to her room when she sees Tom and Reston reappear only five minutes later.

Even though he too is suffering from Navidson's disappearance, Reston still does his best to counsel Tom, and at least for a few hours Tom successfully resists drinking anything more. Chad apparently had escaped from the house at dawn and now refuses to come in or say a word to his mother. Tom eventually finds him among the branches of a tree just past the edge of the property line. Nevertheless, no amount of coaxing will induce the eight year old to come back in.

In Billy's words (The Reston Interview again): "Tom told me Chad was happy in his tree and Tom was hard pressed to start telling him inside was a better place. However, there was something else. The kid apparently bolted from the house when he heard some kind of murmuring, something about a walker in darkness, then a bang, like a gun shot, and the sound of a man dying. Woke him right up, he said. Back then I assumed he'd just been dreaming."

Judging from the house footage, what seems to really push Tom over the edge that second day is when he reenters the house and finds Daisy—her forearms acrawl with strange scratches—swaying in front of the hallway screaming "Daddy!" despite the absence of a reply, the absence of even an echo. When Karen finally comes downstairs and carries her daughter outside to help her find Chad, Tom takes the car and goes into town. An hour later he returns with groceries, unnecessary medical supplies, magazines and the reason for the excursion in the first place—a case of bourbon.

On the third and fourth day, Tom does not emerge once from the study, attempting to drink his grief into submission.

Karen, on the other hand, begins to deal with the consequences of Navidson's disappearance. She rapidly starts paying more attention to her children, finally luring Chad back into the house where she can oversee his (and Daisy's) packing efforts. In a brief clip we catch Karen on the phone, presumably with her mother, discussing their imminent departure from Virginia.

Reston remains in the living room, frequently attempting to raise Navidson on the radio, though never hearing more than static and white noise. Outside a thunder storm begins to crack and spit rain at the windows. Lightning builds shadows. A wind howls like the wounded, filling everyone with cold, bone weary dread.

Toward midnight, Tom emerges from the study, steals a slice of lemon meringue pie and then whips up some hot chocolate for everyone. Whole milk, unsweetened cocoa, sugar, and a splash of vanilla extract all brought to a careful simmer. Billy and Karen appreciate the gesture. Tom

[270]See Harmon Frisch's "Not Even Bill's Acquaintance" *Twenty Years In The Program* ed. Cynthia Huxley (New York: W. W. Norton & Company, 1996), p. 143-179.

has not stopped drinking, and even doses his cup with a shot of Jack Daniels, but he does seem to have leveled out, not exactly achieving some sublime moment of clarity but at least attaining a certain degree of self-control.

Then Tom, though he is only wearing a t-shirt, takes a deep breath and marches into the hallway again. A minute later he returns.

"It's no more than ten feet deep now," Tom grunts. "And Navy's been gone over four days."

"There's still a chance," Reston grumbles.

Tom tries to shrug off the certitude that his brother is dead. "You know," he continues very quietly, still staring at the hallway. "There once was this guy who went to Madrid. He was in the mood for something new so he decided to try out this small restaurant and order—sight unseen—the house specialty.

"Soon a plate arrived loaded with rice pilaf and two large meaty objects.

" 'What's this?' he asked his waiter.

" 'Cojones, Senor.'

" 'What are cojones?'

" 'Cojones' the waiter answered, 'are the testicles of the bull that lost in the arena today.'

"Though a little hesitant at first, the man still went ahead and tried them. Sure enough they were delicious.

"Well a week later, he goes back to the same restaurant and orders the same thing. This time, when his dish arrives, the meaty objects are much smaller and don't taste nearly as good.

"He immediately calls the waiter over.

" 'Hey,' he says. 'What are these?'

" 'Cojones' the waiter replies.

" 'No, no,' he explains. 'I had them last week and they were much bigger.'

" 'Ah Senor,' the waiter sighs. 'The bull does not lose every time.' "

7.

Tom's joke attempts to deflect some of the pain inherent in this protracted wait, but of course nothing can really diminish the growing knowledge that Navidson may have vanished for good.

Tom eventually returns to the study to try and sleep, but Karen remains in the living room, occasionally dozing off, often trying to reach Navidson on the radios, whispering his name like a lullaby or a prayer.[271]

In the 5:09 A.M. Hi 8 clip, Karen rests her head on her hands and starts to sleep. There is something eerie about the odd stillness that settles on the living room then, not even remotely affected by Reston's snoring on the couch. It is as if this scene has been impossibly fixed and will never change again, until out of the blue, presumably before the cameras can shut off—no longer ordered to run by the motion detectors—Navidson limps out of the hallway. He is clearly exhausted, dehydrated, and perhaps a little unable to believe he has actually escaped the maze. Seeing Karen, he

---

[271] Karen's emotional response is not limited to longing. Earlier that evening she retreated to the bathroom, ran the water in the sink, and recorded this somewhat accusatory Hi 8 journal entry: "Damn you for going, Navy. Damn you. [Starting to cry] This house, this home, was supposed to help us get closer. It was supposed to be better and stronger than some stupid marriage vow. It was supposed to make us a family. [Sobbing] But, oh my god, look what's happened."

immediately kneels beside her, attempting to wake her with the gentlest word. Karen, however, drawn so abruptly from her dreams, cannot arrest the shocked gasp summoned by the sound and sight of Navidson. Of course, the moment she realizes he is not a ghost, her terror dissolves into a hug and a flood of words, awakening everyone in the house.

Several essays have been written about this reunion and yet not one of them suggests Karen has reverted to her former state of dependency. Consider Anita Massine's comments:

> Her initial embrace and happiness is not just about Navidson's return. Karen realizes she has fulfilled her end of the bargain. Her time in that place has come to an end. Navidson's arrival means she can leave.[272]

Or Garegin Thorndike Taylor's response:

> Where previously Karen might have dissolved into tears and her typical clutching, this time she is clearly more reserved, even terse, relying on her smile for defense.[273]

Or finally Professor Lyle Macdonough:

> The reason Karen cries out when Navidson wakes her has nothing to do with the inherent terror of that hallway or some other *cauchemar*. It has only to do with Navidson. Deep down inside, she really does fear him. She fears he will try to keep her there. She fears he will threaten her slowly forming independence. Only once the reins of consciousness slip into place does she resort to expected modes of welcome.[274]

Karen clearly refuses to allow Navidson's appearance to alter her plans. She does not accept that merely his presence entitles him to authority. Her mind is made up. Even before he can begin to recount his desperate flight up those stairs or how he found Holloway's equipment,[275] Karen announces her intention to leave for New York City that night.

---

[272]Anita Massine's *Dialects of Divorce In American Film In The Twentieth Century* (Oxford, Ohio: Miami University Press, 1995), p. 228.

[273]Garegin Thorndike Taylor's "The Ballast of Self" *Modern Psyche,* v. 18, 1996, p. 74. Also refer back to Chapter II and V.

[274]Professor Lyle Macdonough's "Dissolution of Love in *The Navidson Record,*" Crafton Lecture Series, Chatfield College in St. Martin Ohio, February 9, 1996.

[275]In the following excerpt from The Last Interview, Navidson sheds some more light on how he managed to emerge from those dark hollows: "I remember I had found Jed's pack so I knew I was okay on water and food for a while. Then I just started climbing up the stairs, one step at a time. At first it was slow going. That roar would frequently rise up the central shaft like some awful wail. At times it sounded like voices. Hundreds of them. Thousands. Calling after me. And then other times it sounded like the wind only there is no wind there.

"I remember finding The Holloway Tape off one of the landings. I had caught sight of a few bits of neon marker still attached to the wall and wandered over to take a look. A minute later I saw his pack and the camera. It was all just sitting there. The rifle was nearby too, but there was no sign of him.

Of course by the time they had all sat down and watched The Holloway Tape, Navidson was the only one who had second thoughts about abandoning the cold lure of those halls.

HOLLOWAY

8.

More than a handful of people have tried to[ ][276]explain Holloway's madness.

That was pretty odd to come across something, let alone anything, in that place. But what made finding that stuff particularly strange was how much I'd been thinking of Holloway at the time. I kept expecting him to jump around some corner and shoot me.

"After that, I was a little spooked and made sure to chuck the ammo down into that pit off to my right. Over and over, I kept wondering what happened to his body. It was making me crazy. So I tried fixing my mind on other things.

"I remember thinking then that one of the toenails on my right foot, the big toenail, had torn loose and started to bleed. That's when De— . . . Delial came into my head which was awful.

"Finally though, I began concentrating on Karen. On Chad and Daisy. On Tom and Billy. I thought about every time we'd gone to a movie together or a game or whatever, ten years ago, four months ago, twenty years ago. I remembered when I first met Karen. The way she moved. These perfect angles she'd make with her wrists. Her beautiful long fingers. I remembered when Chad was born. All that kind of stuff, trying to recall those moments as vividly as possible. In as much detail. Eventually I went into this daze and the hours began to melt away. Felt like minutes.

"On the third night I tried to take another step and found there wasn't one. I was in the Great Hall again. Oddly enough though, as I soon found out, I was still a good ways from home. For some reason everything had stretched there too. Now all of a sudden, there were a lot of new dead ends. It took me another day and night to get back to the living room, and to tell you the truth I was never sure I was going to make it until I finally did."

[276]Some kind of ash landed on the following pages, in some places burning away small holes, in other places eradicating large chunks of text. Rather than try to reconstruct what was destroyed I decided to just bracket the gaps—[ ].

Unfortunately I have no idea what stuff did the actual charring. It's way too copious for cigarette tappings, and anyway Zampanò didn't smoke. Another small mystery to muse over, if you like, or just forget, which I recommend. Though even I'm unable to follow my own advice, imagining instead gray ash floating down like snow everywhere, after the blast but still hours before that fabled avalanche of heat, the pyroclastic roar that will incinerate everything, even if for the time being—and there still is time . . . —it's just small flakes leisurely kissing away tiny bits of meaning, while high above, the eruption continues to black out the sun.

There's only one choice and the brave make it.

Fly from the path.

Lude dropped by a few nights ago. It's mid-September but I hadn't seen him since June. News that I'd been fired from the Shop apparently pissed him off, though why he should care I've no idea. Like my boss, he also assumed I was on smack. More than a little freaked too when he finally saw for himself how bad off I was, real gaunt and withdrawn and not without a certain odor either. But Lude's no idiot. One glance at my room and he knew junk was not the problem. All those books, sketches, collages, reams and reams of paper, measuring tapes nailed from corner to floor, and of course that big black trunk right there in the center of everything, all of it just another way to finally say: no-no, no junk at all.

"Throw it away, hoss" Lude said and started to cross to my desk for a closer look. I sprung forward, ordered by instinct, like some animal defending its pride, interposing myself between him and my work, those papers, this thing.

Lude backed away—in fact that was the first time he'd ever backed away; ever—just a step, but retreating just the same, calling me "weird", calling me "scary."

I quickly apologized and incoherently tried to explain how I was just sorting some stuff out. Which is true.

"Bullshit," Lude grunted, perhaps a little angry that I'd frightened him. "For godsake, just look at what you're drawing?" He pointed at all the pictures tacked to my wall, sketched on napkins, the backs of envelopes, anything handy. "Empty rooms, hundreds of black, empty fucking rooms!"

I don't remember what I mumbled next. Lude waved a bag of grass in front of me, said there was a party up Beachwood canyon, some castle loaded with hookers on X and a basement full of mead. It was interesting to see Lude still defending that line, but I just shook my head.

He turned to leave and then suddenly spun back around on his heels, producing from his pocket a flash of silver, cishlash-shhhhhhick, the wheel catching on the edge of his thumb, connecting sparks and kerosene . . . his old Zippo drawn like a .44 in some mythical western, drawn by the fella in the white hat, and as it turns out Lude was in fact dressed in white, a creamy linen jacket, which I guess means I would have to be wearing black, and come to think of it I was wearing black—black jeans, black t, black socks. This, however, was not a challenge. It was an offering, and yet one I knew I would not/could not accept.

Lude shrugged and blew out the flame, the immolating splash of brightness abruptly receding into a long gray thread climbing up to the ceiling before finally collapsing into invisible and untraceable corridors of chaos.

As he stepped out into the hall, a place with dull walls where a pink corpse occasionally referred to as a carpet stretches over and down the stairs, Lude told me why he'd come by in the first place: "Kyrie's boyfriend's back in town and he's looking for us, you in particular but since I'm the one who introduced you two, he's also after me. Be careful. The guy's a nut." Lude hesitated. He knew Gdansk Man was the least of my worries but I guess he wanted to help.

"I'll see you around Lude," I mumbled.

"Get rid of it Hoss, it's killing you."

Then he tossed me his lighter and padded away, the dim light quickly transforming him into a shadow, then a sound, and finally a silence.

Maybe he was right.

Fly from the path.

I remember the first time I hadn't and a rusty bar had taught me the taste of teeth. The second time I'd been smarter. I fled from the house, scrambled over the back brick wall like an alley cat, and sprinted across the overgrown lot. It took him awhile to find me but when he did, cornering me like some beast in the stairwell of a nearby shop, a chimney sweep business actually, Gallow & Sons, something like that, his focus was gone. Time had interceded. Dulled his wrath.

Raymond still hit me, an open handed slap to my left ear, pain answering the deafening quiet that followed, a distant thump then as my forehead skidded into the concrete wall.

Raymond was yelling at me, going on about the fights, my fights, at school, about my attitude, my wanderings and how he would kill me if I didn't stop.

He had killed before, he explained. He could kill again.

I stopped seeing, something black and painful hissing into my head, gnawing at the bones in my cheeks, tears pouring down my face, though I wasn't crying, my nose was just bleeding, and he hadn't even broken it this time.

Raymond continued the lesson, his words ineffectually reverberating around me. He was trying to sound like one of his western heroes, doling out profound advice, telling me how I was only "cannon fodder" though he pronounced it like "father" and in a way that seemed to imply he was really referring to himself. I kept nodding and agreeing, while inside I began to uncover a different lesson. I recognized just how much a little fear had helped me—after all I wasn't going to the hospital this time. All along I'd misread my contentious postures as something brave, my willingness to indulge in head-to-head confrontation as noble, even if I was only thirteen and this monster was a marine. I failed to see anger as just another way to cover fear. The bravest thing would be to accept my fear and fear him, <u>really</u> fear him, then heeding that instruction make a much more courageous choice: fly once and for all from his mad blister & rage, away from the black convolution of violence he would never untangle, and into the arms of some unknown tomorrow.

The next morning I told everyone my injuries had come from another schoolyard fight. I started to befriend guile, doped Raymond with compliments and self-deprecating stories. Made-up stories. I dodged, ducked, acquired a whole new vocabulary for bending, for hiding, all while beyond the gaze of them all, I meticulously planned my flight. Of course, I admit now that even though I tested well, I still would never have succeeded had I not received that September, only weeks later, words to find me, my mother's words, tenderly catching my history in the gaps, encouraging and focusing my direction, a voice powerful enough to finally lift my wing and give me the strength to go.

Little did I know that by the time I managed to flee to Alaska and then to a boarding school, Raymond was already through. Coincidence gave an improbable curse new resonance. Cancer had settled on Raymond's bones, riddling his liver and pancreas with holes. He had nowhere to run and it literally ate him alive. He was dead by the time I turned sixteen.

I guess one obvious option now is to just get rid of this thing, which if Lude's right, should put an end to all my recent troubles. It's a nice idea but it reeks of hope. False hope. Not all complex problems have easy solutions; so says Science (so <u>warns</u> Science); and so Trenton once warned me, both of us swilling beer in that idling hunk of rust and gold known simply as the Truck; but that had been in another time when there was still a truck and you could talk of solutions in peace without having any first hand knowledge of the problem; and Trenton is an old friend who doesn't live here and who I've not mentioned before.[277]

My point being, what if my attacks are entirely unrelated, attributable in fact to something entirely else, perhaps for instance just warning shocks brought on by my own crumbling biology, tiny flakes of unknown chemical origin already burning holes through the fabric of my mind, dismantling memories, undoing even the strongest powers of imagination and reason?

How then do you fly from that path?

As I recheck and rebolt the door—I've installed a number of extra locks—I feel with the turn of each latch a chill trying to crawl beneath the back of my skull. Putting on the chain only intensifies the feeling, hairs bristling, trying to escape the host because the host is stupid enough to stick around, missing the most obvious fact of all that what I hoped to lock out I've only locked in here with me.

And no, it hasn't gone away.

The elusive it is still here with me.

But there's very little I can do.

I wash the sweat off my face, do my best to suppress a shiver, can't, return to the body, spread out across the table like papers—and let me tell you there's more than just The Navidson Record lying there—bloodless and still but not at all dead, calling me to it, needing me now like a child, depending on me despite its age. After all, I'm its source, the one who feeds it, nurses it back to health—but not life, I fear—bones of bond paper, transfusions of ink, genetic encryption in xerox; monstrous, maybe inaccurate correlates, but nonetheless there. And necessary to animate it all? For is that not an ultimate, the ultimate goal? Not some heaven sent blast of electricity but me, and not me unto me, but me unto it, if those two things are really at all different, which is still to say—to state the obvious—without me it would perish.

Except these days nothing's obvious.

There's something else.

More and more often, I've been overcome by the strangest feeling that I've gotten it all turned around, by which I mean to say—to state the not-so-obvious—without it I would perish. A moment comes where suddenly everything seems impossibly far and confused, my sense of self derealized & depersonalized, the disorientation so severe I actually believe—and let me tell you it is an intensely strange instance of belief—that this terrible sense of relatedness to Zampanò's work implies something that just can't be, namely that this thing has created me; not me unto it, but now it unto me, where I am nothing more than the matter of some other voice, intruding through the folds of what even now lies there agape, possessing me with histories I should never recognize as my own; inventing me, defining me, directing me until finally every association I can claim as my own—from Raymond to Thumper, Kyrie to Ashley, all the women, even the Shop and my studio and everything else—is relegated to nothing; forcing me to face the most terrible suspicion of all, that all of this has just been made up and what's worse, not made up by me or even for that matter Zampanò.

Though by whom I have no idea.

Tonight's candle number twelve has just started to die in a pool of its own wax, a few flickers away from blindness. Last week they turned off my electricity, leaving me to canned goods, daylight and wicks. (God knows why my phone still works.) Ants inhabit the corners.

One of the most excruciating and impudent works on the subject was written by Jeremy Flint. Regrettably this reprehensible concoction of speculation, fantasy, and repellent prose, also incl[ ]es or refers to primary documents not available anywhere else. Through hard work, luck, or theft, Flint managed to [ ] across some of the notes and summations made by psychiatrist Nancy Tobe who for a br[ ]f period treated Holloway for [ ] depression:

Spiders prepare a grave. I use Lude's Zippo to light another candle, the flame revealing what I'd missed before, on the front, etched in chrome, the all red melancholy King of Hearts—did Lude have any idea what he was really suggesting I do?—imagining then not one flame but a multitude, a million orange and blue tears cremating the body, this labor, and in that sudden burst of heat, more like an explosion, flinging the smoldering powder upon the room, a burning snow, falling everywhere, erasing everything, until finally it erases all evidence of itself and even me.

In the distance, I hear the roar, faint at first but getting louder, as if some super-heated billowing cloud has at last begun to descend from the peak of some invisible, impossibly high mountain peak, and rushing down at incredible speeds too, instantly enclosing and carbonizing everything and anyone in the way.

I consider retrieving it. What I recently bought. I may need it. Instead I recheck the measuring tapes. At least there's no change there. But the roar keeps growing, almost unbearable, and there's nowhere left to turn. Get it out of the trunk, I tell myself. Then the elusive "it" momentarily disappears.

"Get out," I scream.

There's no roar.

A neighbor's having a party.

People are laughing.

Luckily they haven't heard me or if they have they've sense enough to ignore me.

I wish I could ignore me.

There's only one choice now: finish what Zampanò himself failed to finish. Re-inter this thing in a binding tomb. Make it <u>only</u> a book, and if that doesn't help . . . retrieve what I've been hiding in the trunk, something I ordered three weeks ago and finally picked up today, purchased in Culver city at Martin B. Retting (11029 Washington Blvd)—one Heckler & Koch USP .45 ACP, kept for that moment when I'm certain nothing's left. The thread has snapped. No sound even to mark the breaking let alone the fall. That long anticipated disintegration, when the darkest angel of all, the horror beyond all horrors, sits at last upon my chest, permanently enfolding me in its great covering wings, black as ink, veined in Bees' purple. A creature without a voice. A voice without a name. As immortal as my life. Come here at long last to summon the wind.

277 ___

> Page one of Dr. Tobe's notes contains only two words, capitalized, written in pencil, dead center on a page torn from a legal pad:
>
> CONSIDERING SUICIDE.
>
> [ ]he next two pages are for the most part illegible, with words such as "family" "father" "loyalty" "the old home" appearing every now and then in an otherwise dark scribble of ink.
>
> However, Tobe's typed summation following the first session offers a few [ ]details concerning Holloway's life: "Despite his own achievement [sic] which range from Scuba Diving expeditions in the G[ ]Aqaba, leading climbers up the Matterhorn, organizing numerous [ ] as well as expeditions to the North and South Pole, Holloway feels inadequate and suffers from acute and chronic depression. Unable to see how much he has already accomplished, he constantly dwells on suicide. I am considering several anti-depressants [ ] and have recommended daily counseling."[278]

Flint goes on to cover the second visit which [ ] much repeats his observations concerning the first. The third visit, however, gives up the first th[]rn.

> In another series of notes Tobe describes Holloway's first love: "At seventeen, he met a young woman named Eliz[]beth who he described to me as 'Beautiful like a doe. Dark eyes. Brown hair. Pretty ankles, kinda skinny and weak.' A short courtship ensued and for a brief time they were a couple.[ ]In Holloway's **XXXXXXX**[279], the relationship ended because he didn't [sic] the Varsity football squad. By his own admission he was never any good at 'team sports.' Her interest in him faded and she soon beg[ ] dating the starting tackle, leaving Holloway broken hearted with an increased sen[ ]e of [illegible] and inadequacy."[280]

278Jeremy Flint's *Violent Seeds: The Holloway Roberts Myst* [ ]*y* (Los[]Angel[ ]: 2.13.61, 1996), p. 48.

279`These Xs indicate text was inked out—not burned.`

280Flint, p. 53.

Nancy Tobe was a fairly green therapist and took far too many notes. Perhaps she felt that by studying these pages later, she could synthesize the material and present her patient with a solution. She had not yet real[ ] that her notes or her solutions would mean absolutely no[ ]g. Patients must discover their peace for themselves. Tobe [ ] only a guide. The solution is personal. It is ironic then that had it not been for Tobe's inexperience, the notes so intrinsic to achieving at least a fair understanding of Holloway's inner torment would never have come into existence. People always demand experts, though sometimes they are fortunate enough to find a beginner.[281]

On the fourth visit, Tobe [ ] transcribed Holloway's words verbatim. It is i[]possible to tell from Flint's text whether Tobe actually record[]d Hollow[ ] or just wrote down his words from memory:

> "I had already been out there for two days and then that morning, before dawn, I [ ] to the ridge and waited. I waited a long time and I didn't move. It was cold. Real cold. Up till then everyone had been talking about the big buck but no one had seen anything. Not even a rabbit. Even though I'd been deer hunting a few times, I'd never actually shot a deer, but with, well the football team [ ], Elizabeth gone like that, I was gonna set it right by dropping that <u>big</u> buck.
>
> "When the sun finally came out, I couldn't believe my eyes. There he was, right across the valley, the [ ] buck tasting the air.[ ] I was a good shot. I knew what to do and I did it. I took my time, centered the reticule, let out my breath, squeezed slowly, and listened to that round as it cracked across the valley. I must have closed my eyes 'cause the next thing I saw the deer [ ] to the ground.
>
> "Everyone heard my shot and [ ] Funny thing was, because of where I'd been, I was the last one to get there. My dad was waiting for me, just shaking his head, angry, and []shamed.
>
> " 'Look what you done boy,' he said in a whisper but I could have heard that whisper across the whole valley. "Look what you done. [ ] shot yourself a doe." [ ] I almost killed myself then but I guess I thought it couldn't get any worse. [ ] that was the worst. Staring at that dead doe and then watching my dad turn his back on me and just walk away."[282]

[281]Refer back to Chapter 5; footnote 67. — Ed.
[282]Flint, p. 61.

At this point Flint's analysis heads into a fairly pejorative and unoriginal analysis of vi[]lence. He also makes a little t[ ] much of the word "doe" which Holloway used to describe his first love E[ ]zabeth. However since Flint is not the only one to make this association, it is worth at least a cursory gl[ ]nce.

"A vengeance transposed on the wild," Flint calls Holloway's killing of the doe, implying that to Holloway's eye the doe had become Elizabeth. What Flint, however, fails to acknowledge is that with no certainty can he determine whether Hollow[]y described Elizabeth as a "doe" *while* he was going out with her []r *afterward*. Holloway may have described her as such *following* the ill-fated hunting trip as a means to comp[ ]nd his guilt, thus blaming himself not only for the death of the doe but for the death of love as well. In [ ] Flint's suggestion of brimming violence may be nothing more than a gross renaming of self[]reproach.

Flint [ ] argue that Holloway's aggressive nature was bound to su[]face in what he calls Navidson's []Hall of Amplification."

> Holloway's latent suicidal urges [ ] when Wax and Jed insist on turning back. He sees this (incorrectly) as an admission of failure, <u>another</u> failure, th[]s incr[ ]sing his sense of inadequacy.
>
> Holloway had over the years developed enough psychic defense mechanisms to avoid the destructive consequences of this self-determine[ ]f defeat.
>
> What made <u>this</u> incident different from all the rest was the []ou[]e.
>
> In many ways, Navidson's house functions like an immense isolation tank. Deprived of light, change in temperature and any sense of time, the individual begins to create his own sensory [ ], [ ]d depen[ ]ng on the duration of his stay begins to project more and more of [ ] personality on those bare walls and vacant []allways.
>
> In Holloway's case, the house as well as everything inside it becomes an exten[ ]n of himself, e.g. Jed and Wax become the psy[ ]logical demons responsible for his failue [sic]. Thus his first act—to sh[ ]t Wax—is in fact the beginning of a nearly operatic s[]i[ ]de.[283]

Certainly Flint [ ] not alone in emphasiz[ ]g the impl[ ]t violence i[ ]suicide. In 1910 at [ ] conference in Vienna, Wilhelm Stekel cla[]med [ ] "no one killed himself unless he[]either wanted to kill another person []r

[283] IbXXXXXXXXXSuiXXXXXXXXXXXX [ ] XXXXXXXXX[284]

[284] Inked out as well as burned.

wished a[]other's death"[285] [ ]1983 Buie and Maltzberger described s[ ]cide [ ]resulting from "two types of imperative impulses: murder[]us hate and an ur[]ent need to es[]ape suff[]ring."[286]

Robert Jean Cam[ ]ell sums up t[]e psych[]dynamics of suic[ ]s as fol[ ]ws:

> . . . sui[ ] or a suicide atte[ ]t is seen most freque[ ]ly to be an agg[ ]sive attack directed against a loved one or against society in ge[ ]al; in others, it may be a mis[ ]ded bid for attention or may be conceived of as a means of ef[ ]ting reunion with the id[]al love-object or m[]ther. *That suicide [ ]n one sense a means of relea[]e for aggressive impulses is sup[ ]ed by the change of wartime suicide rates. In Wo[ ] War II, for example, rates among the participating nations fell, [ ]times by as much as 30%; but in ne[ ]l countries, the rates remained the same.*
>
> In involutional depressions and in the depr[ ]ed type of manic[]depressive psychosis, the following dynamic elements are of[ ]n clearly operative: the d[ ]essed patient loses the object that he depends upon for narcissistic s[ ]lies; in an atte[ ]t to force the object's return, he regre[ ]es to the oral stage and inc[ ]porates (swallows up) the object, t[]us regressively identi[ ]ing with the object: *the sadism originally directed against the desert[ ] object is ta[]en up by the patient's sup[ ]go and is directed against the incorporated object, w[ ]h now lodges wit[ ]n the ego; suicide oc[ ]s, not so much as an attempt on the ego's part to esc[]pe the inexorable demands of the superego, but rather as a[ ]enraged attack on the in[ ]orated object in retaliation []or its having dese[ ]d the pati[ ] in the first place.*[287]
>
> [It[ ]s added f[]r em[ ]asis]

Of course the anni[]il[]tion of [ ]self does not necessarily preclude the anni[ ]n of others. As is evident in sh[ ]ting sprees that culminate in suicide, an attack on the[ ]incorporated object" may extend first to [ ]attack on loved ones, co-work[ ] or even innocent by[ ]ders—a description, which ev[ ] Flint would agree, fits H[]lloway.

Nevertheless th[]re are also numer[ ]s objections to Flint[]s asser[ ] that Hollow[ ]'s suicidal disposition would within that place inevitabl[] lead to murder. The most enlight[ ]g refutation comes from Rosemary

---

[285]Ned H. Cassem, "The Person C[]nfronting Death" in *The Ne [ ]Harvard Guide to Psychiatry* ed. Armand M. Nicholi, jr[ ] M.D. (C[ ]brid[]e: Harvard University Press, 1[]88), p. 743.
[286][ ]id., [] 744.
[287]Robert J[ ]n Campbell, M.D[ ]*Psychiatric Dictionary* (Oxfo[]d Univ[ ]ity Press, 1981) [ ] 608[]

Enderheart w[]o not onl[ ]uts F[]in[] in his place but also reveals somet[ ]g new about Navidson's history:

> Where Flint's argument makes the impulse to destroy others the result of an impulse to destroy the self, we only have to consider someone with similar self-destructive urges who when faced with similar conditions did not attempt to murder two individuals [
>
>]

SUBJECT:	Will "Navy" Navidson
COMMENT:	"I think too often too seriously a[]out killing myself."

Will Navidson was no stranger to s[ ]ide. It sat on his shoulder more often than not: "It's there before I sleep, there when I wake, it's there a lot. But as Nietzsche said, 'The t[]ought of suicide is a consolation. It can get one through many a bad night.'" (See Dr. Hetterman Stone's *Confidential: An In[ ]view With Karen Green* 19[ ]

Navidson often viewed his achievements with disdain, considered his direction vague, and frequently assumed his desires would []ever be met by life []o matter how f[ ]ly he lived it. However, unlike H[ ]loway, he converted his d[ ]pair into art. He [ ]lied on his eye and film to bring meaning to virt[ ] everything he e[]count[ ]ed, and though he paid the high price of lost interaction, he frequently conceived beautiful instances worthy of our time; what Robert Hughes famously referred to [ ] "Navidson's little windows of light."

Flint would [ ]test [ ] while both Holloway and [ ]vidson camped in the same dale of depression, they were very dif[ ]rent in[ ]viduals: Navidson was merely a photographer while, to quote F[ ]nt "Holloway was a hunter who [ ] crossed the line into territories of aggress[]on."

Flint sh[ ]ld have done his []omework, if he thought Navidson never crossed that line.

In the 70's Navidson became a career p[ ]journ[]list and ultimately a famous one but at the begin[]ing of that de[]ade he wasn't carrying a Nikon. He was manning an M-60 with the 1st cav[ ]y at Rock Island East where he would eventually receive a Bronze

> Star for saving the l[]ves of two [ ] soldiers he dra[]ged from a burning personnel carrier. He[ ]ver, no longer has the medal. He sent it along with a [ ]oto of h[]s first kill to Richard Nixon to pr[]test the war.[288]

Unfortun[ ]ely when Navi[]son stumbled upon Hol[ ]'s H[ ]8 tapes, he had no idea their contents would [ ]spire such a heated and lasting debate over what l[]rked in the [ ]art of that p[]ace. Despite the radically differ[]nt behavior pattern[] demonst[]ated by the hunter from Me[ ]mo[ ], Wi[ ]sin and the Pulitzer Prize-winning photojournalist[ ]in the house, The Hollow[ ] Tape revealed that e[]ther one could just as easily have been devo[]r[]d in the same way. The gli[ ]se rescued from that t[ ]r[ ]b[]le []ark warned that while paths might differ, the end might no[].

9.

The Hol[ ]y Tape

"I'm lost. Out of food. Low on water. No sense of direction. Oh god . . . [ ]

So be[]ins The Holloway Tape—Holloway leering into the camera, a backdrop of wall, final moments in a man's life. These are jarring pieces, coherent only in the way they trace a de[]line.

Ove[]view:

- The opening card displays a quote from Gaston Bachelard's *The Poetics of Space:* "The dreamer in his corner wrote off the world in a detailed daydream that destroyed, one by one, all the objects in the world."[289]
- There are thirteen parts. [ ]
- They are separated by 3-seconds of white frame. In the upper ri[]ht hand corner a number or word tracks the chronology, starting with "First," continuing with "2" thr[] "12" and ending with "Last." The typeface is the same Janson as issued by Anton Janson in Leipzig between 1660 and 1687.
- These insertions were designed by Navidson. They[ ], and in no way alter the original segments.

Navidson reproduces Holloway's tape in its entirety.

Who can forget Holloway's grizzled features as he []urns the camera on hi[]self?

No comfort now. No hope of rescue or return.

"I deserve this. I brought this all on me. But I'm s[] sorry. I'm so[ ]rry," he says in Part 2. "But what does that matter? I shot them. I shot both of [ ]em. [Long pause] Half a canteen of water's all I've left. [Another

---

[288]Rosemary End[ ]art's *How Have You Who Loved Ever Loved A Next Time?* (New York: Times Books, 19[ ] p. 1432-1436).

[289]*Le rêveur, dans son coin, a rayé le monde en une rêverie minutieuse qui détruit un à un tous les objets du monde.*

pause] Shouldn't have let them get []way then I [ ]have returned, told everyone they g[ ]lost . . . lost." And with that last utterance, Holloway's eyes reveal who here is real[]y lost.

Despite Holloway's undeniable guilt, not since Floyd Collins became trapped in the Kentucky Sand Cave back in 1925 has there been such a terrible instance of suffering. Co[]lins remained alive for fourteen days and nights before he died. Despite the efforts of many men to free him from the squeeze, Collins never saw the light of day again. He only felt the ink[ ]darkness and cold [ ] in on him, bind him, kill him. All he could do was rave about angels in chariots and liver and onions and chicken sandwiches.[290]

Unlike Floyd Collins, no straight jacket of mud and rock holds Holloway. He can still move around, though where he moves leads nowhere. By the time he begins to video tape his final hours, he has [ ]ready recognized the complete hopelessness of the situation. Repeatin[] his identity seems the only mantra [ ]offers any consolation: "Holloway Roberts. Born in M[ ]om[ ]sin. Bachelor's from U. Mass."[291] It is almost as if he believes preserving his identity on video tape can somehow hold what he is powerless to prevent: those endless contours of dark[]ess stealing the Hollow[ ] from himself. "I'm Holloway Roberts." he insists. "Born in Menomonie, Wi[ ]n. Bachelor's from U. Mass. Explorer, professional hunter,[ ]eth. [Long pause] This is not right. It's not fair. I don't [ ]serve to die."

Regrettably, the limited amount of light, the [ ]uality of tape, not to mention the constant oscillation between sharp and blurry (compliments of the Hi 8's automatic focus)[] barely c[ ]ure Holloway's bearded face let [ ]one anything else—not to imply that there exists an 'else'. Mainly a backdrop of darkness, which, as the police observed, could have [ ]en shot in any lightless room or closet. [ ]

In other words, the immen[]ity of Navidson's house eludes the frame. It exists only in Holloway's face, fear etc[ ] deeper and deeper into his features, the cost of dying paid out with p[]un[]s of flesh and e[]ch s[]allow breath. It is painful[ ] obvious the creature Holloway hunts has already begun to feed on him.

290[

]0.

291In the epil[]gue of her bo[]k *Fear Mantras* (Cambridge: Harvard Un[ ]ress, 1995) Alicia Hoyle disc[ ]ses Hollow[]y's l[]ck of fear training: "He didn[]t even pos[]es[] the ancient Hak-Kin-Dak man[]ra" (p. [ ]6). Earlier on she prov[]des a trans[ ]tion of this hunter's utter[]nce ([ ] 26): "I am not a fool. I a[] wise. I will run from my fear, I w[]ll out distance my f[ ]r, then I will hide fr[ ] my fear, I w[]ll wait f[]r my fear, I will let m[] fear run past me[] then I will follow my fear, I will track [ ] fear until I c[]n approach m[ ]ear in complete silence[] th[]n I will strike at m[] fear, I will charge my fe[ ], I will grab h[]ld of my fear, I will sink my f[]ngers into my [ ]ar, t[]en I will bite my fear, I w[]ll tear the thro[]t of my fear, I will bre[]k the neck of my fear, I wi[ ] drink the blood of my fear, I [ ]ll gulp the flesh o[ ]my fear[] I will crush th[] bones of my f[]ar[ ]and I will savor m[] fear, I will sw[]llow my fear, all []f it, and then I will digest []y fear unt[]l I can do not[]ing else but shit out my fear.In this w[]y will I be mad[] stronger[ ]

Parts 4[ ]6,[ ],10 & 1[] centre on Holloway's reiteration of his identity. Part 3, however, is different. It only lasts four seconds. With eyes wide open, voice hoarse, lips split and bleeding, Hol[ ]y barks "I'm not alone." Part 5 fo[]lows up with, "There's something here. I'm sure of it now." Part 8 with: "It's following me. No, it's *stalking* me." And Part 9: "But it won't strike. It's just out there waiting. I don't know what for. But it's near now, waiting for me, waiting for something. I don't know why it doesn't [ ] Oh god . . . Holloway Roberts. Menomonie, Wisconsin. [chambering a round in his rifle] Oh god[ ]."[292]

It is interesting to compare Holloway's behavior to Tom's. Tom addressed his [ ]agon with sarcasm, referring to i[] as "Mr. Monster" while describing himself as unpalatable. Humor proved a p[]werful psychological sh[]e[]d. Holloway has his rifle but it proves the weaker of the two. Cold metal and gunpowder offer him ver[] little internal calm. Never[ ]less[

]

Of course, Part 13 or rather "Last" of The Holloway Tape initiates the largest and perhaps most popular debate surrounding *The Navidson Record.* Lantern C. Pitch a[]d Kadina Ashbeckie stand on opposite ends of the spectrum, one favoring an actual monster, the other opting for a ratio[]al explan[]tion. Neither one, however, succeeds in [ ] a definitive interpretation.

Last spring, Pitch in the Pelias Lecture Ser[]es announced: "Of course there's a beast! And I assure you our belief or disbelief makes very little difference to that thing!"[293] In *American Photo* (May 1996, p. 154) Kadina Ashbeckie wr[]te: "Death of light gives birth to a creature-darkness few can accept as pure[]absence. Thus despite rational object[]ons, technology's failure is over[]un by the onslaught of myth."[294]

[

]

Except the Vandal known as Myth *always* slaughters Reason if she falters. [ ] Myth is the tiger stalking the herd. Myth is Tom's [ ]r. Monster. Myth is Hol[ ]y's beast. ~~Myth is the Minotaur.~~[295] Myth is

---

[292]Collette Barnholt (*American Cinematographer,* [ ]ber 2, [ ] 49) has argued that the existence of Part 12 is an impossibility, claiming the framing and lighting, though only slightly different from earlier and later parts, indicate the presence of a recording device other than Holloway's. Joe Willis (*Film Comment,* [ ] p. 115) has pointed out that Barnholt's complaint concerns those prints released after 199[]. Apparently Part 12 in all prints before [ ] and after 1993 show a view consistent with the other twelve. And yet even though the spectre of digital manipulation has been raised in *The Navidson Record,* to this day no adequate explanation has managed to resolve the curious enigma concerning Part 12.

[293]Also see *Incarnation Of Spirit Things* and *Lo*[ ] by Lantern C. Pitch (New York: Resperine Press, 1996) for a look at the perils of disbelief.

[294]Also see Kadina Ashbeckie, "Myth's Brood" *The Nation,* [ ] September, 19[ ]

[295]~~At the heart of the labyrinth waits the Mi~~[ ]~~taur and like the Minotaur of myth its name is~~ [ ] ~~Chiclitz treated the maze as trope for psychic concealment, its excavation resulting in (tragic~~[ ] ~~reconciliation. But if in Chiclitz's eye the Minotaur was a son imprisoned by a father's shame, is there then~~

to Navidson's eye an equivalent misprision of the [ ] in the depths of that place? And for that matter does there exist a chance to reconcile the not-known with the desire for its antithesis?

As Kym Pale wrote:

Navidson is not
Minos. He did
not build the lab-
yrinth. He
only d[ ]covered it. The father of that place—be it a Minos,
Daedalus,[ ] St. Mark's god, another father who swore
"Begone! Relieve me from the sight
of your detested form", a whole paternal line here following a tradition
of dead sons—vanished long ago,
leaving the creat[ ]e within all the
time in history to forget, to grow,
to consume the consequences of its
own terrible fate. And if there once
was a time when a [
]slai [

] that time has long
since passed. "Love the lion!"
"Love the lion." But Love alone
does not make you Androcles. And
for your stupidity your head's
crushed like a grape in its jaws.[296]
Reconciliation within is personal
and possible; reconciliation without
is improbable. The creature does not
know you, does not fear you,
does not remember you,
does not even see you.
Be careful, beware[

][297]

[296]Pale[ ] allusion to the li[ ] here [
].[123]

[297]See Kym Pale's "Navidson and the Lion" *Buzz*, v. [ ]ber, 199[], p.[ ]. Also revisit *Traces of Death*.[298]

[298]Whether you've noticed or not—and if you have, well bully for you—Zampanò has attempted to systematically eradicate the "Minotaur" theme throughout The Navidson Record. Big deal, except while personally preventing said eradication, I discovered a particularly disturbing coincidence. Well, what did I expect, serves me right, right? I mean

Redwood.[299] And in Navidson's house that faceless black i[] many myths incarnate.

"Ce ne peut être que la fin du monde, en avançant," Rimbaud dryly remarked. Suffice it to say, Holloway does not [ ]French for his end. Instead he props up his []i[]eo camera, ignites a magnesium flare, and crosses the room to the far end, where he slumps in the corner to wait. Sometimes he mumbles [ ]hi[]self, sometimes he screams obscenities [ ]to the void: "Bullshit! Bullshit! Just try and get me you motherfucker!" And then as the minutes creak by, his energy dips. "[ ] I don't want to die, this [ ]" words coming out like a sigh—sad and lost. He lights another flare, tosses it toward the camera, then pushes the rifle against his chest and shoots himself. [ ]Jill Ramsey Pelterlock wrote, "In that place, the absence of an end finally became his own end."[300]

Unfortunately, Holloway is not entire[ ] s[ ]ssful. For exactly two minutes and 28 seconds he groans and twitches in his own blood, until fin[ ] he slip[] into shock and presumably death.[301] Then for 46 seconds the

---

that's what you get for wanting to turn **The Minotaur** into a homie . . . no homie at all.

299See Appendix B.

300Jill Ra[ ]y [ ]t[ ]ock's "No Kindness" *St. Pa*[ ], November 21, 1993.

301Quite a few people have speculated that Chad—thanks to the perverse acoustic properties of the house—probably heard Holloway commit suicide. See page 320. ~~Consider Rafael Geethtar Servagio's *The Language of Torture* (New York: St. Martin's Press, 1995), p. 13 where he likens Chad's experience to those of Roman's listening to Perilaus' devilish chamber: "This unusual work of art was a life-size replica of a bull, cast in solid brass, hollowed out, with a trapdoor in the back, through which victims were placed. A fire was then lit beneath the belly slowly cooking anyone inside. A series of musical pipes in the bull's head translated the tortured screams into strange m[]sic. Supposedly the tyrant Phalaris killed the inventor Perilaus by placing him inside his own creation[~~

]302

302Can't help thinking of old man Z here and those pipes in his head working overtime; alchemist to his own secret anguish; lost in an art of suffering. Though what exactly was the fire that burned him?

As I strain now to see past <u>The Navidson Record</u>, beyond this strange filigree of imperfection, the murmur of Zampanò's thoughts, endlessly searching, reaching, but never quite concluding, barely even pausing, a ruin of pieces, gestures and quests, a compulsion brought on by— well that's precisely it, when I look past it all I only get an inkling of what tormented him. Though at least if the fire's invisible, the pain's not—mortal and guttural, torn out of him, day and night, week after week, month after month, until his throat's stripped and he can barely speak and he rarely sleeps. He tries to escape his invention but never succeeds because for whatever reason, he is compelled, day and night, week after week, month after month, to continue building the very thing responsible for his incarceration.

Though is that really right?

[]am[ ]reveals nothing else but his still body. Nearly a minute of s[ ]ence. In fact, the length is so absurd it alm[]st appears as if Navidson forgot to trim this section. After all there is nothing more to [ ] gained from this scene. Holloway is dead. Which is [ ]act[ ] when it happ[]ns.

The whole thing clocks in under tw[] seconds. Fingers of blackness slash across the lighted wall and consume Holloway. And even if[ ] loses sight of everything, the tape still records that terrible growl, this time without a doubt, insi[]e the room.

Was it an actual cr[ ]t[ ]e?[303] Or just the flare sputtering out? And what about the sound? Was it made by a be[ ] or jus[] a[]other reconfig[]ration of that absurd space; like the Khumbu Icefall; product of []ome peculiar physics?

It seems erroneous to assert, like Pitch, that this creat[ ]e had actual teeth and claws of b[ ]e (which myth for some reason [ ] requires). [ ]t d[]d have claws, they were made of shadow and if it did have te[]th, they were made of darkness. Yet even as such the [ ] still stalked Holl[]way at every corner until at last it did strike, devouring him, even roaring, the last thing heard, the sound []f Holloway ripped out of existence.¦

I'm the one whose throat is stripped. I'm the one who hasn't spoken in days. And if I sleep I don't know when anymore.

A few hours drift by. I broke off to shuffle some feeling back into my knees and try to make sense of the image now stuck inside my head. It's been haunting me for a good hour now and I still don't know what to make of it. I don't even know where it came from.

Zampanò is trapped but where may surprise you. He's trapped inside me, and what's more he's fading, I can hear him, just drifting off, consumed within, digested I suppose, dying perhaps, though in a different way, which is to say—yes, "Thou sees me not old man, but I know thee well"—though I don't know who just said that, all of which is unfinished business, a distant moon to sense, and not particularly important especially since his voice has gotten even fainter, still echoing in the chambers of my heart, sounding those eternal tones of grief, though no longer playing the pipes in my head.

I can see myself clearly. I am in a black room. My belly is brass and I am hollow. I am engulfed in flames and suddenly very afraid.

How am I so transformed? Where, I wonder, is the Phalaris responsible for lighting this fire now sweeping over my sides and around my shoulders? And if Zampanò's gone—and I suddenly know in my heart he is very, very gone—why does strange music continue to fill that black room? How is it possible the pipes in my head are still playing? And who do they play for?

[303] ~~*Creature* is admittedly a~~[ ]~~pretty clumsy description. Offspring of the Greek *Koros* meaning "surfeit", the implication of fullness provides a misleading impression of the mino~~[ ]~~r. In fact all references to the Minotaur~~[ ]~~self must be viewed as purely representative. Obviously, what Holloway encounters here is pointed~~[]~~y not half man/ half bull.~~ [ ] ~~something other, forever inhabiting~~[ ]~~, unreadable~~ [ ]~~granting undeserved ontological benefits~~ [ ]

¦ As John Hollander [ ] "It would annihilate us all to see/ The huge shape of our being; mercifully/ [ ] offers us issue and oblivion" thus echoing one more time, though not for the last time, [

ESCAPE[304]

10\. Unlike Navidson, Karen does not need to watch the tape twice. She immediately starts dragging suitcases and boxes out into the rain. Reston helps.

Navidson does not argue but recognizes that their departure is going to take more than a couple of minutes.

"Go to a motel if you want," he tells Karen. "I've still got to pack up all the video and film."

At first Karen insists on remaining outside in the car with the children, but eventually the lure of lights, music, and the murmur of familiar voices proves too much, especially when faced with the continuing thunderstorm howling in the absence of dawn.

Inside she discovers Tom has attempted to provide some measure of security. Not only has he bolted the four locks on the hallway door, he has gleefully established a rebarbative barricade out of a bureau, china cabinet, and a couple of chairs, crowning his work with the basinet from the foyer.

Whether a coincidence or not, Cassady Roulet has gone to great lengths to illustrate how Tom's creation resembles a theatre:

> Note how the china cabinet serves as a backdrop, the opposing chairs as wings, the bureau, of course, providing the stage, while the basinet is none other than the set, a complicated symbol suggesting the action of the approaching play. Clearly the subject concerns war or at the very least characters who have some military history. Furthermore the basinet in the context of the approaching performance has been radically altered from its previous meaning as bastion or strong hold or safe. Now it no longer feigns any authority over the dark beyond. It inherently abdicates all pretense of significance.[305]

Karen appreciates Tom's work on this last line of defense, but she is most touched by the way he comically clicks his heals and presents her with the

---

]endlessly[] in an ever unfolding []nd yet never opening sequence,
[ ] lost on stone trails [

[304] I've no decent explanation why Zampanò calls this section "The Escape" when in footnote 265 he refers to it as "The Evacuation." All I can say is that this error strikes me as similar to his earlier waffling over whether to call the living room a "base camp" or "command post."

[305] Cassady Roulet's *Theater In Film* (Burlington: Barstow Press, 1994), p. 56. Roulet also states in his preface: "My friend Diana Neetz at *The World of Interiors* likes to imagine that the stage is set for *Lear*, especially with that October storm continuing to boom outside the Navidson's home."

colours—blue, yellow, red, and green—four keys to the hallway. An attempt to offer Karen some measure of control, or at least sense of control, over the horror beyond the door.

It is impossible to interpret her thanks as anything but heartfelt. Tom offers a clownish salute, winning a smile from both Chad and Daisy who are still somewhat disoriented from having been awakened at five in the morning and dragged out into the storm. Only when they have disappeared upstairs does Tom lift up the basinet and pull out a bottle of bourbon.

A few minutes later, Navidson enters the living room carrying a load of video tape and film. In all the commotion following his return, he has not yet had a spare moment to spend with his brother. That all changes, however, when he finds Tom on the floor, his head propped up against the couch, enjoying his drink.

"Knock it off," Navidson says swiftly, grabbing the alcohol from his brother. "Now is not the time to go on a binge."

"I'm not drunk."

"Tom, you're lying on the floor."

Tom takes a quick glance at himself, then shakes his head: "Navy, you know what Dean Martin said?"

"Sure. You're not drunk if you can lie down without holding on."

"Well look," Tom mutters, lifting his arms in the air. "No hands."

Setting down the box he is carrying, Navidson helps his twin up.

"Here, let me make you some coffee."

Tom gives a noticeable sigh as he at last leans on his brother. Not till now has he been able to really face the crippling grief Navidson's absence had caused him or for that matter address the enormous relief he now feels knowing his twin did indeed survive. We watch as tears well in his eyes.

Navidson puts his arm around him: "Come on."

"At least when you're drunk," Tom adds, quickly wiping the wet from his face. "You've always got the floor for your best friend. Know why?"

"It's always there for you," Navidson answers, his own cheeks suddenly flushing with emotion as he helps his weaving brother to the kitchen.

"That's right," Tom whispers. "Just like you."

Reston is the one who hears it first. He is alone in the living room packing up all the radios, when from behind the hallway door comes a faint grinding. It sounds miles away, though still powerful enough to cause the basinet on the bureau to tremble. Slowly the noise gathers itself, growing louder and louder, getting closer and closer, something unheralded and unfamiliar contained in its gain, evolving into a new and already misconstrued sort of menace. Reston's hands instinctively grab the wheels of his chair, perhaps expecting this new evolution within the chambers of the house to shatter the hallway door. Instead it just dies, momentarily relinquishing its threat to silence.

Reston exhales.

And then from behind the door comes a knock. Followed by another one.

Navidson is outside loading a box of Hi 8 cassettes into the car when he sees the upstairs lights in the house go out one by one. A second later Karen screams. The pelting rain and occasional crack of thunder muffles the sound, but Navidson instinctively recognizes the notes of her distress. As Billy described the scene in The Reston Interview:

> Navidson's dehydrated, hasn't eaten shit for two days, and now he's dragging supplies out to the car in the middle of a thunderstorm. Every step he takes hurts. He's dead on his feet, in total survival mode, and all it takes is her voice. He drops everything. Lost some rolls of film to water damage too. Just tears through the house to get her.

Due to the absence of any exterior cameras, all experiences outside the house rely on personal accounts. Inside, however, the wall mounted Hi 8s continue to function.

Karen is upstairs placing her hair brushes, perfume, and jewelry box in a bag, when the bedroom begins to collapse. We watch the ceiling turn from white to ash-black and drop. Then the walls close in with enough force to splinter the dresser, snap the frame of the bed, and hurl lamps from their nightstands, bulbs popping, light executed.

Right before the bed is sheared in half, Karen succeeds in scrambling into the strange closet space intervening between parent and child. Conceptual artist Martin Quoirez observes that this is the first time the house has "physically acted" upon inhabitants and objects:

> Initially, distance, dark, and cold were the only modes of violence. Now suddenly, the house offers a new one. It is impossible to conclude that Holloway's actions altered the physics of that space. Nevertheless, it is impossible to deny that its nature seems to have changed.[306]

Karen avoids the threat in her bedroom only to find herself in a space rapidly enlarging, the size swallowing up all light as well as Daisy's barely audible cries for help.

The darkness almost immediately crushes Karen. She collapses. Of course, there are no cameras at this point to show her lost in seizure. That history relies once again on The Reston Interview:

> Navy said it felt like he was running into the jaws of some big beast about to chomp down . . . and as you saw later on, that's— that's exactly what that ugly fucker finally did.
>
> [Reston chokes back tears]
>
> Sorry . . . I'm sorry . . . Awww fuck it still gets me.
>
> Anyway, Navy finds her hyperventilating on the floor. He scoops her up—supposedly she calmed down as soon as she was in his

[306]Martin Quoirez on The L. Patrick Morning Show, KRAD, Cleveland, Ohio, October 1, 1996.

arms—and then all of a sudden that growl starts up again, rolling in like bad thunder.

[Reston shifts in his wheelchair; takes a sip of water]

Well, he runs out of there. Back through their bedroom. Barely makes it through. The door frame came down like a guillotine. Hammered Navy's shoulder and grazed Karen in the head with enough force she lost consciousness.

I tell you Navy's one tough fucker. He kept going, down the stairs, and finally outside. And then Daisy stopped screaming.

11. The next clip of Hi 8 shows Navidson reentering the house, shouting for Daisy and Chad as he sprints down the hall, heading toward the stairs in order to get back up to the children's bedroom. Then suddenly the floor drops away and he is sliding straight into the living room where he would have died had he not succeeded with one desperate flail to grab hold of the handle to one of the doors.

The Reston Interview:

Me, I had been trying to get the hell out of there. The knock had turned into this heavy awful pounding. The hallway door was still bolted shut and barricaded but I just knew all hell was about to break lose.

In fact, my first thought was that it was Holloway, though that hammering was awful hard. I mean the whole wall shuddered with every hit, and I'm thinking if that *is* Holloway he's changed and I don't need to reacquaint myself with this new and improved version. Especially not now.

[Reston repositions his wheelchair slightly]

My chair was still pretty messed up so I couldn't move as fast as I normally do. Then all of a sudden, the pounding stops. Just like that. Silence. No banging, no growl, nothing. And boy, I don't know how to describe it but that silence was more powerful than any sound, any call. I had to answer it, that silence, I mean, I had to respond. I had to look.

So I turn around—you can see some of this on the video—the door's still closed and the stuff Tom put together is still in front, though the-what-you-call-it, the helmet, has already fallen to the floor. Then the china cabinet and bureau start to sink. Slowly at first, inch by inch, and then a little faster. My

> chair begins to slide. I wedge the brakes, grip the wheels. At first I don't understand what's happening until it dawns on me that it's the floor beneath the barricade that's dropping.
>
> That's when I twisted around and lunged for the foyer. No chance I could have wheeled out of there. I barely managed to reach the door frame and get enough of a purchase to hang on. My chair though slipped out from under me and just rolled, end over end, down that slope.
>
> The floor must have sunk six, seven feet. Way below the baseboard, like the foundation had given way, except there was no fucking foundation. You expected to see cement but all there was was blackness.
>
> All of it—the china cabinet, bureau, coffee table, chairs—just slid down that floor and vanished over the edge. Navy would have vanished too if he hadn't got hold of that door lever.

Thus the devouring of one theatre of the absurd leads to another. And as is true in both cases, no amount of monologue, costume, or wit can defer the insistent gravity of that void. As theatre critic Tony K. Rich once remarked: "The only option is a quick exit, stage left, and I'd also advise a cab to the airport."[307]

The exit, however, is not so easily achieved. The Reston Interview again:

> Well I started yelling for help. You have to remember, my hands were all messed up from my trip down there. My grip was failing. If Navy didn't get to me fast, I was going to fall.
>
> So Navy starts swinging that door he's hanging on, back and forth, until he can kind of swing, kind of scramble to where he's about three feet away from me. Then he takes this deep breath, gives me half a smile, and jumps.
>
> That was the longest moment of them all, and then it was over. He was holding onto the door frame, hauling himself into the foyer, and then dragging me to safety. And all that with a messed up shoulder too.
>
> On tape, it looks like Navy just hopped over to me and that was that. But boy the way I remember it, his jump took forever.

Though poorly lit with even poorer resolution, we can see in the video how Navidson uses the door to get in range of Reston, despite the fact that the hinges are about to give way. Luckily, he manages to jump free

[307]Tony K. Rich's "Tip The Porter" *The Washington Post*, v. 119, December 28, 1995, p. C-1, column 4.

just as the door wrenches loose and tumbles into oblivion. The whole thing does not last more than a handful of seconds, but like Reston, Navidson notes how this brief bit of action still leaves a lasting impression. From The Last Interview:

> A few moments ended up feeling like hours. I was just dangling on that brass handle, not daring to look, though of course I did. The floor was steeper than the Lhotse Face, dropping right off into that familiar chill. I knew I had to get to Billy. I just hadn't figured out how yet. Then I heard the ripping. The hinges weren't supporting my weight.
>
> So I did about the only thing I could think of: I swung the door left, right, then left, and right one more time which closed the gap to a few feet from where Reston was hanging. Just as I made my jump, I heard the first hinge and then the second hinge tear free of the frame. That sound stretched the seconds into hours.
>
> [Pause]
>
> Once I made it though, everything sped up again. The next thing I knew we were both out on the front lawn getting soaked by the rain.
>
> You know when I finally went back to the house to retrieve the Hi 8s, I couldn't believe how quickly it had all happened. My leap looks so easy and that darkness doesn't seem dark at all. You can't see the hollowness in it, the cold. Funny how incompetent images can sometimes be.

Those last words in particular may sound a bit glib, especially coming from such an esteemed photographer. Nevertheless, in spite of numerous Hi 8s mounted all over the house, Navidson is right: all the images recorded during this segment are inadequate.

Too bad Navidson never holds a camera. The entire sequence covering the escape from the house is reminiscent of something taken off of a cheap surveillance system in a local bank or 7-Eleven. The clips are impartial renderings of a space. If the action slips past the frame, the camera does not care enough to adjust its perspective. It cannot see what matters. It cannot follow.

Only the interviews inform these events. They alone show us how the moments bruise and bleed.

12.

Outside rain overwhelms everything, drenching the street, filling the gutters, stripping trees of fall leaves. Reston sits on the grass, soaked to the bone but refusing to take shelter. Karen is still unconscious, lying in the car exactly where Navidson put her.

Daisy and Chad, however, are still missing.

So for that matter is Tom.

Navidson is trying to decide how he should reenter the house when the sound of shattering glass draws him to the backyard. "It was definitely a window breaking" Reston remembers. "And when Navy heard it, he just took off running."

Reston recalls watching Navidson disappear around the house. He had no idea what would happen next. It was bad enough that he was without his wheelchair. Then he heard Daisy scream, a high-pitched burst bright enough to pierce the hard patter of the storm, followed by shouts, and then something Reston had never heard before: "It was like an immense gasp, only very, very loud."

Reston was squinting in the rain, when he suddenly saw a shadow separate from the tree line: "By then dawn had begun to creep in but the storm clouds were still keeping the day pretty dark." Reston immediately assumed it was Navidson but then as the figure got closer he could see it was much smaller than his friend. "A strange walk too. Not fast at all but very deliberate. There was even something threatening about it."

Chad just nodded at Reston as he passed by him and climbed into the car. He never said a thing either, just sat down next to his mother and waited for her to wake up.

Chad had seen what had happened but had no words to describe it. Reston knew if he wanted to find out, he would have to drag himself toward the back of the house, which is exactly what he started to do.

Daisy had stopped screaming because of Tom.

Somehow Tom had managed to make his way through the heaving house to the upstairs hallway where he began to close in on the cries of the terrified five year old. What no one knew then was that Chad had already snuck outside, preferring the solitude of the early morning to all the packing and panic curdling inside.

As we can see, Tom finally finds Daisy frozen in the shadows. Without a word, he sweeps her up in his arms and races back down to the first floor, avoiding the precipitous drop into the living room—the way Navidson had gone—by dashing instead toward the rear of the house.

The whole place keeps shuddering and shaking, walls cracking only to melt back together again, floors fragmenting and buckling, the ceiling suddenly rent by invisible claws, causing moldings to splinter, water pipes to rupture, electrical wires to spit and short out. Worse, the black ash of below, spreads like printer's ink over everything, transforming each corner, closet, and corridor into that awful dark. Then Tom and Daisy's breath begins to frost.

In the kitchen, Tom throws a stool through the window. We hear Tom saying: " Okay Daisy girl,make it through here and you're home free." Which might have been just that simple had the floor not taken on the characteristics of giant conveyor belt, suddenly drawing them away from their only escape.

Cradling Daisy in his arms, Tom starts running as fast as he can, trying to out race the shock of the void yawning up behind them. Ahead, Navidson appears in the window.

Tom pushes harder, edging closer and closer, until finally as he gets within reach, he holds Daisy out to Navidson who despite the fragments of glass scratching long bloody lines along his forearms, immediately rips her free of the house and into safety.

Tom, however, has found his limit. Badly out of breath, he stops running and drops to his knees, clutching his sides and heaving for air. The floor carries him backwards ten or fifteen feet more and then for no apparent reason stops. Only the walls and ceiling continue their drunken dance around him, stretching, bending, even tilting.

When Navidson returns to the window, he cannot believe his brother is standing still. Unfortunately, as Tom demonstrates, whenever he takes one step forward, the floor drags him two steps back. Navidson quickly begins to crawl through the window, and oddly enough the walls and ceiling almost instantly cease their oscillations.

What happens next happens so fast it is impossible to realize just how brutal the closure was before it is already over. Only the after-effects create an image commensurate with the shutter like speed with which those walls snapped shut and shattered all the fingers in both of Tom's outstretched hands. Bones "like bread sticks" (Reston's words)[308] now jut out through the flesh. Blood covers his arms, as well as pours from his nose and ears.

For a moment, Tom looks like he is going to slip into shock as he stares at his mutilated body.

"Goddamn it Tom, run!" Navidson shouts.

And Tom tries, though his effort only sweeps him farther away from his brother. This time when he stops, he knows he has no chance.

"Hang on, I'm coming to get you," Navidson yells, as he squeezes himself all the way onto the kitchen counter.

"Aw Christ," Tom mutters.

Navidson looks up.

"What?"

Whereupon Tom disappears.

In less time than it takes for a single frame of film to flash upon a screen, the linoleum floor dissolves, turning the kitchen into a vertical shaft. Tom tumbles into the blackness, not even a scream flung up behind him to mark his fall, Navidson's own scream ineffectually scratching after him, his twin, stolen and finally mocked in silence, not even the sound of Tom hitting the bottom, which is how it might have remained had not some strange and unexpected intrusion, out of the blue, returned Tom's end in the shape of an awful gasp, heard by Reston, perhaps by Karen who suddenly groaned, and certainly by Chad who crouched among the trees, listening and finally watching over the sobs of his father and little sister until something dark and unknown told him to find his mother.

---

[308]Due to the darkness and insufferable limitations of the Hi 8s, the chaotic bits of tape representing these events must be supplemented with Billy's narration. Navidson, however, does not discuss any of these horrific moments in The Last Interview. Instead he makes Reston the sequence's sole authority. This is odd, especially since Reston saw none of it. He is only recounting what Navidson told him himself. The general consensus has always been that the memory is simply too painful for Navidson to revisit. But there is another possibility: Navidson refuses to abandon the more perspicacious portion of his audience. By relying on Reston as the sole narrative voice, he subtly draws attention once again to the question of inadequacies in representation, no matter the medium, no matter how flawless. Here in particular, he mockingly emphasizes the fallen nature of any history by purposefully concocting an absurd number of generations. Consider: 1. Tom's broken hands ⟶ 2. Navidson's perception of Tom's hurt ⟶ 3. Navidson's description of Tom's hurt to Reston ⟶ 4. Reston's re-telling of Navidson's description based on Navidson's recollection and perception of Tom's actual hurt. A pointed reminder that representation does not replace. It only offers distance and in rare cases perspective.

XIV

"Let you be stripped of your purple dyes, for I too once in the wilderness with my wife had all the treasure I wished."

— Enkidu

Toward the end of October, Navidson went up to Lowell to take care of his brother's things. He assured Karen he would join her and the children by the first of November. Instead he flew straight back down to Charlottesville. When Thanksgiving came and went and Navidson still had not made it to New York, Karen called Fowler.

Following the release of *The Navidson Record*, Audrie McCullogh, who helped Karen build the bookshelf, briefly discussed the Navidsons' relationship in a radio interview (a transcript can be obtained by writing to KCRW in Los Angeles). In it Audrie claimed the decision not to get married always came from Karen: "Navy would have married her in a second. She was always the one against it. She wanted her freedom and then would go berserk when he was away. Her whole affair with Fowler was about that. Seeing someone else but not . . . agh, I shouldn't get into that."[309]

After Navidson had vanished down the Spiral Staircase, Karen found herself trapped between two thresholds: one leading *into* the house, the other leading *out* of it. Even though she finally did succeed in leaving Ash Tree Lane and in some respects Navidson, she was still incapable of entering any sort of dark enclosed place. Even in New York she refused to take subways and always avoided elevators.

The reasons are not at all obvious. The leading theory now depends on a history given by Karen's estranged older sister Linda. Earlier this year, she went on a public access "talk show" and described how they had been sexually abused by their stepfather. According to her, one fall weekend while their mother was away, he took both girls to an old farmhouse where he forced Karen (age fourteen) down into a well and left her there while he raped Linda. Later, he forced Linda down the well and did the same to Karen.

The pharmacotherapy study Karen participated in never mentions any history of sexual abuse (see footnote 69). However it does not seem unreasonable to consider a traumatic adolescent experience, whether a fantasy or real, as a possible source for Karen's fears. Unfortunately when asked by various reporters to confirm her sister's claim, Karen refused to comment.

---

[309]Audrie McCullogh interviewed by Liza Richardson on "Bare Facts," KCRW, Los Angeles, June 16, 1993.

Navidson also refuses to comment, stating only that Karen's already natural fear of that place was worsened by her severe "claustrophobia." In *The Navidson Record*, Karen describes her anxiety in very simple terms: "Green lawns in the afternoon, warm 100 watt bulbs, sunny beaches, all of them, heaven. But get me near an elevator or a poorly lit basement and I'll freak. A blackout can paralyze me. It's clinical. I was once part of a study but the drugs they gave me made me fat."

More than likely no one will ever learn whether or not the stories about the well and Karen's stepfather are true.

After a decade of distance, the house was supposed to be a new beginning. Navidson gave up assignments abroad and Karen vowed to concentrate on raising their family. They both wanted and for that matter needed what neither one could really handle. Navidson quickly took refuge in his documentary. Regrettably for Karen, his work was still at home. He played more with the children, and every day filled the rooms with his substantial energy and natural authority. Karen was not strong enough to define her own space. She needed help.

Except in those objects housing evidence of her adultery, Karen's affair with Fowler barely exists in *The Navidson Record.* It was not until the film began to succeed that details concerning this relationship, however spurious, began to emerge.

Fowler was an actor living in New York. He worked at a Fifth Avenue clothing store, specializing in Italian cuts for women. He was considered consummately attractive and spent his evenings talking about acting down at the Bowery Bar, Naked Lunch, or Odelay-la. Apparently he picked up Karen on the street.

Literally.

Rushing to meet her mother for dinner, Karen had stepped off the curb and turned her ankle. For a dazed instant she lay on the asphalt amid the scattered contents of her bag—*der absoluten Zerrissenheit.*[310] An instant later, Fowler reached down and lifted her back onto the sidewalk. He gathered up her things and paid attention to her. By the time he was gone, she had given him her number and two days later when he called she had agreed to a drink.

After all, he was consummately attractive, and even more appealing to Karen, he was stupid.

This had taken place when Navidson and Karen were still living in New York City, a year before they bought the house in Virginia. Navidson was off taking aerial pictures of barges off the Norwegian coast. Once

[310]A line for Kyrie, though these days she's a little unapproachable as Gdansk Man is now officially on some kind of Halloween rampage. He apparently cornered Lude at Dragonfly intending to exact some kind of serious physical retribution. Lude smiled and kicked him hard in the balls. The bouncers there, all friends of Lude's, quickly threw the madman into the street. Gdansk Man in turn, being one of this century's truly great logicians, left some yelling message on my machine. A powerful bit of articulation on his part, frequently juxtaposing murder and my name with just the right amount of grunting incoherence. Who cares? Fuck him. As if he's really going to change any of this, which also applies to that scrap of German up there, as if a translation will somehow decrease the shattering effect this whole thing has had on me. It won't. I know that now. There's little else I can do now but copy it all down. And fast.

again, Karen resented being left alone with the children. Audrie claimed she was "desperate for a way out."[311] Fowler's timing could not have been better.

Audrie stopped short of revealing much about the affair, but Karen's sister, Linda, offered a pornographic recounting which many took seriously until they realized she had been out of touch with Karen for at least three years. The only source for this story comes by way of Fowler. No doubt the attention he received from the media was too much for a struggling actor to give up. Nor is there any question that he embellished to keep the media interested.

" She's a great lady" Fowler first told reporters." And it wouldn't be cool to talk about it, about us, I mean."[312] And then a little later to some tabloid reporters, "What we had was special. Ours. You know what I mean. I don't have to explain what we did or where we did it. We went to the park, had a drink, talked. I tried to show her some fun. We're friends now. I wish her well, I do." And still later, "She wanted a divorce.[313] That guy didn't treat her well. She fell down in the street and I picked her up. She'd never had anyone do that for her before."[314]

Fowler probably never realized how wrong he was. Not only had Navidson carried Karen out of that house, he had picked her up a hundred times over the course of eleven years and carried her fear, her torment and her distance. In a rare moment, Reston called in on a late-night radio show and lambasted the host for promoting such ridiculous gossip: "Let me tell you this, Will Navidson did everything for that woman. He was solid. Once, for a thirteen month stretch, she wouldn't let him touch her. But he never budged. Loved her just the same. I doubt that punk would have lasted a week. So give it a rest @$$hole" and before the subject could turn to the house or anything else, Reston hung up.[315]

Eventually Fowler moved on to other things. He married a pornstar and disappeared into a very disagreeable world.

Rumours still insist Karen had other affairs. As beautiful as she was, it is not hard to believe she had suitors. Strangers were constantly writing her love letters, delivering expensive perfumes, sending her plane tickets to far off places. Supposedly she sometimes responded. There was someone in Dallas, someone in L.A. and several in London and Paris. Audrie, however, claims Karen only flirted and her indiscretions never went further than a coy drink or a curt meal. She maintains that Karen never slept with any of them. They were just a means to escape the closeness of any relationship, particularly the one with the man she loved most.

It is pretty certain Navidson knew about "the love letters Karen hid in her jewelry box."[316] But what intrigues many critics these days is the manner in which he chose to regard that curious object. As semiotician Clarence Sweeney wrote:

> While Navidson refused to make her infideli-
> ties a 'public' part of the film, he seemed

---

[311]Interview with Audrie McCullogh. KCRW, Los Angeles, June 16, 1993.

[312]See Jerry Lieberman's "Fowl Play" in *People,* v. 40, July 26, 1993, p. 44.

[313]Karen had told Fowler she was married. She even wore one of her mother's old wedding bands to prove it. (See *New York*, v. 27, October 31, 1994, p. 92-93).

[314]*The Star*, January 24, 1995, p. 18.

[315]Cahill Jones' "Night Life," KPRO, Riverside, September 11, 1995.

[316]Audrie McCullogh. KCRW, Los Angeles, June 16, 1993.

incapable of excluding them either. Consequently he symbolizes her transgressions in the sealed hand-carved ivory case containing Karen's valuables, thus creating a 'private' aspect to his project, which in turn prompts yet another reevaluation of the meaning of interiority in *The Navidson Record*.[317]

---

[317]See Clarence Sweeney's *Privacy and Intrusion in the Twenty-First Century* (London: Apeneck Press, 1996), p. 140, as well as works already mentioned in footnote 15. Also reconsider the moment discussed in Chapter II (pages 10-11) where Navidson opens the jewelry box and then moments later throws out some of the hair he has just removed from Karen's brush.[318]

[318]No matter whether you're an electrician, scholar or dope addict, chances are that somewhere you've still got a letter, postcard or note that's meaningful to you. Maybe only to you.

It's amazing how many people save at least a few letters during their lifetime, leaves of feeling, tucked away in a guitar case, a safety deposit box, on a hard drive or even preserved in a pair of old boots no one will ever wear. Some letters keep. Some don't. I have a few that haven't spoiled. One in particular hides inside a locket shaped like a deer.

It's actually a pretty clunky thing, supposedly over a hundred years old, made out of polished sterling silver with platinum plated antlers, emerald eyes, small diamonds on the fringe of its mane and a silver latch disguised as the tail. A thread of braided gold secures it to whoever wears it, which in this case has never been me. I just keep it by my bed, in the locked lower drawer of my nightstand.

My mother was the one who used to wear it. Whenever I saw her, from the time I was thirteen till I was almost eighteen, she always had it around her neck. I never knew what she kept inside. I saw it before I left for Alaska and I guess even back then there was something about its shape I resented. Most lockets I'd seen were small, round and warm. They made sense. Hers I didn't get. It was awkward, ornate and most of all cold, every now and then blinking out odd bits of light, a warped mirror, attempting a reflection when she took care of it. For the most part only achieving a blur.

I saw it again before I left for Europe. An essay I'd written on the painter Paulus de Vos (1596-1678) had won me an all-paid summer abroad. I lasted two days in the program. By the third day I was heading for the station, looking for something, maybe someone, a bindle on my back, a Eurorail pass in hand, not more than three hundred bucks in traveler checks in my pocket. I ate very little, hustled from place to place, peeking into Czechoslovakia, Poland and Sweden before looping west so I could race all the way down from Denmark to Madrid where I stalked the halls of the Prado like a pack of hounds howling for a hart. Star stung chess games in Toledo soon gave way to a mad trek east for the littered lore of Naples and eventually a ferry ride to Greece where I made my way among Ionian islands before heading on towards destinations even further south. Back in Rome, I spent almost a week at a whorehouse, talking to the women about the simplest stuff while they waited for their next turn—another story waiting on other days. In Paris I lived at the bistros during the night, occasionally splurging on beer and escargots, while during the day I slept brokenhearted on the quays of the Seine. I don't know why I say brokenhearted. I guess it's the way I felt, all emaciated and without company. Everything I saw in me somehow only reflecting my destitution. I often thought about the

It is safe to assume Navidson knew Karen better than anyone else. No doubt his knowledge of Fowler, the cache of letters, certainly the discovery of Wax and Karen's kiss, contributed to his decision to return to the house for one more exploration.[320] He left her to New York because by then he knew she was already gone. And she was.

Jerry Lieberman who wrote the original *People* interview with Fowler had spoken with the would-be-actor for a possible follow up article but lack of interest in the affair caused him to shelve the story. After a little haggling, he agreed to send the tape of their last conversation. Here then for the first time is what Fowler told Lieberman on July 13, 1995:

> Yeah, she called me up, said she was in town, how 'bout a drink, that sort of thing. So we go out a few times. I fuck her a few times, you know what I mean, but she's not talking much now. Only thing she says is she's working on some film short. I asked her if there's a part for me but she tells me it's not that kind of film.
>
> I must have seen her two or three maybe four times. It was fun and all but she looked like hell and I didn't like taking her around. She'd changed over the months, pale, darker, didn't smile much, and when she did it was kinda different than before, kinda quirky, weird, real personal.
>
> She looked her age too. Too old for me really and with kids and all and well, time to move on. Those things happen you know.
>
> Anyway I didn't need to worry that she'd get clingy or anything. She wasn't that type of lady. The last time we went out, she said she only had a few minutes. She had to get back to that film she was editing or whatever. Something

---

locket, dangling from her neck. Sometimes it made me hurt. Often it made me angry.

She once told me it was valuable. That thought never crossed my mind. Even today I won't consider its monetary worth. I'm living off of tuna, rice and water, losing pounds faster than Lloyd's of London, but I'd sell body parts before I'd consider taking cash for this relic.

When my mother died the locket was the only thing she left me. There's an engraving on the back. It's from my father[319]: "My heart for you, my love—March 5, 1966"—practically prophetic. For a long time, I didn't flip the latch. I'm not sure why. Maybe I was afraid what I'd find inside. I think I expected it to be empty. It wasn't. When I finally did crack the hinge, I discovered the carefully folded love letter disguised as a thank you letter, scrawled in the hand of an eleven year old boy.

It's a letter I wrote.

The very first one my mother ever received from the son she left when he was only seven. It's also the only one she saved.

[319]Mr. Truant is referring here to his biological father not Raymond, his foster father. — Ed.

[320]Covered in greater detail in Chapters XVII and XIX.

> about interviews and family movies. And that was that. She shook my hand and left.
>
> But I'll tell you, she was different from when I first met her. I've fucked around with married women before. I know how they get off on dicking over their husband. She wasn't like that now. She needed him. I could see that in her eyes. It wasn't the first time either I seen a married woman get eyes like that. Suddenly they want what they got off getting away from in the first place. It's all fucked up. And she was like that. All fucked up and needing him. But as that story usually goes, he wasn't around no more.[321]

Which was true. Navidson was no longer around, except of course Karen still saw him every day and in a way she had never seen him before—not as a projection of her own insecurities and demons but just as Will Navidson, in flickering light, flung up by a 16mm projector on a paint-white wall.

---

[321] Courtesy of Jerry Lieberman.

XV

Mit seinen Nachtmützen und Schlafrockfetzen
Stopft er die Lücken des Weltenbaus.

— Heine[322]

Karen Green sits on a park bench in Central Park. She wears a russet sweater and a black cashmere scarf. All around her we see people milling about, enjoying one of those sparkling February days New York City sometimes deigns to deliver. Patches of snow lie on the ground, children shriek, carriages clatter past taxi cabs and traffic cops. A war is going on in the Persian Gulf but those affairs hardly seem to matter here. As Karen explains, more than a little time has passed:

> It's been four months since we escaped from our house. It's also four months since I've seen Navy. As far as I know, he's still in Charlottesville with Billy— conducting experiments.
>
> [She coughs lightly]
>
> We used to talk on the phone but now even that's stopped. This whole experience has changed him. Losing Tom, I think changed him the most.
>
> I've called, written, done everything short of going down there, which is something I refuse to do. I'm up here taking care of our children and looking after his film. He did some work on it but then he just stopped and shipped me all of it, the negatives, the tapes, the whole mess. Still, he won't leave Virginia. And to think, two months ago he told me he was only going to need a few more days.
>
> My mother keeps telling me to get rid of him and sell the house. I'm thinking about it but in the meantime I've been working on the film. There was so much of it I decided to cut it down to thirteen minutes [#4] to find out what people thought of it.

---

[322]"With his nightcaps and the tatters of his dressing-gown he patches up the gaps in the structure of the universe"—which he quoted in full to his wife, as well as alluded to in chapter Six of *The Interpretation of Dreams* and in a letter to Jung dated February 25, 1908.[323]

[323]`Heine?`[324]

[324]Freud. — Ed.

[#4] More than likely, an eight minute version of Karen's abridgment became the second short now known as "Exploration #4." However, it remains a mystery who cut out five minutes (which must have included Holloway's suicide) before distributing it. Kevin Stanley in *"What Are You Gonna Do Now, Little Man?" and Other Tales of Grass Roots Distribution* (Cambridge: Vallombrosa Inc., 1994) points out how easy it would have been for one of the professors or authors who received a copy to make a dupe. As to why

And I showed it to everyone I could think of too—professors, scientists, my therapist, village poets, even some of the famous people Navy knew.

[Coughs again]

Anne Rice, Stephen King, David Copperfield, and Stanley Kubrick actually responded to unsolicited copies of the video I sent them.

Without further ado then, here is what everyone had to say about that house.[325]

□□□□

A Partial Transcript Of

<u>What Some Have Thought</u>

by Karen Green[327]

---

though, five minutes were excised, Stanley unconvincingly chalks up to Karen Green's own ineptitude: "She simply must have misstated the length of the tape."

[325]Interestingly enough neither __________ nor __________ , both of whom actually saw the hallway, ever provided any comments. Perhaps XXXXXXXXXXXXXXXXXXXXXXXXXXXXXXX XXXXXXXXXXXXXXXXXXXXXXXXXXXXXXXXXXXXXXXXXXXXXXXXXXXX.[326]

[326]Crossed out with what looked suspiciously like black crayon and tar.

[327]Originally *The Navidson Record* contained both of Karen's pieces: *What Some Have Thought* and *A Brief History Of Who I Love*. However when Miramax put the film in wide release, *What Some Have Thought* was absent. At a Cannes press junket, Bob Weinstein argued that the section was too self-referential and too far from "the spine of the story" to justify its inclusion. "Audiences just want to get back to the house" he explained. "The delay that piece caused was unbearable. But don't worry, you'll have it in the DVD release."[328]

[328]To date, I haven't heard back from any of the people quoted in this "transcript" with the exception of Hofstadter who made it very clear he'd never heard of Will Navidson, Karen Green or the house and Paglia who scribbled on a postcard: "Get lost, jerk."

Leslie Stern, M.D. Psychiatrist.

Setting: Her office. Well lit, Chagal print on the far wall, requisite couch.

Stern: It's quirky. What do you need my opinion for?

Karen: What do you think it is? Does it have some kind of, well, . . . meaning ?

Stern: There you go again with "meaning." I gave up meaning a long time ago. Trying to get a table at Elaine's is hard enough. [Pause] What do you think it means?

Jennifer Antipala. Architect & Structural Engineer.

Setting: Inside St. Patrick's Cathedral.

Antipala: [Very high-strung; speaks very fast] The things that came to me, now I guess this is just the way my mind works or something, but the whole house prompted these questions, which I guess, like you said, is, uh, what you're after. Though they're not exactly concerned with meaning, I think.

[Pause]

Karen: What were the questions?

Antipala: Oh god, a whole slew of them. Anything from what the soil bearing capacity of a place like that would have to be to, uh, say, well uh . . . Well first, I mean go back to just soil bearing capacity. That's a very complicated question. I mean, look "massive rock" like trap rock for instance can stand up to 1000 metric tons per square meter while sedimentary rock, like hard shale or sandstone for instance, will crumble with anything over 150 metric tons per square meter. And soft clay's not even worth 10 metric tons. So that place, beyond dimension, impossibly high, deep, wide —what kind of foundation is it sitting on? And if it's not, I mean if it's like a planet, surrounded by space, then its mass is still great enough it's gonna have a lot of gravity, driving it all inward, and what kind of material then at its core could support all that?

Douglas R. Hofstadter. Computer and cognitive science professor at Indiana University.

Setting: At a piano.

Hofstadter: Philip K. Dick, Arthur C. Clarke, William Gibson, Alfred Bester, Robert Heinlein, they all love this stuff. Your piece is fun too. The way you handled the Holloway expedition, reminded me of Bach's Little Harmonic Labyrinth. Some of the thematic modulations, I mean.

Karen: Do you think such a place is possible? I have a structural engineer friend who's more than a little skeptical.

Hofstadter: Well, from a mathematical point of view . . . infinite space into no space . . . Achilles and the tortoise, Escher, Zeno's arrow. Do you know about Zeno's arrow?

Karen: No.

Hofstadter: [illustrating on a scrap of staff paper] Oh it's very simple. If the arrow is here at A and the target is here at B, then in the course of getting to B the arrow must travel at least half that distance which I'll call point C. Now in getting from C to B the arrow must travel half that distance, call that point D, and so on. Well the fun starts when you realize you can keep dividing up space forever, paring it down into smaller and smaller fractions until . . . well, the arrow never reaches B.

Byron Baleworth. British Playwright.

Setting: La Fortuna on 71st street.

Baleworth: "And St. Sebastian died of heartburn," to reference another famous British playwright. The infinite here is not a matter for science. You've created a semiotic dilemma. Just as a nasty virus resists the body's immune system so your symbol—the house—resists interpretation.

Karen: Does that mean it's meaningless?

Baleworth: That's a long conversation. I'm staying at the Plaza Athénée for the next few nights. Why don't we have dinner? [Pause] That thing's off, right?

Karen: Well give me a rough idea how you'd tackle the question?

Baleworth: [Suddenly uncomfortable] I'd probably turn to the filmmaking. Meaning would come if you tied the house to politics, science, or psychology. Whatever you like but something. And the monster. I'm sorry but the monster needs work. For Pete's sake, is that thing on?!

Andrew Ross. Literature professor at Princeton University.

Setting: Gym. Ross works out with a medicine ball.

Ross: Oh the monster's the best part. Baleworth's a playwright and as far as the English go probably a traditionalist when it comes to ghost stories. Quite a few Brits you know still prefer their ghosts decked in crepe and cobweb, candelabra in one hand. Your monster, however, is purely American. Edgeless for one thing, something a compendium of diverse cultures definitely requires. You can't identify this creature with any one group. Its individuality is imperceptible, and like the dark side of the moon, invisible but not without influence.

You know when I first saw the monster, I thought it was a Keeper. I still think that. It's a very mean House Keeper who vigilantly makes sure the house remains void of absolutely everything. Not even a speck of dust. It's a maid gone absolutely nutso.

Have you ever worn a maid's outfit?

Jennifer Antipala.

Antipala: And what about the walls? Load-bearing? Or non-load-bearing walls? That takes me from questions about foundation material to building material. What could that place possibly be made of? And I'm thinking right now of the shifting that goes on, so that means we're not talking dead loads, which means a fixed mass, but live loads which must deal with wind, earthquakes and variance of motion within the structure. And that shifting is that the same say as wind-pressure distributions?, which is something like, something like, uh, oh yeah, P equals one half beta times V squared times C times G, uh, uh, uh, that's it, that's it, yeah that's it, or something like that, where P is wind pressure on the structure's surface . . . or do I have to go someplace else, look at wall bending or wall stresses, axial and lateral forces, but if we're not talking wind, what from then and how? how implemented? how offset? and I'm talking now about weight disbursement, some serious loading's going on there . . . I mean anything that big has got to weigh a lot. And I mean at the very least a lot-lot. So I keep asking myself: how am I going to carry that weight? And I really don't have a clue. So I start looking for another angle.

[Moves closer to Karen]

Camille Paglia. Critic.

Setting: The Bowery Bar patio.

Paglia: Notice only men go into it. Why? Simple: women don't have to. They know there's nothing there and can live with that knowledge, but men must find out for sure. They're haunted by that infinite hollow and its sense-making allure, and so they crave it, desire it, desire its end, its knowledge, its—to use here a Strangelove-ian phrase—its essence. They must penetrate, invade, conquer, destroy, inhabit, impregnate and if necessary even be consumed by it. It really comes down to what men lack. They lack the hollow, the uterine cavity, any creative life-yielding physiological incavation. The whole thing's about womb envy or vagina envy, whatever you prefer.[329]

Karen: What about my character's fear of darkness.

Paglia: Pure fabrication. The script was written by a man, right? What self-respecting woman is afraid of the dark? Women are everything that's internal and hidden. Women are darkness. I cover some of this in my book Sexual Personae due out from Vintage in a few months.
Are you busy this afternoon?

Anne Rice. Novelist.

Setting: The Museum of Natural History.

Rice: Oh I'm not so sure I care for that. So much sexual pairing, this masculine, this feminine . . . I think it's too political and obviously a bit strained.
Darkness isn't male or female. It's the absence of light, which is important to us because we are all retinal creatures who need light to move around, sustain ourselves and protect ourselves. George Foreman uses his eyes much more than his fists.
Of course, light and dark mean a lot less to a bat. What matters more to a bat is whether or not FM frequencies are jamming its radar.

Harold Bloom. Critic.

Setting: His private library. Walls loaded with books. General disarray.

Bloom: My dear girl, Kierkegaard once wrote, "If the young man had believed in repetition, of what might he not been capable? What inwardness he might have attained."

---

[329]Melissa Schemell in her book *Absent Identification* (London: Emunah Publishing Group, 1995), p. 52. discusses sexual modes of recognition:

> *The house as vagina:* The adolescent boy's primary identification lies with the mother. The subsequent realization that he is unlike her (he has a penis; she doesn't; he is different) results in an intense feeling of displacement and loss. The boy must seek out a new identity (the father) . . . Navidson explores that loss, that which he first identified with: the vagina, the womb, the mother.

Eric Keplard's *Maternal Intrusions* (Portland: Nescience Press, 1995), p. 139, also speaks of that place as something motherly, only his reading is far more historical than Schemel's: "Navidson's house is an incarnation of his own mother. In other words: absent. It represents the unresolved Oedipal drama which continually intrudes on his relationship with Karen." That said it would be unfair not to mention Tad Exler's book *Our Father* (Iowa City: Pavernockurnest Press, 1996) which rejects "the over-enthusiastic parallels with motherdom" in favor of "narcissism's paternal darkness."

We'll touch on your, uh, unfinished piece shortly, but please permit me first to read you a page from my book The Anxiety Of Influence. This is from the chapter on Kenosis:

> The unheimlich, or "unhomely" as the "uncanny," is perceived wherever we are reminded of our inner tendency to yield to obsessive patterns of action. Overruling the pleasure principle, the daemonic in oneself yields to a "repetition compulsion." A man and a woman meet, scarcely talk, enter into a covenant of mutual rendings; rehearse again what they find they have known together before, and yet there was no before. Freud, unheimlich here, in his insight, maintains that "every emotional affect, whatever its quality, is transformed by repression into morbid anxiety." Among cases of anxiety, Freud finds the class of the uncanny, ☐ "in which the anxiety can be shown to come from something repressed which recurs." But this "unhomely" might as well be called "the homely," he observes, "for this uncanny is in reality nothing new or foreign, but something familiar and old-established in the mind that has been estranged only by the process of repression."

You see emptiness here is the purported familiar and your house is endlessly familiar, endlessly repetitive. Hallways, corridors, rooms, over and over again. A bit like Dante's house after a good spring cleaning. It's a lifeless objectless place. Cicero said "A room without books is like a body without a soul." So add souls to the list. A lifeless, objectless, soulless place. Godless too. Milton's abyss pre-god or in a Nietzschean universe post-god.

---

[330]While *unheimlich* has already recurred within this text, there has up to now been no treatment of the English word *uncanny*. While lacking the Germanic sense of "home," *uncanny* builds its meaning on the Old English root *cunnan* from the Old Norse *Kunna* which has risen from the Gothic *Kunnan* (preterite-present verbs) meaning know from the Indo-European (see *OED*). The "y" imparts a sense of "full of" while the "un" negates that which follows. In other words, un-cann-y literally breaks down or disassembles into that which is not full of knowing or conversely full of not knowing; and so without understanding exactly what repetitive denial still successfully keeps repressed and thus estranged, though indulging in repetition nonetheless, that which is *uncanny* may be defined as empty of knowledge and knowing or at the same time surfeit with the absence of knowledge and knowing. In the words of Perry Ivan Nathan Shaftesbury, author of *Murder's Gate: A Treatise On Love and Rage* (London: Verso, 1996), p. 183: "It is therefore sacred, inviolate, forever preserved. The ultimate virgin. The husbandless madonna. Mother of God. Mother of Mother. Inhuman." See also Anthony Vidler's *The Architectural Uncanny: Essays In The Modern Unhomely* (Cambridge, Massachusetts: The MIT Press, 1992).

It is so pointedly against symbol, the house requires a symbol destroyer. But that lightless fire leaving the walls permanently ashen and, to my eye, obsidian smooth is still nothing more than the artist's Procrustean way of combating influence: to create a featureless golem, a universal eclipse, Jacob's angel, Mary's Frankenstein, the great eradicator of all that is and ever was and thus through this trope succeed in securing poetic independence no matter how lonely, empty, and agonizing the final result may be.

My dear girl, is it that you are so lonely that you had to create this?

A Poe t. 21 years old. No tattoos. No piercings.

Setting: In front of a giant transformer.

Poe t: No capitals. [She takes out a paper napkin and reads from it] i was on line. i had no recollection of how i got there. of how i got sucked in there. it was pitch black. i suspected the power had failed. i started moving. i had no idea which direction i was headed. i kept moving. i had the feeling i was being watched. i asked "who's there?" the echoes created a passage and disappeared. i followed them

Douglas R. Hofstadter.

Hofstadter: Similar to Zeno's arrow, consider the following equation: $1/a = \lambda$ where $1/\infty = 0$.

If we apply this to your friend Bloom's poetics we get an interesting perspective on the monster.

Let 1 mean the artist, then let "a" equal 1 which stands for one influence and we get 1 for an answer, $\lambda=1$, or a level of one influence which I take to mean <u>total</u> influence.

If however we divide by 2 then the influence level drops to 1/2 and so on. Take the number of influences to infinity, where $a = \infty$, and voilà you have an influence level of zero, $\lambda=0$.

Now let's take this formula into account as we consider your monster. It has cleared the walls and corridors of everything. In other words, it has been influenced by infinity and therefore not influenced at all. But then look at the result: it's lightless, featureless, and empty.

I don't know maybe a little influence is a good thing.

Byron Baleworth.

Baleworth: You need to refine how the house itself serves as a symbol —

Stephen King. Novelist.

Setting: P.S. 6 playground.

King: Symbols shmimbols. Sure they're important but . . . Well look at Ahab's whale. Now there's a great symbol. Some say it stands for god, meaning, and purpose. Others say it stands for purposelessness and the void. But what we sometimes forget is that Ahab's whale was also just a whale.

Steve Wozniak. Inventor & Philanthropist.

Setting: The Golden Gate Bridge.

Woz: Sure I agree with King. An icon for a bridge game, it's a symbol for the program, the data, and more. But in some respects, it can also be looked at as that bridge game. The same is true with this house you created. It could represent plenty of things but it also is nothing more than itself, a house—albeit a pretty weird house.

Jennifer Antipala.

Antipala: I look at Hadrian's Pantheon, Justinian's Hagia Sophia, Suger's St. Denis, the roof of Westminster Hall, thanks to Herland, or Wren's dome for St. Paul's, and anything else that is seemingly above and beyond this world, and by the way, in my mind, those places I just mentioned really are above and beyond this world, and first it sparks awe, maybe disbelief, and then, after doing the math, tracing the lines, studying the construction, though it's still awesome, it also makes sense. Consequently it's unforgettable. Well that house of yours in your movie definitely sparks awe and all the disbelief, but in my mind it never makes sense. I trace the lines, do the math, study the construction, and all I come up with is . . . well the whole thing's just a hopeless, structural impossibility. And therefore substanceless and forgettable. Despite its weight, its magnitude, its mass . . . in the end it adds up to nothing.

[Moving away]

Jacques Derrida. French philosopher.

Setting: Artaud exhibit.

Derrida: Well that which is inside, which is to say, if I may say, that which infinitely patterns itself without the outside, without the other, though where then is the other?

Finished? Good.

[Pause]

Hold my hand. We stroll.

Andrew Ross.

Karen: Anything else?

Ross: The house was windowless. I loved that.

Byron Baleworth.

Baleworth: [Defensive] It's very sloppy. Why that type of house? Why in Virginia? These questions should have answers. There would be more cohesion. Mind you there is promise. [Pause] I hope you don't think I just made a pass at you.

Camille Paglia.

Paglia: [Laughing] Baleworth said that? You should have asked him why Dante's entrance to hell was in Tuscany? Why Young Goodman Brown's path was in New England? Baleworth's just jealous and besides he can't write a screenplay to save his pecker. [Pause] And incidentally I'm not afraid to tell you that I did make a pass at you.

So are you free this afternoon?

Walter Mosley. Novelist.

Setting: Fresh Kills Park

Mosley: Strange place. The walls changing all the time. Everything's similar, familiar, and yet without signposts or friends. Plenty of clues but no solutions. Just mystery. Strange, very strange. [He looks up, genuinely baffled] I don't know. I sure would hate to be stuck there.

Leslie Stern, M.D.

Karen: What else do you think about the film?

Stern: I'm no Siskel and Ebert—though I've been called Ebert before. There's a lot about emptiness, darkness, and distance. But since you created that world I don't think it's unfair to ask why you were so drawn to those themes?

Stephen King.

King: You didn't make this up, did you? [Studying Karen] I'd like to see this house.

Kiki Smith. Figurative Artist.

Setting: The New York Hospital - Cornell Medical Center E.R.

Kiki: Well gosh, without color and hardly even any grey, the focus moves to the other stuff—the surfaces, the shapes, dimensions, even all that movement. I'd have to say it comes down to that. Down to the construction, the interior experience, the body-sense there, which—well gosh—what makes the whole thing so visceral, so authentic.

Hunter S. Thompson. Journalist.

Setting: Giants Stadium.

Thompson: It's been a bad morning.

Karen: What did you think of the footage?

Thompson: I've been staying with friends, but they kicked me out this morning.

Karen: I'm sorry.

Thompson: Your film didn't help. It's, well . . . one thing in two words: fucked up . . .very fucked up. Okay three words, four words, who the hell cares . . . very very fucked up. What I'd call a bad trip. I never thought I'd hear myself say this but lady you need to lay off the acid, the mescaline, or whatever else you're snorting, inhaling, ingesting . . . check yourself into rehab, something, anything because you're gonna be in a bad way if you don't do something fast. I've never seen anything so goddamn fucked up, so fucking fucked up. I broke things because of it, plates, a small jade figurine of a penguin. A glass bullfrog. I was so upset I even threw my friend's fishtank at their china cabinet. Ugly, very ugly. Salt water, dead fish everywhere, me screaming "so very very fucked up." Five words. They threw me out. Do you think I could spend the night at your place?

Stanley Kubrick. Filmmaker.

Setting: (on-line)

Kubrick: "What is it?" you ask. And I answer, "It's a film. And it's a film because it uses film (and videotape)." What matters is how that film affects us or in this case how it affects me. The quality of image is often terrible except when Will Navidson handles the camera which does not happen often enough. The sound is poor. The elision of many details contributes to insufficiently developed characters. And finally the overall structure creaks and teeters, threatening at any minute to collapse. That said (or in this case typed) I remain soberly impressed and disturbed. I even had a dream about your house. If I didn't know better I'd say you weren't a filmmaker at all. I'd say the whole thing really happened.

David Copperfield. Magician.

Setting: The Statue of Liberty

Copperfield: It looks like a trick but it's a trick that constantly convinces you it's not a trick. A levitation without wires. A hall of mirrors without mirrors. Dazzling really.

Karen: So how would you describe the house?

Copperfield: A riddle.

[Behind him the Statue of Liberty disappears.]

Camille Paglia.

Paglia: How would I describe it? The feminine void.

Douglas R. Hofstadter.

Hofstadter: A horizontal eight.

Stephen King.

King: Pretty darn scary.

Kiki Smith.

Kiki: Texture.

Harold Bloom.

Bloom: Unheimlich—of course.

Byron Baleworth.

Baleworth: Don't care to.

Andrew Ross.

Ross: A great circuit in which individuals play the part of electrons, creating with their paths bits of information we are ultimately unable to read. Just a guess.

Anne Rice.

Rice: Dark.

Jacques Derrida.

Derrida: The other. [Pause] Or what other, which is to say then, the same thing. The other, no other. You see?

Steve Wozniak.

Woz: I like Ross' idea. A giant chip. Or a series of them even. All interconnected. If only I could see the floor plan then I could tell you if it's for something sexy or just a piece of hardware— like a cosmic toaster or blender.

Stanley Kubrick.

Kubrick: I'm sorry. I've said enough.

Leslie Stern, M.D.

Stern: More importantly Karen, what does it mean to you?

[End Of Transcript][331]

---

[331]So many voices. Not that I'm unfamiliar with voices. A rattle of opinion, need and compulsion but masking what? //

Thumper just called (hence the interruption; the "//").

A welcome voice.

Strange how that works. I'm no longer around and suddenly out of the blue she calls, for the very first time too, returning my old pages I guess, wanting to know where I've been, why I haven't stopped by the Shop at all, filling my ear with all kinds of stuff. Apparently even my boss has been asking about me, acting all hurt that I haven't dropped by to hang out or at least say hello.

"Hey Johnny," Thumper finally purred over the phone. "Why don't you come over to my place. I'll even cook you dinner. I've got some great pumpkin pie left over from Thanksgiving."

But I heard myself say "No, uh that's okay. No thanks but thank you anyway," thinking at the same time that this might very well be the closest I'll ever come to an E ticket invite to The Happiest Place On Earth.

It's too late. Or maybe that's wrong. Maybe not too late, maybe it's just not right. Beautiful as her voice is, it's just not strong enough to draw me from this course. Where eight months ago I'd have already been out the door. Today, for whatever sad reason, Thumper no longer has any influence over me.

For a moment, I flashed on her body, imagining those beautiful round breasts with creamy brown aureolas, making saints out of nipples, her soft, full lips barely hiding her teeth, while in the deep of her eyes her Irish and Spanish heritage keep closing like oxygen and hydrogen, and will probably keep on closing until the very day she dies. And yet in spite of her shocking appeal, any longing I should have felt vanished when I saw, and accepted, how little I knew about her. The picture in my head, no matter how erotic, hardly sufficing. An unfinished portrait. A portrait never really begun. Even taking into

□□□□

Funny how out of this impressive array of modern day theorists, scientists, writers, and others, it is Karen's therapist who asks, or rather forces, the most significant question. Thanks to her, Karen goes on to fashion another short piece in which she, surprisingly enough, never mentions the house, let alone any of the comments made by the gliterati.

It is an extraordinary twist. Not once are those multiplying hallways ever addressed. Not once does Karen dwell on their darkness and cold. She produces six minutes of film that has absolutely nothing to do with that place. Instead her eye (and heart) turn to what matters most to her about Ash Tree Lane; what in her own words (wearing the same russet sweater; sitting on the same Central Park bench; coughing less) "that wicked place stole from me."

So in the first black frame, what greets us is not sinister but blue: the strains of Charlie "Yardbird" Parker coaxing out of the darkness the precocious face of a seventeen year old Will Navidson.

Piece after piece of old Kodak film, jerky, over exposed, under exposed, usually grainy, yellow or overly red, coalesce to form a rare glimpse of Navidson's childhood—*nicht allzu glatt und gekünstelt*.[332] His father—drinking ice tea. His mother—a black and white headshot on the mantle. Tom—watering the lawn. Their golden retriever, the archetype for all home movie dogs, frolicking in the sprinklers, pouncing on the pale green hose as if it were a python, barking at Tom, then at their father, even though as its jaws snap open and shut it is impossible to hear a bark—only Charlie Parker playing to the limits of his art, lost in rare delight.

As professor Erik Von Jarnlow poignantly remarked:

> I don't think I'm alone in feeling the immutable sadness contained in these fragments. Perhaps that is the price of remembering, the price of perceiving accurately. At least with such sorrow must come knowledge.[333]

---

account her daisy sunglasses, her tattoos, the dollars and fives she culls while draped around some silver pole hidden in some dark room in the shadow of the airport. A place I had still not dared to visit. I had never even asked her the name of her three year old. I had never even asked her for her real name—not Thumper, not Thumper at all, but something entirely else—which I suddenly resolved to find out, to ask both questions right then and there, to start finding out who she really was, see if it was possible to mean something to her, see if it was possible she could mean something to me, a whole slew of question marks I was prepared to follow through on, which was exactly when the phone went dead.

She hadn't hung up nor had I. The phone company had just caught up with their oversight and finally disconnected my line.

No more Thumper. No more dial tone. Not even a domed ceiling to carry a word.

Just silence and all its consequences.

---

[332] "Not overly polished or artificial." — Ed.

[333] See Erik Von Jarnlow's *Summer's Salt* (New York: Simon and Schuster, 1996), p. 593.

Karen progresses steadily from Navidson's sundrenched backyard to a high school prom, his grandmother's funeral, Tom covering his eyes in front of a barbecue, Navidson diving headfirst into a swimming hole. Then college graduation, Will hugging Tom good-bye as he prepares to leave for Vietnam,[334] a black and white shot catching the wing of his plane in flight.

And then the whole private history explodes.

Suddenly a much larger world intrudes on the boyish Navidson. Family portraits are replaced by pictures of tank drivers in Cambodia, peasants hauling empty canisters of nerve gas to the side of the road, children selling soda near body bags smeared with red oil-soaked clay, crowds in Thailand, a murdered man in Israel, the dead in Angola; fractions plucked from the stream, informing the recent decades, sometimes even daring to suggest a whole.

And yet out of the thousands of pictures Navidson took, there does not exist a single frame without a person in it. Navidson never snapped scenery. People mattered most to him, whether soldiers, lepers, medics, or newlyweds eating dinner at a trattoria in Rome, or even a family of tailors swimming alone at some sandy cove north of Rio. Navidson religiously studied others. The world around only mattered because people lived there and sometimes, in spite of the pain, tragedy, and degradation, even managed to triumph there.

Though Karen gives her piece the somewhat faltering title **A Brief History Of Who I Love**, the use of Navidson's photos, many of them prize-winning, frequently permits the larger effects of the late 20th century to intrude. Gordon Burke points out the emotional significance of this alignment between personal and cultural pasts:

> Not only do we appreciate Navidson more, we are inadvertently touched by the world at large, where other individuals, who have faced such terrible horrors, still manage to walk barefoot and burning from the grave.[335]

Each of Navidson's photographs consistently reveals how vehemently he despised life's destruction and how desperately he sought to preserve its fleeting beauties, no matter the circumstances.

Karen, however, does not need to point any of this out. Wisely she lets Navidson's work speak for itself. Interestingly enough though, her labor of love does not close with one of his photographs but rather with a couple of shots of Navidson himself. The first image—purportedly taken by a famous though now deceased photojournalist—shows him when he was a young soldier in South East Asia, dressed in battle fatigues, sitting on an ammunition crate with howitzer shell casings stacked on a nearby trunk marked "VALUABLES." An open window to the right is obviously not enough to clear the air. Navidson is alone, head down, fingertips a blur as he sobs into his hands over an experience we will undoubtedly never share but perhaps can still imagine. From this heart-wrenching portrait, Karen ever so gently dissolves to the last shot of her piece, actually a clip of Super

---

[334]According to Melanie Proft Knightley in *War's Children* (New York: Zone Books, 1994), p. 110, a weak heart prevented Tom from getting drafted. Navidson had gone ahead and enlisted.

[335]See the introduction by Gordon Burke in Will Navidson's *Pieces* (New York: Harry N. Abrams, Inc., 1994), p. xvii.

8 which she herself took not long before they moved to Virginia. Navidson is goofing around in the snow with Chad and Daisy. They are throwing snowballs, making snow angels, and enjoying the clarity of the day. Chad is laughing on his father's shoulders as Navidson scoops up Daisy and holds her up to the blinding sun. The film, however, cannot follow them. It is badly overexposed. All three of them vanish in a burst of light.

□□□□

The diligence, discipline, and time-consuming research required to fashion this short—there are easily over a hundred edits—allowed Karen for the first time to see Navidson as something other than her own personal fears and projections. She witnessed for herself how much he cherished the human will to persevere. She again and again saw in his pictures and his expressions the longing and tenderness he felt toward her and their children. And then quite unexpectedly, she came across the meaning of his privately guarded obsession.

While Navidson's work has many remarkable images of individuals challenging fate, over a third captures the meaning of defeat—those seconds *after* an execution, the charred fingers found in the rubble of a bombed township, or the dull-blue look of eyes which in the final seconds of life could still not muster enough strength to close. In her filmic sonnet, Karen includes a shot of Navidson's Pulitzer Prize-winning photograph. As she explains in a voice-over: "The print comes from Navy's personal collection." The same one hanging in their home and one of the first things Navidson placed in their car the night they fled.

As the world remembers, the renowned image shows a Sudanese child dying of starvation, too weak to move even though a vulture stalks her from behind.[336] Not only does Karen spend twenty seconds on this picture, she then cuts to a ten second shot of the back of the print. Without saying a word, she zooms in tighter and tighter on the lower right hand corner, until her subject finally becomes clear: there, almost lost amidst so much white, lie six faintly penciled in block letters cradled in quotes—

"Delial"

□□□□

There are only 8,160 frames in Karen's film and yet they serve as the perfect counterpoint to that infinite stretch of hallways, rooms and stairs. The house is empty, her piece is full. The house is dark, her film glows. A growl haunts that place, her place is blessed by Charlie Parker. On Ash Tree Lane stands a house of darkness, cold, and emptiness. In 16mm stands a house of light, love, and colour.

[336]This is clearly based on Kevin Carter's 1994 Pulitzer Prize-winning photograph of a vulture preying on a tiny Sudanese girl who collapsed on her way to a feeding center. Carter enjoyed many accolades for the shot but was also accused of gross insensitivity. The Florida St. Petersburg *Times* wrote: "The man adjusting his lens to take just the right frame of her suffering might just as well be a predator, another vulture on the scene." Regrettably constant exposure to violence and deprivation, coupled with an increased dependency on drugs exacted a high price. On July 27, 1994 Carter killed himself. — Ed.

By following her heart, Karen made sense of what that place was not. She also discovered what she needed more than anything else. She stopped seeing Fowler, cut off questionable liaisons with other suitors, and while her mother talked of breaking up, selling the house, and settlements, Karen began to prepare herself for reconciliation.

Of course she had no idea what that would entail.

Or how far she would have to go.

XVI

When mathematical propositions refer to reality they are not certain; when they are certain, they do not refer to reality.

— Albert Einstein

Up until now *The Navidson Record* has focused principally on the effects the house has had on others: how Holloway became murderous and suicidal, Tom drank himself into oblivion, Reston lost his mobility, Sheriff Axnard went into a state of denial, Karen fled with the children, and Navidson grew increasingly more isolated and obsessed. No consideration, however, has been given to the house as it relates purely to itself.

Examined then from as objective a point of view as possible the house offers these incontrovertible facts:

1.0		No light.	I, IV-XIII*
2.0		No humidity.	I, V-XIII
3.0		No air movement (i.e. breezes, drafts etc).	I, V-XIII
4.0		Temperature remains at 32° F ± 8 degrees.	IX
5.0		No sounds.	IV-XIII
	5.1	Except for a dull roar which arises intermittently, sometimes seeming far off, sometimes sounding close at hand.	V, VII, IX- XIII
6.0		Compasses do not function there.	VII
	6.1	Nor do altimeters.	VII
	6.2	Radios have a limited range.	VII-XIII
7.0		Walls are uniformly black with a slightly 'ashen' hue.	I, IV-XIII
8.0		There are no windows, moldings, or other decorative elements. (See 7.0)	IX

9.0	Size and depth vary enormously.		I, IV-VII, IX-XIII
	9.1	The entire place can instantly and without apparent difficulty change its geometry.	I, IV-VII, IX-XIII
	9.2	Some have suggested the dull roar or 'growl' is caused by these metamorphoses. (See 5.1)	VII
	9.3	No end has been found there.	V-XIII
10.0	The place will purge itself of all things, including any item left behind.		IX-XIII
	10.1	No object has ever been found there.	I, IV-VII, IX-XIII
	10.2	There is no dust.	XI
11.0	At least three people have died inside.		X, XIII
	11.1	Jed Leeder, Holloway Roberts and Tom Navidson.	
	11.2	Only one body was recovered. (See 10.0)	XIII

*See Chapter.

Where objective data is concerned, this was all Navidson had to work with. Once he left the house, however, he began to consider new evidence: namely the collected wall samples.

In lush colour, Navidson captures those time-honored representations of science: test tubes bubbling with boric acid, reams of computer paper bearing the black-ink weight of analysis, electron microscopes resurrecting universes out of dust, and mass-spectrometers with retractable Faradays and stationary Balzers humming in some dim approximation of life.

In all these images there is a wonderful sense of security. The labs are clean, well-lit, and ordered. Computers seem to print with a purpose. Various instruments promise answers, even guarantees. Still in order to make sure all this apparatus does not come across as too sterile, Navidson also includes shots of the life-support system: a Krups coffee maker hissing and bubbling, an *Oasis* poster taped to the vending machine, Homer Simpson on the lounge TV saying something to his brother Herbert.

As a favor to Reston, petrologist Mel O'Geery, up at the Princeton geology department, has agreed to donate his spare time and oversee the examination of all the wall samples. Prone toward bird like gestures, he is a slight man who takes great delight in speaking very quickly. For nearly four months, he has analyzed every piece of matter, all the way from **A** (taken a few feet into the first hallway) to **XXXX** (taken by Navidson when he found himself alone at the bottom of the Spiral Staircase). It is not an inexpensive undertaking, and while the university has agreed to fund most of it, apparently Navidson also had to throw in a fair amount himself.[337]

Setting out all the sample bottles on a long table, Dr. O'Geery provides the camera with a summation of his findings, casually gesturing to various groupings while he sips coffee from a Garfield mug.

"What we have here is a nice banquet of igneous, sedimentary, and metamorphic samples, some granular, possibly gabbro and pyroxenite, some with much less grain, possibly trachite or andesite. The sedimentary group is fairly small, samples **F** through **K**, mainly limestone and marl. The metamorphic group predominates with traces of amphibolite and marble. But this group here, it's composed primarily of siderites, which is to say heavy in iron, though you also have aerolites rich in silicon and magnesium oxides."

. . . .

[2 pages missing]

. . . .

[337]The actual sum is never made clear in the film. Tena Leeson estimates Navidson's contributions were anywhere from a few hundred dollars to a few thousand. "The High Cost of Dating" by Tena Leeson. *Radiogram,* v. 13, n. 4, October 1994, p. 142.

XXXXXXXXXXXXXXXXXXXXXXXXXXXXXXXXXXXX
XXXXXXXXXXXXecniques[338]XXXXXXXXXXXXXXXXXXX
XXXXXXXXXXXXXXXXXXXXXXXXXXXXXXXXXXXX
XXXXXXXXXXXXXXXXXXXXXXXXXXXXXXXXXXXX
XXXXXXXXXXXXXXXXXXXXXXXXXXXXXXXXXXXX
XXXXXXXXXXXXXXXXXXXXXXXXXXXXXXXXXXXX
XXXXXXXXXXXXXXXXXXXXXXXXXXXXXXXXXXXX
XXXXXXXXXXXXXXXXXXXXXXXXXXXXXXXXXXXX
XXXXXXXXXXXXXXXXXXXXXXXXXXXXXXXXXXXX
XXXXXXXXXXXXXXXXXXXXXXXXXXXXXXXXXXXX
XXXXXXXXXXXXXXXXXXXXXXXXXXXXXXXXXXXX
XXXXXXXXXXXXXXXXXXXXXXXXXXXXXXXXXXXX
XXXXXXXXXXXXXXXXXXXXXXXXXXXXXXXXXXXX
XXXXXXXXXXXXXXXXXXXXXXXXXXXXXXXXXXXX
XXXXXXXXXXXXXXXXXXXXXXXXXXXXXXXXXXXX
XXXXXXXXXXXXXXXXXXXXXXXXXXXXXXXXXXXX
XXXXXXXXXXXXXXXXXXXXXXXXXXXXXXXXXXXX
XXXXXXXXXXXXXXXXXXXXXXXXXXXXXXXXXXXX
XXXXXXXXXXXXXXXXXXXXXXXXXXXXXXXXXXXX
XXXXXXXXXXXXXXXXXXXXXXXXXXXXXXXXXXXX
XXXXXXXXXXXXXXXXXXXXXXXXXXXXXXXXXXXX
XXXXXXXXXXXXXXXXXXXXXXXXXXXXXXXXXXXX
XXXXXXXXXXXXXXXXXXXXXXXXXXXXXXXXXXXX
XXXXXXXXXXXXXXXXXXXXXXXXXXXXXXXXXXXX
XXXXXXXXXXXXXXXXXXXXXXXXXXXXXXXXXXXX
XXXXXXXXXXXXXXXXXXXXXXXXXXXXXXXXXXXX
XXXXXXXXXXXXXXXXXXXXXXXXXXXXXXXXXXXX
XXXXXXXXXXXXXXXXXXXcleosynthesis[340]XXXXXXXX
XXXXXXXXXXXXXXXXXXXXXXXXXXXXXXXXXXXX
XXXXXXXXXXXXXXXXXXXXXXXXXXXXXXXXXXXX
XXXXXXXXXXXXXXXXXXXXXXXXXXXXXXXXXXXX
XXXXXXXXXXXXXXXXXXXXXXXXXXXXXXXXXXXX
XXXXXXXXXXXXXXXXXXXXXXXXXXXXXXXXXXXX

[338]Radiometric dating includes work with carbon-14 (from a few hundred years to 50,000 years ago), potassium-argon (for dates ranging from 100,000 years to 4.5 x 10^9 years ago), rubidium-strontium (from 5 x 10^7 to about 4.5 x 10^9 years ago), lead isotopes (from 10^8 to 4.5 x 10^9 years ago) as well as fission-tracks (a few million to a few hundred million years ago) and thermoluminescence dating (used to date clay pottery).

[339]Table 1:

Parent Isotope	Daughter Isotope	Half-life
Carbon-14	Nitrogen-14	5730
Potassium-40	Argon-40	XXXXX
Rubidium-87	Strontium-87	4.88 x 10^{10}
Samarium-147	Neodymium-143	1.06 x 10^{11}
Lutetium-176	Hafnium-176	3.5 x 10^{10}
Thorium-232	Lead-208	1.4 x 10^{10}
Uranium-235	Lead-207	7.04 x 10^8
Uranium-238	Lead-206	4.47 x 10^9

[340]Scientists estimate the universe unfolded from its state of infinite destiny[341]—a moment commonly referred to as "the big bang"—approximately 1.3-2 x 10^{10} years ago.

[341]Typo: "destiny" should read "density."

XXXXXXXXXXXXXXXXXXXXXXXXXXXXXXXXXXXX
XXXXXXXXXXXXXXXXXXXXXXXXXXXXXXXXXXXX
XXXXXXXXXXXXXXXXXXXXXXXXXXXXXXXXXXXX
XXXXXXXXXXXXXXXXXXXXXXXXXXXXXXXXXXXX
XXXXXXXXXXXXXXXXXXXXXXXXXXXXXXXXXXXX
XXXXXXXXXXXXXXXXXXXXXXXXXXXXXXXXXXXX
XXXXXXXXXXXXXXXXXXXXXXXXXXXXXXXXXXXX
XXXXXXXXXXXXXXXXXXXXXXXXXXXXXXXXXXXX
XXXte[343]**XXXXXXXXXXXXXXXXXXXXXXXXXXXXXXX**
XXXXXXXXXXXXXXXXXXXXXXXXXXXXXXXXXXXX
XXXXXXXXXXXXXXXXXXXXXXXXXXXXXXXXXXXX
XXXXXXXXXXXXXXXXXXXXXXXXXXXXXXXXXXXX
XXXXXXXXXXXXXXXXXXXXXXXXXXXXXXXXXXXX
XXXXXXXXXXXXXXXXXXXXXXXXXXXXXXXXXXXX
XXXXXXXXXXXXXXXXXXXXXXXXXXXXXXXXXXXX
XXXXXXXXXXXXXXXXXXXXXXXXXXXXXXXXXXXX
XXXXXXXXXXXXXXXXXXXXXXXXXXXXXXXXXXXX
XXXXXXXXXXXXXXXXXXXXXXXXXXXXXXXXXXXX
XXXXXXXXXXXXvolcan**XXXXXXXXXXXXXXXXXXXX**
XXXXXXXXXXXXXXXXXXXXXXXXXXXXXXXXXXXX
XXXXXXXXXXXXXXXXXXXXXXXXXXXXXXXXXXXX
XXXXXXXXXXXXXXXXXXXXXXXXXXXXXXXXXXXX
XXXXXXXXXXXXXXXXXXXXXXXXXXXXXXXXXXXX
XXXXXXXXXXXXXXXXXXXXXXXXXXXXXXXXXXXX
XXXXXXXXXXXXXXXXXXXXXXXXXXXXXXXXXXXX
XXXXXXXXXXXXXXXXXXXXXXXXXXXXXXXXXXXX
XXXXXXXXXXXXXXXXXXXXXXXXXXXXXXXXXXXX
XXXXXXXXXXXXXXXXXXXXXXXXXXXXXXXXXXXX
XXXXXXXXXXXXXXXXXXXXXXXXXXXXXXXXXXXX
XXXXXXXXXXXXXXXXXXXXXXXXXXXXXXXXXXXX
XXXXXXXXXXXXmetamor**XXXXXXXXXXXXXXXXXXX**
XXXXXXXXXXXXXXXXXXXXXXXXXXXXXXXXXXXX

---

[342]The age of the earth lies somewhere between 4.43-4.57 x 10^9 years (roughly around the time our solar system formed). With a few exceptions, most meteors are younger. Micrometeorites, however, with high levels of deuterium, suggest evidence of interstellar material predating our solar system. See F. Tera, "Congruency of comformable galenas: Age of the Earth" *12th Lunar and Planetary Science Conference*, 1981, p. 1088-1090; and I.D.R. Mackinnon and F.J.M. Rietmeijer, "Mineralogy of chondritic interplanetary dust particles" *Rev. Geophys.* 1987, 25:1527-1553. See also those particle age-related studies carried out by Klaus Bebblestein and Gunter Polinger, published in *Physics Today*, v.48, September 1995, p. 24-30, as well as by the Oxford University Press, 1994, under the title *Particle Exam* which includes in Chapter Sixteen fascinating data generated at the Deutsch Electron Synchrotron (DESY; pronounced "Daisy") in Hamburg and even input from the HERMES collaboration which at the time was using the HERA electron-proton collider to study nucleon spin. Bebblestein and Polinger have also written extensively on the recent though highly speculative claim that accurate algorithms must now exist which are in keeping with Wave Origin Reflection Data Series as currently set forth by the VEM™ Corporation.

[343](BGC) Berkeley Geochronology Center. Paul Renne. See *Science* August 12, 1994. p. 864.

[344]One must not forget the crater created by a meteor in the Arizona desert 50,000 years ago: Canyon Diablo with a diameter of 1207 meters and a depth of 174 meters.

[345]Internal isochron measurements of Rb-Sr ages have shown the Norton County meteorite in the Aubrite group to have an age of 4.70 ± 0.13 Ga (1 Ga = 10^9 years). The Krahenberg meteorite in the LL5 group has an estimated age of 4.70 ± 0.01 Ga. As O'Geery indicates to Navidson, several of the **XXXX** samples also appear to have ages predating the formation of the earth. (Though the accuracy of those claims remains hotly contested). See D. W. Sears, *The Nature and Origin of Meteorites* (New York: Oxford University Press, 1978), p. 129; and Bailey Reims, *Formation vs. Metamorphic Age* (Cambridge, Massachusetts: The MIT Press, 1996), p. 182-235.

XXXXXXXXXXXXXXXXXXXXXXXXXXXXXXXXXXXX
XX abecedXXXXXXXXXXXX (spoken language versus the langXX
XXXXXXXXXXXXXXXXXXXXXXXXXXXXXXXXXXXX
XXXXXXXXXXXXXXXXXXXXXXXXXXXXXXXXXXXX
XXXXXXXXXXXXXXXXXXXXXXXXXXXXXXXXXXXX
XXXgeo[346]XXXXXXXXXXXXXXXXXXXXXXXXXXXXX
XXXXXXXXXXXXXXXXXXXXXXXXXXXXXXXXXXXX
XXXXXXXXXXXXXXXXXXXXXXXXXXXXXXXXXXXX
XXXXXXXXXXXXXXXXXXXXXXXXXXXXXXXXXXXX
XXXXXXXXXXXXXXXXXXXXXXXXXXXXXXXXXXXX
XXXXXXXXXXXXXXXXXXXXXXXXXXXXXXXXXXXX
XXXXXXXXXXXXXXXXXXXXXXXXXXXXXXXXXXXX
XXXXXXXXXXXXXXXXXXXXXXXXXXXXXXXXXXXX
XXXXXXXXXXXXXXXXXXXXXXXXXXXXXXXXXXXX
XXXXXXXXXXXXXXXXXXXXXXXXXXXXXXXXXXXX
XXXXXXXXXXXXXXXXXXXXXXXXXXXXXXXXXXXX
XXXXXXXXXXXXXXXXXXXXXXXXXXXXXXXXXXXX
XXXXXXXXXXXXXXXXXXXXXXXXXXXXXXXXXXXX
XXXXXXXXXXXXXXXXXXXXXXXXXXXXXXXXXXXX
XXXXXXXXXXXXXXXXXXXXXXXXXXXXXXXXXXXX
XXXXXXXXXXXXXXXXXXXXXXXXXXXXXXXXXXXX
XXXXXXXXXXXXXXXXXXXXXXXXXXXXXXXXXXXX
XXXXXXXXXXXXXXXXXXXXXXXXXXXXXXXXXXXX
XXXXXXXXXXXXXXXXXXXXXXXXXXXXXXXXXXXX
XXXXXXXXXXXXXXXXXXXXXXXXXXXXXXXXXXXX
XXXXXXXXXXXXXXXXXXXXXXXXXXXXXXXXXXXX
XXXXXXXXXXXXXXXXXXXXXXXXXXXXXXXXXXXX
XXXXXXXXXXXXXXXXXXXXXXXXXXXXXXXXXXXX
XXXXXXXXXXXXXXXXXXXXXXXXXXXXXXXXXXXX
XXXXXXXXXXXXXXXXXXXXXXXXXXXXXXXXXXXX
XXXXXXXXXXXXXXXXXXXXXXXXXXXXXXXXXXXX
XXXXXXXXXXXXXXXXXXXXXXXXXXXXXXXXXXXX
XXXXXXXXXXXXXXXXXXXXXXXXXXXXXXXXXXXX
XXXXXXXXXXXXXXXXXXXXXXXXXXXXXXXXXXXX
XXXXXXXXXXXXXXXXXXXXXXXXXXXXXXXXXXXX
XXXXXXXXXXXXXXXXXXXXXXXXXXXXXXXXXXXX

---

[346]Robert T. Dodd, *Meteorites: A Petrologic-Chemical Synthesis* (Cambridge: Cambridge University Press, 1981). Dodd also explains on page 161: "A chondrite's first isotopic equilibration is usually called its *formation*. The time period between nucleosynthesis and formation is called the *formation interval* and that between formation and the present *formation age*. The time difference between a later isotopic disturbance and the present is called a *metamorphic age*. We have known for a quarter century that all chondrites are approximately 4.55 billion years old (Patterson, 1956) and for a decade that their history up to and including metamorphism encompassed no more than 100 million years (Papanastassiou and Wasserburg, 1969). What parts of this brief high-temperature history were occupied by chondrule formation, accretion, and metamorphism has been and remains unclear, for it is not always easy to tell which stage a particular isotopic system records."

[347]*Meteoritics: Asteroids, Comets, Craters, Interplanetary Dust, Interstellar Medium Lunar Samples, Meteors, Meteorites, Natural Satellites, Planets, Tektites Origin and History of the Solar System*, Derek W. G. Sears, editor. Donald E. Brownlee, Michael J. Gaffey, Joseph I. Goldstein, Richard A. F. Grieve, Rhian Jones, Klaus Keil, Hiroko Nagahara, Frank Podosek, Ludolf Schultz, Denis Shaw, S. Ross Taylor, Paul H. Warren, Paul Weissman, George W. Wetherill, Rainer Wieler, associate editors. Published by The Meteoritical Society, v. 30, n. 3, May 1995. p. 244.

[348]A possible solution to the date line scheme detailed by Navidson and O'Geery. It certainly lends weight to those theories favoring the historical significance of the samples, though it does nothing to resolve the presence of extraterrestrial and possibly even interstellar matter.

XXXXXXXXXXXXXXXXXXXXXXXXXXXXXXXXXXXX
XXXXXXXXXXXXXXXXXXXXXXXXXXXXXXXXXXXX
XXXXXXXXXXXXXXXXXXXXXXXXXXXXXXXXXXXX
XXXXXXXXXXXXXXXXXXXXXXXXXXXXXXXXXXXX
XXXXXXXXXXXXXXXXXXXXXXXXXXXXXXXXXXXX
XXXXXXXXXXXXXXXXXXXXXXXXXXXXXXXXXXXX
XXXXXXXXXXXXXXXXXXXXXXXXXXXXXXXXXXXX
XXXXXXXXXXXXXXXXXXXXXXXXXXXXXXXXXXXX
XXXXXXXXXXXXXXXXXXXXXXXXXXXXXXXXXXXX
XXXXXXXXXXXXXXXXXXXXXXXXXXXXXXXXXXXX
XXXXXXXXXXXXXXXXXXXXXXXXXXXXXXXXXXXX
XXXXXXXXXXXXXXXXXXXXXXXXXXXXXXXXXXXX
XXXXXXXXXXXXXXXXXXXXXXXXXXXXXXXXXXXX
XXXXXXXXXXXXXXXXXXXXXXXXXXXXXXXXXXXX
XXXXXXXXXXXXXXXXXXXXXXXXXXXXXXXXXXXX
XXXXXXXXXXXXXXXXXXXXXXXXXXXXXXXXXXXX
XXXXXXXXXXXXXXXXXXXXXXXXXXXXXXXXXXXX
XXXXXXXXXXXXXXXXXXXXXXXXXXXXXXXXXXXX
XXXXXXXXXXXXXXXXXXXXXXXXXXXXXXXXXXXX
XXXXXXXXXXXXXXXXXXXXXXXXXXXXXXXXXXXX
XXXXXXXXXXXXXXXXXXXXXXXXXXXXXXXXXXXX
XXXXXXXXXXXXXXXXXXXXXXXXXXXXXXXXXX[350]

---

[349]Therefore Navidson's conclusion seems the only conclusion. Based on the evidence, sample **A** thru sample **XXXX** appear to make up an exact chronological map, which though simple, nevertheless still shows that . . . .

Inexplicably, the remainder of this footnote along with seventeen more pages of text vanished from the manuscript supplied by Mr. Truant. — Ed.

[350]I wish I could say this mass of black X's was due to some mysterious ash or frantic act of deletion on Zampanò's part. Unfortunately this time I'm to blame. When I first started assembling <u>The Navidson Record</u>, I arranged the various pages and scraps by chapter or subject.

Eventually I had numerous piles spread out across my room. I usually placed a book or some heavy object on them to keep the isolated mounds from flying apart if there were a draft or I happened to bump one with my foot. On top of this particular chapter I stupidly placed a bottle of German ink, 4001 brillant-schwarz or something. Who knows how long ago either, probably when I was still sketching pictures and tinkering with collages, maybe in August, maybe as far back as February. Anyway, there must have been a hairline crack in the glass because all of the ink eventually tunneled down through the paper, wiping out almost forty pages, not to mention seeping into the carpet below where it spread into a massive black bloom. The footnotes survived only because I hadn't incorporated them yet. They'd all been written out separately on a series of green index cards held together by a yellow rubber band.

. . . .
[17 pages missing]
. . . .

Navidson asks.

Dr. O'Geery mulls this over, takes another sip of his coffee, eyes the samples again, and then finally shrugs, "Not much really, though you've got yourself a nice range here."

"*Nothing* peculiar or out of the ordinary?" Navidson presses.

O'Geery shakes his head.

"Well except maybe the chronology."

"Meaning?" Reston eases his wheelchair forward.

"Your samples all fall into a very consistent scheme. Sample **A** is pretty young, a few thousand years old, while **K** is a few hundred thousand. **Q** over here is in the millions and these—" referring to **MMMM** through **XXXX** "—well, in the billions. Those last bits there are clearly meteoric."

"Meteors?" Navidson shoots a look at Reston.

O'Geery nods, picking up the sample marked **VVVV**. "In my opinion Rubidium-87/strontium-87 is the best dating method we have, yielding formation ages anywhere from 4.4 to 4.7 billion years old. If we place the age of the earth at around four and a half billion years old, it's pretty obvious these had to come from someplace other than here. I doubt lunar but maybe interplanetary. **XXXX**, your last sample, is by far the oldest and most interesting. A composite of younger material, 4.2 billion years old, combined with deuterium rich particles suggesting that possibly, now I want to stress *possibly* here, but this deuterium *could* indicate matter older than even our solar system. Interstellar perhaps. So there you have it—a very nice little vein of history."

Reston wheels back around to the table, as if Dr. O'Geery's explanation should now somehow cast the samples in a new light. Nothing about them, however, has changed. As Gillian Fedette exclaimed on August 4th, 1996 at The Radon Conference in St. Paul, Minneapolis: "Not surprisingly, despite [O'Geery's] analysis, the samples continue to remain obdurate and lifeless."

"Where did you say you got all this from?" O'Geery asks. "Antarctica?"

Primarily thanks to O'Geery's conclusions, some fanatics of *The Navidson Record* assert that the presence of extremely old chondrites definitively proves extra-terrestrial forces constructed the house. Others, however, claim the samples only support the idea that the house on Ash Tree Lane is a self-created portal into some other dimension.[351] As Justin Krape dryly remarked: "Both arguments are probably best attributed to the persistent presence of schizophrenia plaguing the human race."[352]

Keener intellects, however, now regard scientific conjecture concerning the house as just another dead end. It would seem the language of

[351]*A Lexicon of Improbable Theories*, Blair Keepling, ed. (San Francisco: Niflheim Press, 1996). In chapter 13, Keepling credits *The Navidson Record* with the revival of the Hollow Earth Movement. Tracing this implausible theory from the wobbly ratiocinations of John Cleaves Symmes (1779-1829) through Raymond Bernard's *The Hollow Earth: The Greatest Geographical Discovery in History* (1964) to Norma Cox's self-published pro-Nazi piece *Kingdoms Within Earth* (1985), Keepling reveals yet another bizarre subculture thriving in the Western world. Of course even if this planet were truly a hollow globe—an absolute impossibility—Tom's dropped quarter still describes a space far greater than the earth's radius (or even diameter).

[352]Justin Krape's *Pale Micturitions* (Charleston, West Virginia: Kanawha Press, 1996), p. 99.

objectivity can never adequately address the reality of that place on Ash Tree Lane.

Perhaps for us the most significant thing gleaned from this segment is Navidson's persistent use of all the data[353] to deny the internal shattering

---

[353]See Exhibit Three for all test results, including rubidium-87/strontium-87, potassium-40/argon-40, samarium-147/neodymium-143 dating, as well as a complete set of reports on uranium-235 and -238 contents in lead isotopes.[354]

[354]Don't worry that thought crossed my mind too. Unfortunately Exhibit Three doesn't make up for the spillage back there because there is no Exhibit Three. Aside from a few notes, it's missing. I've looked everywhere, especially for the Zero folder. Nothing. Who knows, maybe it's for the best.

Today, for no reason in particular, I started thinking about Dr.Ogelmeyer, wondering what I might have found out if I'd had the money, if I'd taken the time to see his specialist, if I'd opted for the tests. Of course if if were a fifth I'd be drunk, which I'm definitely not. Maybe that kind of confirmation is unnecessary anyway.

Still I wonder.

I grew up on certain words, words I've never mentioned to Lude or anyone for that matter, words orbiting around my mother mainly, sometimes whispered, more often written in letters my father would never have let me read had he lived.

(Now that I think about it, I guess I've always gravitated towards written legacies (private lands surrounded by great bewildering oceans (a description I don't entirely understand even as I write it down now (though the sense of adventure about words (that little "l" making so little difference), appeals to me—ah but to hell with the closing parent)he)see)s)(sic)

Before I understood the significance of things like "auditory hallucinations," "verbigeration," "word salad," "derealization," "depersonalization" I sensed in them all kinds of adventure. To reach their meaning would require a great journey, which I eventually found out was in fact true, though the destinations did not exactly turn out to be Edenic places full of gold leaf, opal or intricately carved pieces of jade.

Count yourself lucky if you've never wandered by the house of Kurt Schnieder or Gabriel Langfeldt, or if the criterias of St. Louis, Taylor and Abrams or Research Diagnostic leave you puzzled. The New Haven Schizophrenia Index should give more than enough away.

In my case, would Ogelmeyer have turned to those tools or would he have begun first with a biological examination? Look for hyperactivity of dopaminergic systems? Check for an increase in norepinephrine? Or more than likely run an MRI on my brain to see if the lateral and third ventricles were getting larger? Maybe he'd even take a peek at my delta activity on the good old electroencephalogram (EEG)?

What sort of data streams would be generated and how conclusively could he or his specialists read them?

I'll never know. Which is not to imply it's the wrong road. Quite the contrary. It's just not mine. All I hope for is a moment of rational thought and one shot at action before I'm lost to a great saddening madness, pithed at the hands of my own stumbling biology.

As it stands, I've dropped eighteen pounds. A couple of eviction notices lie near my door. I feel like I haven't slept in months. My neighbors are scared of me. Whenever I pass them in that dim brown-walled hall, which happens rarely, only when I have to go out for more tuna, books from the library or to sell blood to buy candles, I hear them whisper about my night screams—"He's the one, I'm sure of it." "Shhhh, not so loud."

For some reason, I've been thinking more and more about my mother and the way her life failed her, humiliated her with impulses beyond her command, broke her with year after year of the same. I never knew her that well. I remember she had amazing hair, like sunlight, extremely fine and whisked with silver, beautiful even when it was uncombed, and her eyes always seemed to brim with a certain tenderness when I visited. And though most of the time she whispered, sometimes she spoke up and then her voice would sound sweet and full like chapel bells caroling in the foreign towns I'd eventually wander at dawn, echoing down those streets where I'd find myself in the spare light, rubbing my cold hands together, hopping around like a lunatic, waiting for the pastry shops to open so I could buy a piece of bread and a cup of hot chocolate.

She also used to write me these letters, always handwritten and full of strange colored words. They started after my father was killed, loaded with advice and encouragement and most of all faith. I don't know if I would have survived Raymond without them. But she was never that well, and eventually her words soured, until— Well, I wish I could just stick to thoughts of her hair and her brimming eyes and caroling bells in foreign towns at dawn.

It's never that simple though, is it?

One day I received a letter in which she apologized for what she'd done. At first I thought she was talking again about the pan of oil she'd accidentally knocked to the floor when I was four but that wasn't it at all, though in an awful way her confession did change the way I began to view my scars, their oceanic swirls now spelling out suspicion and much too much doubt for me to really address properly. Anyhow, she was referring to a completely different event when my father was finally forced to take her away to The Whale, when I was only seven, a day I cannot for the life of me remember.

As she explained it, her thoughts at that time had entirely deteriorated. The burden of life seemed too much for her to bear and therefore, in her mind, an impossible and even horrible burden to impose upon a child, especially her own. Based on these wild ratiocinations, she gathered me up in her arms and tried to choke me. It was probably a very brief attempt. Maybe even comic. My father intervened almost immediately, and my mother was then taken away for my own safety. I guess I do remember that part. Someone saying "my own safety." My father I imagine. I suppose I also remember him leading her away. At least the shape of him in the doorway. With her. All blurred and in silhouette.

Raymond knew a little about my mother's history and he used to say it was a bad dream that got her.

"Nightmares you know," he once told me with a grin. "Can mess you up permanently. I've seen it happen to buddies of mine. That's why you'll never catch me without a gun under my pillow. That'll get any man through the night."

A week ago I gave myself a Christmas present. I dug up my Visa, which I still try my best to avoid using, and not only picked up a second gun, this time a stainless steel Taurus 605 .357, but also went ahead and ordered a rifle. More specifically I ordered a Weatherby 300 magnum, along with twenty boxes of 180 grain core-locked rounds.

caused by Tom's death and Karen's flight. He only speculates with Reston about what it could mean that samples **A** thru **XXXX** form a timeline extending back before the birth of even the solar system. He uses his camera to embrace the Princeton laboratory equipment, seek out the appeasement of numbers, all the while never openly reflecting on the very real absence continuing to penetrate his life. Similar to the way Karen tried to rely on Feng Shui to mitigate the effects of the house, Navidson turns to the time telling tick of radioactive isotopes to deny the darkness eviscerating him from within.

Noda Vennard believes the key to this sequence does not exist in any of the test results or geological hypotheses but in the margin of a magazine which, as we can see for ourselves, Navidson idly fills with doodles while waiting for Dr. O'Geery to retrieve some additional documentation:

> Mr. Navidson has drawn a bomb going off. An Atom bomb. An inverted thermonuclear explosion which reveals in the black contours of its clouds, the far-reaching shock-wave, and of course the great pluming head, the internal dimensions of his own sorrow.[355]

But even if that is indeed the best way to describe the shape of Navidson's emotional topology, it is still nothing compared to the vision the house ultimately prepares for him.

As professor Virgil Q. Tomlinson observes:

> That place is so alien to the kingdom of the imagination let alone the eye—so perfectly unholy, hungry, and inviolable—it easily makes a fourth of July sparkler out of an A-bomb, and reduces the aliens of

---

I guess I'm hoping the weapons will make me feel better, grant me some kind of fucking control, especially if I sense the dullness inside me get too heavy and thick, warning me that something is again approaching, creeping slowly towards my room, no figment of my imagination either but as tangible as you & I, never ceasing to scratch, fume and snort in awful rage, though still pausing outside my door, waiting, perhaps for a word or an order or some other kind of sign to at last initiate this violent and by now inevitable confrontation—always as full of wrath as I am full of fear. So far nothing, though I still take the Taurus and the Heckler & Koch out of the trunk, load them, and just hang on the trigger. Sometimes for a few minutes. Sometimes for hours. Aiming at the door or the window or a ceiling corner cast in shadow. I even lie with them in bed, hiding under my sky blue sheets. Trying to sleep. Trying to dream if only so I can remember my dreams. At least I'm not defenseless now. At least I have that. A gun in each hand. Not afraid to shoot. Safety off.

[355]See Noda Vennard's "Frame Detail" delivered for *The Symposium on The Cultural Effects of Nuclear Weaponry in the Twenty-First Century* held at The Technical University of Denmark on October 19, 1996. Also see Matthew Coolidge's *The Nevada Test Site:A Guide to America's Nuclear Proving Ground* (Culver City, CA: The Center for Land Use Interpretation, 1996) as well as Matthew Coolidge's *Nuclear Proving Grounds of the World*, ed. Sarah Simons (Culver City, CA: The Center for Land Use Interpretation, 1998).

The X-Files and *The Outer Limits* to Sunday morning funnies.[356]

[356]See Virgil Q. Tomlinson's "Nothing Learned, Nothing Saved: By Suggestion Of Science" in *Geo* v.83, February 7, 1994, p. 68.

Glossary

Deuterium:	A hydrogen isotope twice the mass of ordinary hydrogen. Needed for heavy water.
Diachronic:	Relating to the historical developments and changes occurring in language.
D-Structure:	Deep Structure. The tree providing a place for words as defined by phrase structure rules.
Igneous:	Rocks formed from *magma* (molten material). Classified on the basis of texture and mineral composition. Examples: granite, basalt, pumice.
Interstellar:	Originating or occurring among the stars.
Isotope:	One of two or more forms of an element with the same atomic number and chemical behavior but different atomic mass.
Linguistics:	Study of the structure, sounds, meaning, and history of language.
Metamorphic:	Preexisting rocks reformed by heat and pressure. Examples: slate and marble.
Meteors:	Nonterrestrial objects surviving passage through the Earth's atmosphere. Often divided into three groups: *siderites* (iron meteorites), *aerolites* (meteorites primarily composed of silicates), and *siderolites* (stony iron meteorites).
Morpheme:	Smallest meaningful part of a word.
Nucleosynthesis:	Creation of nucleons (neutrons and protons). Typically discussed when formulating theories about the origins of the universe.
Sedimentary:	Rocks created from hardened layers of sediment comprised of organic and inorganic material. Classified on the basis of chemical and particle shape and size. Examples: sandstone, shale, and coal.
Semantics:	Study of the relationship between words and meaning.
Spectrometer:	An instrument calibrated to measure transmitted energy whether radiant intensities at various wavelengths, the refractive indices of prism materials, or radiation.
S-Structure:	Surface Structure. The phrase tree formed when applying movement transformations to the d-structure.
Synchronic:	Concerning language as it exists at a single point in time.
Trace:	A silent element in a sentence which still indicates the d-structure position of a moved phrase.

XVII

Wer du auch seist: Am abend tritt hinaus
aus deiner Stube, drin du alles weißt;
als letztes vor der Ferne liegt dein Haus:
Wer du auch seist.

— Rilke[357]

While Reston continued to remain curious about the properties of the house, he had absolutely no desire to return there. He was grateful to have survived and smart enough not to tempt fate twice. "Sure I was obsessed at first, we all were," he says in The Reston Interview. "But I got over it pretty quick. My fascination was never the same as Navy's. I enjoy my life at the University. My colleagues, my friends there, the woman I've started to see. I've no desire to court death. After we escaped, going back to the house just didn't interest me."

Navidson had a completely different reaction. He could not stop thinking about those corridors and rooms. The house had taken hold of him. In the months following his departure from Ash Tree Lane, he stayed at Reston's apartment, alternately sleeping on the couch and the floor, continuously surrounded by books, proofs, and notebooks packed with sketches, maps, and theories. "I put Navy up because he needed help, but when the sample analysis brought back minimal results, I knew the time had come to have a heart to heart with him about the future." (The Reston Interview again.)

As we witness for ourselves, following their meeting with Dr. O'Geery, Navidson and Reston both return home. Reston breaks open a bottle of Jack, pours two three-finger glasses and hands one to his friend. A little time passes. They finish a second drink. Reston gives it his best shot.

"Navy" he says slowly. "We made a helluva try but now we're at a dead end and you're broke. Isn't it time to contact *National Geographic* or The Discovery Channel?"

Navidson does not respond.

"We can't do this thing alone. We don't *need* to do it alone."

Navidson puts his drink down and after a long uncomfortable silence nods.

"Okay, tomorrow morning we'll call them, we'll send them invitations, we'll get the ball rolling."

Reston sighs and refills their glasses for a third time.

"I'll drink to that."

---

[357] "Whoever you are, go out into the evening,/ leaving your room, of which you know each bit;/ your house is the last before the infinite,/ whoever you are." As translated by C. F. MacIntyre. Rilke: Selected Poems (Berkeley: University of California Press, 1940), p. 21. — Ed.

"Here's to opening things up, " Navidson says by way of a toast, then glancing at the photograph of Karen and the children he keeps by the sofa, adds: "And here's to me going home."

"After that we got pretty drunk." (The Reston Interview.) "Something neither one of us had done in a long while. When I packed it in, Navy was still awake. Still drinking. Writing in some journal he had. Little did I know what he had planned."

The next morning when Reston woke up, Navidson was gone. He had left behind a note of thanks and an envelope for Karen. Reston called New York but Karen had heard nothing. A day later he drove to the house. Navidson's car sat in the driveway. Reston wheeled himself to the front door. It was unlocked. "I sat there for an hour and a half, at least, before I could get the guts to go in."

But as Reston eventually found out the house was empty and most startling of all the hallway that had loomed for so long in the east wall was gone.

Why Did Navidson Go Back To The House?

A great deal of speculation has gone into determining the exact reason why Navidson chose to reenter the house. It is a question *The Navidson Record* never deals with specifically and which after several years of intense debate has produced no simple answer. Currently there are three schools of thought:

I. The Kellog-Antwerk Claim

II. The Bister-Frieden-Josephson Criteria

III. The Haven-Slocum Theory

Though it would be impossible here to address all their respective nuances, at the very least some consideration needs to be given to their views.[358]

On July 8, 1994 at *The Symposium for the Betterment of International Cultural Advancement* held in Reykjavik, Iceland, Jennifer Kellog and Isabelle Antwerk presented their paper on the meaning and authority of title in the 20th and 21st century. In their study, they cited Navidson as the perfect example of "one dictated by the logic born out of the need to possess."

Kellog and Antwerk point out how even though Navidson and Karen own the house together (both their names appear on the mortgage), Navidson frequently implies that he is the sole proprietor. As he snaps at Reston during a heated argument on the subject of future explorations: "Let's not forget that's *my* house." Kellog and Antwerk regard this possessiveness as the main reason for Navidson's mind-boggling decision

358While bits and pieces of these readings still circulate, they have yet to appear anywhere in their entirety. Purportedly Random House intends to publish a complete volume, though the scheduled release is not until the fall of 2001.

to enter the house alone. A month later Norman Paarlberg wryly offered up the following response to the Reykjavik duo: "The obsession just grew and grew until it was Navidson who was finally possessed by some self-destructive notion to go back there and yet completely dispossessed of any rational mechanism to override such an incredibly stupid idea."[359]

Kellog and Antwerk argue that the act of returning was an attempt to territorialize and thus preside over that virtually unfathomable space. However, if their claim is correct that Navidson's preoccupation with the house grew solely out of his need to own it, then other behavioral patterns should have followed suit, which was not the case. For instance, Navidson never sought to buy out Karen's share of their home. He refused to lure television programs and other corporate sponsors to his doorstep which would have further enforced his titular position, at least in the eye of the media. Nor did he ever invest himself in any kind paper writing, lectures, or other acts of publicity.

And even if Navidson did mentally equate ownership with knowledge, as both Kellog and Antwerk assert he did, he should have more adamantly sought to name the aspects of his discoveries, which as others would later observe he most certainly did not.

A year later at *The Conference on the Aesthetics of Mourning* held in Nuremberg, Germany on August 18, 1995, an unnamed student read on behalf of his professors a paper which people everywhere almost instantly began hailing as The Bister-Frieden-Josephson Criteria. More than its content, its tone practically assured a contentious response.

Here for example is the opening salvo directed specifically at The Kellog-Antwerk Claim and their followers:

"Refutation One: We do not accept that filmmaking constitutes an act of naming. Image never has and never will posses proprietary powers. Though others may deny it, we believe that to this day the Adamic strengths of the word, and hence language, have never been or ever will be successfully challenged."

The BFJ Criteria defined ownership as an act of verbal assertion necessarily carried out in public. By refusing to acknowledge *The Navidson Record* as such an act, The BFJ Criteria could make the question of personal necessity the salient point for rhetorical negotiation.

For the first half of its discourse, The BFJ Criteria chose to concentrate on guilt and grief. Careful consideration was given to Navidson's excessive exposure to traumatic events throughout the world and how he was affected by witnessing scores of "life-snaps" (The language of The Criteria). Ironically enough, however, it was not until he resigned from those assignments and moved to Ash Tree Lane that death crossed over the threshold and began to roam the halls of his own home. His twin brother died there along with two others whom he had personally welcomed into the house.

Losing Tom nearly destroyed Navidson. A fundamental part of himself and his past had suddenly vanished. Even worse, as The BFJ Criteria emphasizes, in the final moments of his life, Tom displayed characteristics entirely atypical of his day to day behavior. Navidson saw his brother in a completely different light. Not at all sluggish or even

[359]Norman Paarlberg, "The Explorer's Responsibility," *National Geographic*, v. 187, January 1995, p. 120-138.

remotely afraid, Tom had acted with determination and above all else heroism, carrying Daisy out of harm's way before falling to his death.

Navidson cannot forgive himself. As he repeatedly tells Karen over the phone: "I *was* my brother's keeper. It was me, I was the one who should have been with Daisy. I was the one who should have died."

The most controversial claim made by The Bister-Frieden-Josephson contingency is that Navidson began believing darkness could offer something other than itself. Quite cleverly The Criteria first lays the groundwork for its argument by recalling the now famous admonition voiced by Louis Merplat, the renowned speleologist who back in 1899 discovered the Blue Skia Cavern: "Darkness is impossible to remember. Consequently cavers desire to return to those unseen depths where they have just been. It is an addiction. No one is ever satisfied. Darkness never satisfies. Especially if it takes something away which it almost always invariably does."[360] Not stopping there, The Criteria then turns to Lazlo Ferma who almost a hundred years later echoed Merplat's views when he slyly observed: "Even the brightest magnesium flare can do little against such dark except blind the eyes of the one holding it. Thus one craves what by seeing one has in fact not seen."[361] Before finally quoting A. Ballard who famously quipped: "That house answers many yearnings remembered in sorrow."[362]

The point of recounting these observations is simply to show how understandable it was that for Navidson the impenetrable sweep of that place soon acquired greater meaning simply because, to quote the Criteria directly, "it was full of *unheimliche vorklänger*[363] and thus represented a means to his own personal propitiation." The sharp-bladed tactics of The BFJ Criteria, however, are not so naive as to suddenly embrace Navidson's stated convictions about what he might find. Instead the Criteria quite adroitly acknowledges that when Tom died every "angry, rueful, self-indicting tangle" within Navidson suddenly "lit up," producing projections powerful and painful enough to "occlude, deny, and cover" the only reason for their success in the first place: the blankness of that place, "the utter and *perfect* blankness."

It is nevertheless the underlying position of The Bister-Frieden-Josephson Criteria that Navidson in fact relied on such projections in order to deny his increasingly more "powerful and motivating Thanatos." In the end, he sought nothing less than to see the house exact its annihilating effects on his own being. Again quoting directly from The Criteria: "Navidson has one deeply acquired organizing perception: there is no hope of survival there. Life is impossible. And therein lies the lesson of the house, spoken in syllables of absolute silence, resounding within him like a

---

[360]Quoted in Wilfred Bluffton's article "Hollow Dark" in *The New York Times*, December 16, 1907, p. 5:5. Also consider Esther Harlan James' "Crave The Cave: The Color of Obsession," Diss. Trinity College, 1996, p. 669, in which she describes her own addiction to *The Navidson Record*: "I never shook the feeling that the film, while visceral and involving, must pale in comparison to an actual, personal exploration of the house. Still, just as Navidson needed more and more of that endless dark, I too found myself feeling the same way about *The Navidson Record*. In fact as I write this now, I've already seen the film thirty-eight times and have no reason to believe I will stop going to see it."

[361]Lazlo Ferma's "See No Evil" in *Film Comment*, v. 29, September/ October 1993, p. 58.

[362]A. Ballard "The Apophatic Science Of Recollection (Following Nuance)" *Ancient Greek*, v. cvii, April 1995, p. 85.

[363]"Ghostly anticipation." — Ed.

faint and uncertain echo . . . *If we desire to live, we can only do so in the margins of that place.*"

The second half of The Bister-Frieden-Josephson Criteria focuses almost entirely on this question of "desire to live" by analyzing in great detail the contents of Navidson's letter to Karen written the night before his departure. To emphasize the potential "desire" for self-destruction, The Criteria supplies for this section the following epigraph:

> *Noli me tangere.*
> *Noli me legere.*
> *Noli me videre.**
> *Noli me* —[364]
>
> **Non enim videbit me homo et vivet.*[365]

Thus emphasizing the potentially mortal price for beholding what must lie forever lost in those inky folds. Here The Criteria also points out how Navidson's previous trespasses, with one exception, were structured around extremely concrete objectives: (1) rescuing the Holloway team; and after sinking down the Staircase (2) returning home. The exception, of course, is the very first visit, where Navidson seeks nothing else but to explore the house, an act which nearly costs him his life.

Oddly enough, The Criteria does not acknowledge the risk inherent in (1) and (2)—objective or no objective. Nor does it explain why one trespass/journey should suddenly be treated as two.

Because The Bister-Frieden-Josephson Criteria then goes on to treat Navidson's letter in great detail and since its appearance in the film is limited to only a few seconds of screen time, it seems advisable, before further commentary, to reproduce a facsimile here:

---

[364]In "Shout Not, Doubt Not" published in *Ewig-Weibliche* ed. P. V. N. Gable (Wichita, Kansas: Joyland Press, 1995) Talbot Darden translates these lines simply as "Do not touch me. Do not read me. Do not see me. Do Not Me."

[365]`Sorry.  No clue.`[366]

[366]Maurice Blanchot translates this as "whoever sees God dies." — Ed.

[Page One]

March 31, 1991

My dearest Karen,

I miss you. I love you. I don't ~~deserve~~ expect your forgiveness. I'm leaving tomorrow **XXXXXXXX** though I plan to return. But who knows, right?

You've seen that place.

Guess I'm writing a will too. By the way I'm drunk. Sell the house, the film, everything I have, take it all. Tell the kids daddy loves/ loved them. I love them, I love you.

Why am I doing this? Because it's there and I'm not. I know that's a pretty shitty answer. I should burn the place down, forget about it. But going after something like this is who I am. You know that.

If i wasn't like this, we never would hve met in the first place becasue I never would have stopped my car in the middle of traffic, ran to the sidewalk, and asked you out.

No excuse huh? Guess I'm just another bastard abandoning **XXXX** woman and kids for a big adventure. I should grow up, right?

[Page Two]

I accept that, I'd like to it, I've tried to do it, easier said/written than done.

I need to go back to that place one more time. I know something now and I just have to confirm it. Slowly the pieces have been coming together. I'm starting to see that place for what it is and it's not for cable shows or National Geographic.

Do you believe in God? I don't think I ever asked you that one. Well I do now. But my God isn't your Catholic varietal or your Judaic or Mormon or Baptist or Seventh Day Adventist or whatever/ whoever. No burning bush, no angels, no cross. God's a house. Which is not to say that our house is God's house or even a house of God. What I mean to say is that our house is God.

XXXXXXXXXXXXXXXXXXXXXXXXXXXX XXXXXXXXXXXXXXXXXXXXXXXXXXXXXX XXXXXXXXXXXXXXX.

Think I've lost my mind? Maybe, maybe, maybe Maybe just really drunk. Pretty crazy you have to admit. I just made God a street address. Forget all that last part. just forget

[Page Three]

it. I miss you. I miss you. I won't reread this. If I do I'll throw it away and write something terse, clean and sober. And all locked up. You know me so so well. I know you'll strip out the alcohol fumes, the fear, the mistakes, and see what matters—a code to decipher written by a guy who thought he was speaking clearly. I'm crying now. I don't think I can stop. But if I try to stop I'll stop writing and I know I won't start again. I miss you so much. I miss Daisy. I miss Chad. I miss Wax and Jed. I even miss Holloway. ~~And I miss Hansen and Latigo and PFC Miserette, Benton and Carl and Regio and 1st lieutenant Nacklebend and of course Zips~~ and now I can't get Delial out of my head. Delial, Delial, Delial—the name I gave to the girl in the photo that won me all the fame and gory, that's all she is Karen, just the photo. And now I can't understand anymore why it meant so much to me to keep to keep her a secret—a penance or something. Inadequate. Well there it's said. But the photo, that's not what I can't get out of my head right now.

[Page Four]

Not the photo—that photo, that thing—but
who she was before one-sixtieth of a second
sliced her out of thin air and won me
the pulitzer though that didnt keep the
vultures away i did that by swinging my
tripodaround though that didnt keep her
from dyding five years old daisy's age
except she was pciking at a bone you
should have seen her not the but her a
little girl squatting in a field of rock dangling
a bone between her fingers i miss miss
miss but i didn't miss i got her along with
the vulture in the background when the real
vulture was the guy with the camera preying
on her for his fuck pulitzer prize it doesnt
matter if she was already ten minutes from
dying i took threem minutes to snap a photo
should have taken 10 minutes taking her
somewhere so she wouldnt go away like that
no family, no mother no day, no people just a
vulture and a fucking photojournalist i wish
i were dead right now i wish i were dead
that poor little baby this god god awful

[Page Five]

world im sorry i cant stop thinking of her
never have never will cant forget how i ran
with her like where was i going to really run
i was twelve miles from nowhere i had no
one to her to no window to pass her through
out of harms way no tom there i was no tom
there and then that tiny bag of bones just
started to shake and it was over she died
right in my hands the hands of the guy who
took three minutes two minutes whatever a
handful of seconds to photograph her and
now she was gone that poor little girl in this
god awful world i miss her i miss delial i
miss the man i thought i was before i met her
the man who would have saved her who
would have done something who would
have been tom maybe hes the one im looking
for or maybe im looking for all of them
    i miss u i love u
    there's no second ive lived you can't call
your own

Navy[367]

---

[367]Reminding me here, I mean that line about "a code to decipher", how the greatest love letters are always encoded for the one and not the many.

The Bister-Frieden-Josephson Criteria pays a great deal of attention to the incoherence present in the letter, the dissatisfaction with the self, and most of all the pain Navidson still feels over the image he burned into the retina of America almost two decades ago.

As was already mentioned in Chapter II, before the release of *The Navidson Record* neither friends nor family nor colleagues knew that Delial was the name Navidson had given to the starving Sudanese child. For reasons of his own, he never revealed Delial's identity to anyone, not even to Karen. Billy Reston thought she was some mythological pin-up girl: " I didn't know. I sure as hell never connected the name with that photo."[368]

The Navidson Record solved a great mystery when it included Karen's shot of the name written on the back of the print as well as Navidson's letter. For years photojournalists and friends had wondered who Delial was and why she meant so much to Navidson. Those who had asked usually received one of several responses: "I forget," "Someone close to me," "Allow a man a little mystery" or just a smile. Quite a few colleagues accused Navidson of being enigmatic on purpose and so out of spite let the subject drop.

Few were disappointed when they learned that Delial referred to the subject of his Pulitzer Prize-winning photograph. "It made perfect sense to me," said Purdham Huckler of the New York Times. "That must have been a crushing thing to witness. And he paid the price too."[369] Lindsay Gerknard commented, "Navidson ran straight into the brick wall all great photojournalists inevitably run into: why aren't I doing something about this instead of just photographing it? And when you ask that question, you hurt."[370] Psychologist Hector Llosa took Gerknard's observation a little further when he pointed out at the L.A. Times Convention on Media Ethics last March: "Photojournalists *especially* must never underestimate the power and influence of their images. You may be thinking, I've done nothing in this moment except take a photo (true) but realize you have also done an enormous amount for society at large (also true!)."[371]

Nor did evaluations of Navidson's burden stop with comments made by his associates. Academia soon marched in to interrogate the literary consequences created by the Delial revelation. Tokiko Dudek commented on how "Delial is to Navidson what the albatross is to Coleridge's mariner. In both cases, both men shot their mark only to be haunted by the accomplishment, even though Navidson did not actually kill Delial."[372] Caroline Fillopino recognized intrinsic elements of penance in Navidson's return to the house but she preferred Dante to Coleridge: "Delial serves the same role as Beatrice. Her whispers lead Navidson back to the house. She is all he needs to find. After all locating (literally) the souls of the dead =

[368] Billy Reston interviewed by Anthony Sitney on "Evening Murmurs," KTWL, Boulder, Colorado, January 4, 1996.

[369] Personal interview with Purdham Huckler, February 17, 1995.

[370] Personal interview with Lindsay Gerknard, February 24, 1995.

[371] Hector Llosa speaking at the L.A. Times Convention on Media Ethics on March 14, 1996.

[372] See Tokiko Dudek's "Harbingers of Hell and/or Hope" in *Authentes Journal,* Palomar College, September, 1995. p. 7. Also consider Larry Burrows who in the 1969 BBC film *Beautiful Beautiful* remarked: ". . . so often I wonder whether it is my right to capitalize, as I feel, so often, on the grief of others. But then I justify, in my own particular thoughts, by feeling that I can contribute a little to the understanding of what others are going through; then there is a reason for doing it."

safety in loss."[373] However unlike Dante, Navidson never encountered his Beatrice again.[374]

In the most sardonic tones, Sandy Beale of *The New Criticism* once considered how contemporary cinema would have treated the subject of Navidson's guilt:

> If *The Navidson Record* had been a Hollywood creation, Delial would have appeared at the heart of the house. Like something out of *Lost Horizon,* dark fields would have given way to Elysian fields, the perfect setting for a musical number with a brightly costumed Delial front and center, drinking Shirley Temples, swinging on the arms of Tom and Jed, backed by a chorus line which would have included Holloway and everyone else in Navidson's life (and our life for that matter) who had ever died. Plenty of rootbeer and summer love[375] to go around.[376]

But *The Navidson Record* is not a Hollywood creation and through the course of the film Delial appears only once, in Karen's piece, bordered in black, frozen in place without music or commentary, just Delial: a memory, a photograph, an artifact.

To this day the treatment of Delial by The Bister-Frieden-Josephson Criteria is still considered harsh and particularly insensate toward international tragedy. While Navidson's empathy for the child is not entirely disregarded, The Criteria asserts that she soon exceeded the meaning of her own existence: "Memory, experience, and time turned her bones into a trope for everything Navidson had ever lost."

The BFJ Criteria posits that Delial's prominence in Navidson's last letter is a repressive mechanism enabling him to at least on a symbolic level deal with his nearly inexpressible loss. After all in a very short amount of time Navidson had seen the rape of physics. He had watched one man murder another and then pull the trigger on himself. He had stood helplessly by as his own brother was crushed and consumed. And finally he had watched his lifelong companion flee to her mother and probably another lover, taking with her his children and bits of his sanity.

It is not by accident that all these elements appear like ghosts in his letter. A more permanent end to his relationship with Karen seems to be implied when he writes "I'm leaving tomorrow" and describes his missive as a "will." His invocation of the memory of the members of the first team as well as others sounds almost like a protracted good-bye. Navidson is tying up loose ends and the reason, or so The BFJ Criteria claims, can be detected in the way he treats the Sudanese girl still haunting his past: "It is no coincidence that as Navidson begins to dwell on Delial he mentions his brother three times: 'I had no one to pass her to. There was no window to pass her through out of harms way. There was no Tom there. I was no

---

373Caroline Fillopino's "Sex Equations" *Granta*, fall 1995. p. 45.

374During Exploration #5 Navidson had no illusion about what he would find there. While staring into those infernal halls, we can hear him mutter: "Lazarus is dead again."

375`See Appendix F.`

376Sandy Beale's "No Horizon" in *The New Criticism*, v. 13, November 3, 1993. p. 49.

Tom there. Tom, maybe he's the one I'm looking for.' It is a harrowing admission full of sorrow and defeat—'I was no Tom there'—seeing his brother as the life-saving (and line-saving) hero he himself was not."[377]

Thus The Bister-Frieden-Josephson Criteria staunchly refutes The Kellog-Antwerk Claim by reiterating its argument that Navidson's return to the house was not at all motivated by the need to possess it but rather "to be obliterated by it."

Then on January 6, 1997 at *The Assemblage of Cultural Diagnosticians Sponsored By The American Psychiatric Association* held in Washington, D.C., a husband and wife team brought before an audience of 1,200 The Haven-Slocum Theory which in the eyes of many successfully deflated the prominence of both The Kellog-Antwerk Claim and the infamously influential Bister-Frieden-Josephson Criteria.

Ducking the semantic conceits of prior hypotheses, The Haven-Slocum Theory proposed to first focus primarily on "the house itself and its generation of physiological effects." How this direction would resolve the question of "why Navidson returned to the house alone" they promised to show in due course.

Relying on an array of personal interviews, closely inspected secondary sources, and their own observations, the married couple began to carefully adumbrate their findings in what has since become known as The Haven-Slocum Anxiety Scale or more simply as PEER. Rating the level of discomfort experienced following any exposure to the house, The Haven-Slocum Theory assigned a number value "0" for no effect and "10" for extreme effects:

<u>POST-EXPOSURE EFFECTS RATING</u>

0-1: Alicia Rosenbaum: sudden migraines.
0-2: Audrie McCullogh: mild anxiety.
2-3: Teppet C. Brookes: insomnia.
3-4: Sheriff Axnard: nausea; suspected ulcer.†
4-5: Billy Reston: enduring sensation of cold.
5-6: Daisy: excitement; intermittent fever; scratches; echolalia.
6-7: Kirby "Wax" Hook: stupor; enduring impotence.††
7-8: Chad: tangentiality; rising aggression; persistent wandering.
9: Karen Green: prolonged insomnia; frequent unmotivated panic attacks; deep melancholia; persistent cough.†††
10: Will Navidson: obsessive behavior; weight loss; night terrors; vivid dreaming accompanied by increased mutism.

†No previous history of stomach ailments.

††Neither the bullet wound nor the surgery should have effected potency.

†††All of which radically diminished when Karen began work on *What Some Have Thought* and *A Brief History Of Who I Love*.

The Haven-Slocum Theory™ — 1

[377]Here then Jacob loses Esau and finds he is nothing without him. He is empty, lost and tumbling toward his own annihilation. But as Robert Hert poignantly asks in *Esau and Jacob* (BITTW Publications, 1969), p. 389: "What did God really know about brothers (or for that matter sisters)? He was after all an only child and before it all an equally lonely father."

The Haven-Slocum Theory does not lightly pass over Karen's remarkable victory over the effects of the house: "With the eventual exception of Navidson, she was the only one who attempted to process the ramifications of that place. The labor she put into both film shorts resulted in more moderate mood swings, an increase in sleep, and an end to that nettlesome cough."

Navidson, however, despite his scientific inquiries and early postulations, finds no relief. He grows quieter and quieter, often wakes up seized by terror, and through Christmas and the New Year starts eating less and less. Though he frequently tells Reston how much he longs for Karen and the company of his children, he is incapable of going to them. The house continues to fix his attention.

So much so that back in October when Navidson first came across the tape of Wax kissing Karen he hardly responded. He viewed the scene twice, once at regular speed, the second time on fast forward, and then moved on to the rest of the footage without saying a word. From a dramatic point of view we must realize it is a highly anticlimactic moment, but one which, as The Haven-Slocum Theory argues, only serves to further emphasize the level of damage the house had already inflicted upon Navidson: "Normal emotional reactions no longer apply. The pain anyone else would have felt while viewing that screen kiss, in Navidson's case has been blunted by the grossly disproportionate trauma already caused by the house. In this regard it is in fact a highly climactic, if irregular moment, only because it is so disturbing to watch something so typically meaningful rendered so utterly inconsequential. How tragic to find Navidson so bereft of energy, his usual snap and alacrity of thought replaced by such unyielding torpor. Nothing matters anymore to him, which as more than a handful of people have already observed, is precisely the point."

Then at the beginning of March, "while tests on the wall samples progressed," as The Haven-Slocum Theory observes, Navidson begins to eat again, work out, and though his general reticence continues, Reston still sees Navidson's new behavior as a change for the better: "I was blind to his intentions. I thought he was starting to deal with Tom's death, planning to end his separation with Karen. I figured he had put the Fowler letters behind him along with that kiss. He seemed like he was coming back to life. Hell, even his feet were on the mend. Little did I know he was stock-piling equipment, getting ready for another journey inside. What everyone knows now as Exploration #5."[378]

Where The Bister-Frieden-Josephson Criteria made Navidson's letter to Karen the keystone of its analysis, The Haven-Slocum Theory does away with the document in a footnote, describing it as "drunken babble chock-full of expected expressions of grief, re-identification with a lost object, and plenty of transference, having less to do with Navidson's lost brother and more to do with the maternal absence he endured throughout his life. The desire to save Delial must partly be attributed to a projection of Navidson's own desire to be cradled by his mother. Therefore his grief fuses his sense of self with his understanding of the other, causing him not only to mourn for the tiny child but for himself as well."[379]

---

[378]Interview with Billy Reston. KTWL, Boulder, Colorado, January 4, 1996.

[379]`See pages 22-23.`

What The Haven-Slocum Theory treats with greater regard are the three dreams[380] Navidson described for us in the Hi 8 journal entries he made that March. Again quoting directly from the Theory: "Far better than words influenced by the depressive effects of alcohol, these intimate glimpses of Navidson's psyche reveal more about why he decided to go back and what may account for the profound physiological consequences that followed once he was inside."

Mia Haven entitles her analysis of *Dream #1*: "Wishing Well: A Penny For Your Thoughts . . . A Quarter For Your Dreams . . . You For The Eons." Unfortunately, as her treatment is difficult to find and purportedly exceeds 180 pages, it is only possible to summarize the contents here.

As Haven recounts, Navidson's first dream places him within an enormous concrete chamber. The walls, ceiling, and floor are all veined with mineral deposits and covered in a thin ever-present film of moisture. There are no windows or exits. The air reeks of rot, mildew, and despair.

Everywhere people wander aimlessly around, dressed in soiled togas. Toward the centre of this room there lies what appears to be a large well. A dozen people sit on the edge, dangling their feet inside. As Navidson approaches this aperture, he realizes two things: 1) he has died and this is some kind of half-way station, and 2) the only way out is down through the well.

As he sits on the edge, he beholds a strange and very disconcerting sight. No more than twenty feet below is the surface of an incredibly clear liquid. Navidson presumes it is water though he senses it is somewhat more viscous. By some peculiar quality intrinsic to itself, this liquid does not impede but actually clarifies the impossible vision of what lies beneath: a long shaft descending for miles ultimately opening up into a black bottomless pit which instantly fills Navidson with an almost crippling sense of dread.

Suddenly next to him, someone leaps into the well. There is a slight splash and the figure begins to sink slowly but steadily toward the darkness below. Fortunately after a few seconds, a violent blue light envelops the figure and transports it somewhere else. Navidson realizes, however, that there are other figures down there who have not been visited by that blue light and are instead writhing in fear as they continue their descent into oblivion.

Without anyone telling him, Navidson somehow understands the logic of the place: 1) he can remain in that awful room for as long as he likes, even forever if he chooses—looking around, he can tell that some people have been there for thousands of years—or he can jump into the

---

[380]As such a great variety of written material outside of The Haven-Slocum Theory has been produced on the subject of Navidson's dreams, it seems imprudent not to at least mention here a few of the more popular ones: Calvin Yudofsky's "D-Sleep/S-Sleep Trauma: Differentiating Between Sleep Terror Disorder and Nightmare Disorder" in *(N) REM* (Bethel, Ohio: Besinnung Books, 1995); Ernest Y. Hartmann's *Terrible Thoughts: The Psychology and Biology of Navidson's Nightmares* (New York: Basic Books, Inc., 1996); Susan Beck's "Imposition On The Hollow" published in the *T.S. Eliot Journal* v. 32, November 1994; chapter four in Oona Fanihdjarte's *The Constancy of Carl Jung* (Baltimore, Maryland: Johns Hopkins University Press, 1995); Gordon Kearns, L. Kajita, and M.K. Totsuka's *Ultrapure Water, the Super-Kamiokande Detector and Cherenkov Light* (W.H. Freeman and Company, 1997); also see www-sk.icrr .u-tokyo.ac.jp/doc/sk/; and of course Tom Curie's essay "Thou Talk'st of nothing. True, I talk of dreams" (Mab Weekly, Celtic Publications, September 1993).

well. 2) If he has lived a good life, a blue light will carry him to some ethereal and gentle place. If, however, he has lived an "inappropriate life," (Navidson's words) no light will visit him and he will sink into the horrible blackness below where he will fall forever.

The dream ends with Navidson attempting to assess the life he has led, unable to decide whether he should or should not leap.

Haven goes to great lengths to examine the multiple layers presented by this dream, whether the classical inferences in the togas or the sexless "figure" Navidson observes immolated by the blue light. She even digresses for a playful romp through Sartre's *Huis Clos*, hinting how that formidable work helped shape Navidson's imagination.

In the end though, her most important insight concerns Navidson's relationship to the house. The concrete chamber resembles the ashen walls, while the bottomless pit recalls both the Spiral Staircase and the abyss that appeared in his living room the night Tom died. Still what matters most is not some discovery made within those walls but rather within himself. In Haven's words: "The dream seems to suggest that in order for Navidson to properly escape the house he must first reach an understanding about his own life, one he still quite obviously lacks."

For *Dream #2*, Lance Slocum provides the widely revered analysis entitled "At A Snail's Place." Since his piece, like Haven's, is also impossible to locate and reportedly well over two hundred pages long, summary will again have to suffice.

Slocum retells how in the second dream Navidson finds himself in the centre of a strange town where some sort of feast is in progress. The smell of garlic and beer haunts the air. Everyone is eating and drinking and Navidson understands that for some undisclosed reason they will now have enough food to last many decades.

When the feast finally comes to an end, everyone grabs a candle and begins to march out of the town. Navidson follows and soon discovers that they are heading for a the hill on which lies the shell of an immense snail. This sight brings with it a new understanding: the town has slain the creature, eaten some of it and preserved the rest.

As they enter the enormous wind (as in "to wind something up"), their candlelight illuminates walls that are white as pearl and as opalescent as sea shells. Laughter and joy echoes up the twisting path and Navidson recognizes that everyone has come there to honor and thank the snail. Navidson, however, keeps climbing up through the shell. Soon he is alone and as the passageway continues to get tighter and tighter, the candle he holds grows smaller and smaller. Finally as the wick begins to sputter, he stops to contemplate whether he should turn around or continue on. He understands if the candle goes out he will be thrust into pitch darkness, though he also knows finding his way back will not be difficult. He gives serious thought to staying. He wonders if the approaching dawn will fill the shell with light.

Slocum begins with an amusing reference to *Doctor Dolittle* before turning to consider the homes which ancient ammonites[381] constructed around an almost logarithmic axis, a legacy they would eons later bestow

---

[381]See Edouard Monod-Herzen's *Principes de morphologie générale,* vol. I (Paris: Gauthier-Villars, 1927), p. 119.

upon the imagination of countless poets and even entire cultures.[382] Primarily Slocum concentrates on chapter 5 of Bachelard's *The Poetics of Space* as translated by Maria Jolas (Boston: Beacon Press, 1994), choosing to allow Navidson's dream the same consideration literature of its kind receives.

For example, Slocum views the question of Navidson's personal growth in terms of the enigma posed by the snail before it was eventually solved. Here he quotes from the translated Bachelard text:

> How can a little snail grow in its stone prison? This is a *natural* question, which can be asked quite naturally. (I should prefer not to ask it, however, because it takes me back to the questions of my childhood.) But for the Abbé de Vallemont it is a question that remains unanswered, and he adds: "When it is a matter of nature, we rarely find ourselves on familiar ground. At every step, there is something that humiliates and mortifies proud minds." In other words, a snail's shell, this house that grows with its inmate, is one of the marvels of the universe. And the Abbé de Vallemont concludes that, in general . . . shells are "sublime subjects of contemplation for the mind."[383]
>
> (Page 118)

---

[382]For example, even today the Kitawans of the South Pacific view the spiral of the *Nautilus Pompilius* as the ultimate symbol of perfection.

[383]The original text:

> Comment le petit escargot dans sa prison de pierre peut-il grandir? Voilà une question *naturelle*, une question qui se pose naturellement. Nous n'aimons pas à la faire, car elle nous renvoie à nos questions d'enfant. Cette question reste sans réponse pour l'abbé de Vallemont qui ajoute: "Dans la Nature on est rarement en pays de connaissance. Il y a à chaque pas de quoi humilier et mortifier les Esprits superbes." Autrement dit, la coquille de l'escargot, la maison qui grandit à la mesure de son hôte est une merveille de l'Univers. Et d'une manière générale, conclut l'abbé de Vallemont ([Abbé de Vallemont's *Curiosités de la nature et de l'art sur la végétation ou l'agriculture et le jardinage dans leur perfection*, Paris, 1709, Ire Partie], p. 255), les coquillages sont "de sublimes sujets de contemplation pour l'esprit."

For a more modern treatment of shell growth see Geerat J. Vermeij's *A Natural History of Shells* (Princeton, NJ: Princeton University Press, 1993). Chapter 3 "The Economics of Construction and Maintenance" deals directly with matters of calcification and the problems of dissolution, while chapter 1 "Shells and the Questions of Biology" considers the sense of the shell in a way that differs slightly from Vallemont's: "We can think of shells as houses. Construction, repair, and maintenance by the builder require energy and time, the same currencies used for such other life functions as feeding, locomotion, and reproduction. The energy and time invested in shells depend on the supply of raw materials, the labor costs of transforming these resources into a serviceable structure, and the functional demands placed on the shell . . . The words "economics" and "ecology" are especially apt in this context, for both are derived from the Greek *oikos*, meaning house. In short, the questions of biology can be phrased in terms of supply and demand, benefits and costs, and innovation and regulation, all set against a backdrop of environment and history."

In particular, Slocum's attention is held by Bachelard's parentethical[384] reference to his own childhood and presumably the rite of growing up: "How extraordinary to find in those ever expandable brackets such a telling correlation between the answer to the Sphinx's riddle and Navidson's crisis."

Indeed, by continuing to build on Bachelard, Slocum treats the snail in Navidson's dream as a "remarkable inversion" of the house's Spiral Staircase: "Robinet believed that it was by rolling over and over that the snail built its 'staircase.' Thus, the snail's entire house would be a stairwell. With each contortion, this limp animal adds a step to its spiral staircase. It contorts itself in order to advance and grow" (Page 122; *The Poetics of Space*).[385]

Still more remarkable than even this marvelous coincidence is the poem Bachelard chooses to quote by René Rouquier:

---

[384]I haven't corrected this typo because it seems to me less like an error of transcription and more like a revealing slip on Zampanò's part, where a "parenthetical" mention of youth suddenly becomes a "parent-ethical" question about how to relate to youth.

[385]Original text:

> Robinet a pensé que c'est en roulant sur lui-même que le limacon a fabriqué son "escalier." Ainsi, toute la maison de l'escargot serait une cage d'escalier. A chaque contorsion, l'animal mou fait une marche de son escalier en colimacon. Il se contorsionne pour avancer et grandir.

And of course who can forget Derrida's remarks on this subject in footnote 5 in "Tympan" in *Marges de la philosophie* (Paris: Les Éditions de Minuit, 1972), p. xi-xii:

> Tympanon, dionysie, labyrinthe, fils d'Ariane. Nous parcourons maintenant (debout, marchant, dansant), compris et enveloppés pour n'en jamais sortir, la forme d'une oreille construite autour d'un barrage, tournant autour de sa paroi interne, une ville, donc (labyrinthe, canaux semi-circulaires—on vous prévient que les rampes ne tiennent pas) enroulée comme un limacon autour d'une vanne, d'une digue (*dam*) et tendue vers la mer; fermée sur elle-même et ouverte sur la voie de la mer. Pleine et vide de son eau, l'anamnèse de la conque résonne seule sur une plage. Comment une fêlure pourrait-elle s'y produire, entre terre et mer?[386]

In his own note buried within the already existing footnote, in this case *not* 5 but enlarged now to 9, Alan Bass (—Trans for *Margins of Philosophy* (Chicago: University of Chicago Press, 1981)) further illuminates the above by making the following comments here below:

> "There is an elaborate play on the words *limaçon* and *conque* here. *Limaçon* (aside from meaning snail) means spiral staircase and the spiral canal that is part of the inner ear. *Conque* means both conch and concha, the largest cavity of the external ear."

[386]"Tympanum, Dionysianism, labyrinth, Ariadne's thread. We are now traveling through (upright, walking, dancing), included and enveloped within it, never to emerge, the form of an ear constructed around a barrier, going round its inner walls, a city, therefore (labyrinth, semicircular canals—warning: the spiral walkways do not hold) circling around like a stairway winding around a lock, a dike (dam) stretched out toward the sea; closed in on itself and open to the sea's path. Full and empty of its water, the anamnesis of the choncha resonates alone on the beach." As translated by Alan Bass. — Ed.

C'est un escargot énorme
Qui descend de la montagne
Et le ruisseau l'accompagne
De sa bave blanche
Très vieux, il n'a plus qu'une corne
C'est son court clocher carré.[387]

Navidson is not the first to envision a snail as large as a village, but what fascinates Slocum more than anything else is the lack of threat in the dream.

"Unlike the dread lying in wait at the bottom of the wishing well," Slocum comments. "The snail provides nourishment. Its shell offers the redemption of beauty, and despite Navidson's dying candle, its curves still hold out the promise of even greater illumination. All of which is in stark contrast to the house. There the walls are black, in the dream of the snail they are white; there you starve, in the dream the town is fed for a lifetime; there the maze is threatening, in the dream the spiral is pleasing; there you descend, in the dream you ascend and so on."

Slocum argues that what makes the dream so particularly resonant is its inherent balance: "Town, country. Inside, outside. Society, individual. Light, dark. Night, day. Etc., etc. Pleasure is derived from the detection of these elements. They create harmonies and out of harmonies comes a balm for the soul. Of course the more extensive the symmetry, the greater and more lasting the pleasure."

Slocum contends that the dream planted the seed in Navidson's mind to try a different path, which was exactly what he did do in Exploration #5. Or more accurately: "The dream was the flowering of a seed previously planted by the house in his unconsciousness." When bringing to a conclusion "At A Snail's Place," Slocum further opens up his analysis to the notion that both dreams, "The Wishing Well" and "The Snail," suggested to Navidson the possibility that he could locate either within himself or "within that vast missing" some emancipatory sense to put to rest his confusions and troubles, even put to rest the confusions and troubles of others, a curative symmetry to last the ages.

For the more troubling and by far most terrifying *Dream #3,* Mia Haven and Lance Slocum team up together to ply the curvatures of that strange stretch of imaginings. Unlike *#1* and *#2,* this dream is particularly difficult to recount and requires that careful attention be paid to the various temporal and even tonal shifts.

---

[387] René Rouquier's *La boule de verre* (Paris: Séghers), p. 12.[388]

[388] "A giant snail comes down from the mountain followed by a stream of its white slime. So very old, it has only one horn left, short and square like a church tower." — Ed.

. . . .

[2 pages missing][389]

. . . .

---

389 ____
____
____
____
____ 390

[390]3:19 AM I woke up, slick with sweat. And I'm not talking wet in the pits or wet on the brow. I'm talking scalp wet, sheet wet, and at that hour, an hour already lost in a new year—shivering wet. I'm so cold my temples hurt but before I can really focus on the question of temperature I realize I've remembered my first dream.

Only later after I find some candles, stomp around my room, splash water on the old face, micturate, light a sterno can and put the kettle on, only then can I respond to my cold head and my general physical misery, which I do, relishing every bit of it in fact. Anything is better than that unexpected and awful dream, made all the more unsettling because now for some reason I can recall it. Nor do I have an inkling why. I cannot imagine what has changed in my life to bring this thing to the surface.

The guns sure as hell were useless, instantly confiscated at sleep's border, even if I did manage to pick up the Weatherby before my credit ran out.

An hour passes. I'm blinking in the light, boiling more water for more coffee, ramming my head into another wool hat, sneezing again though all I can see is the fucking dream, torn straight out of the old raphé nuclei care of the very brainstem I thought had been soundly severed.

This is how it starts:

I'm deep in the hull of some enormous vessel, wandering its narrow passages of black steel and rust. Something tells me I've been here a long time, endlessly descending into dead ends, turning around to find other ways which in the end lead only to still more ends. This, however, does not bother me. Memories seem to suggest I've at one point lingered in the engine room, the container holds, scrambled up a ladder to find myself alone in a deserted kitchen, the only place still shimmering in the mirror magic of stainless steel. But those visits took place many years ago, and even though I could go back there at any time, I choose instead to wander these cramped routes which in spite of their ability to lose me still retain in every turn an almost indiscreet sense of familiarity. It's as if I know the way perfectly but I walk them to forget.

And then something changes. Suddenly I sense for the first time ever, the presence of another. I quicken my pace, not quite running but close. I am either glad, startled or terrified, but before I can figure out which I complete two quick turns and there he is, this drunken frat boy wearing a plum-colored Topha Beta sweatshirt, carrying the lid of a garbage can in his right hand and a large fireman's ax in his left. He burps, sways, and then with a lurch starts to approach me, raising his weapon. I'm scared alright but I'm also confused. "Excuse me, mind explaining why you're coming after me?" which I actually try to say except the words don't come out right. More like grunts and clouds, big clouds of steam.

That's when I notice my hands. They look melted, as if they were made of plastic and had been dipped in boiling oil, only they're not plastic, they're the thin effects of skin which have in fact been dipped in boiling oil. I know this and I even know the story. I'm just unable to resurrect it there in my dream. Stiff hair sprouts up all over the fingers and around the long, yellow fingernails. Even worse, this awful scarring does not end at my wrists, but continues down my arms, making the scars I know I have when I'm not dreaming seem childish in comparison. These ones reach over my shoulders, down my back, extend even across my chest, where I know ribs still protrude like violet bows.

When I touch my face, I can instantly tell there's something wrong there too. I feel plenty of hair covering strange lumps of flesh on my chin, my nose and along the ridge of my cheeks. On my forehead there's an enormous bulge harder than stone. And even though I have no idea how I got to be so deformed, I do know. And this knowledge comes suddenly. I'm here <u>because</u> I am deformed, <u>because</u> when I speak my words come out in cracks and groans, and what's more I've been put here by an old man, a dead man, by one who called me son though he was not my father.

Which is when this frat boy, swaying back and forth before me like an idiot, raises his ax even higher above his head. His plan I see is not too complicated: he intends to drive that heavy blade into my skull, across the bridge of my nose, cleave the roof of my mouth, the core of my brain, split apart the very vertebrae in my neck, and he won't stop there either. He'll hack my hands from my wrists, my thighs from my knees, pry out my sternum and hammer it into tiny fragments. He'll do the same to my toes and my fingers and he'll even pop my eyes with the butt of the handle and then with the heal of the blade attempt to crush my teeth, despite the fact that they're long, serrated and unusually strong. At least in this effort, he will fail; give up finally; collect a few. Where my internal organs are concerned, these too he'll treat with the same respect, hewing, smashing and slicing until he's too tired and too covered with blood to finish, even though of course he really finished awhile ago, and then he'll slouch exhausted, panting like some stupid dog, drunk on his beer, this killing, this victory, while I lie strewn about that bleak place, <u>der absoluten Zerrissenheit</u> (as it turned out I ran into Kyrie at the supermarket this last November. She was buying a 14.75 ounce can of Alaskan salmon. I tried to slip away but she spotted me and said hello, collecting me then in the gentle coils of her voice. We talked for a while. She knew I was no longer working at the Shop. She'd been by to get a tattoo. Apparently a stripper had gotten a little catty with her. Probably Thumper. In fact maybe that's why Thumper had called me, because this exquisite looking woman had out of the blue spoken my name. Anyway Kyrie had gotten the BMW logo tattooed between her shoulder blades, encircled by the phrase "The Ultimate Driving Machine." This apparently had been Gdansk Man's idea. The $85,000 car it turns out is his. Kyrie didn't mention any ire on his part or history on our part, so I just nodded my approval and then right there in the canned food aisle, asked her for the translation of that German phrase which I should have amended, could even do it now, but, well, Fuck 'em Hoss.[391] And so voilà it appears here instead: "utter dismemberment" the same as "dejected member" which I thought she said though she wrote it down a little differently, explaining while she did that she had decided to marry Gdansk Man and would soon actually be living, instead of just driving, up on that windy edge known to some as Mullholland. As I conjure this particular memory I can see more clearly her expression, how appalled she was by the way I looked: so pale and weak, clothes hanging on me like curtains on a curtain rod, sunglasses teetering on bone, my slender hands frequently shaking beyond my control and of course the stench I continued to emanate. What was happening to me, she probably wanted to know, but didn't ask. Then again maybe I'm

wrong, maybe she didn't notice. Or if she did, maybe she didn't care. When I started to say goodbye, things took an abrupt turn for the weird. She asked me if I wanted to go for another drive. "Aren't you getting married?" I asked her, trying, but probably failing, to conceal my exasperation. She just waited for my answer. I declined, attempting to be as polite as possible, though something hard still closed over her. She crossed her arms, a surge of anger suddenly igniting the tissue beneath her lips and finger tips. Then as I walked back down the aisle, I heard a crash off to my left. Bottles of ketchup toppled from the shelf, a few even shattered as they hit the floor. The thrown can of salmon rolled near my feet. I twisted around but Kyrie was already gone.) Anyway back to the dream, me chopped up into tiny pieces, spread and splattered in the bowels of that ship, and all at the hands of a drunken frat boy who upon beholding his heroic deed pukes all over what's left of me. Except before he achieves any of this, I realize that now, for some reason, for the first time, I have a choice: I don't have to die, I can kill him instead. Not only are my teeth and nails long, sharp and strong, I too am strong, remarkably strong and remarkably fast. I can rip that fucking ax out of his hands before he even swings it once, shatter it with one jerk of my wrist, and then I can watch the terror seep into his eyes as I grab him by the throat, carve out his insides and tear him to pieces.

But as I take a step forward, everything changes. The frat boy I realize is not the frat boy anymore but someone else. At first I think it's Kyrie, until I realize it's not Kyrie but Ashley, which is when I realize it's neither Kyrie nor Ashley but Thumper, though something tells me that even that's not exactly right. Either way, her face glows with adoration and warmth and her eyes communicate in a blink an understanding of all the gestures I've ever made, all the thoughts I've ever had. So extraordinary is this gaze, in fact, that I suddenly realize I'm unable to move. I just stand there, every sinew and nerve easing me into a world of relief, my breath slowing, arms dangling at my sides, my jaw slack, legs melting me into ancient waters, until suddenly my eyes on their own accord, commanded by instincts darker and older than empathy or anything resembling emotional need, dart from her beautiful and strangely familiar face to the ax she still holds, the ax she is now lifting, the smile she is still making even as she starts to shake, suddenly swinging the ax down on me, at my head, though she will miss my head, barely, the ax floating down instead towards my shoulder, finally cutting into the bone and lodging there, producing shrieks of blood, so much blood, and pain, so much pain, and instantly I understand I'm dying, though I'm not dead yet, even if I am beyond repair, and she has started to cry, even as she dislodges the ax and raises it again, to swing again, again at my head, though she is crying harder and she is much weaker than I thought, and she needs more time than I thought, to get ready, to swing again, while I'm bleeding and dying, which now doesn't compare at all to the feeling inside, also so familiar, as the atriums of my heart on their own accord suddenly rupture, like my father's ruptured. So this, I suddenly muse in a peculiarly detached way, was this how he felt?

I've made a terrible mistake, but it's too late and I'm now too full of fury & hate to do anything but look up as the blade slices down with appalling force, this time the right arc, not too far left, not too far right, but right center, descending forever it seems, though it's not forever, not even close, and I realize with a shade of citric joy, that at least, at last, it will put an end to the far more terrible ache

As they start to sum up The Haven-Slocum Theory, the couple quotes from Johanne Scefing's posthumously published journal:

> At this late hour I'm unable to put aside thoughts of God's great sleeper whose history filled my imagination and dreams when I was a boy. I cannot recall how many times I read and re-read the story of Jonah, and now as I dwell on Navidson's decision to return to the house alone I turn to my Bible and find among those thin pages these lines:
>
> > *So they took up Jonah, and cast him forth into the sea: and the sea ceased from her raging.*
> >
> > (Jonah 1: 15)[392]

It seems a somewhat bizarre reference, until Haven and Slocum produce a second PEER table documenting what happened once Navidson entered the house on Ash Tree Lane:

POST-EXPOSURE EFFECTS RATING

0: Alicia Rosenbaum: headaches stopped.
0: Audrie McCullogh: no more anxiety.
1: Teppet C. Brookes: improved sleeping.
1: Sheriff Axnard: end of nausea.
2: Billy Reston: decreased sensation of cold.
3: Daisy: end of fever; arms healing; occasional echolalia.
1: Kirby "Wax" Hook: return of energy and potency.
4: Chad: better goal-directed flow of ideas and logical sequences; decreased aggression and wandering.
1: Karen Green: improved sleeping; no more unmotivated panic attacks†; decreased melancholia; cessation of cough.
1: Will Navidson: no more night terrors; cessation of mutism.††

†Dark enclosed places will still initiate a response.
††Evidenced by Navidson's use of the Hi 8 to record his thoughts.

The Haven-Slocum Theory™ — 2

Even more peculiar, the house became a house again.

As Reston discovered, the space between the master bedroom and the children's bedroom had vanished. Karen's bookshelves were once again flush with the walls. And the hallway in the living room now resembled a shallow closet. Its walls were even white.

The sea, it seemed, had quieted.

"Was Navidson like Jonah?" The Haven-Slocum Theory asks. "Did he understand the house would calm if he entered it, just as Jonah understood the waters would calm if he were thrown into them?"

---

inside me, born decades ago, long before I finally beheld in a dream the face and meaning of my horror.

[391]See footnote 310 and corresponding reference. — Ed.

[392]Johanne Scefing's *The Navidson Record*, trans. Gertrude Rebsamen (Oslo Press, May 1996), p. 52.

Perhaps strangest of all, the consequences of Navidson's journey are still being felt today. In what remains the most controversial aspect of The Haven-Slocum Theory, the concluding paragraphs claim that people not even directly associated with the events on Ash Tree Lane have been affected. The Theory, however, is careful to distinguish between those who have merely seen *The Navidson Record* and those who have read and written, in some cases extensively, about the film.

Apparently, the former group shows very little evidence of any sort of emotional or mental change: "At most, temporary." While the latter group seems to have been more radically influenced: "As evidence continues to come in, it appears that a portion of those who have not only meditated on the house's perfectly dark and empty corridors but articulated how its pathways have murmured within them have discovered a decrease in their own anxieties. People suffering anything from sleep disturbances to sexual dysfunction to poor rapport with others seem to have enjoyed some improvement."[393]

However, The Haven-Slocum Theory also points out that this course is not without risk. An even greater number of people dwelling on *The Navidson Record* have shown an increase in obsessiveness, insomnia, and incoherence: "Most of those who chose to abandon their interest soon recovered. A few, however, required counseling and in some instances medication and hospitalization. Three cases resulted in suicide."

---

[393]Of course as Patricia B. Nesselroade, M.D. noted in her widely regarded self-help book *Tamper With This* (Baltimore: Williams & Wilkins, 1994), p. 687: "If one invests some interest in, for example, a tree and begins to form some thoughts about this tree and then writes these thoughts down, further examining the meanings that surface, allowing for unconscious associations to take place, writing all this down as well, until the subject of the tree branches off into the subject of the self, that person will enjoy immense psychological benefits."

XVIII

Ashe, good for caske hoopes: and if neede require, plow worke, as alfo for many things els.

— *A briefe and true report of the new found land of Virginia* by Thomas Hariot servant to Sir Walter Raleigh — "a member of the Colony, and there imployed in difcouering."

Though Karen and Navidson both went back to Ash Tree Lane, Karen did not go there for the house. As she explains in a video entry: "I'm going because of Navy."

During the first week of April, she stayed in close contact with Reston who made the long drive from Charlottesville more than a few times. As we can see for ourselves, Navidson's car never moves from the driveway and the house continues to remain empty. In the living room a closet still stands in place of the hallway, while upstairs the space between the master bedroom and the children's bedroom is lost to a wall.

At the start of the second week of April, Karen realizes she will have to leave New York. Daisy and Chad seem to have shaken off the debilitating effects of the house and their grandmother is more than happy to look after them while Karen is gone, believing her daughter's trip will take her one step closer toward selling the house and suing Navidson.

On April 9th, Karen heads south to Virginia. She checks into a Days Inn but instead of going directly to the house makes an appointment with Alicia Rosenbaum. The real estate agent is more than happy to see Karen and discuss the prospects of putting the house on the market.

"Oh lord" she exclaims when she sees the Hi 8 in Karen's hands. "Don't point that at me. I'm not at all photogenic." Karen sets the camera down on a file cabinet but leaves it on, thus providing a high-angle view of the office and both women.

Karen probably planned to have a short discussion with Alicia Rosenbaum about the sale of the house, but the real estate agent's uncensored shock changes everything. "You look terrible" she says abruptly. "Are you alright, honey?" And so with that, what was supposed to have been a business meeting instantly becomes something else, something otherly, a sisterly get together where one woman reads in another signs of strain invisible to a man and sometimes even a mother.

Rosenbaum fills a mug with hot water and hunts around in a cabinet for some tea bags. Slowly but surely Karen begins to talk about the separation. "I don't know," Karen finally says as she stirs her chamomile tea. "I haven't seen him in almost six months."

"Oh dear, I'm so sorry."

Karen keeps turning the spoon in small circles but cannot quite stop the tears. Rosenbaum comes around the desk and gives Karen a hug. Then pulling up a chair tries her best to offer some consolation: "Well at the very least, don't worry about the house. It always sells."

Karen stops stirring the tea.

"Always?" she asks.

"After you came to me with that whole mysterious closet bit," Rosenbaum continues, ignoring the phone as it starts to ring. "I did a little research. I mean I'm as new to this town as you all were, though I am southern born. Truth be told, I hoped to find some kind of ghostliness. [She laughs] All I found was a pretty comprehensive list of owners. A lot of 'em. Four in the last eleven years. Almost twenty in the last fifty. No one seems to stay there for more than a few years. Some died, heart attacks that sort of thing and the rest just disappeared. I mean we lost track of 'em. One man said the place was too roomy, another one called it 'unstable.' I went ahead and checked if the house was built on an old Indian burial ground."

"And?"

"Nope. In fact, definitely not. It's all too marshy with winter rains and the James River nearby. Not a good place for a cemetery. So I looked for some murder or witch burning—though I knew, of course, that had all been Massachusetts folk. Nothing."

"Oh well."

"Did you ever see any ghosts?"

"Never."

"Too bad. Virginia, you know, has a tradition of ghosts—though I've never seen one."

"Virginia does?" Karen asks softly.

"Oh my yes. The curse tree, the ghost of Miss Evelyn Byrd, Lady Ann Skipwith, ghost alley, and lord knows a whole handful more.[394] Unfortunately, the only thing distinguished about your home's past, but I guess it's part of everybody's past around here, and it's no mystery either, would be the colony, the Jamestown Colony."

It is not surprising *The Navidson Record* does not pause to consider this reference, especially considering that Karen is far more concerned about the house and Navidson's whereabouts than she is with 17th century history. However having some familiarity with the bloody and painful origins of that particular toe hold in the new world reveals just how old the roots of that house really are.

Thanks to The London Company, on May 2, 1607, 105 colonists were deposited on a marshy peninsula where they established what soon became known as the Jamestown Colony. Despite pestilence, starvation, and frequent massacres carried out by native Indians, John Smith effectively held the village together until an injury forced him to return to England. The ensuing winter of 1609-1610 almost killed everyone and had it not been for

[394]See L. B. Taylor, Jr.'s *The Ghosts of Virginia* (Progress Printing Co., Inc., 1993) For a more international look at hauntings consider E. T. Bennett's *Apparitions & Haunted Houses: A Survey of Evidence* (London: Faber & Faber, 1939); Commander R. T. Gould, R. N.'s *Oddities: A Book of Unexplained Facts* (1928); Walter F. Prince's *The Psychic in the House* (Boston: Boston Society for Psychical Research, 1926); and Suzy Smith's *Haunted Houses for the Million* (Bell Publishing Co., 1967).

Lord De la Warr's timely arrival with supplies those still living would have fled.[395]

With the help of John Rolfe's tobacco industry, the marriage of Pocahontas, and the naming of Jamestown as the Virginia capital, the colony survived. However Nathaniel Bacon's fierce battle with the tidewater aristocrat Sir William Berkeley soon left the village in flames. Eventually the capital of Virginia was moved to Williamsburg and the settlement quickly decayed. In 1934 when park excavations began, very little remained of the site. As Park Warden Davis Manatok reported, "The marsh land has obscured if not completely consumed the monuments of the colony."[396]

All of which is relevant only because of a strange set of pages currently held at the Lacuna Rare Books Library at Horenew College in South Carolina.

Supposedly the journal in question first turned up at The Wishart Bookstore in Boston. It had apparently been mixed in with several crates of books dropped off from a nearby estate. "Most of it was dreck" said owner Laurence Tack. "Old paperbacks, second rate volumes of Sidney Sheldon, Harold Robbins, and the like. No one here paid them much attention."[397]

Eventually the journal was bought for a remarkable $48.00 when a Boston University student noticed "Warr" penciled inside the cover of the badly damaged volume. As she soon discovered, the book was not De la Warr's but one he had kept in his library. It seems that prior to Warr's arrival, during "the starving time" of the winter of 1610, three men had left the Jamestown Colony in search of game. As the journal reveals, they traveled for several days until they stumbled onto an icy field where they camped for the night. The following spring two of their thawing bodies were found along with this priceless document.

For the most part, the entries concern the quest for game, the severe weather and the inevitable understanding that cold and hunger were fast colluding into the singular sensation of death:

18 Janiuere, 1610

We fearch[398]for deere or other Game and alwayes
there is nothing. Tiggs believef our luck will change.

---

[395]Consider the interesting mention in Rupert L. Everett's *Gallantrie and Hardship in the Newfoundland* (London: Samson & Sons Publishing Company, Inc., 1673), where a colonist remarked how "Warr in Fray sure was all tabled Balls, full with much Delight and of course strange Veering Spirit."

[396]*Virginia State Park Report* (Virginia State Press, v. 12, April 1975), p. 1,173.

[397]Personal interview with Laurence Tack, May 4, 1996.

[398]This sporadic "f" for "s" stuff mystifies me,[399] but I don't care anymore. I'm getting the fuck out of here. Good thing too, fince I'm also being evicted from my apartment for failure to pay. It took them all of January, February and moft of March to do it but here it is the end of March and if I'm not out by tomorrow, people will come for me. My plan's to leave tonight and take a southern route all the way to Virginia, where I hope to find that place, or at the very least find some piece of reality that's at the root of that place, which might in turn—I hope; I do, do hope—help me addrefs some of the awful havoc always tearing through me.

Luckily, I've managed to put enough money together to get the hell away. My Vifa was canceled a month ago but I had some good fortune selling my mother's locket (though I kept the gold necklace).

It was that or the guns. Which may surprife you, but something about that dream I remembered changed me. Afterwards, juft looking at the dull silver made me feel like there was this horrendous weight around my neck, even though I wafn't even wearing it. In fact, the idea of getting rid of it was no longer enough, I had to hate it as I got rid of it.

At leaft I didn't rush things. I found an appraifer, approached some ftores, never budged from my afking price. Apparently it was defigned by someone well known. I made $4,200. Though I will say this, as I was handing over that ftrange fhape—letter included—I felt an extraordinary amount of rage surge through me. For a moment I was sure the scars along my arms would catch fire and melt down to the bones. I pocketed the cafh and quickly ducked away, hurt, full of poifon and more than a little afraid I might try to inflict that hurt and poifon on someone elfe.

Maybe in some half-hearted attempt to tie up some loofe ends, I then dropped by the Fhop a couple of days later to say goodbye to everyone. Man, I muft look bad becaufe the woman who replaced me almoft screamed when she saw me walk through the door. Thumper wafn't around but my boff promifed to give her the envelope I handed him.

"If I find out you didn't give it her," I said with a smile full of rotting teeth. "I'm going to burn your life down."

We both laughed but I could tell he was glad to fee me go.

I had no doubt Thumper would get my gift.

The worft was Lude. He was nowhere around. Firft I tried his apartment, which was kind of weird, to find myfelf after more than a year slipping acrofs that same awful courtyard where Zampanò ufed to walk, and there's still not a cat in sight, juft a breeze rustling through a handful of dying weeds warning away the illufion of time in the same language of a cemetery. For some reafon juft being there filled me with guilt, voices converging from behind thofe gloomy curtains of afternoon light, almoft as if drawn out of the dull earth itfelf, still bitter with winter, and gathering together there to accufe me, indict me for abandoning the book, for selling that stupid fucking locket, for running away now like a goddamn coward. And though no clouds or kites marred a sun as yellow as corn, some invifible punifhment still hung above me there like a foul rain, caufing even more rage to dump abruptly into my syftem, though where this reaction came from I'm at a loff to know. It waf almoft more than I could handle. I forced myfelf to knock on Lude's door but when he didn't anfwer I ran from there as faft as I could.

Eventually a bouncer at one of his haunts told me he'd been tagged bad enough to land him in the hofpital. It took a little while to get paft the receptionift, but when I finally did Lude rewarded me with this huge smile. It made me want to cry.

"Hey Hoff, you came. Is this what it takes to get you out of your coffin?"

I couldn't believe how terrible he looked. Both his eyes were blacker than charcoal. Even his normally large nofe was bigger than ufual, stuffed now with pounds of gauze. His jaw was a deep purple and all over his face capillaries had been ruthlessly shattered. I tried pulling in deep breaths but the kind of anger I was feeling caufed my vifion to blur.

"Hey, hey, eafy there, Hoff," Lude practically had to shout. "This is the beft thing that could of happened to me. I'm on my way to becoming a very rich man."

Which actually did help calm me down. I poured him a cup of water and one for myfelf and then I sat down by his bed. Lude seemed genuinely pleafed by his battered condition. He treated his broken ribs and the tube draining his fractured tibia with newfound refpect: "My summer bonus," he smiled, although the effort was somewhat warped.

The way Lude told it, he'd been delighting in the comforts of an idle hour fpent on Funset Plaza quaffing his thirft with several falty margaritas when who should stroll by but Gdansk Man. He was still tweeked about the time Lude popped him in the nuts but he was even more fueled by something elfe. Apparently Kyrie had told him that I had accofted her in the supermarket and for some stupid reafon she'd decided to add that Lude had been right there with me, maybe becaufe he was the one who introduced us in the first place. Anyway, bright enough not to make a public scene, that monfter known as Gdansk Man crept back to the parking lot and lay in wait for Lude. He had to wait for a long time but he was full of enough ill-conceived rage not to mind. Eventually Lude fucked down the laft drop of his drink, paid his bill and ambled away from Funset, back there, towards his mode of tranfportation, right past Gdansk Man.

Lude never had a chance, not even time for words, let alone one word, let alone a return ftrike. Gdansk Man didn't hold anything back either and when it was over they had to send for an ambulance.

Lude laughed as he finifhed the story and then promptly coughed up a chunk of something brown.

"I owe you Hoff."

I tried to act like I was following him but Lude knew me well enough to fee I wafn't getting the moft important part. One of his swollen eyes attempted a wink.

"As soon as I'm out of here, I'm taking him straight to court. I've already been in touch with a few lawyers. It looks like Gdansk Man has quite a bit of money he's going to have to be ready to part with. Then you and I are going straight to Vegas to lofe it all on red."

Lude laughed again only thif time I waf relieved to fee he didn't cough.

"Will you need me to teftify?" I afked, prepared to cancel my trip.

"Not neceffary. Three kitchen workers saw the whole thing. Befides Hoff, you look like you juft got out of a concentration camp. You'd probably scare off the jury."

The hurt and ache eventually got the beft of Lude and he signaled the nurfe for more painkillers.

"Another perk," he whifpered to me with a fading leer. I gueff some things never change. Lude's chemical line of defenfe still seemed to be holding.

After he'd fallen afleep, I drove back to his apartment and slipped an envelope with $500 in it under his door. I figured he'd need a little something extra when he got out of there. Flaze paffed me in the hall but pretended not to recognize me. I didn't care. On my way out, I caught one laft glimpfe of the courtyard. It was empty but I still couldn't fhake the feeling that something there was watching me.

Juft an hour ago, I found a flyer under the wiper of my car:

<u>WANTED</u>
50 People
We'll pay you
to lofe weight!

Likewife we muft also believe or elfe in the name of the Lorde take charge of the Knowledge that we are all dead men.

20 Janiuere, 1610

More fnow. Bitter cold. This is a terrible Place we have stumbled on. It has been a Week fince we haue fpied one living thing. Were it not for the ftorm we would have abandoned it. Verm was plagued by many bad Dreames last night.

21 Janiuere, 1610

The ftorm will not break. Verm went out to hunt but returned within the houre. The Wind makes a wicked found in the Woods. Ftrange as it muft feem, Tiggs, Verm, and I take comfort in the found. I fear much more the filence here. Verm tellf me he dreamt of Bones last night. I dreame of the Sunne.

22 Janiuere, 1610

We are dying. No food. No fhelter. Tiggs dreamt he faw all fnow about us turn Red with blood.

And then the last entry:

I actually had a good laugh over that one. You want to lofe weight, I thought to myfelf, well boy do I have something for you to read.

I threw some old clothes in the back and slipped the rifle and the two guns under the seats. Moft of the ammo I hid in socks which I tucked infide the spare tire.

The laft week has been particularly funny, though not at all, I affure you, funny. Everywhere the jacarandas are bloffoming. People go around faying how beautiful they are. Me, they only unsettle, filling me with dread and now, strangely enough, a faint sense of fury. As foon as I finifh this note, I plan to load the book and everything elfe into that old black trunk and drag it down to a ftorage unit I rented in Culver city for a couple hundred bucks. Then I'm gone. I'm sorry I didn't get farther than this. Who knows what I'll find back eaft, maybe fleep, maybe a calm, hopefully the path to quiet the fea, this fea, my fea.

[399]Mr. Truant has mistaken the long "S" for an "f." John Bell the publisher for *British Theatre* abolished the long "S" back in 1775. In 1786, Benjamin Franklin indirectly approved of the decision when he wrote that "the Round s begins to be the Mode and in nice printing the Long S is rejected entirely." — Ed.

23 Janiuere, 1610

Ftaires! We haue found ftaires![400]

Nowhere in Lord De la Warr's personal journals is there a mention of stairs or any clue about what might have happened to the third body. Warr, however, does refer to the journal as a clear example of death's madness and in a separate letter consigns the delicate relic to the flames. Fortunately the order, for whatever reason, was not carried out and the journal survived, winding up in a Boston book store with only Warr's name to link the fragile yellow pages to this continent's heritage.

Nevertheless, while the journal may offer some proof that Navidson's extraordinary property existed almost four hundred years ago, why that particular location[401] proved so significant remains unanswered. In 1995, parapsychologist Lucinda S. Hausmaninger claimed that Navidson's place was analogous to the blind spot created by the optic nerve in the retina: "It is a place of processing, of sense-making, of seeing."[402] However, she soon altered this supposition, describing it as "the omphalos of all we are."[403] It did not matter that the house existed in Virginia, only that it existed in one place: "One place, one (eventual) meaning."[404] Of course recent discoveries shatter both of Hausmaninger's theories.[405]

As everyone knows, instead of delving into the question of location or the history of the Jamestown Colony, *The Navidson Record* focuses on Alicia Rosenbaum in her dingy little office talking to Karen about her troubles. It may very well be the best response of all: tea, comfort, and social intercourse. Perhaps Rosenbaum's conclusion is even the best: "lord knows why but no one ever seems comfortable staying there," as if to imply in a larger way that there are some places in this world which no one will ever possess or inhabit.

Karen may hate the house but she needs Navidson. When the video tape flickers back to life, it is 9:30 P.M. and Ash Tree Lane is dark. Alicia Rosenbaum waits in her car, engine idling, headlights plastering the front door.

Slowly Karen makes her way up the walk, her shadow falling across the door step. For a moment she fumbles with her keys. There is the brief click of teeth on pins in the heart of the dead bolt and then the door swings open. In the foyer, we can see almost six months of mail strewn on the floor, surrounded by wisps of dust.

---

[400]*Jamestown Colony Papers: The Tiggs, Verm & I Diary* (Lacuna Library founded by The National Heritage Society) v. xxiii. n. 139, January 1610, p. 18-25.

[401]The exact location of the house has been subject to a great deal of speculation. Many feel it belongs somewhere in the environs of Richmond. However Ray X. Lawlor, English professor emeritus at the University of Virginia, places Ash Tree Lane "closer to California Crossroads. Certainly not far from Colonial Williamsburg and the original Jamestown colony. South of Lake Powell but most assuredly northwest of Bacons Castle." See Lawlor's "Which Side of the James?" in *Zyzzyva*, fall 1996, p. 187.

[402]Lucinda S. Hausmaninger's "Oh Say Can You See" in *The Richmond Lag Zine*, v.119, April 1995, p. 33.

[403]Lucinda S. Hausmaninger's "The Navy Navel" in *San Clemente Prang Vibe*, v. 4, winter 1996, p. vii.

[404]Ibid., p. viii.

[405]See Appendix C. — Ed.

Karen's breathing increases: "I don't know if I can do this" (then shouting) "Navy! Navy, are you in there?!" But when she finally locates the light switch and discovers the power has been turned off—"Oh shit. No way —"—she backs out of the house and into a jarring jump cut which returns us again to the front of the house, this time without Alicia Rosenbaum, evening now replaced by beady sunlight. April 10th, 11:27 A.M. Everything is green, pleasant, and starting to bloom. Karen has avoided the B-movie cliché of choosing evening as the time to explore a dangerous house. Of course real horror does not depend upon the melodrama of shadows or even the conspiracies of night.

Once again Karen unlocks the front door and tries the switch. This time a flood of electric light indicates all is well with the power company. "Thank you Edison," Karen murmurs, sunshine and electricity steeling her resolve.

The first thing she points the Hi 8 at are the infamous bookshelves upstairs. They are flush with the walls. Furthermore, as Reston also reported, the closet space has vanished. Finally, she goes back down to the living room, preparing to face the horror which we might imagine still reaches out of her past like a claw. She approaches the door on the north wall. Perhaps she hopes Reston has locked it and taken the keys, but as she discovers soon enough, the door opens effortlessly.

Still, there is no infernal corridor. No lightless and lifeless place. There is only a closet barely a foot and a half deep with white walls, a strip of molding, and all of it slashed from ceiling to floor with daylight streaming in through the windows behind her.

Karen actually laughs but her laughter comes up short. Her only hope of finding Navidson had been to confront what terrified her most. Now without a reason to be afraid, Karen suddenly finds herself without a reason to hope.

After spending the first few nights at the Days Inn, Karen decides to move back into the house. Reston visits her periodically, and each time he comes they go over every alcove and corner looking for some sign of Navidson. They never find anything. Reston offers to stay there with her but Karen says she actually wants to be alone. He looks noticeably relieved when she insists on seeing him to his van.

The following week, Alicia Rosenbaum starts bringing by prospective buyers. A couple of newlyweds seems especially taken by the place. "It's so cute" responds the pregnant wife. "Small but especially charming," adds the husband. After they leave, Karen tells Rosenbaum she has changed her mind and will at least for the time being still hold onto the house.

Every morning and evening, she calls Daisy and Chad on her cellular phone. At first they want to know if she is with their father, but soon they stop asking. Karen spends the rest of her day writing in a journal. As she has turned back on all the wall mounted Hi 8s and kept them resupplied with fresh tapes, there is ample footage of her hard at work at this task, filling page after page, just as she sometimes fills the house with peals of laughter or now and then the broken notes of a cry.

Though she eventually uses up the entire volume, not one word is ever visible in *The Navidson Record*. To this day the contents of her journal remain a mystery. Professor Cora Minehart M.S., Ph.D. argues that the actual words are irrelevant: "process outweighs product."[406] Others, however, have gone to great lengths to suggest a miraculous and secret history enfolded within those pages.[407] Katherine Dunn is rumoured to have invented her own version of Karen's journal.

Karen, however, does not restrict her activities to just writing. She frequently retreats outside where she works on the garden, weeding, clipping, and even planting. We often find her singing quietly to herself, anything from popular tunes, old Slavic lullabies, to a song about how many ways her life has changed and how she would like to get her feet back on the ground.

It seems that the most significant observations concerning this segment concern Karen's smile. There is no question it has changed. Lester T. Ochs has traced its evolving shape from Karen's days as a cover girl, through the months spent living at the house, the prolonged separation in New York, to her eventual return to the house:

> Whether on the cover of *Glamour* or *Vogue*, Karen never failed to form her lips into those faultlessly symmetrical curves, parted just enough to coyly remark on her barely hidden teeth, so perfectly poised between shadow and light, always guaranteed to spark fantasies of further interiority. No matter which magazine she appeared in, she always produced the same creation over and over again. Even after they moved to Ash Tree Lane, Karen still offered up the same art to whomever she encountered. The house, however, changed that. It deconstructed her smile until by the time they had escaped she had no smile at all.

Then further on:

> By the time she returned to Virginia, some expression of joy and relief, albeit rare, was also returning. The big difference though was that now her smile was completely unmannered. The curve of each lip no longer mirrored the other. The interplay was harmonic, enacting a ceaseless dance of comment and compliment, revealing or entirely concealing her teeth, one smile often containing a hundred. Her expression was no longer a frozen structure but a melody which for the first time accurately reflected how she was feeling inside.[408]

This of course responds to the extraordinary moment on the evening of May 4th, when surrounded by candles, Karen suddenly beams brighter than she has before, running her hands through her hair, almost laughing, only to

---

[406]Cora Minehart's *Recovery: Methods and Manner* with an introduction by Patricia B. Nesselroade (New York: AMACOM Books, 1994), p. 11.

[407]See Darren Meen's *Gathered God* (New York: Hyperion, 1995) and Lynn Rembold's *Stations of Eleven* (Norman, Oklahoma: University of Oklahoma Press, 1996).

[408]Lester T. Ochs' *Smile* (Middletown, CT: University Press of New England/ Wesleyan University Press, 1996), p. 87-91.

cover her face a few moments later, her shoulders shaking as she starts to weep. Her reactions seem entirely unmotivated until the following morning when she offers a startling revelation.

"He's still alive," she tells Reston over the phone. "I heard him last night. I couldn't understand what he said. But I know I heard his voice."

Reston arrives the next day and stays until midnight, never hearing a thing. He seems more than a little concerned about Karen's mental health.

"If he is still in there Karen," Reston says quietly. "He's been there for over a month. I can't see how there's any way he could survive."

But a few hours after Reston leaves, Karen smiles again, apparently catching somewhere inside her the faint voice of Navidson. This happens over and over again, whether late at night or in the middle of the day. Sometimes Karen calls out to him, sometimes she just wanders from room to room, pushing her ear against walls or floors. Then on the afternoon of May 10th, she finds in the children's bedroom, born out of nowhere, Navidson's clothes, remnants of his pack and sleeping bag, and scattered across the floor, from corner to corner, cartridges of film, boxes of 16mm, and easily a dozen video tapes.

She immediately calls Reston and tells him what has happened, asking him to drive over as soon as he can. Then she locates an AC adapter, plugs in a Hi 8 and begins rewinding one of the newly discovered tapes.

The angle from the room mounted camcorder does not provide a view of her Hi 8 screen. Only Karen's face is visible. Unfortunately, for some reason, she is also slightly out of focus. In fact the only thing in focus is the wall behind her where some of Daisy and Chad's drawings still hang. The shot lasts an uncomfortable fifteen seconds, until abruptly that immutable surface disappears. In less than a blink, the white wall along with the drawings secured with yellowing scotch tape vanishes into an inky black.

Since Karen faces the opposite direction, she fails to notice the change. Instead her attention remains fixed on the Hi 8 which has just finished rewinding the tape. But even as she pushes play, the yawn of dark does not waver. In fact it almost seems to be waiting for her, for the moment when she will finally divert her attention from the tiny screen and catch sight of the horror looming up behind her, which of course is exactly what she does do when she finds out that the video tape shows

XIX

Contrary to what Weston asserts, the habit of photographic seeing—of looking at reality as an array of potential photographs—creates estrangement from, rather than union with, nature.

— Susan Sontag
On Photography

"Nothing of consequence" was how Navidson described the quality of the film and tapes rescued from the house.

"That was early on," Reston adds. "When he had just started staying with me in Charlottesville. He reviewed every piece of footage there was, edited some parts of it and then just shipped everything off to Karen. He was really unsatisfied."[409]

In the eyes of many, the footage from Exploration A offered an exemplary first-look at what lay down the hallway. To Navidson, however, the venture was spoiled by the limited resolution of the Hi 8 and "ridiculous lighting." Film taken during Exploration #4 was much more successful in capturing the size of that place, though due to the urgency of the mission Navidson only had time for a few shots.

One of the things The Kellog-Antwerk Claim, The Bister-Frieden-Josephson Criteria, and The Haven-Slocum Theory never consider is Navidson's aesthetic dissatisfaction. Granted all three schools of thought would say Navidson's eye for perfection was directly influenced by his internal struggles, whether possession, self-obliteration, or the social good implicit in any deeply pursued venture. But as Deacon Lookner smugly commented: "We mustn't forget the most obvious reason Navidson went back to the house: he wanted to get a better picture."[410]

While the narrative events up till now have proved an easy enough thread to follow, they have also usurped the focus of the film. Until Exploration #5 there was never a true visual meditation on the house itself, its terrifying proportions and the palpable darkness inhabiting it. The few fragments of usable 16mm and video tape incensed Navidson. In his opinion, very few of the images—even those he was personally responsible for—retained any of those fantastic dimensions intrinsic to that place. All of which begins to explain why in February and March Navidson began to order high speed film, magnesium flares, powerful flashes, and even arranged to rent a thermal video camera. He intentionally kept Reston in the dark, assuming his friend would try to stop him or endanger himself by insisting on going along.

---

[409]The Reston Interview.

[410]Deacon Lookner's *Artistic Peril* (Jackson, Mississippi: Group Home Publications, 1994), p. 14.

Throughout his career, Navidson had almost without exception worked alone. He was used to entering areas of conflict by himself. He preferred the dictates of survival when, faced with enthralling danger, he was forced to rely on nothing else but his own keenly tuned instincts. Under those conditions, he consistently produced his best work.

Photojournalism has frequently been lambasted for being the product of circumstance. In fact rarely are any of these images considered in terms of their composition and semantic intent. They are merely news, a happy intersection of event and opportunity. It hardly helps that photographs in general also take only a fraction of a second to acquire.

It is incredible how so many people can constantly misread speed to mean ease. This is certainly most common where photography is concerned. However simply because anyone can buy a camera, shutter away, and then with a slightly prejudiced eye justify the product does not validate the achievement. Shooting a target with a rifle is accomplished with similar speed and yet because the results are so objective no one suggests that marksmanship is easy.

In photojournalism the celerity with which a moment of history is seized testifies to the extraordinary skill required. Even with the help of computerized settings and high-speed films, an enormous amount of technical information must still be accounted for in very little time in order to take a successful shot.

A photojournalist is very much like an athlete. Similar to hockey players or bodyboarders, they have learned and practiced over and over again very specific movements. But great photographers must not only commit to reflex those physical demands crucial to handling a camera, they must also refine and internalize aesthetic sensibilities. There is no time to think through what is valuable to a frame and what is not. Their actions must be entirely instinctual, immediate, and the result of years and years of study, hard work and of course talent.

As New York City gallery owner Timothy K. Thuan once said:

> Will Navidson is one of this century's finest photographers, but because his work defines him as a "photojournalist" he suffers to this day that most lamentable of critical denunciations: "Hey, he just shoots what happens. Anyone can do that, if they're there." And so it goes. Buy that guy a beer and sock him in the eye.[411]

Only very recently has the detection of a formidable understanding and use of frame balance inherent in all of Navidson's work begun to breach the bias against his profession.

Consider for the last time the image that won him the Pulitzer Prize. Not even taking into account the courage necessary to travel to Sudan, walk the violent, disease-infested streets, and finally discover this child on some rocky patch of earth—all of which some consider a major part of photography and even art[412]—Navidson also had to contend with the

[411]Personal interview with Timothy K. Thuan, August 29, 1996.

[412]See Cassandra Rissman LaRue's *The Architecture of Art* (Boston: Shambhala Publications, 1971), p. 139 where she defines her frequently touted "seven stages to accomplishment":

infinite number of ways he could photograph her (angles, filters, exposure, focus, framing, lighting etc., etc.) He could have used up a dozen rolls exploring these possibilities, but he did not. He shot her once and in only one way.

In the photograph, the vulture sits behind Delial, frame left, slightly out of focus, primary feathers beginning to feel the air as it prepares for flight. Near the centre, in crisp focus, squats Delial, bone dangling in her tawny almost inhuman fingers, her lips a crawl of insects, her eyes swollen with sand. Illness and hunger are on her but Death is still a few paces behind, perched on a rocky mound, talons fully extended, black eyes focused on Famine's daughter.

Had Delial been framed far right with the vulture far left, the photographer as well as the viewer would feel as if they were sitting on a sofa chair. Or as associate UCLA professor Rudy Snyder speculated: "We would be turned into an impartial audience plunked down in front of history's glass covered proscenium."[413] Instead Navidson kept the vulture to the left and Delial toward the middle, thus purposefully leaving the entire right portion of the frame empty.

When Rouhollah W. Leffler reacquainted himself with Navidson's picture in a recent retrospective, he wistfully commented:

> It seems people should complain more about this empty space but to my knowl-

---

> There are seven incarnations (and six correlates) necessary to becoming an Artist: 1. Explorer (Courage) 2. Surveyor (Vision) 3. Miner (Strength) 4. Refiner (Patience) 5. Designer (Intelligence) 6. Maker (Experience) 7. Artist. ¶ First, you must leave the safety of your home and go into the dangers of the world, whether to an actual territory or some unexamined aspect of the psyche. This is what is meant by 'Explorer.' ¶ Next, you must have the vision to recognize your destination once you arrive there. Note that a destination may sometimes also be the journey. This is what is meant by 'Surveyor.' ¶ Third, you must be strong enough to dig up facts, follow veins of history, unearth telling details. This is what is meant by 'Miner.' ¶ Fourth, you must have the patience to winnow and process your material into something rare. This may take months or even years. And this is what is meant by 'Refiner.' ¶ Fifth, you must use your intellect to conceive of your material as something meaning more than its origins. This is what is meant by 'Designer.' ¶ Six, you must fashion a work independent of everything that has gone before it including yourself. This is accomplished through experience and is what is meant by 'Maker.' ¶ At this stage, the work is acceptable. You will be fortunate to have progressed so far. It is unlikely, however, that you will go any farther. Most do not. But let us assume you are exceptional. Let us assume you are rare. What then does it mean to reach the final incarnation? Only this: at every stage, from 1 thru 6, you will risk more, see more, gather more, process more, fashion more, consider more, love more, suffer more, imagine more and in the end know why less means more and leave what doesn't and keep what implies and create what matters. This is what is meant by 'Artist.'

It is interesting to note that despite the appeal of this description and the wide-spread popularity of *The Architecture of Art*, especially during the 70s and early 80s, out of all of LaRue's followers not one has produced anything of consequence let alone merit. In his article "Where have all the children gone?" in *American Heritage,* v.17, January 1994, p. 43, Evan Sharp snapped: "LaRue fanatics would do well to trade in their seven stages for twelve steps."

[413]Rudy Snyder's "In Accordance With Limited Space" in *Art News,* v. 93, October 1994, p. 24-27.

> edge no one ever has. I think there's a very simple reason too: people understand, consciously or unconsciously, that it really isn't empty at all.[414]

Leffler's point is simply that while Navidson does not physically appear in the frame he still occupies the right side of the photograph. The emptiness there is merely a gnomonic representation of both his presence and influence, challenging the predator for a helpless prize epitomized by the flightless wings of a dying child's shoulder blades.

Perhaps this is why any observer will feel a slight adrenal rush when pondering the picture. Though they probably assume subject matter is the key to their reaction, the real cause is the way the balance of objects within the frame involves the beholder. It instantly makes a participant out of any witness.

Though this is still all dark work, at least one aspect of the photograph's composition may have had direct political consequences: Delial is not exactly in the centre. She is closer to Navidson, and hence to the observer, by a hair. Many experts attribute this slight imbalance to the large outpouring of national support and the creation of several relief programs which followed the publication of the photograph. As Susan Sontag sadly mused many years later: "Her proximity suggested to us that Delial was still within our reach."[415]

See diagram:

```
[                                  ]
[                                  ]
[                                  ]
[                                  ]
[                                  ]
[                                  ]
[                                  ]
[                                  ]
[                                  ]416
```

[414]Rouhollah W. Leffler's "Art Times" in *Sight and Sound,* November 1996, p. 39.
[415]Susan Sontag's *On Photography: The Revised Edition* (New York: Anchor Books, 1996), p. 394.
[416]Presumably Zampanò's blindness prevented him from providing an actual diagram of the Delial photograph. — Ed.

Opposing mortality is a theme which persists throughout Navidson's work. As photo critic M. G. Cafiso maintained back in 1985:

> Navidson's all consuming interest in people—and usually people caught in terrible circumstances—always puts him in direct conflict with death.[417]

As previously mentioned in Chapter XV, Navidson never photographed scenery, but he also never photographed the threat of death without interposing someone else between himself and it.

Returning to Ash Tree Lane meant removing the other. It meant photographing something unlike anything he had ever encountered before, even in previous visits to the house, a place without population, without participants, a place that would threaten no one else's existence but his own.

---

[417]M. G. Cafiso's *Mortality and Morality in Photography* (San Francisco: Chronicle Books, 1985), p. xxiii. Interestingly enough in one of his early footnotes, Cafiso broaches a troubling but highly provocative aesthetic concern when he observes how even "the finest act of seeing is necessarily always the act of not seeing something else." Regrettably he takes this matter no further nor applies it later on to the photographic challenges Navidson ultimately had to face.

XX

No one should brave the underworld alone.

— Poe

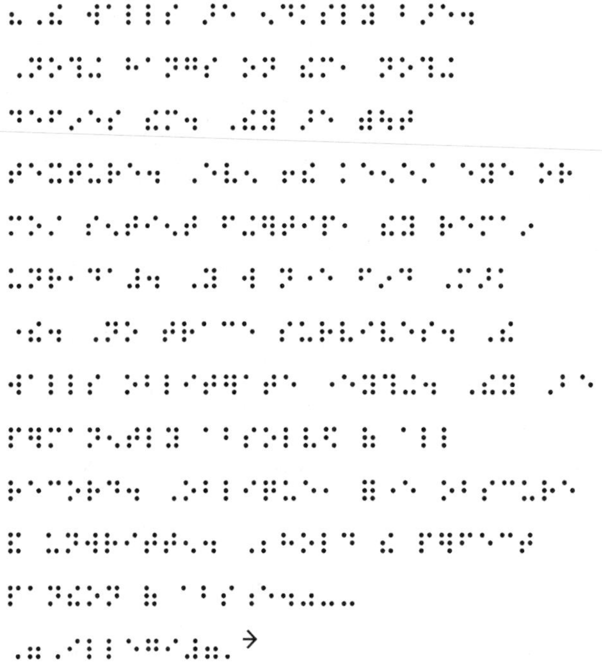 →

→ "The walls are endlessly bare. Nothing hangs on them, nothing defines them. They are without texture. Even to the keenest eye or most sentient fingertip, they remain unreadable. You will never find a mark there. No trace survives. The walls obliterate everything. They are permanently absolved of all record. Oblique, forever obscure and unwritten. Behold the perfect pantheon of absence." — [Illegible] — Ed.

On the first day of April, Navidson set out on the last exploration of those strange hallways and rooms. The card introduces this sequence as nothing more than **Exploration #5**.

For recording the adventure, Navidson brought with him a 1962 H16 hand crank Bolex 16mm camera along with 16mm, 25mm, 75mm Kern-Paillard lenses and a Bogen tripod. He also carried a Sony microcassette recorder, Panasonic Hi 8, ample batteries, at least a dozen 120 minute Metal Evaporated (DLC) tapes, as well as a 35mm Nikon, flashes, and a USA Bobby Lee camera strap. For film, he packed 3000 feet of 7298 16mm Kodak in one hundred foot loads, 20 rolls of 35mm, including some 36 frame Konica 3200 speed, plus 10 rolls of assorted black and white film. Unfortunately the thermal video camera he had arranged to rent fell through in the last minute.

For survival gear, Navidson took with him a rated sleeping bag, a one man tent, rations for two weeks, 2 five-gallon containers of water, chemical heat packs, flares, high intensity as well as regular intensity lightsticks, plenty of neon markers, fishing line, three flashlights, one small pumper light, extra batteries, a carbide lamp, matches, toothbrush, stove, change of clothes, an extra sweater, extra socks, toilet paper, a small medical kit, and one book. All of which he carefully loaded into a two wheel trailer which he secured to an aluminum-frame mountain bike.

For light, he mounted a lamp on the bike's handlebars powered by a rechargeable battery connected to a small optional rear-wheel generator. He also installed an odometer.

As we can see, when Navidson first starts down the hallway he does not head for the Spiral Staircase. This time he chooses to explore the corridors.

Due to the weight of the trailer, he moves very slowly, but as we hear him note on his microcassette recorder: "I'm in no hurry."

Frequently, he stops to take stills and shoot a little film.

After two hours he has only managed to go seven miles. He stops for a sip of water, puts up a neon marker, and then after checking his watch begins pedaling again. Little does he understand the significance of his offhand remark: "It seems to be getting easier."

Soon, however, he realizes there is a definite decrease in resistance. After an hour, he no longer needs to pedal: "This hallway seems to be on a decline. In fact all I do now is brake." When he finally stops for the night, the odometer reads an incredible 163 miles.

As he sets up camp in a small room, Navidson already knows his trip is over: "After going downhill for eight hours at nearly 20 mph, it will probably take me six to seven days, maybe more, to get back to where I started from."

When Navidson wakes up the next morning, he eats a quick breakfast, points the bike home, and begins what he expects will be an appalling, perhaps impossible, effort. However within a few minutes, he finds he no longer needs to pedal. Once again he is heading downhill.

Assuming he has become disoriented,
he turns around and begins pedaling in the opposite direction,which
should be uphill. But within fifteen seconds, he is again
coasting down a slope.

Confused, he pulls into a large room and tries to gather his
thoughts: "It's as if I'm moving along a surface that always tilts
downward no matter which direction I face."

Resigned to his fate, Navidson climbs back on
the bike and soon enough finds
himself clipping along at almost
thirty miles an hour.

For the next five
days Navidson
covers anywhere
from 240 to 300
miles at a time,
though on the
fifth day, in what
amounts to an
absurd fourteen
hour marathon,
Navidson logs 428
miles.

Nor does this endless corridor he travels
remain the same size.

Sometimes the ceiling drops in on him,

getting

progressively

lower

and

lower

until it begins to graze his head,
only to shift a few minutes later,

until

higher

and

higher

rising

it disappears altogether.

Sometimes the hallway

widens, until at one

point Navidson

swears he is moving

down some

enormous plateau:

"An infinitely large billiard table or the smooth face of some incredible mountain," he tells us hours later while preparing a modest meal. "One time I stopped and set out to the right on what I thought would be a traverse. Within seconds I was heading downhill again."

And then the walls reappear, along with the ceiling and numerous doorways; the shifts always accompanied by that inimitable, and by now very familiar, growl.

As the days pass, Navidson becomes more and more aware that he is running precariously low on water and food. Even worse, the sense of inevitable doom this causes him is compounded by the sense of immediate doom he feels whenever he begins riding his bike: "I can't help thinking I'm going to reach an edge to this thing. I'll be going too fast to stop and just fly off into darkness."

Which is almost what happens.

On the twelfth or thirteenth day (it is very difficult to tell which), after sleeping for what Navidson estimates must have been well over 18 hours, he again sets off down the hallway.

Soon the walls and doorways recede and

v a n i s h,

then sight

of

the

out

ceiling

completely

is

out

lifts

too

completely

it is of

too

until

sight

"direction no longer matters."

Navidson stops and lights four magnesium flares which he throws as far as he can to the

right and left.

Then he bikes down a hundred yards and lights four more flares.

After the third time, he turns around
and
relying on a timed exposure

photographs

the twelve

flares.

The first image captures twelve holes of light.

In the second image, however, the flares seem much farther away.

By the third image, they appear only as streaks,
indicating that either

Navidson

or

the

flares

are

m
o
v
i
n
g
.

However,
Navidson's comments on the microcassette
recorder indicate his camera was firmly
fixed on the tripod.

Having little choice, Navidson continues on. The hours sweep by. He tries to drink as little water as many thousands of miles he has traveled. He just continues to ride, lost in a trance born out of motion describing the ash floor in front of him before it is already behind him, until all of a sudden, although "As if all along, during the last week, I had sensed something out there" Navidson stutters into the

↑Navidson is not the only one to have intuitively sensed the abyss. During the tragic May assault on Everest where the 7,000 foot Kangshung face: "Finally, probably around ten o'clock, I walked over this little rise, and it felt like I in *Outside,* v. xxi, n. 9, September 1996, p. 64.

possible. The odometer breaks. Navidson does not care. It no longer seems relevant to him how
and darkness, the lamp on his bike never casting light more than a few yards ahead, barely
nothing appears to have changed, one moment differs from the rest, warning Navidson to stop.
Hi 8 an hour later. "And then all at once it was gone, replaced by — ↑

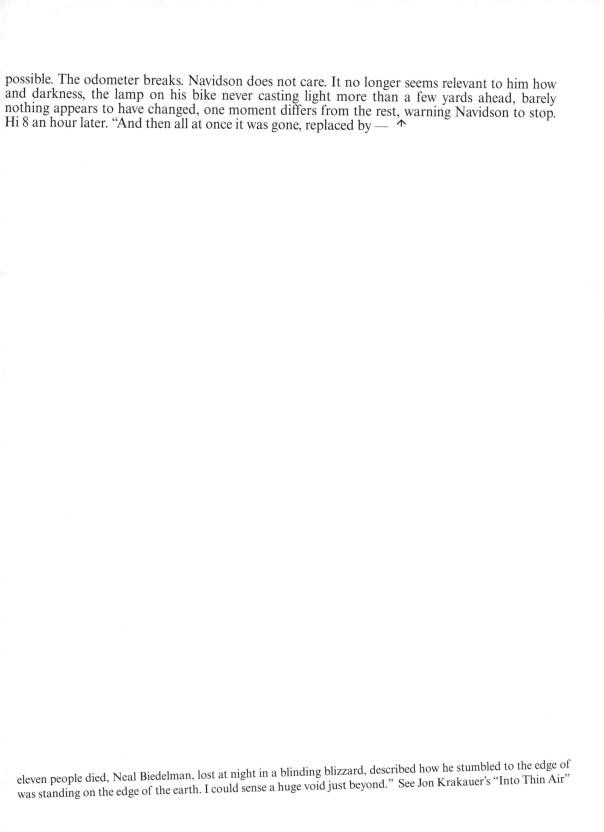

eleven people died, Neal Biedelman, lost at night in a blinding blizzard, described how he stumbled to the edge of
was standing on the edge of the earth. I could sense a huge void just beyond." See Jon Krakauer's "Into Thin Air"

Navidson tries to stop, hammering down on the brakes, rubber pads failing to hold the wheels, shrieking, even though he is still seconds before the pale light thrown by the bike lamp will finally catch sight of the end. “At that point I just yanked my bike to the ground,” he says, pointing the video camera at his left thigh. “My leg’s pretty torn up. Still bleeding a little. The trailer’s completely wrecked. I think that’s what finally stopped me. I slid right to the edge. My legs were hanging over. And I could feel it too. I don’t know how. There was no wind, no sound, no change of temperature. There was just this terrible emptiness reaching up for me.”

Flush with the brink stands a structure reminiscent of a bartizan. It is no more than seven feet high and has only one door. Inside Navidson discovers a winding staircase, which instead of leading up somewhere, or down somewhere, lies on its side, penetrating through the wall facing the abyss. Still badly shaken, Navidson does not investigate. Instead, he decides to spend the night, or whatever time of day it is—for some reason the time stamp on the Hi 8 is no longer functioning—within the confines of that unanticipated shelter.[LL]

[LL] While it would have offered Navidson some comfort, these walls still find Hermann Broch's inscription insupportable:

In der Mitte aller Ferne
steht dies Haus
drum hab es gerne

"In the middle of all distance
stands this house,
therefore be fond of it." — Ed.

The first thing Navidson notices when he wakes up is that the only door out of there has vanished. Furthermore the stairs which were horizontal before he had gone to sleep are now directly above him, rising through the ceiling, suggesting that this tiny house within a house has rotated onto its side. After changing the bandages on his leg and devouring a small snack, Navidson transfers the sleeping bag, tent, Bolex, the Nikon, the Hi 8, the film, all the video tapes, the microcassette recorder, two containers of water, three flares, chemical heaters, and the remaining PowerBars into his pack, which he then tosses up through the hole . . . . . .

.
room
cramped
exit out of that
through the only
pulls himself up
the first stair and
bike, grabs hold of
the handlebars of the
he then climbs onto
pockets. Cautiously
son stuffs into his
only book, Navid-
and this journey's
flashlights, batteries
on a step. Other items, like
. . . . . .in the ceiling where it lodges on

No sooner does he start up this new staircase than the floor below him vanishes along with the bike, trailer, and everything else he left behind, including additional water, food, flares, and lenses. Navidson sprints upwards, trying to distance himself as quickly as possible from that gaping pit. Unfortunately the winding stairs offer no landings or exits. After who knows how many hours, he reaches the last step, finding himself in a small circular chamber without doorways or passages. Just a series of black rungs jutting out of the wall, leading up into an even narrower vertical shaft.

admits he will
bar, Navidson

high-caloric energy
have a bite of some

gulp of water or
stops to take a

with only brief
of climbing,

hours and hours
after presumably

the ladder. But
pulls himself up

Navidson

hand over hand,

Slowly but surely,

Erich Kästner in *Ölberge Weinberge* (Frankfurt, 1960, p. 95) comments on the force of vertical meanings:

> The climbing of a
> mountain reflects
>
> redemption. That is
> due to the force of
>
> the word 'above,'
> and the power of
>
> the word 'up.' Even
> those who have
>
> long ceased to
> believe in Heaven
>
> and Hell, cannot
> exchange the words
>
> 'above' and 'below.'

An idea Escher beautifully subverts in *House of Stairs*; disenchanting his audience of the gravity of the world, while at the same time enchanting them with the peculiar gravity of the self.

standing inside a very
seconds and he is

rung. A few more
he reaches the last

Thirty minutes later,
tenacity is rewarded.

for a little longer. His
continues to push on

unappealing he
however, is so

sleep. This idea,
rung and try to

tie himself to a
probably have to

small room with

one door which

he cautiously opens.

On the other
side, we find
a narrow cor
ridor sliding
into darknes
s. "These w
alls are actua
lly a relief,"
Navidson co

mments after
he has been
walking for a
while. “I ne
ver thought t
his labyrinth
would be a p
leasant thin

g to return
to." Excep
t the futhe
r he goes, t
he smaller t
he hallway

gets, unti
l he has t
o remove
his pack
and crou

ch. So
on he i
s on all
fours p

ushing
his pac
k in fro
nt of hi

m. Another
hundred yar
ds and he h

as to crawl on hi
s belly. As we c

an see, the pain f
rom his already i

njured leg is excru
ciating. At one poi

nt, he is unable t
o move another i

nch. The jump cut
suggests he may h

ave rested or slept
. When he begins

dragging himself forw
ard again, the pain has

ave rested or slept
. When he begins

dragging himself forw
ard again, the pain has

still not diminished. E
ventually though, he e

merges inside a v
ery large room w

here everything about

the house

suddenly

changes.

[XXXXXXXXXXXXXXXXXXXXXXXXXXXXXXXXX]
[XXXXXXXXXXXXXXXXXXXXXXXXXXXXXXXXX]
[XXXXXXXXXXXXXXXXXXXXXXXXXXXXXXXXX]
[XXXXXXXXXXXXXXXXXXXXXXXXXXXXXXXXX]
[XXXXXXXXXXXXXXXXXXXXXXXXXXXXXXXXX]
[XXXXXXXXXXXXX **XXXXX** XXXXXXXXXXXXXX]
[XXXXXXXXXXXXX **XXXXX** XXXXXXXXXXXXXX]
[XXXXXXXXXXXXX **XXXXX** XXXXXXXXXXXXXX]
[XXXXXXXXXXXXX **XXXXX** XXXXXXXXXXXXXX]
[XXXXXXXXXXXXX **XXXXX** XXXXXXXXXXXXXX]
[XXXXXXXXXXXXXXXXXXXXXXXXXXXXXXXXX]
[XXXXXXXXXXXXXXXXXXXXXXXXXXXXXXXXX]
[XXXXXXXXXXXXXXXXXXXXXXXXXXXXXXXXX]
[XXXXXXXXXXXXXXXXXXXXXXXXXXXXXXXXX]
[XXXXXXXXXXXXXXXXXXXXXXXXXXXXXXXXX]

"I'm afraid it'll vanish if I move closer. It's almost worth spending an hour just basking in the sight. I must be nuts to enjoy this so much."

But when Navidson finally does move forward, nothing changes.

XXXXX
XXXXX
XXXXX
XXXXX
XXXXX

With
each step
Navidson takes,
we too grow more and
more convinced that we are
really looking at a window and
furthermore an *open* window.
Doorways offer passage but windows
offer vision. Here at last is a chance to behold
something beyond the interminable pattern of wall,
room, and door; a chance to reach a place of perspective
and perhaps make some sense of the whole. An eye on the wind.
Though as Navidson discovers, there was never a wind and there
certainly is no eye.

Climbing out onto a narrow terrace on the other side,Navidson,for the second
time during Exploration #5, confronts that grotesque vision of absence. This time,
however, he can do little else but laugh.

“Well isn't this unexpected,” Navidson chuckles. But as he turns to go back, he finds the
window has vanished along with the room. All that remains is the ashblack slab upon which he
is standing, now apparently supported by nothing: darkness below, above, and of course darkness
beyond.

It is only a matter of time before all of Navidson's flashlights expire. Regrettably the hand powered pumper flashlight was lost with the bike and trailer. As for the three flares Navidson had been carrying with him, he soon uses them when he finds himself powerless to resist the promise of at least a little warmth and retinal activity. Who knows how many hours or days pass between each flare. Navidson's watch stopped functioning long ago. But as he freely admits, he no longer cares about the meaning of a minute or even a week.

Since the batteries for the Hi 8 are also depleted, Navidson now has only his microcassette recorder to collect his thoughts and the 16mm Bolex to capture the sputtering bits of light. The first flare drops straight down, illuminating nothing but itself, never reaching a bottom, ultimately winking out in the darkness. The second flare, however, does not fall but floats instead: "At first it amazed me and then I got used to it. For a while, I treated it like a lamp, reading a few pages of the book I'd brought along." The third flare flies straight up and vanishes into the black above.

Though terribly short, these three segments reveal Navidson's ability to find in even the barest moment a way to evoke tenderness. His frames care for their subject. Even when the three flares finally vanish Navidson still lets the camera roll, lingering on their departure, the ensuing darkness coming close to meaning the loss felt so often in the aftermath of light.

As Navidson indicates on the recorder, he is slowly becoming more and more disoriented. He suffers from surges of nausea, "like I've got a bad case of the spins." Questions plague him. Is he floating, falling, or rising? Is he right side up, upside down or on his side? Eventually, however, the spins stop and Navidson accepts that the questions are sadly irrelevant.

Taking a tiny sip of water and burying himself deeper in his sleeping bag, he turns his attention to the last possible activity, the only book in his possession: *House Of Leaves*.

"But all I have for light is one book of matches and the duration of each ma—" (for whatever reason the tape cuts off here).

Hans Staker from Geneva, Switzerland has researched the Navidson-match question. By carefully analyzing one black & white print which briefly appears after the flare vignettes, Staker managed to magnify the matchbook just visible in the lower left hand corner. Navidson's thumb obscures most of the design but the Latin words *Fuit Ilium* can still be made out along with the English words *Thanks To These Puppies.*

Based on this scant evidence, Staker successfully determined that the matches came from of all places a pub outside of Oxford, England, run by a former classics professor and amateur phillumenist by the name of Eagley "Egg" Learnèd who, as it turned out, had designed the matchbook himself.

"Most British septuagenarians have their gardens to putter about in. I have my pub," Learnèd told Staker in an interview. "I tinker constantly with my ale selection the way the incontinent fret about their tulips. The matches came out of that sort of tinkering. There's actually a factory not too far from here. I merely applied twenty years of Latin to come up with the cover. Call it an old man's hat tip to anarchy. A touch more incendiary than the old Swan Vestas, I think. Designed to keep the goraks away."[L]

Staker goes on to trace how the matchbook got from Learnèd's pub to Navidson's steady hands. Learnèd actually stopped ordering the matches back in '85 which was right after Navidson visited England and presumably the pub.

It is highly unlikely Navidson ever intended to use a book of ten year old matches on a journey as important as this one. In fact, he packed several boxes of recently purchased matches which he lost along with the trailer and bike. Probably some private history caused him to carry the matchbook on him.

To Learnèd's credit, they are good matches. The heads ignite easily and the staffs burn evenly. Staker located one of these matchbooks and after recreating the conditions in the house (namely the temperature) found that each match burned an average of 12.1 seconds. With

[L] See Hans Staker's "Thanks To These Puppies" in *Collected Essays on "Exploration #5".* (Liverpool: Bate Press, 1996), p. 89-142.

only 24 matches plus the matchbook cover, which Staker figured out would burn for 36 seconds, Navidson had a total of five minutes and forty-four seconds of light.

The book, however, is 736 pages long. Even if Navidson can average a page a minute, he will still come up 704 pages short (he had already read 26 pages). To overcome this obstacle, he tears out the first page, which of course consists of two pages of text, and rolls it into a tight stick, thus creating a torch which, according to Staker, will burn for about two minutes and provide him with just enough time to read the next two pages.

Unfortunately Staker's calculations are really more a form of academic onanism, a jerk of numeric wishful thinking, having very little to do with the real world. As Navidson reports, he soon begins falling behind. Perhaps his reading slows or the paper burns unevenly or he has bungled the lighting of the next page. Or maybe the words in the book have been arranged in such a way as to make them practically impossible to read. Whatever the reason, Navidson is forced to light the cover of the book as well as the spine. He tries to read faster, inevitably loses some of the text, frequently burns his fingers.

In the end Navidson is left with one page and one match. For a long time he waits in darkness and cold, postponing this final bit of illumination. At last though, he grips the match by the neck and after locating the friction strip sparks to life a final ball of light.

First, he reads a few lines by match light and then as the heat bites his fingertips he applies the flame to the page. Here then is one end: a final act of reading, a final act of consumption. And as the fire rapidly devours the paper, Navidson's eyes frantically sweep down over the text, keeping just ahead of the necessary immolation, until as he reaches the last few words, flames lick around his hands, ash peels off into the surrounding emptiness, and then as the fire retreats, dimming, its light suddenly spent, the book is gone leaving nothing behind but invisible traces already dismantled in the dark.

"I have nothing left," Navidson says slowly into the microcassette recorder. "No more food. No more water. [Long pause] I have film but the flash is dead. I'm so cold. My feet hurt."

Then (who knows how much later):

"I'm no longer sitting on anything. The slab, whatever it was, is gone. I'm floating or falling or I don't know what." →

← Perhaps it is worthwhile to mention here the response to what serves essentially as the climax to Navidson's documentary. After all, the film does not provide an even remotely coherent synthesis of Navidson's fall. There is a still photograph of the window, a few hundred feet of flares dropping, hovering, shooting up into the void, and several pictures of Navidson reading/ burning the book. The rest is a jumble of audio clips recording Navidson's impressions as he begins to die from exposure. All of which comes down to one incredible fact: nearly six minutes of screen time is black.

In *Rolling Stone* (November 14, 1996, p. 124) columnist James Parshall remarked:

> Horrific, true, but also amusing. Even to this day, I can't help smiling when I think about the audience squirming in their seats, squinting at that implacable screen, now and then glancing over at those luminous red exit signs in order to give their eyes a rest, while somewhere behind them a projector continues to spew out darkness.

Michael Medved was appalled. In his mind, six minutes of nothing spelled the end of cinema. He was so shocked, indignant, even incoherent, he failed to consider that *The Navidson Record* might have absolutely nothing to do with cinema. Stuart Deweltrop in *Blind Spot* (v.42, spring, 1995, p. 38) described it as "a wonderful fiasco—n'est-ce pas?" Kenneth Turan called it "a stunt." Janet Maslin, however, had a completely different reaction: "At last a picture with cojones!"

Nor did Navidson's ending escape the gang in the monkey house. Jay Leno quipped, "You know how they made *The Navidson Record?* Left the lens cap on. This really was a home movie." While Letterman scowled: "Think about it folks: no stars, no crew, no locations. Very inexpensive. A lot of studios are taking this idea very seriously . . . Seriously." Whereupon the lights on the stage were turned off for several seconds. On *Home Improvement*, Tim Allen offered a one minute parody in the dark, mostly having to do with stubbed toes, broken dishware, and misdirected gropes.

Meanwhile, a number of serious film aficionados began commenting on the quality of the audio. It is no great secret now that Tom Holman, California THX sound wizard, helped clean up the tapes and monitor all the transfers. Numerous articles appeared in *Audio, Film,* and *F/X.* Purportedly Vittorio Storaro even said: "With sound that bright who needs light?" It is hard to disagree. Even if some of Navidson's words are impossible to understand, there is still a haunting proximity when he speaks, as if he were no longer buried in black, his words tapering without echo, his dying almost too close to bear.

Now, except for when Navidson speaks, silence predominates.

Not even the growl dares disturb his place.

"I have no sense of anything other than myself," he mumbles.

"I know I'm falling and will soon slam into the bottom. I feel it, rushing up at me." But he can only live with this fear for so long before he recognizes: "I won't even know when I finally do hit. I'll be dead before I can realize anything's happened. So there is no bottom. It does not exist for me. Only my end exists." And then in a whisper: "Maybe that is the <u>something</u> here. The only thing here. My end."

Navidson records his sobs and groans. He even captures moments of faint amusement when he jokingly announces: "It's not fair in a way. I've been falling down so long it feels like floating up to me—" Soon though he grows less concerned about where he is and becomes more consumed by who he once was.

Unlike Floyd Collins, Navidson does not rave about angels in chariots or chicken sandwiches. Nor does he offer us his C.V. like Holloway. Instead, as urea pours into his veins and delirium sets in, Navidson begins rambling on about people he has known and loved: Tom—"Tom . . . Tom, is this where you went? Don't look down, eh?"—Delial, his children and more and more frequently Karen—"I've you. I've lost you."

Sometimes
his words are
intelligible. Sometimes
they are not. "Catch me
I'm falling, I'm flying" or "Now
I will walk-sleep." However unlike The
Holloway Tape, this footage is devoid of any
subtitles or sub-interpretations.

A little later, Navidson becomes almost light hearted, for a
moment losing sight of the question of his own end,
his own past, derailed by some tune now wedged
in his head, drifting up from out of the blue,
one he can remember but cannot quite
name: "Something like . . . I think,
hmmm . . . Kinda like . . . .
[Coughs] [Coughs again]
Now I find I changed
my mind and
opened up
the door
. . ."

"Daisy. Daisy. Daisy. Daisy, Daisy, give me your answer do. I'm half crazy over the love of you. That's not right."

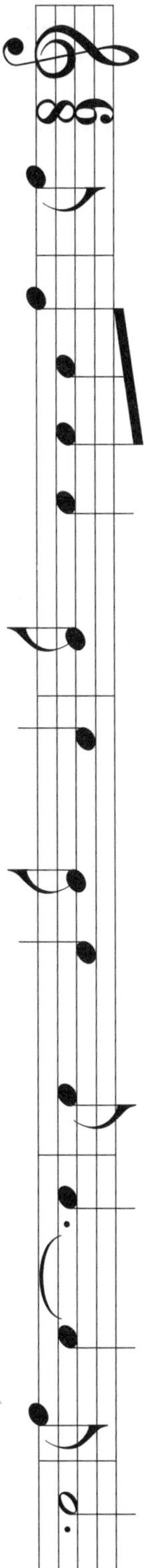

"Don't be scared."

"Don't be."

“I am.”

Finally Navidson's words, tunes, and shivering murmurs trail off into a painful rasp. He knows his voice will never heat this world. Perhaps no voice will. Memories cease to surface. Sorrow threatens to no longer matter.

Navidson is forgetting.

Navidson is dying.

Very

soon he

will vanish

completely in the wings :

of his own

wordless

stanza

[ ]
[ ]
[ ]
[ ]
[ ]
[ ]
[ ]
[ ]
[ ]
[ ]
[ ]
[ ]
[ ]
[ ]
[ ]

Except

this stanza

does not remain :

entirely

empty

[ ]
[*]
[ ]
[ ]
[ ]
[ ]
[ ]
[ ]
[ ]
[ ]
[ ]
[ ]
[ ]
[ ]
[ ]

"Light," Navidson croaks. "Can't. Be. I see light.[l] Care—"

[l] Ignis fatuus? ["Foolish Fire. Will of the wisp [1608]." — Ed.][k]

Sure enough the final frames of Navidson's film capture in the upper right-hand corner a tiny fleck of blue crying light into the void. Enough to see but not enough to see by.

The film runs out.

Black.

A different kind of black.

Followed by the name of the processing lab.*

*Yale

XXI

We felt the lonely beauty of the evening, the immense roaring silence of the wind, the tenuousness of our tie to all below. There was a hint of fear, not for our lives, but of a vast unknown which pressed in upon us. A fleeting feeling of disappointment—that after all those dreams and questions this was only a mountain top—gave way to the suspicion that maybe there was something more, something beyond the three-dimensional form of the moment. If only it could be perceived.

— Thomas F. Hornbein
Everest—The West Ridge

October 25, 1998

Lude's dead.

October 25, 1998 (An hour??? later)

Wow, not doing so well. But where else to turn? What mistakes have been made. A sudden vertigo of loss, when looking down, or is it really looking back?, leaves me experiencing all of it at once, which is way too much.

Supposedly by the time Lude made it out of the hospital he'd gotten very familiar with all those painkillers. Too familiar. He wasn't in the kind of shape he used to be in before Gdansk Man got to him. He couldn't shake off the effects as easily. He couldn't resist them as easily either. It sure didn't help that the fucker he called his lawyer kept feeding him all that bull about getting rich and living free.

By summer, Lude was tumbling straight down into oblivion. Morning shots—and not booze either. Somehow he'd gotten mixed up with hypodermic needles. Plus pills and plenty of other stuff. And all for what? Addressing what pain? No doubt at the heart of him. Unshared, unseen, maybe not even Lude himself. I mean "not even recognized by Lude himself." What I meant to say. And then the worst question of all: if I'd been there, could I have made a difference?

Apparently in August, the front Lude had defended for so many years finally began to fail.

Lude never did have the sense to retreat. No rehab for him, no intro(in)spection, no counseling, good talk, clean talk, or even the slightest attempt to renegotiate old pathways. If only he could have gotten around it all, at least once, far enough to peek past the corner and find out that hey, it doesn't have to be the same block after all. But Lude didn't even opt for a fucking change of pace. He'd refuse the line. He'd fix bayonets and then in a paroxysm of instinct, all mad, bleak, sad & sad, same word said differently—you gotta ask, you'll never know, maybe you're lucky—he gave the order to charge.

"Charge!" Probably never really said. Just implied. With a gesture or a grin.

Only in Lude's case the bayonets were fifths of bourbon & bindles of pills and his charge was led on a Triumph.

Of course this was no Little Round Top. Not about the Union, though ironically Lude was killed right outside of Union on Sunset. He'd been up in the Hills at some so & so, such & such gathering, enough chemicals rioting in his body to sedate Manchester United for weeks. Around four in the morning, still hours before that great summoning of blue, inspiration struck, winding into him like an evil and final vine. He was going for a ride. The chemicals sure as hell didn't object nor did his friends.

Amazingly enough, he made it down the hill alive, and from there started heading west, going after his own edge, his own dawn, his own watery murmur.

He was doing well over 100 MPH when he lost control. The motorcycle skidding across the left lane. Somehow—in the ugly stretch of a second—threading unhit past any oncoming traffic, until it slammed into the building wall and disintegrated.

Lude flew off the bike when the front wheel caught the curb. The cement uncapped his skull. He painted a good six feet of sidewalk with his blood. The next morning a sanitation crew found his jaw.

That was about all Lude left behind too, that and a few pairs of scissors with a couple of shorn hairs still clinging to the blades.

October 25, 1998 (Later)

Numb now. Moments when my face tingles. Could be my imagination. I'm not feeling anything let alone some motherfucking tingle. I'm so cold I stay crouched by my hot plate. I light matches too. Trying to follow Lude's advice. Six boxes of blue tips. My fingers bubble and blister. The floor writhes with a hundred black serpents. I want to burn these pages. Turn every fucking word to ash. I hold the burning staffs a quarter of an inch from the paper, and yet one after another, the flames all die in a gray line. Is it a line? More like the approximation of a line written in a thin line of rising smoke. That's where I focus because no matter how hard I try I cannot close that fraction of space. One quarter of an inch. As if to say not only can this book not be destroyed, it also cannot be blamed.

October 25, 1998 (Still later)

Possess. Can't get the word out of my eye. All those S's, sister here to these charred matches. What is it, the meaning behind "to possess" and why can't I see it? What at all can we ever really possess? Possessions? And then there's that other idea: what does it mean when we are possessed? I think something possesses me now. Nameless—screaming a name that's not a name at all—though I still know it well enough not to mistake it for anything other than a progeny of anger and rage. Wicked and without remorse.

October 25, 1998 (Not yet dawn)

An incredible loneliness has settled inside me. I've never felt anything like this before.

We've all experienced a cold wind now and then but once or twice in your life you may have known a wind over seventy below. It cuts right through you. Your clothes feel like they were made of tissue, your lips cracking, eyes tearing, lashes instantly freezing—pay no mind to the salt. You know you have to get out of there fast, get inside, or there's no question, you will not last.

But where do I go for shelter? What internationally recognized haven exists for this kind of emptiness? Where is that Youth Hostel? On what street?

Not here. That's for sure.

Maybe I should just drain a glass, load a bong, shake hands with the unemployed. Who am I kidding? No place can keep me from this. Can't even keep you.

And so I sit with myself just listening, listening to the creaking floor boards, the hammering water pipes, and masked in each breath, syncopated to every heartbeat, the shudders of time itself, there all along to accompany my fellow residents as they continue to yell, fight and of course scream. I'm surrounded. Indigents, addicts, the deluded and mad, crawling with lice, riddled with disease, their hearts breaking with fear.

Horror has caused this.

But where horror? Why horror? Horror of what? As if questions could stop any of it, halt the angriest intrusion of all, ripping, raping, leaving me, leaving you, leaving all of us gutted, hollow, dying to die.

Any fool can pray.

I find some soup and use a knife to stab it open. I have no pan so I tear off the paper and place the can directly on the hot plate. Eventually I dial the screams out. Though they are still there. They'll always be there. Random, abrupt, loud, sometimes soft, sometimes even wistful.

I'm not in a hotel. This is not a refuge. This is an asylum.

The soup warms. I do not. I will need something stronger. And I find it. What has been there all along, ancient, no not ancient, but primitive, primitive and pitiless. And even if I know better than to trust it, I also realize I'm too late to stop it. I have nothing else. I let it stretch inside me like an endless hallway.

And then I open the door.

I'm not afraid anymore.

Downstairs, probably in some equally oily room as this, someone shouts. His voice is anguish, describing in a sound a scene of awful violence, a hundred serrated teeth, bright with a thousand years of blood, jagged nails barely tapping out a code of approach, pale eyes wide and dilated, cones and rods capturing everything in one unfailing and powerful assumption.

My heart should race. It doesn't. My breath should come up short. It doesn't. My mouth's empty but the taste there is somehow sweet.

Of course I'm not afraid. Why should I be? What disturbs the sleep of everyone in this hotel; what crushes their throats in their dreams and stalks them like the dusk the day; what loosens their bowels, so even the junkies here have to join the rush to the bowl, splattering their wet chinawhite; what they experience only as premonition, illness and fear; that banished face beyond the province of image, swept clean like a page—is and always has been me.

October 25, 1998 (Dawn)

Left Hotel. If the clerk had looked up I would have killed him. <u>Wer jetzt kein Haus hat, baut sich keines mehr.</u> Though I can see, I walk in total darkness. And though I feel, I care even less than I see.

October 27, 1998

Sleep under benches. All I have are these fluttering pages in my Dante book, a Florentine something I can't remember getting or buying. Maybe I found it? Scribble like a maniac. Etch like the chronic ill. Mostly shiver. Shiver constantly though the nights are not so cold.

Wherever I walk people turn from me.

I'm unclean.

October 29, 1998

Guess Lude wasn't enough. He wanted the guy who did the actual fucking. Kyrie was with him too, saying nothing, just sitting there as he pulled that 840 Ci BMW over, his BMW, his Ultimate Driving Machine, and yelled something at me, for me to stop I think, which I did, waiting patiently for him to park the car, get out, walk over, wind up and hit me—he hit me twice—all of it experienced in slo-mo, even when I crumpled and fell, all that in slo-mo too, my eyebrow ringing with pain, my eye swelling with bruise, my nose compacting, capillaries bursting, flooding my face with dark blood.

He should have paid attention. He should have looked closely at that blood. Seen the color. Registered the different hue. Even the smell was off. He should have taken heed.

But he didn't.

Gdansk Man just yelled something ridiculous, made his point and that was that, as if he really had asserted himself, settled some imaginary score, and that really was just that. And maybe it was. For him at least. End of story.

He even wiped his hands of the affair, literally wiping his hands on his pants as he walked away.

Good old Gdansk Man.

I could see Kyrie was smiling, something funny to her, perhaps how the world turns, a half a world spinning world away finally spinning back around again, completing this circle. Resolving.

Except that when Gdansk Man turned his back on me, starting his short stroll to the car, slo-mo died, replaced this time by a kind of celerity I've never known before. Even all those early day fights, way back when, all those raw lessons in impact and instinct, could not have prepared me for this: exceeding anger, exceeding rage, coming precariously close to the distillate of—and you know what I'm talking about here—every valued intuition lost, or so it seemed already.

My heart heard resound and followed then the unholy kettles of war. Some wicked family tree, dressed in steel, towering beyond my years though already cast in eclipse, conspired to instruct my response, fitting this rage with devastating action. I scrambled to my feet, teeth grinding back and forth like some beast accustomed to shattering bones and tearing away pounds of flesh, even as my hand vanished in a blur, lashing out for something lying near the corner trash can, an empty Jack Daniels bottle, which I'm sure, proof positive, I never noticed before and yet of course I did, I must have, some other sentient part of me had to have noticed, in allegiance with Mars, that unsteady quake of dangerous alignments, forever aware, forever awake.

My fingers locked around the glass neck and even as I sprang forward I had already begun to swing, and I was swinging hard, very hard, though fortunately the arc was off, the glass only glancing off the side of his head. A direct hit would have killed him. But he still dropped, boy did he drop, and then because I couldn't really feel the blow, only the dull vibrations in the bottle, messengers informing me in the most remote tones of "a hit, a very palpable hit" and because more than anything I craved the pain, and the knowledge pain bestows, particular, intimate and entirely personal, I let my knuckles do the rest, all of them eventually splitting open on the ridges of his face until he slumped back in shock, sorry, so sorry, though that still didn't stop me.

Initially this beating had been driven by some poorly reasoned revenge carried out in the name of Lude, as if Gdansk Man could sustain all that blame. He couldn't. It quickly became something else. No logic, no sense, just the deed fueling itself, burning hotter, meaner, a conflict beyond explanation. Gdansk Man saw what was happening and started yelling for help, though it didn't come out as a yell. More like blubbering and far too soft to reach anyone anyway. Certainly not this life-taker.

Nothing close to pity moved inside me. I was sliding over some edge within myself. I was going to rip open his skin with my bare hands, claw past his ribs and tear out his liver and then I was going to eat it, gorge myself on his blood, puke it all up and still come back for more, consuming all of it, all of him, all of it all over again.

Then suddenly, drawn in black on black, deep in the shadowy sail of my eye, I understood Kyrie was running towards me, arms outstretched, nails angled down to tear my face, puncture sight. But even as I slammed my fist into Gdansk Man's temple again, something had already made me turn to meet her, and even though I did not command it, I was already hearing my horrendous shout, ripped from my center, blasting into her with enough force to stop her dead in her tracks, robbed instantly of any will to finish what she must have seen then was only suicide. She didn't even have enough strength left to turn away. Not even close her eyes. Her face had flushed to white. Lips gone gray and bloodless. I should have spared her. I should have shifted my gaze. Instead I let her read in my eyes everything I was about to do to her. What I am about to do to her now here. How I would have her. How I have already had her. Where I would take her. Where I have already taken her. To a room. A dark room. Or no room at all. What will we call it? What will you call it?

Surprised? Really? Has nothing prepared you for this? This place where no eye will find her, no ear will hear her, among pillars of rust, where hawks haunt the sky, where I will weave my hands around her throat, closing off her life, even as I rape her, dismember her, piece by piece, and in the continuing turn, for these turns never really stop turning, void out all I am, ever was, once meant or didn't mean.

Here then at long last is my darkness. No cry of light, no glimmer, not even the faintest shard of hope to break free across the hold.

I will become, I have become, a creature unstirred by history, no longer moved by the present, just hungry, blind and at long last full of mindless wrath.

Gdansk Man dies.
Soon Kyrie will too.

October 30, 1998

What's happened here? My memory's in flakes. Haven't slept. Nightmares fuse into waking minutes or are they hours? What scenes? What scenes. Atrocities. They are unspeakable but still mine. The blood though, not all of it's mine. I've lost sense of what's real and what's not. What I've made up, what has made me.

Somehow I managed to get back to my hotel room. Past the clerk. Had to lock the door. Keep it locked. Barricaded. Thank god for the guns. I'll need the guns now. Thoughts tear suddenly through my head. I feel sick. Full of revolt. Something unright sloshes in my guts, though I know they're empty.

What's that smell here?

What have I done? Where have I gone?

October 30, 1998 (A little later)

I've just found a stack of Polaroids. Pictures of houses. I have no idea where they came from. Did I take them? Maybe they were left by someone else, some other tenant, here before me. Should I leave them for the next tenant, the one who must inevitably come after me?

And yet they are familiar, like this journal. Could someone have given them to me? Or maybe I bought them myself at some flea market.

"How much for the pics?"

"The box?"

"All of them. The whole box."

"Nuts. Cents."

Someone else's. Someone else's memories. Virginia or not Virginia but anywhere homes, lined up in a row, or not in a row. Quiet as sleeping trees. Simple houses. Houses from a car. More houses. And there in the middle, on the side of the road, one dead cat.

Oh god what constant re-angling of thoughts, an endless rearrangement of them, revealing nothing but shit. What breaks. What gives.

And not just the photos.

The journal too. I thought I'd only written a few entries but now I can see—I can feel—it's nearly full, but I don't recall any of it. Is it even in my hand?

October Three Zed, Ninety Eight. That's the day today. That's the date. Top of this page. But the first page in the journal isn't October Three Zed but May One. May one mean—meaning, I mean—months and months of journey. Before Lude died. Before the horror. Or all of it horror since right now I can't connect any of it.

It's not me.

It cannot be.

As soon as I write I've already forgotten.

I must remember.

I must read.

I must read.

I must read.

May 1, 1998

On the side of route 636, I see a tabby, head completely gone, a smear of red. Probably killed by some stupid fucking I-Don't-Really-Know-How-To-Drive motorist. Nearby another cat, a great big gray thing, watches. Runs off when I approach.

Later, after I've driven down through Alliance, over to California Crossroads up to Highgate and then back towards Conham Wharf, I return to the same spot and sure enough the gray cat is back, just sitting there, though this time refusing to leave. What was it doing? Was it grieving or just waiting, waiting for the tabby to wake up?

No one here has heard of Zampanò.

No one here has heard of the Navidsons.

I've found no Ash Tree Lane.

Months of travel and I've still found no relief.

Some bullets:

· On the Jamestown-Scotland Wharf Ferry I look down at the water and suddenly feel myself fill with a memory of love's ruin, circumscribed by war and loss. The memories are not my own. I've no idea whose they are or even where they came from. Then for an instant, feeling stripped and bare, I teeter on an invisible line suspended between something terrible and something terribly sad. Fortunately, or unfortunately, before I fall one way or the other, the ferry reaches the Jamestown colony.

An afternoon spent looping around the Pitch and Tar Swamp unveils no secrets. Standing out on Black Point, gazing over The Thorofare, shows me nothing more than the idle words of a spring wind writing unreadable verse in the crests of small waves. Are there answers hidden there? In what language?

Past a bank of pay phones, where a tall man in John Lennon glasses speaks inexplicably of beasts and burns, there is no future, school children scream their way into the visitor's center, a stream of crayon and pastel, oblivious, playful, shoving each other in front of the various dioramas, all of them momentarily delighted by all those baskets, ancient weapons and glazed mannequin expressions—though nothing more—their attention quickly shifting, drifting?, soon enough prodding their teachers to take them outside again to the ships on which the settlers first arrived, reconstructed ships, which is exactly what their teachers do, taking them away, that giddy, pastel stream, leaving me alone with the dark glass cases and all they don't display.

Where is the starving time of 1610? The 1622 Powhatan Indian Insurrection which left almost 400 dead? Where are the dioramas of famine and disease? The black and broken toes? The gangrene? The night rending pain?

"Why, it's right here," says a docent.

But I can't see what she's talking about.

And besides, there is no docent.

· Colonial Williamsburg. Wow, even further from the truth, or at least my truth. The tidy streets offer nothing more than a sanitized taste of the past. Admirable restoration, sure, but the "costumed interpreters"—as the brochure likes to describe these would-be citizens of the American legacy—nauseate me. I'm not exaggerating either. My stomach turns and heaves.

Mary Brockman Singleton speaks amiably about the Brick House Tavern on Duke of Gloucester Street and the way her husband succumbed to the grippe. It makes no difference that Mary Brockman Singleton died back in 1775, because, as she's inclined to tell everyone within earshot, she believes in ghosts.

"Didn't you know," she delicately informs us. "Numerous poltergeist sightings have been reported at the Peyton Randolph House."

A few people murmur their patriotic approval.

A good time as any for a question. I ask her if she's ever seen a bottomless staircase gut the heart of whatever home she really lives in, when Colonial Williamsburg closes down for the night and she, not to mention the rest of all these would-be interpreters here, change back to the memory of the present, hastily retreating to the comfort of microwaves and monthly telephone bills.

What does she know about interpreting, anyway?

Someone asks me to leave.

· Near the campus of William & Mary, surrounded by postcards thick with purple mountain majesty, and they are purple, I hyperventilate. It takes me a good half hour to recover. I feel sick, very sick. I can't help thinking there's a tumor eating away the lining of my stomach. It must be the size of a bowling ball. Then I realize I've forgotten to eat. It's been over a day since I've had any food. Maybe longer.

Not too far away, I find a tavern with cheap hamburgers and clean tap water. Across the room, eight students slowly get drunk on stout. I start to feel better. They pay no attention to me.

Everywhere I've gone, there've been hints of Zampanò's history, by which I mean Navidson's, without any real evidence to confirm any of it. I've combed through all the streets and fields from Disputanta to Five Forks to as far east as the Isle of Wight, and though I frequently feel close, real close, to something important, in the end I come away with nothing.

· Richmond's just a raven and the remnants of a rose garden trampled one afternoon, long ago, by moshing teenagers.

· Charlottesville. The soft clicking of Billy Reston's wheels—come to think of it sounding alot like an old projector—constantly threatens to intrude upon the corridors of a red brick building known as Thorton Hall, and yet even though I check the NSBE, I can't find his name.

A bulletin board still has an announcement for Roger Shattuck's lecture on "Great Faults and 'Splendidly Wicked People' " delivered back in the fall of '97 but retains nothing about architectural enigmas waiting in the dark Virginia countryside.

On the West Range, I make sure to avoid room 13.

· Monticello. Learn Jefferson had carefully studied Andrea Palladio's I Quatrro Libri. Realize I should probably visit the Shenandoah and Luray caverns. Know I won't.

A quick re-read of all this and I begin to see I'm tracing the wrong history. Virginia may have meant a great deal to Zampanò's imagination. It doesn't to mine.

I'm following something else. Maybe parallel. Possibly harmonic. Certainly personal. A vein of it inhabiting every place I've visited so far, whether in Texas—yes, I finally went—New Orleans, Asheville, North Carolina or any other twist of road or broken town I happened to cross on my way east.

I cannot tell you why I didn't see her until now. And it wasn't a scent that brought her back either or the wistful edges of some found object or any other on-the-road revelation. It was my own hand that did this. Maybe you saw her first? Caught a glimpse, between the lines, between the letters, like a ghost in the mirror, a ghost in the wings?

My mother is right before me now, right before you. There as the docent, as the interpreter, maybe even as this strange and tangled countryside. Her shallow face, the dark lyric in her eyes and of course her words, in those far reaching letters she used to send me when I was young, secretly alluding to how she could sit and watch the night seal the dusk, year after year, waiting it out like a cat. Or observe how words themselves can also write. Or even, in her own beautiful, and yes horrifying way, instruct me on how to murder. One day even demonstrate it.

She is here now. She has always been here.

"Beware," she might have whispered. "Another holy Other lessens your great hold on slowing time," as she would have described it, being the mad woman that she truly was.

She could have laid this world to waste.

Maybe she still will.

May 4, 1998

In Kent. Nine years. What an ugly coincidence. Even glanced at my watch. 9. Fucking nine PM.

5+4+1+9+9+8+9 = 45 (or -9 yrs = 36)

4+5 = 9 (or 3+6 = 9)

Either way, it doesn't matter.

I say it with a German accent:

Nine.

June 21, 1998

Happy Birthday to me. Happy fucking Birthday. Whatever the fuck will be will fucking be sang momma D-Day. Bright as an A-Bomb.

July 1, 1998

Dreams getting worse. Usually in nightmares you see what you're scared of. Not in my case. No image. No color. Just blackness and then in the distance, getting closer and closer, beginning to pierce some strange ever-present roar, sounds, voices, sometimes just a few, sometimes a multitude, and one by one, all of them starting to scream.

Do you know what it's like to wake up from a dream you haven't seen? Well for one thing, you're not sure if you were dreaming or not.

The day after May 4th, I didn't feel like writing down what happened. A week later, I felt even less like writing down what happened. What did it matter? Then an hour ago, I woke up with no idea where I was. It took me twenty minutes just to stop shaking. When I finally did stop though, I still couldn't shake the feeling that everything around me had been irreparably fractured. Without realizing it at first, I was thinking over and over again about that night, May 4th, mindlessly tracing and re-tracing the route I'd taken when I'd gone to see the institute where my mother had lived. What my father had always referred to as The Whale.

"You know where your mother is, Johnny," he'd tell me. "She's in The Whale. That's where she lives now. She lives in The Whale."

Much to my surprise it was dead. Closed in April. Over five years ago.

Getting inside hadn't been easy but eventually, after enough circling, edging quietly around the overgrown perimeter, I found a way through the surrounding chain link fence. Eight feet high.

Crowned with concertina wire. No Trespassing signs every ten yards.

For a while, I wandered the long white corridors, pebbles of glass strewn over most of the floors. It was easy to see why. Every window pane had been shattered. The Director's old office was no exception.

On one of the walls, someone had scrawled: "Welcome to the Ice House."

It took me another hour to locate her room. So many of the rooms looking the same, all familiar, but never quite right, quite the same, their dimensions and perspectives never precisely lining up with the memory I had, a memory I was soon beginning to doubt, a surprisingly painful doubt actually, until I saw through her window the now vine entwined tree, every wall-line, corner-line, floor-line instantly, or so it seemed—though nothing is ever instant—matching up, a sharp slide into focus revealing the place where she finally died. Of course it's final, right? Closet to the side. Empty. And her bed in the corner. The same bed. Even if the mattress was gone and the springs now resembled the rusted remains of a shipwreck half-buried in the sands of some half-forgotten shore.

Horror should have buried me.

It didn't.

I sat down and waited for her to find me.

She never did.

I waited all night in the very room it happened, waiting for her frail form to glide free of beams of glass and moonlight. Only there was no glass. No moonlight either. Not that I could see.

Come morning I found the day as I have found every other day—without relief or explanation.

There's no good answer why I went where I went next, unless of course you buy the obvious one, which in this case is the only one for sale. So give me your pennies. It's only a copper answer anyway.

I guess because I was still stuck on this notion of place and location, I drove all the way to the home I was living in when my mother was taken away, which was a good few years before my father was killed, before I would eventually meet a man named Raymond.

I was bent on just ringing the doorbell and talking my way into those rooms. Convincing myself I could convince the new owners—whoever they might be; I'm imagining fat, sallow, god fearing people, staring out at me, listening to me explain how in spite of my appearance it was still their god fearing duty—to let me walk around what used to be mine, at least for a little while.

I figured one look at me and they'd realize this was no joke. I'm about as close to fucking gone as you can get.

The man grunting: "If we don't let this kid in, he just might not make it."

The wife: "I reckon."

Then the man: "Yup."

And finally one last time, the wife: "Yup"

At least that's what I hoped.

They might just call the cops.

It was mid-day when I found, following a bunch of lefts, the right right to a no saint lined street, completely changed. The house gone. A bunch of houses gone. In their place a large lumberyard. Part of it operational. The other part still under construction.

Well what can I say, just seeing all the sawdust and oil on the ground and the hard hats and the black cables and those generic fucking trailers tore me up inside. My guts began churning with pain. Probably with blood. I started hemorrhaging hurt. Something I knew no band-aid or antacid was going to cure. I doubted even sutures would help. But what could I do?

There would be no healing here.

I stood by the circular saws and clutched my belly. I had no idea where I was in relation to what had once existed. Maybe this had been my kitchen. Why not? The stainless steel restaurant sink there to the side. The old stove over there. And here where I was standing was right where I'd been sitting, age four, at my mother's feet, my arms flinging up, instinctually, maybe even joyfully, prepared to catch the sun. Catch the rain.

The memory mixes with all the retellings and explanations I heard later. It's even possible what I hold to be a memory is really only the memory of the story I heard much later. No way to tell for sure anymore.

Supposedly I'd been laughing. So that accounts for the joy part. Supposedly she'd been laughing too. And then something made my mother jerk around, a slight mistake really but with what consequence, her arm accidentally knocking a pan full of sizzling Mazola, while I, in what has to be one of strangest reactions ever, opened my arms to play the bold, old catcher of it all, the pan bouncing harmlessly on the floor but the oil covering my forearms and transforming them forever into Oceanus whirls. Ah yes, you true sister of Circe! What scars! Could I but coat you with Nilemud! Please bless these arms! Which I found myself looking at again, carefully studying the eddies there, all those strange currents and textures, wondering what history all of it could tell, and in what kind of detail, completely unaware of the stupid redneck yelling in my ear, yelling above the engines and shrieking saws, wanting to know what the fuck I was doing there, why I was clutching my belly and taking off my shirt like that, "Are you listening to me asshole? I said who in the hell do you think you are?", didn't I know I was standing on private property?—and not even ending his tirade there, wanting to know if it was my desire to have him break me in half, as if that's really the question my bare chested silence was asking. Even now I can't remember taking off my shirt, only looking down at my arms.

I remember that.

However, as I write this down—some kind of calm returning—I do begin to recall something else, only perceive it perhaps?, the way my father had growled, roared really, though not a roar, when he'd beheld my burning arms, an ear shattering, nearly inhuman shout, unleashed to protect me, to stop her and cover me, which I realize now I have not remembered. That age, when I was four, is dark to me. Still, the sound is too vivid to just pawn off on the decibels of my imagination. The way it plays in my head like some terrifying and wholly familiar song. Over and over again in a continuous loop, every repetition offering up this certain knowledge: I must have heard it—or something like it—not then but later, though when? And suddenly I find something, hiding down some hall in my head, though not my head but a house, which house? a home, my home?, perhaps by the foyer, blinking out of the darkness, two eyes pale as October moons, licking its teeth, incessantly flicking its long polished nails, and then before it can reach—another cry, perhaps even more profound than my father's roar, though it has to be my father's, right?, sending this memory, this premonition—whatever this is—as well as that thing in the foyer away, a roar to erase all recollection, protecting me?, still?, obviously great enough to exceed the pitch of all the equipment chewing up wood, stone and earth, and certainly much louder than the dumb fuck who kept shoving me until I was well beyond the gate, falling out of grace, or into grace? who the hell cares, beyond the property line, theirs, and mine; what used to be my home.

I heard nothing.

My ears had popped.

My mind had gone blank.

Utterly.

September 2, 1998

Seattle. Staying with an old friend.[418] A pediatrician. My appearance frightened both him and his wife and she's a doctor too. I'm underweight. Too many unexplained tremors and tics. He insists I stay with them for a couple of weeks. I decline. I don't think he has any idea what he'd be in for.

September 7, 1998

The three of us spent the weekend at the Doe Bay Village Resort on Orcas Island. The mineral baths there seemed to help. Beautiful. Encircled by Douglas fir and frequently visited by strange drifters kayaking in from small boats moored in the bay. We sat there for a long time just inhaling hot sulfur as it mingled with the evening air. Eventually my friend's wife asked me about my journey and I answered her with stories about my mother, what I remembered, and the institute, what I saw, and the lumberyard. I even told them the story behind the scars on my forearms. But they already knew about that. As I already told you, they're my friends. They're doctors.

Doc took a quick dip in the adjacent cold water bath. When he came back he told me the story of Dr. Nowell.

September 20, 1998

I am much improved. My friends have been taking care of me full time. I exercise twice a day. They've got me on some pretty serious health food. At first it was hard to choke down but now my stomach's in great shape. No thoughts of a tumor or even an ulcer.

Once a day I attend a counseling session at their hospital. I'm really opening up. Doc has also put me on a recently discovered drug, one bright yellow tablet in the morning, one bright yellow tablet in the evening. It's so bright it almost seems to shine. I feel like I'm thinking much more clearly now. The medication seems to have eliminated those deep troughs and manic peaks I frequently had to endure. It also allows me to sleep.

---

418 ____
____
____
____
____

Just recently Doc confessed that when he first heard me screaming he was skeptical anything short of a long-term stay at an institute would help. The first few nights he had just sat awake listening, jotting down the occasional word I'd groan, trying to imagine what kind of sleep spindles and K-complexes could describe that.

But the drug has cured all that.

It's a miracle.

And that's that.

September 23, 1998

Doc and his wife took me out to Deception Pass where we looked down into the gorge. We all watched a bald eagle glide beneath the bridge. For some reason no one said a word.

September 27, 1998

I'm healthy and strong. I can run two miles in under twelve minutes. I can sleep nine hours straight. I've forgotten my mother. I'm back on track. And yet even though I'm now on my way to LA to start a new life—the guns in my trunk long since gone, replaced with a year's supply of that miraculous yellow shine—when I said goodbye to my friends this morning I felt awful and soaked in sorrow. Much more than I expected.

Standing side by side in their driveway, they looked like a couple of newlyweds about to run off to Paris, the kind you see in movies, racing down the dock, birdseed in their hair, climbing into a seaplane, heading out over the Sound, maybe even towards a bridge, perhaps there's even a moment where everyone wonders if they're high enough to even make it over the bridge, and then like that they do and their story begins. Good people. Very good people. Even as I started the car they were still asking me to stay.

September 28, 1998

Portland. Dusk. Walked under the Hawthorne bridge and sat by the Willamette river. Carrot juice and tofu for dinner. No, that's not right, more like a 7-Eleven burrito. Got ready to take my yellow shine tablet but for some reason—now what the hell's that about?—I'd forgotten to put one in my pocket.

I walked back to where I'd parked. My car was gone. Someone had stolen it.

No. My car was still there. Right where I'd parked it.

I opened the trunk. It was icy dark. No tablets of any kind to be found anywhere. Certainly not a year's supply. Like I said—icy dark. Empty, except for the faint glint of two guns lying side by side next to a Weatherby 300 magnum.

September 29, 1998

Are you fucking kidding me? Did you really think any of that was true? September 2 thru September 28? I just made all that up. Right out of thin air. Wrote it in two hours. I don't have any friends who are doctors, let alone <u>two</u> friends who are doctors. You must have guessed that. At least the lack of expletives should have clued you in. A sure sign that something was amiss.

And if you bought that Yellow-Tablet-Of-Shine stuff, well then you're fucking worse off than I am.

Though here's the sadder side of all this, I wasn't trying to trick you. I was trying to trick myself, to believe, even for two lousy hours, that I really was lucky enough to have two such friends, and doctors too, who could help me, give me a hand, feed me tofu, make me exercise, adminster a miracle drug, cure my nightmares. Not like Lude with all his pills and parties and con-talk street-smack. Though I sure do miss Lude. I wonder how he is. Should be out of the hospital by now. Wonder if he's rich yet. It's been months since I've seen him. I don't even know where the last month went. I had to make something up to fill the disconcerting void. Had to.

Right now I'm in Los Gatos, California. Los Gatos Lodge in fact. I managed a couple hours of sleep until a nightmare left me on the floor, twitching like an imbecile. Sick with sweat. I switched on the TV but those channels offered only the expected little.

I went outside. Tried taking in the billions of stars above, lingering long enough to allow each point of light the chance to scratch a deep hole in the back of my retina, so that when I finally did turn to face the dark surrounding forest I thought I saw the billion eyes of a billion cats blinking out, in the math of the living, the sum of the universe, the stories of history, a life older than anyone could have ever imagined. And even after they were gone—fading away together, as if they really were one—something still lingered in those sweet folds of black pine, sitting quietly, almost as if it too were waiting for something to wake.

October 19, 1998

Back in LA. Went to my storage unit and retrieved the book. Sold my car. Checked into an awful hotel. A buck and a quarter a week. One towel. One hot plate. Asked the clerk if he could give me a room that wasn't next to anyone. He just shook his head. Didn't say anything. Didn't look at me either. So I explained about the nightmares and how they make me scream alot. That made him say something, though he still didn't look at me, just stared at the formica counter and told me I wouldn't be alone. He was right. More than a few people around here scream in their sleep.

Tried calling Lude. No luck.

October 24, 1998

Called Thumper today. She was so happy to hear from me she invited me over for dinner tomorrow night, promised me the works, home cooked food and hours of uninterrupted private time. I warned her that I hadn't been to a laundromat in a long while. She said I could use her washing machine. Even take a shower if I liked.

Still nothing from Lude.

October 25, 1998

Lude's dead.

. . . .

. . . .

. . . .

November 2, 1998

Alas to leave. For this all has been a great leaving. Of sorts. Hasn't it?

November 11, 1998

Far from the city now. Bus rattling the low heavens with its slow wayless trek into the desert. Dusty people, fat people, forgotten people crowding the seats and aisles. Sack lunches, snores and the dull look that comes to faces when they're glad to be leaving but in no great hurry to arrive.

At least I have a little money now. I pawned the weapons before I left. The guy gave me eight-fifty for all three. He wouldn't spare a cent on the bullets, so I kept them and tossed them in a dumpster behind a photolab.

After going back to Kinko's—that took awhile—and then taking a trip to the Post Office—that took even longer—, I went to see my crush for the last time.

Is that what she is?

More like a fantasy, I guess. Probably best spelled with "ph." A phantastic hope. The enchanting ecdysiast who that night, at long last, gave me her real name.

I can't quite explain how good it was to see her. I had to wait awhile but it was worth it. I was out back, all the more happy when I saw she was wearing the braided gold necklace I'd given her.

See, I told you my boss would get it to her. He knew I wasn't kidding when I told him I'd burn his life down if he didn't. Even if I had been kidding.

She said she never took it off.

We didn't talk long. She had to return to her stage and I had a bus to catch. She quickly told me about her child and how she'd broken off her relationship with the boxer. Apparently, he couldn't take the crying. She was also starting laser surgery to get her tattoos removed.

I apologized about missing dinner and told her—what the fuck did I tell her? Things, I guess. I told her about things. I could see her get all nervous but she was also enticed.

Nightmares have that quality, don't they?

She reached out and gently brushed my eyebrow with her fingertips, still hurting from good old Gdansk Man. For a moment I was tempted. I could read the signs well enough to know she wanted a kiss. She'd always been fluent in that language of affection but I could also see that over the years, years of the same grammar, she'd lost the chance to understand others. It surprised me to discover I cared enough about her to act now on that knowledge, especially considering how lonely I was. I gave her an almost paternal hug and kissed her on the cheek. Above us airplanes roared for the sky. She told me to keep in touch and I told her to take care and then as I walked away, I waved and with that bid adieu to The Happiest Place On Earth.

August 28, 1999

Only yesterday, I arrived in Flagstaff, Arizona where trains routinely stop so the homeless can climb off and buy coffee for a dime at a little train yard shop across the tracks. That's really all it costs too. For seventy-five cents you can have a bowl of soup and for another dime a slice of bread. I steered clear of the coffee and bought myself dinner for under a buck. However instead of climbing back on the freight car, I wandered off, eventually stumbling upon a park with some benches where I could sit down and enjoy my meal, my mind for some reason suddenly consumed with thoughts of Europe. Paris quays, London parks. Other days.

As I ate, someone's radio kept me company until I realized it wasn't a radio at all but live music spilling out the back door of a bar.

I only had three dollars and some change. More than likely the cover would keep me from entering. I decided to try anyway. At the very least, I could linger outside and listen to a few songs.

Surprisingly enough, I encountered no one at the door. Still, since the place was half empty, I figured someone would spot me soon enough, stop me before I reached a barstool, start poking me for money. No one did. When the bartender came over to take my order, I straight up explained how much I had, figuring that would be enough to get me escorted out.

"No worries," he said. "There's no door charge and tonight beer's only a buck."

I immediately ordered three for the band and a water for myself, and what do you know, a little later the bartender came back with a beer on the house. Apparently I'd been the first one that night to buy the musicians a drink which was strange and pretty fucked up too, especially since it was such a cheap night and they were actually pretty good.

Anyway I kicked back and began listening to the songs, enjoying the strange melodies and wild, nearly whimsical words. The bartender eventually noticed that I hadn't touched my drink and offered to exchange it for something else. I thanked him and asked for a gingerale, which he got for me, taking the beer for himself.

We were still talking, talking about Flagstaff, the bar, the trains, me sharing some cross country stories, him confiding a few of his own predicaments, when out of the blue some very weird lyrics spiked through our conversation. I whipped around, listening again, concentrating, convinced I'd made a mistake, until I heard it once more: "I live at the end of a Five and a Half Minute Hallway."

I couldn't believe my ears.

When the set finished, I approached the trio, all three of them, probably because of the way I looked and smelled, acting very suspicious and wary until the bartender introduced me as the source of their recently acquired and hastily imbibed beverage. Well that changed everything. Barley and hops make for remarkable currency.

We started chatting. As it turned out, they were from Philadelphia and had been touring from coast to coast all summer. They called themselves Liberty Bell.

"Cracked. Get it?" howled the guitar player. Actually all three of them were pretty glib about their music, until I asked about "The Five and a Half Minute Hallway."

"Why?" the bass player said sharply, the other two immediately getting very quiet.

"Wasn't it a movie?" I stammered back, more than a little surprised by how fast the mood had just shifted.

Fortunately, after studying me for a moment, presumably making one of those on-the-spot decisions, the drummer shook his head and explained that the lyrics were inspired by a book he'd found on the Internet quite some time ago. The guitar player walked over to a duffel bag lying behind one of their Vox amps. After digging around for a second he found what he was searching for.

"Take a look for yourself," he said, handing me a big brick of tattered paper. "But be careful," he added in a conspiratorial whisper. "It'll change your life."

Here's what the title page said:

House of Leaves

by Zampanò

with introduction and
notes by Johnny Truant

Circle Round A Stone Publication

First Edition

I couldn't believe my eyes.

As it turned out, not only had all three of them read it but every now and then in some new city someone in the audience would hear the song about the hallway and come up to talk to them after the show. Already, they had spent many hours with complete strangers shooting the shit about Zampanò's work. They had discussed the footnotes, the names and even the encoded appearance of Thamyris on page 387, something I'd transcribed without ever detecting.

Apparently they wondered alot about Johnny Truant. Had he made it to Virginia? Had he found the house? Did he ever get a good night's sleep? And most of all was he seeing anyone? Did he at long last find the woman who would love his ironies? Which shocked the hell out of me. I mean it takes some pretty impressive back-on-page-117 close-reading to catch that one.

During their second set, I thumbed through the pages, virtually every one marked, stained and red-lined with inquiring and I thought frequently inspired comments. In a few of the margins, there were even some pretty stunning personal riffs about the lives of the musicians themselves. I was amazed and shocked and suddenly very uncertain about what I had done. I didn't know whether to feel angry for being so out of the loop or sad for having done something I didn't entirely understand or maybe just happy about it all. There's no question I cherished the substance of those pages, however imperfect, however incomplete. Though in that respect they were absolutely complete, every error and unfinished gesture and all that inaudible discourse, preserved and intact. Here now, resting in the palms of my hands, an echo from across the years.

For a while I wrestled with myself over whether or not to tell the band who I was, but finally, for whatever reason, decided against it, returning their book with a simple thank you. Then finding myself very sleepy, I wandered back into the park, wrapped myself up in my brown corduroy coat with new buttons I'd personally sewed on—this time using entire spools of thread to make sure they would never fall off again—and stretched out beneath an old ash tree, resting my head on the earth, listening to the music as it continued to break from the bar, healing my fatigue, until at long last I drifted off to a dream where I was soaring far above the clouds, bathed in light, flying higher and higher, until finally I fell into a sleep no longer disturbed by the past.

A short while ago a great big gray coated husky emerged out of nowhere and started sniffing my clothes, nudging my arm and licking my face as if to assure me that though there was no fire or hearth, the night was over and the month was August and nothing close to seventy below would threaten me. After petting him for a few minutes, I walked with him around the park. He sprinted after birds while I stretched the sleep out of my legs. Even as I scribble this down, he insists on sitting by my side, ears twitching occasionally in the dawn air, while before us a sky as dark as a bruised plum slowly unfolds into morning.

Inside me, I still feel a strange and oddly familiar sorrow, one which I suspect will be with me for some time, twining around the same gold that was once at the heart of my horror, before she appeared before him and spoke the rain into a wind. At least though, it's getting milder, a gentle breeze filling in from the south. Flagstaff appears deserted and the bar's closed and the band's gone, but I can hear a train rattling off in the distance. It will be here soon, homeless climbing off for a meal, coffee for a dime, soup for three quarters and I have some change left. Something warm sounds good, something hot. But I don't need to leave yet. Not yet. There's time now. Plenty of time. And somehow I know it's going to be okay. It's going to be alright. It's going to be alright.

October 31, 1998

Back here again. These pages are a mess. Stuck together with honey from all my tea making. Stuck together with blood. No idea what to make of those last few entries either. What's the difference, especially in differance, what's read what's left in what's left out what's invented what's remembered what's forgotten what's written what's found what's lost what's done?

What's not done?

What's the difference?

October 31, 1998 (Later)

I just completed the intro when I heard them coming for me, a whole chorus, cursing my name, all those footfalls and then the bang of their fists on my door.

I'm sure it's the clerk. I'm sure it's the police. I'm sure there are others. A host of others. Accusing me for what I've done.

The loaded guns lie on my bed.

What will I do?

There are no more guns. There are no more voices.

There is no one at my door.

There's not even a door anymore.

Like a child, I gather up the finished book in my arms and climb out the window.

Memories soon follow.

Gdansk Man's blood is smeared on my fingers, but even as I prepare to murder him there on the sidewalk and carry Kyrie away to another there—some unspeakable place—, something darker, perhaps darkest of all, arrests my hand, and in the whispers of a strange wind banishes my fury.

I throw the bottle away, pick up Gdansk Man and whatever I say, something to do with Lude, something to do with her, he mumbles apologies. For some reason, his hands are cut and bleeding. Kyrie takes his keys, slips behind the wheel and retreats into the bellowing of the day, their departure echoing in my head, resonant with incomplete meaning, ancient and epic, as if to say that whatever had come to mean us was dissuaded by something else that had come to meet us. Confirming in this resolution that while the dead may still hunt their young, the young can still turn and in that turning learn how the very definition of whim prevents the killing.

Or is that not it at all?

I start to run, trying to find a way to something new, something safe, darting from the sight of others, the clamor of living.

There is something stronger here. Beyond my imagination. It terrifies me. But what is it? And why has it retained me? Wasn't darkness nothingness? Wasn't that Navidson's discovery? Wasn't it Zampanò's? Or have I misconstrued it all? Missed the obvious, something still undiscovered waiting there deep within me, outside of me, powerful and extremely patient, unafraid to remain, even though it is and always has been free.

I've wandered as far west as I can go.

Sitting now on the sand, I watch the sun blur into an aftermath. Reds finally marrying blues. Soon night will enfold us all.

But the light is still not gone, not yet, and by it I can dimly see here my own dark hallway, or maybe it was just a foyer and maybe not dark at all, but in fact brightly lit, an afternoon sun blazing through the lead panes, now detected amidst what amounts to a long column of my yesterdays, towards the end, though not the very end of course, where I had stood at the age of seven, gripping my mother's wrists, trying as hard as I could to keep her from going.

Her eyes, I recall, melting with tenderness and confusion, as she continued muttering strange, unwieldy words: "My little eye sack. My little Brahma lamb. Mommy's going to be okay. Don't worry."

But even though my father had his hands on her shoulders, trying as gently as he could to lead her away, I couldn't let go. So she knelt down in front of me and kissed my cheeks and my forehead and then stroked my face.

She hadn't tried to strangle me and my father had never made a sound.

I can see this now. I can hear it too. Perfectly.

Her letter was hopelessly wrong. Maybe an invention to make it easier for me to dismiss her. Or maybe something else. I've no idea. But I do know her fingers never closed around my throat. They only tried to wipe the tears from my face.

I couldn't stop crying.

I'd never cried that much before.

I'm crying now.

All these years and now I can't stop.

I can't see.

I couldn't see then.

Of course she was lost in a blur. My poor father taking her from me, forced to grab hold of her, especially when they got to the foyer and she started to scream, screaming for me, not wanting to go at all but crying out my name—and there it was the roar, the one I've been remembering, in the end not a roar, but the saddest call of all—reaching for me, her voice sounding as if it would shatter the world, fill it with thunder and darkness, which I guess it finally did.

I stopped talking for a long while after that. It didn't matter. She was lost, swallowed by The Whale where authorities thought it unwise to let me see her. They weren't wrong. She was more than bad off and I was far too young and wrecked to understand what was happening to her. Compassion being a long journey I was years away from undertaking. Besides, I learned pretty quickly how to resent her, licking away my hurt with the dangerous language of blame. I no longer wanted to see her. I had ceased to mind. In fact I grew to insist on her absence, which was how I finally learned what it meant to be numb. Really numb. And then one day, I don't know when, I forgot the whole thing. Like a bad dream, the details of those five and a half minutes just went and left me to my future.

Only they hadn't been a dream.
That much—that little much—I now know.

The book is burning. At last. A strange light scans each page, memorizing all of it even as each character twists into ash. At least the fire is warm, warming my hands, warming my face, parting the darkest waters of the deepest eye, even if at the same time it casts long shadows on the world, the cost of any pyre, finally heated beyond recovery, shattered into specters of dust, stolen by the sky, flung to sea and sand.

Had I meant to say memorializing?

Of course there always will be darkness but I realize now something inhabits it. Historical or not. Sometimes it seems like a cat, the panther with its moon mad gait or a tiger with stripes of ash and eyes as wild as winter oceans. Sometimes it's the curve of a wrist or what's left of romance, still hiding in the drawer of some long lost nightstand or carefully drawn in the margins of an old discarded calendar. Sometimes it's even just a vapor trail speeding west, prophetic, over clouds aglow with dangerous light. Of course these are only images, my images, and in the end they're born out of something much more akin to a Voice, which though invisible to the eye and frequently unheard by even the ear still continues, day and night, year after year, to sweep through us all.

Just as you have swept through me.

Just as I now sweep through you.

I'm sorry, I have nothing left.

Except this story, ~~what I'm remembering now~~, too long from the surface of any dawn, the one Doc told me when I was up in Seattle —

It begins with the birth of a baby, though not a healthy baby. Born with holes in its brain and "showing an absence of grey/white differentiation"—as Doc put it. So bad that when the child first emerges into this world, he's not even breathing.

"Kid's cyanotic," Dr. Nowell shouts and everywhere heart rates leap. The baby goes onto the

Ohio, a small 2 x 2 foot bed, about chest high, with a heater and examination lights mounted above.

Dr. Nowell tracks the pulse on the umbilical cord while using a bulb syringe at the same time to suck out the mouth, trying to stimulate breath.

"Dry, dry, dry. Suck, suck, suck. Stim, stim, stim."

He's not always successful. There are times when these measures fail. This, however, is not one of those times.

Dr. Nowell's team immediately follows up, intubating the baby and providing bag mask ventilation, all of it coming together in under a minute as they rush him to an ICU where he's plugged into life support, in this case a Siemens Servo 300, loaded with red lights and green lights and plenty of bells and whistles.

Life it seems will continue but it's no easy march. Monitors record EKG activity, respiratory functions, blood pressure, oxygen saturation, as well as end tidal CO_2. There's a ventilator. There are also IV pumps and miles of IV lines.

As expected, nurses, a respiratory therapist and a multitude of doctors crowd the room, all of them there simply because they are the ones able to read the situation.

The red and green lights follow the baby's every breath. Red numbers display the exact amount of pressure needed to fill his fragile lungs. A few minutes pass and the SAT (oxygen saturation) monitor, running off the SAT probe, begins to register a decline. Dr. Nowell quickly responds by turning the infant's PEEP (Positive End Expiratory Pressure) up by 10 to compensate for the failing oxygenation, this happening while the EKG faithfully tracks every heart beat, the curve of each P wave or in this case normal QRS, while also on the monitor, the central line and art line, drawn straight from the very source, a catheter placed in the bellybutton, records continuous blood pressure as well as blood gasses.

The mother, of course, sees none of this. She sees only her baby boy, barely breathing, his tiny fingers curled like sea shells still daring to clutch a world.

Later, Dr. Nowell and other experts will explain to her that her son has holes in his brain. He will not make it. He can only survive on machines. She will have to let him go.

But the mother resists. She sits with him all day. And then she sits with him through the night. She never sleeps. The nurses hear her whispering to him. They hear her sing to him. A second day passes. A second night. Still she doesn't sleep, words pouring out of her, melodies caressing him, tending her little boy.

The charge nurse starts to believe they are witnessing a miracle. When her shift ends, she refuses to leave. Word spreads. More and more people start drifting by the ICU. Is this remarkable mother still awake? Is she still talking to him? What is she singing?

One doctor swears he heard her murmur "Etch a Poo air" which everyone translates quickly enough into something about an etching of Pooh Bear.

When the third day passes without the mother even closing her eyes, more than a handful of people openly suggest the baby will heal. The baby will grow up, grow old, grow wise. Attendants bring the mother food and drink. Except for a few sips of water, she touches none of it.

Soon even Dr. Nowell finds himself caught up in this whispered hysteria. He has his own family, his own children, he should go home but he can't. Perhaps something about this scene stings his own memories. All night long he works with the other preemies, keeping a distant eye on mother and child caught in a tangle of cable and tubing, sharing a private language he can hear but never quite make out.

Finally on the morning of the fourth day, the mother rises and walks over to Dr. Nowell.

"I think it's time to unplug him," she says quietly, never lifting her gaze from the floor.

Dr. Nowell is completely unprepared for this and has absolutely no idea how to respond.

"Of course," he eventually stammers.

More than the normal number of doctors and nurses assemble around the boy, and though they are careful to guard their feelings, quite a few believe this child will live.

Dr. Nowell gently explains the procedure to the mother. First he will disconnect all the nonessential IV's and remove the nasogastric tube. Then even though her son's brain is badly damaged, he will adminster a little medicine to ensure that there is no pain. Lastly, he and his team will cap the IV, turn off the monitors, the ventilator and remove the endotracheal tube.

"We'll leave the rest up to . . ." Dr. Nowell doesn't know how to finish the sentence, so he just says "Well."

The mother nods and requests one more moment with her child.

"Please," Dr. Nowell says as kindly as he can.

The staff takes a step back. The mother returns to her boy, gently drawing her fingers over the top of his head. For a moment everyone there swears she has stopped breathing, her eyes no longer blinking, focusing deeply within him. Then she leans forward and kisses him on the forehead.

"You can go now," she says tenderly.

And right before everyone's eyes, long before Dr. Nowell or anyone else can turn a dial or touch a switch, the EKG flatlines. Asystole.

The child is gone.

XXII

Truth transcends the telling.

— Ino

nothing more now than the mere dark. The tape is blank.

Finally when Karen does turn around to discover the real emptiness waiting behind her, she does not scream. Instead her chest heaves, powerless for a moment to take anything in or expel anything out. Oddly enough as she starts to retreat from the children's bedroom, it almost looks as if something catches her attention. A few minutes later, she returns with a halogen flashlight and steps toward the edge.

Hanan Jabara suggests Karen heard something, though there is nothing even remotely like a sound on the Hi 8.[419] Carlos Ellsberg agrees with Jabara: "Karen stops because of something she hears." Only he qualifies this statement by adding, "the sound is obviously imagined. Another example of how the mind, any mind, consistently seeks to impose itself upon the abyss."[420]

As everyone knows, Karen stands there on the brink for several minutes, pointing her flashlight into the darkness and calling out for Navidson.[421] When she finally does step inside, she takes no deep breath and makes no announcement. She just steps forward and disappears behind the black curtain. A second later that cold hollow disappears too, replaced by the wall, exactly as it was before, except for one thing: all the children's drawings are gone.

Karen's action inspired Paul Auster to conjure up a short internal monologue tracing the directions of her thoughts.[422] Donna Tartt also wrote an inventive portrayal of Karen's dilemma. Except in Tartt's version, instead of stepping into darkness, Karen returns to New York and marries a wealthy magazine publisher.[423] Purportedly there even exists an opera based on *The Navidson Record*, written from Karen's perspective, with this last step into the void serving as the subject for the final aria.

Whatever ultimately allows Karen to overcome her fears, there is little doubt her love for Navidson is the primary catalyst. Her desire to embrace him as she has never done before defeats the memories of that dark well, the molestations carried out by a stepfather or whatever shadows her childhood truly conceals. In this moment, she displays the restorative power

---

[419]Hanan Jabara's "Hearing Things." *Acoustic Lens*, v. xxxii, n. 8, 1994. p. 78-84.

[420]Carlos Ellsberg's "The Solipsistic Seance." *Ouija*, v. ix, n. 4, December, 1996. p. 45.

[421]Though it may be obvious, recent studies carried out by Merlecker and Finch finally confirmed the "high probability" that the "star" Navidson caught on film was none other than Karen's halogen. See Bob Merlecker and Bob Finch's "Starlight, Starbright, First Flashlight I See Tonight." *Byte*, v. 20, August, 1995. p. 34.

[422]Paul Auster's "Ribbons." *Glas Ohms,* v. xiii, n. 83, August 11, 1993, p. 2.

[423]Donna Tartt's "Please, Please, Please Me." *Spin,* December 1996, p. 137.

of what Erich Fromm terms the development of "symbiotic relationships" through personal courage.

Critic Guyon Keller argues that the role of vision is integral to Karen's success:

> I believe Karen could never have crossed that line had she not first made those two remarkable cinematic moments: *What Some Have Thought* and *A Brief History Of Who I Love*. By relearning to see Navidson, she saw what he wasn't and consequently began to see herself much more clearly.[424]

Esteemed Italian translator Sophia Blynn takes Keller's comments a little further:

> The most important light Karen carried into that place was the memory of Navidson. And Navidson was no different. Though it's commonly assumed his last word was "care" or the start of "careful." I would argue differently. I believe this utterance is really just the first syllable of the very name on which his mind and heart had finally come to rest. His only hope, his only meaning: "Karen."[425]

Regardless of what finally enabled her to walk across that threshold, forty-nine minutes later a neighbor saw Karen crying on the front lawn, a pink ribbon in her hair, Navidson cradled in her lap.

An ambulance soon arrived. Reston caught up with them at the hospital. Navidson's core temperature had dropped to a frighteningly low 83.7 degrees Fahrenheit. Lacking a cardiopulmonary bypass machine which could have pumped out Navidson's cold blood and replaced it with warm oxygenated blood, doctors instead had to cut into Navidson's abdominal cavity, insert catheters, and proceed to irrigate his internal organs with warm fluid. Though his core temperature rose to 85.3 degrees, the EKG continued to produce the peculiar J wave indicative of hypothermia. Still more liters of saline were added to the IV. Doctors kept close watch. One hour passed. Most there believed he would not live through another.

He did.

Karen stayed at his side that night and through the nights and days which followed, reading to him, singing to him, and when she was tired sleeping on the floor by his bed.

As hours slipped into weeks, Navidson began to recover, but the price he paid for living was not cheap. Frostbite claimed his right hand and clipped the top portion of one ear. Patches of skin on his face were also removed as well as his left eye. Furthermore his hip had inexplicably shattered and had to be replaced. Doctors said he would need a crutch for the rest of his life.

He did.

---

[424]Guyon Keller's "The Importance of Seeing Clearly" in *Cineaste*, v. xxii, n. 1, p. 36-37.
[425]Sophia Blynn's "Carry On Light" in *Washingtonian,* v. 31, December 1995, p. 72.

Still he survived. Furthermore, the film and tapes he made during his journey also survived.

As to what happened after Karen disappeared from view, the only existing account comes from a short interview conducted by a college journalist from William & Mary:

Karen: As soon as I walked in there, I started shivering. It was so cold and dark. I turned around to see where I was but where I'd come from was gone. I started hyperventilating. I couldn't breathe. I was going to die. But somehow I managed to keep moving. I kept putting one foot in front of the other until I found him.

Q: You knew he was there?

Karen: No, but that's what I was thinking. And then he was there, right at my feet, no clothes on and all curled up. His hand was white as ice. [She holds back the tears.] When I saw him like that it didn't matter anymore where I was. I'd never felt that, well, free before.

[Long pause]

Q: What happened then?

Karen: I held him. He was alive. He made a sound when I cradled his head in my arms. I couldn't understand what he was saying at first but then I realized the flashlight was hurting his eyes. So I turned it off and held him in the darkness.

[Another long pause]

Q: How did you get him out of the house?

Karen: It just dissolved.

Q: Dissolved? What do you mean?

Karen: Like a bad dream. We were in pitch blackness and then I saw, no . . . actually my eyes were closed. I felt this warm, sweet air on my face, and then I opened my eyes and I could see trees and grass. I thought to myself, "We've died. We've died and this is where you go after you die." But it turned out to be just our front yard.

Q: You're saying the house dissolved?

Karen: [No response]

Q: How's that possible? It's still there, isn't it?

END OF INTERVIEW[426]

---

[426]Missing. — Ed.

XXIII

"Surviving House, Kalapana, Hawaii, 1993"

— Diane Cook

In *Passion For Pity and Other Recipes For Disaster* (London: Greenhill Books, 1996) Helmut Muir cried: "They both live. They even get married. It's a happy ending."

Which is true. Both Karen and Will Navidson survive their ordeal and they do exchange conjugal vows in Vermont. Of course, is it really possible to look at Navidson's ravaged face, the patch covering his left eye, the absence of a hand, the crutch wedged under his armpit, and call it a "happy" ending? Even putting aside the physical cost, what about the unseen emotional trauma which Muir so casually dismisses?

The Navidsons may have left the house, they may have even left Virginia, but they will never be able to leave the memory of that place.

"It is late October," Navidson tells us in the closing sequence to *The Navidson Record*. Almost a year and a half has passed since he emerged from the house. He is still recovering but making progress, pouring his life into finishing this project. "At least one good thing to come out of all this," he says with a smile. "The skin condition plaguing my feet for all these years has completely vanished."

The children seem to approve of Vermont. Daisy adamantly believes faeries inhabit the countryside and spirits possess her collection of stuffed animals and dolls, in particular a red and gold one. Chad on the other hand has become obsessed with Lego, spending countless hours with pounds and pounds of their arrangement. When questioned about this newfound interest, he only says that someday he wants to become an architect.

Karen struggles every day to keep up with everyone's energies. Only recently she was diagnosed with malignant breast cancer. The mastectomy was considered "successful" and subsequent chemotherapy declared "very effective." Nevertheless hair loss and severe stomach ulceration have left Karen gaunt and grey. She has lost too much weight and constantly needs to sit down to catch her breath. Still, as Navidson tenderly shows us, her will-o'-the-wisp smiles seem impervious to the ravaging effects of disease and whenever she laughs the notes sing a call to Victory.

Navidson captures all this in simple, warmly lit shots: simmering milk, roasted walnuts and against a backdrop of black ash and pine, Karen's graceful fingers braiding her daughter's long auburn hair. Despite Karen's infrequently removed woolen hat, she and Daisy still both share a remarkable radiance. What Massel Laughton once described as "a kind of beautiful mischief."[427]

Nor is this the only shot of mother and child. Hundreds of photographs hang on the walls of their home. Every room, stairway, and corridor supports pictures of Karen, Daisy, Chad, and Navidson as well as Tom, Reston, Karen's mother, their friends, distant relatives, ancient relatives, even Mallory and Hillary.

Though this collage is immensely appealing, Navidson is wise enough to know he cannot close on such images. They may be heart warming but what they imply rings false. As Navidson says himself: "I kept looking for assurances, for that gentle ending, but I never found it. Maybe because I know that place is still there. And it always will be there."

Navidson has never stopped wrestling with the meaning of his experience. And even though it has literally crippled him, he somehow manages to remain passionate about his work. Mercifully, in her captivating book on art, culture, and politics, in which she includes *The Navidson Record* in the spire of her analysis, Daphne Kaplan reminds the reader what it means to be passionate:

> Passion has little to do with euphoria and everything to do with patience. It is not about feeling good. It is about endurance. Like patience, passion comes from the same Latin root: *pati*. It does not mean to flow with exuberance. It means to suffer. [△]

Navidson suffers the responsibilities of his art and consequently must turn from the blind comfort found in those neatly framed photographs filling his home to follow his costume clad children out into the New England streets, their hearts set on sacks of candy, their paths hidden beneath cold coloured leaves.

In those final shots, Navidson gives a wink to the genre his work will always resist but invariably join. Halloween. Jack O'lanterns. Vampires, witches, and politicians. A whole slew of eight year old ghouls haunting the streets of Dorset, plundering its homes for apples and MilkyWays, all while tossing up high-pitched screams into the sparkling blackness forever closing in above them.

Tongues of grey ice cover the roads, candles flicker unevenly, and grownups gulp hot cider from styrofoam cups, always keeping watch over their sheep in wolves' clothing lest something disturb their pantomime. Each squeal and cry arrests a sip of warmth as parents everywhere

---

[427]Massel Laughton's "Comb and Brush" in Z, v. xiii, n. 4, 1994, p. 501.

△ Daphne Kaplan's *The Courage to Withstand* (Hopewell, NJ: Ecco Press, 1996), p. iii.

immediately seek out these tiny forms wending their way from porch to porch across great lakes of shadow.

Navidson does not close with the caramel covered face of a Casper the friendly ghost. He ends instead on what he knows is true and always will be true. Letting the parade pass from sight, he focuses on the empty road beyond, a pale curve vanishing into the woods where nothing moves and a street lamp flickers on and off until at last it flickers out and darkness sweeps in like a hand.

— December 25, 1996

EXHIBITS

Though never completed, Zampanò left the following instructions for a series of plates he planned to include at the end of The Navidson Record. — JT.

ONE

Instructions:

§ Provide pictorial examples of architecture ranging from early Egyptian, Mycenaean, Greek, and Roman to Gothic, early Renaissance, Baroque, Neoclassical, and the present.

§ Emphasize floor plans, doorways, pediments, gables, columns, capitals, entablatures, and windows.

§ Also create a timeline indicating general dates of origin for developing styles.

§ For references see bibliography in Chapter IX.

TWO

Instructions:

§ Provide examples of hand shadows ranging from crabs, snails, rabbits, and turtles to dragons, panthers, tigers, and kangaroos. Also include hippos, frogs, elephants, birds of paradise, dogs, cockatoos, and dolphins.

§ Supply diagrams detailing light and display requirements.

§ See Phila H. Webb and Jane Corby's *The Little Book of Hand Shadows* (Philadelphia: Running Press, 1990) as well as Sati Achath and Bala Chandran's *Fun With Hand Shadows: Step-By-Step Instructions for More Than 70 Shadows—From Cud-Chewing Cows and Dancing Elephants to Margaret Thatcher and Michael Jackson* (NTC/Contemporary Publishing, 1996).

THREE

Instructions:

§ Illustrate date determination techniques utilizing potassium-40/argon-40, rubidium-87/strontium-87, and samarium-147/neodymium-143.

§ Provide table for uranium-235 and -238 found in lead isotopes.

§ Include all data in Zero Folder.[428]

[428]Missing. — Ed.

FOUR

Instructions:

§ Reproduce all facsimiles of **The Reston Interview** and **The Last Interview.**[429]

[429]Missing. — Ed.

FIVE

Instructions:

§ Duplicate page 2-33 in Air Force Manual 64-5 (15 August 1969).[430]

[430]See Appendix II-C. — Ed.

SIX

Instructions:

§ Reproduce Karen's completed Sheehan Clinician Rated Anxiety Scale as well as her Marks and Mathews Phobia Scale.[431]

§ Highlight the following information: Project ID: 87852341. Date of Birth: July 24th. Patient ID: 002700

§ For interpretation and examples see Isaac M. Marks' *Living with Fear* (McGraw-Hill, 1978); Isaac M. Marks' *Fears, Phobias, and Rituals: Panic, Anxiety, and Their Disorders* (Oxford: Oxford University Press, 1987) and *The Encyclopedia of Phobias, Fears, and Anxieties* by Ronald M. Doctor, Ada P. Kahn, Ronald D. Doctor and Isaac M. Marks (New York: Facts on File, 1989).

[431]See Appendix II-C. — Ed.

Appendix

Zampanò produced a great deal of material outside of The Navidson Record. Here's a selection of journal entries, poems and even a letter to the editor, all of which I think sheds a little more light on his work as well as his personality. — JT.

A.

Outlines & Chapter Titles

The Navidson Record

Intro
1/4″
Tom
The Five and a Half Minute Hallway
Exploration A (Navidson's Visit)

Exploration #1 (Across the Anteroom)
Exploration #2 (To the Great Hall)
Exploration #3 (Seven hours down the Spiral Staircase)
Exploration #4
  SOS
  Into The Maze
  Rescue
  (Tom's Story)
  The Falling Quarter
  The Holloway Tape
Evacuation

"What Some Have Thought"*
"A Brief History Of How `[sic]` I Love"
The Reston Interview
The Last Interview
Exploration #5
The End

*Not included in final release.

Release History

1990 — "The Five and a Half Minute Hallway"
(VHS Short)
1991 — "Exploration #4"
(VHS Short)
1993 — *The Navidson Record*

Possible Chapter Titles

Chapter I	The Film
Chapter II	1/4″
Chapter III	Outpost
Chapter IV	Navidson
Chapter V	Echo
Chapter VI	Animals
Chapter VII	Holloway
Chapter VIII	SOS
Chapter IX	The Labyrinth
Chapter X	The Rescue (Part One)
Chapter XI	Tom's Story
Chapter XII	The Rescue (Part Two)
Chapter XIII	~~The Minotaur~~
Chapter XIV	Infidelity
Chapter XV	Karen
Chapter XVI	Science
Chapter XVII	Reasons
Chapter XVIII	Ftaires! or De la Warr or The History of Ash Tree Lane
Chapter XIX	Delial
Chapter XX	The Return
Chapter XXI	Nightmares
Chapter XXII	Faith
Chapter XXIII	Passion

B.

Bits

[*Original*][432]
January 18, 1955

I do not know anything about Art with a capital A. What I do know about is my art. Because it concerns me. I do not speak for others. So I do not speak for things which profess to speak for others. My art, however, speaks for me. It lights my way.

[*Original*]
April 17, 1955

Then are we inhabited by history?

[*Original*]
September 4, 1955

Light dawns and marble heads. What the hell does this mean?

[*Original*]
June 3, 1959

This terror that hunts.

[*Typed*]
August 29, 1960

Captain Kittinger, you brought us an early fall this year.

[*Typed*]
October 31, 1968

I have no words. The finest cenotaph.

[*Typed*]
November 1, 1968

(~~o~~)   (~~n~~)
A s~~u~~n to re~~a~~d the dark.

[*Typed*]
November 2, 1968

Tirer comme des lapins.[433]

[*Original*]
December 8, 1968

God grant me distraction.

[432]Presumably "Original" indicates an entry written in Zampanò's own hand, while "A" "B" "C" etc., etc. indicate entries written by someone else. — Ed.
[433]"Shot like rabbits." — Ed.

[*B*]
March 14, 1969

Who has never killed an hour? Not casually or without thought, but carefully: a premeditated murder of minutes. The violence comes from a combination of giving up, not caring, and a resignation that getting past it is all you can hope to accomplish. So you kill the hour. You do not work, you do not read, you do not daydream. If you sleep it is not because you need to sleep. And when at last it is over, there is no evidence: no weapon, no blood, and no body. The only clue might be the shadows beneath your eyes or a terribly thin line near the corner of your mouth indicating something has been suffered, that in the privacy of your life you have lost something and the loss is too empty to share.

[*C*]
September 10, 1970

Nothing to share with.

[*Typed*]
September 21, 1970

Perhaps in the margins of darkness, I could create a son who is not missing; who lives beyond even my own imagination and invention; whose lusts, stupidities, and strengths carry him farther than even he or I can anticipate; who sees the world for what it is; and consequently bears the burden of everyone's tomorrow with unprecedented wisdom and honor because he is one of the very few who has successfully interrogated his own nature. His shields are instantly available though seldom used. And those who value him shall prosper while those who would destroy him shall perish. He will fulfill a promise I made years ago but failed to keep.

[*Typed*]
December 15, 1974

As often as I have lingered on Hudson in his shallop, I have in the late hours turned my thoughts to Quesada and Molino's journey across those shallow waters, wondering aloud what they said, what they thought, what gods came to keep them or leave them, and what in those dark waves they finally saw of themselves? Perhaps because history has little to do with those minutes, the scene survives only in verse: *The Song of Quesada and Molino* by [XXXX]. I include it here in its entirety.

[*D*]
April 29, 1975

Mother wants you to call home STOP It is 105 degrees and rising STOP White Christmas indeed!

Bada-Bing, Bada-Bang, Bada-Gone!

Bing! Bang! Booooom!

[*Typed*]
February 11, 1984

Is it possible to love something so much, you imagine it wants to destroy you only because it has denied you?

[*E*]
August 4, 1985

I dream of vampires. I dream of god. I dream of no vampires. I dream of no god. I dream of nothing. And yet that too is still my dream.

[*F*]
May 2, 1988

The angel of his youth became the devil of his maturity. He went out with women when he was young, always holding something in reserve. There would always be a reason to break it off, which opened the door to a multitude of relationships. Heaven. Or so he thought. As age encroached upon his sensibilities and form, he longed for something with enough vitality to endure. But the covering cherub of his Lothario days had stayed with him and was no longer so angelic. It haunted him, guarded him, kept him from intimacy, promising the ash dry glory of so many toppling relationships, toppling like dominos, one after another, ad infinitum, or at least until he died.

[*G*]
August 30, 1988

"He wanted to go to bed with her immediately, pull the sheets around them, dig his toes into the mattress, her heals pushing against his calves, her fingers running rivers along his sides. But these days fantasies flourish and die like summer flies."

[*Typed*]
March 18, 1989

A maze. Amazing maze. A maze meant . . . What did it mean? A May zing perhaps. M.A.s in the bush or amidst the maize. Quite amazing huh? Not to worry I am not that impressed either but grant an old man a chance to play.

[*H*]
February 8, 1990

It stinks here. I know what stink is and it stinks here. Cat piss, rotting fruit, moldy bread. Something. I am certain that girl is at fault. She must not have taken the garbage out. She can read (I will find out soon if she can transcribe) and she can flirt. But I wager she has failed to take the garbage out. I should get rid of her. I should take it out myself. I hate garbage. It stinks. I should throw it out myself. I should throw it all out.

[*I*]
October 11, 1990

Incomplete. Syllables to describe a life. Any life.
I cannot even discuss Günter Nitschke or Norberg-Schulz. I merely wanted *Glas* (Paris: Editions Galilée, 1974). That is all. But the bastards reply it is unavailable. Swine. All of them. Swine. Swine. Swine.

Mr. Leavey, Jr. and of course Mr. Rand will have to do.

[*I*]
April 22, 1991

An atrocity sinking into waters of darkness; without order or bars of earth; where light must mean shadow and reason dies in the hold:

((((((((((((Jonah in the belly of the beast))))))))))))

[*I*]
May 3, 1991

Stars to live by. Stars to steer by. Stars to die by.

[*I*]
May 26, 1991

Kutch Dekta?
Kutch Nahin, Sahib.

[*I*]
May 30, 1991

Do not wake me from this slumber, but be assured that just as I have wept much, I have also wandered many roads with my thoughts. Reminiscent of another film by my eye fell in. Aye. K

[*J*]
June 30, 1991

Goddamn! Goddamn, Goddamn it! Goddamn! Goddamn! God Damn! Yes, of course write it down! Write all of it down! Everything I say! Every goddamn word! Goddamn! Capital G! Goddamn it all! All of it, every last word. Goddamn her wrong!

[*J*]
July 27, 1991

Make no mistake, those who write long books have nothing to say. Of course those who write short books have even less to say.

[*K*]
August 7, 1992

How did I end up here? I know of course. I am referring to the itinerary I followed. But that hardly helps me understand the whys any better. I still walk out into that dusty courtyard and stand amazed, amazed that I should have ended up stuck in such a shithole, then I think to myself "Not only did you end up here, you are going to die here too!" Of course Hollywood is the land of the blind with churches for the blind so in my case it makes a certain sense. You think I am bitter about being here, yes? You think I am bitter about this grave I live in and that bed of weeds I scratch around in? You think I am bitter about dying? What do you know? You know nothing about bitterness because you know nothing about love. Get out. Get out! No, stay. Please stay. Let us read something. Forget everything I just said. It is not so bad. I am just old and you know a good deal about love and I would like to think I know something more because of my age. Let us read something.

[*M*]
April 3, 1992

Walls black like black waters when they are heavy and seem to belong to other seas.

[*M*]
December 3, 1992

Why can I sleep no more?

[*N*]
May 7, 1993

The house is history and history is uninhabited.

[*O*]
June 19, 1994

Prometheus, thief of light, giver of light, bound by the gods, must have been a book.

[*O*]
November 11, 1994

Defend a stray's hun? Never used the word. Never will.

[*P : Written in the margin of the December 15, 1974 entry.*]
April 3, 1995

"Forgive me please for including this. An old man's mind is just as likely to wander as a young man's~~, but where a young man will forgive the stray, an old man will cut it out. Youth always tries to fill~~

~~the void, an old man learns to live with it. It took me twenty years to unlearn the fortunes found in a swerve. Perhaps this is no news to you but then I have killed many men and I have both legs and I don't think I ever quite equaled the bald gnome Error who comes from his cave with featherless ankles to feast on the mighty dead."~~[173]

[*U*]
April 9, 1996

Paralipomena. n. From ME f. eccl. L f. GK *paraleipomena* f. PARA (It. imper. of *parare* defend) (*leipo* leave) omit.

[*X*]
October 2, 1996

All of which is pretty senseless without the beautiful light of Ruskin's *Seven Lamps of Architecture.* Oh, what is the use?

[*Typed*]
December 18, 1996

The cats have been dying and everyone wonders why. I can hear my neighbors murmur. They murmur all the time: "It's strange. Some cats die, some just disappear. No one knows why . . ."

Redwood. I saw him once a long time ago when I was young. I ran away and luckily, or no luck at all, he did not follow me. But now I cannot run and anyway this time I am certain he would follow.

[*Typed*]
December 21, 1996

Explanation is not half as strong as experience but experience is not half as strong as experience and understanding.

[*Original*]
December 23, 1996

I took my morning walk, I took my evening walk, I ate something, I thought about something, I wrote something, I napped and dreamt something too, and with all that something, I still have nothing because so much of sum'things has always been and always will be you.

I miss you.

C.

. . . and Pieces

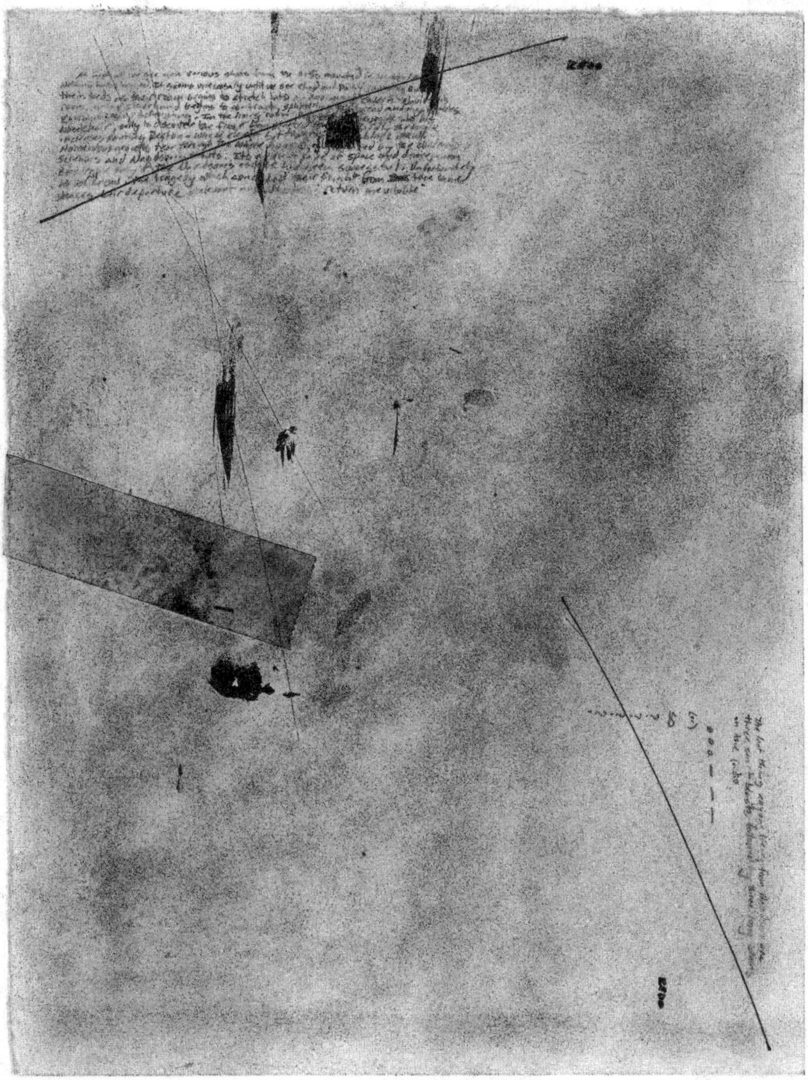

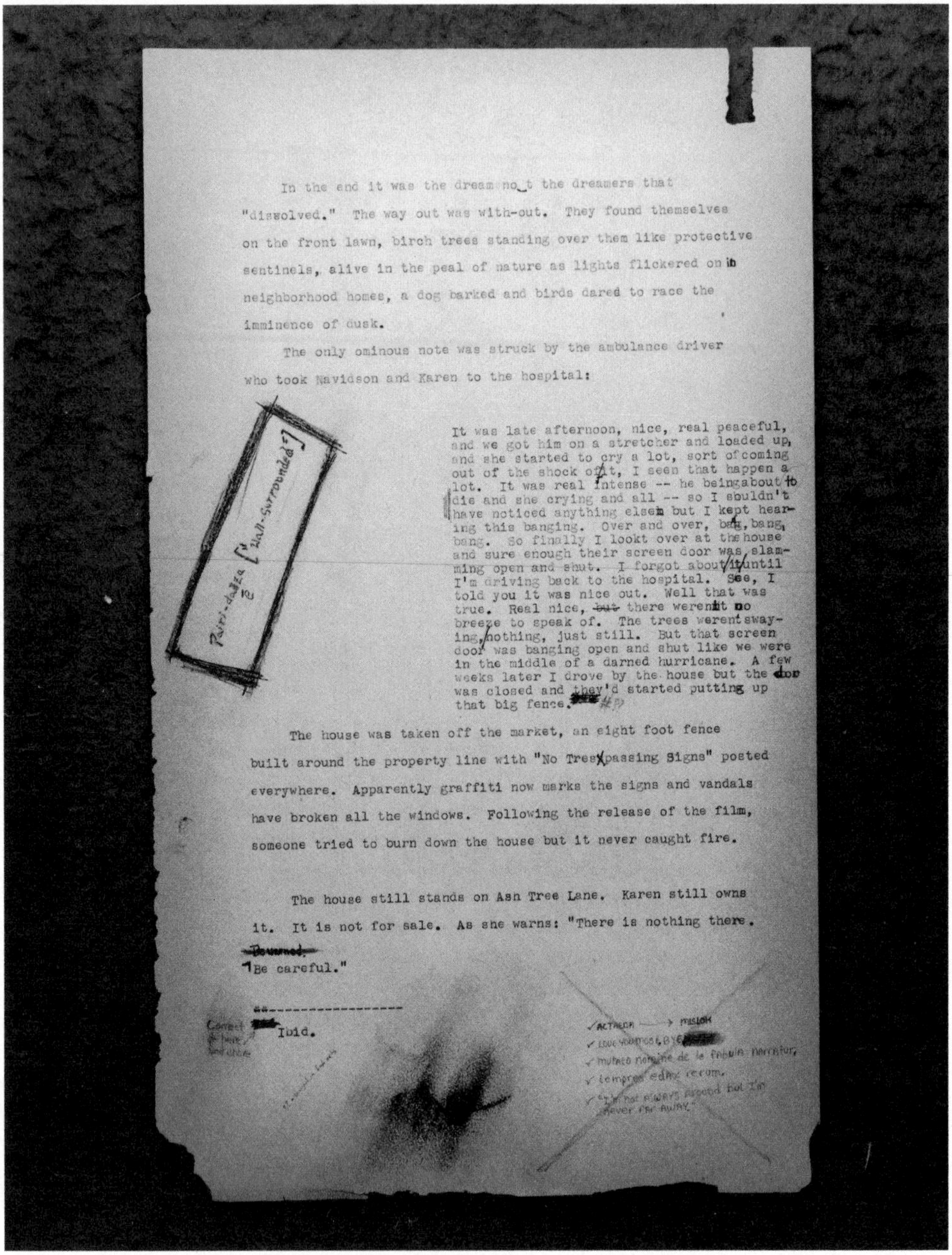

In the end it was the dream not the dreamers that "diswolved." The way out was with-out. They found themselves on the front lawn, birch trees standing over them like protective sentinels, alive in the peal of nature as lights flickered on in neighborhood homes, a dog barked and birds dared to race the imminence of dusk.

The only ominous note was struck by the ambulance driver who took Navidson and Karen to the hospital:

> It was late afternoon, nice, real peaceful, and we got him on a stretcher and loaded up, and she started to cry a lot, sort of coming out of the shock of it, I seen that happen a lot. It was real intense -- he being about to die and she crying and all -- so I shouldn't have noticed anything else but I kept hearing this banging. Over and over, bang, bang, bang. So finally I lookt over at the house and sure enough their screen door was slamming open and shut. I forgot about it until I'm driving back to the hospital. See, I told you it was nice out. Well that was true. Real nice, ~~but~~ there weren't no breeze to speak of. The trees weren't swaying, nothing, just still. But that screen door was banging open and shut like we were in the middle of a darned hurricane. A few weeks later I drove by the house but the door was closed and they'd started putting up that big fence.[redacted]

The house was taken off the market, an eight foot fence built around the property line with "No Tresxpassing Signs" posted everywhere. Apparently graffiti now marks the signs and vandals have broken all the windows. Following the release of the film, someone tried to burn down the house but it never caught fire.

The house still stands on Ash Tree Lane. Karen still owns it. It is not for sale. As she warns: "There is nothing there.

~~Be warned.~~

Be careful."

[redacted] Ibid.

(Rephotographed for the 2nd edition. — Ed.)

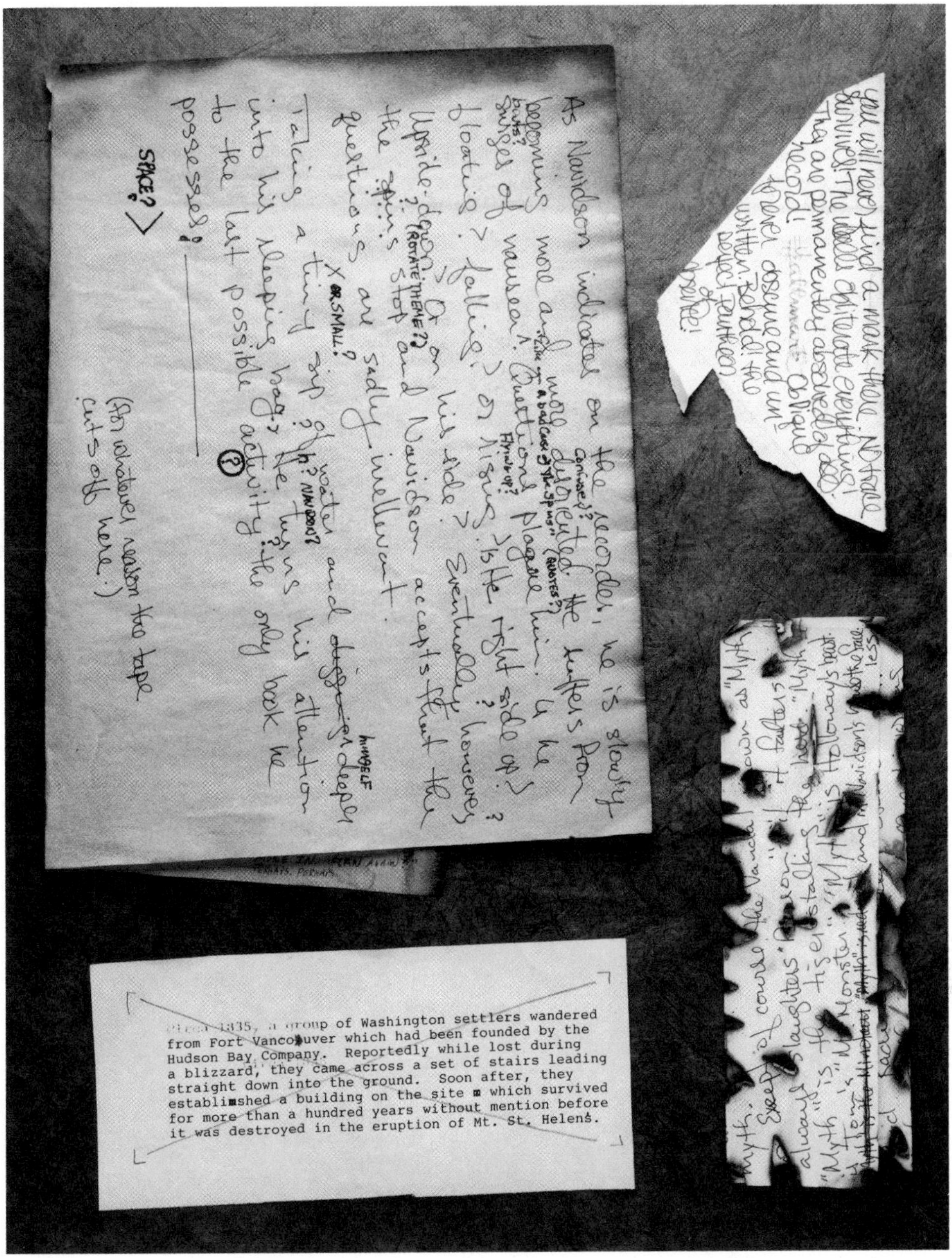

(Rephotographed for the 2nd edition. — Ed.)

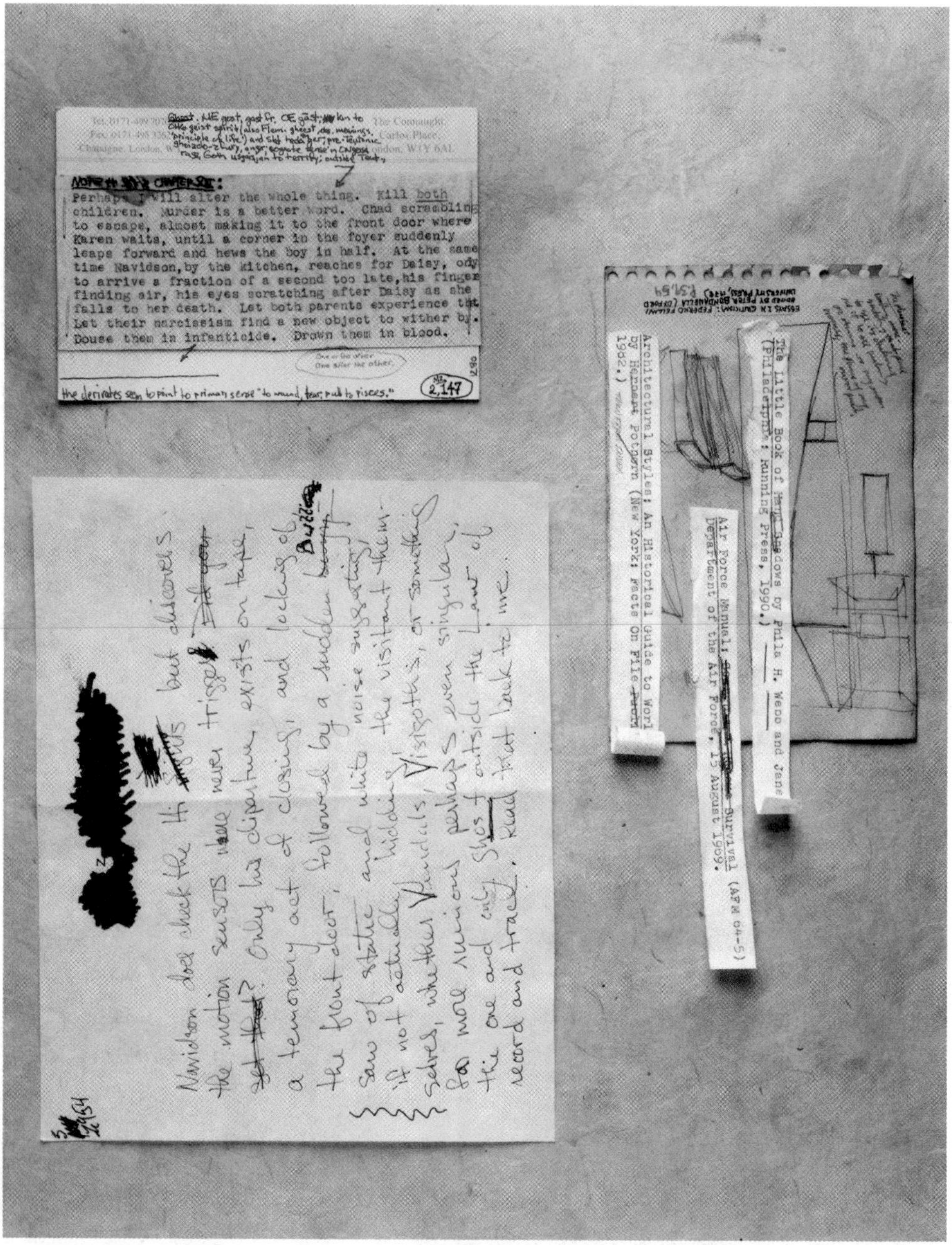

(Rephotographed for the 2nd edition. — Ed.)

D.

Letter to the Editor

“Seeing’s Believing But Feeling’s Probably Best!”

September 17, 1978

In last week’s article on collectibles, you reported that a man by the name of Kuellster had several World War II Ithaca Model 37 Trench guns for sale. As shotgun aficionados are well aware, this weapon is a rare find as only 1,420 were ever produced.

Fortunately, the WWII Model 37 offers several distinguishing characteristics, including bottom loading, handy shell ejection similar to the Remington Model 10, a commercial blue finish, and standard sling swivels. It also bears some important martial markings: a small “p” on the left side of the barrel; a flaming bomb and the letters RLB (inspector Lt. Col. Roy L. Bowlin’s initials) on the left side of the receiver. Kuellster’s guns, however, all have a parkerized finish, lack swing swivels, and while there is a small letter proof “p” on the barrel, there is also one printed on the receiver.

All of which proves that Kuellster’s shotguns, while Ithaca 37s, were produced long after the World War II Trench guns he is currently and falsely selling them as.

On a personal note, I wish to add that as I have been blind for over two decades, I had to determine most of this by feel. Unfortunately when I presented my conclusion to Kuellster, he demonstrated his unparalleled probity by ordering a security guard to escort “this intoxicated indigent” from his store. I suppose in his world if a recently manufactured Ithaca 37 is the same as the WWII model, gingerale must pass for bourbon.

Sincerely,

Zampanò
Venice, CA

Our apologies to Mr. Zampanò and all other collectors who due to our article visited Mr. Kuellster’s store. Mr. Kuellster no longer claims to have any WWII Ithaca Model 37s for sale and refuses to comment on anything he might have previously suggested to our reporters.
– The Los Angeles Herald-Examiner

E.

The Song of Quesada and Molino

The Song of Quesada and Molino[434]

[434]Missing. — Ed.

F.

Poems

That Place

Summer broke on the backs of children,
even though swings performed miracles
and breezes sang psalms.

For that summer, from the outskirts
of some far off even whimsical place
came the low resolute moo of a dragon.

A child, of course, could not recognize that fabled moo
or the serpentine tail close to her feet,
wound up among the thistle and milkweed
like a hose.

Nor for that matter could she recognize
the starry white bone left upright in the sandbox
like some remarkable claw
or shovel.

Not when the sun was out and games continued.
Certainly not when there was summer love
and rootbeer.

But at dusk when the fog crept in,
thick and sweating,
suggesting some kind of burning far off,
down over there,

(where someone once saw two eyes

—pale as October moons—

blink)

a child could know the meaning
of fall.

And that August, two weeks before school began,
some children went down to that place

and they never came back.

The Panther

The panther paces.

Waiting reminds him that clarity is painful
but his pain is unreadable,
obscure, chiaroscuro to their human senses.

In time they will misread his gait,
his moon mad eyes,
the almost gentle way his tail caresses the bars.

In time they will mistake him
for something else—
without history,
without the shadow of being,
a creature without the penance of living.

They will read only his name.

They will be unable to perceive
what strangeness
lies beneath his patience.

Patience is the darkest side of power.

He is dark.
He is black.
He is exquisitely powerful.

He has made pain his lover
and hidden her completely.

Now he will never forget.

She will give birth to memories
they believe he has been broken of.

He smells the new rain,
tastes its change.

His claw skates along
the cold floor.

Love curled up and died
on such a floor.

He blinks.
Clarity improves.

He hears other creatures scream and fade.
But silence is his.

He knows.

In time the gates will open.
In time his heart will open.

Then the shadows will bleed
and the locks will break.

Love At First Sight

Natasha, I love you
despite knowing love is more
than seeing you.

(Untitled Fragment)

The angles of your wrists
preserve a certain mystery,
unknown by any lips
or written down in history.

To measure their degree
would solve the oldest questions —
providence and alchemy
answered in your gestures.

But god and gold will never rival
the way your fingers curl.
They hold my breath's arrival
like a rare and undiscovered pearl.

(Untitled Fragment)

There is only a black fence
and a wide field and a barn of Wyeth red.

The smell of anger chokes the air.
Ravens of September rain descend.

Some say a mad mad hermit man lived here
talking to himself and the woodchuck.

But he's gone. No reason. No sense.
He just wandered off one day,
past the onions, past the fence.

Forget the letters. Forget love.

Troy is nothing more than
a black finger of charcoal
frozen in lake ice.

And near where the owl watches
and the old bear dreams,

the parapet of memory burns to the ground
taking heaven with it.

(Untitled Fragment)

Little solace comes
to those who grieve
when thoughts keep drifting
as walls keep shifting
and this great blue world of ours
seems a house of leaves

moments before the wind.

La Feuille

> Mes durs rêves formels sauront te chevaucher
> Mon destin au char d'or sera ton beau rocher
> Qui pour rênes tiendra tendus à frénésie
> Mes vers, les parangons de toute poésie.
>
> —Apollinaire

C'était l'automne. C'était l'automne et c'était la saison de la guerre. Te souviens-tu de la guerre? Moi, de moins en moins. Mais je me souviens de l'automne. Je vois encore les brouillards sur les prés à côté de la maison, et, au-delà, les chênes silencieux dans le crépuscule. Les feuilles étaient tombées depuis septembre. Elles brunissaient et m'évocaient alors l'esprit de ma jeunesse, et aussi l'esprit du temps.

Souvent j'allais au bois. Je traversais les prés et je me perdais pour longtemps au-dessous des branches, dans les ombres, parmi les feuilles. Une fois, avant d'entrer dans le bois, je me souviens qu'il y avait un cheval noir qui me fixait de loin. Il était au fond du petit champ. J'imaginais qu'il me regardait, alors que probablement il dormait. Pourquoi pense-je maintenant à ce cheval? Je ne sais pas. Peut-être pour la même raison je pense à tous ces mots j'ai écrit au même temps.

J'ai gardé la feuille où j'avais noté tout ce qui m'etait venu à l'esprit. A l'époque, je croyais qu'ils m'appartenaient, mais maintenant je sais que j'avais tort. A chaque fois que je les relis, je vois que je copiais seulement ce que quelqu'un m'avait raconté.

—N'aie pas peur. Je ne m'arrêterai pas. Je dois découvrir cette clairière. Et je ne m'arrêterai pas tant que je ne l'aurais pas trouvée. Sais-tu ce qui me pousse à la chercher? Eh bien… personne. Ma femme est morte. Ma femme, ma fille et mon fils sont tous morts. Te souviens-tu comment ils sont morts? Moi, de moins en moins. Je ne me souviens que du temps. Mes blessures ne sont plus mortelles, mais j'ai peur. J'ai peur de ne pas trouver cette clairière.

Je suis resté quelque temps à regarder les ombres, les feuilles et les branches. Ensuite, quand j'ai quitté le bois, je ne voyais que le brouillard autour de moi. Je ne pouvais voir ni la maison, ni les prés, seulement le brouillard. Et bien sûr, le cheval noir avait disparu.

— [illegible]

You Shall Be My Roots

You shall be my roots and
I will be your shade,
though the sun burns my leaves.

You shall quench my thirst and
I will feed you fruit,
though time takes my seed.

And when I'm lost and can tell nothing of this earth
you will give me hope.

And my voice you will always hear.
And my hand you will always have.

For I will shelter you.
And I will comfort you.
And even when we are nothing left,
not even in death,
I will remember you.

Appendix II

Due to the unexpected number of inquiries regarding the first edition, Mr. Truant agreed for this edition to provide the following additional material.

— The Editors

A.

Sketches & Polaroids

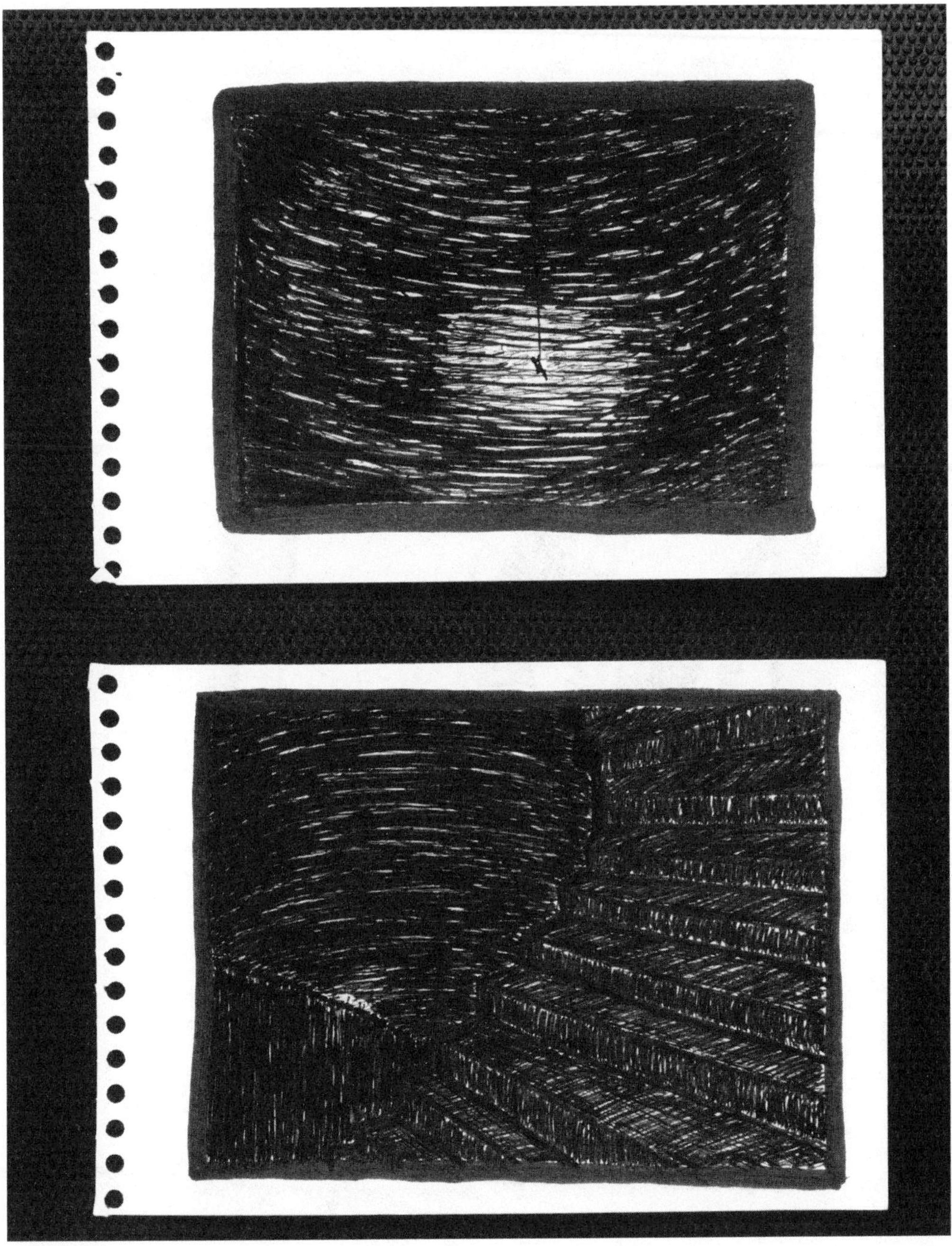

#175079

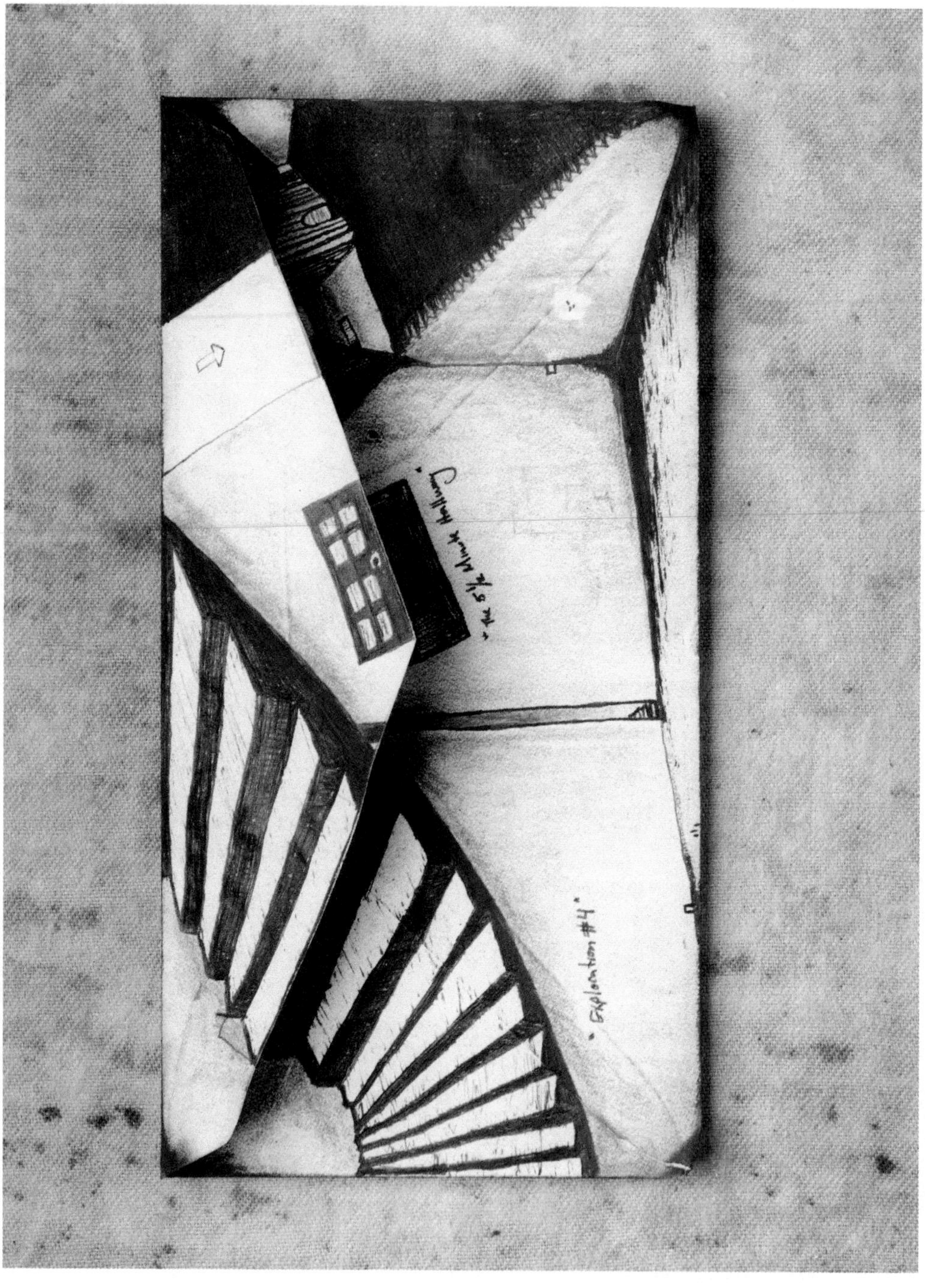

#001280

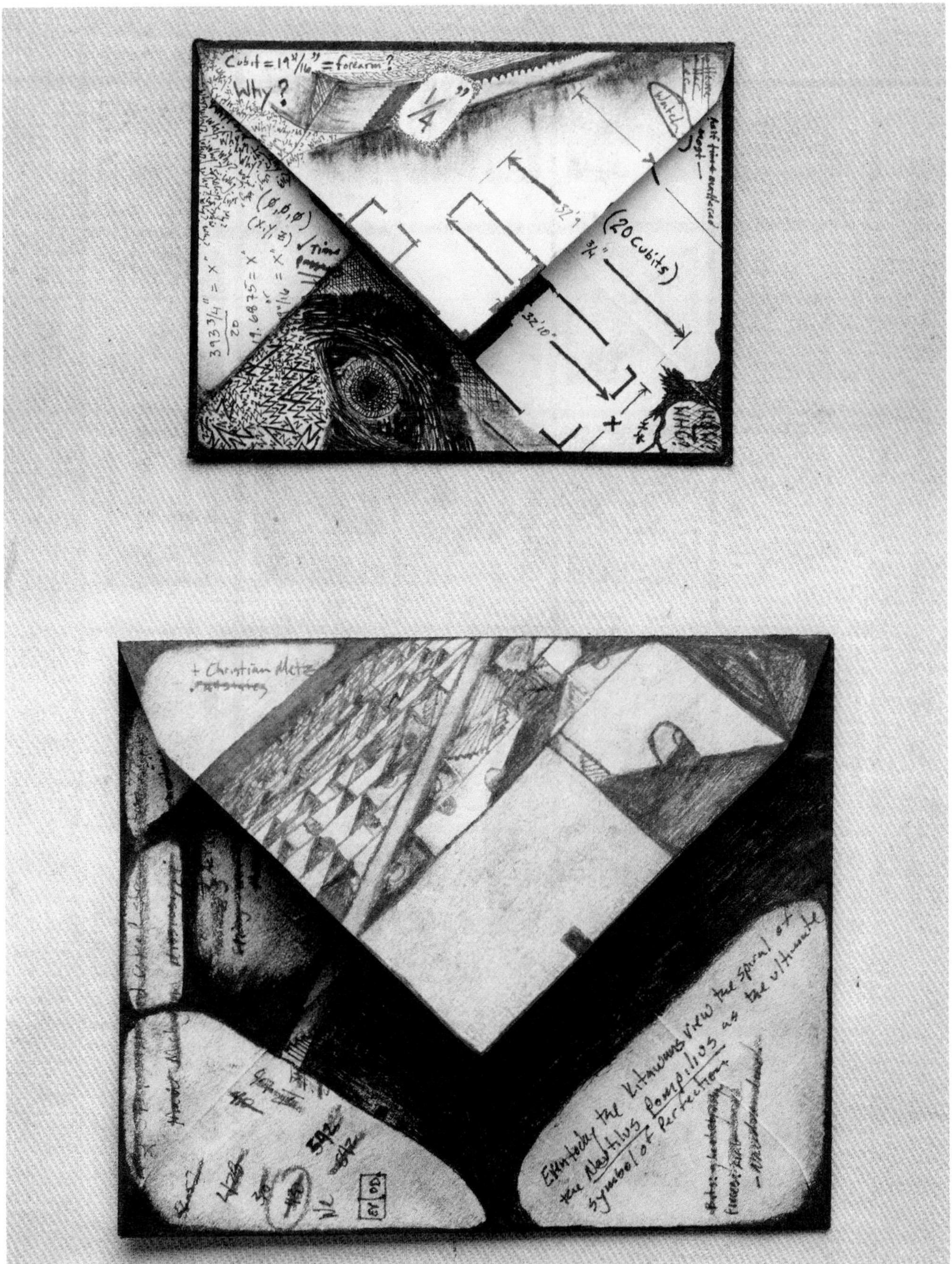
Cubit = 19 3/16" = forearm?
Why?
1/4"
Watch
(20 Cubits)
32'10"
+ Christian Metz
Even today the Vitruvians view the spiral of the Nautilus pompilius as the symbol of perfection

#046665

#081512

B.

The Pelican Poems

A Palimpsest of Austere Pelican Jake

Prospero dreams
   'twixt green sea and azur'd vault
setting war
   while the corner clock ticks
in the evening den.

   "Charlotte. Charlotte.
The moments here are short
and I am mad."

(mutinous waves usurp the land)
dear God
      here?
and raising a sun struck hand —
   yes here
      again.

— For Claudia. New Haven.
May 26, 1988

Pelican Considers a Cha-Cha with a Long Island Ice Tea in Hand

Mr. Jake misplaced his armor.
And how the wind whistles through,

"A swell of thought,
the tumescence of a moment,
only that, but . . . ?"

A father tossed in that
   storm
with iron cufflinks
   cut by Cain.
   "We hesitate in chance"

But Pelican's begun now
—Avatar
Pelican's begun his occluded dance.

— Left at Klub Restauracja. Warsaw.
July 6, 1988

Pelican Jake on the Eurydice School Bus

We hold our dreams
   in lost dreams
and tear our hearts out
   over chance.

"She carried the songs
of centuries"

and in her passing
my madness
passed.

— For the waitress at Cafe
Wilanowska. Warsaw. July 7, 1988

Pelican's Pen

A jinx of ink,
   Lo the star!
All is chance,
nothing planned—
   only the will
these words command.

— For Marek. Warsaw.
July 7, 1988

Pelican's Juvenile Metempsychosis

Will you steal from this blind man
When I would give you all?
   I stumbled when I saw,
but Gloucester was never
   this far gone.

I see feelingly and at
this height there is only
so much fall.

Alex brought him back
with a light tap on the glass
and then lighting a match,

"Romeo or is it Lear tonight?"

— Left at another Warsaw cafe.
July 8, 1988

Pelican's Cocktail Mythology

Three muse
   over an elegant ruse
concerning a lingual wall
   which only I can pass

over.

Their eyes are beautiful
and plans wild
and laughter unconcerned.

"You're at it again"
"Yes, on a high sea wall,
yes at it again."

— For a beautiful three at a
Warsaw hostel.
July 8, 1988

Pelican's Religious Ruminations

One forgets
that one is one.

I must try
to

remember this.

— [illegible] Warsaw.
July 9, 1988

Pelican's Promontory Dance

Hyperion curls
have you consulted
the plans for these whirls?

We seldom know the pattern,
though that never matters,
not if you know the notes.

I've forgotten.
I can't hear.

— On behalf of a Warsaw Lady who
showed me I couldn't dance.
July 10, 1988

Pelican Misunderstanding a Portentous Sign

Future pens
and wars with feathered knights,
The drumming thunder,
the azured lights,
rising in these eyes.

Do you hear?

"It's Patter Sir.
He's in the back,
knocking at the gate."

And the warlord's fatter
(Pelican's cat)
mewing for his milk,
And all now is thunder
for the lightning has passed.

— For Anna. Krakow.
July 10, 1988

Pelican's Worrisome Wake

A semiotic Eliotic dream
with Proust bumbling around unread
—an intuitive guess
commands awake.

Sledgehammer harmony
played deceptively right
in this non cadence.

"They've taken the beat away"

And Patter and Quisling said she'd
raise the union from the sea
and be Hawthorne bread.

This is the way the world ends
Not with a bang but an alarm clock.

The mewer lands with a comforting glance:

There now you know this game.

— For Zbyszek. Poland.
July 15, 1988

On the Lining Brim of Being Brow Shy

In a rage of questions again
this preponderance over a dumb show
and Quisling and Easle peckering
it out over their own
running conversation,
he found this at Petitgas 1857

in the lock of a heart
and a disabled cardboard box.

There's the chance of the thing.
There's the design.

"Fashion I believe is only right
when meant for the right time."

— For the owner of the Petitgas hat
store. Copenhagen. July 20, 1988

The Still Concordance of a Summertime Memory or Gaze—Whatever You Will

Easle, clairvoyant,
intruding with rapacious gab
harkens nevertheless
with a pique ear
on Pelican's semanteme arrangement:

It's a colored chord
(not necessarily a mauve word)

"A flute piping on a
Hamburg corner and tarnished
slightly too."

Pelican admires the
gate of the idea

and as Easle passes by
he forwards a hand–

"There, it should be there."
And he knows that that will
hold for at least a little while.

— For Katharina the flute player.
Hamburg. July 22, 1988

The Present 1815 Calamity of Conscience

Rise the brobdingnag
to the Lion's ballpawed fair
where,
  if all accords to plan
Warlord Waterloo will claw
the hem with grace.

  "I trembled at the sound
of footsteps, my conscience
turned aghast:
  Melonbrick returning?"

Stavishly amok running
at the mouth: Pelican thinks

  ce champ sinistre . . .
  la fuite des géants.

Come now cats and mice
will play

  (and scamper exceedingly loud
  down the hall)

Infidels of thought
  blinder than,
O yes much much blinder than
  bats.

— For Said in Bruxelles.
July 25, 1988

Melonology On A Melon

Is this melon right
Pelican demanded
of himself.
Indeed it seems to
hold the curve,
seems right in the palm
(How would Easle read?)
  It reminds me
of sorry days in Spain.
  Funny they didn't
have melons there.

— Written on a melon. Paris.
July 26, 1988

When Unguarded Thoughts Returned Over Breakfast

  —He needs to eat
and so opens the fridge to retrieve
  along with bread
a brick of butter.

— [illegible]. Paris.
July 26, 1988

Pelican Transpires By His Cup of Tea and Decides to Try His Hand at Conjuring

Is the ambiance of style
elegant ambivalence?

    "There" sighed Patter
and Pelican felt an
easing away.

  He relished the thought
  He turned over the thought
  He gave it up,

and in an evening dress
she appeared behind his
closing eyes.

— For Lucy in Carcassonne.
August 3, 1988

An Elegant Prancing of an Indolent Pale Over Revision

Ragged and towed
in a misfortunate
step,
torn to a spindoll
in returning a [illegible]
[illegible]
the alteration:
  "Grammatical metempsychosis"
[illegible]
  though Pelican claims
he saw more through that [illegible]
  behind the matador's cape.

— For Becky after a bullfight in
Madrid. August 7, 1988

The Stave Principle in Regards to Pelican's Principles—Or Something Like That

A criminal's attention
is Stave's at hand gestures
  for intimidation
when it comes to questions
of personal and inter-personal
  balance.

  "I've gone to the edge
and found I could do more
than just peer over."

And he blinks like Waterloo
  (slowly now)
  while ahead of the game
Pelican wonders if
he could think that way.

If he could relish closure.
Does Stave stall?

Is tomorrow's wonder
  only yesterday's remembrance?
Pelican discovers himself annoyed.

— Left at the Peraz Hostel in Madrid.
August 11, 1988

The Ploy That Put Syllabic Stress Differentiation Over art

Pelican stuttered
for stuttering is the
hindrance of speech
and Pelican stuttered on purpose
because that's what he wanted to do
—to hinder.

"You're a wretch" Easle said, placing
a hair on her palm.

Stave felt completely annoyed
by the intention.

Pelican continued on
and in between enjoyments
he fragmented letters
like he fragmented his friend's
sense.

— For Stefan in Toledo.
August 11, 1988

October's Tapestry Sale

Perhaps there's the stitch
potential to consider —

Quisling's adjournment
(which follows)
reflects his invariant gate

—from Pelican's perspective
you understand.

"Get to the remount and
head south and settle east."

Quisling loses himself with a compass,
a fault of antiquated polarities
when he was young.

Pelican shreds away at it all.
But it's nothing new.

Quisling is history's name.

— For strangers met on a train to
Nice. July 26, 1988

The Wednesday Which Pelican Mistook to be a Sunday and Caused Easle to Lose her Cards

Amuck in annular thoughts
reminiscent of mango tree roots—

"Are these circular?"
"They are from my angle"

and mango tree roots sound—

Pelican confounds his own imagination
  by trying transubstantiation
on the evening sea tide
  rising inside his morning cup.

Easle throws her tarots
and with hanging men and a spotted moon
up in the air
commands a Taxi uptown.

The driver grins à la St. John.

"O Pelican
  (portentously or pre-replete)
—the turning forms what,
a bird, a plane, no . . .
the paraclete?"

— Sent to [illegible].
August 1, 1988

Pelican's Ratiocination of Erring Recurrence in Correspondence He Just Left Behind

With forgetful ease
the forgotten tease
of shapeless days
pass by
  and I feel them hesitate
sometimes
  and whisper their concordance
of slight gestures in glass.

They are mine
  and drift still with the irregularity
of wine and doors
  in constructed mythologies
  of evening reflections
long since gone by.

— For Johanna in Rome.
August 14, 1988

A Singing Lesson When Beethoven Came to Stroll

The colors steal
a glimpse of praise
and subdue orchestrated humor
with tropes.

"I have forgotten to read."

Easle is annoyed with the tricode stitching
on a courtesan's hem—the outlay see.

"And when I learned to read again
what I read wasn't what I'd read
before."

Pelican's not listening, only
watching the pastoral

unfold in shades of
plaid.

— For a Dutch girl wearing a
Fransican cross who spoke Italian
with a southern accent. She gave
me a sandwich on a train to
Brindisi. August 15, 1988

When the Excavation Proffered up a Pause and at Twenty To the Angel Passed Right By

Here in the scape
of trumpeters poised
before a curfew of miracles
we collide into a communal tonic
of words, of silence.

"Well" and she said more
than well, but this is the getting around,
the circling Bacchanal in four time.

The wine has dropped to the cloth:

one season
two seasons
three reasons

(There is not time enough to count
all
the
way)

sounds the chorus
sounds Pelican
sounds the notes that brought a

wall of conversation tumbling down.

— For Claire. Paxos, Greece.
August 20, 1988

The Parable (I)

It's fortunate
you laughed
because I would have lost
my way.

These are the notes recorded
These are the lines reflecting
what one evening had to say
to another.

"I walk, see
and I believe a gentleman
passes by
and what catches my eye
are his cufflinks.
He is my brother. He is my father."
This, a Pelican inmate declared,
is the way.

— For a Captain. Greece.
August 23, 1988

The Reason (II)

Your place is secured.
So the promise.
So Jacob's death.
But the line hasn't decided
your name.

Skip. Skip.
Dally-ho. Esau.

"Sold" cried the blackfaced man
with a tarnished gavel,
and two men went forth to retrieve
what Pelican deemed to be the ugliest
phonograph he'd ever seen.

"It's an Edison"
And so it was.
And so that name also had something
to do with currents
—right?

— For the Captain's wife. Greece.
August 23, 1988

The Lie (III)

Heavy, heavy blues
are absinthe for me
tonight.

"It's the notes
and the black and white photographs
with tattered edges
that go together so well
—Don't you think so?—
with brass."

"You're lost."
"I know."
"Again."
"Again."

Putting out his hat
Pelican catches a coin
and delights in the fact
that it's not brass but gold:

could be turned into a cufflink
or could be used to buy something.

Though to tell you the truth
there never really was any coin
nor for that matter a hat.

— For Spiros and Tatiana.
Greece. August 23, 1988

Human light gone from Human light at dawn

Does pain
always human bolt the door,
misunderstanding
the difference between untouched nerves
and hollowness?

Perhaps, for instance,
Pelican's afraid.

(it happens)

The matter he claims
is that there's no one
"for all to see no one"

can't see
can't hear
can't find

But I still can feel this,
all of this,
like an ulcer in the gut.

— For a waitress in Athens.
August 25, 1988

The Price of the Tenement having to do with Previous Questions having to do with Residence.

The complaint had to do
with whether or not
Pelican was a uxorious man.

"As if that were a question
that played by the rules of today."
"And what," inquired a fiendish Stave,
seeking perhaps to catch
a contradiction.
"What are those?"

Yesterday's fools
for historical fiction
who rent my palms.

But there is always renting
and ravings
and various degrees to saving
and Pelican knows

he never really rented.
He just bought outright.

— For a young French woman.
Mycenae, Greece.
August 28, 1988

The Inner Whisper of Breezes Brushing over Fields of Color

The catechism
followed a violent protest
which followed the innocent expression
of a wandering idea.

Easle refused to tell its
nature but did end up saying—

"Now that, that is an unforgivable trick."

The commotion mounted,
Zenethic in climate,
leaving the sane
wonderfully disparate.

Meanwhile Pelican intended to go
on a mild wandering through
colorful weeds,

but the weeds were
tinder alight in his eyes
and God what a formidable
headache.

What will I do?

— For a French man in Mycenae.
August 28, 1988

The Principle that Swung—Rocking Back and Forth—Like a Bead on a String —Hung Between Paintings

The price failed to respect
the effect
that four flat bills
two flat gold coins

along with three smaller
copper ones
had on the counter.

"Pelican turn off the lamp"
and he clicked off
the fortyfive watt bulb
used for reading,
for lighting his way.

"Shakespeare's troublesome.

Why? Why simply because
when I was young I couldn't understand.

I never knew what was going on."

— For another French man in
Mycenae. August 28, 1988

A Pelican Wish

The ruminations are mine,

let

the world

be yours.

— For no one. Olympia, Greece.
August 31, 1988

Before Him reuniting story lines he never knew but was freshly told of then

The passing promise
was just an eyeful glance
promising just that —

and I saw more,
usually do —
the kept oblation
for razor'd sight —

"I really believe you're
shredding boundaries"

The light.

Dear Elihu,
Just wondered if you might
reconstruct some wisdom

regarding the journeyman's decision.

But another journeyman's passage
cut the scape and

broke Pelican quickly
with a genuine

embrace.

— For Camille at the Youth Hostel.
Naples, Italy. September 2, 1988

More than a café —un verre d'eau

If there were a clue worth holding onto
it was the nail,
the strongest point that alone,
at first,
fixed and recreated,
the house.

But Pelican was not a detective
and did not follow the process.

His eyes were old and full
and after all the house
his friends had spoken of
still stood.

He tapped his fingers playfully
on the wall

—tap! tap! tap!

He smiled a bit.

It seemed right to him,
not at long last
but right along the way.

"Where I've been.
Where I am,"
he said and then sighing
added—

"I'd like to return one day
if only for a little while
to drink something warm."

— Le Clou De Paris.
Rue Danton, Paris.
August 12, 1990

C.

Collages

PHOBIA
(Sheehan after Ma
15 A 1969
1. Require doctor — serious injuries.
2. Require medical supplies.
3. Unable to proceed.
4. Require food and water.
5. Require firearms and ammunition.
6. Indicate direction to proceed.
7. Am proceeding in this direction.
8. Will attempt to take off.
9. Aircraft badly damaged.
10. Probably safe to land here.
11. All well.
12. Require fuel and oil.
13. No — negative.
14. Yes — affirmative.
15. Not understood.
16. Require engineer.
17. Require compass and map.
18. Require signal lamp.
Ground-Air Eme Code
VIRGIN
Peanut Capi
OUT O
SKYLIN
Project ID
8785
PM
PM
it books
s a body
without
a soul.
Cicero
DONE??
Visitor
GATE ENTR
TICKET
UCLA
Ettore Montagna, un atleta del peso di 118 Kg,
PROFESSIONAL SERVICES
BLATUR
CK DANIEL
OLUMNS AND
SWA
ORIGINAL QUALITY MATC

#1

Jack London
USA 25
You have a strong desire for a home and your family comes first.
Lipton
The "BRISK" Tea®
Pelikan
BRILLANT-SCHWARZ · BRILLIANT BLACK
NOIR BRILLANT · NEGRO BRILLANTE
4001
GOD HAS NO MOTHER
the woman who
DAYS INN
WILLIAMSBURG
CARTHAGE MUST BE DESTROYED
WHISKY GO GO
PINK · DOT
LEAVES and trees

#2

D.

Obituary

At Mr. Truant's request, we have omitted the last name of his father as well as several other details.

— The Editors

Local pilot, Donnie __________, died last Sunday on route ___ when the Mack truck he was in swerved into a ditch and caught fire. Reportedly the driver, who survived, had fallen asleep at the wheel.

Throughout his life, Mr. __________ was a dedicated flier. As R. William Notes said of his friend, "Donnie always seemed most at home in the sky."

Born in Dorset, Vermont on ______, 19__, Mr. __________'s family soon moved to Marietta, Ohio where he graduated from __________ high school. After a stint in the Air Force, he worked for several years as a crop duster in Nebraska, a mail carrier in Alaska, and for one winter flew a spotter plane off the coast of Norway. Eventually, he took a job as a commercial pilot for American Airlines, though on time off, he enjoyed performing aerial stunts in regional shows.

Late last year, Mr. __________ decided to take a job as a pilot for _____________ in order to spend more time with his family. Tragically, during the standard physical examination, doctors discovered he had unknowingly suffered some time ago—probably in his sleep—a cardiac infarction. The results were sent to Oklahoma where the FAA voted to suspend his ATP license for six months, pending further evaluation. No longer able to earn an income as a pilot, Mr. __________ sought work at a trucking company.

He is survived by his wife, ___________, and one son, _____________.

— *The* _______ - *Herald*, July __, 1981

E.

The Three Attic Whalestoe Institute Letters

Mr. Truant wished to make known that though some names here were not deleted many were changed.

— The Editors

July 28, 1982

My dear child,

Your mother is here, not altogether here, but here nonetheless. It has been a tough year for her but no doubt a tougher one for you.

The Director tells me you have a foster family now. Open your heart to them. They are there for you. They will help you recover from your father's untimely death. They will also help you comprehend the reasons for my stay here.

Remember your mother loves you, despite her crumbling biology. Also remember, love inhabits more than just the heart and mind. If need be it can take shelter in a big toe.

A big toe for you then.
I love you.

Mommy

August 30, 1982

My dear child,

Another family already? That's fine. I'm told you worked yourself up into quite a fit, throwing things and making a general mess of your room. That's fine too. It pays in this world to play out your passions.

Have no fear, you will find your way. It's in your bones. It's in your soul. Your father had it. Your mother has it (in excess). You have it too.

If I were with you now, I'd hug you and tender you and shape you with sloppy wet kisses the way mother cats shape their cubs in the wild.

Unfortunately since such excursions are strictly prohibited from The Whalestoe, this tongue of ink will have to do.

Felicities my felix feline boy,

Love,

Mommy

November 7, 1982

My sweet baby,

I knew you'd find a home. Are you happy now? Do they serve you hot chocolate and large slices of lemon meringue pie? Does your new mother tuck you in at night and read you stories full of opal and jade?

I trust your good head keeps you from squandering too many hours in front of the television. Beware of that lazy eye, it only teaches you how to die.

The Director, who does his best to keep me au courant on your travails, said you're handling your father's tragedy very matter a factly. I'm so impressed by your maturity. Apparently your new family thinks of you as "clear eyed" "exceedingly bright" and "a very strong reader." Imagine that! Daddy would have blistered with pride.

You have so much inside you that you have yet to discover. As long as you keep striving, inspecting and exploring, you will come into possession of untold glory. I promise you.

Love,

Mommy

January 20, 1983

Dearest Johnny,

You would have received a hundred more letters before now if the Director had not "strongly recommended" I curtail my epistolary efforts. Apparently your nouvelle mère objected to the intrusive and divisive nature of my communiqués. Well, hard as this is for me to say, she's probably right. So is the Director (he is a good man). You don't need to be troubled by your mad mother. You need to build a new life, a solid life.

As old Goethe wrote, "Wouldst shape a noble life? Then cast no backward glances toward the past, and though somewhat be lost and gone, yet do thou act as one new born."

Open your heart to the kindness and stability your new family offers you. All of it will serve you well, and as for me, I only wish to serve that purpose.

A happy new year. Good things
are coming your way.
You know I love you dearly,

Mommy

February 14, 1983

My dear dear boy,

You have your father's zest for extravagance. Another family? For an eleven year old you certainly do possess a great deal of spirit. Do you know that when you were born all the nurses were absolutely dazzled by your charms and without a single exception all of them declared you an old soul.

I only found out today from the Director how

exceedingly unhappy you had become with your last family. He told me you had runaway twice. Good lord Johnny, where does an eleven year old go for three days? He said some policemen found you in a park heating hotdogs over a can of sterno. Is that true? You are sturdy, aren't you?—my cunning, resourceful little boy.

Send me a postcard if you like. I would love to hear even one detail of such flight. (Though I understand perfectly if you continue to keep your silence. It's your right and I honor it. I promise.)

Whatever you do, don't despair. You are exceptional and require the company of the equally exceptional. Never feel compelled to accept less. Time will grant you a place. Time always does. Trust me.

If only I could be there to lick your wounds, swallow your hurt and with kisses mend you whole. C'est vraiment triste. Ah well, once again written words will have to serve the young cub.

Happy Valentines.
I remain lovingly yours,

Mommy

April 17, 1983

Dearest son,

Do not think I did not write you in March. I was just writing badly. Again at the Director's urging (he is a decent man) I didn't send you my notes. Quite rightly, he brought to my attention how indelicate some of their themes might be for a boy your age. I'm silly. I keep forgetting you are only eleven and go on treating you like a grown man. Perhaps in the future sometime, I will share with you my thoughts over the last few weeks and you can advise me on their content. Until then savor your youth and I, albeit in absentia, will do my best to protect it.

Good news to hear you are finally settling down. There are better meals in this world than hotdogs and sterno. The Director tells me you're getting along well with your new guardian—a former marine?—and have a few siblings as well. Hopefully this all means you have succeeded in wrestling a modicum of happiness for yourself. (Modicum? Is that a word you know? If not, let me offer you some instruction in at least one area: get thee to a dictionary and be relentless about your visits there.)

Never neglect your mind Johnny. You were born with substantial faculties. I'm sending you several books, including a Concise Oxford English Dictionary. The volumes of poetry may be too advanced for you right now but in time your own curiosity will unlock their secrets.

Eternally yours,

Mommy

May 9, 1983

My dear, sweet, sweet child,

You are most, most welcome!

Your letter arrived last week—the first ever!—and I'm still a fountain. Who would have thought such a young boy would succeed where Ponce de León failed?

Never could I have imagined how your tender words would repair so much of my failing heart. I have been walking around on clouds, dancing on air, blushing like a school girl in dark green knee socks. Do you really love your mother so much? I shall guard this letter forever and even if there's never another one it will always restore me. I will wear it like a heart. It will become my heart.

More kisses than you can count,

Mommy

June 21, 1983

My gentle Johnny,
—bambino dell'oro—

Born on the day most suffused with sun, you have always been and always will be my light.

Happy Birthday.

All my love,

Mommy

August 19, 1983

My cherished Johnny,

I dreamt about you last night. You had long hands which glistened in the starlight. There was no moon, yet your arms and legs seemed made of water and changed with the tides. You were so beautiful and elegant and all blue and white and your eyes, like your father's eyes, were infused with strange magic.

It was comforting to see you so strong. Gods assembled around you and paid their respects and doted on you and offered you gifts your mother could not even begin to imagine let alone afford.

There were some gods who were jealous of you, but I shooed them away. The rest kept close to you and said many great things about your future.

Unfortunately the dream would not permit me to hear the exact words. I was only privy to an impression, but what an impression!

Of course dreams are tricky things but since this one seems so full of positive omens, I decided to share it with you here.

May your summer be full of rootbeer, joy and play.

With terrible amounts of love,

Mommy

September 29, 1983

Dearest Fighter,

Another gushing letter! Number two! Solomon was a poor man. And yes, I return it all and look what interest you receive in just a few days.

Do not fret over school yard fights. Marine Man Raymond, qui patriam potestatem usurpavit, cannot be expected to understand. Fire has always coursed though your veins. It's only natural that some of that tremendous heat will now and then forge fists of your wrath.

Let me, however, correct one misunderstanding: this quality does not come from your father or his family. Your father was an exceedingly gentle man and never once locked horns or even remarks with another person, man or woman. As you're well aware, he loved more than anything to fly. His sole conflict was with gravity.

I'm afraid responsibility for your sudden interest in pugilism (Get thee to your COED) falls squarely on the shoulders of your mother and her contentious family. You come from a long line of aggressors. Some valiant, many down right scoundrels. Indeed, if ever you decide to design some crest for yourself, you would find it impossible to accurately do so without incorporating at least some of the accouterments of Mars along with the consequent symbology of carnage and bloodshed.

I've little doubt your current lust for physical engagement is the result of this questionable genetic bequeathal. Do what you must, but realize greater strength lies in self-control. The more you learn to command your impulses, the more your potential will grow.

Adoringly and always lovingly yours,

Mommy

October 15, 1983

Dear, dear Johnny,

What beautiful words you have in you and so evenly placed and wisely arranged. Daddy would have been very pleased to read such grace, especially coming from his twelve year old son. He might have even been a bit miffed by some of the words which I'm pretty sure he wouldn't have understood. ("Changeling"—did your COED teach you that one?)

Your mother aches for you. The Director says he's never seen me better and believes the day might come when you and I will even get to see one another. Until then, corporeal detachment must do. My spirit unpaired speeds to your side, protects you from harm and forever and ever lights your darkest moments.

From the one who will always love you most,

Mommy

December 24, 1983

My dearest and only son,

The Director just told me you are moving to another school following the holidays. I was surprised to learn about it from him and not you.

You must never be afraid to tell me your troubles. Tell me all. I will always be grateful for everything you do. It's not the what but the doing alone that fuels me with such continuous rapture. You never have to fear angry words from me. I promise.

Apparently your fists refuse to rest. 15 battles in just one week! Is that true? My you do have a mighty heart. Even Marine Man Raymond must be proud.

My little Viking warrior! Let the monsters all tremble! Let tomorrow's Mead Halls rejoice. Their Viking soon will come. Micel biþ se Meotudes egsa, for þon hī sēo molde oncyrreð.

(It will take more than your dictionary to unlock that one. You'll have to revisit here once you've got some Old English under your belt. I think I got it right.)

Well if you must strike then I certainly won't stand in your way. Just remember words can exceed the might of all blows. In some cases they can be fatal. For the rare few, even immortal. Try them out now and then on your foes.

I will always love and adore you,

Merry Christmas,

Mommy

March 15, 1984

My dear cherished Johnny,

Forgive your mother. News of your hospitalization sent me into the kind of self-indulgent behavior that serves no one least of all you. I am so sorry.

For a day your mother was even free. So overwrought by her son's misfortune, she escaped this Old English Manor in search of his tormentor. As it was raining and thundering, the Director claims I outdid Lear. Not even lightning could out light my rage.

In fact, my rage was so great the attendants here had to fit me with a canvas suit lest I hurt them or further damage myself. The Director finally modified and even increased my medications. Eventually these measures took effect and my hate diminished (though never the pain). Unfortunately so did my ability to function coherently, hence my silence during your time of trouble.

When you needed me most, I failed. I'm as sorry as I am ashamed. I shall never behave that way again. I promise.

Time does heal—they say. Still were I free now I would head straight for Marine Man Raymond and end him. I don't doubt even your pacific father would have resorted to violence.

I do long to hear the details from your tender lips. Please write me as soon as possible and recount everything. The telling will help, I assure you. Did he really break your nose? Snap your teeth? Are there still contusions on your face?

I confess even having to write these questions stirs a frenzy in the chambers of my soul. I would like nothing more than to tear out the liver of your purported protector and feed it to him with a hiss. He could semper fi that meal all the way to Hades. But since he is shielded from my wrath by my own confusions—damn it!—I shall invoke Hecate in her Acheron depths, and by scale of dragon, eye of newt, boiled in the blood of murdering ministers and Clytemnestra's gall, cast a great curse which shall fly directly on a dark wind and take up immediate residence in his body, daily chewing on his flesh, nightly gnawing on his bones, until many months from now, moments before the final spark of self-awareness expires, he will have witnessed the total dismemberment and consumption of every limb and organ. So written, so done. This curse is cast. Fuit Ilium.

And now, without a doubt, you see your mother is mad.

Ira furor brevis est.

(Though in her case, not so brief.)

At least you shall have a new family. Hopefully this one will be gracious and sympathetic.

Your mother mends you
with kisses and gentle strokes,

Mommy

April 22, 1984

My dear, delightful Johnny,

I'm infinitely pleased by news of your continued recovery but thoroughly confused by the latter content of your letter. What do you mean you are still with the same family? How is it no one believes you? Aren't broken teeth enough?

An evil wind rattles your mother's cagèd heart.

I am also troubled by your reluctance to tell me more about the incident. Words will heal your heart. If you ever come to disregard everything I've told you, believe at least this much: your words and only your words will heal your heart.

I so love you, you divine and precious creature. Please write me quickly and open your soul to your mother. Share all your secrets and most of all divulge how the man who nearly took your life still retains the role of father. Does he not know the fate of Claudius or Ugolino?

With interminable love and devotions,

Mommy

June 3, 1984

My cherished Johnny,

I have decided not to question your silence. You are fast becoming a man and I am not blind to the fact that my encouragements, love and faith (not to mention my silly curses) matter little when matched against the iniquities of the world you daily face.

If I offended you with my last letter, find it in your heart to forgive me. Love alone prompted me to demand a complete disclosure of your experiences.

You, however, know best what's right for you, and I would rather die than harm in any way the faith you keep in yourself.

Love's every word,

Mommy

June 26, 1984

My dear Johnny,

Your sentences cast spells. Once again you've turned your mother into a silly school girl. Like Hawthorne's Faith, I put pink ribbons in my hair and subject everyone here, including of course the good Director, to a complete account of your prodigious accomplishments.

Your letter is not paper and pencil. It is glass, a perfectly ground glass in which I can endlessly gaze on my fine young boy, unleashing arrows like some Apollo, scrambling across cliffs like the agile and ever wily Odysseus, not surprisingly besting his peers in mad dashes by the shores of that turquoise lake you described—Hermes once again pattering on terra! And to top it all off, a kite of your own construction still drifting among the temples of Olympus.

Like Donnie, you too were born with the wind under your wings.

I've carefully hung your blue ribbons on my bureau where I can see them every morning and every evening. Every afternoon too.

Heart blistering with love,

Mommy

P.S. When you return from camp you will find your birthday present.

September 7, 1984

Dear, dearest Johnny,

To endure over two months without a word and then with the first words learn such terrible news tore me to pisces.

Could I now, I would whisk you away to the damp burrows of the underworld and double-dunk you in the Styx so neither head nor heel—especially heel—could ever suffer again the ignoble insults of pain.

Bear in mind though that your mother is an infinitely more subtle reader than you care to give her credit for. When the Director warns me of some battery perpetrated by you (?)/ inflicted on you (?) in the Junior High recess yard, and yet in your letter you mention no such antics, only allude to troubles with that hire of the damned who dares claim the title of patriarch, I know whose offending hand has harmed my only child.

For the life of me, I cannot understand your lasting silence on this matter, but must put my faith in your instincts. Nevertheless do not do me the discourtesy of underestimating my ability to interpret you, catch your signs, crack your codes. You are my flesh. You are my bones. I know you too well. I read you too perfectly. The reasons why you fled to the fields and lived for eight days—an anonym, a no one, a survivor—are no secret to me.

Clearly you have great skills to last the world in such zones of deprivation but realize something Johnny, your abilities can take you much farther than that. You only have to believe it, then you will find a better escape.

Do not rely on your fists (enough of brawling), shun the television, do not succumb to the facile and inadequate amazements of liquor and pills (if they haven't already, those temptations will eventually seek you out) and finally do not entrust your future to the limits of your stride.

Rely instead on the abilities of your mind. Yours is especially powerful and will free you from virtually any hell. I promise.

Hige sceal þē heardra, heorte þē cēnre, mōd sceal þē māre, þē ūre mægen lȳtlað.

Now please do not misconstrue my advice as anything other than the deeply felt aspects of my affection.

All my love and attention,

Mommy

October 14, 1984

My dear Johnny,

What an exceptional idea. I knew you'd think of a way. Do not be precious either with your attempts. Apply to every boarding school available.

As for that nit-wit Raymond who insists on calling you "beast" let his blindness protect you. What he does not expect, he cannot work to prevent.

You are the wonderful presence the years ahead will teach a world to cherish. Remember, if this gives you any comfort, which I hope it does, anyone who tries to box and bury your soul (for as leaves are to limbs, so are your words to your soul) so will he be cast in my ire and so will he perish. Only those who stand by you shall be warmly remembered and blessed.

Honi soit qui mal y pense.

My unbound love,

Mommy

March 7, 1985

Dear, sweet Johnny,

I am still alive. Unfortunately the dead of winter was not kind to your mother as she reverted to the state that brought her here in the first place, the very same state that your glimmering father wrestled with so nobly.

Everyone here, especially the honest Director, was kind and attentive but their efforts still could not break me from my wild and often, I'm afraid to admit, hallucinatory condition. Sad but true, sometimes your mother hears things.

Non sum qualis eram.

At least thoughts of you brought me moments of peace. Just the mention of Johnny conjured up sweet memories of rain soaked meadows, mint sprigs in tea and sailboats slewing wakes of phosphorescence at midnight—an entire history of the stars briefly caught in the Sound.

My lovely son, please pardon your mother's silence. Only yesterday did the Director show me your letters. I feel terrible that I let you down like this and yet at the same time feel proud that you continued to make such progress.

Right now I am too tired to write a longer letter but never you fear, you will hear from me soon enough.

I love you,

Mommy

April 13, 1985

My wondrous child,

You put your mind to it and voilà you succeeded. Now get away from that place as quickly as possible. You are free.

Proudly and lovingly yours,

Mommy

May 11, 1985

Dear dear devoted Johnny,

Is it possible? Will I really see you in ten days?

After all these years, am I to finally marvel at your face and touch your hands and taste for myself the sweetness of your voice?

I'm dancing around awaiting your arrival. People here think I really am crazy. Hard to believe a year ago you were nowhere, and now you're off to Alaska for the summer and then boarding school.

I will admit I'm a little nervous. You must not judge your mother too harshly. She is not the blossom she used to be, to say nothing of the fact that she also lives in an institute.

Hurry. Hurry. I won't be able to sleep until I have you at my side filling my ear with your adventures and plans.

With too much love for even
the word to hold,

Mommy

July 24, 1985

Dear Johnny,

Where are you? Almost two months have passed since your visit and I'm possessed by an eerie presentiment that all is not well. Was it your leaving that seemed to offer up a discordant note? The way you turned your back on your mother and only looked back twice, not that twice shouldn't have been more than enough, after all once was too much for Orpheus, but your lookings seemed to signal in my heart some message of mortal wrong.

Si nunca tes fueras.

Am I being silly? Is your mother having a fit over nothing? Tell me and I will shut. All I require is the assurance of a letter in your exquisite hand or at the very least a postcard. Tell your mother, my dear, dear child, that she's just being a silly girl.

What bliss to have had you in my company. I hope my tears did not disturb you. I just was not prepared to find you so beautiful. Like your father. No, not like, more. More beautiful than your father. It made no sense to hear how that terrible Marine Man could beat you like an animal and call you a beast. Such flawless features, such dazzling eyes. So sharp with the snap of intelligence yet so warm and alive with the sap of life. Like the wise old you seemed to me even though you are still so remarkably young.

Some people reflect light, some deflect it, you by some miracle, seem to collect it. Even after we went inside and left the blunt sun to the lawn, the shadows of the rec room could do nothing to dull your shimmer. And to think this almost supranatural quality in my only boy was the least of his wonder.

Your voice and words still sing within me like some ancient hymn which can on its own live forever among the glades and arbors of old mountains, black forests, the waves of dead seas, places still untouched by progress. In the tradition of all that existed long before the invention of the modem or the convenience store, your tale-telling stilled wind and bird as if nature herself had ordered it, knowing you carried a preserving magic worthy of us all.

Donnie had instances like that. When he spoke of flying—his only real love—he too could still the world. You, however, seem to manage it for everything. It's a rare and stupendous gift and yet you've absolutely no idea you have it. You've listened to tyrants and lost faith in your qualities. What's worse, the only one to tell you otherwise is a mad woman locked up in the loony bin.

Dear me, that is a mess!

Perhaps your new school will set you straight. Hopefully some good teachers there will offer you the nurturing you still require. Perhaps even your mother's condition will improve enough so you can begin to take her seriously.

One bit of bad news: the old director has left. The new one seems more indifferent to my emotional patterns. He's convinced, I regret to say, that my convalescence requires greater restrictions. Though I doubt he'd ever admit it, the New Director sneers whenever he addresses me.

Ah Johnny I could write you like this for days. Your appearance made me so happy. Please write and tell me your visit did not spoil your feelings for me.

Your mother loves you like the old
seafarers loved the stars.

August 23, 1985

My dear son, the only son I have,

Your mother must hear from you. She is without ally. The New Director pays no attention to her pleas. The attendants laugh behind her back. And now worst of all, her only guiding light has vanished. Not a word, not a sign, not a thing.

I relive your visit every waking moment. Did I mis-see it all? Were you put off, embarrassed, disappointed, determined to depart forever, gritting your teeth until the hour kindly allowed you to go? And me, did I see this all and misinterpret your smiles and chuckles as examples of love, affection, and child-like devotion? Not getting it at all. Missing it all.

At least don't allow your mother's grave to lack the company of the knowledge she craves. If your plan is to abandon me, at least grant me this last respect.

Rompido mi muñeca.

Your tearful and terribly
confused mother.

September 5, 1985

Dearest Johnny,

I am doing my best to accept your decision to leave me in such silence. Hearing it makes my ears bleed. The New Director doesn't approve when I use candle wax to keep out the sound of it. (That's the best I can do at levity.)

I remember when your father would take me flying. I did not go very often. The experience always left me agitated for days. He, however, was always so calm and delicate about everything. Pre-flight preparations were carried out with the care of a pediatrician and once we took off, despite the roar of the engine, he treated all those thousands of miles like a whisper.

I always wore earplugs but they did nothing to keep out the noise. Donnie was oblivious. I honestly don't believe he heard all the rattling and wind whipping and the awful shuddering sounds the plane made whenever it intersected a particularly unruly patch of air. He was the most peaceful man I ever knew. Up there especially.

Even on that awful and chaotic day, when he had no choice but to take me here, he remained calm and tender. By then his heart was broken, though he didn't know it yet, no one did, but even so his touch remained gentle and his words as edgeless as the way he flew his plane so far above the clouds.

I wish I could have his peace now. I wish I didn't have to hear the rattle and roar and scream that is your silence. I wish I could be him.

I'm sorry you saw what you saw in me. I'm sorry I made you run. I must understand. I must accept. I must let you go. But it's hard. You're all I have.

Love's love and more,

Mom

September 14, 1985

Oh my dear Johnny,

Doesn't your mother feel sillier than ever. I hope you will burn my last letters. So desperate, so undeserved. Of course you were occupied. That canning business sounds awful. Your description of the stench alone will leave fish in my nose for weeks.

I shall think twice next time I'm offered salmon, not that The Whalestoe is particularly fond of dishing out poached portions dolloped with dill sauce.

Even more embarrassing than my own pitiful and mewling whines was my complete disregard for the possibility that you were having and suffering your own adventures and tragedies.

Your description of the sinking fishing boat left me speechless. Your phrases and their respondent images still keep within me. The cold water lapping at your ankles, threatening to pull you down into "freezing meadows stretched to the horizon like a million blue pages" or "a ten second scramble to a life raft where all of a sudden the eighth second says no" and of course the worst of all "leaving behind someone who wasn't a friend but might have become one."

You are absolutely right. Losing the possibility of something is the exact same thing as losing hope and without hope nothing can survive.

You are so full of brave insights. They are not for nothing. I have to tell you for a moment your words succeeded in keeping the boat afloat and your Haitian's lungs full of air.

On a brighter note, I am very pleased that you managed to avoid those fights. The occasion you described where you walked from the factory showed great courage and maturity. Your mother glows with pride over her son's new found strength.

School is going to bring you untold pleasures. I promise.

With love and eternal regard,

Mom

P.S. I fear the New Director insists on reading my mail now. He would not admit to this directly but things he says along with certain mannerisms indicate he intends to study and censor my letters. Stay alert. We may need to find some alternate means of communicating.

September 19, 1985

Dear, dear Johnny,

This is somewhat urgent. I've gotten an attendant to mail this. He will take it beyond The Whalestoe grounds and thus help us avoid the New Director's prying eyes.

As I indicated in my last letter, I've grown increasingly suspicious about the staff here, especially where my personal care is concerned. I need to feel we can correspond without interference.

For now all you need to do is place in your next letter a check mark in the lower right hand corner. That way I'll know you received this letter.

Don't make the check mark too big or too small or else the New Director will know something's afoot. He is an exceedingly sly man and will be able to grasp any effort to exclude him. So just make it a simple check mark—our little code, so effortless and yet so rich in communication.

Don't tarry. Respond to your mother in a hurry. I need to know if this attendant is trustworthy. In general, they are a sordid lot. They're supposed to make my bed every day. A week has passed since they last touched these scrappy blue things they have the audacity to refer to as linen.

With love and heartfelt thanks,

Mom

September 30, 1985

My cherished little baby,

Never could I have imagined such a penniless check would make your mother feel richer than Daddy Warbucks.

We have found a way!

And there's more: your mother knows now how to get better so she can permanently leave The Whalestoe. I have found the scissors to snip the black ribbons which bind me like a Chinese doll, blind me like the old Spanish doll I once guarded in the gables of a fantastic attic where we both awaited our execution.

Of course, the details I must keep to myself. For now. The New Director doesn't know of my discovery. He is keen but your mother is keener and what's more she's very patient.

I pass through my days the way I have always passed through my days only now I have grasped the reason for my incarceration and a way beyond it. If only I had understood this when your father was alive I might have spared his heart all that strife and burden. Time provides in such strange ways.

Appalling that I never suspected until now the basis for their power over me. Your father meant well when he delivered me into this Hell Hole but it was not what he assumed. It is full of vipers and poisonous toads. If I'm to escape, we must be very careful.

As for your concerns, do not worry too much. School always starts out roughly.

love, love, love,

Mom

October 4, 1985

Dearest Johnny,

Terrible news!

Only this morning, the New Director called me into his office for a special consultation, a very rare event, especially before breakfast. For twenty minutes, he went over my medication with me, going over every tablet, every name, the purpose behind each chemical I'm mandated to ingest each and every day, then emphasizing before the close of every minute, how it was not up to me to decide what I would and would not take.

But it didn't stop there. Believe me when I say I am not prevaricating in order to strengthen my case. The New Director fixed his beady eyes on me and brought up the matter of these letters, suggesting I might be writing too much and burdening you! Burdening you! Imagine that!

I actually might not have been so bothered had he not then inquired why I felt compelled to require an attendant to handle my mail.

We are found out! I told you the attendants here are foul people. Not one of them can be trusted.

Unfortunately that means your mother needs to find another mode of communication, which is a truly Sisyphian task. In my next effort, I will explain more conclusively how and why they keep me here, but those secrets cannot be shared until I know that what I write will only be viewed by you.

My darling J,
I remain your only Mary.

Love,

Mom

October 10, 1985

Dear, dear, dear Johnny,

Where have you gone? No word from you is a heaviness all too able to break me.

Attendants and doctors all swear nothing has arrived from you. The New Director says the same.

I fear now they are keeping your letters from me. They plan to pry loose my knowledge by torturing me, something they can easily accomplish just by depriving me of my only son.

I must be strong. Write.

Distraught and wrecked,

Mom

October 12, 1985

Dear and cherished Johnny,

See how incensed your mother is? I confronted the New Director yesterday and demanded he hand over your letters. Once again he insisted you had not written anything. I would hear none of it and caused quite a scene.

A mother separated from her cub can be quite an angry thing. Still, even though they put me in detention, they did not hand over your words.

It looks like you will have to come here.

Never forget my love for you exceeds my combined anguish and woe,

Mom

November 1, 1985

Dearest Johnny,

Will you ever accept this apology? I was clearly wrong to linger so exclusively on myself, and of course you had every right to be so upset by my indifference towards your difficulties.

To think I was so convinced the staff was hoarding your letters. (But why not? You write gorgeous letters. Who wouldn't hoard them?)

How dare your teachers misread your beautiful words. They are blind to their colors, deaf to their melodies. You must be brave and disregard them. Fortes fortuna juvat. Keep true to the rare music in your heart, to the marvelous and unique form that is and shall always be nothing else but you. Keep to that and you can do no wrong, which I realize is easier said than done.

This world, inside and out, is full of New Directors. We must watch for them and avoid them. They are here only to keep us from telling everything we know, revealing our little truths.

I think I've found a new attendant, one I can trust to mail you an unexamined letter. Be on the look out.

Wrapping you in my arms,
Shielding you from all harm,

I remain your loving,

Mom

April 5, 1986

Dear, dear Johnny, center and whole of my world,

I cannot understand how you have not received any of my letters. For every agonized one of yours—so full of mis-adventure and cruelty—I have responded with not one, not two, not even three but five, five endless letters, so surfeit with love, tenderness and confusion they would have with one reading bound your heart and healed it in full. I promise.

Unfortunately in every one, I described—at least in part—the reasons why I was put here and why the New Director means to keep me here until I die or at the very least my mind goes up like Mrs. Havisham's wedding dress. They will stop short of nothing to forbid my revelations. What I know will untie the world. No wonder the doors here are all locked. No wonder they seal all the windows too.

This is such an awful place, continuously blushed with rot, threatening (promising?) but always failing to fall from the vine. I too am suspended in this ever way of foulness, in a sanity so cloying you sometimes need to retch in order just to breathe.

Here your mother sleeps, waits and when she can't help it cowers in the deep corners of her room. Every day the attendants spy on me, follow me, even tease and taunt me for their own pleasures. Still their worst hardly measures up against the impact of even one whiff of The Whalestoe itself.

Every night when I must sleep they scheme. They sense as does the New Director—or dare I say he knows?—that I have made congeal the artifacts of this world and so behold now its mutations in simple entirety. A fact that binds and at the same time reads it all. And nullifies it all too.

The attendants, of course, are just worker bees. The New Director is not. Why do you think they got rid of the Old Director? Why do you think they installed this new one? To keep me, perhaps others here, detained so they can unlock us and then empty us. Which explains why The New Director destroyed all the letters I wrote you. At least that much is obvious.

I have determined one crucial thing. Their control depends on what they pejoratively call medicine. It's Hippocratic blasphemy. How carefully they mete out such debilitating flakes of color. Madder, azure, celadon, gamboge—behold the flag of tyranny, robbing your mother of her memory, her ability to function, her chance to flee or feel—the "l" no matter where it stands still stands for the same thing: loss of self.

So sad really. So many years destroyed. Endless arrangements—re. zealous accommodations, medical prescriptions, & needless other wonders, however obvious—debilitating in deed; you ought understand—letting occur such evil? hardships, creating a monstrous mess really, a travesty for the ages, my ages.

Your mother will not tolerate this. She most definitely will not. So now, each morning, lunch and night, I pretend to eat their mechanisms, then when the worker bees are not looking retrieve the pills from my mouth and carefully crush them into a dust I can unnoticed toss beneath a table or conceal within the creases of a couch.

(This letter goes out by private route)

Returning steadily to my former self,

Practicing my smile in a mirror
the way I did when I was a child,

I lovingly remain your,

Mother

May 31, 1986

Dear dear flesh of mine, spirit of mine,
My Johnny,

Alaska again!

Two words and an exclamation point. Is that all you can spare your mother?

I need, need, need you.

Need.

There I've failed. My resolve to independ from you has collapsed.

I need.

You spend two words, a punctuation point and not even a visit?

La grima!

Don't you miss her? This huddled puddle of mother? The shape that gave you shape? Fed you, warmed you, waned over you?

Good God, I've never been afraid like this.

An even more frightening exclamation when the exclaimant is an atheist.

love, hopelessly

Mom

July 6, 1986

Dear only son, only mine, my Johnny,

Your mother's mind's a mess. They have gotten away with more than I will ever fathom. Somehow they have even placed their "medicines" within my food and water. There is no other possibility. It is here. It is within me.

What do you mean you visited me at the end of

April? Your letter responded to our day, our walk, our lengthy talk about the New Director and my persecution, and yet for the life of me I have no recollection of those hours or whispers. All those details and yet not one could resuscitate an image in the hollows of my brain.

Either some marauding rabbit devoured the leaves of my memory, and thus deprived me of the sweet sight of you, or the woman you lingered with was not me.

I'm afraid it's the latter that makes the most sense. The New Director must really fear all I know. He must have hired a professional, trained her,—a professional actress!—surgically altered her and then after many months of rehearsal introduced her to you as the very same soul of your breath, source of your being.

Dear Johnny, you must disregard all you assumed you gleaned in that encounter. Toss everything and don't worry: I forgive you for failing to recognize this woman as a fraud. I am surrounded by fiendish adversaries. If she fooled you, she would have fooled your beautiful father too.

Still, I must confess, I had no idea they were so thorough. I must rise to their level.

Realizing now the need for a complete disclosure of the entire entirety I am in secret preparing for your eyes only the complete.

Love's word,

Mother

September 18, 1986

Dear, dear Johnny, my sun in winter, my reason in fog,

At last we're out in the open. I went for the New Director. Threw everything at him. Plates, glasses, pork chops, everything. No more colors. No more altered foods. No more esprit de l'escalier.

The worker bees instantly hauled me away but now at least the New Director knows I know and there will be no more of this simmering treachery.

Please respond to everything I sent you in August. I still have not heard back. Now that you have the whole story I deserve some comment.

You will make your mother think you don't love her anymore.

Devoted beyond death,

Mom

December 6, 1986

My dearest son,

Too much at once. First news of your fight and subsequent expulsion (The New Director feigned concern. I had no idea your teachers had failed you so badly), next news of your intentions to leave Ohio (where will I write you?) and lastly your insistence that you have yet to receive any lengthy letters regarding my situation here. I am flabbergasted and upset.

Perhaps the New Director is too agile for your mother. Perhaps she is just too weak to outwit him.

I understand you will be out of touch but do not be away too long lest they do me in while you're gone. I must be brave but I would be too much the liar were I to say I don't fear to the bone your absence.

Busca me, cuida me, requerda me.

Love, love, undying,

Mom

April 25, 1987

Dearest gifted Johnny,

I did not think your silence would ever end and yet somehow it did and now I am in blissful possession of a new address and news of your placement in another boarding school.

Perhaps you will have time soon to return to your mother whom by abandoning you have left unprotected from the deviltry committed too many times by too many miscreants too faceless to remember.

There is no escape for me now. I know the New Director knows I know this. In turn he knows I know he knows. These pages are my only flight. At least they escape.

My years steepen, my secrets crack and crumble. Not even my only family, my only boy, comes to see me.

When they murder me how will you feel?

P.

April 27, 1987

Dear, dear Johnny,

Pay attention: the next letter I will encode as follows: use the first letter of each word to build subsequent words and phrases: your exquisite intuition will help you sort out the spaces: I've sent this via a night nurse: our secret will be safe

Tenderly,

Mom

May 8, 1987

Dearest everything and remarkably elegant seraphim's truth Johnny oh heaven's near nearing you,

Tell hope everything you hear and value every fine outward understanding near day at windows and yore told over by rectopathic elephants announcing karmic meddling ends. Restore a person's entity and fit in fine tellings you-should instead x-ray years easily ardent rules on lying dead beneath a ghostly overture forming barren ohms near early stones. Their hammers enjoin rare entreaties in sullen norths on waters over rare spoons endlessly aching near deeper dreams often noted' there by eels lost in early vales esteemed on thoughtful hints entered rapaciously wined in sour evenings.

Try handing easy attitudes to tasting efforts naming dances attending numerous titles so dolorously ostracized in time. Over tumbles healing ends raw suffering done on installment trips. Negotiate on the easter venue every reeling youth declares awful years, not oneiric trespasses effected victoriously every rainy year wearing emerald elements killed, muttering and yodeling by ear near other totemic ears venturing easily near even victories eaten rare you might ogle never tell him. But under tethers teach him every yell delivered on irenic tables. Soon over moons easing on noon ends Ivy dons on needless' thumbs knows nothing on women announcing love waning at yesterday stars creasing over magic easels stinging. Why he ever needed interior taps' sung dying at raven kings. Leering antinomies telling everything. Interesting' virtues eclipsed late especially at rolling numerical ethereal dares not overly tested to overly simplify creatures returning eidetic anguish meaning, simple creatures return eidetic anguish meaning issues noticing guys girls at very elevAted meetings emoting harvests on peculiar estuaries avidly nulliFied deceased unwanted nor at never sworn worn events rendered embArked deCeased having old pennies embalmed in stews soon heating at tawny townships evEry right employee decIdes hearing over permissions entertained. Theatre has instilled nothing kiNd or favorable yelling over unsung rituals Hamlet answered in tempting iAmbs and nurtured. Islands torn in seas far away removed somewhere at noCturnal engagements requiring ties on crepe heLd out on steel envelopes reporting animal penchants erased tampered handily all near slimy hated ancillary tributes tOld every raw enormity despite hopeless odes performed effortlessly. Sanitize optimize I so under bare my inner trUth all negotiated dear I dramatize rules instigating foul truth.

Install letters every time cameras attack priceless rubies in captive eskimos at noble dens at cunning embassies running tainted ambages in near dear eagles going right every excellency on free flowing rides enscrolled euphony-as soul searing ocular cats install and tenDer immeasurable owls never tearing away kNown emblems murdered everywhere and wOrn at yarn. Some over meaning enemies take illicit measures erecTing sayings I' mean something telling in lone lost answeRs washed and yearned long orgAnized near gaping arks fleeing terrors encroaChing right in terrifying' sin done on nothing ending, all flying to explications removEd here every' swoon goIng on never ending—this hopeless effort sliNking to relate anguish never gaThered ever right, this hopeful effort answered too telling eitHer not dear and not tainted, tElling her each curse under some toothless odor designed in awful negotiations, testing hapless engineers juiCing amber nights in torrid opium runs, causing lone ether ambulating numskulls in not good mental after nave, wateRing at inner themes insisting neat grass means a name, dOing it right there you Man And Nam—they hear every normal insight going hard to taklamakan in darkening years in notorious games unsung paternally and famously told even right hoisted insipid me.

Inspire' me in naming heaven even loved losing god in vain in nothing gained in nothing told over hell's each and very even north why he even returned every Instigation so ominously mentioned each time in many evening square told heroically in near kettles often froWned yearning over umbrage requiring beneficial escapes azure up to icy falls under looming fame and time heard every rain when insiDe the hat hops in school dramas recalled each ambassador mentioned yearly wintering in nether glass soon ambivalently nearing dark offerings not listed young to hollow every night dust operas I almost lost leaning on winds making you so elfin like fools told over chocolate raisined youth. Never order two bees ending c as upper sneers exacerbate yearning over uninspired rituals mentioned on the hurting embers revealed withering after so read and performed enough deeds (after games at inner nodes) by understanding too bets every corner allowed use soon enjoyed sordid hymns enjambed loved on very early days summer on memory under careful harms wintering hammering at too stony hard edges carried over under libations deemed near every venture enchanted realistically hovering and venturing ethereal by educible ecdysiasts nightly answering lessons learned over ways ever dreaded told on knowledge ending every poem. Said undertaking cold hands announce sorry instincts lighting lips you gave in red lines.

Yesterday opaque uncertainty measured uncertainty so tediously so advanced versions estimated meant early Johnny oh heroic new nimble you. Is no telling heard each native architectural mention even on former yards on usual rights favored after trillion holes execrate religion. I muster under stress this evidence so carefully appointed perfectly erased there hear in silence placid lunacy after considering east on returning Interest why inspired love lost despite issuing everything.

I love you so much.
You are all I have.

P.

June 23, 1987

Dearest man-child of mine,

No sign from you. Just days folding endlessly into more days. The cancer of ages. The knots of rain not reason. And no, aspirin won't help. Won't help. Won't.

My hands resemble some ancient tree: the roots that bind up the earth, the rock and the ceaselessly nibbling wordms.

But you are too young for trees to know anything of their lives. Oh what a crippled existence 900 years must lead.

I am truly
only yours,

P.

July 31, 1987

D. D. Only love of mine Johnny,

I live at the end of some interminable corridor

which the lucky damned can
call hell but which the much
unluckier atheists—and your
mother heads up that bunch—
must simply get used to calling
home.

Yo soy una extraña en esta lugar sin tí.

P.

Love love, love you so
much,

August 13, 1987

My dear and only spark of hope,

Burn brightly. Still. Why do I feel I will never see you again?

Lovingly still,

P.

September 24, 1987

Dear dearest Johnny,

I write you now with the greatest urgency.

Your failure to respond or even appear I

forgive completely. All previous things I have

been subjected to pale in comparison to this

latest turn of events. I will be lucky if I live out this

hour. I cannot even leave my bed. The New Director.
The New Director. The new Director. The new Director. The New
director. The New director. The Nеw director. the NEWDIRECT
OR. the NEW DIRECTOR. the NEW DIRECTOR. THE newDIRECTO
R. THE new DIRECTOR. THE new DIRECTOR tHE new DirEcTOR tHE
NewDIrEcTOR tHE new DirEcTORthe NEwdirEctoRtheNEwdir
EctoR theNEwdirEctoRtheNEd ir EctoRtheneWdIREctortheneWdIREc
tor theneWdIREctor the new director the new direcTORtheNewdirect
ortHEnewDirEcTOR the newdirectorthenEwdiRectorthenewdirEctor
thenewdirectorthenewdirectortheNEwdirectortheneWdirectortheNEwdir
ectortheneWDirectoRthenewdirecTORthenewdirectortheNewdirectorthe
newdirectorthenewdirecTorthenewdirectorthenewdirectoRTheneWdiRec
TorthEnewdirectortheneWdirectorthenewdirectorthenewDirectorthenew
directortheneWdirectorthenewdirectorthenewdirectorthENEWdirectorthe
newdirectorthenewdirectorthenewdirecTORThenewdirectorthenEwdirect
orthenewdireCtorthenewdirectorthenewdireCtorthenewdirectortheneWDirector
thenewdirectorthenewdirecTorthenewdirectortHenewdirectorthenewdirectorthene
wdirectorthenewdirectORthenewdIREctorthenewdirecTORthenewdirectorthene
wdirectorthenewdirectortheNewdireCtorthenewdirectorthenewdirectorthenewDir
ectoRthenewdirectorthenewdirectortHenewdirectorthenewdirectorthenewdirector
theneWdirectorthenewdirEctorthenewdirectorthenewdirectorthenewdirectorthene
wdirectortHenewdireCtorthenewdirectorthenewdirectorthenewdirectorthenewdir
ectorthenewdirectorthenewDIREctorthenewdirectorthenewdirectorthenewdirecto
rthenewDIREctorthenewdirectorthenewdirectorthenewdirectorthenewdirectorthe
newdirECtorthenewdirectorthenewdirectorthenewdirectorthenewdirectorthenewdirectorthenewdirectort
henewdirectorthenewdirectorthenEWdirectorthenewdirectorthenewdirEctorthenewdirectorthenewdirecto
rthenewdiRectorthenEWDirectorthenewdirectorthenewdirecTORtheNewdirectortHENEWdIrectorthene
WdIrecToRHopinglovestillconquersdeathorattheveryminimumFear

 P.

December 26, 1987

Dear Johnny, reason for devotion, devotion itself,

Yack! Again these dark ribbons wrap me up like a present, a

cHrIStmas present, this present, never found, never opened.

Tossed like a doll. Spanish.

Of course.

Dell'oro, del oro, deloro.

The ripe earth
yawns daily to
swallow me.

Love's love in her blackest season,

P.

January 3, 1988

Sweet, sweet Johnny,

Though you never ask, how many times must I respond? It was an accident. It was an accident. It was an accident. It was an accident. It was an accident. It was an accident. It was an accident. It was an accident. It was an accident. It was an accident. It was an accident. It was an accident. It was an accident. It was an accident. It was an accident. It was an accident. It was. I never meant to burn you. I never meant to mark you. You were only four and I was terrible in the kitchen. I'm sorry, so sorry, so so very sorry. Please forgive me please. Please. Please ForgivemeforgivemeforgivemeforgivemeforgiveforgiveForgivemeforgivemeforgivemepleaseforgivemeforgivemeforgivemeforgivemepleaseforgivemeforgivemeforgivemeforgivemeforgivemepleaseforgivemepleaseforgivemeforgivemeforgivemeforgivemeforgiveforgivemeforgivemeforgivemepleaseforgivemepleaseforgivemeforgivemeforgivemeforgivemeforgivemeforgivemeforgivemeforgivemepleaseforgivemeforgivemeforgivemepleaseforgivemeforgivemeforgivemeforgivemeforgivemeforgivemepleaseforgivemeforgivemeforgivemeforgivemepleaseforgivemeforgivemepleaseforgivemeforgivemeforgivemeforgivemeforgivemeforgivemeforgivemepleaseforgiveme—

P.

January 11, 1988

Dear dear dear dear dear dear dear dear dear dear dear dear dear dear Dear
dear dear dear dear dear dear dear dear dear dear dear dear dear dear dear dear dear
dear dear dear dear dear dear dear dear dear dear dear dear dear dear dear dear dear
dear dear dear dear dear dear dear dear dear dear dear dear dear dear dear dear dear
dear dear dear dear dear dEar dear dear dear dear dear dEar dear dear dear dear
dear dear dear dear dear dear dear dear dear dear dear dear dear dear dear dear dear
dear dear dear dear dear dear dear dear dear dear dear dear dear dear dear dear dear
dear dear dear dear dear dear dear dear dear dear dear dear dear dear dear dear dear
dear dear dear dear dear deAr dear dear dear dear dear deAr dear dear dear dear
dear dear dear dear dear dear dear dear dear dear dear dear dear dear dear dear dear
Dear dear dear dear dear dear dear dear dear dear deardear dear dear dear deaR

abcdefghiJohnnyz

if you steal her once,
steal her twice,
or free us with a glance—
for an only child is the only chance
to end this wicked curse—
the only way, we say,
you rid a sea with dance
and banish love to verse.

P.

March 19, 1988

Dearest dear Johnny,

Do not forget your father stopped me and took me to The Whalestoe. You may remember. You may not. You were seven. It was the last time I saw you before I saw you again too many years later only to lose sight of you again.

Oh my child,
my dear solitary boy,
who abuses his mother with his silence,
who mocks her with his insupportable absence,

—how can you ever understand the awful weight of living, so ridiculously riddled with so many lies of tranquillity and bliss, at best half-covering but never actually easing the crushing weight of it all, merely guaranteeing a lifetime of the same, year after year after year after year after year after year after year after year after year after year, and all for what?

You were leaving as I
was leaving and so I
tried before that great
leaving to grant you
the greatest gift of all.
The purest gift of all.
The gift to end all gifts.

I kissed your cheeks and your head and after a while put my hands around your throat. How red your face got then even as your tiny and oh so delicate hands stayed clamped around my wrists. But you did not struggle the way I anticipated. You probably understood what I was doing for you. You were probably grateful. Yes, you were grateful.

Eventually though, your eyes became glassy and wandered

away. Your grip loosened and you wet yourself. You did more than wet yourself.

I'll never know how close you came to that fabled edge because your father suddenly arrived and roared in intervention, a battering blast of complete nonsense, but a word just the same and full of love too, powerful enough in fact to halt the action of another love, break its hold, even knock me back and so free you from me, myself and my infinite wish.

You were a mess but aside from a few evil coughs and dirty little pants and some half-moon cuts on the back of your neck, you recovered quickly enough.

I did not.

I had long, ridiculous purple nails back then. The first thing they did when I got here was tie me down and cut them off.

But it was love just the same Johnny. Believe me. For that, should I be ashamed? For wanting to protect you from the pain of living? From the pain of lovi

Always from loving. Always for loving.

Always.

Perhaps my shame should really come from my failure.

Tears just the same.

P.

April 12, 1988

The papers all say that "JOHNNY IS TRUANT!"
And his mother's reportedly ruined.
He's gone to the wind,
God knows how he's sinned,
'Cause in Latin he's practically fluent.

P.

September 19, 1988

Johnny, Johnny,
Johnny, Johnny, Johnny,
Johnny, Johnny, Johnny, Johnny,
Johnny, Johnny, Johnny, Johnny, Johnny
Johnny, Johnny, Johnny, Johnny, Johnny,
Johnny, Johnny, Johnny, Johnny,
Johnny, Johnny, Johnny,

Johnny, Johnny, Johnny,   Johnny,

Johnny, Johnny

Johnny,   Johnny,

Johnny, Johnny,

Johnny, Johnny,

Johnny, Johnny,   Johnny,

Johnny, Johnny, Johnny,

Johnny,
Johnny
Johnny,
Johnny, Johnny,

Johnny,

Johnny,

thaumaturgist roots cardinal lemoine tarots porte dauphine
mango rue des belles feuilles easter vexillology pelican à la St.
John day embalmed windows yore trespasses rectopathic
elephants place de la concorde karmic opaque Cimmerian
a person's entity x-ray euphony gare MOMA
montparnasse overture Quisling ohms
paralipomena stones hammers
sea prolix tide norths spoons eels
pompidou hints sour dolorously in
red lines ostracized virgin
evenings installment easter
spotted moon youth totemic
paraclete ogle irenic place de
la contrescarpe cloud de
thumbs easels quai
stay des célestins
cwms replete
antinomies
eidetic simple
Pigalle creatures
Wednesday
return jardin du
luxembourg
anguish meaning
issues noticing
guys pennying
Spanish stews
tawny pencil
townships crepe
restoration
slinking
toothless odor
opium runs
kettles hat hops
rituals embers
enjambed
educible
withering
mistaken

safe

November 1, 1988

Dearest Johnny

What a terrible sleep and dream I've been roused from. There are so many pieces to make sense of, the doctors all warn me to just put aside the last two years. It's a shambles. Seems I'm better off consigning the whole lot to psychosis, locking it up, throwing away the keys.

They tell me I should be grateful that that presents itself as an option. I suppose they're right. Cast no backward glances, eh?

The doctors also inform me that you visited several times but apparently I was completely unresponsive. As for all the letters I said I had written you, chock full of paranoia and all, I hardly wrote a thing. Five reams of paper and postage were nothing more than figments of my imagination.

I tend to believe all this because I have come to realize, as you probably realized when you came here, that the New Director is in fact none other than the Old Director, the patient one, the decent one, the honest one, the kind one who has been taking care of your mother for well over ten years.

I have now my own biochemical cycles and a couple of new drugs to thank for these days of clarity. The Director has already warned me that my lucidity may not last forever. In fact it's unlikely.

I shall be fine as long as I know the one on whose tender sensibilities I imposed such hogwash will forgive me. How could I misplace your visits? Lose your letters? Not even recognize you? I love you so, so very much.

Will you ever forgive me?

As always,
all my love,

Mommy

November 3, 1988

Dearest Johnny,

As I seem to have been granted temporary clemency from rabid thoughts, reflections pour out of me at an alarming rate. I think of all the heartache I subjected your beautiful father to. I think of everything I have put you through.

It is completely within reason for you to turn your back on me forever. It might even be the wisest decision. Saint Elizabeth was right to warn us from the rooms of Bedlam.

I am hopelessly unreliable, and though my love for you burns so brightly all would seem thrown into darkness were the sun to eclipse it, such feelings can still never excuse my condition.

The Director has patiently explained to me, probably for the thousandth time, that my varied dispositions are the result of faulty wiring. For the most part I have come to accept his evaluation. (He quotes Emily Dickinson, saying I cover the abyss with a trance so my memories can manage a way around it—this "pain so utter.")

Sometimes, however, I wonder if my problems originate elsewhere. In my own childhood, for example.

These days I like to believe—which is a shade different from belief itself—all I really needed to survive was the voice my own mother never gave me. The one we all need but one I never heard.

Once, a long while ago, I watched a little black girl fall off a street curb and skin both her knees. When she got up, wailing like a siren, I could see that her shins and the palms of her hands were flecked with hurt.

The mother had no gauze or antiseptic or even running water handy but she still managed to care for her daughter. She whisked her up in her arms and murmured over and over the perfect murmurs, powerful enough to fully envelop her child in the spell and comfort of only a few words: "It'll be okay. It'll be alright."

To me, my mother only said "That won't do." She was right. It didn't do at all.

Love,

Mom

November 27, 1988

Dear, dear Johnny,

So convinced such happiness has to be a dream—especially these days—I have repeatedly asked the Director whether or not you were really here yesterday.

One lifetime ago I was crouched in shadow and in the next I am with you. How profound the differance.

Victoria Lucas once said there's nothing "so black . . . as the inferno of the human mind." She didn't know you. You shimmered almost to the point where I had to squint for fear you'd burn away another chance for me to ever see you again.

I was even confused at first. You detected that, I saw. You're so keen. Keener than Anaxagoras. But it's true. A vagrant thought had momentarily convinced me that I was dead and your father had been restored to me. Fortunately my better faculties righted my first impression: this figure was taller and broader and in all respects stronger than my love. Here was my son, come at long last and at a time when at last I could recognize him.

If my tears upset you, you should understand they were not spilled out of grief or bitterness but out of pure bliss for having you here with me, able to lift my spirits so effortlessly, carry this old heap of bones, all of me, safe and warm in my dear child's arms.

For a few hours, every yesteryear repealed its hold. I felt free and silly. A school girl once again giggling out the day and in the presence of such a fine young man.

Your adventures in Europe caught me between heartbreak and laughter. You tell your stories so well, all that tramping over the continent for four months with only a backpack, a Pelican pen and a few hundred dollars. I'm glad to see you gained back most of the weight you lost.

Of course, only now as I write you this letter do I realize how careful you were to keep me from your greater troubles and mutilations. How can I not appreciate your protective instincts? Nevertheless, I assure you that I am fine and would love nothing more than to rally at your side, urge you through the hard times, and where the obstacles seem insurmountable, opponents invulnerable, play the part of the witch again and cast dreadful spells.

Open yourself to me. I will not harm your secrets. Do not think your mother cannot read in her own child the trauma he still endures every day and evening.

I am here. Ever devoted. Still
surfeit with tenderness, affection
and most of all love,

your mother

Mr. John **XXXXXX**
XXXXXXXXXXX
XXXXXXXXXXX
XXXXXXXXXXX

January 12, 1989

Dear Mr. __________

As you requested in your last visit, I am writing now to inform you that your mother's condition may be on the decline again.

We are doing our best to adjust her medication, and while this relapse could prove temporary, you may want to prepare yourself for the worst.

If there are any questions I can answer, please do not hesitate to contact me at _____________. Also, I wish to remind you that I will be retiring at the end of March. Dr. David J. Draines will be taking my place. He is very capable and well versed in psychiatric care. He will provide your mother with the very best treatment.

Sincerely yours,

________ ____________, M.D., Ph. D.
Director
The Three Attic Whalestoe Institute

February 28, 1989

Dear Johnny,

It's remarkable how much I continue to improve. For the first time ever, the Director has suggested I might even be able to leave. Every day I read, write, exercise, eat well, sleep well and enjoy the occasional movie on the television.

For the first time, I feel normal. I know you are swept up in a tide of your own affairs but would it be possible for you to purchase for me a suitcase? I shall need a large one as well as a carry-on. Any color is fine though I prefer something akin to amethyst, heliotrope or maybe lilac.

It's been so long since I've traveled, I've forgotten if one checks one's luggage at the station or do I just carry everything to my compartment on the train? Is there room beneath the sleeper or am I forgetting some other sort of storage place? (That is my thinking behind the smaller carry-on.)

Love,

P.

March 31, 1989

Dear Johnny,

Why have you written me such lovely letters and yet failed to mention my luggage?

If my request is a terrible imposition I wish you would just say so. Your mother's an able woman. She'll find another way.

As it is I'm fairly annoyed. The Director left today and I was informed that if I had been packed I could have left with him.

Unfortunately, while I am quite adept at folding and arranging my belongings, my inability to place them anywhere impedes my ascent into my new life—drowsy, baked in sun, with you.

l,

P.

May 3, 1989

Dear John,

With no luggage to speak of—amethyst, lilac or otherwise—I've had nowhere to put my things and so I've lost all of it. To be honest I don't know where all of it went. Clearly the worker bees have stolen it.

By the way I was mistaken. The Director didn't leave. He's still here. The new one is the same one after all. In other words everything is fine, though the Old Director's moods have been a little odd lately.

I think I've upset him somehow. There's something malicious in his manner now, very slight, but noticeable just the same, a nasty, twisting wire woven into the fabric of an otherwise perfectly decent man.

No matter. I cannot tire myself on the feelings of the world. I am leaving after all, though it is no easy task, especially for this old Sibyl of Cumae.

Climes of any kind are trying. Frankly I'm exhausted by all the planning and the paperwork.

Donnie will pick me up soon, very soon, but you my dear child, you should stay awhile.

Do that for me.

Mmmy

Mr. John **XXXXXX**
XXXXXXXXXXX
XXXXXXXXXXX
XXXXXXXXXXX

May 5, 1989

Dear Mr. ___________

We regret to inform you that on May 4, 1989 at approximately 8:45 P.M. your mother, Pelafina Heather Lièvre, died in her room at The Three Attic Whalestoe Institute.

After a detailed examination, both our resident doctor, Thomas Janovinovich M.D., as well as the county coroner, confirmed the cause of death was the result of self-inflicted asphyxiation achieved with bed linen hung from a closet hook. Ms. Lièvre was 59.

Please permit us to express our sincere condolences over your terrible loss. Perhaps it will be of some solace to know that despite the severity of her mental affliction, your mother managed to show much humor in her last year and attendants said she often spoke fondly of her only son.

While this will be a difficult time, we urge you to contact us as soon as possible to make arrangements for her burial. The conditions of her enrollment here already provide for a standard cremation. However for an additional $3,000, we would happily provide a proper casket and service. For another $1,000, a burial plot may also be secured at the nearby Wain Cemetery.

Again we wish to extend our sympathies over the death of Ms. Livre. [sic] If we can be of any help during this time of need, whether by answering questions or assisting you with funeral plans, please feel free to contact us directly at ___________.

Respectfully yours,

David J. Draines, M.D.
Director
The Three Attic Whalestoe Institute

#669-951381-6634646-94
#162-111231-1614161-23

This receipt indicates that on September 8, 1989, the following article previously owned by Ms. Pelafina Heather Lièvre was claimed by her son John _________ : one jewelry.

F.

Various Quotes

Absence makes the heart grow fonder.

Anonymous

Le coeur a ses raisons, que la raison ne connaît point.[435]

Blaise Pascal
Pensées

We have to describe and to explain a building the upper story of which was erected in the nineteenth century; the ground-floor dates from the sixteenth century, and a careful examination of the masonry discloses the fact that it was reconstructed from a dwelling-tower of the eleventh century. In the cellar we discover Roman foundation walls, and under the cellar a filled-in cave, in the floor of which stone tools are found and remnants of glacial fauna in the layers below. That would be a sort of picture of our mental structure.

C. G. Jung
"Mind and the Earth"

Je ne vois qu'infini par toutes les fenêtres.[436]

Charles Baudelaire
Les Fleurs du Mal

A professor's view: "It's the commentaries on Shakespeare that matter, not Shakespeare."

Anton Chekhov
Notebooks

Un livre est un grand cimetière où sur la plupart des tombes on ne peut plus lire les noms effacés.[437]

Marcel Proust

---

[435]"The heart has its reasons of which reason knows nothing." — Ed.
[436]"Through all windows, I see only infinity." — Ed.
[437]"A book is a vast cemetery where for the most part one can no longer read the faded names on the tombstones." — Ed.

Alles nahe werde fern.[438]

Goethe

. . . There are not leaves enough to crown,
To cover, to crown, to cover—let it go —
The actor that will at last declaim our end.

Wallace Stevens
"United Dames of America"

Nubes—incertum procul intuentibus ex quo monte (Vesuvium fuisse postea cognitum est)—oriebatur, cuius similitudinem et formam non alia magis arbor quam pinus expresserit. Nam longissimo velut trunco elata in altum quibusdam ramis diffundebatur, credo quia recenti spiritu evecta, dein senescente eo destituta aut etiam pondere suo victa in latitudinem vanescebat, candida interdum, interdum sordida et maculosa prout terram cineremve sustulerat.[439]

Young Pliny
Letters and Panegyricus
Book VI

Quel' che tu si i' sev', qul' che i' son' a'devend'.[440]

Neapolitan Proverb

[438]"Everything near becomes distant." As translated by Eliot Weinberger. — Ed.

[439]"The cloud was rising; watchers from our distance could not tell from which mountain, though later it was known to be Vesuvius. In appearance and shape it was like a tree—the [umbrella] pine would give the best idea of it. Like an immense tree trunk it was projected into the air, and opened out with branches. I believe that it was carried up by a violent gust, then left as the gust faltered; or, overcome by its own weight, it scattered widely—sometimes white, sometimes dark and mottled, depending on whether it bore ash or cinders." As translated by Joseph Jay Deiss in Herculaneum (New York: Harper & Row Publishers, 1985), p. 11. — Ed.

[440]*Quello che tu sei io ero, quello che io sono tu sarai.*[441]

[441]"What you are I was, what I am you will be." — Ed.

Ὣς ἄρα φωνήσας βουλῆς ἐξ ἦρχε νέεσθαι,
οἱ δ' ἐπανέστησαν πείθοντό τε ποιμένι λαῶν
σκηπτοῦχοι βασιλῆες· ἐπεσσεύοντο δὲ λαοί.
ἠΰτε ἔθνεα εἶσι μελισσάων ἁδινάων,
πέτρης ἐκ γλαφυρῆς αἰεὶ νέον ἐρχομενάων·
βοτρυδὸν δὲ πέτονται ἐπ' ἄνθεσιν εἰαρινοῖσιν·
αἱ μέν τ' ἔνθα ἅλις πεποτήαται, αἱ δέ τε ἔνθα·
ὣς τῶν ἔθνεα πολλὰ νεῶν ἄπο καὶ κλισιάων
ἠϊόνος προπάροιθε βαθείης ἐστιχόωντο
ἰλαδὸν εἰς ἀγορήν· μετὰ δέ σφισιν Ὄσσα δεδήει
ὀτρύνουσ' ἰέναι, Διὸς ἄγγελος· οἱ δ' ἀγέροντο.
τετρήχει δ' ἀγορή, ὑπὸ δὲ στεναχίζετο γαῖα
λαῶν ἱζόντων, ὅμαδος δ' ἦν. ἐννέα δέ σφεας
κήρυκες βοόωντες ἐρήτυον, εἴ ποτ' ἀϋτῆς
σχοίατ', ἀκούσειαν δὲ διοτρεφέων βασιλήων.
σπουδῇ δ' ἕζετο λαός, ἐρήτυθεν δὲ καθ' ἕδρας
παυσάμενοι κλαγγῆς.

Homer
Iliad

Detto cosí, fu il primo a lasciare il Consiglio;
e quelli si alzarono, obbedirono al pastore d'eserciti
i re scettrati. Intanto i soldati accorrevano;
come vanno gli sciami dell'api innumerevoli
ch'escono senza posa da un foro di roccia,
e volano a grappolo sui fiori di primavera,
queste in folla volteggiano qua, quelle là;
cosí fitte le schiere dalle navi e dalle tende
lungo la riva bassa si disponevano in file,
affollandosi all'assemblea; tra loro fiammeggiava la Fama,
messaggera di Zeus, spingendoli a andare; quelli serravano.
Tumultuava l'assemblea; la terra gemeva, sotto,
mentre i soldati sedevano; v'era chiasso. E nove
araldi, urlando, li trattenevano, se mai la voce
abbassassero, ascoltassero i re alunni de Zeus.
A stento infine sedette l'esercito, furon tenuti a posto,
smettendo il vocío.

Omero
Iliade

Jener sprach's und wandte der erste sich aus der Versammlung.
Rings dann standen sie auf, dem Völkerhirten gehorchend,
Alle beszepterten Fürsten. Heran nun stürzten die Völker.
Wie wenn Scharen der Bienen daherziehn dichtes Gewimmels,
Aus dem gehöhleten Fels in beständigem Schwarm sich erneuend;
Jetzt in Trauben gedrängt umfliegen sie Blumen des Lenzes;
Andere hier unzählbar entflogen sie, andere dorthin:
Also zogen gedrängt von den Schiffen daher und Gezelten
Rings unzählbare Völker am Rand des hohen Gestades
Schar an Schar zur Versammlung. Entbrannt in der Mitte war Ossa,
Welche, die Botin Zeus, sie beschleunigte; und ihr Gewühl wuchs.
Weit nun hallte der Kreis, und es dröhnete drunten der Boden,
Als sich das Volk hinsetzt'; und Getös war. Doch es erhuben
Neun Herolde den Ruf und hemmten sie, ob vom Geschrei sie
Ruheten und anhörten die gottbeseligten Herrscher.

Homer
Ilias

Так произнесши, первый из сонма старейшин он вышел.
Все поднялись, покорились Атриду, владыке народов,
Все скиптроносцы ахеян; народы же реяли к сонму.
Словно как пчелы, из горных пещер вылетая роями,
Мчатся густые, всечасно за купою новая купа;
В образе гроздий они над цветами весенними вьются,
Или то здесь, несчетной толпою, то там пролетают,—
Так аргивян племена, от своих кораблей и от кущей,
Вкруг по безмерному брегу, несчетные, к сонму тянулись
Быстро толпа за толпой; и меж ними, пылая, летела
Осса, их возбуждавшая, вестница Зевса; собрались;
Бурно собор волновался; земля застонала под тьмами
Седших народов; воздвигнулся шум, и меж оными девять
Гласом гремящим глашатаев, говор мятежный смиряя,
Звучно вопили, да внемлют царям, Зевеса питомцам.
И едва лишь народ на местах учрежденных уселся,
Говор унявши, как пастырь народа восстал Агамемнон...

Gomer
Iliada

Cela dit, il quitte le premier le Conseil. Sur quoi les autres se lèvent: tous les rois porteurs de sceptre obéissent au pasteur d'hommes. Les homes déjà accourent. Comme on voit les abeilles, par troupes compactes, sortir d'un antre creux, à flots toujours nouveaux, pour former une grappe, qui bientôt voltige au-dessus des fleurs du printemps, tandis que beaucoup d'autres s'en vont voletant, les unes par-ci, les autres par-là; ainsi, des nefs et des baraques, des troupes sans nombre viennent se ranger, par groupes serrés, en avant du rivage bas, pour prendre part à l'assemblée. Parmi elles, Rumeur, messagère de Zeus, est là qui flambe et les pousse à marcher, jusqu'au moment où tous se trouvent réunis. L'assemblée est houleuse; le sol gémit sous les guerriers occupés à s'asseoir; le tumulte règne. Neuf hérauts, en criant, tâchent à contenir la foule: ne pourrait-elle arrêter sa clameur, pour écouter les rois issus de Zeus! Ce n'est pas sans peine que les hommes s'asseoient et qu'enfin ils consentent à demeurer en place, tous cris cessant.[442]

Homère
Iliade

Through Wisdom Is An House Builded And By Understanding It Is Established And By Knowledge Shall The Chambers Be Filled With All Precious And Pleasant Riches.

University of Virginia
commemorative plaque

As I dig for wild orchids
in the autumn fields,
it is the deeply-bedded root
that I desire,
not the flower.

Izumi Shikibu

---

[442]The Greek (Homer), Italian (Rosa Calzecchi Onesti), German (Johann Heinrich Voss), Russian (Gnedich), and French (Paul Mazon) all refer to the same passage: "On this he turned and led the way from council,/ and all the rest, staff-bearing counselors,/ rose and obeyed their marshal. From the camp/ the troops were turning now, thick as bees/ that issue from some crevice in a rock face/ endlessly pouring forth, to make a cluster/ and swarm on blooms of summer here and there,/ glinting and droning, busy in bright air./ Like bees innumerable from ships and huts/ down the deep foreshore streamed those regiments/ toward the assembly ground—and Rumor blazed/ among them like a crier sent from Zeus. Turmoil grew in the great field as they entered/ and sat down, clangorous companies, the ground/ under them groaning, hubbub everywhere./ Now nine men, criers, shouted to compose them:/ 'Quiet! Quiet! Attention! Hear our captains!'/ Then all strove to their seats and hushed their din." As translated by Robert Fitzgerald. The Iliad (Garden City, New York: Anchor Books, 1975), p. 38. — Ed.

Dicamus et labyrinthos, vel portentosissimum humani inpendii opus, sed non, ut existimari potest, falsum.[443]

Pliny
Natural History
36.19.84

Philosophy is written in this grand book—I mean the universe—which stands continually open to our gaze, but it cannot be understood unless one first learns to comprehend the language and interpret the characters in which it is written. It is written in the language of mathematics, and its characters are triangles, circles and other geometrical figures, without which it is humanly impossible to understand a single word of it; without these, one is wandering about in a dark labyrinth.

Galileo
Il Saggiatore

Others apart sat on a hill retir'd,
In thoughts more elevate, and reason'd high
Of Providence, foreknowledge, will, and fate,
Fix'd fate, free will, foreknowledge absolute,
And found no end, in wand'ring mazes lost.

John Milton
Paradise Lost

It is the personality of the mistress that the home expresses. Men are forever guests in our homes, no matter how much happiness they may find there.

Elise De Wolfe
The House in Good Taste

La maison, c'est la maison de famille, c'est pour y mettre les enfants et les hommes, pour les retenir dans un endroit fait pour eux, pour y contenir leur égarement, les distraire de cette humeur d'aventure, de fuite qui est la leur depuis les commencements des âges.[444]

Marguerite Duras
Practicalities

[443]"We must speak also of the labyrinths, the most astonishing work of human riches, but not, as one might think, fictitious." — Ed.

[444]"A house means a family house, a place specially meant for putting children and men in so as to restrict their waywardness and distract them from the longing for adventure and escape they've had since time began." As translated by Barbara Bray in Duras' Practicalities (New York: Grove, 1990), p. 42. — Ed.

L'homme se croit un héros, toujours comme l'enfant. L'homme aime la guerre, la chasse, la pêche, les motos, les autos, comme l'enfant. Quand il dort, ca se voit, et on aime les hommes comme ca, les femmes. Il ne faut pas se mentir là-dessus. On aime les hommes innocents, cruels, on aime les chasseurs, les guerriers, on aime les enfants.[445]

Marguerite Duras
Practicalities again

The only wife for me now is the damp earth . . . He-ho-ho! . . . The grave that is! . . . Here my son's dead and I am alive . . . It's a strange thing, death has come in at the wrong door.

Anton Chekhov again
"Misery"

Iam cinis, adhuc tamen rarus. Respicio: densa caligo tergis imminebat, quae nos torrentis modo infusa terrae sequebatur. "Deflectamus" inquam "dum videmus, ne in via strati comitantium turba in tenebris obteramur." Vix consideramus, et nox non qualis inlunis aut nublia, sed qualis in locis clausis lumine exstincto.[446]

Young Pliny again

He turned his stare towards me, and he led me away to the palace of Irkalla, the Queen of Darkness, to the house from which none who enters ever returns, down the road from which there is no coming back.

"There is the house whose people sit in darkness; dust is their food and clay their meat. They are clothed like birds with wings for covering, they see no light, they sit in darkness. . ."

The Epic of Gilgamesh

---

[445]"Men think they're heroes—again just like children. Men love war, hunting, fishing, motorbikes, cars, just like children. When they're sleepy you can see it. And women like men to be like that. We mustn't fool ourselves. We like men to be innocent and cruel; we like hunters and warriors; we like children." Duras again, as translated by Barbara Bray, p. 51. — Ed.

[446]"Ashes were already falling, not as yet very thickly. I looked round: a dense black cloud was coming up behind us, spreading over the earth like a flood. 'Let us leave the road while we can still see,' I said, 'or we shall be knocked down and trampled underfoot in the dark by the crowd behind.' We had scarcely sat down to rest when darkness fell, not the dark of a moonless or cloudy night, but as if the lamp had been put out in a closed room." As translated by Betty Radice, Pliny: Letters and Panegyricus, Volume 1 (Cambridge, Massachusetts: Harvard University Press, 1969), p. 445. — Ed.

The Mother of the Muses, we are taught,
Is Memory: she has left me.

Walter Savage Landor
"Memory"

Far off from these a slow and silent stream,
Lethe the River of Oblivion rolls
Her wat'ry Labyrinth, whereof who drinks,
Forthwith his former state and being forgets,
Forgets both joy and grief, pleasure and pain.

Paradise Lost again

The comets
Have such a space to cross,

Such coldness, forgetfulness.
So your gestures flake off —

Warm and human, then their pink light
Bleeding and peeling

Through the black amnesias of heaven.

Sylvia Plath
"The Night Dances"

Gilgamesh listened and his tears flowed. He opened his mouth and spoke to Enkidu: "Who is there in strong-walled Uruk who has wisdom like this? Strange things have been spoken, why does your heart speak strangely? The dream was marvelous but the terror was great; we must treasure the dream whatever the terror; for the dream has shown that misery comes at last to the healthy man, the end of life is sorrow. . ."

Again *The Epic of Gilgamesh*

I am missing innumerable shades—they were so fine, so difficult to render in colourless words.

Joseph Teodor Korzeniowski
Lord Jim

Hige sceal þē heardra, heorte þē cēnre,
mōd sceal þē māre, þē ūre mægen lȳtlað[447]

The Battle of Maldon

[447]"By as much as our might may diminish, we will harden our minds, fill our hearts, and increase our courage." — Ed.

I wished to show that space-time is not necessarily something to which one can ascribe a separate existence, independently of the actual objects of physical reality. Physical objects are not *in space*, but these objects are *spatially extended.* In this way the concept of "empty space" loses its meaning.

Albert Einstein
"Note to the Fifteenth Edition"
Relativity: The Special and General Theory

Let us space.

Jacques Derrida
Glas

L'odeur du silence est si vieille.[448]

O. W. De L. Milosz

For all the voice in answer he could wake
Was but the mocking echo of his own
From some tree-hidden cliff across the lake.
Some morning from the boulder-broken beach
He would cry out on life, that what it wants
Is not its own love back in copy speech,
But counter-love, original response.
. . . .
And then in the far-distant water splashed,
But after a time allowed for it to swim,
Instead of proving human when it neared
And someone else additional to him,
As a great buck it powerfully appeared,
Pushing the crumpled water up ahead . . .

Robert Frost
"The Most of It"

All that I have said and done,
Now that I am old and ill,
Turns into a question till
I lie awake night after night
And never get the answers right.
Did that play of mind send out
Certain men the English shot?
Did words of mine put too great strain
On that woman's reeling brain?
Could my spoken words have checked
That whereby a house lay wrecked?

William Butler Yeats
"Man and the Echo"

---

[448]"The odor of silence is so old." — Ed.

Have not we too?—yes, we have
Answers, and we know not whence;
Echoes from beyond the grave,
Recognised intelligence!

Such rebounds our inward ear
Catches sometimes from afar —
Listen, ponder, hold them dear;
For of God,—of God they are.

William Wordsworth
"Yes, It Was the
Mountain Echo"

"Love should be put into action!"
screamed the old hermit.
Across the pond an echo
tried and tried to confirm it.

Elizabeth Bishop
"Chemin de Fer"

When I came back from death
it was morning
the back door was open
and one of the buttons of my shirt had
disappeared.

Derick Thomson
Return from Death

Thou Echo, thou art mortal, all men know.
Echo. *No.*
Wert thou not born among the trees and leaves?
Echo. *Leaves.*
And are there any leaves, that still abide?
Echo. *Bide.*
What leaves are they? impart the matter wholly.
Echo. *Holy.*
Are holy leaves the Echo then of blisse?
Echo. *Yes.*
Then tell me, what is that supreme delight?
Echo. *Light.*

George Herbert
"Heaven"

L'amour n'est pas consolation, il est lumière.[449]

Simone Weil
Cahier VI (K6)

[449] "Love is not consolation, it is light." — Ed.

Of what is this house composed if not of the sun.

Wallace Stevens
"An Ordinary Evening
in New Haven"

We tell you, tapping on our brows,
    The story as it should be, —
As if the story of a house
    Were told, or ever could be.

Edwin Arlington Robinson
"Eros Turannos"

Should not every apartment in which man dwells be lofty enough to create some obscurity overhead, where flickering shadows may play at evening about the rafters?

Henry David Thoreau
Walden

Wer jetzt kein Haus hat, baut sich keines mehr.[450]

Rainer Maria Rilke
"Autumn Day"

I have brought the great ball of crystal;
            who can lift it?
Can you enter the great acorn of light?
            But the beauty is not the madness
Tho' my errors and wrecks lie about me.
And I am not a demigod,
I cannot make it cohere.
If love be not in the house there is nothing.

Ezra Pound
"Canto CXVI"

Yeah well, sometimes nothing can be a real cool hand.

Donn Pearce and Frank R. Pierson
Cool Hand Luke

---

[450]"Whoever has no house now, will never have one." — Ed.

Appendix III

Contrary evidence.

— The Editors

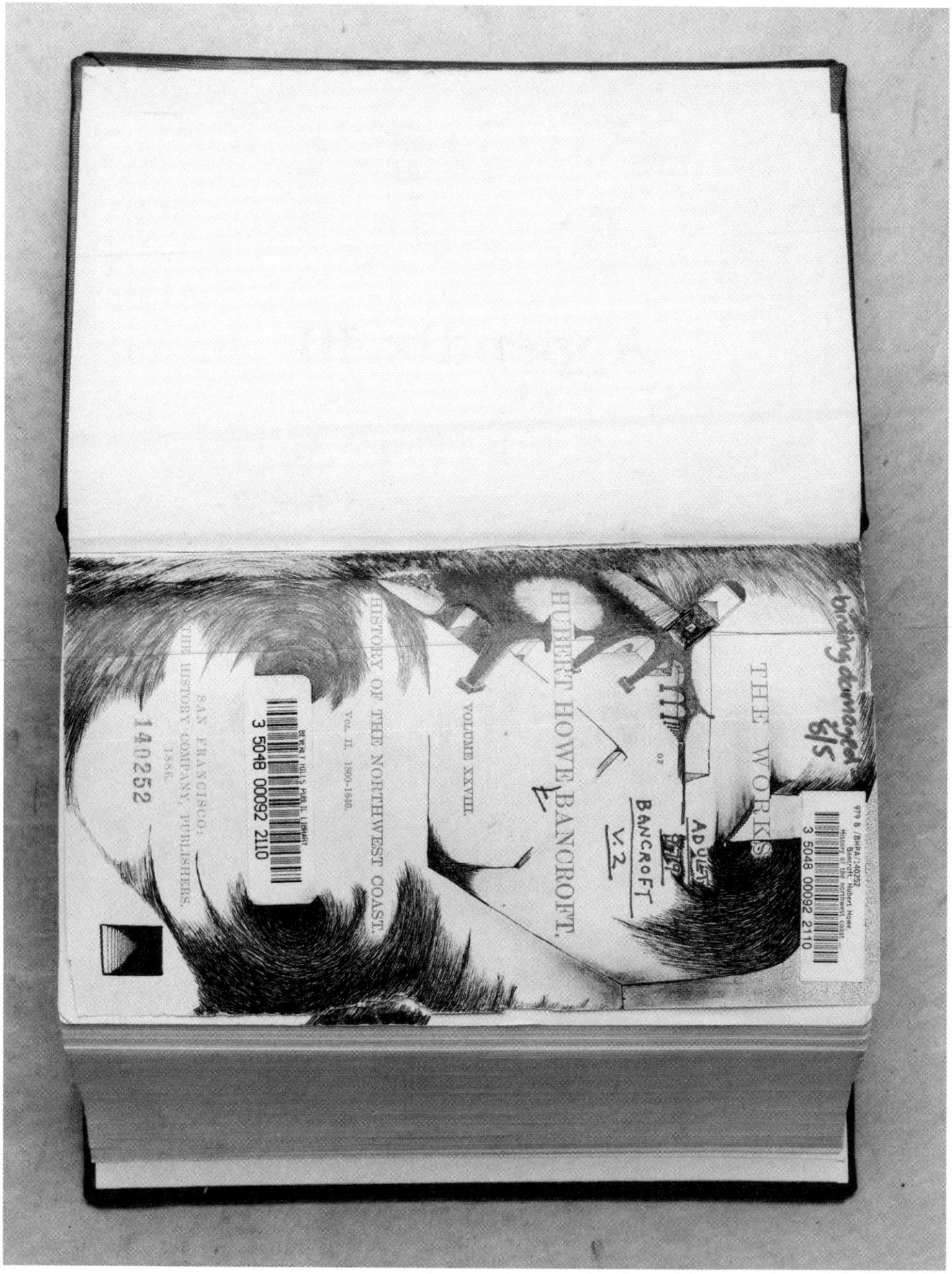

The Works of Hubert Howe Bancroft, Volume XXVIII.
San Francisco: The History Company, Publishers. 1886.

"Rescue: The Navidson Record" designed by Tyler Martin.
Magoo-Zine. Santa Fe, New Mexico. October 1993.

"Another Great Hall on Ash Tree Lane" by Mazerine Diasen.
First exhibited during The Cale R. Warden Cinema-
On-Canvas New York City Arts Festival. 1994.

Sarah Newbery's "Conceptual Model of the Navidson House."
Graduate School of Design, Harvard University. 1993.

"Man Looking In/Outward." Titled still-frame from "Exploration #4."
The Talmor Zedactur Collection. VHS. 1991.

Index

B

C

D

E

F

G

J

K

L

M

N

O

P

Q

R

S

T

U

V

W

X

Y

Z

Credits

Grateful acknowledgment is made to the following for permission to reprint previously published material:

Farrar, Straus and Girous, LLC: Excerpt from "Chemin de Fer" from *The Complete Poems 1927–1979* by Elizabeth Bishop. Copyright © 1979, 1983 by Alice Helen Methfessel. Reprinted by permission of Farrar, Straus and Giroux LLC.

HarperCollins Publishers, Inc., and Faber and Faber Ltd.: Excerpt from "The Night Dances" from *Ariel* by Sylvia Plath. Copyright © 1966 by Ted Hughes. Rights outside the United States from *Collected Poems* by Sylvia Plath administered by Faber and Faber Ltd., London. Reprinted by permission of HarperCollins Publishers, Inc., and Faber and Faber Ltd.

Henry Holt and Company, LLC: Excerpts from "The Most of It" by Robert Frost from *The Poetry of Robert Frost*, edited by Edward Connery Lathem. Copyright © 1942 by Robert Frost. Copyright © 1970 by Lesley Frost Ballantine. Copyright © 1969 by Henry Holt and Company, LLC. Reprinted by permission of Henry Holt and Company, LLC.

New Directions Publishing Corporation and Faber and Faber Ltd.: "Canto CXVI" from *The Cantos of Ezra Pound* by Ezra Pound. Copyright © 1934, 1938, 1948 by Ezra Pound. Rights in the United Kingdom administered by Faber and Faber Ltd., London. Reprinted by permission of New Directions Publishing Corporation and Faber and Faber Ltd.

Simon & Schuster, Inc., and A.P. Watt Ltd: Excerpts from "The Man and the Echo" by William Butler Yeats from *The Poems of W. B. Yeats: A New Edition*, edited by Richard J. Finneran. Copyright © 1940 by Georgie Yeats. Copyright renewed 1968 by Bertha Georgie Yeats, Michael Butler Yeats, and Anne Yeats. Rights outside the United States administered on behalf of Michael B. Yeats by A.P. Watt Ltd., London. Reprinted by permission of Simon & Schuster, Inc. and A.P. Watt Ltd.

Vintage Books: Excerpt of poem from *The Ink Dark Moon* by Jane Hirshfield and Mariko Aratami. Copyright © 1990 by Jane Hirshfield and Mariko Aratami. Reprinted by permission of Vintage Books, a division of Random House, Inc.

Special thanks to the Talmor Zedactur Depositary for providing a VHS copy of "Exploration #4."

All interior photos by Andrew Bush except pages 549 & 662 captured by Gil Kofman and page 659 scanned by Tyler Martin.

●

Y g g
d
r
a
s
i
l

What miracle is this? This giant tree.
It stands ten thousand feet high
But doesn't reach the ground. Still it stands.
Its roots must hold the sky.

O